To me mate —

Stop the piracy!

[signature]

Pirates

of the

Potomac

or

THE SQUID

AN AMERICAN FABLE

 JAMES E. CHURCHES

Green Man Publishing

Published by GREEN MAN PUBLISHING
www.PIRATESOFTHEPOTOMAC.net

©2004 The Studio at Nederland, Ltd.
POBox 3180 Nederland, Colorado 80466 USA

Cover and book design ©2004 Susan Davis Churches

ISBN 0-9762704-0-4

Printed in the USA on recycled paper.
All paper used in the printing of this book has been replanted through the 100% Replanted Program.

Visit them at www.ReplantTrees.org

For Susan,
I feel connected.

Special thanks to John Madden, Jr.,
businessman, benefactor, mentor and friend.
Thanks for believing.

"Grand Contested Election for the
Presidency of the United States"

"WHALING VOYAGE BY ONE ISHMAEL"

"BLOODY BATTLE IN AFFGHANISTAN"

~ HERMAN MELVILLE, 1851
MOBY-DICK OR, THE WHALE

BOOK I

The Fortunate Son

Chapter I

Choose Your Druthers

ALL ME ISHCABIBBLE. I tossed the name off as an alias when I registered for
the big South Texas Pigeon Shoot, August the 3rd of 1882, four months
to the day after my so-called death. Ishcabibble won the contest by hitting
forty-eight out of fifty live pigeons released at thirty yards—quite a show of
fire, blood, and feathers. He became an instant celebrity in Galveston. There
was not a saloon along the dock where he could pay for a drink.

Not very smart, you say? A wanted outlaw getting himself famous when
he was supposed to be *laying low?* Enough of that, Frank. I don't need your
bossy, big brother scolding after all I been through. Besides, I can't help it.
Fame's a bloodhound on me, Frank, you know that. Anyhow, I survived, else
you wouldn't be sitting there right now, reading these words. So just sit back
and listen to the tale of what happened to me out of that dumb name, Ishcabibble. It's your fault I picked it—after burying that imposter's body in my
Kearney, Missouri, grave, I finally had time to read Mr. Melville's outrageous
whaling book, *Moby-Dick.* You insisted it would one day be an American classic, so I figured on improving myself by reading it. Don't think your bookish
ways didn't leave a cocklebur or two stuck in my socks, big brother. Me being
a robber and all, it seemed natural to steal my new name from Mr. Melville's
first line in the book. I changed Ishmael just enough to suit my personality.
Call me Ishcabibble, Frank. What follows is for you.

It was there in Galveston, four days and nights after winning the pigeon
shoot, that I sat in the Squid Roe Tavern, enjoying free glasses of Kentucky
whiskey, minding my own business. It was a dark, heavy timbered tavern,
dimly lit by ponderous chandeliers in the shape of long, twisted tentacles with
squat spermaceti candles at the ends. I sat at a table in the unfriendliest corner

of the place with my new comrade, Tatanka, a Sioux warrior who had taken second place in the contest. His name meant buffalo in the Lakota tongue. I had read in the newspaper only a week prior that the very last one of that once endless buffalo herd had been killed. Thank you, Colonel William Cody and friends. Perhaps this two-legged Indian buffalo was the last of his kind. Typical of his tribe, he couldn't handle liquor and sat at the table with his body weaving and head jerking as if he heard people from many directions calling his name. Any moment I expected his strong, dark face to land with a thud on the beer-soaked planks of the robust oak table.

Just then, the front door burst open and a group of three men and a parrot clambered into the tavern. "*BRACK!*" screeched a portly red parrot perched on the right shoulder of a crisp naval officer I soon learned was Captain Wrong John Silverspoon. "Seen IshcaBible?" the parrot croaked, "marksman and holy crusader?" The oxen one-armed barkeep pointed with his stump to the corner where I sat. I squinted at the newcomers, surprised by the parrot's line—strange words, Frank, for a man to repeat often enough a clever bird could memorize them. Fast too, given I hadn't been using the name Ishcabibble but four days. My hands went instinctively to the pearl handles of Peacemaker and Widowmaker—you know the killers, Frank: my Colts .45 and my .45 Smith and Wesson.

One in the group took an oil lamp from the bar, and the three marched directly to me. "If you're IshcaBible, state it, so we can get on with business," barked an older man from the right side of his mouth. He wore gold hoops the size of dollar coins in his droopy ears, and had two gold canines. Thick spectacles rested on his nose. His nearly bald head and wide face shone with a redness that spoke of impatience and irritability. He was Captain Silverspoon's chief mate, Dagger, and was usually called Chief. I pulled Peacemaker and dinked with her trigger.

"I go by Ishcabibble, as in scribble," I said, without looking at him.

"Your country needs you. We set sail tomorrow morning at 7:00 sharp," Chief Dagger said. Gobs of spit had collected at the corners of his thin lips.

"The Confederacy needs me?" Even though the Civil War ended seventeen years previous, I had still not accepted defeat. I know you thought me mule-headed, Frank, for carrying the grudge nigh on two decades, but who can argue our campaign of terror didn't work? The blue backs pulled out, Reconstruction ended, and Negroes stepped back in line.

"There is no Confederacy! America awaits Captain Wrong John Silverspoon!" Chief roared. I ignored him, opened the revolver and spun the cylinder. It clicked methodically. The captain, with the red parrot on his shoulder, stepped in front of his first mate.

"Let me finesse this thing, Chief," he said. The parrot whispered in his ear. He turned to it and replied, "I know, Krill. You think I just fell under the turnip wagon?" Captain Wrong John Silverspoon looked at me, his sharp nose flared like that of a haughty racehorse entering the gate. His arms hung apishly, as if he dragged his knuckles against the ground to show his dominance. His features in general had an overly sharp aspect—nose, chin, and ears like some rare cactus grown from an inner desert. His gray eyes, though, had a cunning glimmer, a quick, searching, inquisitive quality that constantly assessed the ripeness of the moment.

"Here's the deal, IshcaBible," he said. "I'm runnin' for president and I got one last position to fill on the *Lone Star*—my personal bodyguard and valet. Had me a vision the right fella'd be tough, but also a man of scripture, like me. Then along came news of a pigeon killin' son of a preacherman, name'a IshcaBible. Done deal far as I'm concerned."

"Are you people deaf? It's bibble, as in 'scribble.'" I don't know how they found out my daddy was a preacher. He had little influence on me, though, having got himself killed in the un-Christian pursuit of California gold when I was just two. Momma Zee was the man in my family, and I worshipped at the foot of her butter churn.

A fight broke out at the bar and we all looked over. One of the combatants lifted a bar stool over his head to crack his enemy, but he hit a squid chandelier instead and sent its tentacles spinning. The turning candles cast a parade of shadow and light over the dark wood and musty patrons of Squid Roe. The burly one-armed barkeep climbed over the bar and tossed one fighter, then the other, out of the tavern. Tatanka glanced at the hubbub, wobbly, then passed out, his head clunking against the table.

Another one of Captain Silverspoon's crew slapped a paper and pen on the table. He was a slight African man wearing a brightly flowered silk bandana, a shock of jet-black hair slicing across his forehead and covering his left eye completely. His smooth face had no whiskers save for a thin mustache that appeared drawn with a grease pencil. His ears were pierced with an array of gold hoops and dangling baubles of African design. When he spoke, I imagined he had something stuck in his throat, the voice was so strained. Even a dimwitted Pinkerton detective could have seen that the captain's Second Mate, Basmati Sweet, was a woman pretending to be a man.

"Sign on, IshcaBible. Reserve with us your place in history," she said.

I fiddled with Peacemaker, slowly taking one bullet at a time from the cylinder, examining it with one eye closed, and slipping it back in the chamber. "First of all, I ain't the least bit worried about my place in history. And second, I don't take orders from a nigra."

Before I could right my weapon, she had a gleaming two-edged throwing knife at my throat.

"*Never* call me that again!" she hissed. "I have worked too hard and crossed too many fences to endure that insult one more time." She pressed the cool blade against my Adams apple. I dared not swallow, for she had me so tight the movement of any muscle in my throat would draw blood.

Captain Wrong John Silverspoon reached down to her wrist and pulled it away from my throat. She snorted angrily but did not resist him. She withdrew the knife and thrust it in the sheath at her belt, next to a wrinkled, brown, shrunken head hanging by a length of gold chain screwed into its skull.

The captain spoke to me from the back of his hand. "Bad word, Ish. Our stance is all for one and one for one, kinda like the four musketeers—or however the hell many. You count 'em. I'm the guy, see, and I'm colorblind. Basmati Sweet is just as white as you or me, far as I'm concerned. *Comprende?*"

"No, I don't *comprende*," I said, half a click away from smoking that cheek African. "I got no interest in your journey. Got plans of my own. Leave me be." I shook the barrel of Peacemaker at them and turned back to my whiskey. The black lady stepped forward.

"You don't look like somebody who should pass up a chance at redemption," she said, hands on hips, her long, thin neck jutting forward. I suppose she was right. I had gotten a green and red face tattoo around the eyes and mouth. It was in a Polynesian design, like that character Queequeg in *Moby-Dick*, "who, by those hieroglyphic marks, had written out on his body a complete theory of the heavens and earth." Mine was a little more simple, and said only, "Will kill when necessary." I had shaved my head, and wore a silver hoop in my left ear—all to disguise myself as a salty dog hungry for high seas adventure. I had been drinking for three solid days and hadn't washed or shaved. I looked up at her and our eyes connected, as mine never had with a child of slaves. I saw fierceness and truth in her sharp brown eyes. They chilled me, and warmed me at the same time, as if she knew who I was, the life I lived, and knew in an instant the only prize still had some glitter to me was the one she just mentioned.

"Redemption. Well now." I sat up. "There's a strong box I would'a never thought old Jess—uh, Ishcabibble—would get a chance to bust open. Say a word or two more."

"*BRACK!*" squawked the chubby red parrot, flapping its short wings from the shoulder of the captain. "Redeem the White House from Perversion. Redeem the White House from Perversion. *BRACK!*" It whistled the first few notes of a cavalry charge.

The Chief pushed forward and said, "Join us, IshcaBible. We're going to redeem America. Cash it in like a book of Green Stamps. Join our revolution. We'll rescue America from the liberal horde. Then we'll kick that rat bastard out of Iraq!" Spit flew in the force of his words. His red face reddened and veins stood out on his forehead.

All four of them looked at me with eyes full of yearning, eyes like you and me saw all the time, Frank, when boys in the gang came to us with news of the perfect heist. Looking at Captain Silverspoon's crew, I wasn't, at the time, at all certain what they intended. It was the black woman that sparked my interest in pulling just one more job, the one of reaching down into the fires of Perdition to rescue my forsaken soul.

"Okay. I'll be your IshcaBible. I'll protect your captain from himself. But you got to take my Injun friend here as cook." I elbowed Tatanka. He groaned but didn't lift his head.

"Sorry," said the black lady. "We already have a cook—five-star. The captain is a very fussy eater."

"The Injun goes or I don't. Choose your druthers."

"Is he a cook?" she asked.

"Best in the Dakotas," I lied. Tatanka smacked his lips and started to snore.

The four of them huddled and argued for a minute. I heard the captain mention destiny and his unwillingness to cross thread it. The huddle broke open and Captain Wrong John Silverspoon stuck his hand at me. "Got yerself a deal!" he said. I shook his hand and tipped my black bowler at him. Basmati Sweet gestured at the paper and pen, and I put down my phony autograph. I grabbed Tatanka's limp wrist, shoved a pen in his fingers, grabbed his muscular paw, and marked his shipping papers with an X.

An old hag emerged from a hidden nook in the tavern and loomed over the table holding a crooked quartz crystal. "Let me tell your fortune," she said in a raspy, witchy voice, her thin, bony fingers and sharp, yellowed nails clawlike on the crystal. "The cloudy quartz knows all. For one gold doubloon you can see in advance, act on the knowledge, change the bad into good." She peered into the murky stone with her milky left eye, the right one a caved-in empty socket.

"Already I begin to see. There is a bird, long legged and white—."

"*BRACK!* A stork! There's a leggy stork in my future," said the parrot, crouching, seeming ready to pounce.

"She delivers a bundle, swaddled. It does not cry—but wait! Something is wrong. The child is stillborn. She delivers death—."

"Say it ain't so," croaked the parrot.

"Give me that thing!" blurted Chief Dagger. He lunged for the crystal. The hag anticipated his move, and with a turn of her wrist made the crystal vanish. Captain Silverspoon's eyes grew round and his mouth fell open.

"Where'd it go? Where'd it go?" he asked.

"Never reach directly for the mystery," growled the hag. "For ten years I coaxed it from a Mayan cave by *not* wanting it, begging it to leave me alone. When at last it trusted me, it's charms were mine alone to see. Now you scared it away." She leered at them with her one milky eye. "You have desires. I feel them pulsing in the air. You crave. You crave, but you refuse to read the signs. Blind, blind you find yourself, but even then you cannot admit you are wrong, when you are wrong, when you are wrong."

"Well, you're right about being wrong. Bingo. I'm Wrong John Silverspoon and we got us a country to make right. Let's hit it, gang." The captain turned on his heels and sauntered out of the Squid Roe Tavern, looking left and right as if daring anyone to challenge him.

That's how I signed up with the Pirates of the Potomac, Frank. It was the dingus dangest agreement I had ever made. Maybe that hag's curse was on me too, but I thought it well suited my purposes to be whisked out of town by the Governor of Texas. It was funny, brother, them being so blamed sure I was IshcaBible, no matter how many times I tried to plea-bargain down to bibble. Them going after me for a marksman made good sense, but forcing the .58 caliber bullet of saintliness into the barrel of a .45 caliber outlaw—that showed poor judgment. What they did was stick themselves with the most wanted man in America, your brother, Jesse James.

Being so headstrong, they consigned themselves to having their tale told through the eyes of murderer, a man who robbed and killed without compunction, who believed himself right because he had an injustice to rectify. They wanted it, and they got it—a bushwhacking Southern rebel who lived for the terror he could spread. They chose Jesse James, a man who put every ounce of his gumption against the ideals of democracy, equality, and freedom—and won!—a cloudy, gray victory though it was. Call me IshcaBible. I don't care. I'm still a cagey coyote who can chew a practical joke to the marrow. That's who they picked for witness. It's their own damn fault.

Chapter II

An Undertaker's Wet Dream

I threw a fat sponge soaked in cold water at Tatanka where he lay asleep in a corner of an upstairs room at the Squid Roe Tavern. Through the small window a predawn glow shoved some light into the sullen gray clouds hunkered down over the surly Gulf of Mexico. "Wake up, Injun!" I told him. "You got vittles for 200 to rustle up on the *Lone Star*." Tatanka groaned and rubbed the back of his neck.

"What do you mean, vittles?" He said, voice thick and nasally.

"You're the new cook on Captain Wrong John Silverspoon's campaign ship, the *Lone Star*. You can cook, can't you?"

Tatanka moaned and wiped the water from his face. "Never again. You hear me? On the graves of my ancestors, never again with that *wasichu* poison water." He threw the wet sponge at me. I ducked and it splat against the knotty pine wall. He struggled to his feet and went to the washbasin and splashed more water in his face. "Cook?" he asked. "You mean biscuits and gravy? Huh? Or *food*, like black bear stew, skunk pudding, elk liver pie? Can I cook?" He grunted and dried his face with a towel. I rolled us a couple of smokes, and the two of us grabbed our gear chests, threw them on our shoulders, and walked to the dock. The low clouds spit small rain on us. Our smokes required heavy puffing to keep from being snuffed. We walked toward the dim outline of tall-masted clippers and stout frigates moored to a long jetty, their hulls banging the dock's timber, ropes complaining about old wounds that never heal.

Heavy barrels stuffed with provisions rumbled and thudded as they were loaded on deck. Deep voices shouted orders I could not understand. It was a world completely foreign to me, a lubber, who had never, in all his born days, been to sea. An ill, icy wind crept up my back. Each step closer to the *Lone Star* I felt more stretched out, became somehow thinner, less substantial, less rooted to my own time and place, pulled like an Arabian jinni down into a magic lamp. I came to the gangplank and slowly walked up, each step taking me more deeply into another time, another set of circumstances, unmoored from history. It was a place I did not want to be, and yet had to be. Mr. Melville describes the sensation in *Moby-Dick*, through the voice of Elijah, who spoke to Ishmael and Queequeg before they boarded the Pequod: "Ye've shipped, have ye? Names down on the papers? Well, well, what's signed is signed; and what's to be, will be; and then again, perhaps, it won't be after all. Any how, it's all fixed and arranged a'ready; and some sailors or other must go with him, I suppose; as well these as any other men, God pity 'em!"

Each step closer to the deck of the *Lone Star* made me feel less real, more ghost, more phantom. My escape from death seemed a trick to me. I wondered if all of this was a dead man's dream, and it really *was me* after all, and not

Bobby Ford, lying in the grave of Jesse James. When I put my foot on the deck, I believed, was almost certain, I was dead indeed. I looked around in a stupor and fell over with my trunk. I could not find my balance to regain my feet when a strong arm reached from behind and lifted me. It was Tatanka, my Indian friend who watched out for me, just as Queequeg watched out for Ishmael in *Moby-Dick*. In the pre-dawn light, his skin was a color I had never seen, a shade of purple, deep, sophisticated, the color of an eggplant, almost iridescent. His long straight hair could have been a raven's wing.

"Huh. Not a good sign," said Tatanka, dusting off my back with hard slaps of his big hands—not that there was any dust. The wet deck was spotless. "Already bucked into the prickly pear."

I slapped my cheeks rapidly to knock off the stupor. "Don't you worry yourself about old Dingus—uh, Ishcabibble," I said, slipping up and betraying my true identity through the nickname I had been given in my early days with Quantrill's Raiders. Dingus was a name, thanks to the dime novels, nearly famous as Jesse James. You remember how I got it, Frank? It was twenty years before, March of 1862. I was just fifteen and had yet to take my first ride with you and the bushwhackers. I was loading rounds into the cylinders of the gang's revolvers. For those who don't know, the Colt's Navy .36 we used at the time didn't take independent bullets. You had to pre-load each chamber, almost like a musket—enough revolvers so every man could carry three or four. For a Missouri bushwhacker in the early 1860s there was no such thing as reloading your pistol during a fight.

One of them blamed rounds went off on me and took a chunk of my left middle finger. "Well ain't that the *dingus dangest* thing you ever did see," I said, watching the blood ooze from my fingertip. You, Frank, and all the boys got a big kick out of my reaction, and from then on, I was Dingus. I couldn't tell if Tatanka caught it or not, so I just kept talking, although a part of me wanted him to know me. I wasn't sure yet how far I could trust him. "I can cover my own wagers, Injun. Rode to hell and back more times than Beezelbub."

"Good to hear," Tatanka said in his low, smooth voice. He grabbed me by the shoulders and shook me. "We stick together, right? Sharpshooters." He drew a bead on an imaginary pigeon in the ship's rigging. I nodded at him and he nodded at me, then he turned and descended through the hatch down inside the *Lone Star.*

I stood uneasily on the rocking deck and took in my surroundings, feeling still more spirit than flesh. It was as if that ship existed somewhere outside of time. Well-groomed men in neat white sailor's caps, crisp blue blouses, and spotless knickers scurried about with bundles of wood, sacks of sugar, flour, coffee, boxes of canned fruit and vegetables, bellies of pork, beef jerky, box after box of Belgian chocolates, cases of eggs, live chickens and turkeys, goats and lambs, kegs of gunpowder, coils of hemp rope, harpoons, boxes of rifles, pistols, and bullets, and cannon balls.

Others polished brass fittings and rubbed oil into the railing, or painted red, white, and blue rings around the masts. Everyone appeared set to a task and steadfast in its achievement. I would have guessed them crew for a nobleman's yacht or the contestants at a sculling meet, but never, given my reading of *Treasure Island* and the adventures of Blackbeard and Captain Kidd, would I have imagined these dandies to be a crew of pirates. Only later was I to appreciate the utter genius of their disguise.

I had begun to let my eyes wander up the main mast to the lookout, imagining there might well be a goldsmith up there gilding the crown, when I heard the brash squawks and feathery thuds of the portly red parrot that had been perched on his captain's shoulder in Squid Roe Tavern. It flopped and fussed across the deck toward me, apparently trying to gain flight. It clawed its way onto the helm and lovingly rubbed the binnacle lamp—lit at night to navigate by the compass there—with its cracked, worn beak.

"*BRACK!* Pretty lamp. Pretty lamp. *BRACK!*" said the bird, eyes closed, rubbing one side, then the other, of the glass-encased oil lamp. Its eyes brightened, and it leapt to the helm and hopped to the uppermost arm, put a wing edgewise above its eyes and peered at the sea. "You see that? That a stork off the port? Them black legs go all the way up. Don't they? Just like my sweetie." He gave a wolf whistle. "That's some bird, Ish. Let me tell ya." He gave that wolfish whistle again. "Most loyal fowl in the world, stork—loyal fowl in the world. Builds its nest on a chimney—on a chimney. Delivers babies right down the chimney. Just like Santa. Just like Santa."

I pulled Peacemaker and aimed it at the parrot. "What on earth?" I said. "I heard'a smart parrots that can speak word puzzles for peanuts, but you—you seem to be making it up as you go." I was seriously inclined to blow the little demon's head off. It raised its short red wings in the air.

"The bird in brain stays mainly on the Maine. Mainly on the Maine, *BRACK!* Any idea who you're holding up?"

"I must be dead and this is hell. *You're* a little red demon is all I can figure, and you better stop talking before I deliver you back to the devil," I said, still pointing the long black barrel of Peacemaker straight at its sparsely feathered red head.

"Listen, pal, I'm Krill. Better get to know me. To know me is to love me. I set the tone for this campaign. I lay it out, figure it out, and make it happen—make it happen. Put down the gun, Ish. Put it down."

I wanted to shoot that nasty sprite and get the hell out of there, until, thanks to you, Frank, a calm voice not my own advised me to settle down and put my hat on straight. I kept the gun on Krill, opened the black trunk, took out my favorite black bowler, placed it neatly on my head. "How is it, Krill, you can talk so good?"

"*BRACK!* Magic! Magic! Kissed a frog and turned into a talking parrot." He whistled the first few notes of a cavalry charge.

I holstered my .45 and scratched my head up under the black bowler. You know me, Frank, I can take a joke as well as dish one, but a parrot that talks like a human? I could not imagine what sort of enchanted circus I had wandered into. When in doubt, I've always said, play along. "So if you got turned into a talking parrot, what were you before?"

"I was but a tailor. *BRACK!* A lowly cutter of the cloth. Mute too. I kissed off my humanity for a voice. With that voice, with that voice, I will cut from rough cloth the robe of a king—robe of a king!" Krill danced back and forth on the helm of *Lone Star*, clucking and jabbering in a delighted gabble. He paused, winked at me, and said, "Didn't count on the parrot outfit. Win some, lose some." He scratched himself rapidly under the chin with a scabrous gray claw.

I pushed my hat back, smiled, and shook my head at the strange bird. What, Frank, in God's name was it when the brains of a gang was a bewitched parrot? I felt a tap on the shoulder and turned to find an ashen-faced, jowly man in a preacher's collar and black smock with a silver marshal's badge pinned at the chest. He wore a heavy, black leather belt around his waist, decked with leg irons and a coiled bullwhip. "IshcaBible, I presume," he said, in a stilted, overly precise tenor, his words smooth, calculated, and cold. "We have something in common, both of us the sons of parsons." He eyed me up and down, taking special measure of my sidearms and my face. "It doesn't fit, a man of God tattooed with the idolatrous runes of a savage."

That icy chill I spoke of went more frosty. Damn me! Jesse James, first day of my ocean escape, face-to-face with a marshal. I tipped my black bowler forward and low over my forehead. My hands went slowly to the butts of Peace- and Widowmaker. "I don't believe we've met," I said, looking hard into his pale blue eyes.

"I'm Tosspot, ship's marshal and judge." He extended a pasty, unblemished hand in my direction. I ignored his soft excuse for a man's hand.

"Nice racket, if you can work it." I half smiled, half sneered at him. "And a preacher to boot." Marshal, judge, and priest, I thought. Hunt 'em down and hang 'em high. Absolve yourself on the way back home.

"Comes in handy," he said. "Where you from, IshcaBible?"

"The land of misery."

Krill clucked and muttered from his perch on the helm, but he didn't join the conversation.

"Well," said the marshal, "there you go, another common bond between us. I too am a good Missouri boy."

"Never mentioned good."

"Well you had better behave on this voyage. We don't take to that secesh attitude, do you hear me? Any bushwhacking to be done out here will be sanctioned by the highest law in the land before it begins." He flicked his silver badge with the index finger of his right hand. Boy, Frank, I hadn't heard the term "secesh" in a while—that way we had of shortening the word secession during the Civil War. And bushwhacker, that one too had gone dusty as the term for a Confederate guerilla. Was he onto me already? I wondered.

"Tell me, IshcaBible," the marshal continued, "have you a favorite Biblical passage?"

"Thou shalt not kill." I said slowly, casting him a sour smirk and stroking my holsters.

Krill chuckled in a deep, gizzardly way. "*BRA-HA-HACK!* Bit of a card, Bible? Thou shalt not kill. Oh, man, that's precious. Ooh ha ha ha!"

"You ought to strike that one from your repertoire, IshcaBible," said Tosspot, adjusting his preacher's collar. "Could get you in trouble around here. Wrong John's not disposed to take implied criticism of his judicial policy." I was well aware Captain Silverspoon had sent more men and women to the gallows than any governor in U.S. history. Quite a feat, Frank, given the roughshod story of this nation.

"*BRACK!* They called his hanging tree the undertaker's wet dream— undertaker's wet dream."

"That's crude, Krill. A bit of decorum, please." The bird stood at attention and saluted him with its left wing. He hopped to the deck and waddled away, gabbling to himself. "Enough chitchat," said Marshal Tosspot. "The Chief wants to see you in his quarters. He doesn't like to be kept waiting." I hoisted my black gear chest on a shoulder and walked aft, in the direction the marshal pointed.

Chapter III

Wax and Wick

I found the Chief's quarters located off the poop deck, in a spacious room absent windows except for a small one at the door that could be covered by a sliding wooden panel, and one along the rear wall similarly furnished. Only one picture hung from the wall: a black and white photograph of Chief with a former Captain of *Liberty* known as The Great Communicator. The only furniture in the room were a long, red oak desk neatly stacked with papers and rolled maps bound with raffia, and a single chair in front. Two fat candles burned on either side of him. Thick bifocals perched on the end of Chief Dagger's long, Roman nose. He looked up at me over the rims of his glasses, didn't smile or speak, but motioned me to sit at the small, plain chair in front of his desk. I declined the invitation, preferring to lean against the doorjamb with my right shoulder. Experience had taught me it was best to take on a sidewinder at an angle.

I could not get over the gold hoops in his ears; they seemed completely out of character. Only later would I come to appreciate them as something he couldn't help, like a mole or a wart that had grown on its own from the deep soil of his pirate soul. The gold canines, though, they looked natural as butter on a johnnycake. His coat was dark and well tailored, so perfectly fit I imagined it a second skin, only to be shed when he was over-fed with wrath. By choosing Chief Dagger as first mate, Wrong John showed his cunning, showed that he had studied the mistakes of Captain Wrong John Johnson Silverspoon, his father, whom he judged as having wrongly hiring a first mate his considerable junior. The son of Silverspoon did the opposite, hired a man much his senior both in experience and in bearing. Thus he would skip the ribbing his father took for making a yokel his second in command.

"You have an important position here, IshcaBible," Chief Dagger said. "The captain has a gut feeling about you, and I don't want you to give him indigestion." He took off his glasses, chewed on the end, and leaned back in his chair. "You will not find me the intuitive type. I will judge you by your performance, and it better be spotless." I nodded at him. Chief raised his eyebrows, leaned forward, stuck his neck out, and lifted his hands up as if about to trap a cricket on his desk. I knew what he wanted. Even among bushwhackers the rules of rank required superiors be addressed as "sir." I had been in charge so long it felt like digging up a loved one to address anybody as "sir." Then I heard your voice, Frank, advising me to get my hat on straight. "Yes, sir," I said half-heartedly. It appeared to be enough for him, and he leaned back and chewed on the end of his glasses.

"Good. Now let me give you a briefing on your new boss. He is a man of routines. The daily regimen must be exact. No surprises. Up at 6:00, jog till 7:00, bathe, dress, breakfast 7:30. Eggs, bacon, toast, fresh squeezed orange juice, strong black coffee—a pot of it. Chocolate always on hand. You get him started on the right foot, IshcaBible, or it'll be hell on the rest of us all day long. He's used to a genteel life, and the rigors at sea will be no excuse for him to question his innate right to be pampered. Lunch precisely at noon. Dinner 5:00 p.m. Understand?" He had that expectant look on his face again. "Yes, sir," I gave him. Footsteps of the crew clomped on the poop deck above our heads. Low rumbles slithered through the hull from its grinding on the dock.

"Wrong John Silverspoon is precise, but he is not unplayful. He likes a good joke and is immensely congenial. He is not a practiced leader, but a natural one. He knows his strengths and plays to them. Everything else is up to the rest of us." Dagger paused and took a drink of water. He sucked his teeth loudly and looked back at me.

"He has the enviable gift of single-mindedness. Once he has decided a course, the debate is over. Do not try to change his mind, ever. He is a man of faith who receives guidance from above. Do not attempt to argue with his higher authority. Talk scripture with him. It comforts him. He likes his clothes crisp, underwear starched, pajamas fresh every night. Lights out at 10:00 sharp. No horseplay. No drinking. Discipline, IshcaBible, discipline. Keep your wits. You're a sharpshooter. Let no harm come to him. Clear?" He raised his eyebrows at me. I wasn't going to curtsy to him again. Instead I pulled Widowmaker, spit on her pearl handle, and polished her with a corner of my shirttail.

"Any questions?" asked the Chief. He jerked his head back and looked at the ceiling where a loud bang had just sounded. I imagined someone had dropped a case of chocolates.

"Yeah. What's he up to? What's he really want?" I asked.

"Between you, me, and the yardarm, he's a wayward boy trying to prove himself. He wants to silence his critical mother, outdo his ambitious father, stick it to his detractors. He never took his life too seriously until he almost lost it in a drinking accident with horses. He found Jesus, and his ambition. He gave up drinking. From that point forward he has sought redemption. Classic prodigal son. It's a handy package for us, really, to have a man operating from such basic instincts. Leaves the playing field wide open. Tabula rasa. We've got him trained on saving America. A lot can happen there, a very great deal."

I tipped my bowler at him for the frankness. "What's with the Texas accent? Rings hollow to me."

"His family is blue blood, Ivy League Yankee. They came to Texas for blubber, and have gotten rich off of it."

"So he's a carpetbagger."

"You could say that. His father made the move on blubber. Wrong John isn't cut from the same cloth. He started and bankrupt two or three blubber companies. Bailed on them just in time to make some cash. His claim to fame is baseball. He got a stadium built in Dallas, and the people loved him for it. He cashed in for a tidy profit and moved into the governor's mansion. With his dad the former vice president, then president, he has the pedigree to take the executive chair."

"Guess we'll see."

He nodded at me and said, "Find your bunk in the forecastle. Settle in for twenty minutes. Make ranks on deck when you hear the trumpet call. Dismissed." He had his right hand ready, almost quivering, to return my salute, but I'm sorry, Frank, I just couldn't do it. I opened the door and slipped onto the deck. I wandered through the busy crew hoisting, hauling, polishing, painting, tying down. One thing that surprised me, Frank, was the extent of rope involved in sailing. Everything on deck was tied to something else, or tied down, secured, adjusted, set, or moved, by a length of rope. I couldn't imagine how anyone kept track of all those ropes, and knew what would happened if this one over here was pulled instead of that one over there. It fascinated me, and I spent a while studying the various connections. I slowly wandered toward the hatch, and down into to the cramped, dark, packed galley where I found Tatanka at a small, square butcher-block table rubbing his temples.

"What's for breakfast, Cookie?" I asked him.

"Never again. You hear me? On my ancestors' graves. *Wasichu* poison water." He groaned and squeezed his head in his hands. Goats and sheep bleated from their small pens at the far end of the galley. Chickens clucked and pecked at the wire of their cages.

"I'm trying to find my bunk. Where do they keep the crew?" I asked Tatanka.

Rosy cheeked young men in their crisp white shirts and sharp blue knickers stuffed boxes and bags into the compact shelves of the galley. They asked Tatanka where to put things and he brushed them off with the back of his hand.

"You sleep with me," he told me. "There's an extra bunk behind the galley. Sharpshooters." He slapped his hands together and squeezed them. "Tight." I carried my trunk to a small room at the rear of the kitchen. There I found top and bottom bunks, the top one empty save for a thin feather mattress. I stowed my trunk below, next to his, unbuckled my holster, and draped it over a corner of the bunk. I decided to get my Bible and my *Moby-Dick*, and pulled out the trunk to find them. I climbed into the bunk and lay down.

As I rested in the bunk, rocked by the roaming sea, I tried to look into that hag's creamy crystal. I tried to imagine what was ahead, and to forget what was behind. I kept hearing the Chief's words, about Wrong John being a prodigal son, looking for redemption. What was I if not that? Second Mate Basmati Sweet had tempted me with the very same thing: redemption. Did I and Silverspoon hold the same hope? Maybe we did, I reckon, but from different ends of the candle. He wanted to redeem his wasted youth by doing impressive things. I wanted to redeem myself by somehow *undoing* the terrible things I had done in my unhinged youth. We burned the same candle from opposite ends, and it was a question of wax and wick, brother. Was there enough of both for each of us to be redeemed? Would just one of us have enough light by which to finish his work? Or would our flames meet in the middle, consuming wax and wick in heat and light until there was nothing left of either one of us?

Chapter IV

Gather Around the Try-Works

I had been looking through my Bible, and in *Moby-Dick*, to get ready in case IshcaBible was called to the pulpit, when a flourish of trumpets sounded from the deck. Tatanka walked in from the kitchen and asked if I thought we had to go up there. I told him we probably ought to make a show, and so we climbed out of the hatch to the deck. Wet hemp rope stretched from mast to cleat, from sail to yard, from yard to rail and everywhere in between. A subtle breeze softly flapped the ends of the furled sails. The entire crew had taken rank to starboard and port and stood at attention under the close gray sky. Their faces, in the diffuse light of a cloudy dawn, had the glow of freshly opened rosebuds, and their glistening blue uniforms had, in the drizzle, the appearance of new leaves dappled with dew. I and Tatanka did not have uniforms: he wore an off-white muslin shirt, sleeves cut off below the elbows, brown dungarees cut off below the knees, and no shoes, while I had on a worn leather vest over a denim shirt, my favorite snakeskin pants, and black cowboy boots. An owl feather was tied to the end of a thin braid of hair on the right side of Tatanka's head. I wore the black bowler. Both of us had twin furies holstered to our waists.

We joined the collection of laborers assembled aft around the mizzenmast. Like us, they did not have uniforms, but wore simple, earthy clothes that matched the shades of their skin. Presently, the trumpeters brought their golden horns to their lips and played a fanfare most angelic. Off the gangway strode Captain Wrong John Silverspoon. As he ambled apelike toward the quarterdeck, he winked and grinned at people and pointed his finger at them and pretended to shoot them, which caused those hit by his magic personality bullets to fall immediately and everlastingly in love with him. He was a real Cupid with his pretend six-shooter, making matches with himself that were meant to be forever. I moved forward and butted into the line of sailors to get a better view.

Captain Wrong John Silverspoon stood at the quarterdeck rail in a wide stance that made me think he had always wished he were bowlegged. His pet bird perched on his right shoulder while his officers arrayed into a half-moon behind him. I recalled Ishmael's first impression of Captain Ahab: "There was an infinity of firmest fortitude, a determinate, unsurrenderable willfulness, in the fixed and forward dedication of that glance." Captain Silverspoon also gazed forward willfully, but not with what I would call fortitude. His bearing more reminded me of someone in church who had just recalled an off-color joke and was holding back a smirk. Then it shifted, and his angular, prickly face expressed a sentimental ferocity, the shallow toughness of someone who wants to be taken more seriously than he deserves—a sort of unearned gravity. He took a deep breath and addressed us.

"I think we all know why we're here," he said. "I know why I'm here. Chief Dagger knows why he's here. Second Mate Basmati Sweet knows why he's here. Krill, well, he ain't sure yet, but he'll catch on." He poked the parrot with his left index finger and Krill squawked and ruffled his feathers. The crew laughed quietly. "You see, that's what we're all about, knowing why we're here. That's what makes us unique in America. We know. America needs that. It's hungry for it. America is sick of Captain Bubba and all his never-ending questions—not knowing this, not knowing that, following orders from the little general in his pants." The crew giggled. "When he got caught, he claimed he didn't know—didn't understand the definition of knowing right from wrong. Come on, these are the basics, folks, and we're bringing them back to the White House." The crew erupted in cheers and applause. I had no idea what he was talking about.

He held up his hands to quiet the crew. The breeze picked up, and the corners of the sails flapped louder. The raindrops, smaller than grains of sand, grew to the size of pebbles. "Before you get all hepped up on me, me, me, I want you to meet the officers of the *Lone Star*. This is the team that's going to win me the pennant. They represent my philosophy of hardly working. Each of them has skills beyond me, talent unlike me, experience ahead of me. I got them involved because I'm not a micro manager. I brought in these good people to make the hard decisions, knowing their boss approves of everything they do. That's called *leadership*.

"I'm going to bring them up in reverse order. Least but not last is Pinch, my financial guru. She's gonna make sure my checkbook balances." He turned to his left and motioned Pinch forward. She stumbled from her place at the end of the line, her long, awkward legs moving independent of her body. She found her way to the captain's side, stood a hand taller than he, saluted, and smiled with her long full teeth. Even after she stopped smiling she appeared still to smile a little, her teeth too large for her thin lips to completely cover. Pinch stood at attention and saluted, her eyes shifting rapidly from one side of the ship to the other, and seemed ready to stand there forever, until finally Captain Silverspoon nudged her and she slouched back to her place in line.

"Next to her is Dr. von Shlop, our science officer. He's the magician who can turn any piece of science on its ear, make it look phony, or *shazam!* it's a goat, or a frog, or whatever in the heck we want." The doctor came forward with small precise steps to match his small body and trim gray goatee. He wore a full-length blue robe embroidered with they symbols for dollars and cents, and a pointed blue cap similarly decorated. In his right hand he carried a thin white wand. He raised it, waved it about, and had the trumpeters instantly playing *Hail to the Chief*.

"See what I mean?" said Silverspoon, after Dr. von Shlop cut the music, and Krill stopped clapping his wings. "Maestro's got me president before I even run. That's what we're all about—proactivity." The scientist returned to the officer ranks.

"Next, but not most, is our Oil Czar, Crude." Forward walked a short man who stood not quite at the captain's shoulder, but was considerably wider. He had what seemed but a single hair on his head that he had wrapped and spread like an endless thread to cover his baldness. His pouty lips were red and translucent like those of an infant. He had a broad hawkish nose and wore an elaborate scrimshaw around his neck.

"Crude's key here. He's Mr. Blubber. The Captain of Fat. The Giant of Jiggle. And I'm not talkin' about his body." Wrong John chuckled, as did his officers and crew. Crude gave a small smile that showed only four of his front teeth, making him look like a woodchuck. "Seriously, folks, Crude is key. We may appear to be politicians. We may look like and pretend ourselves to be aspiring public servants. But let me tell you something. We're in the *business* of government. If it ain't profitable, it ain't worth it. Crude here is our cash cow. Get to know him if you're at all attracted to stock options." The crew applauded. Crude bowed, causing his gathered hair to nearly slide off his head, and returned to his place.

"Next up is Sir Yes Sir, the ship's diplomat." A powerful African came forward. His broad shoulders and well-muscled frame filled his blue blazer commandingly. He was the sort of black man who, a generation previous, would have commanded top dollar at the slave auctions. Now, Frank, he stood at attention next to the man who was to be president, and he was to be the president's chief diplomat, the highest position in government ever achieved by a man of his race. What promise he carried in that strong frame! How much hope gleamed in his proud eyes, stood out on his strong chin. Pity that trailblazer earned his stripes on a pirate ship. Isn't it so that a buccaneer's idea of diplomacy is to ask politely before robbing you, and smile before he cuts your throat?

Sir Yes Sir stood at attention, an angular hat in his hand. "This here's a five star general," said the captain. "He's a man who knows combat, knows battle, understands chain of command. He can give orders, but more importantly, he can follow 'em. Best thing though, about havin' a military man your diplomat, is that it scares the snot out of other countries. When a general's runnin' your diplomacy, military idn't a final option, it's a *gotcha* option. Military force could be your third choice, could be second, could be—*gotcha!*" He pulled his left and right finger revolvers and fired a few quick personality bullets across the deck. Sir Yes Sir squinted and crumpled the left edge of his black trousers in his hand. He saluted and turned back to the half-moon line of officers, looking quickly at Basmati Sweet, who slightly raised her eyebrows then bit a corner of her lip.

"In shoot number five we got us a Brahma bull straight out'a the Great Western Ro-day-o. Meet your gunner, Yo Ho Ho!" Out from the line of officers strode a short, robust man with a patch over his left eye and a monocle in his right. He didn't wear the usual black, angular hat of an officer, but instead had a blue scarf tied in a band across his forehead. Like the Chief, he also wore a gold earring, and I wondered if they were in the same club, except that Yo Ho Ho's gold hoop attached between the nostrils of his nose. He did not have any gold teeth. He placed his extended index fingers on either side of his head, lowered, and charged at Captain Silverspoon, who, pretending himself a matador, held out an invisible cape for the gunner to run through. Yo Ho Ho charged through, came around, reached out his hand and gave his captain a solid shake. "Olé!" hollered Wrong John Silverspoon. "Olé!" returned the crew.

"This here's what you call the two of your one-two punch. Sir Yes Sir sets 'em up; Yo Yo knocks 'em down. He's a tough SOB who shoots first and probably never asks questions. He's going to liberate the American military from the powder puff closet of Captain Bubba and restore the services to their former dignity under my dad and The Great Communicator. He minces no words, takes no prisoners, and tolerates no dissent. If you're lookin' for a pay raise, he's your man—but you better prove your case, or he'll walk you down the plank." The gunner revealed his gritted teeth, saluted briskly, and returned to the line next to Sir Yes Sir, whose hands made fists.

Silverspoon introduced the remainder of the officers: Marshal Tosspot, lawman and judge; Basmati Sweet, second mate; Krill, the wonder bird, and Chief Dagger, the only one he invited to speak.

Dagger came at it sideways, golden earrings swaying gently, and spoke from the right side of his mouth. "Open the try-works!" he shouted. Ten Latin American laborers from the back of the boat ran forward to a red brick structure nearly six feet tall halfway between the quarterdeck and the main mast. They surrounded the short, wide, brick structure, and reached up to release the clasps on a square hatch fifteen feet across. They slipped the paneled oak lid behind the try-works to the deck, revealing three huge, round steel pots the shape of silver balls cut in half, polished to a stunning luster. The pots rested in holes on the top plate of a great furnace, so that only the lips of the pots were flush with the iron top plate. This was the place where whale hunters made their money in the fire of rendering whale flesh to oil. Mr. Melville describes one evening around the try-works on the Pequod:

> "the harpooners wildly gesticulated with their huge pronged forks and dippers; as the wind howled on, and the sea leaped, and the ship groaned and dived, and yet steadfastly shot her red hell further and further into the blackness of the sea and the night...freighted with savages and laden with fire, and burning a corpse, and plunging into that blackness of darkness...."

The Chief looked into the untried try-works of the *Lone Star*. "Everyone gather around the try-works!" he shouted in a sonorous voice. "Look deeply into the try-pots. Look until your reflection smiles back at you. Then you will understand." The crew broke ranks in a scuffle of boots and excited shouts on their way to the square, red brick structure.

They shoved the Mexican and Puerto Rican laborers out of their way, gathered round the stout chimney, pulled themselves above the brick ledge, and gawked into the shiny pots, hoping to see themselves. I noticed Captain Silverspoon jealously leaning forward from the quarterdeck rail, craning his neck at the lustrous crucibles, desperate to see his *own* reflection in the shiny silver.

"Look deeply, men," said Chief Dagger. "Find your reflection, or the mission is lost before it begins. These pots are the heart and soul of liberty. This is where we cook the whale fat down to oil, take chunks of flesh and render them into gold." The crew grappled for position on the edge of the try-works. Men, and one or two women, fought for the angle that would reflect their faces, show them how pretty and important they were, assure their belonging in the fate of Silverspoon. One young man with bright red hair was pushed, and he tumbled into a shiny vat. He found his place on all fours at the curved bottom and looked into the sloping silver wall in front of him. He reared back on his knees and clasped his hands toward the sky. "There I am! It's me! Spoon by spoon with our great captain!" He stood, reached up with his arms, and was pulled from the vat. Others tumbled into the try-pots, laughing and shouting praises at their reflections in the silver.

"Attention!" shouted Chief. The crew scrambled out of the pots and back to ranks along both sides of the *Lone Star*. "This is not a game. These pots are the sacred cauldrons of our deeper purpose. We do not just run a campaign. We do not merely seek office. We strive for greatness. We strive to transform America, and the world. Our mission is to render all useless blubber into valuable oil. All riffraff, all scum, all waste and idleness can be rendered, with enough focused power, into useful, contributing, profitable goods. Ours is a system, a deliberate, purposeful, unwavering commitment to the American way, to our enterprise, our work ethic, our efficiency, our single-minded devotion to bottom-line results." Chief saluted and stepped back to his position in the half-moon of officers.

"There it is," said Captain Silverspoon. "What'd I tell you about the help? I hire the best, and let 'em do their job." The officers shifted in stance. I could see Chief Dagger's jaw muscles working. He pulled on the gold hoop in his left ear.

"The beauty of those try-pots reminds me of an old saying," Wrong John said. Krill whispered something in his ear. "Shut up, Krill, I remember this one. It's about trying. One of my favorites. Ahem. If at first you don't—if you can't get it—the, uh, the—if the first time you don't, don't—can't get the damn—if you don't get it right the first time, try, try again. There it is." He bobbed his head and looked back and forth at the crew. "Point is, you don't give up. It's about gumption, sticking with it, hanging tough. Mistakes will be made along the way. Heck, I might even flub up once or twice. We keep pushing on. We keep our focus and our discipline. We stay on task. We stay on message. We stick with what works, and we do not deviate. We pull no prisoners and take no punches. We do whatever it takes, to win. Your job, each and every one of you, is to remember the reflection you saw in that try-pot, and to try harder than you ever tried before. You take personal responsibility for my victory. Do that, and before three months are out, we will stand together at the helm of *Liberty!*" The crew erupted in cheers and applause. Captain Silverspoon bobbed his head and took in the approval as long as it lasted.

"I want to finish with some inspiration. IshcaBible, can you come up here?" I had a hunch that was next. They hadn't rendered my flaccid "bibble" into Grade A Bible without intending to burn it. I sauntered past the rigid sailors, past the exposed try-pots, and up the quarterdeck stairs. Basmati Sweet gave me a slight smile and twitched her grease-pencil mustache. I nodded. Marshal Tosspot curled his lip and looked away from me. I took a position to Silverspoon's right, Krill on his shoulder between us. "This here's IshcaBible, whaler, sharpshooter, man of The Word. He's like me, tough, but compassionate. He'll be by my side most all the time—sort of a Good Book with legs—and a gun. Show 'em what you got, IshcaBible."

I quickly studied the second yardarm of the main mast and figured ten decent shots could produce a little drama. All number of ropes crisscrossed the mast, and I wasn't sure I could pull it off, but the challenge made it interesting. In a flash I pulled Widowmaker and Peacemaker and blasted the knots holding the rolled second mainsail to the yardarm. It unfurled like a giant white flag and popped against the mast from a gust of wind. Everyone cheered. Wrong John Silverspoon clapped and Krill whistled, and when it grew quiet, the captain spoke.

"Nice shootin,' IshcaBible. Looks like it's time to set sail. But just to show us the other side, bag me a Bible quote, would ya, Ish?"

I was prepared for the request. "In Job, Chapter 41, the Lord compares His greatness to that of a whale. He asks Job if he thinks he can catch a whale with a fishhook, or drill a hole in its jaw with a thorn. You think he can?"

"No, sir!" shouted the crew.

"Of course not. The Lord advises small humans to beware of stirring the great leviathan. He is so fierce, like the Lord, that no man may stand before him without being crushed. The Lord advises Job he's not going to take this one with a bridle for a horse. To the whale, He says, iron is as straw, brass as rotten wood. The whale laughs at the shaking of a spear. He is the only creature of the earth made without fear.

"So ya'll think you're gonna subdue God's greatest creature on earth?" I hollered.

A few scattered shouts of "Yea!" returned from the crew. From the captain's shoulder came the hushed voice of Krill. "BRACK. Off message, Ish. Call in the Coast Guard." I could hear muttering from the officers behind me.

"You think you're going to subdue nature and squeeze her for every drop of oil, even as she and God are one?"

The crew was silent.

"Let's turn to another Bible for the answer." I pulled from my pocket a page torn from *Moby-Dick*. "This here's Mr. Melville's bible of the whaling trade, *Moby-Dick*. He's got something to say about the whaler's craft:

> But, though the world scouts at us whale hunters [looks down on them], yet does it unwittingly pay us the profoundest homage; yea, an all-abounding adoration! for almost all the tapers, lamps, and candles that burn round the globe, burn, as before so many shrines to our glory!

"So there's a riddle for you. Only by killing God the whale can you get the candles by which to offer him your prayers. Without you hunting him, he would not be honored. So go off bravely, *Lone Star*, knowing that what you hunt is the Almighty himself!" I tipped my hat and walked to midships next to Tatanka and the Latin laborers. None of the crew said a word or hardly moved a muscle. I liked the tingle it gave me, Frank—like a train holdup. Only the Chief, it seemed, was able to make something out of my conundrum.

He stepped beside the captain and shouted, "Thank you, IshcaBible. We have set for ourselves a lofty goal. Small goals make small men. Only great goals offer greatness." He clapped his hands resolutely. The captain and officers followed, and soon the ship filled with applause.

Tatanka elbowed me and said, "Pretty good response to your buffalo chip." I grinned and threw an arm around his shoulder.

"Hoist the mizzen and frock the mainmast! We got us a country to save!" shouted Wrong John. The crew hollered its approval, broke ranks, and scurried up the rigging to free the sails, set and trim them. Others unleashed the moorings while a third bunch gathered at the handspikes of the capstan, turned it around, and weighed anchor. The breeze freshened, the rain came hard, and the *Lone Star* was on her way.

Chapter V

Terror Worked

Once the pilot had guided the *Lone Star* through the narrow mouth of Galveston Bay and into the open waters of the Gulf (around 8 a.m.) the sailors were ready for breakfast. Captain Silverspoon, of course, had to have his eggs precisely at 7:30. He had returned them twice for being wrongly cooked. I finally had to do it myself, as my friend Tatanka did not understand the concept of sunny-side-up, and kept turning the eggs and breaking the yolks. Even Second Mate Sweet got involved, questioning Tatanka's credentials as a chef. He pulled his big jack knife from his pocket, opened the blade, and showed it to her. "A gift," he said, "after I finished cooking school." She didn't know how to take it and left the galley, advising him to "get it right" this time.

Tatanka did a lot better with the big meal for the crew. He had the help of several laborers, the lead man of which was a Mexican named Roberto Mendoza, who spoke with a slight lisp. Mendoza was so lovestruck with *mi novia*, as he put it, his fiancée, I worried every time he picked up a knife he would carelessly lop a finger. Tatanka broke fifteen dozen eggs and scrambled them on big black skillets over his roaring iron stove. It was an unusual meal for men at sea, and would be the last time they received eggs while campaigning. Tatanka served bacon, grits and fresh oranges along with the eggs. By 10:00, the meal and clean up were done, and Tatanka set Roberto Mendoza to lunch preparations: slicing ham and cheese for sandwiches. I and Tatanka retired to our quarters behind the kitchen and settled in for a nap—at least that's what I intended.

No sooner had we lain our heads in our bunks, when Tatanka asked me a question. "Why are you running, Ishcabibble? Why are you going to sea?"

I sat up, leaned on an elbow, and looked over the edge of the top bunk. Across from me on the floor Tatanka had made a cloth alter in four directions with colors of the four peoples: red, yellow, black, and white. He had his *chanupa*, his sacred redstone pipe, on a stand in the middle. "Who said I was running?" I asked. He didn't answer, just grunted. Somehow, he knew I was trying to escape. "I don't know," I said. "Got into some trouble."

"Me too," he said. "I killed the white Indian agent at Rosebud." He spoke no further for some time. "He said we would have freedom to sun dance. Then he called in the army on us. I could not accept this lie. We have to dance, or all hope dies."

I let his story set a while. "That the first white man you killed?"

"No. I killed many. Not enough. I fought at the Greasy Grass, against Yellow Hair." I knew that was their name for General Custer. "I have killed many. This last one, I shouldn't have. A reservation Indian is already in prison. You kill the warden, you better make a break. I rode south until I reached the sea. Now, I'm on it—can go no farther, unless we sail off the edge of the earth."

I rolled a smoke and offered it to him, then rolled one for myself. I gave us both a light; the rough wooden room filled with gray smoke. The footsteps of sailors on the deck above us felt like being underneath a dancehall. The ribbing of the ship creaked and groaned under the push of wind against the sails and wave against the hull. "What about you, Dingus? You kill a few?"

He had caught the nickname. "Yeah. I killed myself."

"Who am I talking to, the ghost of Jesse James?"

"Maybe. I'm supposed to have died a few months back. One of my gang, a pisser named Bobby Ford, wanted to kill me with his brother Charlie—reward money. I and my wife, Zerelda, planned a trick on them to fake my death and bury one of them as me. We invited them to the house in St. Joe, Missouri,

April 3, 1882. It was a chilly spring day. The maple trees out front had just sprouted their new leaves, and the tulips stood up bright red in the dark flowerbeds. I gave the Fords a false opening by taking off my holster, draping it over a chair, and pretending to find the horse painting above the mantle a little crooked. I stood up there on the wobbly oak chair, my back to the Fords, hoping my guardian demon would nudge one more bullet off fatal for me.

"Sure as thunder, little Bobby Ford shot me in the back, a shade inside my left kidney. I had tucked a third pistol in my pants, and I killed him as I fell from the chair with a blind shot under my left arm. Before Charlie could draw, I tucked and rolled, and pinned him down. I told him he was a dead man if he didn't go along with our story. We dressed his brother in my clothes, with my wedding ring on his finger and my holster around his waist. I and Zerelda doused the floor with oil and set the house on fire. I went into hiding. Zerelda went into grieving.

"That's how we worked it, the charred remains of Bobby Ford laid to rest in the Kearney cemetery, next to my half-wit brother Archie, my wife Zerelda the only person in black who knew I hadn't actually died. I look forward to, and count the days, when I can walk into my Momma Zee's kitchen, find her there with Zerelda, Jesse Jr., Mary, and Frank, and dumbfound them all with my return from the grave."

"Think the trick worked?" Tatanka asked, curls of smoke rising from the end of his cigarette.

"I don't know. I been gone four months. There's no way to know. Ain't seen nothin' in the paper denying Jesse James is dead, but those Pinkertons, they'll track down Charlie Ford, ask him about his brother. He may crack."

The clomping of feet continued above our heads. Every so often a sheep bleated, or a turkey gobbled from its cramped pen in the galley. The ship rocked to and fro in the waves, and groaned, always groaned like it was in pain or never-ending sadness.

"Why'd you do it, Jesse James? Why did you go on robbing and killing all those years?" Tatanka asked.

"It goes way back, Injun. My daddy was a preacher in the times before the Civil War. He came out every Sunday in favor of slavery. He followed the '49 California gold rush and got killed for it. Imagine that: a preacher, a man of God, throwing away his family and farm, not to follow the Lord, but to chase gold. A preacher. Well, he got his comeuppance, hell fire. My momma, though, she grew more attached to Southern ways. She remarried twice and set to with a man named Ruben Samuel, a doctor, and got to growing hemp with the labor of slaves.

"Missouri was a divided state, not sure which way it was leaning in the coming battle over state's rights. Folks was told, 'You're either with us, or you're agin us.' And we Missourians got to choosin' up sides and killin' one another. The Jameses settled hard on the side of secession. Our way of life was more important to us than the Union. To our way of thinking, slaves were our most valuable property, and we weren't about to give 'em up. We figured the only truly free man was the fella had his work done for him by others. Them Northern factory workers were just slaves to their jobs. We wanted no part of it.

"In 1860 the war started and a local Union militia came around the farm looking for bushwhackers. I was just fifteen and got in a fight with them and got beat up. I joined Frank and the bushwhackers—rebel guerillas under Quantrill, in a company with Bloody Bill Anderson and Archie Clement. You'd have liked Arch—he scalped the men he killed. I spent the next five years raising hell against the Union in Missouri. Took a side trip to Texas. That was my introduction to manhood: ambushes, killing, burning, running, hiding, regrouping, and killing again.

"After the war, I thought about pledging loyalty to the Union, but I got shot during their rebel amnesty and almost died. That bullet still sits in my chest, right next to my heart. And sometimes, Injun, it talks to me." I opened my shirt, leaned over the bunk, and showed him the scar. He grunted.

"Well now, that's when we took to robbing. We made a target of carpetbaggers and Missouri Radicals—anyone we associated with the Northern victory. We robbed their banks, their trains, their stagecoaches. It was all designed to punish them, to terrorize them, make them rue their wicked assault on the peaceful farmers of Missouri." The ship lurched unexpectedly and sent me flying from my bunk to the deck. Chickens squawked, turkeys gobbled, lambs and goats bleated. Tatanka laughed at me.

"There you go again," he said, and chuckled. "Bucked off into the prickly pear." I laughed with him, sitting there on my butt again like the first day on *Lone Star*. After our mirth died down he reached out a hand to me. "Sharpshooters. Outlaws. Brothers." He looked me in the eye and nodded his head assertively. I nodded back.

I leaned against the wall. "I went on a twenty-year quest to avenge the South, Injun. Twenty years of payin' down a grudge. It wears on ya. My big brother, Frank, he was done with it years ago, but I pressed on. Then came Northfield, Minnesota—I can't talk about how wrong I figured that one. Anyway, all said and done, it worked. Terror worked. The white hood of the Ku Klux Klan made a frightful disguise. The threat we posed ended black rights in the South before they began. Five years ago, in 1877, President Rutherford B. Hayes pulled his Union troops out of Dixie. We may have lost the war, but we won the battle for race supremacy."

Tatanka looked at me with sullen, dark eyes. "You won. I lost."

I started to speak, to defend myself, to point out the difference between his situation and mine, to speak of the similarity between the red man and the Southerner, both of us attacked and subdued by the Union. I could not speak. I was too far gone, Frank. I was no longer a bushwhacker, but just a stowaway, bunking with an Indian on a strange ship of carnival politics. I could not defend my past. Tatanka had fought for a way of life, for the freedom to roam the plains and hunt and dance and pray. I too had fought for a way of life, but it was a way of life built on the backs of other people, treated as less than human. How could I defend that to a man who lived off the land, made a slave of no one, and was a prisoner in his own country?

I excused myself and went up on the deck. It was raining hard, and the sea rolled with whitecaps. Sailors worked that maze of rope masterfully to keep the ship trained to its course yet able to catch the most wind to push it along. The sails popped and fluttered with the changes in force and direction of the wind. Rope stays creaked under the strain.

I did not know what to do. I did not wish to go below, nor did I want to find the officers and try to sit with them. I had never been to sea, and the sight of it, gray and ghastly, did not encourage me to believe I had missed anything. I could not bear the sight of it, became queasy, and finally went below. Luckily, Tatanka had fallen asleep. I climbed into the upper bunk and did the same.

Chapter VI

Whale Steaks for Dinner

By the following morn the storm had passed—or we passed it. The sky was mottled blue and white, and the fiery sun darted in and out of downy clouds. Just after lunch—a hearty lamb stew with chunks of potato and carrot, and the very freshest lamb—a cry resounded from the crow's nest, "Thar she blows!" All eyes went to the misty puff of a whale spout half a league to starboard. "Two now!" shouted the lookout. "Two spouts!" I took a small telescope from one of the junior officers and spied the two whales, one blowing a large, thick mist of air from its blowhole, a second blowing more frequently with much smaller gusts. "Parmaceti!" shouted the lookout, indicating the spouts were in the distinctive, short, thick shape of the sperm whale—the very family of *Moby-Dick*.

The specksynder, a tall, lanky man with a thin face and hawkish nose, whose arms appeared laced with steel cables, and who was the officer in charge of all matters of whaling, hollered at the whalers racing to their boats, "Stand back! It's a mother and her calf. We won't put in for that. Wait till we find the bull."

Captain Silverspoon's shoulders drooped, and he kicked at the deck with the sharp toe of his brown leather cowboy boot. "Damn!" he said. "Dudn't America have equality of the sexes?" Krill spoke into his ear and Silverspoon brightened and nodded.

"*BRACK!* Take to it anyway. Take to it. Remember the election. Make a great photo, big impression: 'Silverspoon Storms New Orleans, Standing on a Whale'—standing on a whale." Krill walked quickly back and forth on the captain's shoulder as he spoke. The specksynder looked at Chief, pleading with his hands for understanding, but Chief Dagger only sucked his teeth, pulled on an earring, and with a flick of his right index finger directed the specksynder to give chase.

At the specksynder's orders, crew rushed to the three whaleboats, piled inside, and lowered to the rolling sea. They trimmed and set their small sails and heaved to the oars, their bare backs and arms crossed and rippled by sinew and muscle. It was as if each man's back now held the rigging of the ship just below the skin. The skippers of the small crafts stood in the rear at the tillers and lambasted their oarsmen to make their boat first in the race to smite the whale. Just in front of the skippers stood the line-tubs, filled with precisely coiled hemp rope attached to the harpoon, and described by Mr. Melville as follows: "When the painted canvas cover is clapped on the American line-tub, the boat looks as if it were pulling off with a prodigious great wedding-cake to present to the whales."

One of the skippers, a junior officer named Bill, yelled, "Bust a gut, you lazy rascals! This is the time to be heroes!"

The specksynder, who captained the second boat, admonished, "Pull that water as if your life was on the line—and it is!" His lead oarsman, I noticed, was Sir Yes Sir, the diplomat. His broad back pulled mightily at his oar, so much so that the whaleboat coursed his direction with every stroke. I looked closely at the other oarsmen, and one of them had remarkably deep, purple skin and raven-black hair with an owl feather tied at the end. It was Tatanka.

A third skipper spoke in an unnaturally lowered voice that I recognized as that of Second Mate Sweet: "Break your arms, and legs, and hearts, boys! It's a chance at glory! Let's make it ours!"

Captain Wrong John Silverspoon and his officers gathered on the poop deck above the Chief's quarters and sat in chairs to take in the event. Each had a small telescope in his lap, and a glass of fresh lemonade in his hand. "I'll put twenty on the speck," said the captain. He set down his lemonade, pulled a wad of cash from his front pocket, and threw a bill into a round hat on the deck. "He's got Sir Yes Sir on harpoon, and the Injun in there pullin'—that's the team to beat."

"My money's on Sweet," said Pinch, the treasurer, in her throaty, earnest voice. "He's so darned determined. Just look at him. And that shrunken head—yikes! You hit your oar hard, or risk being his next dang trophy." She threw her twenty in the hat.

"I like Bill," said the gunner, Yo Ho Ho. "He's got youth and vigor. Light,

trim, responsive—that boy is the physical embodiment of my new military."
He also tossed twenty into the kitty.

"*BRACK!* My money's on the stork! Just look at her. Sex-y momma!" squawked Krill, looking on the opposite side of ship at a big white bird with black-tipped wings and long red legs and beak, flying low over the blue water. "Deliver me from evil, baby. *BRACK!*"

Wrong John flicked his parrot on the beak. "Get your head in the game, Krill. You're off goggling in the grandstand when there's a pop fly comin' right at your head." Krill shivered his head and neck and pecked himself under the wing. Marshal Tosspot pulled a small leather-bound notebook from his back pocket and scribbled in it, every so often squinting at Krill. Chief Dagger did not partake in the gambling. He took the helm of the *Lone Star* and steered her after the whaleboats. "Bring in the topgallants fore and aft! I don't want to run them over," he yelled. Sailors scrambled up the rat lines and rolled up the topgallant sails on the fore and aft masts.

Captain Silverspoon hit Yo Ho Ho, whom he also called Gunny, on the shoulder with the back of his hand. "Son-of-a-gun's sharp, idn't he, Gunny?" he asked, looking down at his first mate. Gunny looked over, his right eye magnified by his monocle so that it appeared to bug out, the left eye covered with a black patch, blue silk headband around his forehead and tied behind his head, gold ring dangling from his nose.

"He's a good man," the gunner said. "That's why I hired him when he was a junior officer."

"Get out'a town! Chief worked for you?"

"Yes, yes he did. Then he pulled ahead of me." Yo Ho Ho shook his head, then muttered, "The little brownnoser." He touched his nose ring and turned it between his fingers.

Out on the water the three whaleboats sped toward their quarry. They were far enough away now that they appeared as dark bugs floating amid the swells. Through the glass, the whalers assumed human form, and it became clear the specksynder had taken a strong lead and would be first upon the whale. The oars of the boatmen rose and fell in unison. A gathering horde of seabirds—gulls, petrels, gannets, cormorants--circled above the three small boats carrying their rope-wormed wedding cakes to the cow whale and her calf. The officers cheered on their favorite boat as would spectators at a horserace.

Wrong John jumped to his feet and focused his telescope. "The diplomat's up! He's got his harpoon! Bear down, oarsmen! Bear down. He's got it cocked! There it goes! Hell of a pitch! Stee-rike! He's got her fast! Look out fellas! Man, she's peeling off some hemp!" Smoke poured off the whale line where it whizzed around the loggerhead. The specksynder wrapped more turns of hemp around the spindle, trying to slow down the stuck whale. Soon she slowed dramatically and, to everyone's surprise, circled back toward the whaleboats. I could see by the gasping spouts of her calf that it had panicked at the gap between them. Its mother must have sensed its fear and come back to help it.

The specksynder exchanged places with Sir Yes Sir, as it was customary for the skipper to lance the harpooned whale and bring it to its death. The African diplomat took the tiller, and with the oarsmen rowing toward the whale, soon drew close enough that the specksynder could throw in a dart. Then came the call from the crow's nest, "Flukes up!" which meant the tail was in the air; the whale was about to sound. "Two flukes up!" came a second shout, indicating the calf had gone down with her. Sir Yes Sir had to quickly untie the rope from the loggerhead or the boat would be pulled down to the depths by the sounding whale. He managed it just as the prow of the boat began to dip below the surface. Then it was smoking hemp burning against the spindle as the fast whale swam for safety into the darkest deep.

The dive lasted no more than five minutes, a very short dive, most likely because the frightened calf ran out of breath. Mother and child burst through the surface in full-body breaches and splashed down so near the specksynder's boat I thought it would capsize. The splash drenched the crew and knocked the specksynder into the water from his perch on the prow; he had to be fished back in by the crew. After that insult he was dogged in running her down, and smote her hard with five strong darts. A wrathful red foam rose around the desperately thrashing whale. Beyond that, I was not able from the distance to gain a sure picture of her death, but will rely on the accuracy of Mr. Melville's account of a dying bull whale:

And now abating in his flurry, the whale once more rolled out into view; surging from side to side; spasmodically dilating and contracting his spout-hole, with sharp, cracking, agonizing respirations. At last, gush after gush of clotted red gore, as if it had been the purple lees of red wine, shot into the frightened air, and falling back again, ran dripping down his motionless flanks into the sea. His heart had burst!

"Yeehaw!" yelled the captain.

"*BRACK-A-DOODLE-DO!*" Krill screeched. The *Lone Star*'s crew whooped and hollered "Huzzah!" Silverspoon snatched the wagered money from the round hat and stuffed it in his pocket.

"Am I good, or what?" he said.

The other two boats came alongside the dead whale and threw harpoons into her side to help tow the beast back to the *Lone Star*. Her frantic calf swam back and forth behind her, flopping this way and that, lifting its long fins into the air and slapping them on the water, reminding me of rifle shots. Chief Dagger guided the ship to meet the whalers halfway. Somewhere along the way, something unseen jerked Basmati Sweet's tiller and sent her flying into the water. A whaleman extended an oar to her and pulled her in. Sir Yes Sir came on board first and was surrounded by the officers and crew, who lifted him to their shoulders and carried him around the deck, singing the praises of his successful hunt. Wrong John, however, did not join in, but stood amidships at the rail with his arms crossed.

Others tied the whale fast to the side and immediately set to stripping the blubber from her sides before the gathering sharks ripped her to shreds. This operation amazed me. A huge block and tackle was hung from the mainmast with a big hook at the end of a heavy rope. This hook was inserted into the blubber of the whale, which encompassed the exterior of its body, to a thickness of almost two feet. Laborers took spikes of the windlass and pushed against them, winding the rope and putting pressure on the hook in the whale's flesh. This caused the whale to rise and the ship to tip sideways, so much so I imagined I would slide off into the sea, and had to secure myself to the far rail with a lifeline.

Men went to the blubber with sharp, long-handled cleavers, called spades, and cut around the hook, then in lengths alongside it, then went to the membrane that connected the blubber to the muscle and cut the blubber free. This caused the thick fat to peel away from the flesh while the body turned in the water from the pressure brought by the windlass. Just as Mr. Melville writes, it was very much like watching a giant, oblong brown orange peeled of its skin. After a length of blubber ten feet long came away from the body, a man cut it with a long sharp knife called a boarding sword, which sent the body crashing back to the water, and the ship snapping to attention. All the while, the distraught calf swam circles around the ship. Sharks tore at the cow's open wound, angular fins and tails slashing the water.

The grisly butchers on deck dropped their ten-foot lengths of blubber through the hatch into the blubber room for storage until they fired up the try-works. Once the whale had been completely peeled of its private blanket, the specksynder sliced vertically with his spade against the muscle just ahead of the fins, and went about the business of beheading the mother whale. Now that the blubber had been harvested, the only thing left of any value was the spermaceti oil in her head. Sea birds circled the ship, crying urgently for their supper.

"Hey!" shouted the captain at the specksynder. "Get me some nice whale steaks for dinner before you cut loose that carcass." The specksynder passed the order to Tatanka, who sliced slabs of meat from near the tail—considered the tenderest part. I wondered if he was reminded of the buffalo slaughter, millions of them killed for only the tongue and the hump. In half hour's time, the specksynder had cut loose the whale's body from its head and released the body to float away as a feast for sharks. Seagulls and gannets dove at the bloody stump of the whale's head, tearing off pieces of meat they fought over in mid-air, screeching and battering one another with their wings and claws. The baby whale started to follow the body, then swam back toward the head, and back and forth, not seeming to comprehend the growing distance between its once whole mother.

Later that night, after the captain and his officers had finished their meal of whale steak, and the kitchen had been cleaned, and Tatanka and I bedded down, a strange combination of sounds began to haunt us. The first sound I can only describe as chewing. Something, I could not imagine what, worked its way around the hull of the ship, seemingly chewing on it. Tatanka and I speculated what it might be, but neither of us being seamen, we could not begin to identify it. The picture in my mind, based on the sound, was of a giant underwater bird working the hull, as would a blue jay cracking open a pumpkin seed.

The second sound was also a mystery to me, until it became clear the source of it had to be the baby whale. Before that night, I would have guessed the whale mute, as Krill had described himself when he was a tailor before he kissed the frog. It turns out, however, that a whale can speak, but not in words, barks, or growls, or chirps, grunts, or yowls. A whale sings.

The voice of that baby whale passed directly into our heads as we rested them against the hull while lying in our shallow bunks. It was a song like none I had ever heard, a song of endless grief, sang in the eternal salt tears of the sea, a song that had no words, neither ending nor beginning, only wailing, like a watery, howling, windless wind through the broken heart of an orphaned ocean child. Tatanka began to sob along with it, in sympathy with the whale, I imagined, but also in memory of his precious namesake, the buffalo, that had been eliminated from the Great Plains. I felt a sharp pain in my chest, as if that bullet still in me had poked my heart. I could not help myself, Frank, and I too shed tears with that lonely whale and that lost Sioux warrior. I did not realize until then how much sadness I carried in me. I sobbed, brother, until my stomach and throat and face hurt, and my face was streaked with tears.

Chapter VII

How Things Go for Me

Two days later the *Lone Star* arrived off the Mississippi Delta. Low clouds and patchy fog obscured our view. All semblance of a breeze disappeared, and the whaleboats had to be lowered and roped to the ship to pull her through the water. In this deathly calm we encountered a vast acreage of dead fish floating belly-up in the sea. The sickly smell of rotting fish assaulted my nose; the water held an alien, sallow tinge. The fish floated in such quantity that we plowed through them as if breaking ice—jack and mackerel mostly, somebody said. The only life to be found was the occasional flash of rigid dorsal that betrayed a shark supping on the fine slaughter. Then too I noticed the regular huff of air from the baby whale, still following its mother's head tied starboard of the ship.

I and Tatanka added to the fog with cigarettes we smoked. We stood at the prow and watched the oarsmen pull hard at the water to move the heavy clipper, armed with twenty cannon on deck three and four pieces of small artillery on the top deck. The pilot shouted directions to the whaleboats according to the binnacle readings of his man at the helm. The officers had gathered in the roundhouse to plan the campaign route in the run-up to the November election. The sails had been furled in the calm, leaving the yards stark, and they stood against the three masts as tiered crosses. From the white bellies of the innumerable dead fish, the ocean appeared an endless pitcher of chunky buttermilk.

"What you reckon killed them all?" I asked Tatanka.

"Don't know. Spirit says poison. That is all. Some poison from the river. Drainage from the valleys and the plains. All gathered into the great river. It has no choice. It delivers the poison to the sea."

I took a long draw on my smoke. The young whale's back arched through the mass of fish, and it shot out a quick puff of air. It slapped its tail against the water and rolled hard to its right. The whale seemed to be tangled in seaweed. Its breath gurgled and hissed in the sickly, jaundiced graveyard. It thrashed, rolled, and shuddered against the slimy green arms.

"You wouldn't think a whale would get stuck in seaweed like that," I told Tatanka.

"That seaweed can move. Look, it pulls the whale down," he replied, pointing at the struggle.

A slurping, smacking sound arose from the tussle between the whale and the seaweed. In the next instant, the calf slipped beneath the surface and disappeared. For the next little while, here and there large air bubbles burst through the mass of dead fish, rolling them so their dark dorsal fins momentarily showed.

Tatanka sang a quiet song in his native tongue. I took my bowler off and placed it over my heart. The bullet lodged under my breastbone whispered, "You know nothing, nothing, nothing at all." Another of the crew, who had also watched the drowning, spoke unto the water, "Lord, have mercy on our souls." The whalers rowed on, stroke by stroke, pulling their oars through the corpse-ridden water, towing the dead weight of the *Lone Star* out of the fog-bound doldrums.

"Ten degrees to port!" yelled the helmsman.

"Ten degrees to port!" the pilot yelled to the whaleboats.

"Ten degrees port!" returned the whaleboat skippers in turn.

The whaleboats towed the ship past the jutting delta of the Mississippi for a full day and half the night. I passed the night fitfully in the silent void left by the baby whale's drowning, and the absence of whatever had been gnawing at the hull. In my dream, I stormed into a cramped bank that was filling with water. No teller would agree to open the vault, and every one of them I shot did not die but grew seaweed arms that slithered toward me. I ran out the front door to the wood plank sidewalk and into a hard rain, and found my horse drowning in a river of mud, neighing wildly, snorting, nostrils flared, eyes startled, kicking as the thick mud carried it away. Coffins passed by in the frothy current. Their lids opened, and the grim faces of men I had killed looked at me and smiled. They did not have teeth but something wriggling that crept down their chins.

I awoke, terrified, out of breath and cold with sweat. I feared to sleep again, so instead went up on deck and stood silently with the helmsman, who measured the compass by the light of the binnacle lamp. I reached out to rub the lamp, wondering what about it had been so attractive to Krill the first day I met him. I did not return to my bunk until it was almost dawn.

Some time later a great commotion of footfalls on the deck above my head awakened me. I ascended the hatch to find the brick try-works billowing with the black smoke of an ogre's chimney. The smell was so bad I had to wrap a bandana around my nose and mouth. It reminded me of how Ishmael describes the nauseating odor in a chapter of *Moby-Dick* titled "The Try-Works":

Once ignited, the whale supplies his own fuel and burns by

> his own body. Would that he consumed his own smoke! for
> his smoke is horrible to inhale, and inhale it you must.... It
> has an unspeakable, wild, Hindoo odor about it, such as may
> lurk in the vacinity of funereal pyres. It smells like the left
> wing of the day of judgment.

I climbed the quarterdeck, squinting and coughing, and watched the whalers; with long pitchforks they poked at the chunks of blubber jostled in the boiling golden oil. Several men held long-handled ladles they used to scoop oil from the try-pots into wooden barrels on deck.

Krill waddled over and climbed up the quarterdeck rail. "Stick 'em up, IshcaBible," he said, making fun of my mask. "Quite an operation, eh? Blubber to gold, blubber to gold. Cook it up good for New Orleans."

The masts had been fully sheeted and billowed with a goodly breeze. Just after lunch, we came into the port at New Orleans, *Lone Star* shrouded in stinky black smoke. The pilot positioned the ship so the breeze carried the smoke to port, and dropped anchor. Some of the sailors lowered Captain Silverspoon, parrot on his shoulder, harpoon in hand, to the head of the mother whale. He stood there, just in front of a hole that had been bored through her skin, waving and shooting magic finger bullets at the cheering crowd gathered along the industrial waterfront. He held the harpoon up, poised to hurl it, and held the pose for the flashing cameras.

The *Lone Star* weighed anchor and continued along the waterfront to the dock of a blubber-works, where raw oil and spermaceti were refined further and packaged as lamp oil, candles, lubricant, and heating oil. The entire wharf took on a poisonous green hue from sunlight refracted by the sluggish cloud of chartreuse smoke hanging above the factory. America's greatest industry was this, the one of energy, blubber, oil, and it was the captain's first love. The factory continued to operate, punctuating his speech with grinding gears and clanking metal, the thud of wooden implements and massive valves, the hiss of escaping gas and the roar of unending fire. Wrong John addressed the crowd of admirers and reporters that had followed his ship along the waterfront.

"Welcome, Captain Silverspoon, to New Orleans," he said. The parrot whispered in his ear. "I mean welcome, New Orleans, to Captain Silverspoon. You get my drift. We're on a mission to restore decency and honor to the

White House. Let me say this about that: 'This, about, that.'" The crowd applauded. The captain's head bobbed and his chest puffed out. "Take this whale. I took 'er down. It's what I do—sort of guy I am. Opportunity knocks— I knock it off. There's no hesitation. Decisions—it's what I specialize. Making them, and standing on top of them." He jabbed the tip of his harpoon into the head of the whale.

"Here's my point. It's your blubber. You earned it. *You* should decide what to do with it, not a bunch of lazy Washington bureaucrats who never hunted a whale in their lives. My campaign's about one word, and one word only: tax relief." The crowd cheered. A sailor approached the captain and tied a rope to his waist—known in the whale trades as the monkey rope. It ran through a pulley off the first yard of the foremast. Two men on deck pulled the rope, and the captain rose into the air. The sailor on the whale handed Wrong John a metal bucket tied by its handle to a thin rope. The captain, and his bucket, tied to his monkey rope, dropped into the hole that had been bored into the whale's head. Just as his shoulders dropped through, Krill neatly jumped off.

"*BRACK!* Captain will now take questions from the press—questions from the press."

A number of reporters hurried from the dock onto the deck and were lowered to the head of the whale. "What's it like down there?" asked a woman who wrote for a prominent Washington newspaper.

"I stand for the values of working-class Americans," spoke the hollow voice of Silverspoon. The reporters smiled and scribbled in their notebooks. Wrong John gave a couple of tugs on the bucket's rope and it rose through the hole filled with viscous, pale-yellow spermaceti. Blubber was one thing, and had its value, but spermaceti, the mysterious mass of buttery cream that had some unknown purpose in allowing the whale to navigate its deep dives to the lightless depths—that stuff was the whale's blue-ribbon apple pie. Whalers guided the bucket of spermaceti to a barrel on deck, dumped it, and sent it back down the hole.

"What's the main difference between you and your opponent?" shouted another reporter into the black hole.

"I'm in the hole, scooping out the oil, contributing directly to The Economy. He's running around bragging about how he invented the harpoon."

The reporters laughed and scribbled in their books.

"What sort of foreign policy can we expect if you're elected?"

"I'm too busy down here keeping The Economy strong to go meddling in the business of foreign nations." The reporters smiled and wrote.

A small woman leaned down to the hole, cupped her hands, and yelled down, "There are a few unanswered questions about your past. Have you, or have you not, smoked opium? Have you been arrested for riding a horse while drunk? Did you violate securities law by selling stock based on inside information? Were you away without leave during your stint with the home guard?" The other reporters glared at her and then slapped her with their notebooks until she lost her balance and fell into the harbor.

"What?" asked the hollow voice from the hole. "Didn't catch that last one."

"Never mind," yelled a man from a New York newspaper. "How will you win Louisiana and the Deep South?"

"Through colorblindness. In my party, we have no pigment. One American is just as white as the next. Deep down, everybody has white bones. We're all wh—"

"BRACK! Interview over. Interview over." Krill jumped at the reporters and flapped his stunted wings. They climbed from the whale head back onto the Lone Star, and then returned to the dock. Another bucket of spermaceti rose from the hole. The whalers dumped it in the wooden barrel and sent it back down the hole. Next came Silverspoon, rising through the hole, his hair soaked with oil.

"You're anointed, captain!" said Tosspot from the foredeck rail. "Just like the kings of yore." The captain smiled and shot him with a finger bullet. Tosspot threw his hands over his heart, pretending to be hit, and stumbled backward, smiling. Chief Dagger hurried across the deck, slipped on a spill of spermaceti, and landed on his butt.

The reporter who had fallen in the harbor trod water and yelled up to Silverspoon, "What about your service record?"

"There's that liberal media bias Americans are so sick of," he said, the nostrils of his sharp nose red and flared.

"That's not biased. I don't have an opinion about it. I just think

Americans have a right to know," the reporter yelled back.

"*BRACK! Raise the rooster. Raise the rooster, BRACK!*" squawked Krill, hopping up and down on the whale. Sailors on deck pulled on the rope around Wrong John's waist, and he rose quickly into the air above the whale head.

"That's the bias!" He yelled down to the waterlogged reporter. "Side that says there's a fair, unbiased position is *their position*! Don't you get it? We know everybody is either on one side or the other. If you aren't pulling for us, you're pulling for them."

Supporters of Captain Silverspoon threw fish heads from the dock at the reporter to shut her up. Once Captain Silverspoon was safely on board the *Lone Star*, the whalers cut loose the mother's head and let it drop into the harbor. It sank below the surface, then bobbed up and tipped side to side, the unharvested spermaceti draining out and forming a buttery pool that floated on the water. The loose flesh, where the head had been severed, came away in shreds; sea gulls and buzzards fought over the carrion. Sailors set and trimmed the sails, and the ship glided out into Lake Borgne, past Halfmoon Island, and made for the open water of the gulf. I brought the captain a pot of coffee and retired to my cabin.

Later that night, I went to the captain to fulfill my nightly duty to get him tucked into bed. He flossed and brushed his teeth. I turned down his sheets (me, Frank, a damn maid!), and fluffed his feather pillow. His bed was one of those sleigh types with curved mahogany head and footboards polished so they shined. He had a collection of autographed baseballs in a glass case on the wall, next to his letter sweater from Yale.

"Quit a mess of dead fish there at the delta," I said.

"Dead fish?"

"You had to notice. The smell alone could knock over a razorback."

"You workin' up to a Bible story, Ish?"

"I'm talking about real dead fish—millions of them."

"—and not enough loaves of bread," he said. "Yeah, yeah, I get it. Well, you may be right. It may take a miracle for me to take the White House, but I'm kinda lucky that way. Seems like whenever I get into a jam, well, somehow, someway, it just works out for me. Like that time I almost got called into that nasty war. Dad wrote a couple of letters and next thing you know, I'm in the reserves, guarding a supply depot in Dodge City. Or that time I almost went bankrupt, money just showed up—like I closed my eyes and wished for it. That's how things go for me. There's very little I have to do or say. I just have to be *me* and that's about all it takes."

"Must be nice," I said.

"Yes and no. At some point a man's got to prove himself. He's got to carve his own name in the tree trunk."

I inquired of him how he came to be involved in politics. It turns out to have been based on a misunderstanding. His father, Wrong John Johnson Silverspoon, had asked him one afternoon if he wanted to join the party. Wrong John Jr., not one to pass up an invitation to a good time, immediately accepted. His dad brought him to an office where volunteers stuffed envelopes with campaign information. "Where's the keg?" junior asked. His dad informed him this was a different sort of party and that you didn't get to celebrate until *after* winning the election. From that point forward, junior became a slave to the duty of winning—mostly, he said, so he could have a good excuse to tie one on. That was long ago. He had since found the Lord and given up drinking.

Chapter VIII

Full-Out Jim Crow

In the coming weeks, Captain Wrong John Silverspoon campaigned throughout the South. *Lone Star* stopped at the shipyards of Mobile, in fishing towns, and in cane sugar factories along the coast of Florida. Now and then, the captain took a train deeper into the country for a rally in Knoxville or Atlanta. Everywhere he went in the South, he poured on the Texas drawl and preached the gospel of colorblindness. It was a sermon well received by poor whites ready to believe that black civil rights was a program of discrimination against whites. But even as he rounded the Florida Keys and made every effort to dominate the Sunshine State, Wrong John Silverspoon was not able to secure it. His opponent, an abolitionist Tennessean named Foul Bore, had patched together a coalition of Africans, Caribbeans and sympathetic whites, and was gaining ground on the Silverspoon campaign.

Chief Dagger and Krill had determined Florida a likely lynchpin for the entire election, and they called an emergency strategy meeting at a private cove on Great Abaco Island in the Bahamas. *Liberty* dropped anchor along a channel through the coral reef, two hundred yards off the sandy, white crescent beach. It was rumored among the crew that an undiscovered treasure of Captain Kidd's was buried in the cove. Just after dawn the captain went for what was called a "jog," a sort of slow run around the deck of the ship. I could not understand why anyone would run unless a dog or a bear was chasing him, but it was said to be good for his health and disposition. Afterward, at precisely 7:30 a.m., he sat down for a breakfast of sunny-side-up eggs, toast, and bacon—Tatanka had by then perfected the exact, bright-eyed optimism asked of the bare yolks. I cleared his dishes and brought them to the galley. Tatanka and his helpers cooked oatmeal in heavy iron pots for the crew. I returned to the deck when trumpets called us to the morning prayer. The captain asked me to provide inspiration.

I looked out over the blue water of the cove, startled by its dazzling azure color. The ship's sails were furled. A solitary sailor stood watch from the crow's nest atop the main mast. A few cotton clouds dotted the soft blue sky. The gentle surf whispered from its break beyond the reef. Crew stood at ranks along both sides of the ship, and the officers stood behind me in their half-moon circle on the quarterdeck. Among them was a new face: Silverspoon's younger brother, Myturn, the governor of Florida, a hulking man with heavy hands and a pronounced brow. The captain and Krill stood next to me. I cleared my throat to speak.

"In Matthew, Jesus declares the folly of Hebrew law that requires an eye be taken for an eye, and a tooth for a tooth. Jesus doesn't want a world of blind, toothless beggars, groping for love. Does he?"

"No, sir!" shouted the crew.

"In Chapter 5, Verse 39, He says 'But I say unto you, That ye resist not evil: but whosoever shall smite thee on thy right cheek, turn to him the other also.' And in verse 44, He says, 'But I say unto you, Love your enemies, bless them that curse you, do good to them that hate you, and pray for them which despitefully use you, and persecute you.' So with that thought, let us bow our heads in a moment of silence for our opponent, Foul Bore." The crew lowered their heads. After a bit, I said, "Amen."

Ah, Frank, you know I was a complete hypocrite to speak those words. My entire manhood had been devoted to eye gouging and dentistry. But hell fire, brother, it was them insisted on a coyote preacher. What choice did I have but to circle back on them and nip at their heels?

"Very nice, IshcaBible, a prayer for Foul Bore," said Wrong John. "All I can say is he *better* turn the other cheek, 'cause we're gonna kick one side of his butt, then the other, from here to San Francisco!" The crew whistled and cheered. "It's crunch time, folks, bottom of the ninth, tie ballgame, two outs and a man on third. We need a hit, and it's got to come from Florida. Good thing we know the umpire down this way, my brother, Governor Myturn Silverspoon." The crew applauded. Myturn stepped forward. I walked to the far side of the quarterdeck.

"Consider Florida a tired whale, *Lone Star*. Her fat is yours to harvest," said Myturn. The crew whooped and cheered. "It reminds me of a story. There was a grasshopper and an ant. The ant was very—"

"Okay, everybody," the captain interrupted, "back to work. Get this shape ship for the final push to victory!" The crew cheered, broke ranks, and set to scrubbing the deck, polishing the try-pots with sand and soapstone, rubbing oil into the fittings, painting the hull, mending rope and sails. Tatanka sent his kitchen crew out to the reef in a whaleboat to spear fish and hunt lobster and crabs for dinner. Roberto Mendoza handed me the dog-eared photo of his *novia*—a beautiful, many-shaded chocolate woman—and asked me to take good care of it while he went swimming. The captain and his officers adjourned to a golf ball-driving platform made of oak planks covered with a green wool carpet that had been constructed aft, on the poop deck. I and Tatanka sat on the rail on either side of the golf stage.

Myturn stepped to the tee first and placed his ball. They were still using the old feather golf balls, "featheries" they were called, small leather pouches stuffed with goose down and sewn up, over the new rubber ones called "gutties." The feather ones flew much farther. Wrong John called Myturn, and when he turned, Krill waddled to his ball, kicked it off the tee, and hid. Wrong

John pretended to forget what he wanted. Myturn looked back at the tee and replaced his ball, his brother snickering behind his back. Wrong John called him again, and Krill ran out and kicked the ball off the tee and hid. On the third round of the joke, Myturn pretended to turn to Wrong John, but when Krill ran out, Myturn whirled and smacked him on the tail with his driver.

"*BRACK!*" Krill said, flapping his wings and waddling off the far end of the platform. The officers laughed at him. Myturn gave his older brother a condescending smile. Wrong John smiled back at him falsely. The Florida governor hauled back and hit his ball. It flew about twenty yards before I pulled Widowmaker and blew it apart, leaving nothing put a puff of goose feathers floating above the azure water. Myturn looked over at me and frowned, his jaw sticking out. The other officers stifled their laughter with a hand to the mouth. Someone let a snicker escape through his nose. Myturn looked at his brother for support, but Wrong John shrugged. The governor stormed off the platform.

The gunner, Yo Ho Ho, stepped next to the tee. He placed his ball, let his monocle fall from his good eye, hauled back his driver, and swung. He hit the ball low, and it bounced off the bulwark and back at the officers. They ducked and let it fly over their heads. It landed directly in a try-pot.

"Hole in one, Gunny!" shouted Wrong John. "There's *my* military. Laser guided precision." Yo Ho Ho gave a half salute and walked from the platform. Next up came the captain. He teed his ball, reared back and smacked it. After it had sailed about thirty yards, Tatanka pulled his revolver and dusted it.

"Come on you guys!" the captain shouted. "Go on and find your own game. Can't you see we're working here?"

Tatanka smiled at me and holstered his pistol. "Tie. One each," he said. He walked amidships, stripped off his clothes, and dove into the water.

"Public nudity is completely contrary to God's law!" roared Marshal Tosspot.

"Give him a break, marshal. Damn savage don't know any better," I said.

Tosspot walked at me quickly, pulling the bullwhip from his heavy leather belt. "I will flog you for your insolence!" My right hand quivered above Peacemaker. Whip *me*, will you—you pale, jowly creep, I thought.

"Shee-it, marshal, simmer down," said Captain Silverspoon. "IshcaBible's right—heathen ignorance. Besides, it *is* hot out here. I might have to do some skinny dippin' myself." He forced a laugh. Tosspot pulled up and glared at me with something approaching hatred. I went behind the golf platform, leaned against the aft mast, and rolled a smoke. Tatanka and his lobster mob could be heard shouting and splashing over the reef. They sounded angry and surprised by something. The officers went back to their golf game. A Mexican galley worker arrived with a silver tray of lemonade, goose liver pâté, and crackers.

Chief Dagger climbed onto the platform, placed his stitched-up featherie on the tee, addressed the ball, wiggled his butt, hauled back and swung. He missed the ball completely, but placed a hand edgewise over his forehead and looked out over the shimmering sapphire cove.

"Missed it," he said.

"*BRACK!* Boy, I'll say. Whiff city," Krill said. The others laughed. Chief looked down at his ball and frowned. He hauled back and swung again, missing completely. The officers held back their laughter. He looked down at his ball and frowned. One more time, he attempted to hit, but caught only air. He swore, and threw his club over the side, causing his glasses to fall off. He leaned over and groped the platform, the crack of his butt showing above his belt. Everyone tried not to laugh, but they didn't do a very good job. I really wanted to shoot his ball off the tee, but I held back. He found his glasses and stomped off the stage.

"Like I always say, Chief," said the captain, "if at first you can't—if you don't get it right the, uh—get it the whatchamacallit, you know, don't give up. Try again. That's the story. Remember the try-pots?"

"Screw the damn blubber-works," said Dagger, who had turned away from the golf game, arms crossed, sucking his teeth. Silverspoon walked over to him with a tall glass of lemonade and handed it to him. Dagger accepted the drink and guzzled it. He finished by spitting lemon seeds onto the golf stage. He turned to the group with a sneer.

"All right, enough piddling around. Governor Myturn, give us an update on your program. How are you making sure we've got Florida in the bag?"

"*BRACK!* Florida in the bag, Florida in the bag."

Wrong John's bigger little brother shoved his club into his bag and stepped onto the golf platform. He picked up Dagger's featherie from the tee and ripped it in half with his bare hands. He pushed on the leather skin until white feathers fell around him like snow. He strode across the green carpet, reached to the bowl of goose liver pâté, scooped out a glob with his fingers, and shoved it in his mouth. He chewed loudly with his mouth open.

"Scrubbing, swabbies," he said ominously. He licked his fingers. "We're scrubbing the voter lists—ruthlessly."

"Scrubbin'? What the hell does that mean?" asked Wrong John.

"It means, dear brother, that any blemish on a person's record—an unpaid fine, an overdue bill, a criminal record—*strikes* them from the vote. When they go to the poll, a big black X is through their name." He lowered his eyes and stared at the officers one by one.

Wrong John closed his right eye, wrinkled his nose, and shook his head.

"That's pathetic!" bellowed Chief. "We told you to aggressively employ the Southern strategy. Do whatever it takes. And all you've come up with is mopping the kitchen floor?" Chief pulled the dagger from his belt and brushed it back and forth across his cheek.

"Well, I—I didn't want to appear too obvious. I mean, this is America, still—right? I mean, these things have to have deniability, don't they?"

Krill walked over to him and kicked him in the ankle. "*BRACK!* Thank a lot, chump. There goes the election." Wrong John sauntered to his brother and punched him in the shoulder, then punched him again in the exact same spot.

"Ow! That raised a bump. You always do that!" Governor Myturn grabbed his shoulder and grimaced.

"I've got plans, damn you!" yelled Yo Ho Ho, scratching his left eye under the patch. "Twenty years, waiting on the sidelines, biding my time—I've got plans!" He ran at Myturn Silverspoon, but tripped on an edge of the platform and fell on his face.

"Okay, everyone, let's take a deep breath and go about this intelligently," said Sir Yes Sir, stepping forward. "It's a military operation. You come at it with multiple prongs, layered strategy, contingency planning. Scrubbing might be a viable option, but let's flesh out a few more."

Gunny sat, leaning against the golf platform, a bleeding cut on his chin.

He mocked the diplomat, wagging his head and moving his lips as Sir Yes Sir spoke. Chief Dagger's eyes lit up. He walked to the diplomat and put an arm around his shoulder. "That's an excellent idea, Sir Yes Sir. I think you and Second Mate Sweet should retire to my quarters and draw up a plan."

"Us?" asked Sweet, left hand on the hip of her red silk pants, head tilted to the right. She had a length of what I assumed was a rubber hose, stretched half a foot down the inside leg of her white pants. "Why just us? Shouldn't the whole group be involved?"

"It will be, Mr. Second Mate. It will be. We'll stay out here, strategizing, and you two will do the same in parallel. Then we'll come back together and compare notes. Sound good?" He smiled from the right side of his face, beads of sweat on his upper lip.

"I, uh, well, I guess," she said in her strained voice. The two Africans retired to the Chief's quarters on the deck below.

"Okay," said Chief, "now let's get to business." He unbuttoned the cuffs and rolled up the sleeves of his starched white shirt. "Governor Myturn, I hope you're smart enough to realize a random scrubbing of the voter rolls does us absolutely *zero* good."

The governor shook his shoulders, held up his hands, and said, "Well, yeah—."

"No, he idn't smart enough," said Captain Silverspoon. "Go ahead and spell it out for him, Chief."

"*BRACK!*" Spell it out, spell it out," said Krill from the captain's shoulder.

"We *need* stupid white people, Myturn," said Chief. "They're convinced we care about them. You've got to scrub only the black vote. They're the ones that'll go for Foul Bore."

"Okay, but that's, well—you can't discrimi—"

"This is politics, dummy. Got nothing to do with skin color," said Wrong John. "Hell, why do you think I hired two of 'em on my staff?" He scowled at his brother. "Don't screw me, Myturn. It's *not* your turn. It's *mine*."

"Enough, you two," said Chief. "Let's stay on task. Now what else? We can't rely on the scrubbing alone to get us the votes we need. There's got to be more."

"Why not go full-out Jim Crow?" I said with a puff of smoke from where I leaned against the aft mast.

"Excuse me?" Chief said.

"You know, take it all the way. You need to suppress the black vote to win this thing. How do you think we worked it in 1876, to get our man Sam Tilden elected over Ruth Hayes?"

"Tilden didn't win," said Tosspot. "Hayes cried foul, said we blocked the black vote, and he took office, IshcaBible. Everybody knows that." He rolled his eyes.

"Sure he did, marshal. Everybody knows. But who really won? In order for Tilden to cede the victory, Hayes had to give the South everything we wanted. Hayes got the title, but we took the office."

"We don't need a history lesson, Ish. What's your point?" asked the captain.

"Oh, I think you *do* need a history lesson. You aren't going to block the Democrat unless you go full-out Jim Crow after the nigras. That means white hoods and robes, burning torches, dragging uppity black preachers out of their homes at night, a few high-profile beatings, a lynching or two."

"You can't be serious! The KKK?" shouted Chief.

"How bad do you want to win?" I opened the cylinder of Widowmaker and spun it around. It clicked fast, then slower, until it stopped.

"I warned you about that secesh, bushwhacker attitude, IshcaBible!" shouted Marshal Tosspot, using that old word again, "secesh," the chopped off "secession." Tosspot was so angry, his clammy white face had some actual color in it. "I swear, I will—." He reached for his bullwhip as Wrong John broke in.

"Sim-mer down, TP. Good God almighty!" His nostrils flared and he stared at the marshal. He turned to me and said, "He's right this time, Ish. You're out'a line. We've got some standards here. We can't dress up as ghouls and go chasing black folk around at night. That's un-American."

"*BRACK!* I'll do it! Dress me up as the ghost parrot. Spooky bird, spooky bird."

"Krill! This is an election, not Halloween," scolded the captain, knocking his pet bird to the deck with a backhanded punch. Krill landed hard and coughed.

"I know! I know!" said Governor Myturn excitedly. "We'll increase police patrols around the African polling places. We'll randomly search people. We'll raid their settlements and throw a few in jail. Word will get out. People will stay home. We'll change the ballot. Confuse them on exactly how to cast a valid vote, then chuck any that aren't perfect." A flock of sea ravens, black and bawdy, ranged into shore from beyond the break and landed in the upper yards of the ship. They croaked and grumbled and pecked at each other, perched above the meeting.

"Now you're talking, governor," said Dagger, walking to Myturn and putting an arm around his shoulder. The thuggish brother of Wrong John half closed his eyes and smiled without showing his teeth.

"Don't you have something to do?" the marshal said to me, fingering his bullwhip.

"S'pose I do," I said. I slowly undressed until I stood before them butt-naked. The treasurer, Pinch, gasped and covered her eyes. Tosspot showed his teeth and looked away, down and left. I scratched my nuts, pulled the smoke from my lips and flicked it at them, climbed the rail, and dove in the calm blue cove. Okay, Frank, don't start with the scolding. I knew it was a dumb move the minute I hit the water. I should have blended in, played the part of a lap dog, and so on. Tosspot likely noticed the gunshot scar on my chest, and wrote about it in his diary. Even so, I didn't give their reaction a second thought once I started swimming in that cool water. I paddled over to the kitchen crew, casual as an otter, to help them collect dinner.

Chapter IX

A Hump Like a Snow Hill

The reef had been like a graveyard, all white with coral tombstones, oddly shaped grave markers that might belong to mermaids and ocean sprites. Something had happened—no one knew just what (Spirit told Tatanka it was sky poison)—to kill the reef. I had been led to believe by sailors on *Lone Star* that it would be a miraculous underwater garden of color, full of bright blue, yellow, red, orange, white, and green coral, along with plants, fish, eels, octopi, and turtles. The only thing down there were sea urchins, spiny, stiff, blind pin cushions, chewing up the decay. The laborers picked them and threw them into the boat, but no one imagined they would be edible. My chest and throat tightened, and I fought back tears. It was like being back at the Mississippi Delta, in that expanse of dead fish, and that baby whale swimming through and then disappearing in those slimy, green arms.

I could not take much of it and swam back to the ship. I climbed up the rusty anchor chain and over the rail. After the first wet footprint I left on the hot, knotty brown timbers of the *Lone Star* I knew something was wrong. Across the way hunched Tosspot, with my clothes, going through the pockets. He took up my holster—*my holster!*—and strapped it on his waist below his thick belt loaded with leg irons and his bullwhip. He pretended himself in a gunfight and clumsily drew Peacemaker and Widowmaker, nearly dropping them. He holstered them and tried again, nonetheless clumsy, a lawman unaccustomed to firearms—no Wyatt Earp or Bat Masterson by a long shot. Hell, even a pitiful Pinkerton could handle a pistol.

I snuck up behind him, my naked, white skin wet and glimmering in the sunshine, reached into the holster and pulled the two revolvers. I had them hard to his temples before he knew what happened. "Having fun, marshal?" I asked. I clicked back the triggers. I could feel him shaking through the barrels of my guns.

"IshcaBible? I—I didn't think you would mind. I'm just—it's a patriotic act. All for one and one for one, as the captain says, eh?"

"These are my children, lawman, and I don't take to filthy old men pawing them." I jammed the barrels harder into his temples.

"Lovely sermon earlier, *Ish*," he said, attempting familiarity with me. "A good reminder to be merciful, most especially with our enemies. Bravo, I say, bravo."

"Come on, marshal. You know it's impossible to follow that notion in the roughshod world of ambitious men. A fella'd get himself shot in the head before he could turn *one* cheek, let alone the other." I slowly released the triggers and let them tap against the bullets. I holstered the guns where they hung on Tosspot's hips.

"Mind if I get dressed?" I reached down for my snakeskin pants and heard him turn quickly. I did not look up, but slipped on my pants, socks, and black leather cowboy boots. I knew he didn't have the guts to gun me down.

"Disgusting display out there on the reef," he said sourly. "Men should never act that way together. It's immoral," he said.

"Excuse me?" I placed the black bowler on my head but did not put on my shirt.

"That riffraff, out there *touching* one another, cavorting like frisky elk in rut. How vile and repugnant."

"I ain't had so much fun since I was a boy, wrasslin' Frank in the old Missourah River," I said.

"Fun between men should stop at a handshake. You know your Bible, Ishca. God condemns to death men who consort with other men."

"I didn't see no consortin', marshal. I guess you've never been in the army, or with a gang of men. Otherwise you'd understand that fellas need to have fun together, get physical, fight even—just to keep from killing each other."

He ignored me and took to pulling my pistols and examining them. He looked at the silver caps on the end of the pearl handles. I had my initials inscribed in the silver. "What does the JJ stand for?"

"Don't know. Picked them up at a pawn shop." I kicked the horizontal slats of the bulwarks with the tip of my black cowboy boot.

"I can have Mr. Pinkerton do a check on them, if you'd like. Try to figure out where they came from."

"No thanks," I said. "Gun's a gun." I would have guessed he was pals with that son-of-a-bitch Pinkerton. "I'll take those now." I put my hand out for him to give me back the holster. I could not stand another moment of him stroking my babies with his moist, puffy, white fingers. He unclipped the holster, handed it to me, then turned and walked to the Chief's quarters.

Tatanka and the laborers approached, their whaleboat filled with dark sea urchins tap-scratching the hull with their sharp, stiff legs. Tatanka alone rowed the boat, sitting on the stern gunwale, his oar stroking one side, then the other, his helpers still in the water, swimming quietly alongside. Tatanka called to me from the water. "Take a look at this," he said. I stripped again and dove into the cove. That warm blue water sure felt good, considering it was an ocean graveyard. He pointed under the hull, took a deep breath, and dove under the ship. I gulped some air and followed. He pointed to a gouge in the hull, about an inch deep, two inches wide, and almost two feet long, with a gap of about an inch in the middle. I could only imagine that it had been made by a giant, sharp-tipped ice tong. Tatanka swam further and pointed to another gouge, and then another further down the hull. We came to the surface to catch our breath.

"Some *thing*. Chewed on the ship, eh? Had very strange teeth," he said, panting. He shook the water from his long black hair.

"Yeah, only two sharp teeth, scoopers, something from a woodworker's bench."

"Bite of an owl, Ishcabibble."

"Owl?"

"Underwater night eagle."

I could not dispute his claim, for whatever had made those marks was surely not of the world I knew. I climbed back up the anchor and helped the others haul in their catch. Mendoza approached me for his girlfriend's photo, and when I handed it to him, he clutched it to his chest, closed his eyes, and smiled. That night, Tatanka filled the try-pots with water and boiled the black, spiny sea urchins with seaweed on the deck of the ship. He served big bowls of the urchins and provided sharp forks to dig into their undersides and extract the gooey yellow meat. The crew did not find the urchin flesh appetizing and mostly dumped their bowls into the sea. Word came from the captain's roundhouse that the soup was unacceptable. They demanded Tatanka kill chickens and barbecue them immediately. A pitcher of grog might have smoothed tempers, but that was not allowed on Silverspoon's *Lone Star*.

After the mess had been cleared I found Basmati Sweet leaning out over the bowsprit, her brown face shimmering, almost bronze, in the amber rays of dusk. I could not deny my attraction to her, though it went against everything Momma Zee had ever taught me. I had spent my boyhood clothed and fed by black slaves, women and girls, and I had always felt tension between us—but acted on it only once. Momma Zee put her hatchet to that notion like she would to a chicken's neck. That evening, Frank, I felt drawn to the African, felt it rummaging in my guts and in my loins. I rolled two smokes and offered her one. She accepted. I scratched the white tip of a match with my thumbnail and gave her a light. We smoked together without speaking in the amber light over the fading blue cove.

"What did they talk about?" she asked after some time.

"Who?" I said, knowing what she meant, but hoping to wiggle out of the truth.

"The captain, Krill, Chief, the others, when they sent Sir Yes Sir and me below." She blew a thin jet of smoke out over the water, followed by two, perfect round, gray circles.

"It's not my position to say, uh, sir. That's a question for Captain Silverspoon." A breeze pushed her shirt open at the chest, and I caught a glimpse of the bandages wrapped tightly to flatten her breasts.

She turned and looked hard at me. "He won't tell me. He just avoids it. Our plans, our ideas—we worked hard down there crafting a message that would appeal to Africans—and they never asked for them."

I did not know what to say. It was me who suggested full-out Jim Crow. I could not admit that to her. Yet there was an invitation to honesty in the smoke we shared, in the beauty we beheld on that intimate cove. I could have admitted what was done, but I shied away, claiming not to understand the language of politics. She thanked me for the smoke and walked away, her long, lithe gait swaying side-to-side, elegant, supple, alluring.

The sun had set a deeper when Captain Silverspoon suggested a bonfire on the beach. The officers and crew took to shore in the whaleboats. Sailors went about gathering driftwood and making a huge, tangled, sinister pile of wood midway between the surf and the ranks of languid, murmuring palm trees. The blaze went up and a hush settled over the men and women of the *Lone Star*. Only the fire spoke, in roars and pops and hisses. After the flashing red and yellow died down to a bluish orange, the captain turned to me and asked for a story. I wondered if he had a subject in mind, and he requested *Moby-Dick*.

"You mentioned that book about whaling, didn't you?" he asked. "Something about the Bible of whaling. That's a Bible, Ish, we ought to be very familiar with." Dagger, Yo Ho Ho, and Tosspot, wandered off together under the fluted leaves of a palm tree, saying something about "that rat bastard in Iraq." Sir Yes Sir stared to follow, stopped, followed again a few steps, and returned to the fire.

I agreed to tell the story, uncertain though I was how an ignorant farm boy, an unschooled gunslinger and hateful rebel crusader, could ever capture the magnificent breadth of Mr. Melville's masterwork. I agreed, Frank, because I imagined you would have wanted me to try, would have coaxed me to dig deeper and plow up a truth that might challenge my narrow assumptions about life. So I went ahead and tried.

"'Call me Ishmael,' the book begins. That's the name of an orphan from the Bible. He wan an innocent young man, one who had been to sea, but never as a whaler. He met his friend Queequeg, a Fijian cannibal, before they signed on the whaling ship Pequod on Nantucket Island. Queequeg had tattoos like mine." I pointed to my face. I looked something up in the book. "Except his, was 'a mystical treatise on the art of attaining truth,' painted into him by a witch doctor who tried to solve the riddle of the world in his skin. Mine's just for decoration.

The two friends signed on, but a sense of doom that accompanied the. They had the feeling some element of fate was at play in their decision to board the Pequod, captained by one Ahab. There was something about the danger that made it all the more certain they would go with Ahab, all the more enhanced by the news his leg had been bitten off by a whale during his previous voyage.

In and amongst this tense foreboding, Ishmael set about explaining the life of whales. He went through all exhaustions, describing every type of whale, its habits and appearances, its appetites and ranges. All through the book, he dove deeper and deeper into the complexity of whales, their massive size, and the mystery of how they lived. He focused finally on the sperm whale, the most magnificent in Ishmael's view, the most powerful, the most dangerous, the most valuable. He next described the Giant Squid, a sea monster almost never seen that battled sperm whales in the lightless depths.

"Then too he examined in great detail every aspect of a whaling ship at sea. He described the whale hunt, the chase, and the heaving of harpoons. He told of the cook, the carpenter, the blacksmith, and in great detail described the officers and the crew. Ishmael, it seemed, wanted the reader to perceive him as a thorough and trustworthy narrator, one who had spared no effort in understanding his subject, and one then to trust and believe as the story unfolded.

"Not until the book was nearly one-third finished did Ishmael and the crew learn the true purpose of their voyage. Until then, they had assumed it to be a standard whaling expedition, expected to last two, three, perhaps four years, until every spare inch of the ship were filled with barrels of whale oil and the precious spermaceti. Only when Ahab finally removed himself from his quarters did they understand his purpose. He had been, as he said, 'dismasted,' by the white whale, Moby Dick, and he intended to hunt that whale until he found it and killed it for what it had done to him. I paged through the book for a quote.

> What I've dared, I've willed; and what I've willed, I'll do! They think me mad—Starbuck does; but I'm demoniac, I am madness maddened! That wild madness that's only calm to comprehend itself! The prophecy was that I would be dismembered; and—Aye! I lost this leg. I now prophesy that I will dismember my dismemberer.

Ahab demanded of his crew an oath to go with him across the globe in the hunt for Moby Dick. He further demanded their allegiance by having them drink rum together from the same chalice, and then from the cup end of harpoons. He finally secured their ambition by nailing a gold doubloon to the mainmast and promising it to the first man who sighted the white whale.

'With their souls now tethered to him as if *he* were the whale that had wheedled their spears and now towed them relentlessly through the water, Ahab set his course for the exact latitude and longitude of the South Pacific locale at which his leg had been torn asunder by Moby Dick. Along the way, sailors perched at the midnight masthead perceived the phantom jet of a milky whale leading Ahab to their final, fateful encounter. Along the way, to any ship they crossed, Ahab posed the question: "Hast thou seen the White Whale?" To those who had not, he turned a cold shoulder; and to those who had, he inquired of the direction and carried on with his quest.

"Along the way they met many a sailing boat and heard all manner of tales involving plagues, near mutinies and random misfortune. Along the way they met ships of fools who chased useless whales, or tried to harvest rotten ones found floating in the sea. They met the Bachelor, "a full ship homeward bound," disgusting to Ahab in its conceit of success. And then they met the Rachel, whose captain had lost his very son to the white whale, and finally the Delight, which had lost five men to an attack by Moby Dick the day before.

Ahab, despite all warnings, all suffering and death coming to him at all angles, threw every sail he had to catching up with Moby Dick. He forged himself a harpoon out of nail stubs from the shoes of racehorses, the hardest metal, with barbs made of razors and tempered with the blood of pagans, and consecrated in St. Elmo's fire. He had a new leg made from the jawbone of a whale, and every step he took as he paced the deck he walked in the white shoe of his legless enemy. He threatened his first mate, Starbuck, with a loaded musket when the mate tried to talk him out of the hunt. He sailed with a buoy made from the coffin of a cannibal, and yet still he sailed on to meet the great White Whale.

"At last came the cry, made by Ahab himself, "There she blows!—there she blows! A hump like a snowhill! It is Moby Dick!" He rewarded himself the gold doubloon and gave chase to Moby Dick. The whaleboats reached the whale, and he sounded, but not deeply. He rose beneath Ahab's boat and caught it in his jaws, and bit it clean in two. Ahab nearly drowned, but he was revived when he reached the ship; and the following day he lowered a second time for Moby Dick. This time they stuck the brute well with darts but did not reduce his power in the least. He tangled their lines so all the boats seemed caught in a sticky ocean web, and crushed two boats before he flipped Ahab's into the air like a seal playing with a ball—and in so doing, shattered Ahab's newly minted white leg.

Now, at last, it would appear time to call the game and admit defeat, but Ahab, no, he put in a third time for Moby Dick, this time with but a broom handle for a leg, and a harpoon not the least bit special. Even as Starbuck implored him:

'Great God! but for one single instant show thyself; never, never wilt thou capture him, old man—In Jesus' name no more of this, that's worse than devil's madness. Two days chased; twice stove to splinters; thy very leg once more snatched from under thee; thy evil shadow gone—all good angels mobbing thee with warnings;--what more wouldst thou have?—Shall we keep chasing this murderous fish till he swamps the last man? Shall we be dragged by him to the bottom of the sea? Shall we be towed by him to the infernal world? Oh, oh,—Impiety and blasphemy to hunt him more!'

Ahab refused to give up the chase. He thrust oars out a third time and leaped upon the swells to meet his doom. The first two boats were crushed once more, and then Moby Dick turned on the Pequod and built his velocity to ramming speed; thereupon he slammed the ship, split her open, and sank her with all the crew. Ahab, still—no ship to call home, not a leg to stand on—one last time, gave chase to Moby Dick. Sharks snapped at his oars until they were splintered sticks, and still he rowed on. One last time he threw his spear and hit his mark, but this last time the whale line came flying round his neck and dragged him to the wake of Moby Dick's slashing gallows tail. Only Ishmael survived, by using the coffin as a life raft, and floating on it until another ship came by to save him."

I ended the story and left it to bake in the fire. No one spoke. Their faces shone red in the uneven light. I lifted fine sand in my cupped hands and let it run through my fingers. The fire softly cackled at some dark joke it alone consumed, and the surf whispered gibberish to itself like a bum alone on a park bench.

Finally, Captain Silverspoon broke the silence. "Neat story, Ish. That old Ahab, he's like me. Had his white whale. I got mine. Call it the federal bureaucracy. I'm huntin' that fat beast, and I'm gonna strip its blubber and feed it to the sharks!"

"*BRACK!* Meet the harpoon of tax relief—harpoon of tax relief."

"You figure the government dismasted you, captain? Ripped off your leg?" I asked.

"You goddamned right it did! Gubment regulation cost me two nice companies. Crazy whale's runnin' around this whole country, chewing up the entrepreneurial spirit with red-tape teeth." He turned to his parrot. "Hast thou seen the white whale, Krill?"

"*BRACK* yes! Look at the bite he took out of my paycheck!" Krill held up his wing and folded it over, as if the end had been chewed off. The red faces around the fire laughed. Basmati Sweet cleared her throat and spoke in her husky voice.

"I don't know, sir. In some ways the white whale *is* our Moby Dick." She scratched her upper lip and smeared her grease pencil mustache.

"That's deep. Throw some grease on it," said the captain.

"Well, look at the blubber demands of this nation. We have no choice but to relentlessly pursue the whale, to chase it the world over and stop at nothing to keep the blubber coming. Our dominance, our strength, is completely dependent on the steady, cheap supply of whale oil. We have to be like Ahab, or we are doomed."

"*BRACK!* But if we're like Ahab, the whale will, it will——." Krill could not finish his thought but instead began singing, "My bonny lies over the ocean, my bonny lies over the sea, my bonny lies over the ocean, oh bring back my bonny to me." At the chorus the captain and the crew joined in.

After the song, Sir Yes Sir spoke up. "I've always enjoyed that book. Pretty good summary, IshcaBible," he said to me. "It's amazing how Melville predicted the Civil War, foretelling how the leviathan of white supremacy would rise up and shatter our nation."

Wrong John frowned and rubbed his chin. Krill sang another song: "A sailor went to sea, sea, sea, to see what he could see, see, see; but all that he could see, see, see, was the bottom of the deep blue sea, sea, sea!" I walked away from the fire and strolled along the beach. Several crew passed me, speaking excitedly of their plan to spend the night on Great Abaco Island and dig up Captain Kidd's treasure at first light.

Later that night, Tatanka and I lay in our bunks and talked about *Moby-Dick*. "You have a white whale, Tatanka?" I asked. A small oil lamp hung from a hook screwed into the ceiling. It swung idly, along with the ship, rocked by the gentle currents of the cove. The small light spread only a few feet from its source, not reaching the corners of the small cabin.

"White whale?" asked Tatanka. "Huh. More like white snake. Head to tail a thousand miles long. Creeping, crawling, slipping across the Great Plains and over every rock and bush."

"White snake? I don't follow."

"White snake that swallowed white mice. White mice jumping through its skin, running everywhere, eating everything in sight."

"You're goin' pure Injun on me, Tatanka."

"I call it white snake. You call it wagon train."

"Okay, okay." I could picture the settlers as a white snake a thousand miles long.

"My people—no Ahab. We surrendered." Tatanka said. "Our chiefs, they knew: white snake has no end. They said stop, before we all die." Neither of us spoke for a good ten minutes.

"What about you?" he asked. "You Ahab?"

I thought about it a minute. Me, Ahab? Well, I had my obsession, didn't I, Frank? And I chased it all the way to Northfield, Minnesota, where it sunk my ship, but like Ahab, I put in after it a third time. I wasn't Ahab, though, in that I didn't start the fight. He came after the white whale, and it took his leg. I was minding my own business fishing for bullhead when it bit me.

"Yep, Injun," I said. "Union was my white whale."

"That's funny. A white whale hunting a white whale."

I was taken aback by the comment. At first it hit me as an insult, and I was ready to go Old Testament dentist on him. Then I recalled my own words of that morning. I let the slap turn my head and considered its merits. Me, a whale, hunting my own kind. Boy, Frank, if that didn't describe we cannibals in the State of Misery. "You bit off a mighty big plug of chaw, Injun," I admitted. "I'll have to tuck that one in my cheek a day or two."

I blew out the oil lamp and settled into the sparse fluff of my goose-feather mattress. I got to considering Ahab and how his hunger for revenge made him so crazy. How many times had it happened in history, Frank? You're the scholar. And how many other reasons had prodded countless Ahabs to go at a full gallop off a deep cliff? There's our pa, Robert James—threw his harpoon into the '49 California gold rush. Adios. And our ma too, Frank. I can admit it, if you can't. She threw her spear into the backs of those coloreds, and by damn, in the end it tore away her right arm and killed her youngest son. Would she have done like Ahab and made herself a new arm off a black woman? Who can say?

I lay there and thought about it, Frank. How many tragedies had the world endured because of quests like Ahab's? And then there was the other side. What sort of a conquering hero would Ahab have been if he had sailed into Nantucket with the penis bone of Moby Dick? and wearing a heavy necklace strung with his sharp teeth? and the white whale's armor melted and stored in casks to light a thousand Christmas dinners? That's where it gets sticky, don't it, Frank? If a suicide mission pans out, the crazy man or woman (let's not forget Joan of Arc) turns into a hero, or a saint.

I got myself so worked up and confused thinking about it, I had to go topside and throw my questions at the full moon. I received no answer but only the rippling white reflection of her in that tranquil cove.

Chapter X

Pirate? *Pshaw*

The next morning the trumpets called the crew to prayers. Tosspot played parson and delivered a dour warning about the burden of original sin. He concluded the service by singing *Amazing Grace*, with a voice I can honestly say was the worst I had ever heard. It was so off key and overdone with vibrato it drove off the tone-deaf sea ravens resting in the yards. The captain gave the command to set sail, and the crew made ready the sheets, turned the capstan to weigh anchor, and steered toward the gap in the reef, a comely breeze pushing *Lone Star* along. The treasure hunters who had stayed on the island screamed at *Lone Star* to come and pick them up.

"Shee-it, y'all some dumb pirates!" Wrong John hollered. "Only a doofus digs for lost treasure. Smart pirate goes to the bank and takes out a line'a credit." On his command, Gunny went to the cannons and fired a few rounds at the scavengers to drive them into the trees. *Lone Star* navigated the reef and sailed up the Atlantic seaboard to campaign in the final weeks before the election. The captain stumped in Charleston, Wilmington, Philadelphia, New York, and Boston. He took trains to Cincinnati, Detroit, and Chicago, and made a final loop through the South before winding up in Florida to sew up his victory in the Sunshine State.

At last the election happened, and it came out a dead heat. Foul Bore and Wrong John Silverspoon had taken an equal number of states, and Florida would decide the race, just as Krill had predicted. At first it appeared Bore had won Florida. Then Myturn Silverspoon "lost" several thousand ballots from black counties and appeared to have given his brother the slimmest of victories. Foul Bore intercepted the lost ballots before they were burned, loaded them onto *Liberty*—the lead ship of state, loaned to him for the campaign by Captain Bubba—and set sail for Washington to file a complaint with Congress. He had on board with him the black legislators representing the voters of the counties in question.

News of Foul Bore's plan struck Wrong John as a betrayal from his brother. Myturn must have intentionally delayed burning the ballots to sabotage his victory, the captain reasoned. One morning, just after breakfast, Myturn Silverspoon found himself strapped by his wrists to the aft mast of *Lone Star*, facing the golf platform, his shirt ripped and dangling at his waist. Marshal Tosspot had his bullwhip out and warmed it up with loud pops into the open air. Myturn cringed with every snap of the whip. Crewmembers in their sharp white shirts and blue trousers stood at attention on either side of the deck. A single trumpeter played taps.

"Oh, I got ya covered. Don't worry, Florida's a fat whale,' you said. 'Take her blubber,' you said," Wrong John said sarcastically to his brother. "You hosed me, Myturn. Now it's nobody's turn, thanks to you." He turned to the marshal. "How many you reckon, TP? Fifty lashes? Seventy-five?" The marshal popped his whip into the air.

"No, Wrong John! I did everything I could," cried Myturn.

A light steam-driven sailing frigate puffed alongside *Lone Star* and hailed her. Krill perched at the tip of the frigate's bowsprit. "*BRACK!* Here comes the cavalry—the cavalry." He whistled the preamble to *Charge!* Just behind him stood Chief Dagger and Yo Ho Ho. Beyond them on the frigate could be seen four figures dressed in black robes and black hoods, their faces completely obscured. They climbed into a longboat, came alongside *Lone Star*, and were helped on deck.

"Just in time to watch smarty pants get a whuppin'," Wrong John said to Krill and the officers, hands on hips, red nose sharp as a wasp stinger.

"Cut him loose, TP," Chief said to the marshal. "We need him for this operation."

"Thank God," moaned Myturn, his head dropping to his chest. The marshal sliced away his bindings.

"Operation Save the Whale, sir," Gunny told Wrong John, adjusting first his eye patch, then his monocle. "If America isn't smart enough to give us *Liberty*, we'll have to give her death."

The big African diplomat came through the hatch and walked over to the group. "What's going on?" he asked.

"Never you mind, Sir Yes Sir. It doesn't involve hand holding or sending love poems through translators," spoke Yo Ho Ho snidely.

The diplomat stuck out his chest and raised his voice. "Don't condescend to me, Gunny. I'm an officer and I need to know what we're doing. Is there news of the election?"

"You could say that, Sir Yes Sir," Chief said. "There's a controversy in Dade County I need you and Second Mate Sweet to investigate. Gather the intelligence and meet us in Washington."

"Washington?" asked the diplomat.

"Just the two of us, again?" asked Sweet.

"That's right. We've got to get to the capital before Foul Bore—to prepare our arguments against his case before the Congress."

"But shouldn't we help prepare?" said Second Mate Sweet. "We're part of—"

"Of course you are. That's why I want you down here, investigating, preparing a strategy in parallel with ours. We'll rendezvous in D.C. and compare notes."

"Just like before?" asked Sweet, eyes rolled up, brow knitted.

"Just like before," Dagger said. He fingered the handle of the knife at his belt. Sweet swung her shrunken head by its gold chain.

"Let's go, Mr. Second Mate," said Sir Yes Sir. He saluted, and the two

Africans walked to a waiting whaleboat that rowed them to shore.

Krill hopped to the captain's shoulder and spoke rapidly into his ear. Wrong John's eyes grew bright, and a smile parted his lips. "Hot damn! This is my kind'a ballgame. Extra innings, every bat but one broken, pennant on the line." He cupped his hands around his mouth and yelled, "Hang the drapes, boys! Mizen, main and aft! Throw down every hunk of canvas we've got. It's curtains for Foul Bore!"

Sailors scurried up the braces and climbed hand over hand up the halyards. They shinnied out the yardarms and untied the sails, a good thirty of them up in the rigging, flitting along the ropes with the ease of spiders on their webs. *Lone Star* weighed anchor and sailed out of Fort Lauderdale. Storm clouds gathered and whipped up whitecaps on the steel blue Atlantic. Lightning bolts appeared to shoot from the sea into the sky as if attacking the clouds, the thunder behind them announcing a direct hit. Fierce winds out of the east pushed *Lone Star* over, hard to port, and billowed her white drapery to the point of nearly ripping. The pilot threw in the log and line and registered fifteen knots—her maximum hull speed. He accelerated in bursts by positioning *Lone Star* at the crest of storm waves and letting them roll her faster than the wind. The tempest pushed the ship into the night, not letting up until the following day.

Twenty minutes before the next day's dinner the masthead lookout sighted another ship, and shouted, "Three spikes up, two leagues on!" Telescopes revealed her to be *Liberty* by her American flag seconded with a pointed, ribbony blue banner some twenty feet long that declared the ship's top rank. Gunny called all hands to deck, and then to battle stations. The quartermaster lowered the Texas flag and replaced it with a blue banner that flew below the stars and stripes, the same as on *Liberty*. It was a direct, mutinous challenge to the lead ship's authority.

Lone Star raced on, drawing within hailing range of *Liberty*. She announced herself and demanded *Lone Star* lower her blue banner. *Lone Star*, calling herself the Destiny, obligingly lowered her blue pennant, only to replace it with a sullen black banner painted white at the center with a skull and crossbones! She tacked starboard of *Liberty*, enough behind her to eliminate the threat of her cannon, yet at a fine angle for a volley from *Lone*

Star's port cannon battery.

"Let fly a volley in sequence, starting with cannon one to catch her aft mast as we pass by!" demanded Chief Dagger. "Aim high. We don't want to sink her." Wrong John stood next to him at the helm, seeming content to have his first mate in command.

In the next instant came the boom and flash of port cannon one, followed by a cloud of black smoke. Then came the boom of cannon two, a count of ten later, followed by three, four, five, and so forth, until all ten had been fired. The first two shots ripped through *Liberty*'s aft mainsail, leaving strips of cloth flying in the wind. The third shot shattered her aft mast and sent it tumbling into the water. The crew of *Lone Star* yelped and howled. Captain Silverspoon yelled, "Yeehaw!" and waved his long, black, humped captain's hat in the air.

The pull of the downed sails in the water sent *Liberty* hard to port, suddenly positioning her port cannon battery for a direct broadside to *Lone Star*. As she turned, an elegant carving came into view: it was Lady Liberty chiseled into the prow under her bowsprit. The figurehead held a sword in one hand, a torch in the other, her flowing blue gown torn at the chest to reveal abundant, proud, winsome breasts and sharp brown nipples. It occurred to me, as *Liberty* swung sharply round, cutting a smooth swath through the water, her buxom figurehead on the vanguard, that there was something deeply feminine in the spirit of America. She was a country different from so many countries her: one more receptive, more tolerant, more inviting, a country not rigid but open, free, and independent like the wild mother spirit of nature.

Liberty bore down nonetheless fiercely. She was a much larger and better-armed ship than ours, carrying a full forty cannon on two decks, compared to *Lone Star*'s total of twenty. Silverspoon's ship was utterly defenseless, having too soon celebrated and not reloaded forthwith. *Liberty* fired her entire complement of twenty port cannon in a quick burst of explosive fire and gunpowder smoke. The cannonballs flew at us with a loud, roaring, whizzing sound—a terrible world-ending buzz of death-angel wings. I had first heard that noise when I was but a boy of sixteen and encountered an artillery barrage in the hills of Clay County, Missouri. I instinctively dropped to the deck of the ship. Most of the rounds whizzed over us, or splashed into the water, but several, perhaps four or five, blasted into *Lone Star* with loud cracks, sending lethal sprays of wood chips and splinters in all directions. Unnoticed by the crew, Wrong John, Dagger, and Tosspot slink down the hatch.

Sailors cried out in shock and pain. Blood splattered the perfectly polished brass fittings and decorative trim of the upper deck. *Lone Star* managed to fire off just three rounds in response to the attack, but they were enough to slow *Liberty* and allow *Lone Star* to press her advantage of speed—heightened all the more by *Liberty's* fallen aft mast. The tall, gangly treasurer, Pinch, seized the helm and close hauled *Lone Star* to the wind, her sails shuddering and flapping before the crew could reset them. She coursed a tight half circle with amazing speed and precision, positioning the starboard cannon for a full broadside. She caught the front of her shirt on an arm of the wheel and tore it open.

"Let fly the guns, men!" screamed Pinch, looking like Lady Liberty with her sword drawn and cleavage showing from her torn shirt. "Empty hell's fury on them!"

Lone Star delivered her metal in a rage of instant, booming wrath, followed instantly by the sharp cracks of iron balls slamming into *Liberty's* wood. Now, with *Lone Star* close enough to pull in, Pinch ordered grappling hooks out, and the men threw to *Liberty* and quickly drew her tight. I swung over the water on a rope and jumped to the deck. Peace- and Widowmaker seemed to spring from the holster into my hands. I stalked the jungle of frayed rope, ripped white canvas, and shattered lumber. Fires and harsh black smoke made my eyes water. It smelled of sulfur and burning oakum. Shadowy forms ran this way and that, all of them wearing the same blue uniforms. It was impossible to tell friend from foe, and I could not decide who to shoot.

Across the deck I recognized Pinch, who was leading the assault, her cutlass out, parrying and thrusting, blade clashing and clanging against her opponent's. "Behind you, Ish!" she hollered. I spun and shot a sailor who had his cutlass drawn and ready to slice my neck. Along the rail the hawk-nosed specksynder battled by sword, alongside the quartermaster and the junior officer, Bill, who had captained one of the whaleboats. They growled and grunted, blades ringing, boots clomping and grinding, smoke sullenly stalking the deck. Then came the screams of opponents pierced, the tumble of bodies crumpling to the deck, final curses and prayers rasped into the brittle air. An African lad no more than four feet tall jumped from a yard to the specksynder's back and stabbed him with a kitchen knife. I shot the child in the back. He fell to the deck with a thud.

"Cease, pirates!" came a harsh voice from the helm. "*Liberty* surrenders. Let no more blood be shed." Forward walked Foul Bore, his right cheek caked with blood, a square of white canvas tied to the end of musket. A group of Africans stood with him. They did not have looks of surrender on their hard, glistening brown faces.

"Quiet your steel, *Lone Star*! The battle is ours! *Liberty* yields! She yields!" shouted Pinch.

"Huzzah! Huzzah! Huzzah!" shouted the pirates, pumping the air with their swords. I did not join the celebration, but checked the sprawled body of the black boy I had shot. He appeared to be the same age as Jesse Jr., and he was dead.

"*Lone Star?*" asked Bore, looking at Pinch. "Officer Pinch? How can it be?"

Captain Wrong John Silverspoon, Krill on his shoulder, swung from a rope over the starboard rail and landed ahead of the mainmast. "*BRACK!* April Fool. April Fool."

Wrong John strode to Foul Bore and grabbed his white flag. "Nice doin' business with ya," he said. He turned to Pinch, not realizing she had carried the day, and told her, "Search the ship, Pinch. Count up the money and give me a total." She saluted, but when Silverspoon turned back to Bore, dropped her shoulders and shuffled away on her long, clumsy, heroic legs.

"My God, Wrong John. The Jolly Roger? You're a pirate? A pirate?"

"Pirate? Pshaw. We're just funnin' ya, Bore. It's only politics. Don't take it personal."

"Dead men tell no tales, *BRACK!* They tell no tales." Krill looked quickly back and forth. Wrong John handed him a peanut, which he took in his pitted gray beak.

"Don't take it personal? You sacked my ship, murdered my crew, and I'm not supposed to take it personally?" Foul Bore's face wrenched with confused anger. Behind him, *Lone Star*'s crew gathered swords, pistols, and rifles in a big pile, assembled *Liberty*'s crew, and tied their hands behind their backs. They added the black legislators standing behind Foul Bore to the group of bound prisoners.

"Like I said. It's politics. Winner take all. We couldn't let you run off to Washington and raise a big stink about those ballots. It idn't about you or me, Bore. Think about The Economy."

"The economy? To hell with the economy. This is about democracy. Every vote must be counted. It's about fairness and justice, Silverspoon. And now it's about *treason!*"

Wrong John opened his eyes wide and shook his knees. He grinned and flicked the back of his hand at Foul Bore. "Spare us the drama, Bore. Nobody's gonna believe *Liberty* was taken at sea by a pirate named Wrong John Silverspoon."

"There are witnesses! America will believe!"

"America dudn't care. Besides, crime is in the eye of the beholden." From out of the smoke walked Chief Dagger, Yo Ho Ho, and Marshal Tosspot, followed by the four figures in black robes.

"Greetings, Mr. First Mate," said Chief Dagger to Bore. He walked up to him and ripped the epaulets of rank from the shoulders of Bore's sooty blue jacket. "I'll take those."

Bore looked at the group of men in black robes, his furrowed face the picture of woe. "Chief Justice?" he said. "Justices Masters, Wilson, Evans? What are you—? How can—is this—?"

"We, the majority of the United States Supreme Court, do hereby declare this action to be proper, moral, *and legal*. We sanction the intervention as necessary to protect the United States Constitution, and our very way of life," said the Chief Justice.

"We cannot allow your dispute to interrupt the smooth exchange of power in this nation. And so we give *Liberty* to Captain Wrong John Silverspoon and his first mate, Dagger."

Foul Bore shook his head and looked at the deck. "But the votes, the votes," he mumbled. Out from the hatch flew stuffed cotton sacks, one after another, until fifty of them lay strewn over the planks. Crew from the *Lone Star* popped up from the hatch, gathered the cotton sacks, opened them, and dumped their contents into the sea.

"The votes, the votes," mumbled Foul Bore. "I had it in the bag." Behind him, among the prisoners, stood the black legislators who had fought for their constituents. Many of them screamed, some cried. The disputed ballots flew from the sacks, fluttered in the wind, and landed on the water. After all fifty bags had been emptied, a great patch of white bobbed in the water beside the ship. I felt an arm on my shoulder and turned to see Tatanka's dark face, his long nose and prominent cheekbones, his deepest dark eyes, and long black hair waving in the wind. He had a cruel red gash on his wrist and several thick splinters of wood in his forehead and chin, oozing blood. He gazed at the paper littering the sea.

"Better run," he said in his deep, smooth voice. "It's Moby Dick."

Chapter XI

I Link, Therefore, I Am

Liberty limped up the Atlantic seaboard on her way to Washington. Her aft mast had been cut away off the Florida coast, left to drift into the eddying currents of the Sargasso Sea. Wrong John Silverspoon captained her past Cape Fear through a driving rain on the front edge of a fiendish storm. Her war-torn sails slapped the yards and masts as if challenging them again and again to duel. The quartermaster and pilot recommended he put in at Wilmington, North Carolina, and wait out the storm, but Silverspoon would have none of it. He believed America deserving of her president and didn't want to keep her waiting. The pilot battened the fore and mainsails to give *Liberty* stability in the storm. Severe weather pushed the ship all the way to Chesapeake Bay. When at last she made the mouth of the Potomac, the wind abated, though the clouds rolled low and thick along the hills.

The trip up the Potomac was eerily quiet in the grim gray light. When *Liberty* arrived in Washington, the presidential dock was crowded with anxious citizens carrying banners that read: "Welcome President Bore," along with "Count Every Vote—We Can Wait" and "The American Dream Depends on Equality." *Liberty* coasted into the dock, and out walked Foul Bore. The crowd cheered for him. He smiled and waved, trying, it seemed, to appear himself, but something had changed between Florida and Washington.

"Thank you, everyone. As you can see, *Liberty* has been *dismasted*," he said, pointing to the stump of her aft mast. "Off the coast of Florida, she was attacked by pirates." Cries, gasps, and shouts rippled through the crowd. "Luckily, Captain Silverspoon came to our aid in *Lone Star*, and beat back the pirates. He brought with him the justices of the Supreme Court, and we all decided it was best for the nation if I dropped my complaint."

"Boo!" the crowd responded.

"Where are the uncounted votes?" someone yelled.

"They were lost in the battle," said Foul Bore.

"Boo! Boo! Boo!"

Foul Bore raised his hands and smiled. "Hey, I understand your disappointment. I'm disappointed too. I really wanted to be president. I could have taken credit for all sorts of things I didn't do." He laughed at himself. The crowd calmed, and a few people laughed. Wrong John and his officers smiled from where they stood behind Foul Bore, abaft the foremast with the black-robed judges.

"Just remember, this is still America, the beacon of hope for the world. We've got to close ranks and accept this outcome. Wrong John Silverspoon is your new president. It's that simple. The good news is, he's one of us, an American, who believes in the principles that underpin our democracy. Let's put our differences behind us and unite around him. How about it?"

A mixed response of boos and clapping came from the crowd.

"I understand," said Bore, raising his hands. "It will take some time to heal the wounds. For now, though, I want you to open your hearts as good Americans. Welcome your new captain, not as a Republican or a Democrat, but as one of us, an American." He stepped back and applauded. The crew of *Liberty* cheered, and Wrong John's officers clapped. The crowd gave reserved applause.

"Thank you, Foul Bore. That's a good sport there, folks, idn't it?" He applauded for Foul Bore; some in the crowd cheered, some booed. "I think he put it well. There's no point bickering. Heck, we could count those ballots ten more times and get a different result every time. It was a tight, well-fought race, and now it's over." He paused and shot a few people on the crowded dock with magic finger bullets.

"Let's don't let this lack of a fair election thing get in the way of what we do best as Americans. Why let vote tallies, or accounting principles, or civic responsibility get in the way of the American Dream? I'm here to declare a new day in America, a time in which freedom reaches new heights, a time in which nothing and no one can get in the way of good people making a boatload of money. Idn't that what we're all about here in America?"

The crowd responded with some applause, but mostly jeers. Silverspoon shot more love pellets with his bugger wand, then settled into his most sugary drawl. "What I want you to realize is that I'm a bridge builder, not a bridge burner. I'm a guy who connects things." He interlaced his fingers. "Not a tearer aparter." He pulled his hands apart and vibrated his dangling fingers as if they were dying bodies. "I'm a mender of fences, not a buster of the bobbed wire. I link things up, like the links of a chain—the chain of a chain link fence, of—providing safety and linkage for our great nation. I link, therefore, I am." He clasped his hands at his chest and smiled. "Thank you, and may God Test America!"

The new crew of *Liberty* cheered for their captain, as did his officers, and the justices of the court, but the gathered citizens did not. They grumbled and groused, ripped up their banners, threw them to the ground, and slowly drifted away. That was the extent of outrage over the most fraudulent election since Tilden vs. Hayes in 1876. The black suppression had been concealed just enough that almost no one openly contested it. The majority of Americans didn't even know it happened, or, as Silverspoon told Foul Bore, didn't care. *Lone Star*'s attack and capture of *Liberty* never became public, and it came to pass that Wrong John Silverspoon took credit for saving *Liberty* from pirates.

After dropping off the justices and Foul Bore, *Liberty* drew back from the dock and sailed up the Potomac to anchor in a shipyard and make repairs. Ten days later a private yacht picked up Captain Silverspoon and his officers and brought them to Mount Vernon, the estate of President George Washington. There, gathered on the expansive bowling green that yawned before Washington's Mansion House Farm, were several hundred of Silverspoon's most loyal followers. Behind them stood the colonial mansion, a three-story white building of three wings, roofed with burnt orange terra-cotta tile. Ten square pillars stood in perfect symmetry around the front piazza that stretched the entire length of the mansion. A polished bronze Dove of Peace weathervane stood atop an octagonal cupola above the roofline.

News of Wrong John's arrival spread quickly through the crowd. The women in their long white dresses and flowery hats, and the men in black tuxedos and top hats, rushed to the small dock. With the captain's first step on land they erupted in applause. He smiled his smirkish grin, saluted, and shot them with finger bullets. They cheered all the more enthusiastically.

"Heck, it's good to see y'all. It's been a long journey, but now, here we are—the home of our first president with a group of our leading citizens. This is where a boy named George chopped down a cherry tree and admitted he did it. Honesty. That's what we bring back to Washington with us today. Truth. That's our bottom line. You see that Dove of Peace up there?" He pointed to the top of the cupola on Washington's mansion. "That's our weathervane. That's what tells us which way the wind's blowin', and warns us not to stand downwind of a Texan at a chili cook-off." Wrong John chuckled, and laughter spread through the crowd. "I just—thank you—I'm just plain tickled to be here with you. I couldn't have done it without you, and I *never* forget a friend." Strident applause poured from the crowd.

From around a bend a tall, three-masted clipper sailed down the Potomac. She flew the American flag and a long, flowing blue pennant. It was *Liberty*, brightly detailed, fitted with a new aft mast and bright new sails. Her freshly painted figurehead reached out with silver sword, golden torch, creamy brown-tipped breasts. Her refurbishing had been coined "Operation Bubba-Be-Gone" and involved removing all vestiges of the former captain. She coursed gently toward the dock and anchored in deep water thirty feet from shore. The crowd cheered for her, whistled, and shouted. Wrong John saluted her and turned back to his people.

"Now, please join me in the ceremonial raising of the corporate flags." He climbed into a longboat and was rowed to *Liberty*. Eight sailors on board held snare drums from straps over their shoulders and provided a drum roll. The captain came on deck, and approached the mainmast. His crew made ranks on the starboard side of the ship, officers positioned in front of them. He nodded at the officers, whereupon Pinch came forward and handed him a flag.

He attached it by grommets to clips on a rope and raised it up the mainmast. The flag contained a swirling red mark and the words "Anders Arthurson Accounting, *Painting by Numbers.*" I found out later the flags raised were from the companies Captain Silverspoon's officers had worked for before joining him on *Liberty.*

Next came Dr. von Shlop in his blue robe and pointed blue hat. Wrong John raised his flag: Retro Research, *Science Made to Order.* After him walked Crude, the Oil Czar, with a flag that read: BlubbCo., *Blubbering Up for a Better Tomorrow.* Sir Yes Sir followed a flag proclaiming Mercy Nary, *Pirate Security for the Public Good.* Yo Ho Ho hoisted Cannon Fodder, Inc., *Safety Is in the Numbers.* Tosspot advanced with Holy Dollars, Inc., *Take Stock in Salvation.* Basmati Sweet presented Money Lynch, *Let Us Hang Your Pension High.* Krill added Dirty Pool, Inc., *The Politics of Smear.* Chief Dagger came with Hellbent Industries, *The Whaleman's Best Friend.*

I wandered to the new golf stage erected at the stern of *Liberty* and found Tatanka there, sitting on the platform, playing with an Indian toy. The cuts on his face from the cannon splinters had scabbed over black. His toy consisted of a button in a loop of string held between his hands. As he pulled his hands apart, the button spun one direction; then he relaxed his hands and it spun the other way, faster and faster the harder he pulled on the loop, making a high-pitched whizzing sound. I looked at the new flags up the masthead, and something about the angle of the setting sun, or some reflection off the Potomac, got my eyes a little crossed. The company marks on those flags turned ghoulish on me, went all black and white with skulls and hourglasses, crossed cutlasses and arm bones. For a second it looked as if *Liberty* was flying the Jolly Roger of every pirate who ever sailed.

After all the officers had raised a flag up the mainmast to just below the crow's nest, Wrong John wrung his hands and looked with a knitted brow at his officers. "*BRACK!* Captain's got no company. He's got no company," called Krill. The other officers looked sidelong at one another. Captain Silverspoon turned to the audience on shore and shouted, " Hey, Slick!" A tall man with a hound-dog face loped to the riverside and cupped a hand behind his long right ear. "Can I borrow your company?" asked Silverspoon. "Gubment regulation done killed all the ones I had."

"You bet, old buddy!" shouted Slick, his voice coated with Texas barbecue sauce. "But it'll cost ya!" The well-heeled audience laughed, as did the captain and his officers. Slick climbed on his yacht and retrieved something from below, and then had a crewmember row him to *Liberty*. Sailors helped him on deck, and he handed Captain Silverspoon a flag, which he promptly raised: Endrun Energy, *Whoa, Is It Hot Out There!*

With so many flags in the rigging, Old Glory could no longer be seen, but those gathered felt for their tickers with a right hand on the chest, looked up into the rigging, and together sang *God Bless America*, led by Tosspot in his trilling tenor that could have cracked a pewter beer stein.

I looked over at Mr. Washington's mansion and saw in a window of the cupola a candelabrum with seven long candles burning. I tapped Tatanka on the shoulder to have him take a look, but when we turned back at the red-roofed white mansion, the candelabrum was gone.

A commotion on deck brought my attention back to the ceremony. Tosspot had apparently tripped while carrying an urn of oil to the captain. "What in the hell are you doing?" asked Wrong John, looking down at the mess on his chest.

"It's oil, Sire, spermaceti." He turned to the crowd on shore. "Shouldn't he be anointed?" Tosspot cried. "Do we not deserve a king, at last, in America?" The crowd was silent. "George Washington could have set things right from the beginning. He could have taken the crown. It was there for him, but he turned it down, and look at all the trouble it has caused us, this aristocratic void making all of us commoners."

"Cuckoo! Cuckoo!" squawked Krill, poking his head forward and back like a toy bird in a clock.

"Damn it, TP! Stick to the script, would you?" said Silverspoon. The marshal backed away, turned, and hurried down the hatch. A kitchen laborer came forward with a white towel and began to rub the oil out of the captain's stained blue blazer. Dagger cued the trumpets and they began to play *Hail to the Chief*. The captain waved at the crowd while Chief ordered the anchor up, sails set, and sent *Liberty* down the river.

After dinner that night, I found Basmati Sweet leaning over the stem rail with a lamp and looking at the carving of Lady Liberty. "I'd say that artist had a very fine eye for detail," I said to her. She straightened her back and smiled at me. I offered her a smoke and she accepted. I gave her a light.

"Yes," she said, forgetting to lower her voice an octave, "the lines are exquisite." She set her glowing lamp on a bench.

"Curves are pretty, too." I glanced at her bound and flattened breasts, then down at the shrunken head hanging from her belt.

She smiled at me, took a pull on her smoke, and blew a jet of gray through her brown, pillow lips, followed by two perfect circles of smoke. "IshcaBible?" she asked. "I'm still not clear on the pirate battle. What happened to the pirates? Why didn't we capture any of them?"

There I was again, Frank, offered by the shared smoke a chance to clear the air. There I was again, preferring to duck in the shadows. I could not consider the dead African I had shot—a boy the same age as my own son. I told her the pirates escaped on their ship, taking the bodies of those we had killed with them.

"That doesn't sound like pirates. Why would they take the bodies? Why would they care?"

"Don't know." We finished our smokes. She thanked me and strolled away in that long, smooth, swaying gait of hers. I had to look away, Frank. Momma Zee's voice came into my head, shaming me for gawking that way at a slave. But momma, I thought, that's no slave, that's a woman, and she is lovely.

Chapter XII

Al Quota

Next morning the sun attempted a dawn but was mostly denied by a thick haze of smoke lying low and tight against the Potomac. All the sun could manage for well over an hour was a sickly yellow halo drifting slowly higher into the sky. No one could explain the smoke—it didn't seem to come from a particular source—except to guess that a few million blubber fires in the vicinity of the capital may have been contributors. Long about 8:00 a.m. the semblance of a day had begun and the trumpets called the crew to prayers. Basmati Sweet approached the quarterdeck rail wearing a bright blue silk blouse with pleated sleeves tight at the wrist, and her customary red bandana—with a shock of jet-black hair sharp along her forehead, nearly covering her left eye. Woven leather sandals embraced her feet, and from her thick brown leather belt hung her throwing knife and shrunken head. She also wore her manly trappings of a grease pencil mustache, and a length of rubber hose down the inside of her pant leg. She gave a lovely rendition of the Lord's Prayer in song. Hers was a voice—unlike the marshal's frog spit—that could launch a ship or two.

Just as Sweet's pretty voice trailed off from the final "amen," Pinch looked up into the sky and pointed at a solitary turkey vulture circling overhead, its broad black wings unmoving as it soared. "Look!" shouted Pinch, her long nose wrinkled, horse teeth exposed. "An eagle!"

We all looked skyward. I and Tatanka shook our heads. The redheaded deathmonger was *all* buzzard. No one else appeared to know the difference, and they formed a chorus of reverent ooh and ahs.

"Got us a sign, boys and girls," said the captain, taking off his new presidential hat, a fore-and-aft rigged, blue-humped monster with red and white plumes on the butt end. He gazed skyward and placed the flamboyant headgear over his heart. The officers and crew doffed their hats and likewise tented their left nipples. "Right there—boom—first day on the job, is there any doubt who's on our side, huh?" said Silverspoon. "Kinda says it all when the great symbol of *Liberty* herself does a fly by—that's a technical term, kids, flyin' term—ahem—as you embark on a historic voyage to restore faith in your nation."

Everyone nodded and murmured their assent. "That's no eagle," I said flatly. "That's a damn turkey vulture. Look at that scrap of a red head. Looks like a dog's dick." The crew stared at me with uniform scorn. I shrugged and pointed up in the sky. "Well it is," I said. Marshal Tosspot pulled his bullwhip from his medieval black belt, jangled his collection of leg irons, slapped the coiled whip against his leg, and sneered at me.

The captain laughed. "Good one, Ish. The scavenger class is always circling, always waiting for a handout. But don't go all Golgotha on me, Ish, not today." He looked up at the soaring bird, blocking the sun with his hand.

"I ain't a professional bird watcher, but them's the wings of an eagle, far as I'm concerned. Proud and beautiful." He saluted at the buzzard, and his crew followed suit, all except for Sir Yes Sir, Tatanka, and myself.

Krill scrambled and flapped and flopped across the deck, smacked square into a belaying pin, and nearly knocked himself unconscious. He shook his head, waddled his tail, and clambered on toward the captain, whereupon he clawed his way up Wrong John's trousers and jacket to his place on the captain's right shoulder.

"*BRACK!* Set the tone. Stick to principle, *BRACK!* Stick to principle," Krill screeched.

"You're late," said Wrong John. He flicked Krill on the beak. The parrot shook his head and grumbled in his gizzardly way. The captain looked out over the ship, across the newly installed blubber try-works amidships, bricked in presidential red with white masonry lines, its mahogany hatch precisely inlaid with an ivory presidential seal. He bobbed his head and looked back and forth at his crew assembled on either side of the deck. He licked his lips and scratched his head, placed his right index finger over his lips, and frowned.

"So, uh—ahem—look at us, huh? We tried, and we tried, and we blew his house down. Got ourselves a porky little boat, didn't we?" He held out his hands and looked around *Liberty*. Some of the sailors asserted, "Yea!" others stared at the deck, not knowing the proper response to his question. He turned to Krill and spoke from the back of his right hand. "What in the heck am I supposed to be on about?" Krill whispered in his ear. Silverspoon nodded and smiled. He pointed to the corporate flags flying at the masthead. "See those flags up there? We didn't just hang 'em 'cause they looked purty. We begin today the hard work of tax reform and regulatory dismemberment. Keep your eye on the ball. Deliverables, people, on time and under budget, hear me? And remember, like that eagle showed us, God is on our side."

He turned to Krill again and spoke behind his hand. "Is that it? They look a sorta confused."

Krill ruffled his feathers and beat the air with his wings. "*BRACK!* Attention! Review of the troops. Review of the troops." The captain tipped his head back, opened his mouth, and seemed to say, "Ah." He ambled down the quarterdeck stairs, his officers in tow, and slowly walked past the crew.

"Wipe that smile off your face, sailor," he said sternly, then smiled and poked him in the stomach. He walked slowly on, pulled a sailor's cutlass from its scabbard, held it up and examined its blade. "Get that thing sharpened! It's a disgrace." He ran his finger along the edge and drew blood. "Ow! Damn it!" He sucked his finger and handed back the cutlass. He continued his slow stroll along the ranks. "Tie those shoes, boy!" The sailor looked down, but his shoes were not untied. "Gotcha!" said the captain, and shot him in the gut with a finger bullet.

The captain strolled on, adjusting a crewman's hat, polishing a button with a little spit on his finger, brushing lint off a shoulder. A crewman jumped from the line, spun the captain around, knocking Krill to the deck, and had Silverspoon by the throat in a chokehold. I pulled Peacemaker and aimed her at his head. Several other sailors burst from ranks, drew pistols, and aimed them at the officers. Sir Yes Sir drew his pistol and pointed it from one to the other of the mutineers. Dagger and Sweet drew their knives. Pinch drew her cutlass. Yo Ho Ho attempted to pull his, but it was stuck and he couldn't get it out of his scabbard.

I eyeballed the uprising, astounded that a rebellion had occurred so early in Wrong John's voyage. Bad news, though, for the rebels—they had trapped themselves in a stalemate, and there was no way they could win. "Drop your weapons!" shouted Sir Yes Sir. "Drop them now or you will hang from the yardarms!" Hell, I thought, they're gonna hang no matter what they do.

The sailor who had the captain by the throat spun him and pushed him at us. He was a robust man with long, curly blond hair, stood average height but was wide, face ruddy and deeply lined. He laughed heartily and held his round belly. He reached out and shook Wrong John's limp hand. "Little," he said. "Dick Little. I'm your Terrorism Czar. What you have just witnessed is the porousness of America's defenses against a terrorist attack." His men dropped their arms and holstered their weapons. They walked over and stood with their commander.

Little put his hands on his hips and glared at the captain and his officers. "Terrorism, gentlemen. It will be your biggest challenge, your biggest danger, your most pressing issue. How you handle it will define your administration."

Krill ruffled his feathers, walked in a small circle, and muttered, "Our greatest opportunity, greatest opportunity."

Dagger pushed his way to the front of the officers. "Well, if it isn't Chicken Little." He looked up at the hazy sky and held his hands out as if testing for rain. "Is it the sky, Little, falling yet again?"

Wrong John's nostrils flared, and he frowned at the ruddy Terrorism Czar. "So you're Little. Well that was a pretty chicken trick. I ought'a string you up just on principle."

"*BRACK!* Stick to principle. Stick to principle."

"Gentlemen, forget about me. Call me chicken, call me hawk, it matters not." He shook back his long, golden locks. "Sight your guns and aim your cannons at Al Quota. We're convinced he is planning a major attack against our citizens on American soil. Seems they've got to knock off a good many of us to make their quota for the year."

"What'd you say?" asked Wrong John. "Al's Pizza?" He raised his head and looked around the ship. "Anybody order a delivery?" He snickered and stroked his nose.

"Good one, sir. Eat, drink, and be merry... but do not underestimate Quota. He's working by some arcane Koranic salvation formula. It requires a set number of infidel souls to be traded in hell for some old friends of the family. Apparently they've got a prisoner exchange clause down in Jahannum—their word for Satan's domain."

Dagger's face appeared ready to explode. "I'm glad you and Bubba could sit around all day and eat your Quota sardines on oyster crackers. We've got another fish to fry—and it's a whopper!" Gobs of spit had formed at the corners of his mouth. His golden earrings jiggled with his words. "Evil exists in the world, Chicken Little. It is not the fantasy of a disoriented egg layer. It goes by the name of Shalong. It has built its palace in the sands of Iraq—the soft sands, accommodating of its penchant for digging mass graves. Shalong has killed millions, tortured thousands, personally raped hundreds!" Spit flew from the right side of his mouth.

"And," said Gunny, leaning forward, gawking through his monocle, his eye magnified to appear that of a lizard, "he just so happens to sit on the biggest blubber reserves in the world. I think the smart money's on that guy. What's yours got?"

"A band of lunatics who will gladly die for his cause. They will stop at nothing, commit any atrocity, in the service of his holy mission."

"Well whoop-dee-doo," said the captain. "You call that an enemy? Shee-it, I ain't even got Quota in my baseball card collection."

Officer Dick Little stared at Wrong John. His ruddy, wrinkled face drew down into a frown. I half expected him to pull a gun. Second Mate Sweet came forward, her right hand raised tentatively beside her face, as if asking a question at school. "Excuse me, I, uh, I believe Mr. Little reports to me, and, I'm not sure we should completely discount his claims." She looked quickly at Sir Yes Sir who pressed his lips tightly and nodded. Gunny made fists and blinked his eye behind his monocle.

"Basma's right," said the captain. "He reports to her. Now y'all run on over to the roundhouse and report. And when you're done, gimme a report. *Comprende?*" He scooted the air with his hands toward the stem of *Liberty*. "Shoo."

Basmati Sweet looked quickly at Sir Yes Sir. He motioned with his head for her to go where she was ordered. She glanced quickly at me. I shrugged my shoulders. She walked slowly toward the roundhouse just abaft the prow, Officer Little and his gang following. I have to give them credit, Frank; Little's boys pulled a pretty slick job. It was a classic bushwhacking: get into your enemy's ranks, blend in, and when he's half nodding off—pounce!

After Basma and Little got out of earshot, Dagger dismissed the crew and stepped before the officers. "Let's be very clear about something. We have waited through eight years of Bubba to restore the dream of the Great Communicator and Wrong John Johnson. We cannot afford the luxury of distractions. Chicken Little is Sweet's boy. Keep him there—out of the loop. Whatever he says, just imagine it came from the greasy lips of Bubba. No difference. And never forget, Chicken Little voted for Foul Bore." Gunny punched his hand with his fist. Tosspot jangled his irons.

"That's right, men—and Pinch," said Silverspoon. "There's a few things more important than Chicken Little's little chicken—such as—as—well, lots of things, like, uh—"

"*BRACK!*" called Krill from where he had been knocked to the deck. "Quick! Somebody throw him cracker. Throw him a cracker."

The good Missouri boy, Tosspot, obliged. "The sanctity of unborn life, of marriage as an eternal bond between a man and a woman, our mission to join the Ten Commandments with our schools," said Tosspot, his voice like flypaper.

"Yeah! That's what I said." Silverspoon stuck out his chin and looked quickly around the group.

"Right, Mr. Captain. Absolutely," said Chief, giving him a half smile. "So let's get to work. TP, you mollycoddle the religos right away. Get rid of Bubba's program encouraging adolescents to have premarital sex. Come up with some wholesome way to stop the bastard children. And get to work with the states to shut down the liberal, baby slaughterhouses." The marshal saluted and marched off.

"Sir Yes Sir," Chief continued. The diplomat came to attention and saluted. "Put an end to Bubba's pathetic, self-centered attempt to bring peace to Israel. We don't need his phony heroics trying to distract everybody from his whoring. And get rid of his slick flim-flam to trade good American wheat for the obedience of that North Korean tyrant."

"I loathe that inbred heathen," fumed Wrong John, lip curled, head shaking.

"You don't influence a thug by kissing his butt," said Gunny. "You let his people starve. You ridicule him, mock and humiliate him, and then, maybe he actually *does* something about his evil weapons program."

"Exactly. You've got your orders, SYS." The diplomat saluted and marched away.

"Now, Yo Yo, get to work on a war plan. I want that rat bastard out of Iraq!" The gunner saluted. He winked at Captain Silverspoon, pulled on his gold nose ring, placed his index fingers on either side of his head, lowered, and charged off. The captain smiled and put his index fingers against the sides of his head.

"Pinch, crunch the numbers on a tax rebate. I want it top heavy or it's useless to me," Chief demanded. She worked her long, bony fingers on the red and white beads of an abacus, dexterous as a Chinese rice merchant.

"Don't worry, sir. We'll report it as an average. It sounds nice, everybody getting an *average* of a thousand bucks. Nobody will know our pals are getting fifty G, while the riff-raff gets a buck or two." She rubbed her long thin hands together.

"Good! We earned it. Now go!" Chief exclaimed. Pinch saluted and shambled away. "Crude! America is dying for an energy policy. Get the blubber barons together and design one." The chubby Energy Czar saluted and marched away.

"Dr. von Shlop! We've got that Japanese worm Kyoto coming with his treaty of economic suicide. Brew us up some alternate science. If you can't lick them, baffle the crap out of them."

The science officer saluted with his white wand. "Eye of frog, wing of a stork, arm of a squid, ear of a bat," the scientist muttered as he walked away with small, precise steps.

The only ones left were the captain, Chief, myself, and Krill. Dagger sucked his teeth and fiddled with his earrings. I pulled Widowmaker and checked her cylinder. Odd, I thought, there's a bullet missing. The captain crossed his arms and tapped his foot on the deck.

"I'm sorry, sir. Did you need an assignment?" Dagger asked.

"Listen, Chief. Do you see 'Captain' written anywhere on your person?" He reached back and ran his fingers through the red and white plumes of his humped blue hat.

"Sir?"

"Jeez, Chief, don't just bark out the orders like that. You're treatin' me like a deckhand."

"A deckhand, sir?" Dagger sucked on his teeth, drew his knife, and cleaned his fingernails with the sharp tip.

"You got to pause every now and then, see. Ask for my approval. I'll nod at you, or grunt, or whatever. These are my decisions you're making. I want that to be clear in the future." Chief saluted and sauntered to his quarters.

"I need a cup'a coffee, Ish," said Wrong John, "somethin' fierce." I tipped my bowler and went to the galley for his Joe.

Chapter XIII

Butterflies Might Also Fly

Tatanka and I spent a fitful night in our small cabin next to the galley. One of the goats got the jitters just as our heads went down and would not stop bleating. I put a gun to its head, but that didn't influence it in the slightest— if anything, it scared it even more. A few minutes later we understood the animal had sensed danger: that chewing sound started again, working its way around the ship, gnawing at the hull. Having seen the marks it made on *Lone Star*, I now had a picture of some grisly monster with two pincher teeth, or some sort of whetted lobster claw, or a giant beak, working us like a walnut. It moved over right next to our heads. The sound so grated and scratched I began to feel it against my skull, grinding through my scalp to get at my darkest, most tasty thoughts, deep inside my brain.

I pounded hard on the boards next to my head. "Leave us alone, you damn monster!" I yelled.

"Shh," said Tatanka. "Night eagle feeds off your rage. Chew on your anger, Dingus. Swallow it to your heart. Temper it with fierce love."

I tried to do what he said, Frank, but damn was that Sioux asking a lot. My entire life had been fueled by rage. I had almost never felt anger and not made somebody pay for it. I wanted that *thing* to go away, so I worked my jaw that night in the upper bunk, as if I had a chunk of rawhide in my mouth. That critter kept grinding; I kept chewing; Tatanka started singing. A voice from the deck above us shouted, "Agh! Something's got my leg! A headless snake! Help!" A gun went off, and I heard a slippery sliding sound on the boards above us, then a slurpy splash next to my head. I chewed harder on my rage, and swallowed bits of it that went down like white-hot tacks. I wanted to scream, to shoot somebody. That rusty, beat-up bullet camped out next to my heart whispered to me, "Kill yourself, Jess. End the pain." I agreed. *I wanted to kill myself!*

Tatanka stood and grabbed me by the shoulders and shook me. "Swallow it, Jesse. It's your rage and nobody else's. Don't give it to the night eagle. It's *your* medicine."

I gulped down that sharp hatred and screamed from the fire of it in my chest. "God! Help me! Please!" I curled in a ball and moaned and tore at my chest—I don't know for how long. When the pain subsided and I stopped moaning, I could hear the critter no more, and did not hear it again for quite some time.

Next morning we both slept in and received a sharp jostling from Basmati Sweet, who rousted us and scolded us for being late with Silverspoon's eggs. "It's a big day, IshcaBible, and now he's going to be crabby." She stomped out of the cabin and grumbled, "Don't break his yolks, Tatanka, not today."

Tatanka stood, stretched and yawned, and shuffled into the kitchen. I climbed down from my bunk, leaned back, and rubbed my aching lower spine. From the galley came the sound of a heavy frying pan banging on the floor. "Oops," said Tatanka, "Sorry, sir, I dropped your eggs. What's that, sir? No, sir, that is *not* rat dung in your eggs, sir. That is special *Injun* spice. You want more?" He razzed his tongue as if blowing his nose.

I started laughing, and Tatanka joined in. Then the young helper, Roberto Mendoza, got to giggling, as did a few of the Puerto Ricans too. We were still laughing when Basmati Sweet leaned her head into the galley. "It's not going to be funny when Tosspot comes down here with his bullwhip," she said menacingly.

"Oh no," I said between guffaws. "Not the big bad marshal. Please, anything but that." We all bust a gut and Basma got taken in by it too.

"Eggs, red man," she said as she giggled. "Happy yellow ones, pronto!" She retreated up the hatch, still laughing.

After we got breakfast handled, the dishes cleaned and the captain dressed, the trumpets sounded for morning prayers. I came on deck and stood aft with Tatanka and the laborers. That same wool blanket of smoke from yesterday hunkered down over the coffee-colored water of the river. Marshal Tosspot stepped forward in his black tunic with the silver star over his heart and started into *Onward Christian Soldiers*, but the captain cut him off. "I don't need a June bug in my ear today, marshal. Thanks but no thanks." He stuck his finger in his ear, turned it back and forth, and closed his left eye. "IshcaBible, send us off right, would you? I got some Japanese enviro-kook comin' round here and I need something to calm my nerves."

The vulture from the previous day had come back with a couple of friends, and the three circled overhead. Pinch showed her teeth and pointed at them with her nose and the index finger of her extended right arm. "Look!' she cried. "Three eagles today. Oh joy, sir. It's another omen."

Wrong John glanced at the sky and scowled. "Wake up, Pinch. Can't you tell a damn buzzard from an eagle?" She dropped her arm and head, scuffed her heels on the deck, and wrung her hands. I wanted to walk up and comfort that brave woman—and punch Wrong John Silverspoon for being rude to the lady who saved my life.

Tatanka elbowed me in the ribs. "Oops. Somebody dropped the eggs," he said. We both grinned.

I took a step forward and spoke from the book of Revelations. "As you know, the Bible ends with Judgment Day. We ought to all prepare for that time. Who knows when we will be called before the heavenly court? So be on the ready, brothers and sisters. Don't take for granted your time here on earth. Chose your actions wisely. Tend your souls and cleanse your hearts by passionate fire. Do not cast hate upon the world, but claim each his own.

"As He says in Chapter 21, Verse 6, 'I am the Alpha and the Omega, the beginning and the end. I will give unto him that is athirst of the fountain of the water of life freely.' And in Verse 8, 'But the fearful, and unbelieving, and the abominable, and murderers, and whoremongers, and sorcerers, and idolaters, and all liars, shall have their part in the lake which burneth with fire and brimstone; which is the second death." I tipped my hat and stepped back in line.

It was quiet for a minute, and then the captain spoke. "Nice, Ish. Very uplifting," he said, voice tart with sarcasm. He pressed his lips tightly and puffed them out with air. "Is this entire day going to be one long piss in the wind?" He paced back and forth in a tight circle.

"My bonny lies over the ocean," sang Krill. "My bonny lies—"

"Cut it, Krill. You sing about as good as the lawman." The bird seemed to choke on something, coughed, and rolled its head. Chief stepped forward and put his hand on Wrong John's shoulder.

"Cheer up, Captain. Look, your buddy Slick brought you a present." The same yacht that had taken us to Washington's estate came alongside with a narwhale tied to starboard. The gray- and brown-spotted whale spanned half the length of the forty-foot yacht. Its dark, spiral horn stuck out ten feet from its nose, out beyond the yacht's prow.

Silverspoon walked to the port rail and hailed the yacht. "Yo, Slick! That dang unicorn got any blubber on it?"

Slick gave a narrow but deep hound-dog smile and waved from the helm. "Hey, buddy. This here's a narwhale. Got him up Greenland way. He's an ice cap swimmer— coat of blubber three feet thick!" Slick held out his big hands just beyond the width of his shoulders.

"Oughtta cook up like a nice chunk'a pork rind."

"Tell you what."

"Speck!" the captain shouted. "Fire up the try-works." The specksynder saluted and trotted off to clear the hatch and light the furnaces. He ordered his whalers to bring the narwhale fast to *Liberty* and set to peeling the bull of his rubbery blanket. The crew heaved to in a bustle of activity: wood hauled up from the hold; grappling hooks thrown to the yacht, pulling it in; the whale cut free; and a huge block and tackle hung from the mainmast. A harpooner inserted the big metal hook in the whale's side just behind his fin, and up they hoisted him. The ship rolled some to starboard from the weight, but nothing like *Lone Star* had when she had raised that sperm whale cow— which was four times the size of the narwhale. Spades sliced the whale's flesh. Thick sheets of milky fat peeled away from its body. These went immediately into the try-pots, where they sizzled and steamed.

The smell wasn't so bad at first with the hickory wood fire. It reminded me of the smell in those caves, Frank, in eastern Missouri, that we used to hide in after a robbery. It wasn't until the cooked chunks of fat, called "fritters," began to stoke the works that it took on that stench of a pyre.

Crude, Dagger, and Gunny went over on Slick's boat for a meeting. Wrong John invited the other officers to hit some golf balls off the aft deck. A couple of hours later the lookout hollered, "Thar be the ship of one flying the Rising Sun!"

Second Mate Sweet called the crew to ranks. In a rumble of boots against the deck they took their positions on either side of the mainmast. The officers formed their half-moon curve behind Captain Silverspoon on the quarterdeck. Meanwhile, the whalers continued to peel the narwhale and render his fat. Their pitchforks and ladles clanged against the try-pots. Black, deathly smoke enveloped *Liberty*. It was a terrible day for trying blubber: no wind to carry off the smoke. Crewmembers were advised not to cough—that it would make a bad impression—but it was impossible for them not to.

The sixty-foot Japanese cruiser sailed beside *Liberty* and hailed her. "Is it safe to come aboard? You appear to be on fire," yelled an attendant from the Jap ship. "You dang right we're on fire!" Silverspoon shouted in return. "Come on over and witness American enterprise at work!"

The Japanese lowered a boat and paddled over to *Liberty*. We helped Ambassador Kyoto and his five attendants on deck. Kyoto stood a head lower than the captain and was of much slighter build. He wore a thin, drooping moustache and formal Japanese attire, with black silk robe, knotted hair, and wooden sandals on his stocking feet. He carried an ornate wooden scroll in his left hand. The two cylinders of the scroll had dragon heads carved at the ends and were bound together with a delicate golden ribbon. He covered his mouth and nose against the putrid smell with a black silk scarf. Beside him on his left and right, slightly behind, stood his five attendants, also dressed formally, not in black but red robes. They bowed together at Wrong John, who bowed back. Krill slipped from his shoulder and flopped on the deck.

"*BRACK* it! That smarts," he said. He shook off the fall and scrambled up Wrong John's leg and torso to his shoulder.

Kyoto bowed to all of the officers in turn, but only Sir Yes Sir and Basmati Sweet bowed back; the others barely tipped their heads. Crude started to bow but the string of dark spaghetti that covered his bald head began to slip off and was almost at his eyebrows before he recovered it and placed it back on his head. Kyoto completed his formalities and stood with his arms at his side, preparing to address the captain. His eyes watered from the thick black smoke that enveloped us. His brown face turned a sickly shade of green, and it looked as if he would get sick. Tatanka and Robert, dressed in crisp white smocks, offered hors d'oeuvres and fresh orange juice to the diplomats. Ambassador Kyoto shook his head and his hand at the platter of food. He coughed and prepared to speak.

"As you know, the great industrialized nations of the world have agreed for some time that something must be done about the dangerous—," he covered his mouth with his black handkerchief and coughed.

Kyoto cleared his throat. "Something must be done, we have all agreed, about the excessive burning of blubber." He coughed again. "No one can help but notice that everywhere, the earth is continually enveloped in a haze of grey smoke, in rich countries and poor alike. It is causing health problems. And the world's scientific community is united in the belief that the blubber burning is causing major shifts in the earth's climate, with consequences we can't possibly anticipate, but which could be catastrophic."

"Gimme a fer instance," Wrong John requested.

"There is good evidence the polar ice cap is melting at an alarming rate. Some predict this could disrupt the flow of the warm southern current into the north Atlantic. The lack of this warm current could send Europe and the northeastern United States into a sudden and prolonged ice age."

"No kiddin'?" the captain wondered. "And do you think butterflies might also fly out of my butt?"

The crew tittered at his comment. The captain chuckled, slapped his thigh, and said to Crude in a stage whisper, "That's what you call chaos theory." The try-works fire roared in the furnace.

Ambassador Kyoto tried to recover. "This is a very serious matter, Captain Silverspoon. One cannot burn the entire latent energy of the world—a dense mass of black blubber accumulated over millions and millions of years—in less than two centuries, and not expect extreme consequences. It's a matter of the most elementary physics."

"Elementary, is it? Well I've got a plan for how to revitalize elementary education in America, so don't come in here with your 'Japan's ahead of America educationwise' thing," said the captain indignantly. "Besides, everybody knows that peace and stability are dependent on The Economy. What's your plan for powering industry if we slow down on the blubber?"

"We believe the wind could be harnessed as a source of much of our power, as well as the sun."

"Really?" asked Dagger. "Do you honestly believe the juggernaut of industry and the capitalist ideal can be powered by a few puffs of air and a puny golden ball in the sky?" Kind of a low blow from the Chief, I thought, to a man whose national symbol was the rising sun.

"There is no force more powerful than the sun!" fumed Kyoto, his wooden sandals clapping against the deck.

"The problem with your theory," intoned our Oil Czar, "is that even if it could work, what's the incentive? Who's going to hunt the sun? What are we supposed to do with the billions of dollars invested in the blubber infrastructure, the blubber economy, the blubber plutocracy? There's a lot of harpoons floating around out there. Besides, you can't package the sun and market it. It's just too easy to come by to have any value. That, my friend, is *elementary* economics."

"I'm gettin' a sunburn right now, Komodo. It idn't costin' me a dime," said Wrong John. He pushed his thumb into his forearm and showed Kyoto the white mark turning red. As Kyoto looked at his arm, Silverspoon lunged at the scroll in his hand. "Lemme see that thing." His move reminded me of Dagger's attempt to capture the one-eyed hag's quartz crystal in Squid Roe Tavern. This time she wasn't quick enough.

Silverspoon cut the gold ribbon. One cylinder of the scroll fell past his feet and rolled several feet across the deck. Earlier, Basmati Sweet had informed me it contained a detailed procedure for reducing blubber consumption over the course of the next several decades and had been signed by the leaders of the most powerful nations on earth, all save one. Wrong John read the scroll very quickly—so quickly, in fact, it seemed impossible he could have read or comprehended any of it. The paper piled at his feet as he reeled through hand over hand. Kyoto strained forward, holding himself back, it appeared, with immense self-discipline, from catching his sacred pact in his arms so it wouldn't be stepped on.

"Holy cow!" said Silverspoon. "Gotta be a few thousand lawyers at the trough to crank out that many rules. Damn thing's got more greasy fingerprints on it than a lawsuit against a tobacky company." He turned to his officers. "Von Shlop, can you throw some science at this thing, see if it holds water?"

The small man in his shiny blue robe and pointed blue hat, decorated with the magic symbols of dollars and cents, came forward holding a smooth, forked twig of a tree, the two ends in his hand and a single stem pointing in front of him. I had seen diving rods like it used by farmers to decide where to dig a well.

He ran the pointed end of the twig over the length of the treaty lying in folds along the deck, his eyes half closed, muttering some incantation. The divining rod did not dip or even twitch in the direction of the treaty. He opened his eyes, tucked the rod under his arm, and said, "The parchment is drier than a cactus needle in the Mojave. It does not hold water, not even a drop." The science officer bowed and returned to the half moon of officers.

"There you go," said Silverspoon to Kyoto. "That's the considered opinion of the highest scientific authority in the land. Guess your scientific community's got itself a little question mark." He coughed and cleared his throat. "I'm sorry, Kabuki, but even if we could bless the science in this deal, you've got it so lawyered up it's pert near useless." Kyoto stood at attention, his limp moustache twitching, as the captain carelessly stepped on the scroll at his feet.

"You ever seen a try-works, ambassador?" asked the captain.

"No, I've not—it hasn't been something that interested me." Kyoto bowed slightly.

"Never seen one, yet you want to shut 'em all down. Let's take a walk here." He strode down the quarterdeck stairs, the ambassador and his attendants behind him, Silverspoon's officers next. The tour must have been planned: there was a platform set up on one side of the try-works with stairs leading up to it. Everyone climbed the platform and looked into the bubbling silver try-pots. There was actually less smoke on the platform than there had been on the quarterdeck. Along the way, I overheard the marshal sing an odd tune to himself, something about "If sex is on your mind it's better to go blind." I wrote it off as more evidence of his dementia.

"Now take a look down in that oil, Kimono. Look long and hard, try, try to see your reflection in the surface." Wrong John looked back and winked at Dagger, who gave him a small wave of his hand. "Do you see yourself?"

"I'm sorry, Captain Silverspoon, the oil is not a good reflective surface."

"Exactly. That's my point. You can't see yourself in the oil, and yet, you're in there. All the achievements of the modern world are in there. Our whole way'a life is in that blubber, Mr. Kabuki, and so is yours. What's *Moby-Dick* got to say about it, Ish?"

I had torn a dozen or so sheets from the novel and stuffed them in my snakeskin pants. I uncrumpled them and looked through to find one that might apply. "Well, it says here, Chapter 24, Verse 7, 'The high and mighty business of whaling, one way and another, has begotten events so remarkable in themselves and so continuously momentous...that whaling may well be regarded as that Egyptian mother who bore offspring themselves pregnant from her womb.'"

Liberty's whalemen, reaching out with their long pitchforks, poked at the chunks of blubber jiggling in the boiling oil. Grease and soot covered their faces and arms. As the pieces became crisp, they stabbed them and threw them into the furnace. Other whalers, with their long ladles, scooped out the golden oil and poured it into wooden barrels on deck. Kyoto observed the activity with a scarf over his mouth.

"Thanks, Ish. That's from the Bible of whaling, ambassador. I think the point is clear. Blubber is the source of life. Right there in another Bible, Job states it plainly. Blubber and God is one. We have to honor our creator by hunting whales and taking their oil."

"You are mistaken, captain," Kyoto says. "Our creator asks us to stop the killing and find another way to survive."

"Guess we got us a differ'nce of opinion. Chief, you got that improvement handy?" Dagger walked to the front of the platform.

"We've taken the initiative to draft our own version of your manifesto, Kyoto," said Chief. "This one addresses the smoke illusion without unduly punishing the great countries of the world who are responsible for all prosperity and everything good."

The captain leaned toward Kyoto and spoke to him from the back of his hand. "Pursuit of happiness, 'bassador Kabuki. Constitution guarantees it." Wrong John winked at the Japanese, but something in Kyoto's gaze caused him to pause.

He scratched his head and whispered to Krill, who whispered back. "Hold on a second," the captain said. "Maybe we shouldn't be so hasty about all this. Might be something to gain by signing on," said Silverspoon. Dagger grunted and winced, as if he had been punched in the gut. Basma's mouth dropped open. Kyoto, however, opened his eyes wide and clasped his hands together at his chest. Sir Yes Sir leaned forward.

"What do you think, Krill?" asked Silverspoon. "Tell the world to take a hike, or sign the damn treaty and then blow it off? Which gets us more political mileage?" asked the captain.

"*BRACK!* Don't be a Bubba. No compromises, no fudging. Stick to principle, stick to principle," answered Krill, followed by low whistles and clicks. Kyoto's shoulders dropped.

"God, I don't want to get Bubba'd on," said Wrong John. He shook his hands and turned up his nose. "Lemme see that thing, Chief." Dagger handed a sheet of paper, smudged with greasy fingerprints, to the captain. He held it out away from his face and adjusted it back and forth until he could focus on it clearly. "Let's see, here. Hmm. Uh-huh. Yep. Yep. Concur. Yep. Got it. Got it. Yep. Great. Great." He handed the sheet to Ambassador Kyoto. The try-works furnace rumbled. The oil bubbled. "This'un's a lot better, ambassador." He coughed and wiped the soot from his brow. "It's just much simpler and way more workable."

Basma blurted, "And what's the point of having yet another treaty or resolution that nobody adheres to?"

"Like that rat bastard, Shalong!" spewed Dagger, spit flying, wheezing, his face instantly red and swollen. "Mocking us for ten years, promising this, promising that, and all the while planning a horrific attack against freedom at some unknown but certain date in the future!"

Captain Wrong John and the other officers gawked at Dagger. He wiped the grimy sweat from his forehead and licked his dry cracked lips. Kyoto bowed and accepted the paper from Wrong John. His eyes passed quickly over it. "There's only one sentence," he said, looking up from the paper. "This can't be your complete proposal."

"Oh yes, it can be," said Captain Silverspoon. "We like to start with a win-win, then win from there."

"But all it says is, 'Burn fires only when the need for energy outweighs the fear of smoke.' That's—it's—there's no substance. It doesn't require anything of anyone."

"Boom. You're a quick study, Kobe. Best of all, it's voluntary. Give our business leaders the benefit of the doubt, I always say. Don't I, Krill?" The red parrot nuzzled his cheek, and Wrong John gave him a peanut.

Kyoto's fist closed on the new treaty. Hot oil spilled from one of the ladles and landed on his stocking foot. Damn! I thought. That's got to hurt like hell. Kyoto closed his eyes and gritted his teeth but did not let out a sound.

"Now," Wrong John said, "just take that with you and get everybody's John Hancock and partner, we'll be in business!" He looked around at his officers, smiling and nodding. Dagger stepped forward to deliver the coup de grâce.

"Given the choice," Chief said condescendingly, "between saving a few newts from acid rain or having heat and light in their homes, people will choose heat and light every time."

Kyoto bowed, his eyes watering—from the smoke? or was it sadness?— and returned quickly to his ship. The captain patted his officers on the back "This bein' president ain't all that hard." He turned to Kyoto. "Don't worry, Komodo, we'll take good care of your treaty for you."

Krill repeated his message of the day. "Set the tone, *BRACK!* Stick to principle."

As Kyoto sailed away with *Liberty's* new treaty, the officers retired to the golf platform. Crude carried the original scroll in a disorderly pile. Wrong John took one end of the treaty and scanned it, his lips moving.

"Listen to this: 'The United States, as the world's leading consumer of blubber, must reduce its gas emissions by fifty percent over the next ten years.' Shee-it, boys. Might as well just hang up the 'Goin' Out of Business' sign." The officers laughed, except for Basmati, who hung back and watched Kyoto's ship sail down the river, white sails billowed by the thick breeze.

Silverspoon lifted his leg and farted. "That's a violation of the treaty, America," he said, voice lowered mockingly. "That'll cost you five grand." He chuckled and looked around at his officers, who laughed along with him. He stepped to the tee, placed a featherie, hauled back his club, and sent it flying. I pulled Peacemaker and dusted it.

"Damn it, Bible! Stop bustin' my balls!" shouted Silverspoon, shaking his golf club at me, nostrils of his sharp nose grew red and flared. I ignored him and looked over the side of the ship at the skinned narwhale, his long, spiral horn sticking straight out from his bloody carcass. I thought of the baby whale's song in the gulf, and wondered if the narwhale was a father, and if his calves were singing for him. I wondered if there was a market, in Silverspoon's America, for his magic horn.

Speck arrived with a burning stick. Crude picked up the jumble of rice paper. Speck put his flame to Kyoto's scroll, and Crude threw it from the stern of the ship. It arched through the air in the graceful flight of a dragon, breathing the fire that would consume it.

I found out later that Ambassador Kyoto had committed *seppuku*—ritual disembowelment—rather than return from his assignment with Wrong John's counterfeit treaty. One night, as I brought Captain Silverspoon his evening coffee and chocolate, I asked him if it disturbed him that Mr. Kyoto had resorted to seppuku.

"That's an individual choice, Ish—result of the freedom we gave Japan by conquering them." He took a big bite of Belgian chocolate, then a slurp of coffee. "Personally, I'm not fond of raw fish, but the Japanese, they can eat seppuku for breakfast, lunch, and dinner. I honestly don't mind, long as he don't come around here with any more stupid agreements. They've got to realize that if we want a treaty, we'll ask for one. Otherwise, get the hell out of our way."

I thought about asking him if he had heard the night eagle gnawing on the ship, or if he ever chewed his hatred and savored the bitter taste, but there didn't seem any point. He hadn't heard the news of Kyoto's death, and he never would. He was not the sort to bother himself with things that didn't fit neatly into his jewelry box of ideas. Anything that wasn't small and didn't sparkle didn't belong.

You tell me, Frank, if I'm plumb off my rocker here, but I thought about that old Greek story of Pandora and her box. Well now, isn't it just possible that it could go the other way? That if you kept your box too tightly sealed the demons would try to find a way *in*? Maybe that was Pandora's problem all along. She had herself what she thought was a collection of pretty rings and bracelets, and she kept them tight in her box, but when she opened it to take a peak, out flew every pestilence known to man. They had found a way in, and she could not stop them. Well now, Frank, you can hold your jewels, or you can hold your demons, but one stormy day the creek's gonna rise and carry them away, just the same.

I excused myself from Silverspoon to go have a smoke. Out on the deck I found Tatanka smoking his *chanupa.* I didn't interrupt him. When he smoked that redstone pipe it wasn't for an escape, but as a way to go deeply into prayer—just like Queequeg, Ishmael's friend in *Moby-Dick.* The stars flickered in the moonless sky, and one of them threw itself across the glittering black in a bright arc toward the earth.

Chapter XIV

Star-Spangled Jolly Roger

A week or so later on a cool spring eve, I found Pinch sitting on the foredeck sewing a flag. She hummed the same odd tune Tosspot had been singing when Kyoto was on board. She worked her needle and thread in and out of the patchwork of colors. Her background was blue with a white skull in the middle. The skull had red stars for eyes and jagged teeth. Underneath the jawbone, two blood-red leg bones crossed. On either side of the skull stood two white Christian crosses. Pinch concentrated so hard she didn't notice me, her tongue half out sweeping back and forth between her long upper teeth and lower lip, and her humming that odd tune of the marshal's.

"Whatcha doin', Pinch?" I asked, pausing to scratch the white tip of a match with my thumbnail, and lighting my smoke.

"Oh, Ish," she said, looking up at me with her small, narrow bright blue eyes. "Didn't see you there." She smiled at me. "This? Well, it's our very own Jolly Roger. I call it the Star-Spangled Jolly Roger. I figured we might need one. There might be another raid some day, like the one on *Liberty.* Gosh, that was fun!"

"You figurin' on another attack?" I remembered what you had told me about the national anthem, Frank, its tune taken from the drinking song of a London fraternity dedicated to debauchery. Maybe it was destiny that the "The Star-Spangled Banner" end up the emblem for a band of pirates.

"There's talk of another attack," she said. "Now that we scuttled Kyoto's treaty, we got the taste of blood on our lips."

"I know the flavor." I licked my lips and swallowed. A company of bats darted low along the water, calling out in shrill voices, shooting rapidly this way and that.

"Anyway, I didn't like our pirate flag that first time. It was just a copy. Didn't have our stamp on it. This one, though, says it all." I asked her to explain it to me. "Well," she said, "first of all, it's got the national colors. Red stands for hardiness and valor—and it's in the eyes, see—we see red and fearlessly pursue our mission. Blue represents valiance, perseverance, justice, which is in the background there. And white, well, that's purity and innocence, which is our country, trusting, good-hearted, expecting the best out of everybody."

"Don't you find it strange to have your purity and innocence stood for by a skull?" I asked. "And them teeth—pretty vicious."

She scratched her chin and looked skyward. "You got me there, Ish. Could be a slight contradiction—but I think the crosses more than make up for it." She added a few more stitches to her quilt. "It's a rare combination, really: Patriotic pirates, also pious. Hey, I like that—PPP. Your average pirate has no loyalty, and he's not pious until his head's in a noose." She ran a few more loops with her needle and thread. "Gosh, IshcaBible! I feel just like Betsy Ross!" She gave me a big smile.

"Dagger was talking the other day," she continued. "He said we've got a rare opportunity here—leaders of the free world who just happen to be pirates; it provides us the ultimate cover. It's going to take everybody a long, long time to recognize the Jolly Roger hidden in our red, white, and blue skull and crossbones. That's what gave me the idea for the new flag.

"Even if somebody does figure it out, he said, lots of people will still argue that we aren't pirates—that only a deluded conspiracy theorist would ever believe pirates could take over America."

It turned out Pinch's new flag would be called into service more quickly than she anticipated. The very next afternoon the officers were hitting golf balls when the subject turned to the recently built Court of Earthly Justice at The Hague. Nations of the world had banded together to create a legal system to try people for crimes against humanity that could not, or would not, be tried in the country of origin. I guess they hoped to discourage the most brutal and barbaric attacks against innocent people. I sure hoped they didn't have *my* address.

"So what's this Earthly Justice thing?" asked Silverspoon, leaning on his driver with his left hand. He took a sip of lemonade. He wore his commander's hat, blue-humped, fore-and-aft, red and white plumes off the poop deck. "Far as I can throw this new court, it splats against the wall like a buttinsky Euro-lawyer orgy."

"Well put, sir," said Chief. "It's got the paw marks of Bubba all over it. Can you imagine? consigning the national security interests of America to the gutless liberals of Europe?" Gobs of spit hung like spider nests in the corners of his mouth.

"Bubba. That fingers. Sounds like it's time for a Boston Tea Party." He slapped his hands together and rubbed them vigorously. Gunny pulled on his nose ring and placed his index fingers alongside his head. Wrong John mirrored him and they exchanged grunts. Sir Yes Sir crossed him arms and frowned.

"It's a fait accompli, gentlemen," said the diplomat in his deep, stern voice. "Bubba already signed the treaty. Our hands are tied."

"Shee-it. We'll just *unsign* it," said Wrong John.

"You can't do that. America has given its solemn vow. That's gospel."

"Who's side you on, Sir Yes Sir? I intend to *unsign* just about every law or agreement that pervert put his name to. Was I not elected to restore dignity?"

Sir Yes Sir turned away and crossed his arms. Wrong John regarded his diplomat, and said, "Okay, okay, maybe you're right. Let's hit a few balls and knock this thing around."

Chief stepped onto the platform and placed his featherie. "It's a violation of our sovereignty, Mr. Captain. Can you imagine these do-gooders trying to extradite the Great Communicator for liberating Nicaragua?" Silverspoon grunted and shook his head. Chief addressed his golf ball with a big wooden driver. He took a swing and completely missed the ball. Even so, he looked out over the Potomac, hand over his eyebrows, as if waiting to see where it landed.

"Damn, lost it in the reflection." He looked down at the tee, where his ball still sat. "Well look at that. Teeing one up for the next guy, Mr. IshcaBible, how thoughtful."

"*BRACK!*—." Before Krill could comment, the captain grabbed his beak. I tried to make eye contact with the other officers, to see if anybody else thought Chief's B.S. should be called, but only Sir Yes Sir would look at me. *So it comes to this, does it?* I thought. *We're all supposed to pretend you didn't whiff? I couldn't swallow that one, Frank, not me.* "You missed, Chief. That's *your* ball still sitting there."

He narrowed his eyes at me and sucked his teeth as if a T-bone steak were stuck in his molars. I stared right back at him. Tosspot studied my defiance and made some notes in his book.

"Good swing, anyway, Mr. First Mate," said the captain, stepping between us. He addressed the ball, hauled back, and spanked it far out across the broad, brown Potomac. I quickly pulled Widowmaker with my left hand but didn't fire. Wrong John wagged his finger at me. I winked at him and holstered my gun.

Robert Mendoza walked in with a bowl of freshly boiled shrimp. A cast-iron pot of warm spermaceti, that ambrosial blubber of the sperm whale, hung over his forearm. "Shrimp, anyone?" he asked, his lispy voice making the "sh" of shrimp sound like "th." Tosspot gave him a dirty look and scribbled in his book.

The captain peeled a shrimp and dipped it into the oil. "Man, I do love the taste of sperm!" the captain said, smacking his lips. Eyebrows went up all around. Tosspot made a note in his book.

"It's sperm-aceti, captain. The stuff is called spermaceti," said Dagger, his upper lip curled.

"I know, but you know how I like to shorten things and stuff."

"Don't shorten that one, sir, or you're liable to make me ralph."

"Ease up, Dagger. Nobody's gonna wax your knob." He shook his head, looked over at Yo Yo, stuck his finger in his mouth, and pretended to gag. The gunner smirked behind his hand.

Gunny stepped up to the tee box next, placed his ball, scratched under his eye patch, and positioned his monocle. He turned to the group. "We can't let this court stand," he said, "not if we hope to fix the Shalong mistake." He faced his ball, hauled back and hit. It didn't make it over the rail, hit a post, and ricocheted back at us. Everyone ducked and watched it plop into the water to our left.

"Jeez, Gunny, give us a warning next time before you attack, would ya? One finger if by land, two if by sea," said Silverspoon. He held up his hand and wiggled two fingers. He turned to his second mate and said, "Basma?" She looked away and cleared her throat. She preferred to give her counsel to the captain in private, rather than in front of the others. "Basma?" the captain said again, sounding irritated.

"Ahem. I agree with Chief. The court is an insult. Lady Liberty, who gracefully points the way for us at the head of our prow, provides more than enough illumination for this great country. We don't need anybody keeping us honest about justice."

"There you go."

"I disagree wholeheartedly," said Tosspot, raising his driver as if it were a gavel. "This nation is not inspired by a pornographic icon passed off as art."

Basmati pulled a niblick from her golf bag. "There's nothing the least bit pornographic in that carving," she said. The baubles hanging from her ears jangled with the ferocity of her voice. "It's a symbol of *freedom* that her breasts have burst forth from her shirt. She's a feminine warrior, and a powerful expression of the womanly mysteries of birth and life-giving mother's milk— the milk of freedom, the only nourishment that feeds the soul of democracy." As she spoke, Basmati's breasts strained against their binding, but she did not acknowledge them. Instead she reached down and adjusted the length of rubber hose in her pants.

"The Bible is very clear that one is not to gaze upon the nudity of any woman other than his wife. To do so otherwise is a sin." TossPot adjusted *himself* in turn.

"It's not a woman, you idiot, it's a *carving* of a woman—a figurehead."

"Well it's vile and dirty—and watch your tongue with me!"

"What's the matter with you?" She shook her niblick at him. "She's Lady Liberty! Our national symbol." Watch out, marshal, I thought, she'll have your head hanging by a gold chain from her belt.

"A'right, enough bickering," the captain said. "Now I misplaced my train of thought."

"Toot, toot! All board!" Krill interjected.

" Never mind. Are we against this lawyer orgy, or not?"

A small two-masted sloop approached us from downstream. It carried a flag none of us recognized. The ship hailed *Liberty* and asked permission to come aboard. Gunny requested a statement of purpose. "We've got a subpoena from the Court of Earthly Justice."

The Chief rushed at the rail, swearing, his driver raised as a war club, apparently intending to jump in the water, swim over and bludgeon the messenger. Sir Yes Sir and Yo Ho Ho held him back. The captain tried to calm him down, but nothing seemed to work until Krill hopped from the captain's shoulder and onto his, and whispered something in his ear. Dagger's fury instantly abated. He wiped the spit from his chin and smiled from the side of his mouth. He shook himself free from the grasp of the gunner and diplomat. "Invite them aboard," he said calmly.

An envoy from the court came on deck and delivered the subpoena, sealed with red wax in a linen envelope. Pinch strolled over with her new flag wrapped around herself like a big towel, the patriotic skull and crossbones over her stomach, pious white crosses over her breasts. The court's envoy stared at her flag. "What do you think, guys? Pretty spiffy, isn't it?" She extended her leg and touched the deck with the tip of her toe. She turned side to side, looked down on her wicked quilt, and brushed it with her hand.

"Good God, Pinch! What in the hell—," Dagger cried, rushing at her and escorting her away. "You'll have us all arrested parading around in that thing," he told her under his breath.

Krill flapped his wings madly at the court envoy. "*BRACK!* Just a costume, only a costume. Big dress-up ball tonight. You want to stay?" The envoy declined the invitation, looking, it seemed, perplexed at being invited by a parrot. He saluted and returned to his ship.

The captain looked at the subpoena, tore the end of the envelope, blew into it, and said, "And the winner is..." as he pulled out the subpoena. "Dr. Henchman!" he cried. Everyone except me seemed to recognize the name; I alone needed to be told that Dr. Henchman had been the lead diplomat under

Captain Crook.

"Dang it, Chief," said Wrong John, "why'd you let that jerk come aboard? Idn't Dr. Henchman one of our greatest living patriots? We can't deliver him to that lawyer orgy for war crimes."

"Absolutely not," said the Chief, having returned from his lecture to Pinch. He walked over to Krill, who perched on the rail, and patted him on the head.

"Pretty ploy, pretty ploy," Krill said. He clucked and whistled happily.

"As our friend Peckerhead pointed out to me, we only *pretend* to go along with them. We visit The Hague, all contrite and humble, present ourselves to the court, and then we flush that putrid Limburger down the toilet!"

"That mean we're not really gonna give him up?" said Wrong John, pretending to address an imaginary ball with his fat one wood.

"Never. He's one of the greatest American statesmen in history. If he hadn't been born in Germany, he would probably have become president."

"You damn right!" piped up Yo Ho Ho, pulling on his nose ring. "He understood the difficult choices required of a true leader, and he never let decency or the suffering of innocent people stand in his way of doing what was best for his country."

"And he worked tirelessly behind the scenes to stop the red tide, while at the same time pulling strings in every conceivable way to ensure the re-election of his president," added Chief.

"Priority one, re-election—*BRACK!*—most important thing."

"And, might I add," said Yo Yo, "he's a doctor, a man of science, who answers to the hypocritic oath. How can a man trained to save lives be called a killer?"

Sir Yes Sir gave a heavy sigh. "But it is true that he could be implicated in the death of thousands, perhaps millions of innocent people. That's not exactly a legacy to be proud of. And, by the way, he's not a medical doctor. He's a Ph.D."

"Oh let's split hairs, why don't we!" screamed the gunner. "The point is, did you go to war for your country?"

"That's not the point at all. But yes, I did. You know that," answered the African. "What about you?"

Gunny's eye became huge behind his monocle. His face reddened, and the veins on his bullish neck stuck out. "I have—you—I served. I was ready. My life, all I've done has been in the service of—"

"But did you fight for your country? Go to war for her?"

I couldn't tell what Yo Yo was going to do. He snorted, as if he were about to charge. Chief Dagger came to his aid.

"The *point*, Mr. Sir Yes Sir, is that collateral damage is unavoidable in the pursuit of a greater mission. It is the burden great leaders must always bear."

"What do you know? You've never been in battle either," the diplomat said, defiantly crossing his arms, jaw muscles flexing.

"That's enough! Remove yourself to quarters, Sir Yes Sir, or I will have the military police take you!" roared Chief.

"Yes sir," said the diplomat, saluting slowly. "I want to go on record as saying that as *Liberty's* diplomat I would never endorse a military objective that would cause a million citizens to die—or even a hundred. And if I did, I would deserve to be tried for war crimes." He walked away and disappeared down the hatch.

Captain Silverspoon rubbed his hands together and said, "Boy, there for a second I thought they was gonna have to take it outside."

"Captain, we're already outside," said Crude.

The captain put his hands on his hips and wagged his head side to side. "It's a figment of speech, dummy. Point is, Dr. Henchman's a friend of the family, a good man. This kangaroo court has bounced right into a nest 'a hornets, tell you what!"

Chapter XV

Killing Animals

A week later we sailed across the Atlantic, toward the North Sea, and The Netherlands, home of The Hague and the Court of Earthly Justice. We were not on *Liberty*, but a steam and sail frigate, the *Preemption*, that would cover the distance in half the time of a sailing vessel. Tatanka and I had been sent along as personal bodyguards of Chief Dagger and Tosspot. When we were given the assignment, Tatanka grabbed my shoulders and looked me in the eyes, "Sharpshooters," he said. "Brothers."

We enjoyed fine weather down the Potomac to Chesapeake Bay, but once we crossed into the open water of the Atlantic a gale set in. Great streaks of horizontal lightening passed between dark clouds. Thunder roared and rattled, but it did not rain. This kept on for many days, and made for a fast but uncomfortable ride. Finally the wind abated and we enjoyed a few days of sunshine before another storm fell in around us, this time with bayonet thrusts of lightning into the watery skin of the gray Atlantic, explosive thunder, and driving sheets of icy rain. Around this time, the carpenter set about building a coffin.

Tatanka and I took a great interest in the project, neither of us having watched a death box built, and both of us having come (more than once) a bullet's breadth away from lying in one. When it was completed, we took turns lying in it in the dark tool-infested workshop of the trollish carpenter —the hairiest man I had ever met, Frank. There wasn't an inch of his body wasn't dark with his pelt.

I looked down on the Lakota lying in the box with his eyes closed and hands crossed over his chest. "Here lies Too-tanked, good for nothing Sioux savage," I said, my black bowler over my heart. "Broke the law, killed good white folk, and got what he deserved—a bullet in the back."

We switched places, and I climbed into the casket. "Here lies IshcaBiscuit. Low-down mongrel. Skunk-breath bushwhacker. Killed his own kind. Got betrayed for money. Shot in the back of the head. About time." I pretended to rise from the dead and aimed my pistol at him. He aimed at me.

"Two won't fit," he said. We both lowered our guns and smiled fiendishly at one another.

Later that night, when I lay in my bunk, it hit me how our game had been strangely similar to the scene in *Moby-Dick* when the cannibal Queequeg fell ill and requested a coffin be made for him. When it was completed, as he lay dying in his hammock, he asked to try out the casket:

Leaning over in his hammock, Queequeg long regarded the

coffin with an attentive eye. He then called for his harpoon, had the wooden stock drawn from it, and then had the iron part placed in the coffin along with one of the paddles of his boat....Queequeg now entreated to be lifted into his final bed, that he might make trial of its comforts, if any it had.

Not long after, Queequeg made a fast recovery, having decided he was not yet ready to die. It was *his* coffin that would later serve as a lifeboat for Ishmael after the white whale sunk the ship. Ishmael, floating on his friend's coffin, became the journey's soul survivor.

In our case, no one on board was down with a deathly illness, and I could not imagine for whom the death box had been built. Chief Dagger requested the coffin be brought to the bridge and placed beside the helm. Did he have some notion a dead man would steer the ship? Had he become Ahab, and was he guiding us by the hand of a ghost to our death from the White Whale of Earthly Justice? Was our pickle the same as Starbuck's when he asked Ahab, "Shall we keep chasing this murderous fish till he swamps the last man?" I could not say, but will only note that thereafter I strictly avoided the black box resting ill at the helm. It did not seem the least bit funny to me as it had in the carpenter's workshop—out there in the elements, that dark lid on top of it.

We passed the Shetland Islands and dropped into the North Sea. The steamer chugged into dense fog and drizzle. The sea was fairly calm, with swells of three feet and less. I found myself on the foredeck, looking out over the bow, enjoying a smoke in the early evening, finding it a pleasurable sensation to peer into the gray and have no idea what might be ahead.

The hard barrel of a rifle pressed into the middle of my back. I heard the click of several other guns being cocked. Ambushed, Frank, in the middle of the North Sea. Can you imagine it, brother? Half a world away from any bank I ever robbed, and caught like that?

"Don't move, IshcaBible—or whatever your real name is." It was the voice of the marshal. "It would bring me great joy to kill you now, but the Chief has plans for you."

"Hey, *Ish*," said Chief, close to my left ear. "Have you enjoyed flaunting the rules? Acting tough? Pulling guns on people? Misquoting the Bible?"

"Shooting our golf balls and showing your privates!" cried the marshal.

"Sure, Chief," I said. "The rules always beg a good stretchin'."

Tosspot's bullwhip went over my head and tight across my neck. I could not breathe. "You cocky, insolent bushwhacker! We don't know your *real* name yet—rebel boy—but we know you're running from the law. If it wasn't for Silverspoon, I'd have arrested you a long time ago," he hissed.

"What we're doing, this whole caper with Silverspoon: this is *my* immortality project, *Ish*," Chief said sullenly. "One can sense when the reaper is circling, don't you think?" I felt the cold, sharp edge of his dagger against my left ear. "I won't have some two-bit outlaw screw up *my* legacy." Two-bit? I thought. Who you calling two-bit?

"Now, *Ish*. You've got an assignment," Chief said. "How you perform it will determine your fate. The liberals of Europe think they're going to arrest one of our leading statesmen. They might as well dig up the grave of John Adams and spit in it. Hell will see snowfall before Dr. Henchman stands trial for nobly serving his country." I could hear him sucking gold canines and imagined the spit gobs tucked in his lips. I was about to pass out from lack of wind.

"You, *Ish*, will stand in his place. We've got a few days until we reach Holland. Practice a German accent, and prepare yourself to answer questions about the brave actions of Dr. Henchman. You will come before the bench in a coffin. There will be holes drilled in the lid, and you will speak through them. At my signal, you will burst through the lid, send guns blazing, and break us out of there. If you fail, we will frame you, and you will take the fall for impersonating Dr. Henchman. If you succeed, our company achieves the greatest pirate coup in history."

"And Wrong John gets to keep his toy outlaw until next Christmas," added the marshal. After that, I blacked out. Sometime later, I don't know how long, I woke up in my bunk, sailors snoring all around me, the steam engine clanging rhythmically. I felt a hand on my cheek.

"Dingus? You okay?" whispered Tatanka.

"I reckon so," I whispered back, rubbing my throat where the marshal's whip had bruised me.

"What happened to you?"

"Ambushed. Turns out the coffin is for me."

"What? They going to kill you? Not while I stand." His fingers curled tight on the lapel of my shirt and twisted.

"Nah. They ain't gonna kill me yet. Not till old Jess pulls one more job for 'em. I'll tell you about it in the morning. Bed down, Injun." He turned, but I caught his shoulder. "Just one thing. The marshal's a dead man."

Dagger tutored me over the following days on the proper answer to questions that might be posed to me. A crewmember whose family had come over from Germany when he was a boy schooled me in a German accent. Tatanka thought my German voice extremely bad and laughed at me whenever I practiced. The German, however, believed it would get me by.

We came to the port of Gravenhag and anchored the *Preemption* at the dock. The timing was such that we had to lower immediately in a long boat and complete our journey to the court via canal. A complement of ten sailors manned the oars and fell to pulling us into the city. Dagger and Tosspot stood at the bow, wearing long blue capes and black, humped, front-to-back officers hats. There was a smell in that port, in addition to the usual saltwater and fish smell, that I could not identify. I looked around at the brick and limestone buildings, one connected to the other, the extravagantly carved church spires, the streets of cobbled stone, and believed the smell to be age, something that did not occur in American cities.

"Climb in the coffin, IshcaBible," said Chief, without looking back.

I stared down at the black box. Though I had lain in it when Tatanka and I played our game in the carpenter's shop, it now seemed deeper. I resisted, fearing the darkness had no bottom.

Tosspot turned to look at me and shouted, "Do as you're told, bushwhacker!"

I shook my head at him and rolled my eyes sideways. Could the idiot not see I was packing iron? I would have much preferred to plug Tosspot and throw him in the coffin than to go in there myself. I felt Tatanka's hand on my shoulder. He spoke to me with his deep, reassuring voice. "Chew your fear. Make friends with the darkness. We all meet it one day." He helped me into the coffin and placed the lid on top. It was as if I had gone underwater. I could her the splash of the oars but little of what happened above the surface. I felt an ill, icy shiver up my back, and that same sense of smokiness about me that had caused me nearly to faint that first day on the *Lone Star*. I lost my bearings and believed my whole time with Silverspoon had been nothing more than a death dream. I really had perished by the bullet of Bobby Ford and was on my way to the cemetery in Kearney, Missouri, to be buried next to my little brother Archie.

That's when I heard the voice of my brother swearing to kill Bob and Charlie Ford. I heard my wife, Zerelda, blaming herself for not getting there sooner and stopping them. I heard Jesse Jr. and Mary sobbing, then Momma Zee's sharp, mean voice saying, "He was a fine son, and fought till the end for our right to keep our black property." God help me, I thought. Is that what I'll be remembered for? what will be engraved on my tombstone? "Jesse James died for his momma's bitterness at losing her slaves." God help me for the killing I done out of those shallow pools of greed and retribution.

I breathed hard and fast. I could feel my heart drumming my chest. Icould hear that dented bullet whispering, "Die, killer, die. You deserve to die." Sweat rolled down my forehead and cheeks. My feet twitched and tapped against the end of the box.

"We are close to the court," came the voice of Tatanka, pulling me from the brink. "There are thick round columns. A light colored wood. Gray slate roof. The dome is gold. Four towers rise tall into the sky. They have pointed peaks, round metal platforms on top. Nests are built on them. Large white birds. Storks. One of the rowers says the people here invite them. The stork is a blessing. It returns like the sun with spring. It brings new life.

"Marble steps lead to large wooden doors under an arch. There is a carving in wood above the doors. It is a battle, raging on the left; then to the right it changes to a scene of peace, farming, people feasting."

I felt the bump of the prow against something hard. "We are at the dock," Tatanka said. "They will lift you, carry you up many stairs and through the doors. There are four guards with tall hats and red uniforms. That is all I can say. I do not go in with you. I am to wait outside. When I hear your gunshots I am to take out the guards. Good luck, brother."

I felt myself rise in the air and the jostle of being lifted out of the boat. My head tipped against the box as the pallbearers carried me up the stairs.

I heard the creak of heavy doors, and then the slam. Boots clicked against the floor, then I heard a second set of creaking doors, and heard them slam shut. Had I entered a court, or a mausoleum? I passed through a shroud of murmuring voices, all in an alien tongue I could not comprehend, except to hear the emotion in them, the surprise, the shock, the outrage, the fear. I landed on the floor with a thud. I felt for Peace- and Widowmaker; they were there against my sides.

I had never been in court, and here I was, in the highest court in the entire world, expected to lay out a bunch of horse crap, then jump up and shoot my way out. The thought of it raised goose bumps on my arms. My heart started drumming my breastbone again, and that bullet whispered something, but I refused to listen. I heard the groan of the wooden pews and the concerned, frightened, shocked voices, now behind me.

Bang!

It must have been the judge's gavel.

"Who addresses the Court of Earthly Justice?" said the judge, her voice stern and accented with French.

"I am Dagger, first mate of *Liberty*, answering to your subpoena of Dr. Henchman, former lead diplomat of the United States." His knife-edged voice dripped with false sincerity. I could picture him removing his hat and bowing, a little *too* deeply. "We acquiesce to the power of this court, which we concede has jurisdiction over the affairs of the world's most powerful and honorable state. And so in respect of your paramount authority, we hand over our country's most honored statesmen of the last century, the venerable peacemaker Dr. Henchman."

"A coffin? What is this? Where is Dr. Henchman? Has he died?"

"No, he is inside. We have presented him thus to indicate the death of treachery like his in Silverspoon's America."

"This is highly unorthodox. Get him out of there. Defendants *stand* before this court when answering for their crimes."

"I'm afraid that will be impossible. The lid is glued and nailed shut."

"Do you intend to let him die like that?"

"That's *our* business. Do you want to question him, or not?

I heard the voices of several judges conferring, and the voices of the spectators behind me, frightened, angry, confused.

"We will proceed, but you must know that *we* will decide Dr. Henchman's innocence or guilt, and we will decide the punishment, should any be required." Dagger did not reply. Then the judge addressed me.

"Dr. Henchman. Have you ordered the assassination of a democratically elected foreign leader?"

"I don't sink so," I said.

"What do you mean, you don't think so?"

"I cannot remember."

"You cannot remember if you ordered the leader of a free nation to be assassinated?"

"No. I am an olt man. Zoz tings happened a long time ago."

"That is no excuse," said the chief judge. "Time is no shield for your crimes against humanity."

"Objection!" shouted Tosspot.

"I was zhust doing my job," I said.

"Overruled. Dr. Henchman, do you consider yourself to be a terrorist?" It was the deep voice of a man with a British accent. I got confused by the question, and forgot I was pretending to be Henchman. I took the question as if it had been asked of Jesse James.

"You asking me if I scared people to get my way?" I said, forgetting my German voice.

"I'm asking if you used subversive and violent means to achieve a political objective," said the British judge.

"Hell yeah."

"And you felt that was proper conduct for the lead diplomat of a democratic nation?"

"Our way of life was threatened."

"Your way of life? Seriously? By a tiny country thousands of miles away?

I was confused. What country? "I didn't know better. I was just a farm boy."

"A farm boy, with a doctorate?" The judges laughed, as did those in attendance. I couldn't think of anything to say.

"Do you feel it was acceptable to murder thousands of people in order to insure Captain Crook won his bid for reelection?" It was a different voice, a gruff German woman. I assumed she was talking about Tilden vs. Hayes in 1876, and the lynching of uppity nigras.

"It's not murder when you're killing animals!" I shouted. Did I believe that? Did I really believe that anymore?

"Animals? Is that how you comfort yourself? Telling yourself people in a country other than your own are less than human?"

"Do you not believe in the precepts of your own Constitution?" shouted the French judge.

"Can you be trusted at any level on the world stage when you have acted so basely?" shouted the Briton.

"Have you any right whatsoever to condemn the terrorist acts of other nations, or other causes, when you yourself have used the same means whenever you deemed it politically expedient?" shouted the German.

That was it. Party over. I burst from the coffin and faced the dark wooden bench where five judges sat. The judge in the middle looked exactly like my mother. I was stunned. There sat the twin of Momma Zee, staring at me with those same pale eyes, that same jowly face, the thin lips and stout nose. There sat Momma Zee in the black robe of a judge, burning a hole in me like she did that time she found me and a slave girl kissing in the barn.

To hesitate would have been fatal. I shot her straight between the eyes, spun, and smoked the two guards at the door. I could hear shots out front from Tatanka taking out the guards on the front steps. Smoke and flames filled the courtroom. Panic ensued, and everyone scrambled for the door. I jumped from the coffin and fired a half a dozen shots into the air. Someone in the courtroom fired back at me. Tosspot and Chief used the black death box as a ram and plowed through the terrified people running for the door. I fell in behind them. A bullet whizzed past my head. I turned and fired twice in the direction it had come.

Our company burst through the burning foyer, red flames darting and dancing off the walls, smoke billowing out the front door. We charged through the conflagration, clambered aboard the longboat, and rowed full out to the harbor. We hastily boarded The *Preemption*, raised full sheet on all three masts, fired up the steam engine, and cut away from our anchors, having no time to weigh them.

Dagger ran to his quarters and returned with a flag. He cackled and shouted insults to shore while he raised the Star-Spangled Jolly Roger. "Position us lengthwise the garrison and let fly the starboard cannon!" he shouted. The ship turned and blasted the stone outpost with a rapid burst of artillery. The cannonballs hummed through the air and slammed into the stone outpost. Flashes of return fire burst from the fort, and cannonballs zoomed over, roaring, buzzing. Others splashed into the water around us.

Away we plowed into the cold North Sea. "Rum all around!" sang the first mate. He approached me and put out his hand. I accepted it and we shook as comrades who had won a battle. "I don't know who you are, IshcaBible. Right now, I don't care. All I know is you're a gunslinging American freedom fighter. And that's all I need to know."

I found Tatanka at the stern rail, sitting on a bench, chin on his crossed hands resting on the rail. I offered him a cup of rum. He waved me off. "I meant it, Dingus. No more of that *wasichu* poison water." I poured his rum into my tin cup.

"Well, here's to victory," I said, raising my cup.

"Victory? For who?"

"For us, for freedom from persecution, freedom from justice. We're outlaws, remember? How about that for turning the tables on them? Take us to court? We'll burn you down! It's great, brother. The outlaws put the court on trial! Hot damn! Put that in your pipe, Mr. Pinkerton, and choke on it!"

"Happy? Really? I bet all the pirates in hell are dancing a jig with you."

"What do you mean?"

"They would love to take, to take everything, whatever they wanted, the Black Hills, Devil's Tower. Yeah, it's great to take and not have to answer for it. Just great."

The Indian had shut me up again. Instead of drinking my rum, I poured it in the North Sea. What's the matter with me, Frank? I had just shot the supreme judge of the world right between the eyes, and added two other souls to the ghost posse hunting me. I was supposed to be done killing. I was supposed to be laying low. What's the matter with me, Frank? Will I ever be able to stop?

Chapter XVI

The Buzzard Has Landed

The trip back to Washington from The Hague seemed to go on forever. The winds were unfavorable and the sea rough. On top of that I was an uneasy hero with Chief and Tosspot. Every time we crossed paths they got all chummy with me, which was uncomfortable, especially with the marshal, who I imagined killing a different way every time I saw him. I got no comfort from Tatanka, who went deep into himself and spoke next to no words. He smoked his pipe and sang quiet songs by himself late at night up on deck. I didn't know why he would be mad at me. I had only killed three, and he had killed four. He should have been happy. He won the sharpshooter contest, but I reckon that wasn't really the point.

When we reached the States, we found out that while we had been gone, Wrong John and Krill had gone about the country setting the tone of his presidency. They had toured various government-funded programs and done to them what came to be known as the Silverspoon Curse. It was something like the pirate trick of inviting an old hand out for dinner and drinks, showing him a jolly good time, and at the end of the evening, handing him a white piece of paper with a black spot on it. The black spot, of course, was the pirate code for an impending execution. Whoever received the black spot had been marked for death.

Let's not forget, brother Frank, that Captain Silverspoon had earlier declared *his* Moby Dick to be the federal government. "I'm gonna strip its blubber and feed it to the sharks!" he had said. His trail of Silverspoon Curses appeared to be evidence of Wrong John Ahab's fervor to hunt and kill his bureaucratic white whale.

He and Krill visited a cornfield in Iowa where corn was being turned into fuel that could supplement America's blubber affliction. "This," he had said, "is a fine example of how we will bring American enterprise to bear on the need for independence from foreign sources of blubber." When he returned to

Washington, however, funding for the corn fuel distillery disappeared into a giant vault, three-feet-thick with cement walls—a vault called Tax Relief.

He toured an inner-city neighborhood in Montgomery, Alabama, that had taken federal grants and spruced up its skid row. It was Silverspoon at his silver-tongued finest, working the crowd, slapping backs, teasing, shooting his finger bullets. "It's inspiring to see the transformation here in Montgomery," he said. "I could not be prouder of your effort." A few days later the grant money disappeared and no one could find it. Wrong John stuck to principle, stuck to the pirate code, and delivered his charming black spot.

He visited a gold mill in Colorado that had ruined the local water supply. The mill was being cleaned up and the water purified and filtered through an ingenious system of gravel and sand, combined with swamp plants that drew the poisons from the water. Funding came from Uncle Sam. Silverspoon toured the site, dressed up as a miner, wearing a metal hat with a housed candle in front, and he said, "It boggles the mind what Americans can do when they put their mind to it. This is an outstanding achievement." But when he got back to the Potomac, funding for the cleanup was diverted to the vault of Tax Relief. He did save *some* of the clean-up money: set it aside to develop a new leasing program for mining companies. The program invited them to prospect on public land without conducting studies to see if their mines would pollute the water supply.

He and Krill traveled all over America praising government programs they intended to give the black spot to. Word about the Silverspoon Curse spread throughout the country. When employees in a program funded by Uncle Sam heard he was to pay them a visit, they got right to looking for new jobs.

These and other stories got swapped over coffee and chocolates in Wrong John's roundhouse when he was reunited with his first mate. The tale of our razing the Court of Earthly Justice brought the captain great pleasure. I was given credit for impersonating Dr. Henchman, but in the retelling, Tosspot and Dagger blasted the judges and the guards and led us to safety. I didn't try to clarify. By then I was not of a mind to feel heroic about murder. Pinch started crying when she heard they had flown her Star-Spangled Jolly Roger during the getaway. "You must have felt just like Francis Scott Key," she said, blubbering.

I got the captain tucked in at his usual 10:00 p.m., and was enjoying a smoke with Tatanka on the deck when I noticed a company of skiffs silently approach us a'port and take several from *Liberty* into their company. We snuffed our cigarettes, looked at each other, and nodded. We waited for them to get a distance away, lowered a whaleboat, and followed the party, stroking the river with smooth, quiet paddles through the dark water.

Had it not been for their lamps and torches burning with great light and smoke, we would have been lost in the great river on such a dark, dark night. "A butt with legs could track these white men," Tatanka said. The party came ashore on a small island in the Potomac, an island that had the actual name of Pirate Island.

"The buzzard has landed," I said.

As we approached the shore of Pirate Island I heard a shot and the brief squeal of a pig. Our whaleboat ground into the silted shore of the island and came to a stop. We tucked the oars quietly in the boat, rolled up our pant legs (Tatanka was already barefoot, but I had to slip off my cowboy boots), and stepped gingerly into the cool water. We hunched low and snuck into the thick bank of shoreline trees, some of which must have been magnolia from the perfume in the air. As we got closer to a clearing lit up from a big fire, we went down on all fours and crawled through the vines and spider webs on our way like moths to the bright yellow light. Crickets all around us parted in silence as we came past, then filled in where we had been and kicked up their chirping ruckus.

A freshly gutted boar hung on a spit over a smaller cooking fire. One of *Liberty*'s kitchen laborers turned it by a crank. The fire sizzled from the drip of pork fat. The aroma of the roasting pig crawled into my nose and down my gullet and got the natives in my stomach to arguing about who would get the biggest piece. I licked my lips, poked Tatanka in the shoulder, and nodded sideways at the roasting boar. He nodded at me with a slight smile.

Behind the cooking fire, wooden kegs were stacked three high, end to end. A kitchen laborer pounded the tap into a keg with a wooden mallet. The keg hissed, and a frothy spray shot out. Other laborers came around with trays of pewter beer mugs, filled them with the brew, and served them to a gathering of at least fifty people, positioned at tables in a half circle on the far side of the bonfire. Rounds of yellow and white cheeses and hearty loaves of shepherd's bread had been laid out on the thick tables, recently hewn, I guessed, from the island's forest. A heavy cast-iron cauldron hung over the main fire by chains attached to metal posts on either end of the blaze. It steamed and put out a smell I related to being sick—a medicinal potion of some kind.

From somewhere in the bushes behind the group of tables, a hound dog began to bay, calling several others to its chorus. Tatanka nodded at me. My stomach knotted up; I knew that sound all too well, had been tracked by those infernal noses with legs too many times. A heavy-set bald man stood in the center of the half-circle of tables. It was Chief Dagger, and he called the meeting to order.

"Well, here we are, together again as we had hoped," he said, his tankard raised high and overflowing with suds. "I think I speak for everyone when I say we have achieved something unprecedented in modern times—a president that is, essentially, the most influential corporate lobbyist in the history of the world. In our plan to *piratize* America, we have started at the top. We have *piratized* the presidency. Wrong John understands his bailiwick, appreciates the assignment, not as a public servant, but a pirate businessman pretending to be a politician—and not a very good one." He smiled from the right side of his mouth. The gathered crowd laughed.

"So finally, at long last, we can do what needs to be done to ensure the mighty American economic machine runs on at full speed with no interruptions. We don't have to pretend any longer that we have some humanitarian obligation to save the world. We can come out with the truth, the glory, and the passion that is our dedication to wealth, to power, to growth, to control and dominance in the world!" He raised his tankard and took a long draught, as did the others.

Tatanka and I worked our away around the clearing, opposite the dogs, closer to the sizzling pig on a spit, it's pink skin growing dark and shiny as it cooked. The crickets continued to quiet and part before our path. The moonless sky was hazy and caused the stars of the Big Dipper to look like tiny balls of bright, twinkling fuzz. The dogs were silent, for now.

Dagger introduced Crude, the Oil Czar, who really needed no

introduction with this crowd, who were, it turns out, his cronies from a career of service to the blubber trade. Crude explained that modern times demanded a foreign policy that was an energy policy. There could be no division between the two. Every action in the world had to be linked directly to the blubber requirements of the nation.

"We can't waste our attention on countries or issues that don't add up to, in the end, more blubber in our tanks. We simply need too much of the stuff in a continual and uninterrupted flow for there to be any hesitation to locate and protect our supply. Nothing can get in the way of this policy, for without it, our economy, the envy of the world, will go tits up in a heartbeat." That was Crude's sense of humor, well tailored to his name, and to his business, and to this, his finest hour. Across the fire, the laborer's wooden hammer banged a tap into another keg, received with a gurgling hiss.

The chairman of Endrun Energy, Silverspoon's buddy, Slick, stood and spoke in his Texas barbecue sauce voice. "I'm just glad to see a couple of my employees finally amount to something." The crowd giggled and applauded. Crude and Chief nodded their heads and smiled, then raised their tankards toward the chairman. They all took a long pulls from their mugs.

Slick snapped his fingers, and a pert young woman handed him a heavy scroll. "Myself and a few of the other blubber moguls have taken the liberty— no pun intended—to draft a set of policies and procedures that nicely direct the fortunes of our country into our pockets for the foreseeable future and beyond. We'd like you to embrace these guidelines as a substrate to foreign and domestic policy." He walked over and handed the scroll to the Chief, who accepted it with a bow. The crowd applauded, clanged frothy mugs of beer together, and deeply drank.

"Read us a few!" shouted someone in the group. Many others chimed in.

Chief held up a hand and opened the scroll. "Okay, okay. Ahem. Rule One: All pollution regulations are voluntary." The people applauded. "Rule Two: The notion of *protected* public land is extinct." More applause followed. "Rule Three: The American military is your private security firm." The group cheered. "Rule Four: All tax liability is suspended for patriotic blubber companies. Rule Five: All blubber related R&D will be funded by the

American taxpayer."

Crude jumped up excitedly. "We are watched! We are hounded every day by the hard hand of the free market."

"Yeah!" the group shouted.

"Who needs a bunch of stupid busybodies sticking their noses in our business? Price, quality, distribution, these are the forces that continually keep us in line."

"Yeah!" They shouted, then cheered.

Then the president of Fat Co. stood and spoke. "My only concern is that the proceedings of this meeting become public knowledge and come back to bite us in the ass."

Dagger held up his hands. "Please, don't insult me. I've been working this game in Washington for a long time. I know the liability we're all under, and I can assure you, in my capacity as first mate of the executive branch, no one will ever know who was here and what was discussed."

"How can you be so sure?" said the man from Fat Co. defiantly.

"Because there's finally a CEO running the government. His priority is that of a businessman, not a politician who feels obligated to inform the public of what he's doing. As a man of privilege, he *appreciates* executive privilege, and he doesn't believe the private advice he receives is anybody's damn business. He also knows that the only value of a scum-sucking lawyer is as a human shield against an enemy attack."

"What about the Congress?"

"Mostly our friends; shouldn't be a problem. Christ, guys, you can't get elected in America anymore unless you're stinking rich." A murmur of assent passed through the crowd. Tatanka and I had worked our way around so that we were directly behind the roasting pig. We slinked out of the bushes and positioned ourselves behind the stack of kegs.

"What about this whole thing with Kyoto?" asked a woman wearing a full-length mink coat. "His suicide was a calculated publicity stunt—and it worked. Now everybody thinks we're monsters for turning him down on the deal. We need some science of our own to combat the eco-liberal academic onslaught."

Slick from Endrun Energy stood and responded. "You've got a point about the science, and I think Crude has something for you on that. I just wanted to say something about Kyoto and the eco-yahoos. Are these people really as stupid as they sound? Crying about 'Peak Oil' as if it's a bad thing and we need to find alternatives. Find alternatives? Chief Dagger holds America's new energy policy, and it's all about the great opportunity we have to corner the market at a time in history when demand outstrips supply—and these armadilla huggers want to seek alternatives? The money to be made here as these whales start to run rare is absolutely staggering. It's the best time in history, bar none, to be involved in blubber. Thank God our boys on *Liberty* understand." The group cheered and whistled.

"Thank you, Slick," said Crude. "That's why *you* authored the energy policy, and not some federal energy department incompetent who wouldn't know an opportunity if it bit him in his entitlement." The group clapped and hooted. "Now, to answer the question about science. Not to worry. This isn't our first trip to the cathouse—and it won't be our last. Let me present to you Mr. Science with an attitude, Grand Wizard von Shlop"

From out of the forest strode the highest scientific authority in the land, *Liberty's* short man in a tall blue robe, his neat white goatee sharp as a pitchfork tine, the smaller, inverted twin of his pointed hat. He walked into the clearing and stood before the fire. The flames rose, and sparks flew with loud pops, as the fire responded to his powerful presence. He raised his wand and his free hand, the billowing sleeves of his gown appearing as wings, and spoke an incantation.

"Eye of a frog, wing of a stork, arm of a squid, ear of a bat," said the wizard, reaching into his black bag and throwing various substances into the fire. It hissed and flared with each cast he made. He held the group instantly spellbound. "Oh great mysteries of nature, oh great alchemy of the elements, give forth your guidance, give forth your wisdom, teach us the truth of man's place in the world." He threw something on the fire—it smelled like gunpowder to me—that caused a billowing tower of smoke and flames to rise from the bonfire. Several in the crowd whooped.

"Ask me your questions, oh titans of industry, about the science of faith, deeper, more profound, more lasting, and more powerful than the puny experimental fictions of the laboratory."

"Can you tell us the unexpected advantages of accelerating the burning of blubber oil?" asked Slick.

The scientist threw something into the fire that put out a blast of red smoke. "Yes, the surprises are many, but the most exciting, as proven by the placement of bald lab rats into a concentrated environment of carbon dioxide, is the prolific, abundant, almost instantaneous growth of new hair."

Dagger rubbed his bald head and smiled wistfully. The woman who wore the mink coat spoke up. "Certainly there must be some proof that harvesting whales north of Alaska is good for polar bears and fur seals."

The magician threw a potion that caused a blue smoke to rise. "I have a study produced by the University of Blubber that proves conclusively the major cause of polar ice melting is not 'global warming' but horny arctic whales blowing hot air on the ice and melting it. The more they do it, the more whales are born, the faster the ice cap melts. The UB study recommends the immediate removal of fifty to seventy-five percent of arctic whales to save the ice for polar bears and seals."

"But is it a credible study? I've never heard of UB," the woman said.

"Credibility is in the eye of the beholder. The point is, UB's study refutes their study, which opens the debate and puts doubt in the mind of the public. They say ours is phony, we call theirs nonsense, everybody gets confused, nobody acts, and the blubber barons gets a cakewalk."

"Their scientists have all the credentials, the fancy degrees from the best universities; how can you stand up to them?" asked the short, chubby chief of Fat Co.

"By magic, of course. Science is a grand illusion. It presumes to study only facts, and by its nature can be manipulated beyond recognition. Science is a magic word that we can recite whenever and however it suits us. Because it is magic, only another scientist has the courage to examine it. We use our influence with the press to get our magical studies presented in a very positive light, and before you know it, nobody knows what to believe."

The crowd burst into applause. The wizard took off his hat and bowed. Beer steins clanked, and everyone cheered the wizard.

"What about the solid fuel industry?" shouted a burly man with a thick dark beard. "Let's not forget coal, our precious 'black blubber'—petrified blubber, actually—buried for us here in America by Almighty God, on, I believe, the fourth day of creation."

Dagger stood and answered the question. "The men of blubber and petrified blubber are brothers in our eyes," he said solemnly. "If one rises, so shall the other. If one enjoys a subsidy, so shall his brother."

"Just write up your policy," added Crude, "we'll make sure it gets adopted. Blubber is the one area where being dark actually *helps* your career." The group laughed. "Our dream is for equality in America, where all blubber, black, white, red, and yellow, walk together as one, each an equal, and sacred in the eyes of corporate profitability."

"So let's buckle down and kick that rat bastard out of Iraq!" the Chief yelled. Everyone cheered.

"And if you need some science to back up your prospectus, give me a jingle and I'll cook something up for you," added the wizard. While the crowd was distracted, Tatanka and I snuck from behind the kegs, threw our shirts over the roasting pig, and ran with it through the woods to our whaleboat. We chucked the pig into the wide boat, pushed off, and rowed like mad downstream, both of us laughing, the boat tipping side to side with every stroke. If it had been a canoe, we'd have tipped it over. Hounds bayed at us from shore, and there was the splash of dogs jumping into the water. Deep voices shouted; a few people whistled; someone blew a horn.

I really don't know if they took after us in boats. I never heard or saw one—but it was a very dark and hazy night. Regardless, there's no way they would have ever caught us. You know I'm right, Frank. There was never a posse, or a detective agency, or a militia—not even the entire damn Union Army—that could catch Jesse James on a getaway. That feeling, Frank, rowing away, the stolen prize lying between us, still bubbling, was the feeling I loved above all others. There may have been political causes, grudges to settle, enemies to punish, but down deep, the real reason for all the thieving and killing was to get that thrill.

After some twenty minutes of hard rowing, we settled back and took to peeling off strips of pork with our fingers. We had passed Liberty, closer than we should have, and saw Krill at the binnacle lamp again, rubbing it with his beak and singing it a song. We lounged in that whaleboat I don't know how long, tearing meat and feasting on Chief's corporate party pig. By the time we were done we were stuffed, belching and greasy, and had no idea where we were, so we pulled the boat over and fell asleep. Thank goodness the Sioux woke up at first light and got us back to Liberty before the captain set off on his jog. Otherwise, it would have been us roasting on the spit.

The next day Tosspot came snooping around, asking questions about the night before. It was plain as a peacock he wanted to find out if someone on Liberty had stolen their fat pig last night, but he didn't want to give away what they had been up to. He came around Tatanka and me in the kitchen preparing Wrong John's sunny eggs.

"You boys have a good night?" he asked.

"Turned in early," I said.

"My ribs were killing me," said the Indian. We both had toothpicks in our mouth and worked them hard between our teeth.

"My hams ached from all that lifting," I said.

"Yep. Oh, Ish, hand me the bacon, would you?"

"Sure, Injun." I reached over for a hunk of pork belly hanging off a hook and slapped it down on his squat butcher-block table. "How 'bout you, marshal. Get a good night's rest, did you?"

"You could say that." He walked off, twiddling with his bullwhip.

Chapter XVII

Here I Sit, Buns a'Flexin'

A few mornings later I came into the galley for a cup of joe and found Tatanka sitting on his squatty table, barefooted, no shirt, carving on a sperm whale tooth with his long, yellow jackknife. The scrape of steel against hard tooth sent my tongue directly to an old cavity that had been giving me trouble. I poured myself some coffee in a tin mug and leaned against the wall. He must have just fed the fowl—turkeys, chickens, and geese pecked at the floor of their pens and ground their seed.

"Could be trouble ahead," he told me in his deep, flat Lakota voice.

"Would it be of the type to interest me?"

"No money in it." He continued to scratch a scrimshaw into his whale tooth.

"Why bother?" I sipped my coffee.

"Bushwhacker raid. Keep them guessing."

"Always a good idea."

I didn't give it much thought until lunchtime. I was in Wrong John's roundhouse serving his ham-and-cheese sandwich when Tosspot rushed into his quarters.

"Quick, Sire. You must come with me at once. There has been a terrible breach of protocol on board. You must see it for yourself to believe the extent of insubordination that has occurred," Tosspot cried.

"I just got my lunch here, TP. Gimme half an hour for vittles."

"I believe you will want to save your *vittles* for later, Sire. If you will want them at all after you witness the abomination that has taken place."

Krill stood on the captain's table eating a plate of sliced banana, grapes, and pomegranate seeds. "*BRACK!*" he squawked, bits of fruit flying from his worn gray beak. "Disrupt his schedule at your own peril—your own peril. *BRACK!*"

"Don't smart off to me, you filthy bird," snapped the marshal.

"Whoa." said Wrong John. "That's the bird wonder you're talkin' to there, partner."

"Please, Sire. There's a mutiny in the works and I've got a parrot advising me to save it for later. Well I won't—I can't!"

Wrong John scowled and threw his napkin onto his plate. He followed Tosspot out of his cabin. They climbed down the hatch to a corner of deck three at the far end of the starboard cannon battery. A patrol of armed sailors stood at the wooden door, painted with a black crescent moon. Several round spermaceti candles floated in a tub of water and provided a shifting yellow light. Tosspot opened the door and, inside, Crude held a lamp next to the wooden wall beside the commode.

"It's pretty bad," said the oil czar.

"I warned you 'bout them dang Itralian sausages," said Silverspoon, holding his nose. He snickered and looked to his right shoulder, seeming to expect Krill to be there. He thrust two fingers in his mouth and whistled. In the distance came the small echo of his parrot returning the note.

"Look for yourself at this disgrace," Tosspot said snidely.

The captain leaned down toward the light and read what had been carved into the wooden wall. "What's this? 'Here I sit buns a'flexin', givin' birth to another Texan.' What in *the* hell?" he said, his hand held over his mouth to conceal his amusement.

"Shameful, isn't it, Sire?"

"Really bad—really bad joke," the captain said, trying to keep a straight face. "You screwed up my lunch over a little bathroom humor? Good God, marshal, toughen up."

"When something like this happens, it is a precursor to mutiny, and must be curtailed fiercely and thoroughly."

"It is? It must?"

Krill, out of breath and panting, flopped and waddled into the latrine. "*BRACK!*" he cried, breathing hard. "What's the hubbub?"

Basmati Sweet had appeared and stood next to the door, seemingly unable to enter the men's latrine with actual men in it. "TP thinks the bathroom graffiti is a precursor to mutiny," she said, rolling her eyes.

Krill looked at the words carved in the wall. "Bye-bye present from Bubba?"

"It certainly displays *his* lack of discipline, but the carving is undoubtedly recent. Notice the light color of the freshly cut wood," TP said.

"I don't know, marshal," said the captain. "I just don't think it's worth making a big stink over." He realized the pun and laughed, as did Krill, Basmati, and Crude.

"Neither do I," said Basma. "I think it's the same attitude that can't recognize Lady Liberty as a symbol of freedom."

"Mr. Second Mate, I'll not have you start again on that perverse harlot," snarled Tosspot, causing the leg irons strapped to his thick black belt to jangle.

"Harlot? How can you—harlot? She's the only pure and natural beauty on this entire ship." I had to wonder, Frank, if the marshal wasn't so bothered by the sculpture because its bare breasts made him randy, and he was embarrassed by it.

Gunny had just arrived and heard her last remark. "Hold it, Basma. My cannons are works of art." He pointed to his starboard battery dropping away into shadow.

"A weapon is not a work of art. It's a work of destruction," she retorted.

"And that, in terms of national defense, is a thing of beauty," Yo Ho countered.

Basmati turned away from him and walked to the farthest cannons, into the dark. I could hear her down there moving cannonballs. Did I hear one roll down a barrel?

"Regardless of anyone's opinion, the wheels of justice have already begun to turn. I will convene the Buns a'Flexin' Tribunal in twenty minutes. I have already made an arrest." He had his bullwhip in his hand and tapped it against his thigh.

From the stairs I heard pounding feet and arguing voices, one of them high-pitched, spewing Gatling-gun Spanish. I turned to see young Roberto Mendoza in the arms of Tosspot's military police, followed by Tatanka, who demanded they tell him why his assistant had been arrested. No one responded to him until they reached us, when Tosspot said, "Mr. Tatanka, you had better return to the galley at once or you will also be arrested." Tatanka looked at me with fierce, searching eyes, seeming to ask if I thought he should obey. I tipped my head quickly a couple of times to tell him he should do as he was told. He turned defiantly and strode back to deck two. Tosspot's men took Roberto topside and tied him to the mainmast to await his trial. The marshal went about gathering the officers for an emergency tribunal.

Twenty minutes, later, the officers had assembled behind several tables on the quarterdeck. They waited awhile for Basma to show up, then decided to go forward without her. The junior officer, Bill, untied Roberto Mendoza and brought him forward to stand before the marshal, who now wore a black judge's robe, but had his U.S. Marshal badge pinned at the chest.

"You may find it cute, Lisp, to make anal humor jokes at the expense of the captain, but it is an offense that is felonious," said Tosspot.

"I would tend to think of it as more of a prank, actually," interjected Sir

Yes Sir. "As a former military officer, I can tell you the men need to let off some steam to keep their spirits up."

"And I suppose you would condone nigger jokes if it boosted morale?" threw out Yo Ho Ho. Wrong John and the officers turned quickly toward him.

The proud African stood, jaw set, and strode toward Yo Yo with his chest out and fists clenched. Two junior officers held him back, but I didn't think two was enough. Yo Yo sat at his chair and grinned, but would not look at Sir Yes Sir.

"Stand down, SYS," said the Chief. "I can't have the two of you at loggerheads over every little incident." The diplomat jerked away from the junior officer and returned to his seat.

"This 'incident' does not, under any reading of military law, call for a tribunal. The marshal's 'case' is petty, and a waste of our time," growled the diplomat. "Sand the damn joke off the wall if it bothers you that much."

"No!" cried Tosspot. "It's an act of rebellion. It's an insult to our leader. It's a serious offense against the mission of *Liberty* and I won't be satisfied until somebody is flogged for it!"

"Judge not that ye not be judged. For as ye judge, so too shall ye be judged in return.'" said Pinch, surprising everyone with a quote from Matthew.

Tosspot drew back and shook his head. "Well, if you know your scripture, Pinch, Leviticus is very clear in 20:13, 'If a man lie with another man as he would a woman, both of them have committed an abomination; they shall surely be put to death; their blood shall be upon them.'"

"What proof have you that any men have 'lain' with any other men?" asked Sir Yes Sir in his deep, intimidating voice.

"I have—it's, when somebody—," the marshal stammered. "There's a protocol we use, and it's clear that—"

"Hold on there," said the captain. "I won't have the Bible tossed back and forth like a horny toad. Where's this goin' anyway, TP?"

Tosspot turned on the young assistant cook. "Do you think this is some continuation of the Bubba military, where you people can get away with your perversions so long as you lie about them?"

"*No se*, Mr. Marshal, sir. I no understand," said Roberto hesitantly, his lisp more pronounced than usual. He looked at me with fear in his brown eyes. I held up my hand, trying to tell him to sit tight.

"Don't think I haven't seen you and the cook frolicking in the sea like two frisky colts. Now you're scrawling crude references to flexing buns in the officers' latrine. That what stirs the loins, is it? Hm? The back door?" He fiddled with the leg irons at his waist.

"Back door? No, no, is a mistake," he said. "I did not do it. I want to get married. See, *es mi novia*." He pulled a tattered photo from his back pocket and tried to show it to the marshal.

Tosspot stood from his chair, rushed around the table, and grabbed Roberto by the lapel. "There will be no weddings for queers so long as I'm running the churches in this country!" I thought TP had completely lost his mind. I had seen the photo of Roberto's fiancée, and she was the furthest thing from a man. I could not sit back and allow the fanatic's witch hunt to continue.

"Marshal, I know I'm not an officer, or a judge, but I think you've got the wrong man here. Roberto Mendoza is engaged to a fine young woman. I've seen her picture. He talks about her all the time."

Tosspot pointed his fully extended arm and index finger at me. "IshcaBible—or whoever you are—you are in contempt of court, and will be taken to the brig along with Lisp to await sentencing!" he thundered.

BOOM!

A cannon fired from the aft end of the starboard cannon battery. It whizzed across the water and crashed into the far shore, taking down a tall, thin tree. Sweet *did* roll a cannonball down the barrel, I thought. Gunny jumped up and yelled, "That's a direct violation of dep-con, alpha-bravo-charlie niner! I'll get you somebody to flog, marshal!" He ran for the hatch, tangled his foot in a coil of rope, and nearly fell to the deck before he freed himself and ran on.

"Have a nice trip," muttered Sir Yes Sir.

The captain closed his left eye and scratched his head. By the look on his face, he had decided he was angry. "Damn it, TP, now you're coming after my holy gunslinger? No sir. IshcaBible's scriptural to me. I can't have you throwing the Good Book in the hoosegow. If he says Lisp has a girlfriend, done deal. And P.S., I ain't exactly tickled by your suggestion that a Texas turd is automatically queer.

"Next time, why don't *you* go to the toilet with the newspaper, and sit there and think for a good long while before you *ruin* my lunch again!"

"*BRACK!* Mess the schedule at your own peril, your own peril." Krill stuck his black tongue out at the marshal.

Wrong John stood and walked away from the table. "Somebody grab my lunch from the roundhouse and bring it to the driving range. Who wants to hit some balls with me?" Pinch joined him. "And *not you*, sharpshooter," he said, pointing at me. Tosspot sulked away to Chief's quarters. The first mate followed him in.

I walked to Bill, who held Roberto, and winked at him as I took the Mexican from him. He jerked his head away from me and stormed off in the direction of the marshal. I and Roberto and I went down the hatch and into the galley. Tatanka stood anxiously by the door and broke into a big smile when he saw the two of us together.

"Roberto," he said, and embraced the small Mexican. "I'm sorry, friend. All my fault."

I scratched my head up under the black bowler. "That toilet carving your bushwhacker raid?"

"Yep. Got 'em good." Tatanka shook his yellow jackknife at me.

"Got them? What about me? *Cabrón!*" Roberto said, doubling his fists at the Sioux.

"Collateral damage. Right, Dingus?" he said, reciting the term Chief had used to justify the crimes of Dr. Henchman. Then he spoke from the side of his mouth and changed his voice into a bad impression of Dagger's sharp, clipped speech. "It is a burden great leader must always bear." I rushed him and tackled him to the floor. Roberto piled on and the three of us wrassled in the kitchen for a good ten minutes, grunting and laughing.

Chapter XVIII

Uncle Samuel J. Fatass

Roberto Mendoza settled into the kitchen and stayed out of Tosspot's way. Basmati Sweet did not get flogged for firing Gunny's cannon. She had disappeared—hidden away by a sympathetic Lakota rebel—and was never charged with the crime. Wrong John Silverspoon and his officers tried to forget the marshal's potty tribunal, but every time he filed off the carving it showed up again a few days later. He became so angry and frustrated he posted a guard outside the officer's latrine twenty-four-hours a day—and still, the carving magically reappeared. "Injun bushwhacker," said Tatanka, cleaning his nails with his jackknife. "Makes himself invisible." The captain eventually told the guard to find another job, that he didn't need somebody eavesdropping while he did his business. Every few days the marshal had the carving removed. Every few days it reappeared. By the nasty looks Tosspot gave me, I was pretty certain who was his prime suspect. I didn't give him any reason to doubt it.

The other officers turned their attention to planning a big shindig to fulfill Silverspoon's number-one campaign promise: tax relief. At first they looked at a standard Washington pageant, complete with a gala ball, important speeches, and a parade, but the formality of it all didn't dovetail with Wrong John's down-home style. Instead they chose a Texas theme: The Uncle Samuel J. Fatass Ceremonial Rodeo and Tax Rebate. It would take place on the National Mall, dead square in the center of the recovered swampland that had been General George McClellan's training ground for Union troops before the Civil War. President George Washington's partially completed monument (the obelisk rose some four hundred of its intended five-hundred-fifty feet) had been chosen to mark the eastern boundary of the rodeo grounds. A ring of wooden bleachers fifty feet high surrounded the grounds—set up in an oval about the same size as a mile-and-a-quarter racetrack. Tatanka and I had been assigned to ride the arena and help cowboys who got in trouble during the event, or, if necessary, to shoot anybody who threatened the captain from the stands.

The extravaganza took place on a sultry mid-July day, hazy from Kyoto's blubber smoke, humid from the nature of Virginia bottomland, but an otherwise ordinary, hot summer day. Pinch's trio of redheaded eagles soared above the capital. Tens of thousands of people packed the bleachers, and thousands upon thousands more filled the National Mall. The atmosphere reminded me of a huge state fair, with unending booths selling canned goods, fresh pies, ice cream, saltwater taffy, needlepoint, knitting, skirts and blouses, straw hats and top hats and bowlers, boots, shoes, silk stockings, corned beef and cabbages, sausage sandwiches, turkey legs, frothy mugs of beer, and a hundred other things. Politicians, preachers, fortune tellers, snake oil salesmen, and all manner of con men and quacks bellowed their pitches unto the crowd. Brass bands played, people shouted, sang, danced, fought, and, more than anything, gossiped and speculated about how much money Captain Silverspoon was going to give them.

The Uncle Samuel J. Fatass Ceremonial Rodeo and Tax Rebate began with a company of twenty trumpeters holding long, golden horns, galloping into the arena standing on brilliant white stallions. They played what to me could have been the musical fanfare for an event in the Roman Coliseum, riding in two separate lines in a figure eight that crisscrossed in the middle.

The trumpeters rode off, and a big, armored wagon rolled in stacked with a pyramid of gold bars ten feet tall, pulled by a team of snorting black Belgian draft horses twenty-five hands high, driven by a massive, baldheaded man wearing a white shirt and black vest. He held a megaphone five feet long with an opening nearly three feet across. He put the small end to his mouth and hollered through, his voice spreading out and filling the arena like a spray of grapeshot from a cannon. "Welcome, welcome, one and all, to the Uncle Samuel J. Fatass Ceremonial Rodeo and Tax Rebate. When Wrong John Silverspoon rode into town he promised to rob the robbers and give your money back to you. That's what we are here to celebrate today!" The crowd roared its approval.

"Sit back and enjoy the show, folks. We've got a couple hours of Wild West fun in store for you, followed by the greatest tax refund in American history. So without further ado, let's get right to the first event: Bureaucrat

Bulldogging!" He paused to let the cheering die down.

"Comin' outta chute number one, put your hands together for a cowboy out of the corporate offices of Gonzo Railroad, Chief Financial Officer Bud Winkins! He'll be chasing down a varmint called White Lightning from the Federal Antitrust Department." A short, man wearing a tee shirt and boxers, waddled out from a stall and ran clumsily across the grounds. He got a thirty-foot head start before the financial officer burst forth from his chute on a stocky brown and white palomino and bore down on the bureaucrat. In seconds the rider was next to the ponderous government employee, slipped from his horse, and landed on the other man's shoulders. He rolled the chubby guy over, grabbed his hands and feet, and threw a few quick turns of rope around his wrists and ankles. The cowboy finished off his knot with a dramatic fling of his hands in the air, and left the bureaucrat lying in the dirt.

"How 'bout that, folks? Eight seconds flat; that'll be hard to beat." The audience whooped and shouted and waved little American flags in the air (or were they Star-Spangled Jolly Rogers? I couldn't tell). "Imagine a critter, folks, using *your money* to punish a great company like Gonzo Railroad for growing. Give that Washington parasite his pink slip and get him out of here!" Tatanka rode over, untied the bureaucrat, and led him out of the arena.

"Next up is a slippery varmint from the Agency for Counter-Terrorism. Ooh, sounds scary doesn't it? These Bubba leftovers are asking for another million dollars of *our money* to run around in the dark chasing geese. But there's a wrangler from Pinkerton Detective Agency who can bring him down."

A robust man with broad shoulders flew from a stall and ran across the grounds, zigzagging. A cowboy flew from his chute on a bay quarter horse and bore down on the government employee. When the rider came alongside, the employee stopped, and the cowboy slipped from his horse onto the ground. The counter-terrorist kicked him in the ribs, grabbed his rope, and tied his legs. He threw back his arms and walked out of the arena.

The crowd booed, and the announcer bellowed, "These bureaucrats are slippery, aren't they? Will do almost anything to keep their easy jobs and their expense accounts fat with *our money*." I threw a rope around the Pinkerton and dragged him off the grounds with my horse.

"Let's get back in the saddle here. Comin' up outta chute four is a tough hombre from Money Lynch Investment Services, up against a mangy dog called Quick Silver from the bloated agency of Social Security." A short, stout woman, barefooted and wearing a blue polka-dotted hoop skirt, ran out of a stall for about thirty feet before a cowboy galloped out after her. He reached her side, fell upon her, and flipped her over so that her bloomers showed. The crowd gasped. He threw a few wraps of rope around her wrists and ankles, then jerked up and away from her, his arms flung back.

"How 'bout that cowboy, ladies and gentlemen? Do you think its time we put our retirement future in the hands of a real wrangler, instead of leaving it in the desk drawer of a frightened schoolmarm?" A few scattered cheers and whistles came from the audience. Tatanka cut her binding, helped the woman to her feet and escorted her from the arena. I looked over at the flat top of the incomplete monument to our first president. I wondered if he would be proud of what his country had come to. I tipped my hat to his partly-done white tower, thinking, you'll never get your capstone, sir. That'd just be another useless government handout.

"Now we got us a good one, folks. It's the Chief Operating Officer of Winknod Chemical on a black Morgan named Thunder, goin' after a ripsnortin' steer from the EPA, goes by Cow Bite."

A small man in blue jeans and no shirt, wearing glasses, ran with quick, small steps out of his stall. The cowboy rushed out on black Thunder and almost ran him down before the wrangler fell onto the small man and attempted to throw him over. The little guy was tougher than he looked and put up quite a fight. The two began to grapple until finally the COO punched the bureaucrat and knocked him to the ground. He tied him up, but didn't bother to throw his hands back—just walked off shaking his head under his big gray cowboy hat.

"Nobody ever said Silverspoon had an easy job, did they? These agencies have made a fortune out of attacking American business. You think they're going to roll over without a fight?" I went over and untied the man and helped him find his eyeglasses. They were broken. He turned, squinting, and yelled at the crowd.

"I'm trying to protect you! Don't you see? They're only interested in money, not your welfare!" The crowd booed and threw sausages and pickles and rutabagas at him. I pulled him halfway up my horse and got him out of there.

The rodeo continued with the team roping of bureaucrats, lasso tricks, the bureaucrat barrel race, and horse team precision drilling, until it reached the finale, Bareback Bureaucrat Riding. "Are you ready for some fun?" the gargantuan announcer boomed. The crowd applauded mildly. I imagined they were ready for their tax rebate by then. The sun was dropping into the haze, throwing a softer golden light over the grounds, but not much diminishing the heat.

"Outta chute number two we got us a tough old rodeo bull called Dynamite, runs outta the Department of Labor. The cowboy who drew him is the VP of Marketing for WongMart, Lou Billings. Go get 'im, Lou!"

An old man with patchy gray hair above the ears and a heavy belly hanging down crawled out of his chute with a handsome, powerful cowboy in a leather vest and a white hat sitting on his back. The contestant leaned back on a rope through the bureaucrat's teeth and raised his knees up next to his chestnut cowboy hat. He kicked the old man in the ribs with his spurs. The old guy reared back feebly, and the cowboy kicked him again and again. Blood began to drip from the bureaucrat's sides until he fell over, exhausted.

"That's what you get, you naughty bull, for trying to block a smart businessman from lowerin' his overhead." Tatanka helped the old man out of the ring.

"This next one ought to be good, folks. It's a big old Brahma bull called Fury, ridin' in from the ranch of the Internal Revenue Service. He'll have to dismount our Grand National champ, the Chief Executive Officer of Oregon Trail Wagon Company, Buck Snort!"

A smallish man in a brown ten-gallon hat sat on the broad back of a hairy dude with a muscled neck and thick, bulging arms. Buck spurred him once, and the big man rumbled out of the chute. Buck Snort lifted his legs high and spurred the bull a second time. He reared back, twisted hard to the left, and tipped the cowboy over. Fury spit the rope from his mouth and tied the CEO up like he was a cow in the bulldogging contest. He threw his arms back and stormed out of the arena amidst scattered boos.

"Somebody help Buck out there. Hey, I'm sorry, old buddy. Silverspoon hasn't fixed everything yet. You still got to ante up a *little*, just to make it look fair."

The big announcer paused and guzzled a foamy tankard of beer. "Ah, mighty nice. Now, our final varmint is a Black Angus heifer from Affirmative Action, bucks to the name of Lock Jaw. Don't let her get those teeth on your leg, cowboy, she'll *never* let go. Dude that's got to tame her goes by El Rancho and is the Director of Human Resources at Cannon Fodder Incorporated. Here they come outta chute number three!"

A slovenly cowboy whose belly stuck out of his shirt and whose butt spilled out of his pants sat atop a wiry African woman who gamely trotted out on all fours, and attempted one buck before her back gave out. The fat cowboy rode her down and sat on her back grinning and waving his hat in the air before he slowly climbed off of her. Her tongue lolled from her mouth, and she attempted to breath but could not. Tatanka had to spend several minutes finding her wind before she could stagger off the field.

"I don't blame El Rancho for riding her a little hard," asserted the announcer. "He's tired of her terrorizin' talented white folk just to meet her skin pigment quota. In Silverspoon's colorblind America, her function is history!"

The announcer pulled his wagon to the opposite side of the arena, tight against the fence boards. The sun began to set into the haze of blubber fumes and cast shades of pink and amber across the arena. Twenty trumpeters on their white stallions rode in and played another regal fanfare. They wove cloverleaf patterns and figure eights with their galloping steeds, then filed out of the arena.

"Ladies and Gentlemen," bellowed the enormous announcer, "it is my great honor and privilege to present to you Captain Wrong John Silverspoon and the officers of *Liberty*!"

Two-by-two stalked the team of hitched black Belgians into the arena. Twenty of the powerful chargers passed through the gate before the sharp tip of a spiral narwhale horn could be seen. The whale lay on a platform of heavy timber and rolled on iron wheels five feet tall and nearly a foot wide. The entire length of the fifteen-foot whale horn passed into the arena before the figure of Captain Silverspoon could be seen standing just behind the blowhole, balanced on the back of the narwhale, whose body was taller than two big men. It was half again as big a fish as the one Slick had brought to *Liberty*.

Silverspoon had a long harpoon plunged into the back of the whale, and from the end of the wooden shaft, an arms length above his head, flew an American flag. Wrong John smiled and waved his white cowboy hat in the other hand. Krill stood on his right shoulder, smiling as much as a toothless, lipless bird can, waving a tiny, parrot-sized white cowboy hat. Behind him, with his harpoon stuck in the opposite side of the whale, flag flying, gold hoop earrings swaying, stood Chief Dagger, smiling his half smile, also waving a white cowboy hat. Next stood Second Mate Sweet, her flag opposite Dagger's, waving her white hat, followed by Marshal Tosspot, Sir Yes Sir, Gunny, Yo Yo, Dr. von Shlop, Crude the Oil Czar, and Treasurer Pinch. All of them wore crisp blue naval uniforms.

The crowd cheered enthusiastically. From one of the rodeo chutes, a flock of at least a hundred white doves was freed and flew into the pink sunset. A brass band walked through the gate to one side of the heavy wagon and played *America the Beautiful*. Silverspoon and his officers rode into the arena, smiling and waving their white cowboy hats, and were followed by freight wagons also pulled by mighty draft horses, loaded with tall pyramids of gold ingots. One after another of the wagons followed Silverspoon's narwhale, until the entire arena was chock full of gold-laden wagons. There must have been a hundred of them. Imagine it, Frank, just imagine it.

There's me and you, and that gang of bushwhackers pulling into Richmond, Missouri, in 1867, led by a brass band and greeted by the entire town, cheering and waving, who load our wagon with the contents of their bank and hail us heroes as we ride away with their savings. That's what I recalled when I saw the rodeo arena laid out like a Thanksgiving table with shining platters of gold. I thought of you, Frank, and how many times you got shot at and chased out of town, and there stood Silverspoon on the back of his unicorn whale, protected somehow by that magic horn, receiving the adulation of the people whose national treasury he had just emptied. *America the Beautiful* played loud and gloriously from those brass horns as it slowly went dark.

Midget rodeo clowns came into the arena and carried backpacks full of gold and silver coins. Groups of three spread around the grounds. Two in each group held the rubber ends of a giant slingshot while a third filled the pouch with coins and let fly the tax rebate into the stands. The crowd seethed as some titanic oceanic current, swirling and yawning, pushing, pulling, drawing, cresting, and roaring, first with a painful, hungry excitement, then a terrible lustful urgency, soon interspersed with a desperate shrieking and wailing as citizens fought with each other to get as much loot as they could. The wooden bleachers creaked, groaned, and popped, and I feared they would collapse.

The rain of gold showered down on them for five minutes before the midget clowns ran out of the arena and into the surrounding crowd, throwing gold and silver coins and darting through the booths, bands, stages, tents, and picnic tables. The current of madness that had started in the arena followed them as if they were the vanguard of a flood.

Fireworks flew into the sky above the arena. There must have been twenty staging areas across the mall, firing hundreds of rockets simultaneously. They exploded in glittering blossoms of vibrant blue, scarlet, gold, silver, and lime green. The people slowly abandoned their scramble for tax booty to the captivating display of beatific war lighting the night sky. Rockets glared red, bombs burst in the air, and yea, through the night, not one single gold-laden coach was still there.

Under the cover of the fireworks, the sharp horn of a narwhale leading the way, Wrong John and the pirates stole out of Washington and loaded their gold into barges waiting at the presidential dock. The long, flat, black barges, dark except for the small lamp at their binnacle compasses, chugged away for a rendezvous on Pirate Island, taking with them America's bridges, her roads, her parks, her forests, her public beaches, rivers and lakes, her veterans' hospitals, her pensions, her scholarships, her loans, her rainy day reserve.

We followed later in a whaleboat, just Tatanka and I, arriving as we had not so long ago to the shore of Pirate Island, to steal Dagger's fatted pig. This time we were invited, and the gathering was much larger. By the moonlight I saw a line of yachts extending as far as I could see in both directions. We walked into the clearing, and in the center stood a pyramid of gold fifty feet tall. I did not hear a single cricket chirp. Seven hungry bonfires flared around the pyramid, licking at it with red and yellow tongues, and spitting hot, flashing light against the neatly stacked gold bullion. Above the pyramid a banner hung, tied off by long ropes to tall oaks on either side of the clearing, and the banner read, "E Pluribus Unum," which was translated for me by Crude (who was already drunk) to mean, "Out of many taxpayers, one big pile of gold for us to divvy up."

Dainty Chinese maidens on tiny bound feet carried platters of food and drink to the tables arranged in a circle around the pyramid. The conversation was loud, guttural, impatient, marked by the continuous clang of toasting beer mugs. The guests appeared to be royalty in their formal clothes, glittering jewelry, and servants in attendance. White teeth gnashed at barbecued ribs like sharks tearing into the flesh of a stuck whale. Basmati Sweet sat at a huge pipe organ and pounded out sinister church hymns. The tiny rodeo clowns who had distributed to the citizens their tax relief now juggled flaming torches on the edge of the shadowed forest. Other clowns formed a marching band with kazoos, small drums, and cymbals, and paraded through the tables of revelers. I looked up again and there was Wrong John, atop the tower of gold. The firelight coming from below gave him an ominous, demonic appearance, made him seem a giant, all powerful, too mighty and distant to be touched by mere mortals.

"Talk about your tax relief. Hoodoggies! Can you live with it?" he shouted, stomping his foot on the peak of the golden pyramid. By the response of howls, whistles, shrieks, and cries, I would have thought he had just raised the severed head of a dreaded swamp dragon that had eaten a thousand of their young'uns over the last hundred years.

"Fact is, for y'all—my supporters, my friends, my people—tax relief isn't the correct term. This here's a return on investment. You purchased stock in Silverspoon Enterprises—took a gamble on the village idiot, some would say—well guess what, dodo wadn't as dumb as he looked, and dodo don't forget his pals—never!" The crowd cheered wildly, backed by the ugly pounding on the massive pipe organ by Second Mate Sweet. Chief was the first to stand and raise his tankard to his captain. Quickly, the rest of the crowd of wealthy business leaders and heirs stood and raised their tankards high to their heroic comrade.

"Can you live with a tenfold return after six months in the CEO's chair?" Dagger hollered. The group whistled, shouted, clapped, slammed their beer mugs rhythmically on the rough wooden tables. The bonfires flicked their fiery red and yellow tongues up the sides of the golden pyramid. "Let the liberals believe in the myth of politics and races and counting the votes. That man up there isn't a politician. He's your outsourced hired gun, running the government as a taxpayer-funded corporate procurement department." Dagger pointed to the top of the heap. Silverspoon took a big bow, once again drawing zealous cheers, applause, and beer-mug table pounding.

"Ish!" he yelled. "Throw a little Bible on this party!"

I just so happened to have a verse handy. I took off my black bowler, placed it over my heart, and held it there with both hands. "Boy oh boy! That is one fine haul!" I exclaimed, truly impressed—and more than a little jealous. The crowd clapped and whooped. "The gospel makes it clear that when you got a treasure like this tempting you, there's a choice to be made. Luke 16:13: 'No servant can serve two masters: for either he will hate the one, and love the other, or else he will hold to the one and despise the other. Ye cannot serve God and mammon.'"

"Mammon falling from heaven. Beautiful!" cried Silverspoon. "A snowstorm of sacred golden cornflakes. Breakfast of champions." He pulled off his shirt and struck a he-man pose with his bicep and pectoral muscles flexed. The onlookers went wild: screamed, shouted, banged and clanged tankards, whistled, cried, hugged, hooked elbows and pranced in circles, and chanted, "Sil-ver-spoon! Sil-ver-spoon!"

Wrong John smiled, waved, flexed his muscles, and shot various admirers with his .38-caliber finger six-shooters. After the chanting died down, he passed gold ingots down the slope along a spontaneous bucket brigade that had formed on the pyramid. Tatanka nudged me in the shoulder and said, "That Bible. Makes a good bushwhacker, eh?" I slapped him on the back and grinned.

Silverspoon passed down bars of gold and broke into an old slave spiritual: "Nobody knows the trouble I seen. Nobody knows my sorrow," he sang. Sweet accompanied him on the organ, and the entire crowd joined in. "Nobody knows the trouble I seen. Glory hallelu." The crowd raised it voice as one, passing around the savings of their country. "One morning I was a'walkin', O yes, Lord. I saw some berries a'hangin' down, O yes, Lord. I pick the berry and I suck the juice. Just as sweet as the honey in the comb. Sometimes I'm up. Sometimes I'm down, O yes, Lord. Sometimes I'm almost in the ground. What makes ole Satan hate me so? Because he got me once and he let me go. Nobody knows the trouble I seen. Nobody knows my sorrow."

Chapter XIX

A Nice Long Vacation

I had just returned to the galley from the captain's roundhouse the morning after he portioned the loot with his gang on Pirate Island. Tatanka, Roberto and three other laborers grilled up flapjacks and fried bacon for the crew. The Sioux had traded a goat for some good maple syrup, and my mouth watered for a slab of butter melting on a stack of cakes drenched in that sweet elixir. I sipped black coffee and smoked my first cigarette of the day. Basmati Sweet ran in with the captain's breakfast plate, its big yellow frog-eyed eggs unblinking and unbroken. "He doesn't want eggs today," she said, her voice shaking. Everybody stopped what he was doing and stared at her.

"No *huevos?*" said Mendoza. "*Caramba!* Help us, *Santo Antonio.* Something bad gonna happen today." He crossed himself and kissed his closed right thumb and index finger.

"Relax," I told her, taking the plate. "I'll take him up some flapjacks here in a minute." She put her warm hand on my wrist and smiled nervously.

"He *does not* disrupt his routines. This could be bad." She brushed her shock of jet black hair away from her left eye, licked her lips, and hurried off. A few minutes later I came through the hatch with a nice stack of jacks, all buttered and syrup-soaked, five crisp slices of pork belly beside. Chief, Tosspot, Gunny, and Pinch stood outside Silverspoon's door discussing something under their breath.

As I approached, Dagger looked up and motioned me closer. "Trouble in paradise, Ish. The captain seems to have a little hangover from playing God last night. Talk scripture with him, Bible. Try to get him on track."

"And no more of that smarmy Matthew," snarled the marshal. "Give him some meaty John or a nice cut of Ezekiel."

I nodded and entered his cabin. He stood at his collection of baseballs, took one out, rolled it over in his hands, replaced it, examined another.

"Brought you some hotcakes, Wrong John. Fresh butter and maple syrup." He didn't bother to look at me.

"Set them on the table there, Ish."

"Anything the matter?" I asked.

"Oh, I don't know." He closed the glass door on his collection of autographed baseballs hanging on the wall. "I guess this is what it feels like the day after you take the pennant. You wake up, and you think to yourself, what next? How can anything ever matter again?" He walked to the table, cut into his cakes, and took a bite. I still hadn't had breakfast, and my mouth watered like an old trough after a hard rain.

"I mean, heck. I done my big thing last night, what I was elected for. Drove in the winning run. What am I gonna do for an encore?" He placed his elbows on the table, held his face in his hands, and stared glumly at the gorgeous stack of buttered flapjacks.

I had no sympathy for him whatsoever. How could anybody be blue after a haul like that? I tell you, Frank, there's something wrong with a man who doesn't enjoy even one day of satisfaction after pulling the biggest heist ever. Dagger poked his head in the door, and noticing Wrong John's posture, pursed his lips at me, tilted his head, and waved his hands as if trying to raise a flame in a bed of embers. I gestured with my hands for him to back away.

I walked over to Wrong John, pulled Widowmaker, opened the cylinder, and gave it a spin. "Take a look in there, Wrong John. How many bullets do you count?" He pointed at the chambers one by one with his right index finger, tongue sticking out the side of his mouth.

"Five."

"Wrong, John. It's a *six*-shooter. Why do you think there's only six?"

"Wouldn't know, Ish. Don't do the speculation thing."

"Think about it. A man should only shoot six people at a time. Then he should rest—just like God did." I dug in my brain for a hunk of Genesis. "'And on the seventh day God ended his work which he had made; and he rested on the seventh day.' You been huntin' whales and peeling government blubber, robbin' banks, and burning down courts. Hell, Silverspoon, you deserve a nice long vacation."

His eyes brightened, and he took a big bite of hotcakes. "Dang, them are good! You're right, Ish. Let's get back to Texas, get us in a little fishin', chop down some trees, kick back, do some ridin'. If God rested one day out of seven, it's only proper for me to rest one month out of seven."

I walked out and tipped my bowler at the nervous officers. Pinch didn't seem able to decide whether to continue biting her lip or smile at me. Dagger opened the door, saw his captain plowing through his flapjacks, and gave me a pat on the back. I winked at the surprised marshal and said, "Genesis, preacher. Let there be light." He turned his head abruptly away from me. I rushed off to the kitchen for some grub before I went coyote and started chewing my own arm.

Within the hour *Liberty* dropped full sail, weighed anchor, and joined the river's current down to Chesapeake Bay. She enjoyed fair weather and a comely breeze around the tip of Florida and across the gulf to Galveston, Texas. She did not give chase to any whales though several spouts were sighted and Speck was anxious to get his men into a good hunt. Wrong John had a horse's nose for the corral and did not want to pause to piss in his rush to get back home.

My stomach got a little wobbly cruising the mouth of Galveston Bay. I had not enjoyed the ghostly feeling that first day on *Lone Star* and did not wish to get that thin again. We cruised in to the same dock that had moored *Lone Star*. The wharf was a lot prettier than it had been that drizzly day we embarked on the campaign. In the sunshine the warehouses, saloons, stores, and hotels looked bright and cheerful. Wrong John stood at the prow and looked on his fair Texas shore. He breathed deeply and smiled.

"Hey, Silverspoon!" yelled a leather-faced man with gray hair and a thick moustache, unloading a lobster pot from his faded boat. "Where's my tax rebate?"

Wrong John's nostrils flared, and he hollered back. "It's pay for performance, ya bum. Don't shove in a mackerel head and expect to pull out a lobster!" He frowned, shook his head, and muttered to Pinch, "Greedy buzzard thinks he should get a handout."

The captain and officers traveled by military coach with an escort of cavalry to his ranch in the high-plains scrub land of West Texas. Tatanka and I stayed back to get their gear unloaded and take it for them to the ranch. It gave us a chance to stop in the waterfront saloons and see if our keen shootin' eyes were still worth a glass of whiskey. Turns out we were even more famous than we had been before. Word had gotten back to Galveston that we were now cheek by jowl with America's commander-in-chief. We couldn't have paid for a drink if we wanted.

I twisted the Sioux's arm but he still refused to take another sip of "*wasichu* poison water." We ended up that first night back in Squid Roe Tavern, telling stories of our exploits with Captain Silverspoon. The Lakota didn't speak but continued to carve on his whale-tooth scrimshaw. The best stories of piracy—sacking *Liberty* and razing the Earthly Court—I couldn't tell because the truth of them was not publicly known. Still, there were stories of secret meetings, narwhales given as presents, nefarious tribunals, singing baby whales. All-in-all more than enough to keep the drunken swabbies and hookers entertained.

Late at night, after the crowd dispersed, I asked the one-armed oxen bartender if he had seen that hag oracle lately. He said she had gone blind in her one good eye, lost her crystal, and went back to Guatemala to try *not* to find another one. "You mean crystal, or eyeball?" I asked. "Both," he told me. I could see her in my mind as if she was standing before me, gazing into that cloudy quartz, seeing a stork delivering a baby, a *stillborn* baby. The barkeep filled a mug with suds and slid it down the bar for a nightcap. Tatanka excused himself to the bedroom, and I tried to compose a letter to my mamma, by the spermaceti candlelight hanging from the squid chandeliers. Then I realized I *wanted* her to think I was dead. I *needed* to be dead to her. Otherwise, how would I *ever* be free of her spell? I wadded up that letter and threw it in a dark corner.

Two days later Tatanka and I arrived at Silverspoon Acres hauling three wagons of the officers' gear. The captain's ranch had been built as a pueblo out of rough piñon logs, blonde sandstone, and adobe. The walls were three feet thick. Out in front stood a bronze sculpture of a sperm whale twenty feet long, almost the exact size of the calf that had followed us to New Orleans. Somebody alerted Wrong John to our arrival, and he came out to say hello. "Thought you boys might head for the hills," he said. "Half considered it myself." He laughed and punched me in the shoulder. I punched him back and nodded at his whale sculpture.

"Where'd you get that?" I asked.

"I been a nature lover all my life, Ish. Idn't that a dandy? Came to me as a present from some A-rabs in the blubber trade, friends of my daddy. Tell you what. Over in Saudi the whales is so thick they find a few hundred beached every day, 'cause of overcrowding in the Persian Gulf. That place'd give ol' Ahab a woody, wouldn't it?"

"Would give him a *whale bone*," Tatanka said.

Wrong John offered to show us around. We walked through the entry to a rounded foyer, the *saltillo* tile floor covered with a geometric Navajo rug in patterns of brown, red, and gray. On the walls hung the heads of trophy white-tail bucks, pronghorns, buffalo, and a black bear laid flat out. He took us into the living room filled with puffy leather couches and chairs, a coffee table made of a thick piece of red sandstone, a fireplace in the same rock, and more hunting trophies on the walls: the full body of a skunk standing on a piece of fallen wood with its tail raised; a big, stuffed largemouth bass caught "in the pond, right out back here"; the body of an armadillo with a horned toad on its back; and, over the mantle, a huge longhorn bull head with a spread of horns the length of a man.

Tatanka told me later that a member of the kitchen staff said Silverspoon hadn't shot most of the animals himself. He had hired hunters to bring the trophies in for him. I never heard him admit the taxidermy was not stuffed by his own valor.

Silverspoon advised us to get settled in our room upstairs and to meet him on the back veranda for some skeet shooting. We found our room with two double beds next to a big window overlooking a draw green with mesquite, juniper, and cedar. Neither of us could resist running and diving in the fluffy beds. We laughed and cleaned up in our personal bathroom. Tatanka put on a white shirt and a bolo tie. He tied his owl feather in a thin braid on the right side of his head. I threw on the snakeskins, as usual—they were just like a real snake, and never got dirty. I wore a denim shirt and left my freshly shaved head open to the air for a change.

When we got to the veranda, the officers were there next to a rack of shotguns, partaking of quail egg hors d'oeuvres topped with black caviar, and drinking white wine, or in the captain's case, strong coffee. We did not join them, and nobody called us over. Instead we went to the stone rail of the veranda and studied the shooting blind. From the looks of it, they would be going after live birds released at twenty yards. Beyond the blind lay a stretch of Texas scrubland, stretching to the far horizon. Stands of mesquite broke it up now and then, as did a swath here and there of dusty green buffalo grass. A solitary gray windmill stood about a mile off, its round water trough surrounded by fifty or so head of longhorn.

Tatanka turned to the officers and said, "Windy water. Good, no?" He pointed to the windmill. They all looked at him as if he had just held up his collection of paleface scalps. He tried again. "No fire that way, eh? No engine, windy water no smoke." He might as well have offered a skunk hide in trade, for all his words brought him.

Captain Silverspoon set down his coffee, stuffed a quail egg in his mouth, picked up his shotgun, and stepped to the rail. Krill stood on his shoulder, wearing tiny muffs to protect his ears. Wrong John hollered, "Pull!" A white dove flapped madly and flew straight out from the blind. The captain trained his shotgun barrel on its flight path and blew it from the sky, leaving a puff of downy feathers to drift in the mild breeze. The captain's golden retriever ran out and snatched up the dove and brought it to its master, tail wagging. "Good dog, Bilbo! That's my boy," the captain said, petting the big golden.

"Excellent shot, captain," congratulated Dagger, as did the other officers. The captain flashed them a broad grin.

"God, this is unbelievable," said the diplomat. He chuckled, shook his head, and added, "Imagine if the press saw us out here shooting doves."

"What about it?" asked Gunny. He glowered at Sir Yes Sir, and so did Dagger, the captain, and Crude.

"Well, it would just be—it would look like—. Never mind. Excellent shot, excellent, sir."

Dagger gave Sir Yes Sir an icy stare and stepped up to the rail with his shotgun. "Pull!" he hollered. Another dove flew from the blind, but this one lurched left and his spray of shot went wide right.

"Swing and a miss," said Wrong John.

"Well, that just shows you," said the first mate, turning toward the group with a half smile, "never trust a left leaning dove." The others chuckled. Well, I thought, at least the guns forced a *little* honesty on the Chief, as opposed to the golf game. Yo Yo stepped up next with a double barrel in his arms.

"That's not fair," said the captain. "Gunner ought to have a handicap of some kind. Hell, that's all he does all day is shoot things."

"You can't further handicap a blind man," mumbled the diplomat.

"Hey, I got it!" said Silverspoon. "We'll make him shoot with a pistol instead of a shotgun. That'll be a challenge for him. Ish, loan him one of your guns, would you?" I reluctantly handed him Widowmaker, butt first. He turned his nose up at it but took it anyway.

I noticed some movement in a large peach tree loaded with fuzzy golden and pink peaches to the left of the skeet range. "Pull!" yelled Gunny. He turned and fired into the air without looking, completely missing the dove. In the same moment, I pulled out Peacemaker and shot what I was afraid might be an assassin taking aim at Wrong John. Whoever was in the tree yelped and crashed through the branches and landed with a "fwump" on the ground, followed by the "bap bap bap" of falling peaches, and a bushel basket.

"Great shot!" Dagger said to Yo Yo, and slapped him on the back. Gunny placed his monocle in his right eye to see what had happened. Doves cooed quietly from the blind. Somewhere out on the range a coyote howled. A few cowboys stirred up some dust in the distance. Gunny saw the body on the ground, ran down the stairs of the plaza and turned the man over onto his back. "Just as I suspected," he informed us loudly, "a spy trying to gather intelligence on us for a foreign enemy."

"How can you tell?" asked the captain, straining his neck to see.

"The skin is dark, the face unshaven—and he doesn't speak English."

"Got it," answered the captain. He placed his left index finger on the side of his nose, turned to the other officers, and said, "Boy, this foreign affairs stuff is exciting, idn't it?"

"Looks to me like he was just up there picking fruit," said Basma sourly, left hand on her hip, right hand swinging her shrunken head in a circle from its chain.

"Sir," said the diplomat angrily, "if the man is dead, how can anyone know whether he speaks English or not?"

The gunner reached into the man's pocket and withdrew a piece of paper. "These papers confirm he's an Iraqi. Wait, here's a wallet. Probably has pictures of Shalong's grandkids in it."

"My God, Sire, an assassination plot!" screamed Tosspot. "Kill him! Kill him!"

"He's already dead," said Sir Yes Sir through clenched teeth.

"Then kill him again! And post his entrails about the lands to dissuade other murderers from their villainy!" Tosspot rushed to stand in front of the captain, threw his arms back, thrust out his chest, closed his eyes, and grimaced, as if hoping an assassin's bullet would strike and make him a willing martyr.

"What a cracker," Basma muttered to Sir Yes Sir.

"*BRACK!* Loony on the loose. Stir up a posse. Loony on the loose." Krill pulled his head back, raised it high, looked side to side, and scratched himself under the chin.

"Take a breath, TP. No assassination plot," said Dagger. Captain Silverspoon smacked Tosspot on the back of the head. He frowned and rubbed his head. Krill whistled *Taps* forlornly. Dagger continued, "He doesn't have a weapon, but certainly he provides a trail, TP. No weapon, but a smoking gun that stinks all the way to Baghdad and that rat bastard, Shalong!"

"Can we see the papers?" called Sir Yes Sir.

"Oh no you don't!" replied Yo Yo. He stuffed the papers into his pocket and pulled on his nose ring. "This is a *military* investigation now. If we need any handholding, we'll let you know."

Yo Yo returned to the veranda and got a big kiss on the lips from Pinch. "Deadeye Gunny, that's your new nickname!" Yo Yo scratched beneath his eye patch. "God, it makes me safe knowing you're at the trigger," Pinch said, then kissed him again, turned radish red, and backed away, holding her hands.

The other officers congratulated Gunny Yo Yo like a hero. Chief slapped Yo Yo's shoulder. TP went down on one knee. Crude extended his hand for a shake, and as Yo Yo reached out, pulled his hand back and scratched his head. Gunny laughed and pulled him in for a hug. Wrong John placed finger horns alongside his head, and lowered for a charge. Gunny mirrored him and the two came together and bumped heads, then drew away laughing. Sir Yes Sir and Basma walked to the far side of the veranda and got a glass of wine. TP led the others in *For He's a Jolly Good Fellow*. I noticed Basmati Sweet look at Sir Yes Sir and shake her head. He rolled his eyes.

After the song I approached Yo Yo and held out my hand. "Gun," I said. He jerked his head back and drew down his mouth as if offended, but handed me the gun, barrel first. That evening after dinner, one of the maids told me the spy's name was Pedro Salazar, and he was on the captain's gardening staff. He had been in the tree, as Sweet suggested, picking peaches. It turned out I hadn't killed the Mexican, thank goodness, Frank—I didn't need another soul swooping at me like a screech owl) but had only grazed him with the bullet; he fell and was knocked unconscious when he hit the ground.

The dove shoot continued until several birds had been downed—all of them by the captain and Sir Yes Sir. The men then adjourned for dinner. The two Mexicans inside the blind crawled out with several cages of white doves. They began to reach into the cages and pull out doves and wring their necks. I told them to let us take care of it, to just let all the doves go at once and the sharpshooters would step in. The two Mexicans shrugged their shoulders, opened the cages, and let out the doves. They flew out in a tight bunch and then spread—must have been twenty or more.

Tatanka and I pulled our revolvers and shot every dove but one. It flew straight up into the darkening powder-blue sky and disappeared. The Mexicans picked up the dead birds, cut open the breastbones, and pulled out their hearts, about the size of a fingertip. They placed them into a bowl along with the breast meat.

I went to the room to clean up, and when I arrived in the dining hall the officers were gathered round a stack of paper half a foot thick. Tosspot had his hand resting on the top of the stack and smugly spoke to the other officers.

"I call it the God Arrest America Act. It's a little number we whipped up as a 'just in case' measure," said the marshal, brushing the front of his black smock with the backs of his hands.

"Just in case what?" asked Wrong John.

"In case there should be a national emergency. An instance of treason or grave danger in the homeland."

Dagger took off his thick glasses and chewed on the end. "We live in dangerous times, Mr. Captain, and we've got to be prepared for the worst."

"Like that spy today?"

"Peaches, I think, was his name," said Basma, smirking.

"Yes," said Sir Yes Sir. "He's on the FBI's list of Top Ten Most Wanted migrant workers, isn't he, TP?" The marshal half-closed his eyes and scowled at the diplomat. Gunny snorted and pulled on his nose ring.

Dagger cast Sweet and Sir Yes Sir an icy glare. "Precisely, captain, like the spy."

"Supposin' I sign off on God Arrest America. What's in it fer me?"

"Power, Sire. Let me read a few of the provisions," said the marshal. He opened a case hanging from his belt and placed a pair of thin reading glasses on his nose. "'Federal investigators may invite themselves to dinner and take the dessert if national security interests are at stake. Persons involved, or suspected of involvement, in actions deemed harmful to the United States, may be arrested and detained, and insulted for an unspecified period of time. Persons who show sympathy for America's enemies may enemies may be have their pants pulled down in public and be fired from their jobs. Individuals who question the value of additional police, and/or troops, on the streets of their cities shall be subject to noogies.'"

"These are the sorts of things we're looking at," the marshal said, peering over his glasses.

"Why not just suspend the entire Bill of Rights?" Sweet scoffed.

"There are almost six hundred pages here, Mr. Sweet, and if you read the fine print, most of your so-called 'rights' are dealt with."

I leaned in to the captain and said, "Looks like your Moby Dick just grew a second hump." He wrinkled his nose and twiddled his thumbs.

Dagger motioned for Tosspot to put the document away. "It's really pie in the sky, Mr. Captain. Not an *actual* document you would ever hope to use, but a think piece for planning purposes."

"Look, I'm out here to relax, not to think about parts and pieces. I done got my tax relief, so whatever else we do is extra stuffing in the turkey, *comprende?*" He looked from the marshal to Chief. Tosspot nodded at him. Dagger turned away and sucked his teeth.

Two waiters carried in covered plates of food and set them before the officers. Wrong John lifted his cover, closed his eyes over the steaming food, and smelled deeply. "That's nice. What we got, fellas?" The waiter told him it was breast of dove in a saffron ginger demiglaze, with wild rice and truffles. "What're these little things on the side?" The waiter said they were dove hearts. The captain picked one up in his fingers and popped it in his mouth. "Boy," he said, chewing hard, "for the symbol of peace, critter's got a tough heart."

Chapter XX

Anti-Balloon Missile Treaty

The next week involved little else but fishing for bass in the captain's pond, eating three square meals a day, taking long *siestas* in the afternoon, going swimming, rattlesnake hunting by horseback, and chasing armadillos with the captain's golden retriever, Bilbo. I got to tell ya, Frank, it was the longest stretch of relaxation in my entire life. Hand it to old Jehovah for that bit of wisdom about the seventh day. Silverspoon one-upped him and made the Sabbath every day!

I can't say how much Wrong John needed it, or deserved it, but Jesse James had waited a *long* time for that rest, a very long time. By slowing down I came to appreciate the desert in ways I wouldn't have imagined: the odd, prickly plants; the speedy gray speckled lizards; the jackrabbits, mice, bull- and rattlesnakes; the bright yellow birds. There was so much life that had found ways to survive in the most unusual disguises. The weather was equally mysterious, disappearing behind a powder-blue curtain for days on end, then suddenly jumping onto stage as a dust devil, swirling a brown tower of debris fifty feet high in a zigzag across the scrubland, or, in Act II, building of a sudden into a solitary thunderhead, tracking the land like a bounty hunter, shooting bolts of lightning at the targets with the biggest reward money. And rain, well, it fell from clouds like the fringe off a curtain but never quite reached the ground.

Given the captain's large house staff, there was little for me to do but make sure no more Mexican Arabs tried to shoot him from a peach tree. I had a pleasant conversation here and there with Second Mate Sweet, but she didn't seem to trust me past five minutes. She was more inclined to seek Silverspoon's attention and enjoyed her special status as his partner in evening prayers.

Tatanka and I went hunting together, one time for deer, once for pronghorn. That Lakota could read game sign like nobody I had ever known. Even if the wind had blown away all tracks, he could tell where the antelope had been by broken twigs, overturned rocks, or traces of hair left on a cactus needle. And he could smell—always kept himself downwind—and could tell the difference between a buck and a doe white-tail, or a coyote and a fox. I was sure thankful he had never been employed by the Pinkerton Detective Agency. We brought home fresh game both trips, and gained status with the officers from the wild game dishes the chef prepared.

It was so peaceful and quiet, broad, expansive, and empty out there in West Texas, it was impossible to believe Chicken Little's ghost story about Al Quota. Out there, Al Quota was just another tumbleweed, rolling along and falling apart on its way to drown in the Rio Grande.

About ten days into it, Gunny Yo Yo requested a gathering at the fishing pond to demonstrate a new weapons system he had been perfecting. He called it Wrath of God, and believed it the most important national defense priority of the nation. So it was agreed that after dinner we would all gather at the pond to watch what Yo Yo promised would be "an impressive display of American firepower."

We had a hearty meal of barbecued pork ribs, cornbread, collard greens, okra, sweet potato pie, and coleslaw. "Comfort food," said the captain. "Real live Texas vittles." After our plates had been cleared, Yo Yo announced that the demonstration was ready, and we all moseyed out to the fishing pond. The sun lingered on the horizon like a stubborn fire that refused to go out, leaving us, even at 8 o'clock at night, warmed to discomfort. Black-capped vireos scolded us from the rough branches of mesquite. A rafter of wild turkeys crossed our path and trotted into the tall gramma grass, broomweed, and prickly pear. When we reached the pond, a few deep-throated bullfrogs croaked from the far side, out in the bulrushes and the swamp grass. Wrong John cocked his head and listened to the frogs calling, almost seeming to be hypnotized by their deep, rhythmic song.

Green dragonflies darted above the still water, and higher up floated a couple dozen balloons of different shapes and sizes, at different altitudes coordinated by color. A string tethered each balloon to a series of buoys floating in the middle of the pond. A stick of dynamite hung from a string tied to the knot of each balloon.

Yo Yo stood on the dock and addressed us. He had exchanged his uniform for a black bathing suit of one piece that covered his torso and thighs. In that outfit it was clear his nose ring well matched his bullish physique. He stood with his arms pulled back, stomach tucked, and chin jutting out.

"Poised above this pond, gentlemen," Gunny said, "is the most technologically advanced weapons system ever devised by man. In its sophistication, reliability, precision, and infallibility it surpasses by a factor of ten anything that has ever been conceived, let alone developed and brought to fruition."

Wrong John put his hand above his eyebrows and looked up at the balloons. "Idn't there some kinda Anti-Balloon Missile Treaty floatin' around out there?"

"Yes, sir, there is," answered Sir Yes Sir. "Captain Crook signed it many years ago."

"He's one of us, sir," added Sweet. "Dr. Henchman's boss."

"He is *not* one of us!" yelled Gunny. "Captain Crook ran around holding the Russians' hands, kissing up to the Chinese. He was practically a commie!" He snorted, took small steps forward and backward, fists on his hips. "I worked for that closet liberal. I should know."

"That's right," interjected Chief. "Captain Crook nearly preempted the Great Communicator's domination of Russia with his insipid treaty, but luckily for us—and the free world—the Great Communicator didn't let a stupid agreement stop him from doing what was right, and neither will we!"

Crude held up a rolled, faded parchment, tied with a red ribbon, and tapped it against his round, soft belly.

"Here's the antiquated birdcage liner!" cried Chief. He grabbed the parchment from Crude.

"*BRACK!* Put that thing in *my* cage, will you? They call me the shredder—the shredder," Krill screeched, snapping his beak at the parchment.

Chief leered at Sir Yes Sir, and tore off a chunk of the treaty with the molars on the right side of his jaw.

"You can't do that!" shouted Sir Yes Sir, running over to Chief. "These agreements are the basis of trust that binds the international community!"

The Chief chewed slowly and swallowed hard. He took another bite. "You're right, SYS, it will probably give me constipation, but I'm willing to take that risk in the interest of national security." He continued to tear and chew and grind and gulp, the veins on his forehead bulging, face bright red.

"Hey, don't be a treaty hog," said Wrong John, putting out his hand. Dagger tore off a chunk of the treaty and gave it to him. Silverspoon chewed it, nodding his head and turning side-to-side. "Not bad. Tastes like chicken—a little." He slapped his thigh and chortled at his pun.

The two of them ripped and tore and snorted and gobbled until they had eaten the entire Anti-Balloon Missile Treaty. Chief licked his fingers, hit his stomach, and belched. Basmati Sweet grimaced and stuck out her tongue.

"Chew the rage, eh, Injun?" I said to Tatanka.

"Huh," Tatanka said. "We always wondered what they did with those things."

"Ol' Chief's got him some cast-iron *cojones!* Don't he?" said Wrong John, licking the front of his teeth with his tongue. He pulled a pocketknife and cut a notch in his thick, bull-hide belt. "There's an old saying about rules, one of my favorites. Rules was meant to be—ought to—they should—. No, it was treaties. Yeah: 'Treaties are made to be eaten.' That was it."

"*BRACK!* Get out a press release. Silverspoon throws Boston Tea Party at Texas ranch. Defends American independence. Let freedom ring." The parrot imitated a bell.

"Sometime tomorrow, I will deposit the remains of this useless shackle where it rightfully belongs," said Dagger with a sideways smirk, his right hand over his lower abdomen. "Somewhere in the same vicinity as Kyoto's paper dragon and the Court of Earthly Nonsense." He brushed his hands together as if removing dirt from them. Sir Yes Sir walked off, turned toward the open scrubland, and rubbed his temples.

"A'right then, I guess it's back to your demo, Gunny." Wrong John took the stance of a baseball pitcher and threw an imaginary pitch. Yo Yo caught it and smiled at him.

"Thank you, sir. Now then, let us imagine, for demonstration effect, that this pond is thick with enemy combatants. They may look like catfish, bluegill and bass, but they are evil incarnate, and they intend to invade our sacred shores." He waved his hands in front of himself, palms down and spreading like a glass of spilt milk.

Tatanka leaned down to my ear and whispered, "All those Moby Dicklets, swimming around down there." I smiled.

"Simply put, Mr. Captain," said Chief, picking pieces of parchment from his teeth with his dagger, "*these fish* are the biggest single threat in America today. They want to destroy us, and in various sundry and insidious ways, negatively impact The Economy."

"And floating above me, appearing to be harmless balloons, is their Armageddon." Gunny cleared his throat and bounced on the balls of his feet. The bullfrogs continued to croak while the sun dropped halfway below the horizon. Tatanka pulled on my sleeve and pointed to a subtle movement in the reeds across the pond. "Bushwhacker," he whispered.

Krill jumped off Silverspoon's shoulder, flapped his stunted red wings, and flew about three feet toward the edge of the pond. "You see that! Leggy stork at four o'clock. Don't try to hold me back, boys!" he cried. "A bird's gotta do what a bird's gotta do. *BRACK!*" He flapped his wings and jumped up and down. I could see what he was talking about, but it was a blue heron, not a stork. I let him have his fantasy.

Pinch made goo-goo eyes at Yo Yo and said, "Gosh he's good. Isn't he, Mr. Captain? I just look at him in that tight black bathing suit, and all I can think is *safety*, and *bulge*—uh, Battle of the Bulge." Her face flushed crimson. Yo Yo coughed and adjusted his manhood.

"Now, to further illuminate the approaching live demo, alpha niner bravo charlie," he continued, "the 'trial balloons' are filled with a highly flammable gas called Hydrogen-240. They are tethered at the exact height that corresponds to the length of the fuse on the TNT. The green balloons are positioned at thirty feet, the blue balloons at forty feet, yellow at fifty, orange at sixty, and way up there at the severe height of seventy feet, the enforcer—your red balloon." He saluted the ranks balloons in the sky. They tipped back and forth in the soft breeze, their dynamite payloads bouncing lightly.

"Oh say can you seeee," sang Krill off key.

"Precision ordinance like this is detonated by a precisely calibrated fuse, matched by the micron to the floating height of the balloon. Your green balloon has the shortest fuse, followed by the blue, yellow, and so on. The length of the fuse naturally corresponds to the burn time required for the falling TNT to reach a position at or just below the water line."

"Gol dang it, Gunny!" enthused Pinch. "The technology of the thing is so darn advanced. Next thing we know you'll be flying one of those balloon busters to the moon." She pressed her long, thin hands against the front of her thighs, as if holding herself back from running out on the dock and kissing Yo Yo.

"Brings a whole new meaning to Fourth of July fireworks, don't it?" said the captain, his narrow eyes bright and boyish. "I can just see all them purty balloons, floating above the city parks of America, and then—blam! blam! blam!" His hands opened and closed in front of him in concert with his explosion sounds.

Dagger raised his eyebrows, gave Wrong John a tight-lipped smile, and laughed softly through his nose. "My goodness, Mr. Captain, we wouldn't want to bomb our own people, now would we?" Silverspoon looked at him with a blank expression.

"So, in this case," Yo Yo went on, "our enemy is in a submersible, a—for demonstration effect—self-contained, fully-operational underwater survival and sabotage apparatus."

"That'd be a *fish* in layman's terms, wouldn't it?" asked the captain.

"Yes, it would be, as we speak, a fish, but to gain the full impact of the niner-one-fiver Alpha Tango Vulva continuum, it's better to imagine the enemy not a mere school of fish, but a highly motivated submersible strike force invading the shores of our blessed nation."

"Please, can we stop with the schools already—fish or otherwise. I'm already the education president, so get over it," said the captain, his eyes rolled skyward.

Tatanka pointed to something coursing through the water. It was a thin, brown rod of some kind, sticking about two inches above the surface, moving slowly toward the dock, and leaving a slight wake in its path. The bullfrogs had grown quiet. The sun had nearly been snuffed for the day. The green dragonflies darted after gnats emerging from the water.

"Probably a good idea to throw some science at this thing, don't ya think?" asked Silverspoon. "von Shlop, get over here and scare up a study of something."

The compact scientist stepped forward precisely on his small feet. He reached into a black leather satchel and pulled out several red toadstools specked with black spots and held them in his palm. He waved his white wand over them. "Safety, danger, evil stranger. Courage, coward, freedom soured. Help me, hurt me, don't desert me. Hocus-pocus, feed us, stroke us." He threw the red toadstools at the gray-brown pond. They sat on the surface, umbrella caps high in the film. "They float," said Dr. von Shlop in his mousy voice. "The science is good. The threat of God's Wrath will be as effective as ever." He bowed at the captain.

"Thanks, doc. I like your science," said Wrong John. He pointed at his gunner. "*Toro, toro*, Gunny. Fire it up."

Yo Yo handed out color-coded rifles to each of us. He instructed us to line up along the shore and shoot the balloon closest to us that was the same color as our rifle. Filled with highly flammable Hydrogen-240, he explained, the exploding balloon would ignite the fuse of the falling stick of dynamite. He dove into the water and swam to a rowboat in the middle of the pond, directly toward whatever had been coming in from the other shore. Gunny made it to the rowboat and climbed in. I questioned the wisdom of standing below twenty-five sticks of dynamite, but he was the expert, Frank, not me.

He raised his hands above his head and was about to speak when something grabbed the edge of his rowboat, yanked down, and tipped the gunner into the water. A man with drenched curly blonde hair, wearing a red swim suit, climbed into the boat. All at once, seven color-coded Winchester rifles aimed at him.

He stood and raised his arms. "Don't shoot. It's only me, Dick Little, your Terrorism Czar." Some of us lowered our weapons, but Chief, Crude, and Wrong John kept theirs trained on him. "I don't mean to state the obvious, but your sophisticated aerial defense system did not stop a crazy man breathing through a reed from crashing your top-secret party." He held up the thin brown rod Tatanka had detected.

"Not bad for a white man," Tatanka said.

"Cute trick, Little, but pretty chicken if you ask me—sneakin' around like that," shouted Wrong John.

"I've got to report, Mr. Captain, that we have conclusive evidence Al Quota is plotting a major attack on American soil. He's got a company of suicide storks, hungry for the martyrdom that can only come from the killing of infidels. Quota's got a shipment of souls to make to hell, and he doesn't intend to get caught short." Chief continued to aim his rifle at Little's head. I expected to hear its report any second.

Krill leaped into the pond, madly flapping his wings and kicking his claws, swimming for Dick Little. "How dare you?" he said when his head came out of the water. "*BRACK!* Talk about—," he went under, then resurfaced—"storks like that. There is no animal—so loyal, and loving—such a symbol of new life." He got about five feet into the pond before he began to sink. Tatanka waded into the water and picked him up. He continued to flap and kick and hurl insults at Little. Tosspot drew out his diary and made some notes in it. He hunched over it with his too-sharp pencil, scratching and looking, scratching and looking. I wanted to shoot that puny book right out of his hands.

"That's precisely it, Krill," said Little, shaking back his wet hair. "Quota is devious. He will attack us with our own fertility, with the vehicle that brings our loved ones to us. It is a diabolical, but also ingenious deception." I noticed Basma hanging back from the group, pacing in a small circle, glancing nervously in the direction of Little.

Gunny had made his way back to the rowboat, yanked on the gunwale, and sent Little flying into the water. He did not come up for air. Tatanka spotted his piece of reed moving off quickly to the far shore. "Forget that Cassandra!" Yo Yo roared. "Let's set off some bombs!" He raised his arms.

"Hold it, Gunny," said the captain. "Where are we with this whole Little business? Basma? You got if figured yet?"

"I'm—it's not entirely—yes, yes, I've—there's a study nearly done. It looks like he may be correct, that something devastating is being planned." She brushed her hair back from her left eye, pushed her sleeves up, smoothed the front of her white cotton pants. She walked in quick, short steps, forward, backward, forward. Chief Dagger stepped in front of her.

"Mr. Captain," he said. "I think we've got to keep our eye on the ball. The prize here is not to capture and jail, or simply kill, a few outlaws." I turned away at the mention of killling outlaws. Dagger pulled on an earring and pushed his bifocals up on his nose with his middle finger. "The *prize* is to take your father's legacy and achieve its full conclusion. It's about New World Borders, redrawing maps and rewriting constitutions in our own image. It's about finishing up that loud-mouthed asshole, Shalong, once and for all, so that everybody understands America means business. It's about reorganizing that tribal cesspool in the Middle East, so our Hebrew satellite isn't under so much pressure and we can be comfortable in the blubber supply for the next hundred years."

"Those Quota bums would be doing us a favor if they attacked," shouted Gunny from the rowboat. "I say bring on his storks, or carrier pigeons, or parrots—."

"*BRACK!* Not the noble spokesman of the animal kingdom," Krill squawked, shaking himself like a wet dog.

Gunny pointed at Krill and shot him with a finger bullet. "Quota's pin prick would wake a sleeping giant, and that giant would not stop walking until it crushed his puny little gang, and the entire matrix of evil from which it had sprung."

"These boots were made for walkin'..." said Wrong John.

"The God Arrest America Act is standing by to serve, Majesty," said Tosspot, bowing.

Sir Yes Sir stood with his left arm across his chest and his right hand gripping his face over his mouth. He has muzzled himself, I thought.

"A'right then. Let's not table this until the dishes are cleared. Get me?" Basma stopped her pacing and saluted. Chief grunted. Gunny put his finger horns next to his head and lowered. Wrong John mirrored him.

"All right then!" shouted Yo Yo. "Let's do this thing. Man your weapons. Ready, aim, fire!" he cried, and dropped his arms.

We all began shooting at our balloons. Many missed on the first shot and tried several shots before they connected. I hit my red balloon first shot, and picked off three orange and a yellow, but a lot of balloons never got hit. Of the balloons that were shot, about two-thirds did not ignite their fuses, and the dynamite fell with a plop to the water. Most of the remainder blew up too far above the pond to do any damage, although they were close enough to the rowboat to knock Yo Yo unconscious and into the water. I wondered if they were just going to let him drown. Of the twenty-five or so balloon bombs from the sophisticated Wrath of God missile defense system that had been floated, only one exploded below the surface of the pond. That one explosion was, however, of sufficient concussive force to kill, it seemed, every fish in the pond. The collected floating white bellies took me immediately back to the Mississippi Delta.

Among them lay a dozen silver pan fish with striking orange stripes and spiny dorsal fins. "Isn't that something," said Pinch softly. "The orange-striped stickleback was thought to be extinct."

"It is now," said Tatanka.

"Well boys," said Wrong John, "looks like we gonna have us a big old Cajun fish fry after all. Yeehaa!"

"As you can see," said Chief dryly, "it isn't so much that every bomb hit its target precisely, but that our strike ratios remained within the margin of error allowed for by the statistical paradigm." Wrong John scratched his head.

Sir Yes Sir shook his head at Dagger, made a hollow fist with his hand, and shook it slowly up and down in the universal symbol for jerking off. "Go rescue the imbecile, Ish," said Sir Yes Sir, pointing to Yo Yo floating face-down in the pond. I stripped naked and dove in the water.

"Blasphemy!" shouted Tosspot.

"*BRACK!* Call the Clown Criers," crowed Krill, now perched on Tatanka's right shoulder. "Silverspoon tests Wrath of God. Makes it work. Makes it work. Fulfills dream of Great Communicator. Just seven months—seven months—after taking *Liberty*."

I pulled the unconscious, half-blind gunner out of the pond and pumped the water from his lungs by stepping on his back. Honestly, Frank, I felt like chucking him back in the drink and leaving him there. Yo Yo indeed. After a minute, he started coughing and coming to. I slapped him in the face a few times. Looking back, and knowing what was about to hit our country, the whole Wrath of God hornswoggle is almost beyond belief—especially with Chicken Little braying about Al Quota and his suicide storks. I can only conclude from my own experience as a bushwhacker that the officers of *Liberty* understood, as we did, Frank, that there was more to be gained politically through terror than there was through peace.

Chapter XXI

The Masturbation Corps

I had a smoke on the veranda before breakfast. The sun had just climbed a few rungs of the day's ladder, and already it had splashed hot yellow paint across the high plains. I heard gentle footsteps behind me and turned to see Sweet approaching, her brow knit, grease pencil mustache drawn a little crooked. She wore a thin white cotton shirt, sleeves rolled up, and black silk pants that draped nicely on her form—and showed that foolish rubber dick of hers. I offered her a hit from my smoke. She took it in and blew out like she always did, a thin jet of smoke and two perfect, spreading rings.

"I'm worried," she said.

"Oh?" I replied. A pair of mourning doves cooed back and forth in their distinctive call of "hoo-oo oo-oo." A big green iguana sat in the peach tree chewing on a ripe fruit, its flesh bright orange and juicy.

"I just wonder—about Dick Little. He's very convincing, but—well, Chief and Gunny, they just won't—I guess *I'm* not very convincing." She reached out her hand for another pull from my smoke. I handed it to her and watched her place it in her voluptuous lips, draw in her cheeks, and blow out a jet of smoke and rings.

"There's more mileage in retaliating to an attack than preventing one," I said. Out beyond the grass yard I noticed Tatanka and Sir Yes Sir walking together. The Sioux, as usual, did the listening, had his head bent and held his hands behind his back, his long black hair hanging down beside his face, while the diplomat slashed at the air with his big brown hands and moved his head in passionate speech.

"But we should stop Quota if we can," said Sweet. "That's the *right thing* to do."

"It ain't always a matter of right and wrong. Things have a way of ripening. Terror, well, it's a powerful weapon, sister, maybe the most powerful there is—and it cuts both ways. Counterattacking in fear, retreating in fear— it all works to the bushwhacker's advantage. It's all his game when he puts you on your heels, gets you swinging your sword in the dark. The more seriously you take him, the more power he has over you." I pulled Peacemaker, opened her cylinder, and checked her chambers—another bullet missing.

"You folks like to call it terrorism, but it goes by many names: intimidation, violence, brutality, tyranny, ruthlessness. We called it bushwhacking. The magic in terror is the way it can make a little man big. Anyone—and I mean *anyone*—who is crazy enough to set off a bomb, or, I don't know, rob a bank and shoot up the town, can influence things in his direction—way more than he could by honest means. A desperado will choose terror over humiliation every time."

She listened to me thoughtfully. "Sounds like you speak from experience."

"Been up to my ass in blood a time or two." She cleared her throat and looked away. "Pardon, ma'am, that was rude." She didn't ask further, but thanked me and walked away in her slow swaying way. I insisted it was she who deserved the thanks.

Silverspoon's chef served a tasty omelet for breakfast, with white cheddar, ham, green chili, onions, and mushrooms drenched in a creamy, basil-tomato sauce. I visited with Pinch afterward, picked my teeth, and listened to her chatter about how she could move some money out of the national education fund to pay for Gunny's weapon program. She ran her bony fingers quickly over the red and white beads of her abacus. "It's got to happen, Ish. If we don't get those balloons up, and get 'em up quick, the American dream, well, it could turn into a *bad* dream." I told here I didn't know if color-coded balloons were the answer.

Basmati Sweet walked in from the front driveway and said, "You gotta see this." We followed her past the gallery of mounted trophies on the wall, outside across the dirt road that circled through the entry, past the bronze of the whale calf, and out to a rock fence made of blonde sandstone that opened to the road. Four tall saguaro cacti, brought over from Arizona, stood in a group near Wrong John's front gate. The captain and his officers were gathered among them. The long, upward curving, spiny outstretched arms seeming to beseech heaven for some kind of sign. It came to them in the form of the marshal, riding a caramel and vanilla donkey sidesaddle, leading a group of some fifty teenagers down the road toward the gate. He led them in *Onward Christian Soldiers* with his tremulous tenor voice, and belted it out so badly that Silverspoon's dog, Bilbo, began to howl.

Silverspoon covered his ears, and looked down at his golden retriever. "I agree, Bilbo. Arooo! Aa-aa-arooo!" he howled, then laughed, bounced up and down, and looked around at the others. None of them joined him in his wolf's chorus. Basmati Sweet and Sir Yes Sir stood together away from the group, under the tallest cactus, with their arms crossed.

Tosspot approached the gate, sidesaddle on his donkey, his hymn complete, and cued his youthful entourage to begin a chant. When I first hear what they were saying, I could not believe it, and picked at my ear thinking something must have gotten stuck in it. No, they were saying it, marching in place and chanting:

> "We are the Masturbation Corps
> When we feel lust we do not whore.

If sex is on our mind
It's better to go blind
Than to say God won't mind
If two of us entwine.

We are the Masturbation Bunch
Sex isn't safe, that's not a hunch.

It's never okay
Without that vow.
Only a pervert
Would teach you how.
Don't take the bait
No way, no how.
Touching another
Is not allowed!

We are the Masturbation Herd
We please ourselves, don't say a word
If we need love before its time
We do ourselves, it's not a crime.

The sin of sex is surely very bad
But to kill an unborn child is more than very sad
It's murder, kids, and it will drive you mad!
So when you get too hot to abstain
Tend to yourself, that's our refrain
Tend to yourself, that's our refrain."

"Captain Silverspoon, officers of *Liberty*, may I present to you the Masturbation Corps, America's new sexual education service!" said TP. He swept his arm over the tail of his donkey and gestured with his palm up at the bright faces of his team. The girls wore proper blue skirts, white blouses with little American flags embroidered on the chest. The boys had on blue slacks, leather bolo ties, and starched white shirts also patriotically flagged. Boys and girls wore angular black sailors' caps with a fig leaf of green cloth sewn on each side, containing the letters TMC. They stood at attention shoulder-to-shoulder in five rows of ten, prim and eager, their white faces flushed with a pink glow.

No one seemed to know what to say. Dagger sucked his teeth, and Krill gabbled to himself and whistled softly. "Oh, my God," Basma muttered. Gunny turned his ring in his nose and cleared his throat. Only Pinch had the courage to step unto the breach. She started clapping resolutely. The rest of us joined her.

"That's great!" she said, "just super. The Masturbation Corps—golly! I wish they'd have had something like this when I was a girl. Heck, I didn't even know you could do it—till I was twenty and just about wore a pop bottle down to—never mind." Her face went bright red. She looked sheepishly at Gunny and backed away, wringing her long, thin hands.

Tosspot opened his arms to us and bowed slightly at his captain. "Thank you, Pinch. Thank you all. This is a very exciting day in the salvation of our great nation. For many, many years, we have been sliding into the cesspool of promiscuity and moral decay. We have allowed a decadent anti-religious secularism to kidnap our adolescents and young adults and convince them sex is not only inevitable outside of wedlock, not only permissible, but preferable." His donkey curled its lip away from its long upper teeth and brayed.

A bright, slim blonde-haired with curly locks spilling from her hat stepped forward from her line. "They have provided all sorts of incentives for us to have premarital sex, whether it be pornographic entertainment, easy access to drugs and alcohol, oodles of information about how to have sex without causing pregnancy, medications that prevent fertilization, free rubber balloons that collect semen, and worst of all, murdering surgeries that kill our unborn children while they are still in the womb."

She returned to her place in line, and a gangly, pimple-faced boy stepped forward. "These sinful approaches to temptation are corrupting our souls, and rotting the future of our great nation. And so it is with great pride, sure of our mission and calling, that we march forth to spread masturbation across the land!" The boy stepped back in line. Tosspot smiled upon the boy and nodded slowly.

"These young moral warriors will replace all decadent so-called sex education programs that we have all come to understand as primers in promiscuity," TP said, his voice inflated with pomp.

"My God," I said quietly to Tatanka, "it's another Ahab. This one thinks he's going to hunt down and kill the monster of sex."

"Better run," he said in his deep, flat voice. "It's Moby's dick." He pointed between the donkey's back legs, at the beast's huge red pecker growing hard. I covered my mouth to keep from laughing out loud. I didn't see a jenny nearby, but there must have been one in heat somewhere. The jack donkey curled his lip and brayed again.

"Okay. Well, uh, so that's our program?" asked the captain. "That's how we're going to stop teen pregnancy and syphilis and abortion? Wow. The, uh, the Masturbation Corps—sort of like the Marine Corps for nasty. I like it—I think. I mean, it's better than the alternative, right?"

"I'm sorry, but this is not right *at all*," said Sweet. "The Bible does not advocate masturbation as a valid alternative to abstinence. Back me up on this, IshcaBible." She looked over at me. I pulled Widowmaker, spit on the barrel, and rubbed it with my shirttail. I flicked the gun in the direction of the marshal, come to Bethlehem on a donkey's back.

"She's right, lawman. You remember what happened to Onan, don't you? Says right there in Genesis 38, you spill your seed on the ground, God's gonna kill ya." I noticed some of the boys in the corps gulp nervously, adjust their collars, and reach quickly into their pockets.

"That's not confirmed, IshcaBible. Theologians still debate the exact nature of Onan's crime." He looked at the captain and Chief, who stood next to him. "The Bible doesn't *specifically* say masturbation is a sin. It's a loophole, Sire. Rather like an off-shore tax shelter for lust—not the ideal use of one's money, but an option, a viable, legal option."

"Prayer is the viable option," Basma asserted. "Giving in to lust—regardless of your *loopholes*—teaches spiritual laziness. Young people must fight the urge by seeking help from God through prayer. They must transmute lust into agape."

"That's right," I added, spitting again on the barrel of Widowmaker, rubbing it in with my shirt, and giving Sweet a roguish look. "Sex all alone just doesn't cut it." She looked away from me. Her left hand reached for the shrunken head.

Pinch noticed the donkey's boner and started giggling. She poked Gunny in the shoulder with the tip of her long index finger. "Dem-con, alpha-*boner*-charlie," she said, pointing under the burro's belly. Yo Yo saw it and laughed. "Maybe the marshal will give us a demo," he said.

Krill must have seen the hard-on too. "*BRACK!* Call the taxidermist." He whispered in the captain's ear. Silverspoon saw the thing and started laughing.

"You're off message here, TP," said Chief. He pushed his thick bifocals up his nose with his middle finger. "The religious right wants abstinence, period. No loopholes."

"But this is just part of it. I've got a whole program." He reached into the briefcase over his shoulder and drew out a thick stack of paper, about half the thickness of his God Arrest America Act. He waved it as us, the pages spreading and fanning the air. "I've got a whole system. It's the God Sex America Act—an addendum to the other one."

"Don't you have better things to do?" asked Sir Yes Sir gruffly. "Dick Little is pretty adamant about the threat of Al Quota. I hope you have your investigators looking into it." He crossed his arms and glared at the marshal.

"Wait! This is good. It's full of juicy stuff about curtailing immorality in our nation. Listen: 'If a man is seen holding another man's hand in public, that hand shall be cut off. If a man shall place the penis of another man in his mouth, his tongue shall be cut off. If a woman touches another woman's breast, hand *and* breast shall be severed. If a man has relations with a sheep, that man shall eat lamb chops.' Here's one about—"

"You got anything in there about relations with a jackass?" the captain asked, laughing and pointing between the animal's legs. Those that hadn't noticed now saw the red hard on and started pointing and laughing. Tosspot squirmed on the donkey's back and rubbed his chest.

"*BRACK!* Help me, captain!" Krill put the edges of his wings on either side of his neck and acted as if his head was stuck between them. "My head's stuck in the barbed wire. Help! Here comes the *donkey. BRACK!* He's got that look in his eye. And what's that between his legs? Lord have mercy!" Krill jumped up and down on the captain's shoulders, screeching. That gave us all a good chuckle.

"Too bad Roberto Mendoza isn't here," I told Tatanka. "He would have enjoyed this." The Sioux grunted.

"Oh, so now it's funny? You think it's *funny?*" His jowly, ashen face jiggled indignantly. "You think abstinence is the only way. Well it isn't. It's too hard." We all burst out laughing. "Oh, I see. And is it funny when you're young, and you have *urges?*" He gestured at the Masturbation Corps, which seemed to blush all at once. "You fight them off and you fight them off. And they build inside of you like a volcano, and then—it bursts, you can't hold them back, you're screwing like a rabbit every night—then she gets pregnant, there's a scandal, your family has to move. It's, I just—. That was a hypothetical, purely a hypothetical." He coughed and scratched the back of his head.

The female donkey in heat must have put off a stronger scent. That randy jack curled his lip and brayed, kicked up his back legs, bucked TP off, and galloped off to sin.

"Hell, marshal," said the captain between guffaws. "You ought to be able to ride a liberal bureaucrat better than *that!*"

We laughed at the sanctimonious lawman sitting in the dirt for a good five minutes—I mean all of us, the kids as well—until finally Pinch had a heart and told him about his donkey dick. He smiled gamely and stood up. "Murphy's law, I guess." Dagger brushed the dust off him and advised him to get over it, there was important work still ahead.

A week later it was time to go back to Washington. Silverspoon decided to take the train rather than sail, which was fine with me. I could handle the gentle sideways rocking of a train a lot better than that damn ocean—like ridin' a rope swing in a tornado. Tatanka and I had to split up, though. Chief said he was needed on *Liberty* to cook for the crew on the way back to Washington. We said our good-byes and parted company.

I got a sleeper car all to myself. It had a comfortable couch and with a single bed above, its own small window, place to stow my gear. I had a chance to think some in there, about what had happened the first year with Silverspoon. It had been quite a run of piracy, sacking *Liberty* like that, razing the Earthly Court, pulling that heist of the national treasury. I had died yet again, and this time got laid in a coffin—but I'm Jesse James. I rose, by damn,

I rose. I was still haunted by that pitiful song of the baby whale. My mind had got it crossways with my babies, Jesse Jr. and Mary, and I had dreams of them crying out to me in a whale song, begging me to come home.

Ah, Frank, and I had killed again. There was that sailor, and the black boy, on *Liberty*—and then the judge that was the spit outta momma's mouth, and the two guards in Gravenhage. How did I end up a killer again, brother? What's that? I never *stopped* being one. Well, I *wanted* to stop, but so what? Life needs brutal men who will murder when necessary. Once you show the ability, it seeks you out. That'll hold water for now, won't it?

Oh, and one more thing. I did mention something about redemption, didn't I? The only hope for that seemed to rest deep in the dark brown eyes and skin of Basmati Sweet. Something about her looked like hope—though hope was a distant cousin I hadn't seen since I was a boy.

Most of all, Frank, riding across the country in that train, I watched America go by. I watched the cattle yards, the wheat fields, the factories, the paddleboats on the big rivers, the small towns with their simple depots and their water towers and their church steeples. I saw Americans, Frank, red, yellow, black, and white, working in fields, driving cattle, hauling coal and lumber and grain. I saw mothers nursing their babies and grandmothers hobbling on crutches. I heard nails pounded, horses whipped, wagons rattle, cattle low, dogs bark, guns fire. I smelled fire, beer brewing, bread baking, and garbage rotting.

All the way across America I saw life going on, every day, just like it always had. None of them could have guessed what was about to happen, how their innocence was about to be shattered, the white lines in their flag run through with red. They were all just going on, pretending like we do that life goes on forever, and that the little concerns we have about a broken fence, or a squeaky door, or a sliver in our toe will always be important. One day, though, for every one of us, it changes. We look around and shake our heads and say, "Now where did that come from?"

BOOK II

The Silverspoon Mandate

Chapter XXII

The Very Hungry Scorpion

WRONG JOHN SEEMED to have a hard time accepting that his vacation was over. He walked around the train in his leather slippers and baby blue, terry cloth robe the entire time, skipped shaving days on end, combed his hair if he felt like it. He didn't want to talk about Washington, and the work ahead, but preferred to reminisce about our time on the ranch: the big bass, the wild game dinners, the horseshoes. He could not stop teasing Tosspot about his donkey.

Basmati Sweet knocked on my cabin door every other day, pointing out to me that he was a man of routines, and this sloppiness was not normal. I told her he'd get over it, that he was feeling like a kid who missed his carefree days of summer, chewing on a length of grass, watching his bobber on the pond, taking *siesta* during the heat of the day, the smell of ribs barbecuing over hot coals, tall glasses of lemonade sweating in the sun, inspirational hymns sung around the fire at night.

"He's the leader of the free world," she said. "Not some punk pining for an all-day game of marbles."

I shrugged. Somehow he was both. I had my own feelings to wrassle with, Frank, on that long train ride across America. Mine resembled those I had after robbing a bank. Somehow, the long sojourn at Silverspoon Acres settled into my gut as a theft. I had that familiar tingle of excitement, of having gotten away with something, accompanied by the gnawing fear of getting caught, and a low, steady rasping, a quiet sandpaper of shame about the sin I had just committed. You remember the feeling, Frank, when we rode through those towns, our saddlebags heavy with loot, ready to shoot the first person that looked at us more than a glance? I trusted no one at those times—not even you, Frank, I'll have you know.

The feeling perplexed me. What had I stolen? What was my sin? The feeling corkscrewed into me all the way to Louisville before I began to taste some truth. I should have known the foul flavor would be too familiar, like a sour, stringy red stem of Missouri rhubarb growing out behind Momma Zee's kitchen. I was ashamed of myself for taking a month off and doing almost nothing. It was contrary to the Missouri work ethic and everything I had ever been taught. It sure as hell didn't help matters to have Chicken Little hopping around with his head cut off. Why should I have cared if nobody did anything about it? Why should I get rubbed raw with guilt? The first time in my life I could sit back and do nothing and not flinch at every cracking twig and I couldn't just enjoy it. Damn it, brother! I thought I shot that judge through the head at the Court of Maternal Shame over in Holland.

I was relieved when the journey ended on the banks of the Potomac. I gladly got on board a military cutter to intercept *Liberty* on her way to meet us, which we did right around Cape Charles. The sight of Liberty's buxom figurehead, reaching forward with sword, torch, and breasts—carved from native oak beneath the bowsprit—reminded me there was a noble purpose out ahead of those whipping corporate flags. I and the Captain, Krill, Basmati Sweet, Pinch, Tatanka, and the crew of *Liberty* continued on to Philadelphia for the unveiling of Silverspoon's education initiative, called No Child's Behind. The other officers went about their separate business in Washington and Boston. All engagements in New York City were cancelled for some reason.

I surprised myself at the way I took to being back at sea. I volunteered for night watch in the crow's nest, and got to where I liked flitting through that maze of spider ropes that guided our ship. I happily took the helm for hours at a time, navigated by the binnacle compass, and steered her true, despite that dotty bird rubbing and talking to the binnacle lamp half the time.

"What is your fascination with the lamp, Peckerhead?" I asked him one evening.

"Like I told ya, Ish. Long time ago, made a deal with a frog. Remember? The mute tailor? Traded his humanity for a voice? I want my body back." He clucked and whistled to himself, rubbing the lamp with his beak.

"What's the lamp got to do with getting back your arms and legs?"

"Heard of *1001 Arabian Nights?*"

"Nope."

"Aladdin and his magic lamp?" I shook my head. "Well, Ish, Arabia has magic in it—magic. I'll get there someday. That's for sure. That's for sure." He babbled and burbled to himself, hopped to the deck, and waddled off.

Liberty stalked into Delaware Bay under the cover of a dense fog that nearly swallowed the beacon shining from Cape May's lighthouse. I had not been through such a pea-soup sky since passing the Shetland Islands in the North Sea, on our way to raze a court of law. The similarity made me jumpy. I kept looking behind my back expecting to see a rifle barrel coming at me, or a coffin with my name on it. We must have nearly run down a fisherman in a small boat, because someone yelled up to us with a soft but firm voice and said, "It is not safe to be small under a sky like tonight." I didn't reckon it was safe to be *any* size under such gloom.

Liberty sailed up the Delaware River, sounding every quarter mile to make sure she was in the channel, on up to the Marine Terminal in Philadelphia, where she moored. I don't know how late we arrived, but the city was so quiet I wondered if there was a living soul in it. Somebody ring the Liberty Bell, I thought, ring it at least once so we know we're still alive. The hull ground against the dock, and the mooring lines groaned their God-awful lament. I lay in my bunk that night and could not sleep—could not sleep, Frank, because I was scared—not that I would get arrested, or tortured, or hung. I was scared that chewing thing, whatever it was, would come back, and start burrowing a hole in my brain. I did not want those old, bitter acorns dug up again.

Tatanka read my mind, or was having the same thought. "It is near. The night eagle is near. But it will leave us alone tonight. It has another hunger. Its stomach burns, burns for the other hunger."

Not exactly a lullaby.

He blew out the small oil lamp hanging from the ceiling. I never did hear him breathe like he was asleep. I don't think he heard me breathe that way either, but one, the other, or both of us must have done so. Next thing I knew, the sound of clomping feet above me proved another day had dawned, and Wrong John Silverspoon was up as always for an early jog.

After breakfast we packed up and traveled by coach to an elementary school in the city. It was 8:00 the morning of October 10, 1883. We arrived at a brown brick schoolhouse that had three old oak trees out front shedding their tired leaves and their helmeted acorns in the bitter wind. Tatanka and I,, Wrong John, Krill, Basma, Dr. von Shlop, and Pinch hurried up the sidewalk, and crunched the dry leaves under foot. "Early for them to be coming down like this," commented Pinch, looking into the twisted branches, her long, pointed nose wrinkled, and her big teeth showing.

The Negro principal met us in the hallway and walked us down the empty, echoing corridor lined with bleak drawings of Halloween goblins. "Early for Halloween too, isn't it?" Pinch commented. We came to a small wooden door. The principal walked in before us and made grand pronouncements about the beneficent Mr. Captain Silverspoon who had decided on this, of all days, to visit their school. Wrong John sauntered in, parrot in its place, and was greeted with the tiny applause of small hands. He smiled and waved, drew his personality gun briefly, holstered it without firing, and sat at a child's desk chair next to a blackboard. Krill bowed and gave the claws-up sign with his right foot. Behind them had been written in white chalk the words "Welcome Mr. Captain, We Love Your Hair."

"We love your hair?" Krill muttered. Reporters and photographers crowded the back of the room. The bare branch of a twisted oak, shook by the bitter wind, tapped against the window. Dismal light from the cloudy sky fell on the stained oak floor of the classroom.

The teacher's name was Ben Green, and he was a tall, husky African with a surprisingly gentle voice and small hands that waved in the air like butterflies when he spoke. "It's a very special day, children, when the captain of *Liberty* takes time out of his *very* busy day to read you a story. Now put on your *very* best listening ears and make our president proud." The children, whom I guessed were six or seven, pretended to attach special ears to the sides of their heads. They had their names printed on big cards standing on their desks. Mr. Green handed Wrong John a copy of a large, illustrated book titled *The Very Hungry Scorpion*.

The captain licked his lips and began to read. "'The very hungry scorpion baked in the desert sun. It baked and thought. It thought and baked. It was hungry. *Very* hungry. It wanted something *big* to eat." He raised his eyebrows and curled his arm up and behind his head, and formed his first two fingers into the shape of a stinger. The children squealed with delight. The captain smiled and showed them the drawing of the very hungry scorpion. I thought it a sinister portrayal for a child's book.

"'The very hungry scorpion sharpened its stinger. It sharpened it and sharpened it. It rubbed a sandstone. That made its stinger sharper than a needle.' Now, Johnny, who do you think the scorpion was thinking of as it sharpened its deadly stinger?" asked the captain, his attention directed at a towhead boy in the front row.

"Weaker bugs that can't protect thereselves?" asked the boy.

"Correct," said Silverspoon, "which is why your nation is, as we speak, deploying a phosisticated interlocking missile defense system—'Wrath of God,' we call it, 'cause it's up there in the clouds, invisible and deadly—that makes it impossible for enemies to breach our sacred borders." He interlaced his fingers and acted as if he could not pull them apart. Basmati handed the captain a certificate, which he presented to the boy.

"Here's something called a *voucher*, Johnny, that provides you the economic freedom to attend the school of your choice, public or *private*, courtesy of Uncle Samuel

J. Fat—uh, Uncle Sam." The class and teacher applauded quietly. Johnny returned to his seat, a smile on his face and his voucher held against his chest.

Silverspoon smiled at the boy. He licked his thin lips and read. "Okay, next passage. 'That scorpion baked and thought. It thought and baked. It was hot. The scorpion got *very* hot. It baked day after day. It thought week after week. It baked month after month, after month." He turned the book around and showed a picture of the sinister scorpion sitting on a red rock, under a piercing yellow sun. "Ooh," the children murmured.

"'At last, it was ready to go hunting. Ready for something *big* to eat. First it came upon a dog. Do you think that was big enough for it?'" He showed a drawing of the scorpion next to a dog's leg. "No," said the children. "'Then it came to a cow. Do you think that was big enough?'" He showed the picture. "No," they answered. "'Then it came to a giraffe. Do you think that was big enough?'" The children said no. "'Then it came to an elephant. Do you think *that* was big enough.'"

"Yes!" They knew the story.

"That's right. The scorpion came to an elephant and thought it could eat it. Carlita, do you think a scorpion could *really* eat an elephant?"

A little Cuban girl in the third row stood and stepped on one small foot with the other, and wrung her hands. She hesitated, cleared her throat and spoke, "Um, well, I—I think it could."

"Wrong. A scorpion never could, and never would, try to eat an elephant."

"*BRACK!* Crush the bug. Crush the bug." Krill stomped up and down on the captain's shoulder.

The hefty black man waved his butterfly hands. "You're right of course, sir. But, well, it's a silly children's book. And in the book the scorpion actually *does* eat the elephant." The oak branch tapped on the window. News reporters murmured in the back of the classroom.

"There's the problem, then. Your curriculum's off. I'm sorry, Camila, but I'll have to ask you to come forward with your textbooks." The girl gathered her books in her arms and walked slowly to the front of the classroom, head down studying her small feet. When she reached the captain he took her books, set them down, and bent her over his knee.

"I promised America I was gonna turn education around, and that begins today with the No Child's Behind Act." He posed for the cameras with his hand poised over the little girl's bottom. "Don't worry, honey," he said quietly to the girl. "I'm not *actually* going to spank you. It's all for show." She lay over his knee, whimpering as a child will in that position, regardless of what she's told. The cameras flashed, and when they were done, Silverspoon stood the girl up.

"In Silverspoon America, No Child's Behind will remain unspanked if that child fails to answer correctly certain obvious questions." He called Dr. von Shlop over. The scientist stepped quickly and precisely beside his captain, wearing his blue robe, pointed blue hat, and pointed gray goatee. Silverspoon went on. "These tests have been scientistically codified and calibrated to accurately and precisely measure the scholastic attitude of your student's body."

Dr. von Shlop waved his white wand over the classroom, reached into his black satchel, and threw a glittering dust in the air. "The signs are clear. The truth is known. Standard tests will set the tone. They make you wise. They judge you well. Mark them right, or go to—Helen, did you have a question?" He pointed with his wand to a girl in the third row. "No? Okay. Sharpen your pencils, kids." He bowed and returned to his position against the wall by the door.

"Thanks, doc. So kids, life's tough. You fail the test, you get fired. Unless, of course, you're like Johnny over there with his *voucher*, which entitles him to do whatever the heck he wants." He smiled at the girl and patted her head. Her upper lip trembled, and tears welled in her big brown eyes.

"My No Behind measure applies to you as well, Mr. Green." The big man's small hands fluttered to his chest and landed on it, and his face seemed to say, "What? You're going to spank *me?*"

"Public schools have got to be run like a business. That means pay for performance. Your kids don't pass the test, Mr. Greed, your taxpayer-funded cakewalk is over. We'll board this school up and send these students to boot camp in a heartbeat." He spanked his left hand with his right—pop! The little girl jumped, and the big teacher flinched.

Silverspoon scooted the girl back to her desk. He opened the book and started reading again. "Oh, here it is." He smiled. 'The *very* hungry scorpion stung the giant elephant in its big, fat foot.' I'll be danged." He turned the book to the children and showed them the drawing of the grim scorpion piercing the gray mass of the elephant's foot, bright red poison spreading from the stinger. "Owww," murmured the children.

The classroom door opened quickly. A large woman stood waving a telegram. Basma walked over slowly and took it from her. She scanned it quickly. Her hands shook, mouth dropped open, eyes widened. She rushed to the captain and whispered in his ear. All color left his face. He half smiled, searched the room with his small, darting eyes, bounced his legs nervously. He turned the book around and continued to read. "The scorpion stung, and it stung, and it stung." He turned the book to show the many red marks on the elephant's foot, and the stinger sharp and deep inside.

Sweet walked to where I stood next to the door. "The sky is falling," she whispered.

"A stork flew at the New York Stock Exchange." Her voice was shaking. "Just before the opening bell. It carried a bomb in a cotton baby blanket. Christ almighty!" She tried to put her hands together in prayer, but they closed instead into tight fists. She shut her mouth and eyes hard, and banged her fists on her forehead. I stopped her. She opened her dark, beautiful eyes and looked at me. Her long thick lashes blinked, and her eyes filled with tears.

"The bomb exploded at the entrance. It destroyed a newspaper stand. No fatalities—thank God—but I'm afraid this is just the beginning." She wadded up a document that was in her right hand, threw it on the floor and ground it into the stained oak with her black boot. "I was supposed to deliver this speech later about Wrath of God. Jesus help us—floating balloons? That's what was on our minds? Jesus help us."

Pinch marched over to us, arms and legs coordinated like a toy soldier, and said quietly, "We *are* the Masturbation Corps. Got some future recruits out there, don't you think?" She had no idea what was going on. Sweet shook her head and covered her face in her hands.

Silverspoon continued to read. "The elephant went to its knees. It trumpeted in pain from its long trunk. Still, the scorpion stung, and stung, and stung." He turned the book around and showed the drawing of a wrinkled gray elephant, on its knees, bellowing into the air with its long trunk, red welts all over its feet, and a big tear falling from its eye. The scorpion crawled up its side, much, much bigger than it had been before.

Urgent footsteps came from the hallway. We opened the door to find the large woman running, panting, waving another telegram, one hand over her heart. Second Mate Basmati Sweet walked across the hallway, kicked the wall, turned and slipped down against it until she sat on the worn, red tile floor. She dropped her head to her knees. I took the telegram from the big woman, her face pale, lips trembling. I slowly read the message.

"It's from Chief. 'Extreme danger. Stop. Suicide storks attack New York. Stop. They attack military command in Washington. Stop. Swaddled bombs destroy buildings. Stop. Thousands killed. Stop. Impossible to know how many more will strike. Stop. Al Quota. Stop. It is war. Stop. Run, captain, run. Stop.'" Sweet burst into tears. My eyes immediately filled, throat tightened, stomach twisted into a fierce knot. I tore the telegram in two and threw it to the floor. My hands went to retribution waiting in my holsters. I wanted to kill something, anything, right then and there. Sweet sat there weeping. My lips and fingertips went numb. I rubbed the black leather of my gun holsters.

The big woman had gone from classroom to classroom, spreading the news. Teachers wandered into the halls like the walking dead. Some cried, others threw incoherent questions and accusations down the long hall; some walked back and forth with their heads in their hands; some sat like Basma, and looked around as if awaiting news of a loved one having surgery.

I wandered into the classroom. Tatanka saw my expression and grabbed my arm. I just shook my head. Pinch stared at me like a girlfriend who knows you're about to end it with her. I meandered across the room to Captain Silverspoon. He looked up from the book, at first with a smile, then a frown when he saw my face. Krill stood stock still on his shoulder. I leaned down to his left ear and told him the news. The bare oak branch unevenly tapped at the windowpane.

"The bushwhackers got us, sir," I told him. "Chicken Little was right. They pulled a stork trick—bombs disguised as babies. Thousands are dead, and it's not over. Chief wants you to hightail out of here." Wrong John dropped the book to the floor. It opened to a page with the elephant lying on its side, covered with red, poison stings. The *very* hungry scorpion stood on top, wearing a wicked, fanged spider smile.

Chapter XXIII

Show Me Some Pepper

We rushed the rubber-legged captain of *Liberty* to the Marine Terminal of Philadelphia and carried him onto the ship. Pinch, Tatanka and I, and the sailors scrambled up the ratline and dropped every canvas curtain in the house from its yard, trying not to get tangled in the corporate flags that whipped in our faces. We unmoored the ship, weighed anchor at the capstan, trimmed and set sail to catch the bitter wind out of the northwest. *Liberty* glided into the swirling current of the Delaware River at low tide and coursed for the bay. Any bird that came within a hundred yards of *Liberty* got vaporized.

I took the helm. No one else could do it, so stricken were they with grief. I guided us past Cape May and into open water just after dusk, on a course south by southeast for the Sargasso Sea. Around midnight I heard from the try-works what sounded like a cat in heat ringing a muffled bell. I turned over the wheel to Speck, walked to the furnace door, opened it, and shoved a lamp inside. There stood Krill, wailing pitifully and banging his little red head against a try-pot. "Not storks," he cried. "It can't be storks. There must be some mistake. Please, no. Noooo." I reached in and pulled the little fritter out. I set him down on a bench and got him a small bowl of water. He slurped at it and calmed down.

"It can't be, Ish. Not storks. It had to be a trick. The storks thought they were babies. Somebody switched them. Those Quota barbarians!"

"What is it with you and storks? Did your darlin' kiss that same frog and turn into a stork?"

He cocked his head and looked at me sideways through wide eyes. "BRACK! How'd you know that?" I told him it was a guess. He shook his head at me. "Pretty good guess." He pecked at his upper right wing. "We were drunk. It sounded like fun. We had flaws. BRACK! I couldn't talk. She was shy and nervous. We wanted to be different, better. So we puckered up. Smooched the slimy thing. And it worked! It worked! Except she turned into a stork. Me a parrot. But a *brave* stork! A *talking* parrot! She flew off to see the world." He ruffled his feathers and shook himself.

"Haven't seen her. Haven't seen her. Almost ten years now. Ten years. Now this? Quota using storks? Maybe she's one of them." He pecked at his claws nervously and whined. "Maybe she's already dead. Already dead."

"There's a lot of storks in the world, Krill. She's probably okay."

"No, Ish. You don't know pirates like I do. Even if she's alive, they'll hunt down the storks. TP, Chief, Yo Yo: they'll blame storks. Forget who trained them. Forget Al Quota. Storks will be the enemy." He shook himself, stretched his wings, and waddled away. "Check on the captain. Check on the captain. BRACK!"

I relieved the specksynder from the wheel and steered *Liberty* deeper into the darkness, south by southeast, and on to the flotsam of Sargasso. The fleeting light of the binnacle lamp cast a spell on me and I drifted into a trance. I had a feeling like Ishmael, that one night when he steered the Pequod by the try-works fire.

> "Uppermost was the impression that whatever swift, rushing thing I stood on was not so much bound to any haven ahead as rushing from havens astern. A stark, bewildering feeling, as of death, came over me. Convulsively my hands grasped the tiller, but with the crazy conceit that the tiller was, somehow, in some enchanted way, inverted. My God! what is the matter with me? thought I. Lo! in my brief sleep I had turned myself about, and was fronting the ship's stern, with my back to her prow and the compass."

And so, as with Ishmael, I became turned around, and had the feeling I was steering the ship *backward*. I was looking ahead as if going towards something, pursuing some goal, eager to get *somewhere*, but was, in fact, running away. I snapped from my trance and nearly fell over when I realized that, *exactly*, had been my life: running, always running, *away*. I told myself there was a quest, a score to settle, a redress of oppression. Lies! And the thrill of it—deception! Everything I had done, every murder, every theft had been an excuse to run, and to hide, to slink, and to lurk, and pretend to be anybody but myself. I wasn't running from the posse, or Union dominance, or the Pinkertons, I was running from that loathsome killer, Jesse James.

I looked down at the binnacle lamp: north by northwest. I was steering *Liberty* into a broach, and without resetting the sails, would capsize her in the contrary wind. I pulled the wheel back to a southerly course and continued on to Sargasso.

The ship splashed through the rolling water, and I got to wondering what would happen next. Al Quota had attacked, and it was being framed as an act of war. I did not *at all* comprehend this reasoning. How had a renegade bushwhacker, a cult leader without a country of his own, committed an act of war? What was to be gained by giving Quota and his despicable backhanded swindle the status of a belligerent nation? Talk about making a little man big—lordy!—they had made a termite into a tiger shark. Imagine the status, renown, and allegiance we would have gained, Frank, if the Union had declared war on the James and Younger Gang. There would have been a hundred of us overnight, robbing banks and trains across the South.

Foolishness, I thought, as I steered *Liberty* deeper into the darkness of blackness. No quest in it. No forward thrusting Ahab: confusion only, standing backward at the helm, boldly charging at absolute retreat. Whatever cheap victory that villain had got with his bewitched flock of brainwashed fowl, Chief Dagger and the others had compounded for him tenfold by declaring war.

Days passed and Silverspoon did not emerge from his roundhouse. Plates of food put inside his door remained untouched. He allowed no one to see him, and even shot at Pinch once when she tried to force a meeting. Only gibberish came from in there, punctuated now and again by the words: "War! An act of war!"

Basmati Sweet spent much of her time in the galley with me, Tatanka, Roberto, and the other Latin laborers. She continued to scribble a mustache above her lip but stopped wearing that ridiculous hose down her trousers. She seemed comfortable inside the rough, curved sides of the ship's belly with us regular folk. All of us put heads together on the problem of Silverspoon. He was headed for the rocks; how would we get him turned around?

"We could lie to him," Sweet said. "Tell him his mother is ill or something."

"Try it," said Tatanka, sharpening his big cleaver on a whetstone. Four fat turkeys roasted in his black iron stove. They bubbled and put out the most delicious aroma.

I rolled a few smokes and offered them around. Tatanka, Basma, Roberto and I lit up and laced the roasting turkey smell with tobacco smoke.

"Hey. We could slip a Bible quote in with his *huevos*," said Roberto.

Everybody liked the idea. Next morning we gave it a go with a verse from Matthew 17:20: "Verily I say unto you, If you have faith as a grain of mustard seed, ye shall say unto this mountain, Remove hence to yonder place; and it shall remove; and nothing shall be impossible unto you."

"Faith that can move mountains. That ought to get him," said Basma, setting his breakfast plate of sunny-side-up eggs inside the door. She lay on her belly to listen if he took the bait. The metal plate slid along the floor. "He took it!" she whispered.

We all gathered around to see what he did. It was quiet for a minute, now two, now three. Basma winked at Roberto and nodded sideways at the door. Then the plate crashed into the wall and he roared, "Faith? Faith? Is that what the Bible says? Will faith bring back the dead Americans? Can I have faith ever again, after my most trusted officers betrayed me?"

The next morning we tried Basma's lie. She scribbled a note that his mother was deathly ill. If he didn't turn the ship at once, he would never see her again. We gathered at his door, leaned toward it, and waited. A minute later the plate crashed into the door. "Don't lie to me!" he yelled. "That battle-ax will outlive us all."

For a few days after, we did not know what to do. Speck pointed out to us the utter darkness of a storm ahead, and advised that if we continued southeast, we would likely never see land again. I hadn't come all this way to end up in Davey Jones's locker! I pulled the twin furies from my hips and strode hard after Wrong John Silverspoon. He would either take the helm of *Liberty* or take a slug in the gut.

When I got to his door a great commotion came from within. I kicked the door open to find Pinch on her back, pinned to the deck by Silverspoon sitting on her chest and holding down her arms. He looked hideous with his cheeks hollow and jaundiced, a week's growth of beard and his gray-streaked black hair sticking up wildly off his head. "I told you to leave me alone, didn't I," he wailed at Pinch. "Let me starve. Just leave me alone!"

Pinch struggled, kicking her long, heavy legs up and bucked with her stomach. "No, captain! I won't let you do it."

"Why? Why can't you leave me alone? I was supposed to protect them, and I failed. I failed."

"It's crunch time, sir, bottom of the ninth, we're up by one. We've got two outs but there's a man on third. We need a closer, sir. Somebody who can come in and save this ball game!" she cried. "Chief can't do it. Gunny's got a rag arm. Tosspot's a belly itcher. Who's gonna come in and throw, captain?

Tell me! Who?"

Silverspoon loosened his grip. Pinch bucked him off onto the floor. She went to his closet and dug in it for two mitts and a baseball. She threw a mitt at him with the ball tucked in it. "Show me some pepper, sir." She walked out of the cabin and squatted in a catcher's stance in front of the aft mast. We all watched Silverspoon's quarters to see if he would come out. Not long after, he did emerge, slowly, looking thin, weak, hair and eyes wild. He saw Pinch squatting on the deck and walked at her. He stopped, took a pitcher's stance, put the ball behind his back, raised, kicked, and threw.

"That's the stuff, captain. Give 'em the pepper," said Pinch, catching the ball and throwing it back to him. It bounced off his glove to the deck. He stared at it rolling to and fro with the wave-tossed ship. The darkness of the storm ahead drew closer, kicked up whitecaps and popped the sails. The corporate flags got all tangled together and appeared to be in a wrassling match off the masthead. Basma sent Roberto to the galley to get the captain a bowl of chicken soup.

Pinch encouraged Wrong John from her catcher's stance. "Quota can't hit your fastball, sir. Let's give him the pepper. What do you say?" She showed her long teeth and nodded decisively at him.

He looked at her, at me, and at Basma. Krill flapped his wings and cooed at him from his perch on the try-works. Silverspoon cast a wan smile out to the sea, reached down and picked up the ball. He dropped into stance, kicked, and threw hard at his treasurer.

"Stee-rike three!" Pinch crowed. "You're outta her, Quota!" She threw her extended right thumb back over her shoulder. "Take your sorry ass to the bush leagues."

He glanced around at us, lips tight and pulled down at the edges, and bobbed his head. Basma tugged on my arm. "Look! He's back. He's back."

Roberto arrived with a bowl of steaming chicken soup. Tatanka followed him up the hatch. He looked at me, pointed at Wrong John, raised his eyebrows, and nodded. The captain blew on the soup and dug in. He finished it while standing there on the swaying deck. He handed the bowl to Roberto. "Let's play some ball!"

Basma brought a bat from Wrong John's cabin. We took up positions on the cramped oblong diamond of *Liberty*. Silverspoon pitched to Tatanka, who handled the bat like a pro and knocked a single off the try-works on the second pitch. Basma came to bat and bunted, advancing the Sioux to third. Silverspoon struck out Speck. With two outs and a man on third, Jesse James stepped to the plate.

Wrong John stared me down, placed the ball on his lower back, rose, kicked, and threw. Ball one. Four more pitches and the count was full. I tapped the heels of my cowboy boots with the bat. I tucked it between the legs of my snakeskin pants, spit into my hands, rubbed them together, and adjusted my bowler. I lifted the bat over my right shoulder and nodded slowly at him. He nodded back. A bolt of lightning struck just ahead and sudden sheets of rain slashed at the ship. Wrong John turned and looked into the teeth of the storm.

"What in the hell!" he cried. "Rain delay! Speck, bring the ship around and steer us straight to Washington. I got a score to settle." The specksynder hollered the orders to bring her around, and sailors scrambled into the rigging and reset the sails. *Liberty* came sharply about and headed for home.

Later that evening, well after ten, several us sat in the galley, sipping cocoa, smoking cigarettes, and idly visiting. Silverspoon walked in unexpectedly with a pillowcase over his shoulder. He had cleaned up, shaven, combed his hair. Basma and Pinch stood quickly and saluted. He waved his hand at them from the hip and shook his head. "No need for that, girls. We're all equals tonight." He sat at the table across from Roberto, emptied the oranges from a metal bowl, and poured in the contents of his pillowcase. I recognized his collection of baseballs. Tatanka poured him a mug of cocoa. The storm buffeted *Liberty*, wailed at her, slapped her with rain.

Wrong John tossed a ball at Tatanka, who caught it in his big brown hands. "Thatn's signed by Kid Nichols of the St. Louis Cards. The Kid's one of the all-time great pitchers. Has already won thirty games in a season, seven times."

Wrong John rolled a ball across the table to Roberto. "Nap Lajoie, Lisp, Cleveland Bronchos. He hits the ball like a rocket. Runs like a quarter horse." Roberto got a tear in his eye, sniffled, and turned the ball over in his small hands. Silverspoon tossed a ball to Sweet. "Mike 'King' Kelly of the Boston

Beaneaters. I can picture his big old handlebar mustache. His bat is golden."

He threw a ball to me. I looked at the signature. "Buck Ewing," said Wrong John, "catcher for the New York Gothams. Could throw a man out at second from a full squat."

He turned and tossed one to Pinch, who leaned against the doorway to our cabin, eyes teary and red, nose dripping. She caught the ball and brought it between her full breasts. "Dan Brouthers, Pinch. From your hometown, I believe."

She wept, and said, "Big Dan, oh my gosh. Detroit Wolverines. He's my hero. You know he hit *ten* homers last year. Can you believe it? Ten in one season."

"That's the sorta folks come from Detroit, Pinch." He smiled at her resolutely. She saluted, wiped her eyes and blew her nose. Krill clucked and whistled from where he had been flirting with a chicken. "Sorry, Krill, bird's haven't made it to the big leagues yet." Basma stared at the deck and scuffed it with her heel. Wrong John took an orange, threw it in the air, and nabbed it.

"Thanks, Pinch. Thank you all, for standing by me through this. I'm not very good at—it's not in my nature to say I'm—to admit a fault, or take the blame for something going wrong. I just—I want y'all to know how much I appreciate you helping me through this. Now let's get back to Washington and put this thing right." He took a sip of cocoa, commented on how tasty it was, stood, and left the galley. A week later we were back in the capital.

Chapter XXIV

Open for Business

We arrived on *Liberty* to our usual anchoring in Washington outside of the Tidal Basin. In *Liberty*'s place sat the *Preemption*, Chief Dagger's fifty-gun steam and sail dreadnought we had taken to Europe. He flew the Star-Spangled Jolly Roger. Wrong John Silverspoon hailed him and said he was coming aboard. "Permission denied," Chief replied. Silverspoon's sharp ears went red and his nostrils flared. "Only kidding, sir. You're welcome aboard the *Preemption* anytime."

Liberty drew near, and Silverspoon crossed onto Dagger's ship, along with Basmati Sweet, Pinch, and me —Krill, of course, sat on Wrong John's right shoulder. Silverspoon winced every time the crew on *Preemption* addressed Chief as "captain," and confronted him about it. "You may have promoted yourself while I was gone, but I'll take the sheriff's badge back now, thank you." Dagger scowled and looked away. "And what is the matter with you, flying the Jolly Roger in Washington? And in broad daylight?"

Chief pulled his dagger and rubbed it across the white stubble on his cheek. "Nothing to hide," he said matter-of-factly. "America wants us to be pirates now, Mr. Captain. They want us go off pillaging and slaughtering to avenge them for 10-10. Blood is what they want, sir. And we're the right pirates for the job."

"Good. I'm glad to hear it. But unless you're planning a mutiny, I still give the orders around here. Take down that pirate flag. It's completely *off message*, Chief. Y'all got to be some dumb pirates to run around showing your colors like that." He put his hands on his hips and cocked his head to the side. "Now give me an update on the war. Who's it against?"

Pinch set her jaw, winked at me, raised her thumb, and threw her arm over her shoulder like an umpire calling a batter out. A whip cracked from the foremast of *Preemption*, and a man cried out in pain. Dagger tried to direct the captain to his quarters at the stern, but he forced his way toward the bow. There he found Tosspot flogging a man tied to the foremast. "Where are you hiding the storks?" he screamed. "We know you've got a training camp in America. Where is it?" He lashed him across the back, leaving another long red welt to match the crisscross of marks already there.

"What did I tell ya, Ish," Krill said to me as an aside. "Blame the storks, blame the storks."

"I know nothing about storks," said the prisoner in a thick Arabian accent. "I am a chicken farmer. That is all."

"Marshal!" the captain cried. "Why are you beating that man? What are the charges?"

Tosspot, winded, and having some actual color on his jowly face, replied,

"Oh, Sire. You're alive. Nobody knew." He breathed hard to catch his breath. "There aren't any charges, Majesty. Things have move along while you were gone. My God Arrest America Act is now the law of the land, passed almost unanimously by the Congress. I can do this to anybody I wish—no arrest warrant or charges necessary."

"It ain't the friggin' law till it's got my John Hancock on it!" growled Wrong John.

"Well, no, Sire. Actually it is. You were gone—nobody knew where—or if you had been killed. Chief had to assume executive powers. His signature is on the act. Do you want to see?"

"No! I do not want to see!"

Chief looked away and sucked his gold canines. Gunny walked out of the hatch wearing a gray bird on his left shoulder. The bird had the sharp eyes and lean body of a hawk, but the beak and short wings of a parrot. When Yo Yo saw the captain he started and his monocle popped out. He collected himself, placed his finger horns against his head, and smiled. Wrong John gave him the middle finger horn of his right hand and smiled in return.

"ATTACK!" screeched Gunny's gray parrot, its voice a little lower and smoother than Krill's.

"BRACK! Hey, what's the big idea?" challenged Krill.

"ATTACK! Hey, what's the big idea?" parroted his rival.

"Cool it, pal. I'm the bird-in-chief around here."

"Cool it, pal. I'm the bird-in-chief around here." Yo Yo stuffed a green grape in his parrot's mouth. Krill ruffled his feathers and grumbled.

"A'right. Let's get something clear. I been gone, and it's been painful. I'm glad you moved things along, but I'm back, and I'm hotter than a hornet. Y'all may have plans, ideas, ambitions, and all that's great. Just get one thing straight: this here's *my* calling. I'm the one's been chosen by God to lead America through this mess. Any whupin' gets done, I get the credit for it. Any blood spills, I'm the fella gets to weigh it and put it on his trophy case. Is that thick as Texas toast for everybody?" He looked at Gunny, Tosspot, and Chief in turn.

"Where's the diplomat?" the captain asked sharply.

"He's not really part of—" Gunny began.

"The hell he idn't. We're about to play Pick the Enemy, and I want him in on it. Find Sir Yes Sir, and all of you report to *Liberty* in one hour sharp. *Comprende?*" Gunny and Tosspot saluted. Dagger turned his back and strolled to his cabin. I remembered him telling me, in the North Sea fog: "This whole caper with Silverspoon: this is *my* immortality project." Looked like some destinies were getting cross-threaded.

An hour later the offices of *Liberty* had gathered in Silverspoon's roundhouse. Roberto served hot cups of coffee all around. Silverspoon took a deep slurp, cleared his throat, and began. "A'right. America's losing its patience with me. They want blood. You said in your telegram, Chief, that we're at war. Who might that be against?"

"Storks, we're thinking. That's who hit us. That's who we tackle," Chief said, pushing his glasses up on his nose. "It's a War on Storks."

Krill flapped his wings madly. It had gone exactly as he predicted. Knowing him, though, I expected he had a trick up his wing. "No can do, *BRACK!* No can do."

"*ATTACK!*" crowed Gunny's gray parrot, who we had been introduced to as Neo. "No can do. *ATTACK!* No can do."

"Shut up, you little copycat!"

"Shut up, you little copycat!"

Krill hopped off Silverspoon's shoulder, flapped his wings, and scooted across the table to the other bird. He jumped at it, caught a hold of its left eye, pulled the orb right out of its head, and left it to dangle by a nerve against Neo's cheek. The gray parrot screeched and jumped in the air. It flew blindly forward, smashed into a wall, and fell to the floor. Gunny scowled at Krill and drew back his fist.

"Don't you dare, Yo Yo," the captain warned. Krill hopped back across the table and onto Wrong John's shoulder.

"Can't touch the stork," he said. "Can't touch her. National bird of Saudi Arabia. National bird."

"What? That can't be!" Chief exclaimed, shooting Gunny and Tosspot with hate bullets from his eye guns.

"Damn it! He's right," Yo Yo realized. "Now what are we going to do with all those 'War on Storks' buttons and posters?" He held his blinded parrot, pitifully moaning in his arms, and stroked its face with the back of two fingers.

"Burn them in the try-works! And while you're at it, we'll throw your fat heads in the rendering vats!" Chief had gone ripe red, neck and forehead veins bulging, spit collected at his lip edges.

Tosspot's sagging pale face fell even more ashen. "Who cares if it's Saudi Arabia's bird?" he asked. "Deuteronomy makes it clear that whomsoever shall attack you must be utterly and completely annihilated. We've got to hunt down and kill every stork on the planet!—along with related waterfowl such as whooping cranes, great blue herons, pink flamingos, snowy egrets, the scarlet ibis, and—parrots *possibly*." He cast a wry smile at Krill. "They attacked us. We must attack them!"

"*BRACK!* No! No! Stay away from my stork!" Krill snapped his beak menacingly at the marshal.

Wrong John, Chief, and several other officers lowered their eyes at Tosspot and shook their heads. "Forget it, TP," said Wrong John. "Saudis are like family to us. We can't go attacking their symbol of abundant blubber. That'd be like them butchering bald eagles. Just wouldn't fly."

"It's too late. We're already rounding them up. I've got an avian detention center in—"

"Shut it down, Tosspot," said Chief. "If the sheiks like storks, they get a pass. It's that simple."

"Don't worry, marshal," added Wrong John. "We'll cook up a good enemy for ya. Get to work on it, everybody, and leave me alone. I need some solo time to work up my speech to America. Folks need comfort and reassurance from me. I want to do it up right." He adjourned the meeting.

Silverspoon went straight to work. An hour later, I approached him with a warm up for his cup of joe, and casually reminded him of the story of *Moby-Dick*. He looked up from his notes, and took his reading glasses from the end of his sharp nose. Krill also removed his glasses— silly bird-sized spectacles.

"That's right, Ish. The Bible of whaling. I like ol' Ahab—mean, nasty *hombre* like me," said Wrong John.

"*BRACK!* Lost his leg to Moby Dick. Bit it off, *BRACK!* Wore a whale bone on his stump." The bird hopped from Silverspoon's shoulder to the dark oak table, and limped back and forth among the pages of notes as if he had a peg leg.

"That's the one," I said. "Remember how he put in a third time after the White Whale, even though his peg leg was torn off and his whaleboat twice sunk?" They both nodded. "That's what you call commitment, boys. Now *you've* been 'dismasted,' Wrong John. Al Quota's chewed off your leg, now he's your Moby Dick. Might be a handy yarn to weave into your speech."

"Yeah! That's right! I'm the guy—whaler-in-chief—gonna kill that friggin' monster with my bare hands!" He grabbed Krill and began choking the plump red bird. Krill stuck out his black tongue and rolled his eyes back. He flapped his wings madly, which snapped Wrong John from his fantasy. He dropped the bird to the table and looked up at the rough ceiling beams. Krill coughed a few times, breathed hard, then spoke to Silverspoon from the stack of notes on the table. He pulled the quill pen from the ink well and held it in his claw.

"*BRACK!* Not a good fit, boss. Whaling man can't have a whale for his enemy. Be like making war on blubber. *BRACK!* Wave bye-bye to the base." He shook the pen at Wrong John, sending droplets of ink onto his notes.

"He's right, Ish. Besides, I already got my White Whale—federal bureaucracy—'member the ro-deo? *Real whale*, that's a whole 'nuther kettle a fish. I hunt the buggers 'cause I love 'em, not 'cause I hate 'em. I almost feel like I'm one of 'em sometimes—and you can't hunt yourself, now can ya? Ain't you got somebody 'sides the White Whale for me to go after?"

I turned away and pretended to be ruminating on his idea. Damn! I thought, he didn't take the bait. Maybe it was arrogant of me to think I could steer them, but Ahab seemed the perfect hero—one of the all-time grand lunatics of literature. They had already outrun Ahab by declaring war on the bushwhackers. A chase for the White Whale of terror would have been the *perfect* framework for them. Why hadn't they taken it?

I pulled Widowmaker, spit on her pearl handle, and rubbed her with my shirttail. I ran through Mr. Melville's book in my mind. There was no other monster except for Moby Dick. The whole blamed book was a chase for the domineering brute. I looked out the small window of the roundhouse and saw a sailor untangling a jumble of hemp. Then I remembered another monster.

I'm sorry, big brother, for not understanding *Moby-Dick* better. Out of my ignorance, I gave Wrong John and Krill the notion for another monster, one that fit their purposes much better than a While Whale.

"There was a Giant Squid," I said quietly. They both looked up at me from over the rims of their reading glasses. "At first the crew of the Pequod thought it was Moby Dick, but when they lowered boats to give chase, they found out it was a giant Squid—just about as big as the whale, but horrible to look at."

"*BRACK!* Get the book. Read all about it." Krill flapped his stubby wings. I went to my quarters and found my copy of *Moby-Dick*. I thumbed through the index to find the chapter called "Squid," returned to the roundhouse, and read them the following quote:

> "We now gazed at the most wondrous phenomenon which the seas have hitherto revealed to mankind. A vast pulpy mass, furlongs in length and breadth... innumerable long arms radiating from its centre, curling and twisting like a nest of anacondas, as if blindly to clutch at any hapless object within reach.... As with a low sucking sound it slowly disappeared again. 'The great live squid, which, they say, few whale-ships ever beheld, and returned to their ports to tell of it.'"

"*BRACK!* It's perfect! Perfect!" Krill hopped up and down on the table and got so excited he spilled the inkwell, and yet he kept hopping around, leaving claw prints all over Silverspoon's speech.

"Damn it, Krill, look at the mess you're making," Wrong John scolded.

"I'll be back. I'll be back." Krill hopped off the table and left his footprints all the way out the roundhouse.

"Sloppy little Peckerhead," said the captain. "Get Mendoza to wipe this up, would ya, Ish." I left for the galley and saw Krill to starboard in a whaleboat being rowed to shore.

A few hours later he returned, and the two wrote a new version of the captain's speech. Later that afternoon, we disembarked the ship and traveled by coach to the largest cathedral in Washington, where there was gathered the entire Congress and their families, and reporters from the most important newspapers in the nation. Stained glass windows let in a muted rainbow of evening light from the west side of the cathedral. A stark white cross hung on the wall, towering above the simple hickory altar. Dark beams curved across the dome of the ceiling as ribs coming off a whale spine. The captain stepped to the lectern and looked about the crowd, his lips a razor line below his nose, his eyebrows sharp and angled toward the deep furrows between his eyes.

"First of all, let me say, from the bottom of my heart, to all Americans who have suffered these last days, America is open for business!" His words reverberated through the empty, ribbed belly of the cathedral. "Don't let these barbarians keep you from doing your patriotic duty, which is to spend and purchase and buy in support of our sacred trust, The Economy. If we slow down on our consumer confidence for even one day to feel sorry for ourselves, they win. If we stop to ponder why, or shed too many tears, or ask ourselves how this could have happened, they win. If, on the other hand, we continue to do what we do best—which is to work our butts off and spend every last penny—then, differ'nt story. We win, and we get the last laugh all the way to the bank." He looked over the audience in the church, to some unseen force at the far back.

"You may recall Herman Melville's *Moby-Dick,* a book destined to become an American classic, and the main character, Captain Ahab, who would stop at nothing until he hunted and killed the White Whale. Some might say we got us a White Whale now, and he's called Al Quota. It's a nice idea, something Bubba might go for, but it ain't Silverspoon caliber. I got me a sea monster too, but a bigger, badder, nastier one than an innocent whale. In America, we *love* the White Whale. It represents the goodness of our generous colorblindness, our godliness and purity, as spoken of in the Bible by Job. No way in a million years we're gonna hunt that white beauty. What I got, fellow Americans, is a squid—not just any squid, but a *GIANT* one." He paused and looked about the crowd, and seemed to notice, as I did, that his monster had everyone confused. He shifted side to side and bit his lips. Sighs, coughs, and a few harrumphs came from the congregation.

"Ahab had his Moby Dick, I've got my Shalong—Al Quota—Shalong Quota, see, but it's not a whale—they're the good guys, providers of energy, our great blubber way of life—mine's, see, it's a squid—it's—it's got all these

arms—ten of 'em to be exact—and they're always reaching out to grab
you—got suction cups on the end, hundreds of them suckers, each one lined
with shark teeth—and there's so many a'them tentacles, see, you can't tell
where they're coming from. Those arms are everywhere! reaching out to grab
you and pull you down! You yank one off—she just grows back a new one!
One day its Al Quota, next it's Shalong, then it's the evil Colonel Coffee, or
Ill Kim Dung—you never know, who or when, 'cause, see, squid can change
color—change color!—get any color it wants to blend in. Master of disguise,
see." A low murmur passed through the church.

"There's more! You get close to the gruesome thing and it shoots out a
cloud of ink in the shape of its body, but its *real body* jets away! ZOOM! And
it changes color to see-through—disappears, jets off, gone like a ghost." He
waved his hands out in front of him as if doing a magic trick. The murmur in
the church was louder, full of awe. "Deep down inside that mass of writhin'
goo, there's a beak, like a bird, except it's a solid set'a bolt cutters, strong
enough to cut even a good ship away from its anchor." He made his arms into
big pliers and moved them up and down. His eyes got big and he roared, "And
the monster's got eyes *this big!*" He made a full circle around his head with his
arms. "Always looking for an opening, a weakness, sensing the slightest hint
of light, movement, freedom—and she *pounces!*" He lunged forward, almost
knocking over his podium. A collective gasp filled the cathedral.

"The Giant Squid, like Al Quota, has almost never been seen. All you
get is a chunk of tentacle floating to the surface now and then. Squid's down
in the deep, deep, dark, dark, unseen depths of the coldest sea. Down there
layin' eggs, ladies and germs. One pregnant giant squid lays ten million—
count 'em—ten million eggs. People suppose only the Great Godly White
Whale, Moby Dick, has the guts to go down there and hunt her—and it's true.
Even with all his courage and strength, the odds are not good for Moby Dick.
One out of two times that snake-legged thing slaps tentacles on him and kisses
him bloody in a hundred places with those shark-toothed suction cups. The
squid sucks onto the good giver of light, Moby Dick, down there to bravely
attack that evil, dark, inky-black, slimy beast. The Giant Squid attacks him
with those fifty-foot long tentacles, wraps him up in them and pulls him down,
pulls him down, pulls him down." He slowly bent his knees until he kneeled

on the ground. Everyone in the church went to their knees.

He lowered his voice, made it growly and sincere, like a skilled preacher tugging heartstrings. "The White Whale, my fellow Americans, gets covered by the suction-cup arms and tries with all his might to struggle free, or to bite and destroy the evil squid—and sometimes he does. But you see, folks, the Giant Squid has a *terrible* advantage over our heroic White Whale. The whale, like us, is made in God's image, and is human, and like us, it's got to breathe." He took in a deep breath. The congregation took in a deep breath with him. "The squid, though, she's like the dark one, inhuman, otherworldly, in disguise. *She does not need to breathe.* She can stay down there forever, waiting, plotting, planning for just the right moment to rise up and attack us for our goodness.

"This is my mission, my calling, to hunt down and kill the Giant Squid. Call it evil, call it a mollusk—call it what you will. You better pick sides, that's all I got to say. You're either with me or you're with the squid. It's a simple matter of simplicity. I call it war, a war on evil, a war on darkness, a war on terror. I call it a War on Squid, and I will not stop until I rid the world of calamari!"

The applause started slowly, and grew, until it was a thunder more like a charge of cavalry than applause. I stood there in that storming cathedral damning myself. Damn me, Frank, for the ignorant, farm-boy, gunslinging, idiot that I am. Damn me, brother, for giving Silverspoon his monster, giving it to him because I didn't know better.

You tried to educate me, Frank, get my head out of the skirts and into a book, but I couldn't be bothered. You said there were lessons to be found in history, and I ought to learn them, or I would repeat some old mistake for the thousandth time. Pshaw, I told you. My natural instincts are far superior to a crusty old book. I had my cause. It was us against them, right or wrong, no matter what. I did not have to think about it, or worry about it, or wonder if I was doing the right thing. It was simple, efficient, unwavering, absolute. Damn me, Frank. You said knowledge was power, and I had just enough of it that day on *Liberty* to be dangerous. I knew just enough of Mr. Melville's work to betray him, so that Wrong John Silverspoon could turn the villain, Moby Dick, the Great White Whale, into the hero of his modern tale.

Chapter XXV

In on a Camel

Leaders and envoys from the great nations of the world paid their respects to *Liberty* over the following weeks. They expressed their condolences, and spoke in one voice that all free people of the world were now Americans, one with us in our grief. They expressed too their resolve to help us track down the killers, and punish them to the full extent of the law. Wrong John and Dagger smiled and accepted the well wishes, but theirs was an American flag starred and striped with skull and crossbones. It wouldn't take them but an afternoon on a porch swing to whittle the world's sympathy down to a nub of hatred.

Immediately after Wrong John's Sermon on the Mollusk, the officers of *Liberty* set about planning their first response to the attack of October 10. Throughout the land, "10-10" had already become the name for the attacks that day by suicide storks. I thought it odd that such an important and tragic event would not be given a name, but only a number, as if it were the tally on an accountant's ledger. It lacked heart and soul to me, and I could not imagine it inspiring anyone to heroism. "10-10!" they yelled as they charged the hill to vanquish their enemy. It didn't *quite* make the blood boil.

Be that as it may, 10-10 needed a response, and one crisp afternoon the officers threw a football around the deck of *Liberty* and devised a strategy. Wrong John rolled back with the football and pointed to Gunny, who stood atop the try-works on the ivory presidential seal. His gray parrot, Neo, perched on his left shoulder, and wore a small eye patch over its left eye, just as its master wore one over his. Arms of icy fog crawled along the blue-brown surface of the Potomac. The shoreline trees stood naked of leaves, their bare branches standing out, waiting, it seemed, for snow, or the return of birds.

I sat on the first yardarm of the mizzenmast with Tatanka, who continued to carve on his whale tooth with his long, yellow jackknife. I could not yet tell what it would be. We sat up there and took in the game. Four crewmembers manned the four small artillery guns on the main deck, while another dozen stood by the gunwales, hung in the rigging, or stood in the crow's nest, loaded to the teeth with rifles and pistols. Everyone understood that more storks, or possibly scarlet ibis, could attack at any moment.

"Gunny, America has its coals in the barbecue. They are red hot and ready for raw meat." Wrong John's words came out as vapor in the cold air. He lofted the ball to his gunner. "The people of this nation have asked me for a dripping slab of goat flesh. Why have I not provided them any?"

Yo Yo caught the ball. He ran as if evading a defender, but seemed to forget where he was and ran right off the edge of the try-works. His parrot, which, unlike Krill, could fly, hopped from his shoulder, flapped its wings, and landed on the boomvang. *"ATTACK!"* It screeched. Gunny, however, who could not fly, fell on his face and gave himself a screaming bloody nose. He sat on the deck, shook his head, checked himself for broken bones, and stuffed strips of cloth from his shirt up his nose. He crawled to the football and threw if from his knees back to Silverspoon.

"Targets, sir, that's the problem," he said in a nasally voice. "AQ may be hiding in Afghanistan, but it's hardly worth our trouble to go in there and get him. Blowing up tents is not exactly an impressive display of our awesome military might."

Wrong John caught Gunny's wobbly pass. "I want something spectacular, people," said Silverspoon. "I want fireworks and big impressive vengeance— shock and awe. I want it to be clear that America is not only open for business, but it *means* business." He threw a rocket at Chief. The ball landed against his ham hands and fell to the deck. He kicked it and it flew at Pinch, hit her in the stomach, and knocked the wind from her.

"There's no question AQ and Shalong were in this together," said Dagger. "Remember the Iraqi assassin at the ranch?" The captain nodded and pushed out his cheek with his tongue.

"Do you mean Peaches?" asked Sir Yes Sir.

Dagger shot him a dirty look. "We're talking about a web of deceit that stretches throughout the Middle East, much of Africa, and Southeast Asia."

"But not Saudi Arabia," added the captain.

"That's right. Not the blubber Mecca."

"*BRACK!* Protect the national bird," said Krill.

"*ATTACK!* The national bird," Neo croaked from the boomvang rope.

Pinch had recovered herself and did not look happy. She picked up the ball and threw it at Dagger's head, narrowly missing his crooked face. He opened his eyes wide and raised his eyebrows in her direction. She waved her fingers as if tickling him and gave him a tight-lipped smile.

Chief coughed, pushed up his glasses, and continued. "Now the War on Squid is an international battleground. Just because Quota is supposed to be hiding in Afghanistan doesn't mean we have to hit him there. It's a Giant Squid, remember, tentacles reaching all over the globe. Let's hit it where it will hurt the most, and give us the nicest cut of blubber."

"I can already hear the sizzle," said Wrong John. "Where you thinkin'?"

"Afghanistan is a wasteland. Iraq, on the other hand, has some actual buildings, many of them historical, that would make for a showy demolition. Then there are Shalong's palaces—the rat bastard's got a palace for every day of the year, each of them stocked with a gourmet harem, storks galore, the son-of-a-bitch living like a king despite everything we've done to ruin his country."

Krill perked up and jumped from Wrong John's right shoulder onto my left. "Maybe Shalong's got my sweetie. My sweetie and my magic lamp," he whispered in my ear.

"Let's get him," said the captain, rubbing his hands together.

Sir Yes Sir picked up the football, tossed it up, and caught it. "Let's not be hasty. The world community is not yet *fully invested* in the Giant Squid paradigm. It sees the situation as a more *isolated* mollusk—an infestation of slugs in the cabbage patch. They'll back us if we stick to the slug that slimed us, but if we go freelance harpooning for bigger squid, we might loose our coalition." He tossed the ball to Sweet, who ran a few steps and caught it nicely in her fingertips.

"Yes, I—I think Sir Yes Sir may be on to something. I love the whole Giant Squid project—really. It is truly thinking outside the lobster pot. But, well—." She looked up at me sitting in the yardarm, polishing my iron. "Well, we might not want to give the terrorists more status than they deserve."

"*BRACK!* The pirate revolution cannot ride on the back of a slug—the back of a slug," Krill squawked. Neo's muffled voice parroted Krill's. I wondered what was the matter with the gray bird. Did it want to be blind in both eyes?

Basma threw the ball back to Sir Yes Sir. He caught it against his chest. "We have recently received word the Afghans have located AQ and can arrest him whenever we give the word."

Gunny got into a three-point stance, stood, and jogged in place. "What a load of crap!" he shouted, nose stuffed with cloth, dropping back down into his stance. He stood and jogged in place. "We're not going to convince the world of our resolve by arresting people. That's so Bubba it makes me want to puke! We need decisive action, boots on the ground, death and dismemberment of our enemies. We need cities on fire and screaming people and terror far worse than anything a skinny white bird can deliver in a diaper!" He ran at Sir Yes Sir, stripped him of the ball, and tossed a lateral to Chief. Gunny ran interference, blocked Basma on her butt, and the two ran to the aft mast. Dagger spiked the ball against the deck.

"Touchdown!" shouted Wrong John.

"Death and dismemberment, like it says in Deuteronomy," said Tosspot. He unfolded his bullwhip and gave it a pop.

"We need to send the terrorist regimes of the world a Western Union," Dagger said, speaking sideways in his crablike way. "'If you swim with the squid. Stop. You *are* the squid. Stop. You can call yourself an eel. Stop. Or even a porpoise. Stop. But once the squid is in your waters. Stop. His tentacles reach into all things. Stop. He wraps around you, draws you in, and swallows you. Stop.' That's the message we need to send them."

Wrong John looked up to me on the yard and yelled, "Man, Ish, this squid thing is gettin' good, idn't it?" I ignored him. Every mention of the squid felt like a splinter going under a fingernail. I'm sorry, Mr. Melville.

Wrong John jogged across the deck and reached out with his hand. "Hit me. I'm open," he called to Yo Yo, who had picked up the football. Gunny threw in a nice pass and Silverspoon wrapped his arms around it. "Hey! I could go in there on a camel—actually balance on the back of a camel with a knife in my teeth."

"Now that's *politics*, BRACK!" screeched Krill. "Guaranteed second term. Guaranteed second term. Redeem the Silverspoon name. Redeem the name." He danced back and forth on Wrong John's shoulder. Silverspoon gave him a peanut and peeled one for himself.

"No go on the camel trick," said Chief. "Too dangerous."

Wrong John snapped his fingers and jerked his head to the side.

"You go into the Middle East with guns blazing and it could inflame the entire region," said the diplomat. "We've got to be smart about this so that we can build on the sympathy of the world to fight the global war on terror!"

"Screw their sympathy!" returned Yo Yo. "Who needs it! This is America talking. We don't need those saps feeling sorry for us. Whether they like it or not, we're going to get our revenge! We'll do a little slash and burn, show 'em what we're made of. Then we a set up a nice democratic confederation, a healthy home for happy people and good, old-fashioned blubber harvesting!"

"You can't harvest blubber when the whales are on fire!"

"All right. All right. You both have valid points," Chief said. "We can't go straight to Baghdad, but an arrest is hardly the cut of meat America is hungry for. No, this barbecue calls for regime change, nothing less. We take out the Afghans and butcher AQ. The world will entirely understand."

Gunny jumped in. "Then I think it's incumbent upon us to deal with Iraq. Shalong has been thumbing his nose at us for eight years while Bubba grinned and lobbed pop bottle rockets over the border. It's been humiliating. And now look what's happened." He held his hands out and looked back and forth, as if sitting at ground zero. His parrot flew over from the boomvang and landed on his left shoulder.

"ATTACK!" Neo screeched.

"Shalong and Al Quota, were," Yo Yo continued, "if memory serves, on the same debate team in high school, winning contests together all over the Middle East, arguing for the total and complete annihilation of the United States. They played polo together, and, as you know is the Arab tradition, kissed after every victory. They traded sisters to each other's harems as if building a baseball dynasty. If I'm not mistaken, the Butcher of Baghdad and AQ—every day, sir, several times a day—lay out their prayer rugs in the exact same direction and kneel on them and pray to a god not even called 'God,' but some idolatrous name like, *Allah*."

"Well I'll be God damned!" shouted Silverspoon, spiking the football into the deck. It bounced wildly and flew into the water. One of the jumpy artillerymen must have thought it was a dive-bombing stork and shot it with his cannon. The other gunners turned and fired, and the men in the rigging unloaded a hundred or more rounds in the floating football.

"Time out, boys!" shouted the captain. "That's my favorite pigskin you just blew to smithereens." He turned to his gunner and placed his finger horns alongside his head. "Lose the parrot, Yo Yo. There's only one Wrong John Silverspoon. He's the one with a polly. Period."

"BRACK! ATTACK! YOU'RE SACKED!!" Krill crowed, flapping his wings and jumping up and down on Silverspoon's shoulder.

Sir Yes Sir shook his head. He squeezed his temples with his big hand, then looked up at Tatanka. The Sioux nodded at him and struck his chest twice with his fist. Sir Yes Sir struck his own chest and nodded back.

Then Dagger stepped to the center of the group, cleared his throat, sucked his teeth, and quietly spoke. "Your enthusiasm is truly warranted, Mr. Captain. It's imperative that we go about, from this moment forward, building a case against Shalong. SYS, I want you to take the lead on this. No arguments." He threw the full weight of his countenance at the diplomat, who turned away. Yo Yo grinned behind the back of his hand. "Pinch, do you think we can pull some money from the Afghan combat fund to pay for our Iraq planning without getting caught?"

Pinch worked the red and white beads of her abacus as if deducing the profit margin on bolts of silk. "Oh, yes, sir. I'll cook the numbers to the perfection of a nice beef Wellington, lightly browned on top—impossible to trace the individual ingredients."

Dagger went on, "Excellent. Now, Mr. Captain, I'd like to suggest something even bolder."

"Bold? I like bold," replied the captain. "Does it involve riding camels or landing hot air balloons on battleships or anything?"

"It could certainly lead to a number of interesting possibilities," said Chief. He sucked his gold canines loudly and tugged on a gold hoop earring, then continued to speak from the far right side of his mouth. "I'd like you to consider a broader initiative than just knocking off Shalong Quota. I'd like you to consider staking your claim to history by setting forth a grand doctrine, a philosophy all your own, that establishes once and for all the supremacy of the United States as the greatest power the world has ever know."

No one spoke or moved. Puffs of breath made brief clouds in the air, and disappeared as unspoken thoughts. We all looked without blinking on the man who was about to make Wrong John Silverspoon famous, or, more in keeping with the place in history reserved for infamous pirates.

Dagger paced methodically back and forth along a five-foot line. "Events, tragic as they no doubt are, give you license to demand the authority of an absolute ruler, made even more absolute by his elected status in the most democratic of nations. More than license, these events provide you a *mandate*—the people *want* you to take vengeance in their name. In short, sir, you may now, if you wish, claim the just right, the—if I may—*divine right*, to attack and subdue any individual, any organization, any body, any nation, any state, any person, principle, cause, ideology, or religion, for any reason you see fit. *Any reason*."

Wrong John's jaw went slack and he grabbed a hold of a halyard to keep his balance. Dagger went on. He pulled his dagger and stroked his cheek. "Not only may you now do what you wish, but you may, out of self defense, take action to *prevent and preempt* aggression. You may attack before anything happens, at home or abroad, your mandate is so strong. You may do so for any reason—probable, possible, or fabricated—in the name of national security. It is, Mr. Captain, in terms of raw power, a very enviable position."

Wrong John blinked his eyes and slowly shook his head. His eyes brightened and he winked at me. He reached into his pocket and dug around, I supposed, for a coin. He must have remembered my telling of *Moby-Dick*, and the part when Ahab challenges his shipmates to join his quest to capture the White Whale, then inspires them by nailing a gold doubloon to the main mast.

> "Aye, aye! and I'll chase him round Good Hope, and round the Horn, and round the Norway Maelstrom, and round perdition's flames before I give him up. And this is what ye have shipped for, men! to chase that white whale on both sides of land, and over all sides of earth, till he spouts black blood and rolls fin out. What say ye, men, will ye splice hands on it, now? I think ye do look brave...."
>
> "Whosoever of ye raises me a white-headed whale with a

wrinkled brow and a crooked jaw; whosoever of ye raises me
that white headed whale with three holes punctured in his
starboard fluke—look you, whosoever of ye raises me that
same white whale shall have this gold ounce, my boys!"
"Huzza! Huzza!" cried the seamen....
"Skin your eyes for him, men; look sharp for white water; if ye
see but a bubble, sing out."

Wrong John dug around in his pocket, but all he could come up with
was a wooden nickel. "Fetch me the claw hammer, Speck!" he called. The
specksynder shortly handed him the hammer and a ten-penny nail. Wrong
John held the wooden nickel aloft dramatically, looking at it as if it were
the holy grail. "This here's for the first man who slaps eyeballs on the Giant
Squid!" He went to the mainmast and nailed the hickory nickel to the round
timber. He turned and threw his arms back as if expecting a grand ovation and
pledges of undying devotion. Instead there was silence.

Thus was born the Silverspoon Mandate.

Chapter XXVI

Batguano Castle

In *Liberty's* dithering over just exactly *who* we were at war with, and *how* we
would most impressively attack them, Al Quota disappeared into the maze of
canyons, caves and remote villages along the Afghan border with Pakistan.
I knew he would be impossible to find, having nothing to do with magical
attributes of the shape-shifting squid. It would be impossible to find him
for the same reason it had been impossible to find the James gang among
our Missouri friends and kin, and the landscape we knew so well. The law
will never find an outlaw who is looked on by his people as a hero. He lives
among them undercover, like a moth in the parlor draperies. Not only would
his people never say where he was, at every opportunity they would send the
posse down a game trail leading to a mud hole.

But they would have to call him Ishcabibble. No one could ever again know who Al Quota really was. He would have to hide, become invisible, aught—live an assumed life under an assumed identity. That was his curse for running his political ambition through the bobbed wire like he had. He would be like Jesse James, not remembered for his cause, the *reason* that sanctioned barbarity, but for his robbing and his killing. History, it seems, does not remember your reasons, your excuses, even your mandates—it only remembers *what you did*, and judges you by that.

I can go on and on about the stance I took against the inevitable destruction of the Old South. I was a victim. They started the fight. We Southerners were innocent and pure, attacked for no reason by wicked oppression. Out of that I justified a life of getting even, a ride on a backward horse, crupper under the tail instead of reins to the head—all my hopes forever receding away from me. The only way out of the despair was to mount up and seek further vengeance, and wind up further away than when I started. On and on we robbed and murdered, and for what? the right to keep black men and women as slaves? Was it really worth all that? Was it really worth fighting for so viciously? the right to treat other men and women as animals, no different than cattle and chickens? How did I presume myself an innocent victim of Northern aggressors? attacked and vilified for no damn reason? How did I suppose myself a Christian, and an American, believing it good and proper for us white folk to tear Negroes from their African homes and make them our slaves? me, a free man in a country founded on the principles of equality? When did Jesus ever encourage his followers to go forth and become rich by making a slave of the world? How did I go about all those years believing I was victim, persecuted for no damn reason? You tell me, Frank, because I surely have forgotten.

After 10-10, I watched Americans slide into that victim quicksand, believing themselves innocent and pure, attacked for no reason, deserving of bloody revenge for the senseless and savage attack against them.

They gladly handed over their rights and duties as citizens of a free and democratic republic to those who promised to get even for them. Almost the entire membership of Congress threw in with the pirates as well, casting aside their duty to balance and check the powers of the Executive. The Silverspoon

Mandate ruled the land, and it should have come as no surprise to them when, before wielding his sword against a single foreign enemy, Wrong John turned his blade first on his fellow Americans. Why would he do that, you might ask. Because his mandate was a lie. What he really had was a dereliction of duty to cover up, and chaos was the best means by which to do it. Then he would be free to follow his one true calling—to disembowel his "White Whale" of government by and for the people.

It was left to Tosspot to make the first impression of the Silverspoon Mandate a lasting one. His God Arrest America Act, that "pie in the sky legislation" Chief Dagger described when first seen back on the ranch, was now the law of the land. Tosspot had previewed it for us with the flogging we witnessed on *Preemption*.

The marshal referred to his Cheshire-cat Act as "A slight modification of the Constitution, suspending for reasons of national security just a few insignificant details pertaining to privacy, free speech, and habeas corpus— puffed up Latin for an unnecessary impediment to dynamic law enforcement. Patriotic, law-abiding Americans have nothing to fear," he said. Congress passed the act almost unanimously, and so fast, it seems impossible any of them could have read the bill, let alone studied it and formed an opinion. But, as I said, acquiescence was the mood of the land. Joined with blood lust—it is a lethal combination. The crew of *Liberty* understood, and understood well, the very rare opportunity history had presented.

In support of the new legislation, TP purchased Batguano Castle, a colonial Spanish castle in Cuba. He somehow cajoled the Cuban government into selling him the castle and its lands as a nongovernmental autonomous zone, bound by no international agreements and beholden to no body politic. Wrong John insisted on a tour of the new facility. TP warned him it could be uncomfortable, his agencies having already rounded up several hundred suspects in the terror attacks and sent them to Batguano Castle for interrogation.

"Good," said Wrong John. "I want to look the killers in the whites of their eyes—dead or alive."

Liberty sliced into the port of Batguano, a deep-water bay surrounded by dark, steep granite cliffs at the western tip of Cuba. At the very edge of the highest cliff stood Batguano Castle, built from the same granite as the cliff, and appearing to grow directly from it. It was clear by the bulky unadorned style, and by the turreted walls and bartizans heavily armed with cannon, that this had been no vacation home for the Spanish royalty. Captain Silverspoon and Tosspot stood at the prow of the ship and looked up at the castle. Wrong John ducked and swatted at the air whenever a seagull came within ten yards of the ship. TP pointed up at the castle with a white-gloved hand, then gestured toward the captain with his other hand while he explained the strategic advantages of the new acquisition.

We anchored at a rock jetty and climbed off the ship. At the end of the jetty, a small Cuban man in a white straw hat waited with horses for us to ride up to the castle. Pinch, Basma, Wrong John, and I mounted and rode with Tosspot, and an escort of cavalry, up the winding dirt trial to the castle. When we reached the granite parapet a cool breeze rose off the Caribbean, and I looked down into the water so clear and turquoise blue I could see to the reef on the bottom. It was another graveyard, all white with coral tombstones. I imagined sea urchins crawling all over it with their spiny black pincushion bodies, chewing up the decay. On the rocks near the mouth of the bay lay a shipwreck. I blinked my eyes and focused on some huge *thing* groping it. Whatever it was did not have a distinct color and seemed some part of the wreck, come to life from down inside. Before I could study it, the thing was gone, and all that remained was a dark cloud.

"Welcome to Batguano," said Tosspot, turning away from the sea and gesturing toward the interior of the castle, filled with structures, passageways, towers, and arched doorways dark with shadow. Armed soldiers patrolled the walkways and stood guard atop the turrets and towers. From somewhere deep in the castle came the distant moans and cries of the prisoners.

"This is our first line of defense against another stork attack. Anybody who poses a threat to our great nation ends up here." He turned and walked down a winding stone stairway lit with torches standing in metal cages along the walls.

"How deep does this thing go?" asked Silverspoon.

"Nine floors. Nine floors, down." He drew his words out and pointed into the black abyss. We entered a narrow corridor that held a single small cell on one side, enclosed by rusted iron bars an inch thick and lit by a smoky torch on the wall. The cell contained a variety of Americans, ten or fifteen, many of them white, a few black, red, or brown, but all still, it seemed, Americans, undergoing what TP described as an "information extraction methodology." All of the prisoners held knitting needles. The smell of freshly baked cookies fought for air with a less attractive aroma: that of vomit.

"These first couple of floors we call the Treasonous Utterings Ward. It's reserved for Americans who criticize us, Majesty, and in so doing, encourage our enemies," he said, addressing the captain. He placed his index finger over his lips and motioned for us to look into the cell.

A slight old woman with a hump in her back, gray hair in a bun, and wire glasses on her small wrinkled nose walked around the cell carrying a tray of chocolate chip cookies. She wore a long gray skirt and a white shirt emblazoned with the same flag as one that flew as a corporate sponsor in the masthead of *Liberty*: Mercy Nary, *Pirate Security for the Public Good*. Her name was stitched on the left breast pocket: Agent Gran.

"Knit one, stitch two. Knit one, stitch two," announced Gran, her wrinkled face hiding a cruel smile. Knitting needles clicked as the prisoners worked on what appeared to be shawls with words stitched into them.

"What do they say?" asked Basmati Sweet.

"A simple confession: 'I sinned against my country, and God Arrested me,'" said Tosspot.

"Which God is it that wanders the streets of America carrying leg irons?"

"The one in which we trust."

Basma grunted and turned quickly away. Agent Gran supervised the needlework. After a minute she came around with a platter of chocolate chip cookies. "Time for a treat, kiddies," she said in a voice dripping with molasses. The prisoners groaned, and one or two in the back of the cell became sick. Even as they got sick, Agent Gran forced them to take another cookie.

"What's the matter, kiddies? Get too much of a good thing, did we? I'm sorry to spoil your appetite for free speech, but, well, granny knows best. Maybe next time you'll think twice before you open your naughty mouth. It's not nice to back talk to your government when it's trying to protect you from evil. Eat those cookies, kiddies! Yum, yum, yum." Several other prisoners threw up.

Tosspot held his nose and nodded toward the dark passage. He led us further down the dark, narrow, winding stone stairwell. Our footsteps echoed. Water dripped. We entered another corridor with a small cell on one side. Rusty iron bars stood locked in mortar and stone as they had for two hundred years.

"Those in here are mostly librarians," said Tosspot. He held his hands together, then opened them as if opening a book. "And we're throwing the book at them."

"Librarians?" asked Wrong John.

"Yes, Sire, they seem to have the unpatriotic assumption that the contents of a potential terrorist's library card are none of our business."

"Do we think the bad guys are checking out books on animal magnetism or whatever?"

"Well, they certainly could be. Almanacs, for example, are one of the most deadly books out there, Majesty. An excellent resource for plotting vulnerable targets." He called an agent over who showed a copy of *Poor Richard's Almanac* with many passages underlined, and prodigious marginalia. He showed the book to the captain. I noticed on the spine it said, "by Benjamin Franklin."

"This'un belong to a terrorist?" asked Silverspoon, his eyebrows raised.

"We believe so. But librarians don't think it's any of our business. Can you imagine?" He shrugged his shoulders and held out his hands. "They'd rather see terrorists use an almanac like this *Poor Richard* to plot their evil intentions—to delay the squash harvest or cause a terrifying lunar eclipse—than to get on board with us and break the back of these heathens."

From somewhere inside the chamber, a smallish woman in a plain dress—now drenched from some sort of water torture, her hair also soaked and partially broken free of its neat bun to dangle limply on her shoulders—cried out in anguish, "Okay! Okay! I checked out a copy of the *Koran* to David Irvin, a high school teacher in Peoria, Illinois. He—he claimed it was important to understand the religious experience of Islam so we not make the mistake of assuming they are all bad people. I know I should have called you, but, I just was just too frightened!"

"Find this 'Irvin' and get him down here immediately!" shouted the marshal. Four strong guards scurried out of the room. Tosspot leaned over to the captain and said, "You see how it works, Sire? Without the help of a simple librarian, that teacher could remain loose among our children, corrupting their minds with un-Christian dogma, when what he should be doing is Bible study—right Ish?" he said to me.

"Beats me, marshal," I said flatly. "This is your parish, not mine."

"You don't seem shocked by the proceeding, Mr. Bible. I get the impression you've seen worse."

"May have seen worse, but didn't have the cheek to play holy man in the middle of it." That was a lie. I preached in many a similar situation. My favorite verse was from the Book of Jesse, 2:13: "Open the goddamned safe now or I will see you in hell." I carried the Good Book strapped to my waist disguised as a .45 Colt Peacemaker. Many a convert saw the light.

"Where did you see worse, *Ish?* Vicksburg? Shiloh? Louisville?" he said in that snotty voice of his. I know I shouldn't have, Frank, but I decided to push him. "Centralia," I said, citing the most terrible of our exploits with Bloody Bill, the one in which we did the most atrocious murdering things: cutting off heads and such.

"Oh, that's right. Bible the bushwhacker. Well, if you were part of the butchery at Centralia, you must have known the James brothers."

"Don't recall them," I replied.

"Okay, what is this, old home week? Let's get on with the friggin' tour," whined Silverspoon. Tosspot bowed and led us again into those narrow winding stairs that smelled of pitch and human waste. Down the next corridor we found a cell holding a dark-skinned man, shaved bald on every part of his body and strapped to a small wooden chair. His eyes had somehow been glued or taped open: he could not blink. In front of him stood a brawny interrogator wearing camouflage pants and the same shirt as Agent Gram: Mercy Nary, *Pirate Security for the Public Good.* He held in his hands a stack of lewd photos. The one on top showed a naked woman lying on a rug, touching herself between the legs. The prisoner tried not to look at it, but his head was strapped, eyelids held open. Whatever direction he rolled his eyeballs, the interrogator moved the picture in front of them.

"No, please, no!" said the man, his voice strong with an Arabic accent. "It is a sin for me to look at such a thing."

"No kiddin'?" said the interrogator. "I'll stop—if you tell me how long you've been a member of Al Quota."

"I am not a member," answered the prisoner. "Please, I'm an American. I moved here from Egypt seven years ago. I am a citizen now."

"Sure you are." The soldier flipped to the next photo in the stack. This one showed two naked men holding one another's peckers.

"No! Please. It is forbidden."

"What were you doing with a stork in your backyard?"

"That was a peacock. I will get rid of it. They are pretty, but noisy. I will sell it."

"So now you're starting a black market in terrorist storks?" The soldier looked over at us and winked. He flipped to the next photo: two naked women and a St. Bernard.

Tosspot ushered us along. "It's very powerful to use their heathen faith against them like that," he said, his voice hollow and ominous in the stone stairwell. "They'll tell us anything we want to hear."

"But do their answers lead anywhere?" asked Basma. "Do you get closer to the source of the attack?"

"They lead to more arrests, and, as I think is obvious, that *is* the purpose of God Arrest America." Tosspot turned, jangling the sets of leg irons strapped to his waist. He led us down deeper, to another level in the dungeon.

In the next cell four men sat strapped to chairs around a table. In front of them was a plate stacked with what looked to me like tasty sandwiches. "This one is brilliant," said the marshal, rubbing his hands together. "We call it The Bacon Lettuce Tomato Treatment." He put his right index finger to his lips.

An interrogator approached the men. He stalked around the table slowly, wearing camouflage pants and the Mercy Nary t-shirt, and sneered at each man in turn. Then he turned to one and asked, "How long have you been a stork hypnotist?"

"I—I don't know what you mean; I'm—I am a baker, that is all," the man said, straining against the bindings on his head and arms.

"Is that what they call you? The 'Baker'? Well, you're getting a rise out of me, you filthy raghead!" the interrogator yelled. "Open wide, Quota boy. It's BLT time." He grabbed one of the sandwiches, squeezed the man's jaw open with his vice-like hand, and shoved the sandwich into his mouth. The man tried to spit it out, but the interrogator held his mouth closed with one hand on the top of his head and the other beneath his jaw. Eventually the man chewed and swallowed.

"I will be sick. I must be sick. I have never eaten pork in my life. It is awful," the prisoner wailed, then gagged. The others at the tables moaned and mumbled prayers.

"It's your choice, Baker," said the interrogator, getting nose-to-nose with the prisoner. "Take the bacon, or tell me where you're brainwashing the storks!" The prisoner begged for mercy and swore he knew nothing about storks.

"Heck, TP, what's the guy's problem?" asked Wrong John, grabbing a hold of the cell's iron bars and looking through them. "I'm just about ready to grab one'a them BLTs for myself." He licked his lips.

"Muslims have some religious edict against eating pork. As I said before, the threat of committing a sin is one of the best ways to get confessions from them." The corners of his soft mouth curled up, and he looked down his nose with eyes half closed.

"Gosh, marshal," said Pinch, "using their religious devotion against them like that. Sorta funny—like one sin forcing another."

"The 'Baker' isn't in here for burning the toast, Pinch. These are desperate times, and Deuteronomy commands us."

Basmati Sweet crossed her arms tightly over her bound chest and shook her head. Tosspot walked to the stairs and took us down the echoing chamber. He continued on, down the musty passageway dripping with water, thick with the smoke of burning torches. We reached another corridor and another cell. Krill sniffed the air. He lifted his head and leaned it forward, left, then right, and sniffed quickly like a tracking dog, in the direction of a the dark stairwell at the end of the chamber. I looked over and could hear something coming from wherever those stairs led—a muffled croaking sound. Krill jumped off the captain's shoulder and waddled toward the stairs. Tosspot, enamored with the "information extraction methodology," didn't notice Krill.

In the cell stood four naked men that had been shaved and collared, and were held with leashes by specialists from Mercy Nary. The prisoners leaned forward, squatting slightly, straightened arms resting on their knees.

"This one's *got* to be a Tosspot original," I remarked to Silverspoon. "Probably came to him when he was ridin' that horny jackass." Wrong John grinned and shook his head. The marshal leaned toward us, trying to hear what I had said, but missed it, I think.

The honcho interrogator stood before the men and paced back and forth, slapping his left hand with a pair of leather gloves. "Did you think you could come to America and murder our people and just go home and have a good laugh with your sick pals?" came the shouted question.

"No! No! I beg of you," said the first man in line, his English, once again, thick with an Arab accent. "I am a rug merchant. My family has done honest trade with your country for five generations. Please, please spare me!"

"Wrong answer, you fu—," the ramrod broke off, having noticed the captain watching from outside the cell, "you dang sand-person of color!" He slapped his hand with his gloves and nodded at the handlers. "Leap frog!"

The handlers pulled on their prisoners' leashes, and each placed his hands on the back of the man in front of him and leaped over. "Allah be merciful! His penis touched my back! Allah be merciful!" screamed one of the prisoners. Others wept and said, "Allahu akbar," over and over, followed by, "la ilaha illa llah."

"This is sick, Tosspot," Sweet hissed. "You're torturing these men."

"Torture? That's a very strong word, Mr. Sweet. Define torture."

"What you're doing. Humiliating, degrading, abusing other people. That's torture."

"Leap frog is a child's game, Mr. Second Mate. I think you're overreacting." Basma raised her hand, index finger pointed, and was about to reply when the captain stepped in.

"He's right, Basma. I've been clear. Do what it takes to get the intelligence. If that means leap frog, so be it. If it means paddy cake, or blind man's bluff, or hide and go seek, I can deal with that."

"And if it means pulling off fingernails or dipping appendages in boiling oil?"

"Don't go sissy on me, Sweet. This is war. Nobody said it would be purty." He turned away from her and back to the marshal. "So, these must be the really *bad*, bad guys, huh?" asked Wrong John.

"Worst of the worst, Your Majesty," answered Tosspot, shaking his head gravely.

"Pretty sure these are the ones who planned it?"

"Almost certain."

"Boy, it's amazing how convincing they sound. One guy's a baker, 'nother says he's a rug merchant; how can you tell when they're telling the truth?"

"It's hard work, Sire, but your mandate helps. The presumption of guilt gives us a nice edge."

"Amazing discipline, gotta give 'em credit for that."

"I don't know, sir," said Pinch, working her long fingers on an invisible abacus. "I just hope—not to be a sissy—but I just hope we know what we're doing. I would hate to see us do *this* to innocent Americans or foreigners who really didn't have anything to do with 10-10. You've got good evidence, right marshal? I mean, you know for sure before you, well, make them do leap frog and such?" A deep frown crossed her forehead, and she worked her imaginary abacus as if trying to make the numbers add up to some version of American justice.

"At this point, we're keeping the criteria quite broad," Tosspot said magisterially.

"What is it?" asked Basma.

"Well, uh, it's partially based on our Skin Pigment and Facial Hair Algorithm, but mostly, it's a matter of faith. It's a matter of, if you're a Muslim—a faith devoted to little else but violence—you're a suspect, and we bring you to Batguano."

"Here? To this room?" asked Pinch.

"Some, yes, many."

"Good God!" said Basma, her voice cracking, becoming very much the voice of a woman. "Just because they're Muslim?"

"No, of course not. Only the ones who have acted suspiciously."

"See?" Wrong John said to Basma. He turned to the marshal and asked, "What else ya got?"

Tosspot clasped his hands in front of his chest. The corners of his lips curled up. He turned and was about to lead us back to the arched corridor by which we hand entered, when Krill waddled up, coughing and covered in blood.

"Krill, old buddy! Look at you. What happened? You take a line drive in the kisser?" asked Silverspoon, scooping his pet bird in his arms. Krill moaned, and his legs jerked randomly.

"I knew it. Knew they wouldn't listen," the parrot said. "Storks, captain. They've got them—hundreds of them."

"Storks? That's not part of the ballgame." He gave TP a dirty look.

"Killing the storks. Killing the storks. Horribly killing them." Krill wailed, his scabrous gray claws twitching.

"Tosspot?" said the captain, pursing his lips and frowning at the marshal. "This here's supposed to be a War on Squid."

The marshal quickly smiled, his lips trembling. He threw his hands up. "They attacked us, Sire. It's my job to find out why and how."

"Ripping off wings. BRACK. Cutting off heads," Krill moaned.

"They—they've taken a vow of silence," said TP, quickly. "Some pact they've made with that devil, Quota. We haven't gotten a single confession."

"Storks can't talk. They can't talk. She got her courage but lost her voice," said Krill. I remembered the story about his girlfriend, what she had lost in the deal with the frog.

"Something's off here, marshal," said Basmati Sweet, twirling her shrunken head by its golden chain. "Persecution based on religion. Random killing based on race."

"Race? What do you mean? They're not people. They're animals!" His pale face flashed red with fury. There it was again, Frank—that word "animal," the one that invited horror.

"Are you talking about the storks, or the Arabs?" asked Pinch.

"Both—neither! What's the difference? They attacked us, and we can't stop killing until they are *all dead!*"

"All the Arabs?" asked Basma.

"All the storks?" asked Pinch.

"The birds! Kill them all! They've got no business flying. Only angels should fly."

"*BRACK*. Storks *are* angels. They bring the babies. Somebody tricked them. Switched their babies with bombs. They didn't know. They didn't know." Krill whimpered in Wrong John's arms. Tosspot looked away, fidgeted with his bullwhip, and rubbed his jowly cheeks.

"You're gun barrel's got a kink in it, marshal," said Wrong John. "Our war's on squid, namely the Giant Squid. Now you better get this war right. *Comprende?* No storks, no kids—no kids, no consumers. It'll put China right outta business."

"We can outsource the baby thing to crows or something. Probably save some money." The words spilled from Tosspot's mouth. "It's war, Sire! Many of our cherished traditions have to be sacrificed for safety and security. That's just the way it is."

"What *is* this war on terror?" cried Basma.

"Who *is* the enemy?" added Pinch.

"Are we really going to kill all the storks?" asked Sweet. "We're going to destroy the source of life to save ourselves from death?"

"Chief Dagger signed off on it!" Tosspot confessed.

"Chief?" asked Wrong John. "Who's he? I'm still the big kahuna around here, 'member? Now, I'm all for ridding the world of calamari, but that's where it ends. There's lots of *good* appetizers, like buffalo wings, japaleno poppers, artichoke dip, those little mushroom dealies stuffed with cheese and sausage. May you take my order?"

The marshal nodded and began to reply, but Wrong John cut him off with a slice of his hand in the air. Tosspot took the first step down to another level of the dungeon, but Silverspoon grabbed his arm and steered him up. "Can't you take a hint? Lunch, *amigo*, *pronto*."

Chapter XXVII

No Boobs

The following morning I was helping Silverspoon on with his shirt when I noticed a bump in the middle of his back, about the size of a child's fist, lighter by a shade than the surrounding skin. I touched it and Silverspoon giggled. "Stop, ticklin' me, Ish," he said. I told him about the bump, but he refused to believe me. He tried to reach behind himself to feel it, but it was in a place he couldn't touch. I slipped his shirt around his shoulder and he put his arm through the sleeve. Even as he put his coat on, the bump stood out on his back, as if he had a second, larger Adams apple in his back.

Immediately after breakfast we set the sail—running out the spars on the topgallants to best capture the following wind—and made way for Washington. I kept to the galley most of the way, preferring the company of Tatanka and Roberto to that of the officers. It was cozy down below, and Tatanka made me one of his button-twisting Indian toys. This one's button was made out of a brilliant abalone shell, pearly and emerald with brown stripes. The thing was hard to get started, but once it got going, it became some form of perpetual energy.

Such a simple toy: pull your hands apart and the button spins. You relax your hands and it spins the other direction. Then you stretch the string, relax, stretch, and the button goes faster and faster until it's spinning and pulsating, and the rotating power forces your hands in and out. It mesmerized me completely, and reminded me of how a rock, once it starts down a hill, doesn't want to stop.

The whole way home from Batguano Castle, Tosspot brooded and sulked. He spoke to no one except the captain—in private. The rest of us, especially Basma and Pinch, he cast resentful looks whenever we walked by. Once, when I found the officer's toilet occupied, I waited outside and heard the voice of the marshal. "There it is again. That crude rhyme. 'Here I sit, buns a'flexin—.' Who keeps doing this?" He ground something savagely against the wall. "Out, perversion! Out, depravity!" he snarled. "It's Sweet, and that woman, Pinch.

They worship that lewd goddess at the prow, and defile the masculine throne! Pinch and her monthly gush of blood. Her craven howling at the moon. It's a bad smell, vile, filthy— it has no place on a ship of state. None! Yes, Lord, I shall eradicate it. I shall, Lord. I shall!" I ducked in the shadows, waited for him to pass, crept into the john, and gouged the saying back onto the wall.

The very night of our return, by the light of a full moon, Tatanka and I, up on deck for a late smoke, discovered Marshal Tosspot hanging from the bowsprit in the bos'n's chair—a snarl of ropes and tackle that held sailors while they worked on the hull—hacking with a machete at the bare breasts of Lady Liberty. With the ripe moon as his beacon, he rendered her generous, full, abundant breasts a flattened wasteland of chipped, splintered, bare brown wood.

All the while, he ranted, "I'll not have pagan black magic on the vanguard of *Liberty* one moment longer. Vile orbs of temptation! Vulgar nipples beckoning hungry lips. Animal longing! Bestial passion! Primal yearning! Leviticus makes it clear, abundantly clear. This abomination must be destroyed!" He swung his machete with righteous gusto and began to sing *The Battle Hymn of the Republic* in his tremulous tenor.

> "Mine eyes have seen the glory of the coming of the Lord
> He is trampling out the vintage where the grapes
> of wrath are stored,
> He has loosed the fateful lightening of His terrible swift sword
> His truth is marching on.
>
> Glory! Glory! Hallelujah!
> Glory! Glory! Hallelujah!
> Glory! Glory! Hallelujah!
> His truth is marching on."

He sang, and hacked, and he chopped, and wailed, shouted scripture, swung in his snare of ropes, cackled, growled and shook his gleaming machete at the moon. Watching him there, in that tangle of hemp, gleefully dismembering the symbol of freedom, I thought of *Moby-Dick*, and Ishmael's insight in the chapter called, "The Line": "All men live enveloped in whale-lines. All are born with halters round their necks; but it is only when caught in the swift, sudden turn of death, that mortals realize the silent, subtle, ever-present perils of life." How easy it would have been for me remind him, in a flash of gunpowder, of his birthday noose.

The next morning, by the light of the dawn, Lady Liberty's eyes, formerly determined and optimistic, seemed also diminished, wistful, and empty due to the sloppy obliteration of her breasts. The torch of hope in her right hand, painted bright gold, had been carelessly chipped and appeared to be flickering. Second Mate Sweet, having heard about the act just after breakfast, stormed into the captain's cabin, to tell him of the atrocity.

"It's time to court marshal the marshal!" she yelled, her fists clenched so hard the soft brown skin on her knuckles became starkly white. "He had his little 'Buns'a-flexin' witch hunt, which was sick—but fine, indulge him if you want to, he's an officer. Now, though, sir, he's—he's desecrated Lady Liberty. She's our guiding light, the principle that underpins everything we do. She's hope and promise and courage. She is fullness, abundance, generosity, kindness—and now she's got no boobs!"

"No boobs?" the captain asked drowsily, his head slowly turning away from his baseball card collection. "What? Who's got no boobs?"

"Lady Liberty, sir! TP has butchered her. He has, in a word, *raped* her, sir, and destroyed the spirit of our vessel, and the very spirit of our cause."

"Hold on there, partner," said the captain. "Them's fightin' words." He yawned and held out his arms—my cue to adorn him with his perfect blue jacket. Krill hopped up to his usual place on Silverspoon's right shoulder. We walked to the starboard of the ship where Basma had a whaleboat ready to be lowered. Pinch already sat inside. The try-works had been fired up to cook down the blubber of a small narwhale that had been given Wrong John as a welcome-home present. Black smoke, horrible in the nose, billowed from the stout red brick chimney. Fat sizzled and oil boiled. Whalers shouted directions to one another, ran hither and yon with their long pitchforks, cutting spades and ladles, hauled slabs of blubber from the carcass, rolled barrels across the deck.

I looked above the starboard gunwale and shuddered, then grabbed

Tatanka's arm to keep from falling over. There, hanging by a hemp whale line from a tackle off the foremast yard, swung the black coffin in which I had lain at the Court of Earthly Justice. Someone had painted on the side in stark white letters: "Free Speech Zone." Tatanka braced me and slapped my back.

"It's okay, Dingus. Two won't fit." He grabbed my shoulders and looked deeply into my eyes. "Sharpshooters. Tight. One goes. Both go." I nodded at him, glanced at the black death box, shuddered once more, and continued toward the whaleboat.

I, Wrong John, Krill, and Basma joined Pinch in the whaleboat, and Speck lowered us into the brackish brown water of the Potomac, from whence I rowed to the bow of *Liberty* and the scene of rape described by Basmati Sweet. Someone, likely the marshal, had taken the spiral horn from the narwhale and strapped it to the tip of the bowsprit, giving it another ten feet in length beyond the prow of the ship. A colony of eight buzzards circled overhead. They soared, wobbly, drunk it seemed on the billowing smoke of burning whale flesh.

Pinch looked skyward, and pointed with her long finger and nose. "Oh, heavens. What a blessing. There must be ten eagles. Look, sir, it's—never mind." She clamped her hand over her mouth. Wrong John gave her a half frown and shook his head. He looked up at the figurehead, squinting, his right hand over his eyes to block the harsh late morning sun.

"Shiver me timbers!" said the captain with an exaggerated pirate accent. "It's a clear-cut. The woman's been dismasted, and now she's a man!"

"*BRACK!* Shiver me timbers. Shiver me timbers."

"Oh, it's terrible, sir, isn't it," said Pinch, protecting her own breasts with her long hands. "Who could do such a thing?"

"Who else but Marshal Bullwhip?" asked Sweet, brushing back the shock of black hair from her left eye. "Here we have the one place where feminine power is honored, where we can view liberty as a bastion not just for men, but emboldened, even consecrated, by the determination of the feminine, and that bastard had to destroy it!"

"Here here!" exclaimed Pinch.

Sweet held the seams of her white blouse at the buttons on her chest, appearing, I imagined, to want to free her own breasts, which seemed to strain at the bindings that held them flat against her heaving chest, lost, as had been Liberty's, in the charade of fraudulent manhood.

I have to tell you, Frank, I had never seen anything like Tosspot's hack job: an act of terrorism, surely, part of his Ahab crusade to hunt and destroy the White Whale of carnal desire, but mutilating a wooden carving? I could only make some sense of it with the help of Mr. Melville. He describes, in a chapter titled, "The Chart," the way in which Ahab's obsession about the whale had actually grown into a separate creature, something independent of him, yet that lived within him. "God help thee, old man," says Ishmael, "thy thoughts have created a creature in thee." A creature impossible to live with, that has to be rooted out and put somewhere less painful. "Ah God! what trances and torments does that man endure who is consumed with one unachieved revengeful desire. He sleeps with clenched hands; and wakes with his own bloody nails in his palms." A man like that, Frank, a man like Tosspot, finds a home for his monster outside of himself, and wherever it is that he has placed his monster to live, that place, he destroys.

"A'right, a'right, simmer down, Basma," said Silverspoon. He turned to me at the oars. "Take us back aboard, Ish. Let's see if my mandate covers stuff like this." He looked down absently into the murky water. I slipped one of the oars under the keel and banged the boat. He jerked his head up and looked around. "What was that? Did you feel that? Get us out of this nasty river, Ish. Row, man, row!" I put my back into the oars.

"BRACK!" said Krill. "Anybody for calamari?" He nibbled at Silverspoon's ear.

"Shut up, Krill." Wrong John flicked him on the beak. He leaned with his elbows on his knees, and his profile, with the bump on his back, and his sharp nose and chin, he looked like a narwhale, ready to sprout a new horn.

Basmati Sweet sat on the edge of the front bench, leaned forward, and fussed with her hair and the baubles hanging from her ears. I rowed us to where Speck had lowered a rope ladder. Wrong John stepped over his second mate clumsily, rocking the boat. He lost his balance and kicked Sweet in the shoulder with his heel as he lunged for the rope and clambered up it. He ordered the specksynder to summon Tosspot to the bridge. Second Mate Basmati Sweet gathered several of the marshal's own security staff to join the captain, Krill, Pinch and me on the bridge. TP arrived presently, out of uniform, his white shirt untucked, reading glasses perched on the end of his nose. "Sire? More sickening graffiti in the men's room?" He raised his eyebrows, and thick lines formed across his forehead.

The try-works smoked and threw out the most disgusting stench. Whalers speared hunks of blubber and tossed them in the pots. They threw brown, cooked fritters into the furnace—the flame roaring every time the door opened. The turkey vultures circled lower, drinking in the burnt offering, soaring in and out of the black smoke as sharks would a spill of whale blood.

"There's graffiti all right, you son-of-a-bitch!" exclaimed Basma, moving directly in front of his face. Tosspot lurched backward and covered his chest with his hands. Something in the severity of her anger told me it cut both ways. It went at the marshal, yes, but also back at herself, for the way she had covered and bound her own breasts and had disowned her own femininity. Still, it seemed to cut even deeper, at some buried memory, some lost hope, something related, perhaps, to the shrunken head at her waist.

"YOU are the Masturbation Corps!" she bellowed. "What profanity did your sword carve into her heart while your excited *buns* were flexing?" she asked savagely. "What sick words did you write in her womb while you raped Liberty?" Sweet stretched her neck, tendons tight as piano wire, and put her wrathful countenance just inches from his.

Tosspot looked away from her and wiped her spit from his face. "I'm afraid I haven't the vaguest idea what you're talking about," he said. He turned to the captain, shrugged quickly, frowned, pursed his lips, and shook his head.

"You mean it wasn't you that took the tits off Liberty?" asked the captain. Krill walked back and forth on his shoulder, attacking an imaginary opponent with karate.

"No! Absolutely not! I'm sure it was the same prankster who takes endless pleasure from desecrating the men's room."

Basmati Sweet grabbed him by the throat and squeezed. He struggled to free her hands but was clearly no match for her fury. His face got red, eyes wide, and he tried to scream but nothing came out. "There were witnesses, you lying bastard!" she bellowed. "I'll kill you for this! I'll have your head!" The dark shrunken head at her waist rocked and swung, and made me believe she was ready to expand her collection.

The security team pulled her off of Tosspot and held her while she continued to lunge at him, scream profanities, and call him a liar. The captain stepped back and watched the scrap like he was viewing a boxing match. He seemed a little disappointed when it was over so quickly. After a minute, he realized everyone expected him to say something.

"Well, Basma, I have to trust the integrity of my officers." He adjusted the collar of his shirt and stretched his neck. "If TP says he didn't do it, end of story." He turned and walked back to his cabin. Tosspot rubbed his throat and looked down his nose at Basmati Sweet, whose muted rage had now gone inward and seemed to be draining the life from her, as if she were a balloon with a slow leak. She shook the security guards from herself and walked to the fore of the ship and leaned out over the water. From the angle I viewed her from it appeared the narwhale horn and impaled her through the pelvis.

Wasn't there some story, Frank, from grade school about the unicorn? how it's horn had magical healing powers—could very well bestow eternal life—and was hunted by greedy lords? The only way to get near it was to lure it with a virgin maiden. The greedy lords bewitched it with womanly innocence and purity, then killed it and cut off its magic horn. Looking at Second Mate Sweet, I remembered the legend.

That evening, after dinner, I found Sweet in the bos'n's chair, hanging down from the bowsprit. She had a bucket of white paint and brushed a thick bandage over the amputated breasts of Lady Liberty. I lit a smoke and tossed it down to her. She juggled it, nabbed it between her fingers, took a long draw, and blew out her gray jet and twin rings. I wanted to ask her if the bandages she painted matched the ones she wore, but that seemed a mean thing to say. Instead, I asked, "How's the patient?"

"I doubt she'll make it. You can't hack off a woman's breasts without intending to kill her." She looked up at me and smiled for a moment, then frowned.

"It's a shame when a woman can't just be a woman, and be respected for it," I said softly. I took a long pull from my smoke. The end glowed bright red. Sweet looked up at me and smiled briefly, then her face contorted in pain and she wept. I tried to understand her, Frank, as she hung there in that chair of ropes and spilled her tears into that river of grief that ran on deep and ceaseless with a thousand years of womanly lament. Into that ceaseless flow she gave her tithing, as had those countless mothers who lost their children to disease and war, those wives who lost their husbands to battles—all fought for good reasons—bringing death no less random than a rock slide. On that waterway altar she shed her sorrow for the ways in which she and her sisters had suffered because they were the ones blessed and cursed with a womb, blessed and cursed with soft breasts, able to sustain life, blessed and cursed with gentle curves, smaller muscles, a bigger heart, and inner strength far greater than a man's.

Chapter XXVIII

Coconut

In the days that followed, Basmati Sweet was little to be seen. She took her meals alone in her cabin, and did not come out, not even for morning prayers. Pinch tried to be helpful and encourage her with news that she wanted to commission a new sculpture—"one with even bigger boobs, three of them! and pregnant to boot"—but it did not raise Sweet from her melancholy. With or without her, plans moved forward for an attack against Shalong of Iraq. Sir Yes Sir informed the officers one evening at dinner that he had exhausted all intelligence assets, and wanted to give his report. Gunny suggested a secret meeting on the cannon deck the next morning.

Tatanka and I spent another fitful night, thanks to some new sound vibrating through the water and into the planks of our cabin wall. This one woke us just ahead of midnight and provided the sounds of a metal smith, scoring, bending, twisting, rubbing on a stubborn piece of iron. It lasted about half an hour. Then there was silence. I could not sleep for hours, anticipating what might be next. Tatanka's voice spoke in my mind, saying what he had said on the eve of the stork attack as we moored in Philadelphia: "It is near. The night eagle is near. But it will leave us alone tonight. It has another hunger."

Now here it was, or something, nearby, rubbing in a high-pitched squeal, as of metal against metal. It was near, and I was afraid it wouldn't leave us alone (wouldn't leave *me* alone). After hours of shallow breathing, rolling over and over in my thin, cramped, feather bed, I finally accepted that it *was* going to leave us alone, and I nodded off to sleep. Morning came and the sound of urgent footfalls above my head woke me up yet again. I slipped on the snakeskins and my holster and trotted up the hatch barefoot and shirtless.

Pinch greeted me next to the try-works, cleaned and covered with its mahogany lid after reducing the recent narwhale to a few barrels of heating oil. Its horn was still lashed to the tip of the bowsprit, sticking out over the water, the amputated figurehead of Lady Liberty hanging beneath it. And there, aback and starboard, hung that grisly black coffin, lynched from the foremast yard, a truly hated thing to be hung after it was already dead.

Liberty floated sideways, slowly turning, down the Potomac. I did not recognize the surroundings, except for the familiar haze of blubber smoke, and the thick shoreline forest of dogwood, sumac, and mulberry bushes, red maple trees, shag bark hickory, black walnut—and a great many varieties I couldn't name.

"Somebody cut the anchor last night," she said. "We must have drifted ten miles downstream."

"Tatanka and I heard it last night, something underwater grinding at the iron. Why didn't the lookouts notice we were adrift?"

"Asleep on the job. Silverspoon was the first to notice during his early jog. He's got a bee in his bonnet."

I walked over to the capstan where Silverspoon tapped his foot quickly on the deck and watched the anchor chain reeling in. In front of him stood the two sailors responsible for the night watch. "All I ask for is basic discipline," he said testily. "Following orders. Completing your assignments on time and under budget. Now this? Falling asleep on your watch? Bunch of lazy bureaucrats. I oughta ride you like a Brahma bull." The sailors hung their heads.

From his shoulder, Krill threw his wings back and humped the air as if he were fighting to stay on a bucking bull. Tosspot stood on the opposite side of the capstan and popped his bullwhip in the air. "Out of uniform, aren't we,

IshcaBible?" He snapped the whip again.

"I don't know, marshal. Was thinkin' about taking a dive. See what's down there. You want to come?" He wriggled his whip along the deck of the ship. I knew he wanted to flog me. Do it, I thought, just give me an excuse, you jowly creep. My hands rubbed the polished leather of my holsters.

The anchor chain wound in, showing abrasions on the metal for at least thirty feet before it reached the cut. The specksynder and the chief engineer examined the break in the two-inch-thick link of iron chain. "It's not been sawed," said the engineer in a saucy Irish accent. "More like a squeeze—but my God! there's never been a bolt cutter made that's large enough, or powerful enough, to cut a rod of that girth."

Wrong John cringed at the words "bolt cutter." He reached behind his back and tried to scratch his lump, but couldn't touch it. He spun and walked to his roundhouse. "Pot of coffee, Ish. Strong."

A couple of hours later, the war council convened on the cannon deck of *Liberty*. I got there early and found Sir Yes Sir setting up a tall easel at the narrow bow end of the deck, in between cannons nineteen and twenty. Tatanka was with him. The Lakota hung oil lamps from wire off the rough ceiling beams, one every five feet or so. The yellow light of the lamps illuminated the rows of cannon on either side of the deck, rolled back from their closed firing bays, chained in position, and held fast by cleats in the decking. Stacked between each gun was a pyramid of cannonballs, a keg of gunpowder, wadding, fuse, and a tamping rod leaning against the shiny black barrel.

Sir Yes Sir spoke to Tatanka, who listened and grunted. "I can't do it, Tatanka," said the diplomat, placing various exhibits around his easel. "I can't go to the Common Countries and make a case for war based on what we've got. It's just absurd."

"Don't do it," Tatanka said, reaching up to light a lamp.

"Don't do it. Don't do it. Wouldn't that be nice? I really shouldn't. It's unbelievable. Dick Little presents credible evidence of a real threat, and we do nothing. Now I've got innuendo and nursery rhymes, and they'll want to start a war over it."

The other officers and captain Silverspoon arrived and took up various positions of recline among the cannon. Silverspoon wore his flouncy blue hat, long over his face and back, plumes of red and white off the poop deck. Krill stood on his shoulder, clucking to himself. Yo Yo wore his eye patch, his monocle in his right eye, a red silk headband across his forehead, and his customary gold nose ring. Dagger had on his blue tunic that fit him like an outer skin. Dagger had on his blue tunic that fit him like an outer skin. Pinch wore a plain blue dress and her fore-and-aft black officers hat. She sat on a cannon and crossed a long, ungainly leg over her knee. Tatanka left the room.

Chief put the full force of his icy gaze on Sir Yes Sir. "I would hope that by now our case for invading Iraq is all but concluded. Show us what you've got."

The diplomat walked to his easel at the narrow end of the deck. His head bumped an oil lamp, sending his shadow left, then right of his body. He reached down and placed his first exhibit on the easel. Mounted to a board was a chunk of coconut with a dark stain on the husk. "Exhibit A," he said, gesturing at the easel with a wooden pointer. "A fragment of exploding coconut found on the palace grounds of Shalong's primary residence. Laboratory analysis has confirmed the substance on the husk to be a volatile explosive compound."

Sir Yes Sir removed from his easel the board that held his fragment of exploding coconut. He reached behind the easel for the next exhibit: a thick strand of rubber mounted to a board. "You've seen the weapon, gentlemen, now observe the delivery system." He touched the black rubber cord with the tip of his wooden pointer. "Exhibit B: a section of flexible rubber, the sort forbidden in Iraq by Resolution 221 of the Common Countries. The discovery of this rubber launching cable, clearly of a recent vintage, demonstrates not only the will, gentlemen, but the capacity to launch one of the world's most destructive—well, not *the most*, but certainly a dangerous weapon, in the direction of America." Sir Yes Sir cleared his throat, and tapped the easel with his pointer. Gunny harrumphed. Dagger sucked his teeth and crossed his arms.

"Would that be called—in layman's terms—a big ass rubber band?" asked the captain. SYS nodded. Wrong John closed his eyes and nodded quickly in return. "Well, there you go. Got him dead to rights. I can already see his prize sword hangin' right here." He slapped his left hip. "Daddy couldn't take it from him, but sonny boy, he'll damn sure strip the butcher of his cleaver—mark it." He slapped his hip again. Dagger coughed falsely. He stood and walked in front of the cannon near him, holding a small wooden keg. He tipped it and poured black powder into the barrel.

Crude raised his hand a few inches past the top of his head. Wrong John nodded at him. "I was just wondering what the launch distance of these exploding coconuts would be, if, let's say, Shalong were to put them in the hands of his partner, aka AQ, the evildoer."

"The range is approximately three hundred yards," said Sir Yes Sir, looking up at the rafters. The officers shifted on their cannon; some coughed and cleared their throats.

"*BRACK!* But in a strong wing, in a strong wind, it'll carry."

It didn't take a military expert to recognize the tomfoolery of any claim Iraq's weapons posed a threat to America or its allies. Let's face it, Frank, they were talking about glorified slingshots and exploding coconuts. Give them credit, though, for the good bushwhacker sense to know fear is a much more potent weapon than any top-secret artillery hidden in the sands of Arabia. A convincing yarn rains fear like grapeshot falling from the skies.

"Have you nailed down the union between Shalong and Quota?" asked Dagger, tamping a wad into the barrel with the ramrod.

"I've tried. Believe me, I've tried. There just doesn't seem to be one," Sir Yes Sir confessed. "Shalong's brand of secular tyranny—throwing on the robes, so to speak, only when it suits his political will—is reprehensible to Quota. Shalong persecutes his own people—devout Muslims, most of them. Quota may hate Shalong worse than we do."

"Bull dust!" shouted Silverspoon. "I am the most hateful man in the world!"

"This is *very* disappointing, SYS," Chief shook his head and dug in his ear with his pinkie. "The AQ/Shalong marriage is fundamental, fundamental to our entire future. I'm looking for them in bed together, and you have them hurling camel dung at one another across the desert. Whew. Pretty disappointing." He rolled a cannonball down the barrel. Tatanka arrived with a big metal bowl full of freshly steamed mussels. He set them directly in the center of the twin cannon batteries. "Fresh mussels," he said, turned and walked away.

"Mussels? Shee-it," said Silverspoon. He raised his fists above his shoulders and flexed his biceps. "Read 'em & weep, boys."

"Impressive ordnance, sir," Yo Yo said. He placed his finger horns next to his head and smiled. Silverspoon mirrored him. He grabbed a mussel and threw it at Yo Yo. The blind gunner didn't see it coming and it bounced off his head.

"That'll go in your stats as an error, Yo Yo," Silverspoon chided.

Pinch opened a mussel and dug the flesh out with her long upper teeth. "Those little black gems with a hunk'a meat inside remind me of a certain somebody in a black bathing suit," she said, casting a sly look at Yo Yo. He smiled, picked the mussel up off the floor and threw it at her. She caught it easily.

"Detroit Wolverines," said Wrong John, giving her a thumbs up.

Sir Yes Sir removed the exhibit of his rubber launcher exhibit and set it on the deck. He picked up a corkboard onto which several crude sketches had been tacked. The pencil drawings showed explosions in cities, people with their hair on fire, an American flag torn in half, collapsed buildings. "We discovered these drawings in Shalong's main palace. They may be plans for an attack by Iraq against America."

"Boy," said the captain, "have we got some intelligence capacity or have we got some intelligence capacity? Or, have *we* got some intelligence capacity?" Pinch and Crude nodded. Dagger prepared a fuse for his cannon. "God," Silverspoon continued, "the man is a terrible artist. My five-year-old granddaughter could do better than that."

"I didn't realize your daughter had a child," said Crude.

Wrong John wrinkled his nose at the Oil Czar and gave him a dirty look. "It's a figment of speech, dummy." Crude put his hands up and nodded quickly.

"We're not entirely sure he drew the plans, sir," the diplomat said. "These were found in the nursery—but, by comparing the pencil strokes to known writings of Shalong, we're up to fifty-five percent sure they were drawn by him."

Dagger sucked his teeth ominously, sounding as if he had a second and third row of choppers behind the front ones. "I gave you an assignment, Mr. Sir Yes Sir, and this is the best you can come up with? Exploding coconuts? Giant rubber bands? Stick figures from the nursery?"

"I realize it's not much, sir. None of it would stand up in court—not that we believe in the institution." He backed up a step and held up his hands. "I think we've got to face facts. Shalong is a bad guy who lost all his toys. Ten years of sanctions and inspections completely declawed him. We should redouble our effort in Afghanistan. Go all out to get your squid, Mr. Captain. Bring in AQ and every organization slimed by his tentacles. That's where the real progress will be had in the war on terror."

"Isn't that sweet," said Gunny, placing his clasped hands over his heart and batting his eyes. "Can we call up Bubba and his liberal Europe toads to see if they want us to smooch anybody's butt for them?" He stood and kicked the cannon, then pretended it didn't hurt.

Silverspoon stood, slapped his hands, and rubbed them together. "Well, that was easier than I thought. War on Squid got itself done pronto. Get out my sticks, Ish. Time to hit the links."

"I wouldn't make my tee time just yet, Mr. Captain," said Chief. Wrong John crossed his arms and frowned. "In the intelligence game, it's all about your sources," Dagger went on. "Everybody sees the situation through a different lens. You just have to keep looking until you find one that fits your preference."

"It's like the Bible, isn't it, Ish?" said the marshal slowly, in his most superior tone. "It can be twisted to make just about any point you want it to."

"That how you read it, marshal?" I replied.

Up from behind the cannon Dagger had been loading, rose a small figure in a dark robe and a white turban. He had bushy brown eyebrows, a long, sharp nose, double chin, and a wide amphibian mouth. I could not believe it, Frank—another character from *Moby-Dick*. This one Mr. Melville called the Parsee, from a sect of the Persians known as Zoroastrian. The Parsee's name was Fedallah, and Ishmael described him thus:

"The figure that now stood by its bows was tall and swart, with one white tooth evilly protruding from its steel-like lips. A rumpled Chinese jacket of black cotton funereally investing him, with wide black trowsers of the same dark stuff. But strangely crowning this ebonness was a glistening white plaited turban, the living hair braided and coiled round and round atop his head."

Starbuck, the first mate, was less kind in his description, saying, "I take that Fedallah to be the devil in disguise... The reason why you don't see his tail, is because he tucks it up out of sight; he carries it coiled away in his pocket, I guess... Why, do you see, the old man is hard bent after that White Whale, and the devil there is trying to come round him, and get him to swap away his silver watch, or his soul, or something of that sort, and then he'll surrender Moby Dick."

Dagger's Parsee stepped from behind the cannon, waved his right arm in small circles, and bowed deeply. "I think most of you know Makmoud Cherubic, don't you?" asked Chief.

"Know 'im? Hell, he's practically part of the family. How's it hangin', Mak?" asked the captain. Makmoud smiled and bowed slightly.

"For those of you who aren't as familiar, Mr. Cherubic is an exiled Iraqi who has worked with us for years to remove the tyrant Shalong. He heads the largest expatriate Iraqi resistance organization in the world, and, if the Silverspoon Mandate is served, will be the next Shah of Iraq." Makmoud Cherubic waved his right hand in a circle and bowed deeply.

Pinch elbowed me and whispered from behind her hand. "Biggest pirate in Arabia. Calls himself a banker—the sort who embezzles more shekels than he deposits."

"Now, if you don't mind, SYS, step aside and behold some of the most damning intelligence I've ever seen—and I've been in the game a *long* time." Dagger struck a flint against the fuse in his cannon. It hissed, sparked, and smoked. Chief ran to the other side of the deck and ducked behind a cannon, like a boy who had lit a Fourth of July firecracker.

"The panel!" cried Sir Yes Sir, reaching out with his big hands. "You forgot to open—"

BOOM!

The cannon ball exploded from the barrel, shattered the closed wooden bay and sent shards of wood and thick black sulfur smoke throughout the deck. Gunny, who had been sitting closest, had several long splinters sticking from his face. Pinch ran over and tended to him. Out of the smoke walked Makmoud Cherubic, holding in the palms of his hands an object covered by a red and blue Persian scarf, on top of which was perched an oily crow. It cawed and flew away out the smoky, jagged hole as Cherubic placed the object on the barrel of a shiny black cannon. A perfect crystal ball sat before us. He waved his hands over the ball and spoke incantations to it. He peered deeply into it, concentrating so that his thick eyebrows nearly touched.

"I see yellow cake bakeries, mixing the explosive dessert, in the desert. They cover it with venom of the Amazon poison-dart frog—huge, steaming cake tins, great, bubbling pots of poison, each the size of a spermaceti rendering vat." The Parsee seemed to go into a trance, and stood before the crystal ball shaking. I noticed something etched in the side of his ball: "Made in Tehran."

"What's up with the frog-frosted birthday cake?" asked Wrong John, scratching his cheek.

Chief rose from his hiding place behind the port cannon battery and brushed his shiny dagger against the gray stubble of his cheek. "The yellow cake is a compound perfected by the pygmies of the Congo. It is ten, perhaps a hundred times more explosive than regular gunpowder. The venom of the Amazon poison-dart frog is the most lethal in the world. One drop the size of a pinhead is enough to paralyze or kill a hundred strapping young men."

"Alas," interjected Tosspot, "even those chaste youth protected from the sin of fornication by healthy self-pleasuring."

"Hee-haw! Hee-haw!' brayed Krill. Wrong John chuckled and poked his parrot in the belly. Tosspot looked away and curled down the corners of his mouth. Smoke from Dagger's blast slowly escaped through the jagged hole in the ship.

"Shalong has dreamed of getting his hands on the frog cakes for years," said Dagger. "And now, based on the intelligence the Shah has provided, it looks like his dream has come true. Shalong is creating a weapon of unimaginable mass hysteria."

"*BRACK!* Spin potential off the charts—off the charts! Weapons of Mass Hysteria. Weapons of Mass Hysteria." Krill hopped from Wrong John's shoulder to a cannon. He jumped up and down. "Everybody will be saying it. Shaking in their shoes. Get out a press release: 'Shalong builds Weapons of Mass Hysteria. Terror! Terror! Squid! Giant Squid! Exploding tentacles everywhere! Thank God for the Silverspoon Mandate. Safety is at hand! Preemptive measures, swift and sure. Silverspoon Mandate! Safety from evil! *BRACK!*'" Krill danced across the black back of the cannon, whistling a short phrase from *Dixie.* Wrong John pried open a mussel and dug with his teeth the meat from the shell.

The Arab in a black robe and white turban snapped from his trance. He looked again into the crystal and spoke, " I see, I see, Shalong and Al Quota, soaking together in a hot tub, playing footsy underwater and plotting their next move. I see, I see, the two of them choosing targets in America. I see huge explosions in Boston, Houston, Denver, Detroit, and Miami, people choking, bleeding from the mouths and ears, dying by the thousands, and—and Shalong and AQ, hugging and smooching, dancing together like dervishes. I see—"

"That's enough, Shah," said the Chief. He had gone over to Silverspoon, whose head hung down and shook slowly side-to-side.

"God no, not again. I can't take another hungry scorpion," moaned Wrong John. Chief rubbed his shoulders. Krill flapped and waddled over and hummed *Pop Goes the Weasel.*

"We get the picture, Makmoud," said the Chief. "I just have to tell you, this is some of the most actionable intelligence I've ever seen. Superb, Shah, just superb." The Arab bowed deeply. Chief looked over at the black diplomat. "You see, SYS, the Shalong/AQ connect is even stronger than we thought. And those weapons—talk about spooky: dead ringer for the Giant Squid."

"Don't forget that gold doubloon I nailed to the mainmast. Goes to the first sucker cries out, "Thar she wriggles! Thar be none other than Wrong John's Giant Squid!" cried the captain. Gold doubloon? I thought. Now there's some alchemy.

"You can't be serious," said Sir Yes Sir. "Crystal ball gazing from the most vindictive Iraqi on the planet? Uh-uh." He shook his head firmly. "I can't go to the Common Countries and make our case without concrete evidence." The diplomat stood with his arms on his hips, a fierce tension lacing his bony brow and forehead.

"Wake up man!" shouted Chief Dagger, spit flying from his dry, red lips. "We already *have* the goddamned mandate! It just needs a little window-dressing!"

"Please," said the Parsee, holding up his hands and patting the air with them. "I have. I have." He reached into some bag hidden under his black robe and pulled out what looked like a johnnycake, sitting on the palm of his hand. "Observe the yellow cake, baked, as are hundreds every day in mobile yellow cake labs on the street corners of Baghdad." He reached into his robe with his other hand and produced a photo of a food stall on the street of an Arab town. "Behold. Shalong mobile weapons lab."

"Pictures! Pretty pictures. *BRACK!*"

"That's not intelligence!" yelled Sir Yes Sir.

"Hey! It ain't based on IQ. It's based on AQ!" shouted Silverspoon.

"No more arguments, Sir Yes Sir," said Dagger, lowering his eyes and flicking his blade back and forth over his Adam's apple as if sharpening a razor on a leather strop. "We took a huge risk on you—a real test of our colorblindness. You knew the conditions that came with your *race distinction*. I would hate to see a whole people fall from grace because you were pig-headed and refused your duty. Follow orders, man!"

Sir Yes Sir turned away from Chief and exhaled hard. He rubbed his temples with his left hand. Suddenly he stood straight and walked quickly out of the cannon battery and up the hatch.

Chapter XXIX

Johnny Edwards

Over the next few days, Sir Yes Sir frequently visited the kitchen and joined in meal preparations with Tatanka. The two big, dark-skinned men chopped carrots, peeled potatoes, trimmed fat, soaked beans, and did not speak for long stretches of time. I sometimes watched them and smoked, imagining they were two black walnut trees, moving about as people, yet having the voices of trees. The short conversations they had were spoken in code, and I did not fully grasp their meaning.

"Peel the carrots?" asked the diplomat.

"No. Better protection," Tatanka answered, filling a pot with water.

"Stove, wood?" Sir Yes Sir held up a length of oak.

"Too hot already."

"Bowls I think, not plates."

"Yes. Plates spill too easy."

I was unable to break the code and didn't feel it my place to ask questions. I could only assume Tatanka was advising Sir Yes Sir on the guerilla strike he was about to make on the Common Countries. Dagger had nicely fitted his blade between the diplomat's ribs, and twisted expertly, so that Sir Yes Sir, wincing and bloody, nevertheless accepted his orders. Armed with the "most actionable intelligence I've ever seen," as Chief put it, Sir Yes Sir embarked on his bushwhacker holdup of Common Countries. He wanted one simple certificate they held deep in their safe: a resolution sanctioning force against Iraq.

On the night of his expected return from the mission, *Liberty* hosted a party called "African Nights." It was a celebration in the style of the Silverspoon Mandate—a preemptive whoopdedo in advance of an assumed victory. Dagger chose the African theme to "give the negro a warm fuzzy for the honor he has brought his people." Wrong John, being a self proclaimed "nature lover," ordered the ship made into a barnyard of African animals for the shindig.

Two bull elephants were chained to the fore and mizzenmasts. A giraffe wandered loose and nibbled on the furled sails. A troop of chimpanzees swung in the rigging, yowling, screaming and hooting. A dark-maned lion paced in a metal cage on the foredeck. Torches dipped in spermaceti burned from metal holders off the masts and rails, lighting the deck with a cannibal glow. Tatanka had the try-works going with a wood fire; the try-pots boiled a stew of whole lambs, goats, and calves, meant, I was told, to invoke the feeling of a tribal African conquest orgy. A group of Africans dressed in bright robes and feathered headgear banged on drums, shook bone rattles. Dancers wore skimpy zebra-skin outfits and pranced about on the aft deck.

The party guests that evening were not members of Congress but rather friends from business who had their corporate flags flying off the masthead. Silverspoon wandered among them, well within his comfort zone, telling jokes, slapping backs, shooting love puffs from his finger guns. Upon his head sat the front-to-back, blue-humped hat with its flowery red and white entrails wafting out the rear. He adorned the guests with nicknames only he could use—and they had given him one of their own: "Spoons," they called him, because their fit with him was like spoons in a drawer of silver. I stepped into one after another conversation extolling the virtues of the newly minted Silverspoon Mandate. By this time no one commented on my Polynesian face tattoos. I reckon it was understood a quick-drawing savage was a good and welcome addition to a crew of ambitious pirates.

"This here mandate's a humdinger. Best thing ever happened to business," gushed Slick of Endrun Energy, holding a tankard of beer and smoking a fat stogy. "The days of profit margins based on actual performance are *gone.* Nowadays you just decide in advance how much you want to make and you rig the markets to guarantee you hit your numbers."

"Sure," added Blastcap, president of Cannon Fodder, Inc., taking a big puff from his cigar. "And if something doesn't go just like you planned, send in your commandos from accounting to preempt the quarterly report."

"Don't forget to bust those terrorist unions before they send in the storks after your net profits," commented a man from FatCo.

"Cut vacation time, increase the workweek, lower health benefits, discontinue pensions, boot the fed safety inspectors—," bubbled a woman in

238 Ⓢ *James E. Churches*

a full-length mink coat.

"Damn right!" enthused Slick. "You got to hit them *before* they hit you."

"We got us a *mandate* to do it!" shouted Blastcap.

"Just wait'll this war gets cookin'. Goot God almighty!" Slick boomed, raising his beer and saying a toast to Wrong John Silverspoon, their patron saint. One of the elephants trumpeted. The other answered, and the lion roared. The African drummers pounded out a driving rhythm for their gyrating dancers, whose smooth black skin glistened in the pulsating torch light.

Tosspot, Dagger, Yo Yo and Silverspoon stood in front of the lion on the quarterdeck and took in the gala. Krill dug his talons into the right shoulder of his boss's blue blazer. They all smoked cigars, even Krill, who had one parrot-sized. Wrong John didn't light his. I could not understand a man who would smoke a cigar without smoking it. He just chewed on it and spit it out, slobbery piece by piece. A big orange moon, only a few days from full, rose over the shoreline forest, casting a rippling arrow of light across the river.

"It's a great night for *Liberty*, gentlemen, a great night," Dagger opined softly, taking a big puff from his stogy and blowing a cloud of smoke at the orange disk low in the sky.

"Warms the cockles of the old ticker," said Gunny. "Knowing the world community has bowed to our dominance."

"Mandate mambo! *BRACK!* Mandate mambo!" Krill danced back and forth on Wrong John's shoulder, to the rhythm of the African drummers, kicking his stubby legs like a cancan dancer. Wrong John and the officers laughed at him.

"Thanks to 10-10, who in their right mind could possibly deny us the sovereign right—nay, the duty—to attack aggressive and dangerous regimes before they attack us?" added Tosspot.

Wrong John chewed off the sloppy end of his cold cigar and spit it to the planks, grinding it into the oak as if it were a cockroach. "We didn't pick this fight, but we're damn sure gonna start it."

I wandered to the bow, thinking I might find Sweet up there—if she were anywhere but holed up in her cabin, grieving the rape of Lady Liberty. It was a little dark up that way, and at first I didn't see her. The end of a cigarette glowed red. It was her.

"Come up for air finally?" I asked her, sidling up quietly.

"I wouldn't quite call it breathing, but yeah, I had to get out of that tomb. When's the diplomat due?" She pulled on her smoke and exhaled her trademark.

"Any time, I guess." I placed a smoke in my lips, drug the white tip of a match against my jagged thumbnail; it popped and hissed alive with fire. "I do fear for him, though."

"Oh?"

"He's going in there armed with spit wads and a slingshot. I can't see him getting out of it without them tying him at the ankles behind his horse, slapping it on the butt, and having him drug clean outta town."

"You don't think we've got a strong case to attack Shalong?"

"Ma'am, I don't think this is about a 'case' at all."

"What's it about?" A couple of chimps scampered over us, playing in the jib boom, jabbering and cackling. Sweet looked up at them and smiled. The flickering golden light of the torches revealed the curves of her graceful neck.

"It's plain bullying. I know how it works. You go in and take what you want. Then you make it sound like you had to do it because of the horrible way you'd been treated. You get some newspaperman to run a story about your heroic effort to confront tyranny—like we did all those years with Johnny Edwards. It's the biggest flimflam since Mug-Wump's pill for preventing gonorrhea."

"Who's Johnny Edwards?"

Uh-oh, I had revealed another part of my identity: the long and fruitful relationship I had with the newspaperman John Edwards, who wrote of us in the *St. Louis Dispatch,* in February of 1875: "They are outlaws through no fault or crime other than participating in a civil war that was not successful, and are now so wantonly and unjustly hunted and denounced by all who have partisan passions to gratify." We figured out pretty early on that you can't remain a popular and heroic Robin Hood figure without a constant and unending stream of propaganda in the newspaper.

"Edwards? Oh, he was this clown used to juggle for us at parties." I doubt if she bought the fib, but she didn't ask about if further. I was about to inquire of her feelings concerning the marshal, and what he had done to her figurehead, when Sir Yes Sir steamed up in a small dreadnought and came aboard. He looked extremely weary to me, shocked and bewildered by the circus on board *Liberty*. Tatanka came up out of the galley and clapped a hand on the diplomat's shoulder. Sir Yes Sir clapped a hand on his in return. "Can't peel a potato with a soup spoon," he said to the Sioux, speaking in that code of theirs. One of the elephants rose on its hind legs and landed hard on the deck, sending a shudder through the whole ship.

The drumming stopped. Wrong John and the other officers hurried to Sir Yes Sir's side. Pinch had a gaudy African headdress made of ostrich plumes, blue parrot feathers, and red ibis feathers. She removed the diplomat's angular black officer's cap and placed the outlandish headdress on his head. He smiled weakly.

Dagger stepped forward and shook Sir Yes Sir's hand. "You make us proud of our colorblindness tonight, Sir Yes Sir. You pave the way for all Negroes who may some day aspire to the heights of power."

"I think we should meet—in private. There are a few things—" Sir Yes Sir began.

"Nonsense," the captain interrupted. "We're among friends here. Any good news you have to share is more than welcome among this grape of groot—er, group of great American patriots." He waved his arm and the drummers pounded a furious beat. The women dancers cavorted to the diplomat, swept him up, and danced him to the try-works. They spun around him in a flowing, pulsing, sensual weave of long black arms and legs, shining by the light of the torches. He turned slowly, half smiling, half grimacing, moving his head a little to the beat. The gathered business leaders formed a tight half moon in front of the try-works. Then the drumming stopped.

The circle of African women opened, and in walked tall, lanky Speck with the leg of a goat on the end of a whaleman's pitchfork. He shoved it at Sir Yes Sir. He slowly reached out and pulled it from the tines.

"Tell us now, Mr. Sir Yes Sir. How soon can we invade Iraq?" Dagger asked. The business leaders roared their approval.

Sir Yes Sir stared at the naked brown boiled leg of goat in his hand. He threw it to the deck. "There will be no invasion. The Common Countries turned us down."

The moment froze. No one moved or spoke, except that I could sense something like a leak, a slow drain, or a fast rot, as of a pumpkin that collapses in on itself on a warm day after a hard freeze. Finally, one of the business leaders broke the spell.

"No invasion? What do you mean no invasion? I thought we had a mandate for war profits," came an unsteady but rising angry voice from the rear of the half circle.

Another business leader spoke up. "We were promised a war—a *real war*—not this crappy little thing in Afghanistan."

"My stock went up ten points based on projected sales of my Combat Ouch Kit. What am I supposed to tell the shareholders?" asked the small, bespectacled president of A-1 Medical.

"Which are *all of us*," growled Yo Yo. Angry murmuring passed through the crowd.

"We were promised a *global war* on squid," someone shouted.

"A never-ending money grab from the public till," hollered another.

"Tentacles reaching everywhere, huge monster eyes, always looking for an opening."

"Rid the world of calamari, you said."

Wrong John shrunk back into the darkness.

"We want our war, god damn it!"

"Yeah!" roared the crowd.

The giraffe pushed its way through the crowd, lowered its long neck, and picked up the goat leg. It carried it to the side of the ship and dropped it in the water. A thrashing, splashing sound, as of crocodiles, came from the water after it landed.

Sir Yes Sir raised his head and looked around, seeming to notice he was surrounded—angry mob on one side, boiling pots of whole goats and calves on the other. He made eye contact with Tatanka, who hit his chest twice. Sir Yes Sir tapped himself once in return, his eyes shifting nervously about the crowd.

Chief glared at him, his dagger out in front of his face, turning and flashing in the golden light. I couldn't tell if he was going to use it on Sir Yes

242 ～ James E. Churches

Sir or gouge his own eye out as a sacrifice to the hungry entrepreneurs. "You are a *failure*," he hissed. "You didn't make the case, because you *didn't believe!* You sold us out because your soft, liberal heart wanted evidence, wanted proof, wanted to be fair and reasonable."

"I think we can figure out what went wrong—down in Batguano Castle," snarled Tosspot. He slung his whip over Sir Yes Sir's head and snapped it fiercely. I could see by Tatanka's taut arms and his flexing jaw that he was about to pounce. I felt Basma's hand on my arm, squeezing. My left hand went to Widowmaker. My right arm went around her waist.

Then, from out of the darkness came the parrot, Krill, flapping his little wings madly—and actually flying, over the try-pots to land of Sir Yes Sir's shoulder. Out of breath, the bird's chest rapidly heaved. After a minute, he calmed down and spoke.

"*BRACK!* Carpe diem, gentlemen. Carpe diem. Seize the day. This is no setback. What's that? What's that? The diplomat didn't fail. No. No. He paved the way for the mandate. Forced us to embrace it. Forced us to *act on it.*" Krill flapped his wings and whistled three shrill notes.

"Is this a mandate? or is it a *mandate?* Do we really believe? or are we looking for a permission slip from the Common Countries? *BRACK* almighty! The CC says no. The CC says yes. The CC says fish for breakfast. So what? We are America. We do whatever the hell we want! Got God. Got God. Got God."

Dagger sheathed his knife, smiled his sideways half smile, and began to clap. He stepped into the circle and put his arm around Krill and Sir Yes Sir. "He's pretty good, for a parrot. And he's right. We don't need the CC to give us a *mandate.* We already got the damn thing. Al Quota and his suicide squid handed it to us on a silver platter. The Silverspoon Mandate is our Manifest Destiny. It is our right, our duty, our privilege, our passion, and there is nothing we cannot make conform to it."

"We are challenged to act on God's will," offered Tosspot. "His desire for us is to spread, as did the pioneers before us, beyond the continent, out across the world. New World Borders, He asks of us, and it would be impious of us not to obey."

"Were we defeated today by the Common Countries?" asked Yo Yo. Some nodded to the question, others shrugged, most stood still, not wanting to react until the correct reaction was revealed. "I hardly think so. The Europeans betrayed their cowardice. The CC expressed its irrelevance. The *United States*, as it has had to do so many times in its glorious history, stood alone, a solitary vestige of courage against the faceless, omnipresent Giant Squid of Terror. In its weakness, its lack of resolve, its desire never to hurt anyone's feelings, socialist Europe gave us no choice today but to take history by the scruff of the neck and shove it forward in accord with our own designs." Murmurs of approval moved through the crowd.

"The Silverspoon Mandate is much more than a doctrine of national defense," said Chief happily. "It is the total conviction in the truth of our cause, and the courage to do whatever it takes to achieve our ends. Nothing that happens, whether it was our original desire or not, whether it stands utterly contrary to our stated goals, whether it is the complete opposite of what we said just the day before, *nothing* cannot, and should not, be turned to our advantage."

"*BRACK!* Power of conviction. Power of conviction. UN says no. Pretty Bubba says, 'Sorry, I won't do it then.' Wrong! Never show weakness! Never! Encourages the enemy. Encourages the enemy. UN committed terrorism. *BRACK!* Terrorism!" Krill leaped from Sir Yes Sir's shoulder, landed on the deck with a flop, rolled on his back, and trembled with spasms as if he had been poisoned.

Dagger laughed and shook his head. "Oh, you *are* good." He clapped his hands slowly. "He's absolutely right, ladies and gentlemen. The Common Countries have attempted to sabotage our mandate to rid the world of calamari, and in so doing have sided with evil. Conviction. Conviction. It is the confidence that we are right, and anyone who tries to stop us is not just an obstacle, not just a hindrance, but is, in fact, *a terrorist*, and subject to our unmitigated wrath." He waved at the captain, who emerged from the shadows to stand at his side. Tosspot picked up Krill and softly sang his new anthem, *The Battle Hymn of the Republic*, while standing at attention and saluting.

"This man here, Wrong John Silverspoon, our captain, is perhaps the only man, the only man ever to captain *Liberty*, who has the resolve, the tenacity, and the shrewdness to bring his own mandate to its fullest fruition,"

Chief said. Silverspoon smiled as Dagger put his hand on his shoulder. Everyone applauded. I couldn't tell if Wrong John yet understood what was being asked of him, but he had an uncanny ability to divine the emotional tenor of any situation, and an inflatable head that ballooned easily from the praise of others.

"Let's talk about a game plan," he said, his Texas twang a little higher strung than usual. "I'm going to speak my mind to the world, friends. I see evil, I'm calling it out. I see weakness, I'm going to shame it. I see any wavering, any doubt, any question of our motives, I'm going to ridicule it. I see any criticism here at home, I'll call it for the treason that it is. I see evil, I'll stomp on it. It's Silverspoon time, and I will not stand for anything less than absolute devotion to this flag here." He gestured toward the top of the mast, where the flags representing all of the corporations flew, obscuring America's flag. "That one, there—up in there—with the red and white thingies and the stars." He laughed lightly.

"Let's hear it for the diplomat!" shouted someone in the crowd.

"Hip, hip, hurray. Hip, hip, hurray!" The group yelled.

Some of them grabbed Sir Yes Sir, hoisted him on their shoulders, and carried him around the ship. Wrong John turned, crossed his arms, and kicked the try-works with the tip of his black cowboy boot. The drummers pounded on their skins, dancers cavorted behind the entourage, lions roared. Sir Yes Sir sat on his perch, wearing his African headdress, a confused look on his face. I recalled the last time he rode like that, after he had harpooned the mother whale in the Gulf of Mexico. Now, here he was, riding high, saluted for having *completely missed.*

The crowd fell in line and began to chant. "Thank you for failing, the mandate always wins. Thank you for failing, the mandate always wins."

I scratched my shaved head up under my bowler. An odd thing had happened that night. Something got turned on its head: apes in the rigging, a meat-eating giraffe, failure now success. I recognized it as a threshold, something that once crossed cannot be returned from, like a bridge that is burnt behind you. It keeps the enemy at bay, but it also prevents you from ever going back the way you came. Something had changed that night. I recognized it—had made a similar crossing at some point in my bushwhacking career. That thing we called reality, the common understanding that holds us together as a people, had been turned over on its back like a stinkbug, and no matter how hard it wriggled its long, fork-toed legs, it would not be able to right itself again.

Chapter XXX

Squid Alert

Ah, Frank, you know how boys are. Once they get a stinkbug on its back they can't keep from poking it with hot matches and tearing off its legs with tweezers. After Silverspoon and his brigands understood they could flip that pest called reality, and it couldn't turn back over, they set about rebuilding it with the number of legs, the color of skin, and the smell that suited them. Theirs was still a stinkbug, it just went by another name—but that didn't mean it smelled any better.

In order to consolidate their failure with the United Nations, Yo Yo, Sir Yes Sir, and Crude went on a victory tour of the world. Yo Yo took the European leg, calculated to humiliate and belittle our traditional allies for choosing squid over hamburgers. The diplomat took a trip to Israel, and hand delivered a gift-wrapped defense of aggression. Crude embarked to the Far East, preaching the gospel of energy conservation to the Chinese, who, if they got going in the blubber game, could soak up all the extra fat in one dim sum dumpling. He was also to threaten rogue states with the dire consequences of disobeying the Silverspoon Mandate.

In the meantime, Chief, Krill, and Tosspot prepared a grand domestic offensive to deploy the Silverspoon Mandate. After weeks of preparation, they held their *Congreso Mandato* at a giant underground aquarium deep beneath the capital. Pinch described the installation as a "conservative fish tank," dedicated to capturing and breeding marine mollusks of all varieties and distributing them throughout America.

The night of the gala Tatanka and I walked down flights of stairs for five minutes before we reached the floor where the aquarium stood. My black cowboy boots clicked on the white marble, cast over with a rippling blue light from the aquarium. The only illumination came from the fish tank, which had banks of gas lamps above its surface. We walked to the tank, twenty feet tall, a hundred feet wide, and equally as long. The bottom was covered with large round granite boulders in shades of pink, yellow, and brown, lying in a bed of white sand. A booklet provided at the door contained illustrations and names of all the critters inside.

All manner of octopi—in mottled patterns of rust red, blotchy emerald green, deep black, blue ringed golden circles, with tentacle like the edges of lace, all sizes, each with big, lumpy eyes—slunk and slithered along the boulders. Colonies of green-lipped mussels, oysters, and big, brown-striped clams clung to the rocks or were half buried in the sand. Red cuttlefish with black zigzag stripes flew through the water on undulating wings, their tentacles stretched out behind them. Spiral-shelled nautilus floated and wiggled their innumerable legs. Swimming clams eked through the water like puffs of orange hair. Angelic tooth snails crawled through the cracks in the rocks. Sea slugs, bright purple, red, and green, some with wormed lines of white or yellow across their oval bodies, lay among the rocks like underwater lichen. Giant clams sat on the bottom, their rough, fluted shells five feet across. Nudibranch floated in a clump, reminding me of a handful of white-tipped, see-through ash leaves. There were chiton, scallops, limpet, and squid—thousands of squid.

Some of the squid were long and brown with dark spots. Others were golden, or blue, striped like a tiger, or a zebra, or spotted like a jaguar. They swam with fanlike pectoral fins that undulated and rippled through the water, moving them along slowly, until, for some reason they detected danger, and they changed color, or jetted away and left an outline of their bodies in dark ink. One of them, the jet-black vampire squid, shot out glowing gobs of mucus that left a confusing light show—and disappeared. All of them seemed to be hunting, and every so often a larger one shot out tentacles at a small one, pulled it in, and ripped it to pieces.

"I always wondered what the night eagle looked like when it dove," said Tatanka, tapping the glass with his finger.

"My God, Tatanka, all these things are related—like people and monkeys—all part of the same bizarre family." I scratched my head up under the black bowler. "Look at the size of this place. And a hundred feet underground, all done in concrete and glass. There's no way they built this thing *after* 10-10. This here's been in the ground a *long time*."

People filed down the stairs in a steady stream until there must have been seven hundred of us gathered around the aquarium. Someone shouted from the podium on a stage that had been set up at one end of the aquarium, near the stairs. It was Captain Wrong John Silverspoon.

"Welcome everyone, to *Congreso Mandato*," he said, greeted by hearty applause. "There may be *that* Congress, over on the Hill, making its laws and acting smart, but we know who *really* runs this country." He nodded and waved to the cheering, whistles, and applause.

"That dummy Al Quota fell right into our trap. Now we got us the mandate to fling squid all across America. Battin' cleanup for us is one'a the all-time great sea slug sluggers, former freak show superstar Tommy Thumb," He broadcast his impish smile and welcomed on stage the tiniest man I had ever seen, who had to stand on a bar stool to be seen above the podium. Blue rippling light fell on the stage and gave the little man a magical, gnomish aspect.

"Can you hear me?" asked the tiny man in the most booming baritone I had ever heard. Laughter came from the crowd. "I'll take that as a yes. Thank you, Mr. Captain. It's a great honor and a privilege to join the Silverspoon team. As the captain said, I'm Tom Thumb, coming off a great run with P.T. Barnum—the greatest showman on earth." He received a big round of applause. He held up his small hands in white gloves and continued in his deep, booming voice.

"I learned a few things from the master, not the least of which is that there is a sucker born every minute. P.T. also knew that 'the masses' are really 'them asses.' You all remember his Feejee Mermaid, don't you?" Hoots of approval rose from the chamber. "Millions of suckers paid two bits to come look at his mermaid—a monkey head sewed to a carp body, dried and coated with shellac.

"In the grand tradition of the master humbug, Phineas T. Barnum, I am pleased to announce our new, post-10-10 Feejee Mermaid, the Department of Homemade Insecurity. What we've done here, friends, is sewn the head

248 ~ James E. Churches

of a security guard on the body of an undertaker. We've given it a uniform, and a weapon, and let it loose on the streets of America. Its primary function is to implement the national Squid Alert system. Let me provide a demonstration."

A fat balding man in a shirt and blue pants, a pistol and baton strapped to his waist, walked on stage. His white shirt had the letters "HS" printed within cupped hands on the breast. A bandoleer crossed his chest in an "X," but instead of being loaded with bullets, it contained a dozen small, purple squid, dangling from hooks. A referee's whistle hung around his neck. He carried an aquarium the size of a milk box containing a green-spotted squid, about a foot long, undulating with its rippling, fringed, pectoral fin in a small circle through the tank. The man set a corner of the aquarium on the podium.

"Now here ya got yer squid, harmless and green, which is the lowest level on yer Squid Alert. Code Green, we call it—which means no worries, go about yer shoppin' without fear," the agent of Homemade Insecurity said, and blew his whistle. "Now yer squid's a sensitive bugger. He belongs to the collective *squid mind*, which is, of course, the mind of evil, what ya call yer terror, and he senses when the tentacles are reaching out—anywhere in the world, you know, anywhere—and reacts by changing color." The fat balding insecurity agent dropped a veil over the tank, then pulled it away. The squid had changed to a vibrant blue.

"Uh-oh, somethin's fishy in paradise. Now we're up to yer blue." He tooted the whistle. "Little bit a danger floatin' around out there. Some squid, somewhere in the dark waters, is thinkin' a bad thought." He put his hand to his head and closed his eyes. "No big deal, though. Go about yer shoppin', but remain 'guarded', on the lookout fer—uh, fer stuff." He dropped his black veil over the tank again. He removed it and the squid was now bright yellow. His whistle trilled.

"Whoopsie, things are gettin' a little sticky. Yer squid's gone yella, which means you oughta go yella too. Time to get a little scared. Time to start lookin' suspiciously at people whose skin color could resemble that of yer A-rab terrorist. But, you know, other than that, continue yer shoppin'." He lowered the veil. When he removed it the squid was bright orange.

"Hello! Orange alert! Orange alert!" The agent picked up the tank and walked haphazardly around the stage, bumping into Wrong John, and almost knocking over Tom Thumb, slopping water out of the tank, his bandoleer squids wiggling. He tooted his whistle over and over. A ripple of fearful murmuring passed through the crowd. "There's a squid out there somewhere, maybe close, maybe far, *ready to pounce!*"

"Got those huge black eyes," added Silverspoon, "that *never* blink, and those lungs that *never* need to breathe, and he's stalking the pure White Whale, threatening the blubber trade and our sacred trust, The Economy."

"Hello, Dolly. *BRACK!* Hello Dolly," screeched Krill, hopping up and down on Silverspoon's shoulder.

Tom Thumb held up his small white-gloved hands. "Now, there is *another* level, Code Red. We've never seen a squid turn red, and we don't want to. That means we have failed. We are about to get hit. It's too late, and there's nothing we can do." He hung his head and shook it side-to-side. Presently, he raised his head and motioned the insecurity agent over.

"These Squid Alert tanks will be placed in prominent locations throughout the nation," said the midget. "Every city, every town, every village will have its tank or two of squid. Now, I got a little secret for you. The public believes the squid is of a common mind, that the wicked thoughts of the Giant Squid are felt by all squid, and cause them to change color. That's the *myth* we intend to spread."

The insecurity agent pulled from behind his back, tucked into his pants, colored gelatin sheets of green, blue, yellow, and orange. He smiled and held them up in his pale, puffy fingers. "Fact is, yer squid is color sensitive. We slip the blue sheet into the concealed glass slot in the bottom of his tank, he's gonna turn blue. That's the nature of yer squid. He wants to blend in, to be hidden, so he changes to the color we stick in there." The agent slipped the different colors in and out, and the squid went blue, then yellow, then green.

"There is no red, friends," said Tom Thumb. "The Squid Alert will *never* go there. If we put out a red alert, and the Giant Squid hits, we've lost our deniability. People can say, 'You knew it was going to hit, and you didn't stop it.' If the alert stops at orange, we can always say, 'Well, we expected something, we just couldn't be sure exactly what, or where. There just weren't any specific targets.' We can say, 'Oops,' and it will be forgiven."

Tosspot had come on stage. He brushed his marshal's badge with the back of his white-gloved hand, then reached out and shook the hand of Tom Thumb, white glove to white glove. "In the marriage of Homemade Insecurity and the God Arrest America Act," the marshal said, "we have a *very* powerful means of controlling opposition to the mandate. The key, though, to making this whole thing hum, is to EXPAND the definition of terrorism. It is many more things than a savage attack from a radical Islamic political organization.

"Terrorism is a petition refuting the God Arrest America Act, or a scientific report scaring people about global climate change. We must now rewrite the dictionaries, give a whole page to 'terrorism,' sub-definitions in the hundreds. If a teachers union questions our No Child's Behind Act: terrorism. If a civil liberties organization challenges our right to sit in on Thanksgiving dinner and conduct an interrogation over pumpkin pie: terrorism. If an individual attempts to confront our president with an negative opinion about the global War on Squid: terrorism."

The crowd cheered. The bright mollusks in the large tank continued to glide about, leaving puffs of ink where they had shot away from danger. They changed color at will, became exactly like whatever rock they were on, or the sand. Tentacles shot out, nabbed a smaller species, drew it in, and sliced it up. The rippling blue light fell on the white marble floor of the chamber. Tatanka did not pay attention to the speeches; but instead stared into the tank in a daze.

Dagger stepped to the podium. "The final major element to make the mandate all but law is a program from the private sector, which, as the mandate evolves, will become the *only* sector. Let's bring Slick up here. You know Slick, CEO of Endrun Energy. Come on up, Slick." The tall, slow Texan ambled onto the stage.

"Howdy, folks. Yep, that's a fine combination, God Arrest America Squid Alert. Just about gives me the willies." He exaggerated a shudder. "Now this here mandate, well, this idn't exactly the first day it bloomed. We been workin' at this a good long while. We been buildin' these conservative fish tanks for years, puttin slugs and limpets and clams out all across America. Slowly, but surely, like a snail workin' its way across a razorblade, we been settin' the debate in this country, turning the subject, in a hundred different ways, back to mollusks. Is there an issue with poverty? No, it's really a clam problem. Is there a shortage of housing for the poor? Not really. What we have is an infestation of zebra mussels. Are the bridges in disrepair? Nope. Cuttlefish are swimming up the Mississippi."

"What's he talking about?" I asked Tatanka. "I thought the squid was the source of evil. He makes it sound like they've been puttin' 'em out on purpose."

"Dingus, you're a bushwhacker, no? It's called a trick," he said, not looking away from his collection of shocking night eagles.

"A trick? Well, if it's a trick, who's bein' fooled?"

"You fooled yourself, so they could fool themselves." There he was with that damn Injun code again. I may have partially broken it, though, and I felt better about my offer of the Giant Squid to Silverspoon and Krill. Maybe it wasn't a betrayal of Mr. Melville after all.

"We control the message, folks," Slick continued. "We control the research. We control the studies. We provide the funding, so we set the agenda. And it's a business- friendly agenda, a mollusk agenda, as it should be. We've taken over the state legislatures, the courts, the town councils. It's been a tidy little revolution—gone virtually unnoticed. There's been a little sticky issue, though, still sort of a bur in our saddles. All this democracy talk, and freedom of the press, has left people with the impression it's still a good idea to disagree with us. They continue to buy and read their local rags, and often find opinions challenging our octopi. That's got to stop.

"Over the course of the last few years, my subsidiary, Mandate Media, has, in partnership with two or three other key players, bought up ninety percent of the independent newspapers in America. My papers are out there, friends, to print the news best suited to the mollusk way—the Silverspoon way. The same story, about, for example, the oppression of taxes, will appear in a thousand newspapers across the country, same day, page one, no counterpoint."

A loud ruckus came from the stairwell—yelling, the clash of swords, wooden clubs clunking together. Into the chamber clambered a gang of clowns, maybe a hundred, bustling, pushing, hollering, slapping the white marble with their oversized clown shoes. They tweaked one another's red rubber noses, pulled down each other's polka-dotted pants, slapped each other's white painted faces, smudging the black lines around their mouths and eyes. They pushed aside the audience and surrounded the stage.

Slick held up his hands as if being robbed. "Looks like it's over for us boys. The clown posse has arrived." Ten or so clowns came on stage. A big one with a round belly picked up Tom Thumb and gave him a kiss on the forehead. He set him down on his bar stool and turned to the group.

"Hey ho, we're the Clown Criers. Yep yep yep, that's us us us. We'll be spreading out to the street corners of every town in America, beatin' the tar out of the 'hear ye, hear ye' locals, taking their bells and taking over the jobs. Our message will be a simple one. Give it to 'em, boys." All of the gathered clowns chanted in unison.

"Hear me! Hear me! Attention good citizens of Podunk, USA. The Squid Alert is ORANGE! Danger! Code Orange! Danger! Shalong of Iraq is about to attack us with Weapons of Mass Hysteria. Beware of exploding cornbread frosted with frog venom. Trust no one. God Arrest America. Seek shelter. Squid Alert ORANGE! Danger! Danger! Bring on the Silverspoon Mandate. We must attack Shalong of Iraq before he attacks us!"

The chamber echoed with applause, whistles, cheering, hoots, hurrahs. Wrong John and his officers clapped and nodded, and shook one another's hands.

I was confused, Frank. What *exactly* was happening? I could understand the newspaper takeover. Shoot, we had our Johnny Edwards, and he put out the heroic stories on us. That's part of the reason we dodged the law for twenty years. Who's going to turn in a local hero, savior of the people, kindhearted Robin Hood, stealing from the rich carpetbaggers and giving to poor downtrodden Southerners? Silverspoon was just rustling our game of newspaper lies into a whole herd of loud-mouthed hypocrites making him a hero. He had a thousand Johnny Edwards out there, and a thousand more Clown Criers, blabbing on every street corner in America about how good and wise was the Silverspoon Mandate. From the standpoint of pure bushwhacking, hell, my hat was off to him.

The part I didn't get was their love affair with mollusks. They had a mollusk agenda, a whole movement to put fish tanks with clams and slugs and snails all over America, shaping the debate into an argument about their bait. But then there was the War on Squid. Was it only the squid that was bad? or just the *Giant Squid?* How could you be friends with something on the one hand and on the other profess to call it evil, and wish to rid the world of it? Tatanka said it was a trick, but a trick on who?

Chapter XXXI

Code Yellow

The next day, Chief ordered Basmati Sweet to head up the launch of the Squid Alert system. She was to go on a tour of the nation with Tom Thumb, Makmoud "Shah of Iraq" Cherubic, and agents of Homemade Insecurity, to place fish-tanked squid in prominent locations along the Main Streets of America. They were to whip the nation's hunger for revenge into a war fury to invade Iraq. If rage could not be achieved, fear was an acceptable alternative. The mandate was about *Preemption*, and public opinion was the first target.

"We also hear rumblings the liberals are preparing a terrorist strike against us," said the Chief, tugging on his gold earring and sucking his teeth. "They're spreading a rumor that we knew 10-10 was coming and that we did nothing to stop it. You've got to foil that garbage, Sweet."

She frowned and bit her lip. "But how?" she asked, her voice so deeply lowered her throat looked ready to crack.

"Deny it, of course. Tell them there is no way in a million years we could have ever predicted it. Suicide storks delivering swaddled bombs disguised as babies? Impossible! Outrageous! We could *never* have anticipated such evil."

"But Chicken Little—he said, he told us—and I tried to get you to—"

"Oh, Christ, Sweet! You and the diplomat are *really* challenging my colorblindness. Is there something inherently softhearted about being a Negro? If I didn't see that snake running down your leg I'd say you were acting like a woman too. Now, do you want to ruin forever the advancement of your people? or do you want to follow orders?"

She saluted weakly, turned, and walked to her cabin. Twenty minutes later she found me in the galley, preparing an afternoon snack for Silverspoon: pickled red herring, his favorite. She carried a brown leather suitcase and wore a flowery, red silk bandana, and at least five different sets of gold and silver earrings on each ear. Her eyes were moist, as if she were about to cry. She brought me into the mess hall and held my hands.

"Well, off I go!" she said, trying to sound enthusiastic. "Wish me luck."

"You don't have to lie for them, Basma." I looked into her deep, glimmering brown eyes.

"Yes I do, Ish. That's my job."

"Quit."

"And do what? Don't you see? I have to make this work. I *have* to succeed. I can't let my people down." She squeezed my hands.

"So you're going to lie for the pirates? And that won't disappoint your people?"

She looked down, drew her lips into her mouth, and bit down. Then she returned her gaze to mine, tears in her eyes, kissed me quickly on the cheek, and walked away, long, slow, and swaying her hips.

I delivered Wrong John his snack and returned to the galley to find Roberto and Tatanka looking at a flier and laughing. Roberto had found it on Chief's desk and had lifted it. The fliers were apparently to be distributed by Clown Criers ahead of the Homemade Insecurity rollout and its Squid Alert system. The flier read as follows:

Shah & Basma's
Frog-Gob Liniment
Poison-dart Frog Anti-venom
Cures warts, fungus, rashes, hives, dandruff, snakebite,
stinging nettle, poison ivy,
AND THE DEADLY TOXIN OF THE AMAZON
POISON-DART FROG!!
Win the War on Squid!
Learn to identify carriers of deadly yellowcake bombs, and other

WEAPONS OF MASS HYSTERIA (WMHs)
*Crystal ball readings from the Shah of Iraq will predict the chances
you will be* <u>killed</u> *in an attack by the Giant Squid.*
MAKE YOUR TOWN SAFE!!
WITH A FOOLPROOF, EARLY WARNING SYSTEM
--CALLED--
SQUID ALERT!
*Meet P.T. Barnum's former freak show star, Tom Thumb,
the littlest guy with the biggest mouth, your new guardian,
your protector, your savior, and director of the new agency,*
THE DEPARTMENT OF HOMEMADE INSECURITY!!
*See the screaming LUNATIC LIBERAL, chained to a post,
foaming at the mouth like a rabid raccoon,
spewing her hatred of America, and
defending the rights of terrorists*
(unshaven, braless, barefooted, wearing a pentagram instead of a crucifix!)
COMING SOON TO YOUR HOMETOWN!!

"They need Sitting Bull, riding around waving a scalp," said Tatanka, shaking his head at the flier.

"And Buffalo Bill chasing him on a white stallion, shooting feathers out of his war bonnet," I added.

"And P.T. Barnum's *elefante gigante*. What is its name?" asked Roberto. "Jumbo, right?"

I felt a little sorry for Sweet, being sent out with a circus act like that, running around the country selling snake oil and squid bait. She made her choice, though. I understood it. When you're part of a gang, it's a big risk to go against the leaders. You better be ready—like that pisser Bobby Ford—to shoot them in the back and hightail it. Otherwise they're just as likely to string you up on general suspicion.

Chief was right about the bushwhacker strike against *Liberty* for ignoring the terror threat ahead of 10-10. A few days after Sweet went on her road show with the shah and Tom Thumb, a longboat full of legislators pulled up alongside *Liberty*, demanding an investigation into the attack. The boat bobbed in the waves brought up by a brewing thunderstorm. Its American flag shook and snapped in the wind, as did *Liberty's* corporate flags flying from the masthead. The boat hailed and asked permission to come aboard but was told to state its reasons first.

"The families who lost loved ones in the attacks want an investigation. They want to be sure we did everything possible to prevent them," said one of the Congressmen in the boat.

"It's important to address the rumor that the officers of *Liberty* avoided travel in New York City on the day of the attack. That needs to be cleared up," another shouted.

"We also hear from many former Bubba officials that they tried repeatedly to warn you of a major attack in America from Al Quota, and that you ignored them," said a senator from California.

"*BRACK!* Investigate. Hate. Must hate America. Must hate America," Krill screeched from the captain's shoulder.

Wrong John turned around and showed his back to the legislators. He spoke to them over his shoulder, his head adorned in his flouncy, humped presidential hat, his back also humped—and growing—with the pale lump that had formed between his shoulder blades. "It's easy to look backward, idn't it? Shee-it, I know exactly what I should'a done, now that it's over. Like they say in Texas, hindsight is—it's, uh—easy, when you're wearing rose-colored — when you've got on twenty, or, twenty pair of—hindsight, well, if my butt had eyes, I could'a seen the mess comin', couldn't I? 'Here I sit, buns a'flexin.' But since I don't, I don't, which means I didn't. That's why we couldn't, and you shouldn't, and the water under the bridge is—well, it's not there anymore."

Chief showed up, face flushed red, and scowling. He pointed to the black coffin hanging from the yardarm, painted in white with the words "Free Speech Zone."

"There's a special place reserved for those who have the effrontery to speak out against their country," Chief said.

"Nice prop, Chief Dagger. There were a lot of boxes like that one filled after 10-10," said one of the Congressmen.

"Free speech zone?" yelled another. "Isn't that *everywhere* in this country?"

"We're not speaking *against* our country," screamed a woman in the longboat. "We're speaking *for* the open and honest examination of the worst tragedy in our nation's history." The gathering storm flashed lightning. Thunder boomed. Sheets of rain fell to the north and headed our way.

"You people don't get it," said Wrong John. He had turned around, face pinched and reddened. "You just have no idea what it means to run a company—a country, that's also a company—like one—do you? I'm out on the front line trying to combat evil and you gutless career bureaucrats have nothing better to do than conduct a damn investigation?"

Tosspot, who had just arrived, out of uniform again, approached the rail and hollered, "Your accusations only serve to comfort our enemies. We must stand united in every sense, or the agents of destruction will be emboldened by our disunity."

"Aiding the enemy? Are you serious? Accusing us of treason for trying to understand the truth behind the attacks," said a legislator. "It's beginning to look like you've got something to hide."

A bird flew in low off the mizzenmast. "Stork!" someone shouted. TP pulled a pistol from his pocket, shot at and missed the bird. It swooped in and landed on the rail. "Yes, it's just a carrier pigeon," he said. "I, uh, I recognized that and spared its life." He blew across the barrel of his gun and shoved it in his pocket.

Speck pulled the message from the pigeon's leg. He handed it to Dagger. Chief read it quickly, a smile spreading over the right side of his face. He leaned over and whispered something to Wrong John and Krill. The bird laughed his throaty, gizzardly laugh. Wrong John smirked and closed his eyes halfway. "I changed my mind," he announced. "I applaud your concerns, truly. I'm the guy that's got to dry the tears, and wipe the noses, so I—it's tough on me too."

"There's a little more involved than drying eyes and blowing noses," shouted a black woman in the boat.

"Oh really? Such as mouthing off to your commander-in-chief?" He turned and stomped away. The junior officer, Bill, walked over holding a fish tank. The mollusk inside had turned bright yellow.

"Sorry, the Squid Alert has been elevated to Code Yellow," said Tosspot, pointing at the squid with the end of his bullwhip. "I suggest you get out of the open water. Remain vigilant against Satan and his minions." The storm hit fiercely, slicing the Potomac with rain, shooting lightning, blowing and booming. The legislators rowed away, hunched over, coats over their heads, pummeled by rain.

"See what we mean!" the marshal yelled.

In the shelter of the captain's roundhouse, Dagger read the note from the carrier pigeon:

"Dear *Liberty*,

I have been informed the liberals are circling about 10-10. As usual, they would rather attack America than deal with our foreign enemies. Let me offer my services to conduct an "investigation" into the matter. I believe I can support the Silverspoon Mandate by assuring your innocence before I begin.

Yours truly,

Dr. Henchman."

A few days later, Tosspot commandeered *Liberty's* black coffin for another mission. I was relieved when he didn't ask me to get inside, but instead brought it to the Capitol filled with another body. Tatanka, Roberto, Pinch, Speck, Bill, and I acted as pallbearers and carried the coffin into the senate chambers. The legislators shouted and fumed, demanding an explanation, but Dagger, as president of the senate, pounded his gavel and demanded silence.

"We know this trick," a senator yelled. "You've got a gunslinger in there. He's going to pop out and start shooting us!"

Dagger gave his sidewinder smile and shook his head. "Liberals, liberals … they imagine danger where there is none, and refuse to act when it is slithering up their leg. There's no gunslinger in the box. Nor is there squid, nor stork, nor lunatic jihadist. Inside, in fact, is a concession, an olive branch, a demonstration of our shared concern as Americans over Bubba's intelligence failure prior to 10-10."

The lid popped open, and up rose Dr. Henchman, his head thick with wavy gray hair, nose a rack for heavy black glasses, wearing a black suit and a black bow tie. Senators shouted, slapped their desks, booed and whistled. "I have been asked to investigate 10-10. I vil do zis, in service of my country, as I did wis love, all zoz years for Captain Crook. Of course I will be impartial, unbiased, and fair. Zee only motivation for my taking zis job is truth—which has been my solitary ambition in everysing I have done for my country."

Chapter XXXII

Spermaceti Spaghetti

Shah & Basma's traveling salvation show spread across the nation, filling the streets of every town, big and small, with talk of squid: green, blue, yellow, orange, and red. Glowing articles appeared in the *Chicago Mandate*, the *Houston Mandate*, the *San Francisco Mandate*, and the entire *Mandate* chain, praising the new Department of Homemade Insecurity and its sophisticated early warning system against terror. Agents of the department ran around with their squid-laden bandoleers, blew their shrill whistles, and hurled small mollusks at suspicious people. They searched old women before they were allowed to board trains, and confiscated their dangerous knitting needles. They stopped boys who carried marble sacks from their belts, and took the hard, round ballistic missiles.

Clown Criers filled the town squares and rang their bells and cried out about impending doom. Day and night they clanged and shouted: "Danger! Code Orange! Danger! Shalong of Iraq is about to attack. Weapons of Mass Hysteria. Remain vigilant. Continue shopping!" Citizens became outraged at the United Nations for leaving America so vulnerable. They demanded of their legislators an immediate approval of Wrong John's authority to go to war—and they got it.

With the return of Gunny Yo Yo, Sir Yes Sir, and Crude, from their missions abroad, it became clear that *Liberty* had completely shaken off the shameful burden of the world's sympathy and replaced it with the scorn upon which pirates thrive. Still, the invasion had to wait on a few details involving supplies, and the assembly of a coalition of patsies willing to support the American aggression with the blood of their young warriors. That left time for other aspects of the Silverspoon Mandate to flower.

The first blossom burst forth in a scheme hatched by Pinch, Krill, and several of their top economic advisers. A few weeks later, the garden was ready for viewing on a barge outside the U.S. territorial waters off Long Island, on the newly christened Commune of Corporatocracy. *Liberty* weighed anchor one mild July afternoon off the Tidal Basin and sailed through the smaze lingering over the Potomac. Lively commerce passed up and down river on long steamer barges, loaded with tobacco, cotton, rice, and, of course, blubber, always blubber. Favorable winds pushed *Liberty* to the Chesapeake and out into the open waters of the Atlantic. A few days later, under a moonless sky filled with stars, *Liberty* approached her destination.

She pulled up alongside the long, gray iron sides of the brightly lit facility rocking in the ocean swells. Oil lamps hung off of stays strung from the steam and smoke vents to the railing, and from a heavy windlass bolted off the aft deck. Torches stood in metal stands attached to the bridge and the collection of stalls spread out over the barge. Pinch pointed to the well-lit flag flying from a pole above the bridge. "Look!" she cried. "It's my Roger, my Star-Spangled Jolly Roger." She clutched her red-and-white beaded abacus to her chest.

Wrong John walked aboard as if returning home for Thanksgiving dinner. He shook hands and slapped backs and ladled nicknames with absolute ease. Everyone called him "Spoons" and marveled at the masterful way he had taken control of the country. Long tables covered in white linen tablecloths held platters of food: entire roast pigs, apple-mouthed and all, hunks of roast beef, legs of lamb, smoked salmon and eel, sliced mango, kiwi, and candied yams. I noticed no squid and wondered if it wasn't some mistake.

"Don't you figure the man chosen by God to rid the world of calamari would want to eat some squid?" I asked Tatanka, who stood to my right.

"Huh. Nobody could be *that* hungry," he said, wrinkling his nose. "A nice chunk of raw buffalo liver. That's an evil I could stomach."

In the center of one table sat a big bowl of spaghetti soaking in a creamy, yellow sauce, and labeled "spermaceti spaghetti." Wrong John served himself a big bowl and dug in. He sucked in the noodles until the ends popped into his mouth in a spray of oil. "Doggone good!" he said with his mouth full. "God I love the blubber trade. Name me one other business where you can burn it, eat it, take a bath in it, and all three ways rake in a nice pile of cash. Name one!" He slurped in another long noodle. Krill stood on the table beside him, gobbling up grapes.

All about us scurried small, bespectacled men wearing funny white hats and sharp pencils behind their ears, and carrying notepads of grid paper. The sheets were filled with lines of mathematical formulas I could not comprehend. The small men showed the calculations to paunchy fellows in three-piece suits, smoking cigars and sipping brandy. I assumed the precise little men were accountants, reporting their bosses the latest tally of winners and losers, but Pinch told me they were actually chefs.

"Those aren't accountants, Ish. Gosh, they're *way* more creative than that. They're actually chefs, showing their captains recipes for cooking the books."

"Come on, Pinch. My momma used to accuse me of eatin' my school books instead of readin' 'em, but there's no way to really *cook* a book and make it taste good," I said, betraying my ignorance.

"Just look at the CEO's, Ish. Do they look happy?" She pointed at the paunches jiggling with glee. "I'd say they're downright, giddy. Oh, these are some tasty entreés they're cooking out here tonight—yes indeedee." She looked up at her red, white, and blue skull and crossbones and gave it a salute.

Tatanka, Pinch, and I wandered over the dark, flat surface of the barge, where booth after booth had been set up, each bearing a plaque that identified it as the worldwide headquarters of some major American company. Some of the names I recognized as those with flags flying up the mainmast of *Liberty*: Mercy Nary, BlubCo, Money Lynch, Retro Research, Hellbent Industries, Cannon Fodder, Inc., Endrun Energy.

"How in the heck can any of these big 'ol companies get any work done in a tiny booth floatin' on a barge in the middle of the ocean?" I blurted to nobody in particular. Pinch smiled and winked at a chubby chef wearing a very tall white hat.

"This is a rare dish, sir. Our specialty: stuffed carp with mashed turnips," said the chef in a sugary Louisiana accent. "It's a dish that well feeds the eye, and is light on the stomach." He closed his eyes and bowed a little.

"What in *the* hell are you talkin' about?" I replied.

"Pierre, he's not one of us," said Pinch, poking the chef with her long index finger. "Ish, these are gourmet recipes for tax evasion. Nobody does any work out here. The HQ just floats like a buoy, marking a position. It establishes an off-shore address that excludes the company from paying corporate taxes to Uncle Samuel J. Fatass—silly!" She poked me with her long finger.

"Why would a company want to do that?" I asked.

The fat chef scratched his belly. "If you could have an eight ounce filet or a ten ounce filet for the same price, which would you choose?"

"I ain't stupid, chef. 'Course I'd take the thicker cut."

"So would your corporation, sir. It will come to this restaurant because we give a thicker filet of carp for the same price—and our turnips are tender and fresh, lightly buttered, sprinkled with a touch of wolfsbane."

Tatanka sniffed the air. "I sense the night eagle."

Wrong John walked up with a group of CEOs in their three-piece dark suits. A tall drink of water came up behind him and put his long hands over the captain's eyes. "Guess who?"

"Smells like a rotten Texas steer, dropped dead twenty feet from the water hole," answered the captain, peeling away the man's hands and turning on him.

"Hey, you old hound dog," said the man. I recognized him as Slick from Endrun Energy.

"I thought I felt a bump in the road, you lazy armadilla."

"Hang on a second, I got somethin' to show ya." Slick waved over a chef who carried an especially thick pad of paper. Slick asked him to show the recipe to Wrong John. He flipped through the pages and began to explain the ingredients.

"Whoa, Nelly!" said the captain, pushing away the pad of scribbling. "The president is not a number cruncher. Just tell me if it tastes good."

"It's yummy, old buddy," said Slick with a slap on Silverspoon's back. "Ain't you read your new federal energy policy? I handed it to Chief Dagger months ago."

"Shee-it, Slick, you know I'm too busy to read all them damn re-ports." Wrong John gave him a friendly punch in the stomach.

"You illiterate damn cowboy. Let me explain this'un to ya." He took a pair of reading glasses from his breast pocket and placed them on his long, wide nose. "You start out with a whale steak." He pointed at the recipe pad. "You tenderize it through half a dozen dummy corporations. After it's been left out in the sun for a few days, it stinks clear to Amarillo. That's when it really gets good. Our rotten fish has created a false shortage—a diddle of supply and demand, Spoons—basic economics."

"Don't talk to me about basic. I done my military service, fair and square."

"Easy, *hombre*, I'm talking about the price of an essential commodity when it can't be had. People will pay *anything* to get a slice'a blubber. Then, shazaam! we throw that whale steak into the try-works and let the blubber flow, runnin' at ten times the fair market value!"

"Fair?" asked Pinch. "Did I hear somebody say *fair?*" She covered her mouth and chuckled breathily.

Slick smiled, looked closer at the recipe, and pointed out a line to his chef. The chef nodded and smiled at Wrong John. "Well lookie here!" exclaimed Slick. "Says we got an extra half cup sugar to spare now that our HQ is no longer in America, payin' through the nose for those useless welfare programs. By gum, I think this half cup might just find its way to Silverspoon, Ltd."

"I didn't here you say that, Gopher Guts." Wrong John placed his hands over his ears and backed away a few steps. "And if you get caught, we almost can't remember each other's names. You got it, uh, uh—damn, I plumb forgot you already!"

"*BRACK!* Any morsels in there for Parrot Mutual? *BRACK!* Holding company in peanut futures? Take a look. Take a look."

Slick saluted and wandered off to exchange more recipes with his chef. Wrong John shouted after him, "And make that two cups, Tightass—don't gimme that 'cup's half full' malarkey."

We wandered around for a while when the captain of the barge approached us. He wore a crisp white uniform and a white officers hat with a black skull and crossbones stitched into the fabric. Captain Silverspoon admired his hat, then scolded him for being "a little too obvious," at which the barge's captain turned the insignia to the rear. They began to discuss the success of the program along with Pinch and the economic team. Everyone agreed it was a fine way to way to skin Uncle Sam Fatass.

I'm a southern boy, so I'm not opposed to a rebellion against unfair taxes. That's what we hated about the Union. We never asked for a big, expensive central government, and didn't like giving our earnings to something that did us no good and had only the potential to harm us—which, by God, is just exactly what it did! Even so, Frank, there was something in this scheme of theres that didn't sit right with me.

They called themselves patriots, modeled after the American Revolution. They talked about Boston Tea Parties and standing up to the corrupt imperial power. Something about it just smelled rotten to me, Frank, that's all I know. How could it be patriotic for the government to steal from itself and give the money to its friends? I'm just a hayseed from Missouri, but that didn't seem patriotic to me. It *was* revolutionary, but not in the spirit of some lofty dream of liberty. These pirates didn't want the America of Tom Jefferson or Jim Madison. What they wanted I couldn't be sure, but it put off the stench of spoiled squid, that's all I know. I could see them standing backwards at the tiller, going full tilt away from something, away, away, into some other time, long before common people would have demanded a say in their lives.

"I apologize for stating the obvious, but do you think this is a good time to withdraw the financial support of our largest corporations?" wondered Crude, who had been quietly observing the recipes. "We *are* at war, and, well, wars can be expensive, and, well, traditionally in America, our corporate leaders have shown great civic leadership in times of crisis and have made tremendous sacrifices to serve their country. I just, well, was a little concerned about the timing of the whole, you know, Corporate Commune swindle."

Captain Silverspoon glowered at Crude with such fire in his eyes I imagined the Oil Czar would spontaneously combust. "FYI, any actual wars we fight will be financed by the natural resources of the country we conquer. If they ain't got resources they can keep their evil. Number three, if you can't help your friends when you're cookin' like we are, when can you do it?" He reached out and flicked Crude in the forehead.

"Silverspoon Mandate! Silverspoon Mandate!" called Krill, followed by a series of sharp whistles as he paced the captain's shoulder. "A flick in time saves nine—saves nine!" Wrong John flicked the bird too. Krill shook his head and grumbled under his breath.

Suddenly the barge began to shake, and a high-pitched scraping sound came up from the hold. Something had hold of the boat and was either toying with it, like a dog on a stuffed animal, or was giving it the death shake of a coyote with a rabbit in its teeth. The trembler lasted no more than twenty seconds, and was followed by a smacking sound, as of big lips kissing, and a series of splashes all around the barge. Anyone who hadn't been holding on to a rope or the edge of a booth got knocked to the deck. Many of the corporate headquarters were leveled.

Pinch and Crude helped Wrong John up from the deck. "Lord of peace and mercy, what in the heck was that?" he asked. His officers shrugged their shoulders.

"Your enemy accepts your challenge," said Tatanka, looking at him sternly.

"My enemy? What enemy? We're all among friends here."

"The deep unseen one. The creeping shape-shifter. The dark unknowable mystery. It comes up to meet you."

Wrong John screwed up his face at the Lakota. "Who are you, the CEO of Wampum, Incorporated?"

"Um, sir, that's your cook—*Liberty's* cook," said Pinch.

"Well then get over there and whip me up a budget soufflé or somethin'. Stop jabberin' about deep, dark oogie-boogies, fer cryin' out loud." He turned and walked back toward the spermaceti spaghetti, now in a pile on the deck, looking like a giant's spilled bait box.

A fleet of Chinese junks came within range of the light on the starboard side. They weren't flying the flag of China, but an odd banner that looked like a shopping bag, with the word "WongMart" printed on it. The Chinese came alongside the barge, threw out lines to draw in, and scampered over them like baby spiders bursting from a nest. They went straight to work at the windlass, raising cargo from the hold.

I nudged Tatanka, and he grunted and nodded at the Chinese stevedores. The cargo rising from the barge's hold was unlike any I had seen. I walked to the edge of the deck above the open hatch that led to the hold. The Chinese sailors wore tight-fitting black silk skullcaps with tassels on top. Long tails of black hair lay along their backs. They loaded *something*, I know not what, into a big square of canvas tied to the windlass by ropes through grommets along the edges. The windlass rose and synched the canvas tarp hanging from the arm. Whatever they had in there jostled and pushed against the canvas as if a litter of large kittens. The operator lowered the canvas to the deck of the Chinese junk and out erupted the contents, a strange gaggle of indistinguishable oddities, which the sailors scurried to capture. Even as they grabbed and stowed the industrious creatures, I was hard pressed to identify them.

It was almost as if the things had no set form, but existed as a combination of sound and movement, with a shape only discernable as result of the movement, like something passing quickly in the corner of your eye, and yet they were very real and could be grabbed and thrown into cotton rice sacks by the sailors. I would have been completely lost for an explanation had not one of the financial chefs arrived and offered us cigars. We accepted and he lit our stogies, looked down with us on the commerce with China, and explained a little more about the menu.

"You're watching history out there today, boys," he said, introducing himself as T. Shelter, a roly-poly man with a shaved head that he rubbed frequently with his free hand. I told him Tatanka and I were sharpshooters working for Captain Silverspoon.

He walked backward a few paces and pretended to pull a pistol. "Draw," he said. I, of course, instantly had Peacemaker out and aimed at his heart. "That's a word you better mean when you say it, Mister Shelter," I informed him.

He held his hands up and laughed through the un-cigared side of his mouth. "Just kiddin'. Good to know ol' Spoons has some topnotch guardians." He came over and tried to put his arms around us, but we shook them off.

"We call this little operation Ellis Outland. Biggest emigration project in the history of the country, and we can thank your captain for making it possible."

"Emigration? You mean folks moving away from America?" I inquired.

"Just as good as," said T. Shelter, his right hand rubbing his head, a big puff of gray smoke shooting from his mouth. "What we're shipping out tonight, son, are jobs. You see that little one there, jerking sideways and up and down with the hammering and sawing sounds? That's a toy maker's job. And you see that long one with the big swinging motion and the 'ka-chunk' sound? That's a weaver's job. And that one there—Look out!" he called down to the sailors, "That'n'll burn you but good!—that's a foundry job." He stuck his cigar in the side of his mouth and smiled down on the activity. "Ain't they the cutest damn things you ever did see?"

I didn't fully understand his explanation. I puffed on my cigar and inquired further. "You mean these fellas that's moved their headquarters out here are also shipping American jobs to China? What for?"

"The purpose? My God, boy! What's the purpose of life? What the hell are any of us doing here at all? Haven't they told you about your boss's new mandate?"

"God, don't start up with that squidified discombobulation of horse manure." I opened the cylinder of Peacemaker and slowly turned it. Huh, I thought, as it clicked around, another bullet missing. Tatanka cleared his throat and spit on the deck.

"Nice way of putting it, Mr. IshcaBible. Sounds like you're familiar with the philosophy. Well our Ellis Outland comes right out of the War on Squid, and the mandate to hit them before they hit us. You could call it a hidden cost advantage of doing business in Silverspoon America." He puffed on his cigar.

"The whole squid thing—deep, dark, never been seen, tentacles everywhere, changing color, could be anybody or anything—what a bunch of hooey! But the *perfect* hooey. Keep everybody watching for tentacles up from the sewer while we quietly shanghai their jobs and ship them off to, well, to Shanghai. Why should we let terrorist labor groups attack our bottom line with overpriced demands for safer working conditions, more vacation, better medical care, higher wages? No, sir! We preempt that nonsense by gathering up our marbles and going to play in a country where none of that matters. Fifty million Chinese laborers are standing by to do for a penny a day what will cost us two bucks a day in America." He shoved his stogy in his mouth, put a dollar in one hand and a penny in the other, then pretended to weigh them. The hand with the dollar dropped and the penny went way up.

"Wages aren't the only things that're low in China. Raw materials, energy, machinery, construction—all go for pennies on the dollar. We manufacture it over there, ship it back here, and the Silverspoon profit margin—well it's like missing your two front teeth!"

I threw what was left of my cigar into the water. I couldn't believe what I was hearing. After all the righteous indignation of the North about our Negro slaves, and now come to find out the wealth of modern America rested almost entirely on Chinese slaves. Can you imagine, Frank? After all that stink and fuss about human dignity and civil rights and equality, all the death and burning and hatred of the war, and when it's all said and done, they're just as willing to use slaves for profit as we were.

And don't go tellin' me it's okay to do it to foreigners, that it's not your problem how workers get treated in their own country, and whether or not they get paid. You can't call yourself a democracy, devoted above all else to liberty and freedom and justice, and let some godless country like China house your slaves for you. Don't go tellin' me that, by damn.

I'm no accountant, that I'll grant ya, but I did enough robbery splits to gain a little math smarts, and from what I heard of the wages they paid those Chinese workers, they were actually *cheaper* than holding African slaves. Why, they didn't hardly make enough to cover room and board. At least *our* slaves got that much.

Never mind what I thought. The Chinese continued to bag American jobs and stow them below. All manner of livelihood clattered, pounded, sanded, cranked, scraped, shook, squealed, and whined from the deck of that junk.

"So what you're telling me, Mr. Shelter, is that not only is an American's job being stolen, but he's being replaced with a Chinese slave on top of it. Do you think it would make America proud to know its greatest companies had resorted to tax dodging and slavery to increase their profits?"

"Well, sir, that's a very bold statement." T. Shelter rubbed his head and chewed on his cigar. "A bold statement, and one that I would never have expected from an adherent to the Silverspoon Mandate."

"I never signed on for that damnable mandate of his! It's worse than anything we *ever* tried to do in the South. It's worse because it's dishonest. It pretends to be something good, something to benefit the world. At least we Southerners had the good graces to call our slaves slaves, and the decency to admit straight out we intended to keep them for our property!"

Mr. Shelter frowned hard at me and walked off with that sort of smug face I saw all the time on Marshal Tosspot when he was scribbling in his little notebook. It was another "hidden advantage" of the new mandate— something about "mind your manners or I'm going to turn you in." I could not stomach the way this mandate seemed to be pushing everybody in the same small corral, all of us expected to act the same, dress the same, talk the same, everybody ready to slap his neighbor back in line if he acted on his own free will.

I found out a few weeks later that people all across the land could be found wandering the streets of their cities and towns, calling out the names of their lost jobs, not knowing where they had vanished. "Here, Groceries, here, girl," they would say, or, "Come home, Bacon. Come on home now," or, "It's another day, where's my dollar? where are ya, boy?"

If too many of the dangerous job seekers got out on the streets at once, the Squid Alert suddenly went to Code Yellow. Homemade Insecurity agents flung their mollusks, blew their whistles, sent everybody inside, and called for a blackout.

Signs began to appear posted on street corners throughout the country; many of them read like this:

Lost!

ONE GOOD JOB

Last scene at Murphy's Shoe Factory
Answers to the name of Cobby or Tack
Can be identified by cash in her tool belt
Smells of rawhide and tanning
Arrives at 8 a.m., Monday-Saturday, a smile on her face
Likes good company and is always on the go
Runs with a pit bull called Mortgage

Wears the tag *Made in America,*
which used to stand for quality
unmatched in the world.
Any information, please contact
Jack or Jill Uphill, #8 Sycamore Road
We miss her so much.

Chapter XXXIII

E Pluribus Unum

The Pirates of the Potomac continued to race along in the full flame of their swindle, acting with impunity to carry out their modern American Revolution. They had spared their patriotic corporate sponsors the burden of unfair taxes to support their country and society. They had worked out a handy job emigration program at Ellis Outland to pacify the dangerously innumerable Chinese, and raise corporate earnings (now completely tax free) without any political fallout at home. No one hardly noticed the economic hardship. They were just thankful to be alive in a world of immeasurable threat from Giant Squid and Weapons of Mass Hysteria. Thanks to Shah & Basma's Frog-Gob Liniment, TP's God Arrest America Act, the incessant blather of a thousand outraged Clown Criers, unending calls to war in the Mandate Media, and the heroic slapstick of Tom Thumb's Department of Homemade Insecurity and its legion of squid-slinging Feejee Mermaids—and, of course, the catalyst for it all: the devastating attack by suicide storks—America was more frightened than she had ever been before.

It was masterful piracy, Frank, I had to admit. Had they been actual public servants dedicated to the welfare of the people, Silverspoon's mob would surely have been the most abject failures ever to hold higher office— but as hired guns for the corporate pirates, they had no equal.

Still, there was work to be done. They believed their pals were still being punished, penalized, and discriminated against for their success. The prejudice was expressed though all sorts of unfair taxes on their brave capitalist spirit. Righting this wrong became the subject of lengthy debate among the officers. But just *how* to pull it off became the issue.

After the Uncle Samuel J. Fatass Ceremonial Rodeo and Tax Rebate, the economic blow from the 10-10 attack, the expensive new terror heightening programs, and the costly global War on Squid, the federal piggy bank rang hollow. That was a sound, among pirates, next in the line of tragedies to the gallows door popping open. One evening, after the captain retired early because of a backache and sinus congestion, Pinch, Krill, and Dagger lounged around the deck of *Liberty*, clandestinely sipping brandy on a warm summer evening. Swarms of monarch butterflies crossed the Potomac on their way to a field of red poppies in bloom across the Potomac. The setting sun cast a vivid golden light on the masts, furled sails, and shrouds of the ship.

They continued to kick around the idea of how to get more money for their rich friends. Krill idly pecked at a corner of the Bill of Rights, when he suddenly jumped in the air, spilled his bird dish of brandy, and spit out his parrot-sized cigar.

"*EUREEKA!* We borrow the booty, borrow the booty!" He flapped so hard he flews several feet before he got tangled in a halyard and fell to the deck.

Pinch flopped her long legs from the hammock in which she lounged, went over to Krill, picked him up, and stroked his downy cheeks. "Gosh, Krill, borrow the booty? What do you mean, borrow the booty?"

"We go by caravan to ancient Cathay. Just like Marco Polo! Just like Marco Polo! Find the Silk Road. *BRACK!* Pearls of the Orient." Pinch set Krill down on the edge of the try-works and filled his saucer with brandy. She took a sip from her snifter and scratched her head. She had let her long brown hair down for the first time I could remember, and, in the dusk, struck a handsome pose. "Silk Road? Pearls of the Orient? Aren't we already harvesting them? Their labor rate is outright robbery as it is."

Dagger sat up from his recline on the ivory presidential seal in the try-works hatch. "That's right, Pinch. We're fleecing them—and they owe us for it—big time!" He shook his head and tugged on a gold ear hoop. "Damn you, birdbrain, you are the most conniving little camp robber I've ever come across." He leaned over and patted Krill's small red head. The parrot ruffled his feathers and scratched quickly under his chin.

"How many jobs have we shipped to China?" Chief asked Pinch. She ran her fingers over the red and white beads of her abacus. They clicked rapidly, like a telegram office receiving and urgent message. "Oh, gosh, I'd say, roughly, a million-five, plus or minus fifty G."

"That's a lot of factories and a lot of American capital coming into that backward country. We simply ask for a bit of it back, in the form of a loan. Then we can get on with the Silverspoon Mandate, and continue murdering these taxes before they *kill* The Economy." Dagger took a loud sip of brandy and handed fresh cigars around.

Tatanka and I smoked our cigarettes and pretended not to notice. Tatanka pointed to a large wake in the water about thirty yards to port. "It follows us," he said in his slow, deep voice. I did not want to hear that. I felt immediate pressure in my head and could hear that rasping, pecking, scraping sound against the wall of my bunk.

Pinch snickered and covered her mouth with the back of her hand. "Oh, Chief Dagger, you are devious, sir." She continued to snigger in a hissing snakelike way. Dagger lit her cigar and she took a big inhale of smoke, then blew out three big rings and took a long drink of brandy. "Ah! The money game. God I love it!"

After a few weeks of orchestration, Chief, Krill, and Pinch managed a massive transfer of gold ingots from the foundries of Chengdu to the thick cement vault of tax relief somewhere deep beneath Silverspoon's pillow. Then they set the stage for a freebooting spree up the Barbary Coast. Krill's first move—aligned with his obsession that *Liberty* remain "on message" at all times—was to send a personal note to the most influential members of the press:

"In the midst of our nation's greatest crisis, a time when all good Americans should stand together against evil, there has been discovered among us a band of wanton thieves, thieves so villainous, they can be described only as *pirates*."

This, what was called a "tip," instantly became headline news. All of America became enamored of the unfolding scandal, and off Krill went to create the rest of the story.

A little credit, Frank. You always chastised me for my letters to the editor after we pulled a job. You said nobody would ever believe me when I blamed the Union or traitorous Missouri Radicals for the crime we had just committed. Ah, but I knew, brother, just as Wrong John's parrot did, the power of planting poison seeds. Doubt, like the poison seed, grows by the water of further doubt, sprouting into mistrust, qualms, reservations, and eventually, if you work it right, outright hatred.

The first stop on Krill's campaign to get his hands on the borrowed Chinese gold was Granary Burying Ground in Central Boston, a colonial graveyard off of School and Tremont Streets. I learned it was the final resting place of such revolutionary heroes as Paul Revere, John Hancock, and Samuel Adams. There was also a story, many would say a false one, that a Mary Goose, buried at Granary, was the author of the Mother Goose nursery rhymes. We came upon the cemetery after an evening shower, the waxing moon well onto full, and darting playfully in and out of winnowing clouds. A pleasant breeze rattled the leaves in the knobby oak and ash trees holding court among the tired headstones, carved with round heads and square shoulders, leaning forward, back, and sideways in the spongy soil.

Wrong John, Krill, Tosspot, Pinch, Bill, Speck, and I came to the iron gate, dressed as gravediggers, with shovels, picks, rakes, and coils of rope over our shoulders, swinging lanterns in our hands. Wrong John palmed the caretaker his pieces of eight to let us in and keep a lookout for us. We slouched through the heavy black iron gate and shambled toward the grave of a Gretta Misclud, who had been buried two days previously. The gate groaned behind us until it closed with a heavy clang. In the long puddle just ahead the bright moon reflected briefly on the mirrored stillness, then hid in the posy clouds and went away for quite some time.

"Lookie here," said Wrong John in a hushed voice, his lamp down at a worn headstone. "There lies old Paul Revere. 'The Squidish are coming! The Squidish are coming!'"

"Famous quotes by Simple Simon," Krill whispered. I heard Silverspoon's fingernail flick against his beak.

"Hey," I said, "there *is* a Mary Goose buried out here." The wan light of my lantern illuminated the marker, tipped back and leaning a'port. "My momma used to like to tell me that one about Little Boy Blue. 'Little Boy Blue come blow your horn. The sheep's in the meadow, the cow's in the corn. Where's the little boy who looks after the sheep? Under the haystack fast asleep.'"

"It's about the captain, before 10-10," muttered Krill. "Squid's in the meadow. Quota's in the corn."

"Cute, Peckerhead. I'll give you a horn to blow."

"Can we stop playing around?" said the marshal in his sour voice. "It's risky digging up the dead behind enemy lines here in Boston." He led us into the newer section of Granary.

After some twenty minutes wandering the rows in the direction the caretaker had pointed us, past a group of graves belonging to people killed in the 10-10 attack, we found the marker for Gretta Misclud. Bill and Speck took robustly to their shovels against the dark wet earth. In no more than five minutes they were down in the hole, hoisting up the coffin. A loamy, damp smell hung in the air.

"Man, this espionage is spookier'n all get out," said the captain, rubbing his hands together in front of his chin. "Who's got the necklace?" Pinch dug a stunning diamond necklace from the leather satchel over her shoulder. Speck used the tip of his shovel to pry open the rosewood casket. He and Bill lifted their lamps to shine on the ashen, drawn face of Gretta Misclud. She wore a frilly, faded white wedding dress.

"*BRACK!*" screeched Krill, immediately cut off by Wrong John's hand grabbing his beak.

"Christ, Krill," he hissed. "You trying to wake the dead?"

"Look at this one," I said, lantern next to a headstone. "'R.I.P. Tosspot. Went to bed and bumped his head, and couldn't get up in the morning.'" Pinch laughed softly. Tosspot didn't say anything, just fidgeted with his leg irons.

At arm's length, her head pulled back and to the side, Pinch slipped the necklace around Gretta Misclud's dank misshapen neck. Pinch jerked away from the corpse and threw down the coffin lid so abruptly several in the party cried out. Bill and Speck lowered the casket into the ground by rope and quickly covered it with dirt.

"Neatness, gentlemen," intoned Tosspot, "is the imperative of a successful crime. I want every speck of dirt exactly where it was before our arrival." What do you know, I wondered, about getting away with a crime?—goody two-shoes Missouri turncoat.

Speck and Bill looked at one another quizzically and raked the loose soil from around the grave in toward the mound. After not more than a couple of strokes, the captain interrupted them. "A'right, let's vamoose, pronto," he said, and we all turned and galumphed out of the graveyard, shovels, picks, and rakes banging together every few steps. The plan from that point was to plant a poison seed in the office of Boston Congressman Ben Nedal—a despised liberal spendthrift—news of a tax-dodging heiress hiding the rightful treasure of America's underprivileged in her coffin six-feet-under at Granary Burying Ground.

Tosspot recruited his confidence man the following night when he cornered Congressman Nedal's chief of staff ducking out the alley door of a brothel, wobbly, smelling of liquor. A greasy rat crossed his path and darted between barrels of rotting garbage. TP collared the rosy Irishman, John McTeague, and slammed him against the damp red brick wall of the alley, leg irons ringing from his belt. He raised his lantern up to the Irishman's face, smeared with red lipstick.

"Well, if it isn't John the john, still up to his old tricks," said Tosspot through clenched teeth to the fat Irishman, a full head shorter than he.

"Tosspot, you dirty bastard. What're you doing skulking around the Boston red light? Haven't you got a War on Shrimp to fight?" said McTeague in a voice choked by TP's hard grip against his throat.

"You Boston Catholics just can't seem to get that one about adultery, can you?" snarled the marshal. "Now if you know what's good for you and don't want news of your adventures reaching the missus, you'll serve your country and deliver a bit of intelligence to your boss." John McTeague protested the assignment, but Tosspot made clear his intent to ruin McTeague's life. It was not long before he agreed to win the confidence of Congressman Nedal concerning the tax scandal of Gretta Misclud.

Not long thereafter, John McTeague informed us his boss had taken the bait and was planning that night to rob the grave of Gretta Misclud. Congressman Nedal, the crusading champion of the downtrodden, intended to exhume the priceless necklace and confront the Misclud family with their criminal plot to defraud the federal government of millions in estate taxes. McTeague and the congressman, along with several "tax collecting parasites," as Pinch described them, were to visit Granary Burying Ground after attending the annual charity costume ball of Lady von Munchen. As one final assurance on the preservation of his good name, McTeague was to convince his boss and crew to attend the costume ball dressed as pirates, and to remain in costume on their excursion to the graveyard.

That night we lay in wait behind a hedgerow for Krill's "grave-robbing liberal pirates." You can't imagine the glee, dear Frank, of well-disguised pirates out on the warpath to, of all things, *root out piracy!* Our company included Tosspot and a cadre of Pinkerton detectives. God, how I loathed those Pinkertons, hunting us all those years, ambushing mamma and Archie on the farm, killing him and blowing off her arm. I wanted to gun them all down, truly I did.

Reporters from the nation's most prestigious newspapers, plus the Mandate Media, and leadership of the Clown Criers, all waited for the despicable pirates. Also among us were members of the Misclud family—stalwart Republicans one and all, unflinching in their resolve to serve their country (and also quite generous with their campaign contributions).

Congressman Nadel, John McTeague, and their retinue of parasites were all dressed to the nines as corsair rogues, complete with bright red and gold bandanas; some also wore triangular leather hats, a few were barefooted while others donned knee-high leather boots, and they all boasted holsters loaded with pistols and knives and long cutlasses at their hips. McTeague had gone above the call by leading the group with a silken black-and-white Jolly Roger flying from a pole.

"Look at 'em," whispered Wrong John. "Don't know the first thing about pirating."

"Heck no," answered Pinch softly. "No discipline. Acting like a bunch of unruly humanists—typical. Boisterous, clumsy, and *drunk*."

"Bubba would no doubt be proud," the marshal added.

They landed on Gretta Misclud's grave in a flurry of shovels, picks, hoes, and rakes, banging as often against the other tools as they did against the ground. Nevertheless, it wasn't long before they had the soiled rosewood casket once again among the living. Behind the hedgerow it was all hot breath and quiet anticipation rustling in clothes. The moon, full and bright white, gave a clear view of the action.

With some difficulty we held back the incensed Misclud children until Nadel himself pried open the casket with a crowbar, removed the string of gemstones, and went beyond Krill's wildest hopes by stupidly hanging the necklace around his own neck! "What do you think, boys?" he asked, brushing the necklace with his fingertips. McTeague laughed nervously and leaned into the casket as if looking for more jewelry, but he lost his balance and almost fell in the box. At that moment, Tosspot and his filthy Pinkertons burst from the hedgerow.

"Stand away from the casket, you craven necrophile!" TP shouted at McTeague, a pistol in one hand and a flaring, just lit torch in the other. McTeague regained his balance and jumped back from the open casket, hands in the air, mouth wide, eyebrows arched. The tax-collecting parasites scattered in all directions, as would kitchen cockroaches in a sudden light. The sons of Gretta Misclud, hearing TP advertise McTeague's vile intentions on their mother's corpse, roared from the hedge and bludgeoned him with clubs.

"Stop! Please, I did what you asked! I did what you said! Please!" cried McTeague with his arms and legs flailing to block the rain of blows.

"Yes, but did you do what the Lord commanded?" growled Tosspot, who had moved next to him and looked down hard upon him. "You cannot redeem your adulterous sins by betraying your friends."

"You son-of-a-bitch!" screamed Congressman Nadel in a full run at his chief of staff. He dove on McTeague, scattering the Misclud sons, and pounded on his face with his fists. The journalists scribbled in their notebooks so fiercely I imagined them starving coyotes scratching at the gate of a henhouse. Photographers flashed their pans and lit up the graveyard, but I can hardly imagine they captured anything more than a blur. Congressman Nadel did not seem likely to strike a willing pose for the cameras. Maybe, though, a photo of blurry, ghostly pirates robbing graves, well suited their purposes.

Captain Silverspoon wandered out from behind the hedge and sauntered up to the brawling Democrats. He wore the prim blue dress uniform of a ship's commander and his flouncy, humped hat.

"Not a pretty sight at all," he said, looking down his nose at them. Hearing his voice, Nadel pulled himself off the ground and gawked at the leader of the free world. "I wouldn't have imagined even a rabid liberal such as you, Representative Nadel, would stoop to piracy in order to stuff his own pockets." Wrong John gave him the "for shame" sign by brushing his left index finger over his right. "Tsk, tsk, tsk," he said, shaking his head.

"But, sir, Mr. Captain, sir, you know I'm not a *pirate*," said Nadel. "This is just a costume. I was just trying to do my duty—to protect the shared wealth of the people, to—"

"Uh-huh. And I suppose you were going to give that little beauty around your neck to an orphanage." Nadel clutched at his throat and tried to tear the diamond necklace off, tried to explain, but Captain Silverspoon sliced the air horizontally with his hand and leered at him. Mandate Media photographers captured Nadel wearing the stolen prize. Wrong John turned away from the congressman and addressed the entire group. "You know, folks, it's just—it plain breaks my heart when good, hard-working American patriots, like the Miscluds here, are forced to send their family treasure to the grave in order to avoid the punitive death tax that would force them to sell the family business." He rubbed his lips and chin.

"We love our country!" yelled one of the Misclud boys. "Why are they punishing us?"

"I'm just—it's—there's something very, very wrong in our great nation when political leaders will rob a grave to steal the rightful inheritance of honest heirs. It's not just un-American to punalize success like this, it's—there's—you know, there's no other way to characterize it than *racism*. Successful white folk like the Miscluds have been singled out for abuse by a representative of our very own Congress. Can you imagine? And he's white, too. What do you call that? Cannibalism? It's sick. It's class warfare. It's—it's *death tax terrorism*, that's what it is. What next? Lynching somebody for having a stock portfolio? Taking the caviar straight from the mouths of our babes—er, our children?

"It's sick, and it's the sort of racial profiling that we witnessed tonight, the criminal abuse and outright robbery of wealthy, overpriviliged white folk, burdened by the thankless yoke to keep The Economy strong, that *will not stand* in Silverspoon America. If black and brown, yellow, and red people have rights and deserve justice in this nation, then by God so do the good white folk suffering with wealth and privilege." He walked slowly around the hole that had once, and would soon again, hold the body of Gretta Misclud.

"What makes this most painful of all—to me, your commander-in-chief—is that it took place while we are at war," he shook his head grimly and stared into the blackness of the empty grave. "If I were a terrorist, I don't suppose there's anything that would make me more happier than to hear of American's robbing and spitting on the graves of her loved ones. I'm sure Al Quota and Shalong are having a good chuckle together seeing how they turned us against ourselves."

In the days that followed, news spread across the nation of the despicable act of piracy by an elected representative and employees of the federal government. Clown Criers rang their bells and shouted: "Robbery! Villainy! Liberal grave-robbing tax collectors! *Pirates* stealing from *patriots* while their country is at *WAR!*" Agents of Homemade Insecurity raised the Squid Alert to Code Orange, because, as Tom Thumb was quoted on page one of the entire Mandate newspaper chain, "When the Giant Squid sees your society losing its values like this, that's when she rises up and strikes." TP created No Flower lists of dangerous liberals who were to be arrested if they attempted to put bouquets on the graves of their relatives.

Outrage over the grave robbery at Granary Burying Ground inspired a massive tax revolt, in which Americans of every stripe demanded tax cuts from the greedy, wasteful, all but useless Washington bureaucracy. They didn't seem to realize the "death tax" only applied to the very wealthiest Americas. Instead, they took it on as a personal attack of their right to bequeath inheritance to their children. *Liberty* obliged their mandate by raiding the treasury as she had the year before. Armored carriages by the dozen pulled up to the public vault and were loaded with the gold bars recently minted in the foundries of China. Unto the incensed peasantry of America—many of whom no longer paid taxes at all, given they had no jobs or wages to tax—Wrong John showered handfuls of silver and gold, while the glimmering ingots went straight to Pirate Island to be divvied up among his friends.

Imagine it, Frank, just imagine it! We and the Youngers riding into Northfield, Minnesota, September 7, 1876, and when we get to the bank, there's no money in the vault. The good folks of Northfield tell us to come back in a month, that they'll *borrow* the money from some other bank for us to steal. We come back in four weeks, and sure enough, the Bank of Northfield is loaded up with fifty grand in borrowed cash—and the people just open the vault, tell us to help ourselves, and sing My Country 'Tis of Thee to us on the way out of town.

Of course you know that's not how it went. The citizens of Northfield, Minnesota, rose up against us and killed Clel Miller, Billy Stiles, and Charlie Pitts. They captured Cole, Bob and Jimmy Younger, all of them badly wounded, and chased me and you, Frank, clean to Tennessee. We had gone out of bounds, reaching all the way to Minnesota to punish that old Union man Adelbert Ames. If the Union was my Moby Dick, as Tatanka had said, Northfield was me putting in a second time after the whale. I got pretty much the same treatment as Captain Ahab:

> "Ahab's yet unstricken boat seemed to rise up towards heaven by invisible wires,—as, arrow-like, shooting perpendicularly from the sea, the White Whale dashed his broad forehead against its bottom, and sent it, turning over and over, into the air; till it fell again—gunwale downwards— and Ahab and his men struggled out from under it, like seals from a seaside cave."

The night of the second tax rebate festival on Pirate Island, the clearing again burned with hot bonfires, hungrily licking the pyramid of gold standing at the center. Women in mink coats and diamond necklaces sipped champagne and nibbled truffles with their husbands dressed in tails and sporting gold watches in their fobs. The atmosphere, though jubilant, lacked the patina of certainty that had accompanied the previous festival. A sort of pall hung over the clearing, as blubber smoke on the water, making it a little stuffy, tense, hard to breathe, and riddled slightly by termites of guilt, the evidence around the perimeter in careless piles of sawdust.

Instead of the agreeable voice and gentle hands of Basmati Sweet on the pipe organ, Tosspot groped the keys and bellowed an off-key church hymn:

> **Faith of our brothers, suffering sore,**
> **Enduring prison, famine, and sword,**
> **O Holy Spirit, give comfort, we pray,**
> **May they this day find strength in thy Word.**
> **Faith of our brothers, holy faith,**
> **May they be true to thee till death.**

When it was time to divide the spoils, everyone waited for Silverspoon to get up on the pyramid of gold and hand down the booty. They urged him on to sing *Swing Low Sweet Chariot*, or some fitting spiritual. He sat in his chair and gave them a disinterested eye roll. "Do I look like a charity?" he asked. "Get up off your butts and get your own gold."

Chapter XXXIV

Bait and Switch Debate

After destroying Congressman Nadel's career, the mood of *Liberty* was buoyant heading into the mid-term congressional elections. This was usually a time in presidential politics, Pinch informed me, in which the incumbent often lost his House or Senate majority—if he had one—and was left hamstrung politically for his last two years, forced to exercise his power mostly by veto. Krill's goal was for Captain Silverspoon *never* to be insulted by having a piece of legislation come across his desk that he had not pre-approved. Wrong John wasn't going to sit back and wait for squid to slither up America's toilet, and he damn sure wasn't going to let the legislature sneak one in on him either. The legislative branch, in Chief Dagger's opinion, was best understood as a collection of vassals, more in the business of paying tribute than of risking the ire of their king. And so, as I said, Congressman Nadel's infamy, orchestrated masterfully by the parrot savant, provided great confidence that liberals—who were naturally of little backbone—would run like sheep to the slaughter, if you but opened the proper gate.

One afternoon, while the captain and his officers hit golf balls from the driving platform, everyone kicked around ideas for how most effectively to eviscerate the Democrats. As floating targets, Gunny had several enemy combatants from Batguano tied up in row boats and anchored in the river at one-hundred, one-fifty, and two-hundred yards, the yardages marked by heavy signs the prisoners held between their bare legs while they stood on their heads. There was little wind, a mild haze, and a few small clouds on the eastern horizon. A well-armed lookout manned the crow's nest, up among *Liberty's* collection of flags, and other sailors stood at the small cannon on deck. A sailor had shinnied out the bowsprit and was polishing the spiral narwhale horn.

Basmati Sweet and Tom Thumb had returned from their tour and joined the officers for the first time in several weeks. They received updates on the Commune of Corporatocracy, practicing its Ellis Outland off the territorial waters of America. Chief apprised them of Dr. Henchman's new role as "independent investigator" of the 10-10 disaster. "He knows his mandate," Chief said.

"We saw all the articles about Representative Nadel's piracy," said Basma. "That was quite a set up."

"BRACKs a lot," said Krill, taking a bow from the captain's shoulder.

"So how's the squid situation out there, Tommy?" asked Wrong John, leaning on his driver, dabbing the sweat from his forehead with a hanky.

"Damn slippery!" said the dwarf in his deep voice. The officers chuckled. "The jiggly things are flying everywhere, blushing, getting green around the gills. I got a letter from P.T. Barnum—mad as a tick that we got onto the squid before he did."

"If P.T. likes it, you know we're onto a winner," said Gunny, pulling on his nose ring.

"Prince of the Humbugs. Prince of the Humbugs," Krill chattered.

Dagger, who was flying high after the latest tax rebate, stepped up and addressed his ball, hauled back, swung mightily, and, just as before, whiffed;

the only things to move were his gold hoop earrings rocking in his floppy earlobes. He placed his hand above his eyebrows as if sighting a well-hit ball. "Ouch, that's gotta hurt," he said. I wasn't sure what he was talking about, until he yelled, "You want to tell us where Quota's hiding now, or do I paste you with another?"

"That's telling him, Mr. First Mate," said Sweet.

"Got the sweet spot that time, sir," said Tosspot.

"Straight arrow," said Yo Yo, "that's our Chief."

He lowered his eyes at me, waiting, I'm sure, to see if I would let his B.S. slide. I looked back at him, and saw in those sharp blue eyes, behind his thick glasses, a calm savagery. I hadn't seen a look like that since Bloody Bill Anderson lit out after Cox's boys along the Fishing River, October 27, 1864. It was his last ride. A man like that, on his way into the final battle, was not wise to challenge, so I decided (for once in my life) to play along. "Killed that one, Chief. That Arab's balls will be aching for a month." He smiled at me and returned his driver to the bag.

Captain Silverspoon slapped Dagger on the back and said, "Thanks for teeing it up for me, buddy." He addressed the featherie Dagger had whiffed, and smacked it well past the farthest boat. The force of the swing knocked Krill from his perch and sent him tumbling over the rail and into the coffee river water. The officers cheered at the captain's shot. Nobody seemed to notice the mishap of the mouthy bird. Wrong John grinned broadly and did a little strutting chicken dance. "You can run," he hollered, "but you can't hide!" I could just hear Krill splashing in the water below, squawking about how he couldn't swim, and could picture his stubby wings flapping madly to keep his head above water.

Yo Yo approached the tee box next, but before he could place his ball, Tatanka came by with iced tea. The thirsty officers gathered around him. Gunny took a big drink of tea, and I set a baked white cookie in the shape of a golf ball on his tee. He set the tea down, looked at the tee box, and seemed to forget he hadn't yet placed his ball. He addressed it, waggled his butt, and took a big swing. On impact with the ball, it exploded into white dust.

"Whoa-ho, Gunny!" said the captain. "That's what I call power golf."

"You tell Shalong the American military is coming!" shouted Dagger to the prisoners standing on their heads in the dinghies on the river. "We're going to dust him!" He slapped Yo Yo hard on the back and shook his hand. Pinch rushed over and kissed him on the lips. He squeezed her butt and wiggled his eyebrows up and down.

"Ashes to ashes, you heathen thugs!" Tosspot yelled. Sir Yes Sir and Basma said nothing.

"Boy, I guess that says it all. Is the American military ready, or is the American military ready? Or is the American military *really* ready—or is it?" said Wrong John. "Now where's that damn bird? All morning he's been pestering me that we gotta focus on the midterms. Now he's off raiding the pantry or something. So what do you think? We've got 'em on the ropes. How do we deliver the KO? Thirty words, tops."

"Arrest them for having sex with children, Sire," said TP.

"A crisp eight words. I like it," said the captain, relaxing his extended counting fingers to their normal position. The others stared at him, and he eventually realized a reaction to TP's suggestion was in order. "Sex with children—that disgusts me. Tell me who's doing it and I will personally poke him in the nose."

"It's not that I know at this moment precisely who's doing it, Majesty. It's more a matter of suspecting it and—under the terms of the mandate—stopping it before it happens."

"*Dos palabras* over the limit, but sure, well, as we all know, thinking about doing a bad thing is as bad as actually doing something bad—which is very bad and should be punished with a good thumping. Bible even says that, don't it Ish?"

"Not exactly, captain," I said.

"See, told ya," Wrong John said, pointing at TP. He pulled his putter from his bag and began idly knocking balls at a cup on the far side of the platform.

"I like where he's going, sir," said Dagger, pushing his glasses up on his nose. "Even if they categorically deny ever sleeping with a minor, we've got them out there in a close election talking about themselves *not* sleeping with minors. Damage done, count the votes, chock one up for the good guys." The captain counted Dagger's words too (I could tell by the way his lips moved) but he never chastised him for going over the limit, Dagger having earned bonus words, I guess, by running the country for his boss.

I could barely hear Krill, in the river, splashing and wailing about his imminent drowning. No one seemed to hear him or to notice he was gone. Silverspoon pointed to Basmati Sweet, who looked down and shook her head, while her hands spoke a sign language the captain apparently understood— though no one else did, as far as I could tell. I was accustomed by now to understand that she would tell him later what she thought, when no one else was around to question her. Wrong John pointed to Pinch.

"How about if we plant some phony documents on them, linking them to a charity that has donated heavily to Al Quota?" she said, unable as usual, to fully tuck her oversized upper incisors behind her lips.

"Six to spare, Pinch. You want to hold them or trade for the right to piss in the river?"

"I'll hold. I don't get quite the thrill out of sticking my ass over the rail as you guys do whipping it out and showering your generosity on the capital's water supply."

"Up to you." The captain seemed ready to move on to the next person, when, again, he realized there was more required of him than just to count how many words his staff had used. "Yeah, yeah, I kinda like that'un. Everybody's too scared to question us on anything, so, boom, slow boat to Cuba."

"You're right, captain. Absence of evidence is not evidence of absence," said Yo Yo.

"Whoa, Nellie! Good one, Gunny. You didn't just make that one up, did you?"

"Well, yes, I mean, it was—the, the Greeks used to play around with, with logic, and little—yes, yes I did."

"I like it. Let's keep that one in the hopper, Basma, run it up the flagpole a time or two if we ever need to blow smoke up somebody's butt." She wrote the saying into a small book.

The tiny director of Homemade Insecurity stepped to the tee. He placed his featherie on a tee and addressed it with a short driver, not quite two feet long. He pulled back quickly and hit it squarely, out off the stern deck.

"Squid Alert!" I yelled. "Code Red!"

Tatanka pulled his revolver and pulverized the feathered golf ball. The officers clapped and nodded at their longhaired cook. The little man turned on him and scowled. He raised his golf club and walked at the Sioux. Wrong John caught him by the shoulder and held him back. "Easy, Big Tom. We all went through it. Just a little initiation into the club. Don't sweat it." Tom Thumb slammed his driver against the platform, turned, and stormed to the port gunwale.

Silverspoon looked around the golf platform. "Okay, who's left?"

Sweet raised her slender hand. "I haven't hit yet."

"Shee-it, Basma. You swing like a girl, and we ain't got women's tees."

"I want to hit. Everybody else hits. I want to hit." Her face trembled with a sudden rage. "I run around this country, talking out both sides of my mouth as if I was a two-headed snake. I want to hit! I've earned a crack at the little white ball, damn it! I won't do your dirty work and *still* not get to hit!—and nobody shoots it!" She glared at Tatanka and me. Sweet placed her ball, hauled back, and hit a straight shot over the water, nearly hitting the one hundred yard marker in the ass. No one commented. Sir Yes Sir alone clapped. He brought her a glass of iced tea and walked her off the platform.

Crude raised his small, pinkish, chubby hand.

"That counts as a word," said Wrong John.

"I think we should accuse them of using bad science about global climate change to sabotage The Economy," he blurted.

"Twelve words to spare, not counting the raised hand. Way to go, Crude." Wrong John caught himself rather quickly this time, and commented further. "I don't like it though, Ink Blot. Nobody's worried about The Economy right now. They've got a pocket full of silver from the big tax break, and that'll keep them happy until they blow it. Thing is, Americans don't care about jobs, or privacy, or freedom of expression, or any of that junk right now. What they care about is safety. Is their children safe? Those are the questions they want asked."

Tom Thumb reached in his pocket, pulled out a small purple squid, and tossed it on the green wool surface. "Encroachment. Five yard penalty. Repeat third down," he said.

Wrong John looked around. "Where's that bird? I can't usually shut him up and here we are practically in a crisis and he's got nothing?" He put two fingers in his mouth and whistled.

Krill had by then, the lookout told us later, all but expired, and was just keeping his head above the water. "Man—uh, bird overboard!" he cried from the masthead. The captain and his staff rushed to the rail, leaned over and spotted Krill soaked, his red-feathered body in the drink. "Stork!" yelled Tosspot, drew his gun, and aimed at Krill. Basma grabbed his arm. "That's not a stork, and you know it." Officer Bill tore off his shirt and made a perfect swan dive into the water. He gathered Krill up and held onto a rope Speck had thrown to him. Speck pulled him up.

When Bill came over the rail with Krill, who coughed up water and tried to catch his breath, Tosspot was there to congratulate him. Bill, for some reason, kissed the marshal on the lips. The officers looked at one another from the corners of their eyes. Hands went into pockets. Throats were cleared. Mistakes were made. Basma stuck out her tongue as if she had bitten into a rotten apple. Silverspoon and Chief stared intently at Bill and TP, hands on hips. Bill knew he was in trouble. "I'm so sorry, Marshal Tosspot. I was just—I was so completely overcome with relief at the rescue of our chief—our head of—." Bill was clearly at a loss to name Krill's actual position on the ship, which, I must admit, was something I don't think any of us could have done.

"I was just so happy our great, important, um, parrot was safe, I—I lost my head." He looked at us all quickly, licked his lips, smiled falsely, then said, "Three cheers for Krill! Hip hip, hurrah! Hip hip, hurrah! Hip, hurrah!" The officers joined in the cheer halfheartedly. Tosspot's pallid face had blushed, and he frowned, lips tight and wrinkled. Bill attempted to cover his tracks. He bent over Krill, picked him up, and gave him mouth-to-mouth resuscitation. This quickly revived Krill, who pecked Bill's lower lip so hard it bled. Bill jumped back, yelped, and dropped Krill to the deck, where he landed with a thud. The impact brought him completely back to his normal self.

"BRACK! Don't you ever touch me like that again. I'll chop off your balls for crab bait—balls for crab bait," Krill barked. Bill held his hand to his bleeding lip and nodded quickly. The other officers laughed and the captain picked up Krill, placed him on his shoulder, and fed him a salted peanut. TP, however, did not so much as smile. He dragged the junior officer to the mainmast, locked him in leg irons, tied his wrists to the mast, and pulled out his bullwhip. He lashed Bill severely, roaring quotes from Leviticus, and promising an immediate trip to Batguano Castle for his act of "homoerotic terrorism."

Wrong John crossed the deck and grabbed his marshal's arm, just as he was about to deliver another blow. "Let it go, Tosspot. Go wash your face with soap. I'll have Bill reassigned, but I don't think we need to send him to Guano."

"But he!—didn't you see what he—"

"Go and wash your face. Say three Hail Mary's, take a couple of aspirin, and call me in the morning." He slapped TP on the back. The marshal stomped to the hatch and disappeared inside. Wrong John walked back to the golf platform and idly putted balls at the cup lying on its side.

Krill had either been able to hear and assimilate the conversation that had taken place on deck while he was drowning, or had divined the content, but one way or the other, he was able to sum up what had been said and craft it into a wicked stratagem.

"*BRACK!* Public debates. Challenge the liberals to public debates. *BRACK!*"

"Hey, that's not bad. I'm purty good at debates myself," said the captain. Sir Yes Sir and Dagger rolled their eyes. Yo Yo sneezed falsely to cover up his guffaw.

"I'm not with you on this one, Peckerhead," said Dagger, his lip twitching involuntarily. "Our people are not at their best in an open forum. The damn liberals are natural tap dancers and spontaneous prevaricators. We work best with exhaustive pre-planning and tightly scripted events before audiences of our admirers."

"True, Chief. True, very true," Krill replied. He whistled like a quick doorbell. "Who-who. Who-who. Who says we don't script it?"

"Go on," Dagger said, drawing out the words.

"Fake debate. Fake debate. Oh, it is scripted. It's scripted. Humiliate the liberals. Humiliate the liberals." He whistled the preamble to *Charge!* and said. "Bait and Switch Debate, *BRACK!* Bait and Switch Debate." Dagger stuck his tongue in his cheek and winked at Krill. Captain Silverspoon shook his head in amazement, stroked his parrot's beak, and fed him a live, wriggling worm (where he got it from I have no idea—perhaps he had a wormy apple in his pocket). The other officers nodded knowingly. Several crossed their arms, as if the game was already won—à la the Silverspoon Mandate. At this point in the voyage, there was no reason to doubt it.

Chapter XXXV

The Jihadist Charity Ball

Krill's bait-and-switch debates became the leading strategy in Wrong John's push to consolidate power around his mandate during the mid-term elections. It was easy enough to rig the debates without much notice, the country finding itself bombarded with a continuous stream of Squid Alerts, God Arrest America raids, Clown Crier sputum, threats of WMH's, and jingoist articles in the Mandate Media conglomerate. More than thirty of the debatable debates were set up without the Democrats realizing what they had wandered into.

Tatanka and I found ourselves recruited for security at a debate in North Carolina between the incumbent Democratic Senator of North Carolina, Jack Droxford, and his Republican challenger, Bob Broder. Krill informed us the format was the same in the other debates he had organized around the country. The one I attended was considered among the more interesting of the contests, pitting a popular Confederate veteran, the incumbent Droxford, against a man whose war record was in question, but was generally believed a rebel deserter. If the Republicans could unseat this Democrat, word had it, they were a lock to steal the entire election, and could put another notch in their Florida gator belt.

The crew of *Liberty* set the stage in a clearing among the rolling hills of Winston-Salem. Two dark oak lecterns had been placed on either side of the stage, while a long table in front seated the moderator and the panel. An American flag stood at one end of the stage, while the North Carolina flag graced the other. Beneath the state flag, a fish tank held a zebra-striped squid, Code Blue: guarded. An agent of Homemade Insecurity stood on the ground next to the tank. Several photographers waited at their camera tripods in front of the stage. About two hundred people sat in wooden folding chairs set up in neat rows in front of the stage. A dense forest surrounded the clearing, made up of coffee and chestnut trees, sycamore, red oak, alder, and larch, falling away to long leaf pine down the holler. A rugged outcropping of gray granite stood along the hillside behind the stage. A pair of red-crested cardinals sang from the forest edge, flitting among the dogwood.

As the debate neared its start, a boy in bib overalls released a gray, bare-nosed possum that walked a tightrope strung ten feet up at the back of the stage. A pair of black hawks danced in the sky below puffy gray clouds edged in white. Sweet corn and chicken roasted on a nearby grill. A brass band played the North Carolina state song *Old North State*, and the audience sang along, though somewhat "guarded" from the warning of the blue squid.

> **"Carolina! Carolina! heaven's blessings attend her,**
> **While we live we will cherish, protect and defend her,**
> **Tho' the scorner may sneer at and witlings defame her,**
> **Still our hearts swell with gladness whenever we name her.**
>
> **Hurrah! Hurrah! the Old North State forever,**
> **Hurrah! Hurrah! the good Old North State.**

From a tent left of the stage the moderator and panel filed out to the table in front of the stage. The moderator of the debate was the same massive, baldheaded guy who played master of ceremonies at the Fatass Rodeo. His two panel members were dressed in clown suits and sat to his left. From a tent on the other side of the stage, the Republican challenger bounded to the stage, wearing (much to my amazement) the uniform of a Confederate officer, and took the lectern closest to him. The crowd came to its feet, cheered, and whistled.

A moment later, the incumbent emerged from a smaller white tent next to the challenger's, rolling slowly in a wooden wheelchair. The crowd was completely silent. Droxford reached the edge of the stage and stopped. There was no ramp, and he could not get onto the stage—and nobody moved to help him. He had no legs, and only one arm; he looked around for help. No one came to his aid, or offered crutches, and in the heavy silence and strange acrobatics of the trained possum on the tightrope, the pressure mounted until finally Senator Droxford tried to pull himself on stage. I couldn't let a war veteran of the Confederacy be insulted like that and walked over and lifted him (with Tatanka's help), wheelchair and all, onto the stage. The challenger scowled at me, and the moderator uttered a low growl, but damn them, this man had given half his body for the cause, and I knew full well the imposter wearing a Confederate uniform had been a deserter.

"Thank you, Tarheels," the big man boomed, "for hosting this important discussion. I'm Big Jim Crumwell, and I'll be the moderator today. I will have the first question on each topic, and the last, and I will keep time and make sure both participants adhere to the rules. Okay, so the first question is for the challenger. Mr. Broder, what will you do to protect America from terror?"

"Thank you, Big Jim," he said, smiling with perfect white teeth, then quickly frowning. "Unlike my opponent, I believe terror is a threat we must aggressively pursue. I'm not going to cut funds for the military and question the president's actions prior to 10-10, as did the senator. I'm going to support the president and his Silverspoon Mandate that says, 'Hit them before they hit you.'"

The senator attempted to rebut his challenger, but Big Jim cut him off. "I have a new question for you, Senator Droxford." He produced a photo of the senator with his arms around Shalong on one side and Al Quota on the other. "Senator, can you explain to us what you were doing at the Jihadist Charity Ball with Shalong and Al Quota?"

"Ooh," responded the crowd.

Tatanka leaned over to me and said, "Ambush."

Droxford's face flushed red with anger. "I was never at an event with those two! This is an outrage! How can a rodeo announcer run a debate? This is a sham. No one will believe that falsified image. Informed voters know by now that Quota and Shalong were never seen together. The two are bitter enemies, occupying polar opposites in terms of faith and political agenda. Anyone who knows a speck about international relations knows that AQ would have been just as happy to send his storks against Shalong as he did against us."

"Uh-huh," said Big Jim in a condescending tone. He scratched his ear with a big left paw. "I'm sorry, senator, but the people count on me for The Truth, and so I must ask you, once again, how does any of that explain your presence at the jihad awards banquet?"

I noticed Krill behind the audience, perched on the back of a chair, shadow boxing, his wings as fists, clucking and whistling to himself as he punched the air.

"That's not an authentic photo," said Droxford, waving the back of his one good hand at the moderator. "That's all I can say. It's been doctored somehow."

The chief scientist from *Liberty*, Dr. von Shlop, dressed in his usual pointed blue hat and robe, appeared out of the crowd and examined the photo with a large magnifying glass. "The Chief Scientist of *Liberty*, ladies and gentlemen—highest authority in the land, mind you," said Big Jim. "Verify for us, Dr. von Shlop, the authenticity of this photo."

"I can tell by the positioning of the photographic juices, the way in which they are smooshed by the chemicals and such—silver mostly—that this image is from one camera, and a single piece of film," the doctor said in his high squeaky voice.

"What is this, a debate or a trial? What sort of impartial panel are you? Don't you all work for Silverspoon?" demanded the senator.

"We resent the implication, senator," said Big Jim. "Objectivity is the standard to which we are bound as members of the free press in America."

"Press? You're not journalists. You're just showmen!" shouted the senator, shifting in his squeaky wheelchair.

The insecurity agent pulled a small purple squid from his bandoleer and threw it at Droxford's wheel chair. It landed in the spokes, dangled there, and wiggled. He blew his whistle and said, "Illegal use of the hands. Ten yard penalty. Loss of down." Droxford crossed his good left arm with the stump of his right.

Big Jim continued. "Unlike the liberal media that unceasingly pushes the far left perspective, we simply tell it like it is. And to answer your question, it is indeed a debate, and a debate we shall have. Mr. Broder, would you care to rebut the senator's answer?"

"Hey! I didn't get to rebut his answer."

"Bitch, bitch, bitch. Can't you find one positive thing to say about your country? Mr. Broder, rebuttal." The gray possum on stage curled its tail around the rope and stared down on the contestants with its big eyes, its bare, pointed nose quivering. I'm sure the little fella just wanted to find the hollow of a tree to sleep in; they aren't normally active until after dark.

"Thank you, Big Jim." Broder smiled, then fell away to a frown. He grabbed the lapels of his confederate coat. "Yes, yes, I would care to rebut the hollow denials of my challenger—"

"Challenger? *You're* the challenger. I'm the current senator." Droxford leaned forward, his chair creaking, seeming ready to break from the weight of his outrage.

Broder held up his hands at Big Jim. "I can't carry on an intelligent debate if he's going to interrupt me every five seconds."

The moderator shook his big bald head at Broder. "Senator, the American people don't need another Foul Bore apple-polisher trying to prove how smart he is. Challenger, incumbent, what's the differ'nce? Just stop playing your elitist games and let the man respond."

"Thank you, Jim," said Broder, smiling broadly for an instant, then dropping into a deep frown. "I believe that it is wrong to attend the fundraising events of our enemies. I just think it shows bad judgment, and typifies the moral bankruptcy of the far left. It's the same attitude that says homosexuality is good, pornography is free speech, premarital sex is natural, killing unborn children is healthy. I think that instead of propping up terrorists and tyrants, we ought to go after them; we ought to wipe them off the face of the earth before they can do us more harm."

"So you support the captain in his courageous crusade to preempt Shalong Quota's evil Weapons of Mass Hysteria by invading Iraq?"

"Yes, yes I do. Unlike my competitor, I believe that in times of war, you stand together as a people. You stand with your captain and your troops and you don't run around undermining them by voting to cut military spending, and partying with thugs and criminals."

"That's absolutely absurd!" exclaimed Droxford. "I never attended their—those pictures are—I would never attend—. And to insinuate I'm not a patriot... I gave both of my legs and half an arm fighting for the South. We may have lost, and we may have been wrong, but I was a patriot to my people and our ways. Broder didn't have the guts to engage one battle—disappeared before the first bullet was fired. Quite frankly, I'm insulted that he would wear the rebel gray. He's got no business."

"Let's not let this degenerate into a personal attack, senator. Just answer the hard questions America demands that I ask on their behalf." One of the Clown Criers stood on his chair toward the audience and motioned someone forward with a wave of his white-gloved hand. A light-skinned African girl, about eight, walked shyly forward. "Why haven't you been straight with the voters about your bastard daughter?" the Clown Crier asked Senator Droxford.

The senator shook with rage. "My daughter? I've never seen that girl in my life. I've been happily and faithfully married for thirty years. What the hell is going on here? Poor child. Who put you up to this?" The girl began to cry.

"*BRACK! BRACK!* Shocking revelations!" screeched Krill from the rear of the crowd. "Immorality! Sex scandal! Liberal decadence!" Several reporters in the back row scribbled furiously in their notebooks.

Dr. von Shlop took some implements from his black bag and examined the girl. He looked into her eyes, her ears, up her nose, listened to her heart with a stethoscope, and tapped on her ribs with the index and middle finger of his right hand. "Well, doctor?" asked Big Jim. "All of America in on pins and needles, awaiting the diagnosis of the highest authority in the land."

"Pitter, patter, what's the matter? Muzzle, fuzzle, got a nuzzle. Father, mother, there's no other." Dr. von Shlop reached into his medicine bag and threw out a cloud of glittering dust. "This child is, based on the very best science available to us, almost surely the daughter of Senator Droxford."

"How can you possibly determine that? It's preposterous. I've never heard of such a—"

A purple squid landed in the senator's lap. "Unsportsmanlike conduct," the insecurity agent said, and blew his whistle. "Fifteen yards. Automatic first down."

"You see, Big Jim," interrupted Broder. He pulled on the lapels of his

Confederate uniform and tilted his head to the side. "That's the sort of left-wing rebellion that only serves to comfort and encourage the enemies of freedom. When you can't even go along with the opinion of the highest scientific authority in the land, I mean, what good are these politicians who have more interest in arguing about obvious facts than turning their attention to the real business of fighting the War on Squid?"

"Senator?" asked Big Jim.

"This is just—it's just pure insanity. How does my disputing your claim about an illegitimate daughter have even the remotest connection to fighting terror? It's just—it's utterly crazy. Crazy—"

"That will do, senator," said Big Jim. "The next question is from our eminent Clowns Criers."

The two clowns got up and began juggling unlit torches. They threw them back and forth: first two, then three, four, five, six, until there were eight unlit torches flying back and forth in the air. The possum, balancing on its tightrope with its feet and tail, walked to the senator's side of the stage, stopped and scolded him in a high-pitched, chattering voice. The brass band played a bouncy circus tune, and the audience clapped in time with it, as did Broder, smiling. The senator watched the act with his mouth open, eyebrows knitted and raised in disbelief. An assistant from the audience rose from her seat and grabbed one of the torches in mid-air. She lit it on fire and returned it with perfect timing to the juggling act, where it quickly caught the other well-oiled torches on fire until they were all burning.

Without any warning, the clowns turned to the stage and tossed the burning torches at the one-armed, legless senator. Two flaming torches hit his one good arm that he held up to protect his face. Others bounced off of the lectern and fell to the stage and caught the front drape of blue and red fabric on fire. Droxford's wheelchair caught fire, as did his lectern. His shock and outrage constricted his face into a grotesque confusion of wrinkles, and he fell hard to the floor.

Suddenly, there was Broder with a bucket of water in each hand. He dumped both of them on the senator, who was not himself on fire, but lying helplessly on his side. One of the clowns put out the actual fire with a canvas backpack pump hose. Senator Droxford sputtered and tried to catch his breath. The band continued to play their bouncy, circus tune and the audience clapped in time. The smell of chicken and roasting corn mixed in the air with the smoke of burnt oil. The possum's trainer threw a chunk of apple from the side of the stage. It caught the fruit in its small human-looking hands. Broder leaned down to the senator and said something to him I could not make out, but caused Droxford to swear at him and punch him in the mouth. Cameras flashed, as if they had been waiting for the moment. Broder put his hand to his bleeding lip and returned to his lectern. The senator struggled to sit up and leaned against his podium. The band stopped playing and the audience fell silent.

"It would appear, senator," said the clown, sitting on the edge of the moderator's table, "by your response to a mock terrorist strike that you are not only ill prepared to handle the attack, you are also more inclined to strike a friend and colleague—an American—who tries to help you, than you are inclined to defend your nation against evil."

"Oh for God's sake!" said the senator, trying to keep from falling over, the stubs of his legs out in front of him, and what remained of his right arm hanging by his side. "If you heard what he said to me, you would—you can't compare a bad clown act with the diabolical plotting of a disciplined terrorist organization. These people are not fooling around. They're calculating and deliberate, and while we're planning for an unnecessary war against Iraq, they're preparing for the next attack against America. Let's get our attention focused on what really matters."

"Senator Broder?" asked Big Jim, interlacing his fingers.

"Thank you, Big Jim." He smiled again, then frowned. He dabbed at his cut lip with a white handkerchief. "I don't think this will need a stitch." He showed the bloodstained cloth to the audience.

"Oh my!" said an old woman near the front. "Heavens!" exclaimed another. "Cheap shot, Droxford," added a middle-aged man.

Two purple squid landed in front of the senator. A whistle blew. "Personal foul. Unnecessary roughness. Half the distance to the goal."

"But let me tell you something," Broder went on. "America cannot sit idly by as our elected officials go about punching their fellow Americans and doing nothing about the threat from squid. What just happened here illustrates better than any point I could make just exactly and precisely the difference between my opponent and I. He falls apart and catches on fire in the face of terror, while I keep my composure, almost having—in a Silverspoon sort of way—anticipated the intentions of our enemy and responded without hesitation to the threat. Rather than thank me for defending our country, or congratulate me for thwarting a wicked plot, he attacks *me* and completely ignores those that would attack *us.*"

"Thank you, gentlemen," said Big Jim, unlacing his fingers and pushing his hands, palm up, at the candidates. "A lively and informative debate is still the best way to judge a man's character. It's good to know your position on what matters most to Americans, what is the central and *biblical* question before us as a nation. I'm sure—"

"You've got to be kidding," interrupted the dripping senator. "You call this a debate? What about healthcare? What about education? What about the destruction of our forests and the pollution of our water supplies? What about the national debt? The unanswered questions about 10-10? The hemorrhaging of jobs? We haven't begun to address the issues here." The possum jumped from the wire onto Droxford's podium and scattered his notes onto the stage. The insecurity agent placed a veil over the squid tank, and when he took it off the blue squid had turned bright yellow.

"Whoops," said Big Jim, standing quickly and turning to the audience. "Code Yellow! There must be a squid slinking up the holler. Remain calm, but vigilant. Debate's over. The picnic's canceled. Thank you, Tarheels! Don't forget to vote." Big Jim rumbled to his coach. The boy in bib overalls ran on stage and scooped up his pet possum.

The short insecurity agent, his big belly hanging over his belt, addressed the crowd. "In situations like this, we suggest you go home, climb into a gunny sack, and disguise yourself as a bag of corn. Do not move till the threat has passed." The audience jumped from their seats and disbursed in a flurry, racing to coaches and horses tied up in the field. They shouted "Hyaa!" and whipped their horses. Mothers scolded children to get along before the squid got them.

In short order the only people left in the clearing were Tatanka, me, Senator Droxford, and his alleged daughter. We walked onto the stage and helped him into his wheelchair. We wheeled him to his buggy, lifted him up, and set him on the front seat. We placed his wheelchair in the back. The chicken and sweet corn had been left on the grill, so we got him a plate and gave it to him. The little mulatto girl walked up with two glasses of lemonade. "You want a ride home?" he asked her. She nodded, and we helped her into the seat next to him. The two rode off, chatting and munching chicken and corn.

Tatanka and I shrugged at one another, went to the grill, and loaded up with food. We sat and had a good feed, not saying a word. Up from the holler came the sound of two gray squirrels, scampering through the forest, jabbering and chattering. A black hawk soared over, then out of sight into the west.

Chapter XXXVI

The Preemptive Pre-rade

Krill's string of bait-and-switch debates achieved a degree of success beyond even his most optimistic projections. Senator Droxford's drubbing testified to the potency of the format. It raised enough doubts that sprouted into mistrust, qualms, reservations, and eventually, votes for Republicans that resulted in close races going to them. Just for good measure, Krill and the boys reformed the voting process in many states by encouraging the use of disappearing ink on the ballots. This completely solved the sticky issue of contentious recounts, and left close races in the hands of election officials, state legislators, and the courts—each of which were generally infested with partisan mollusks.

When the mid-term election results had been counted, Republicans had solid majorities in both the House and the Senate. They now controlled the executive, legislative and judicial branches of government (Wrong John called it "a trifecta") at the federal level, while on the state level they had captured the majority of governorships and statehouses. With the support of the U.S. Chamber of Piracy, they had systematically replaced liberal activist judges with those who understood that businesses couldn't be successful if they were constantly harried by crippling government regulations and rapacious trial lawyers suing them every time some nincompoop cut himself with a widget. Through the state legislative advantage, Krill was able to redraw the voting precincts state by state, so that in future elections, the Republican congressional majority would continue to grow. By all accounts, Wrong John Silverspoon was the undisputed heavyweight champion of the world, thanks to his masterful parlay of the 10-10 crisis into the Silverspoon Mandate. Who could have ever imagined *Liberty* would achieve such overwhelming dominance by allowing the worst disaster in American history to take place right under its nose? Who indeed, Frank, who indeed.

To celebrate, Krill threw a Mexican fiesta on *Liberty* with all of the newly elected legislators and their wives and husbands. All the officers wore big black sombreros, decorated with silver floral designs. A mariachi band of several guitars, a trumpet, an accordion, and a drummer wandered the ship, singing Mexican ballads. Roberto had filled the try-pots with water, and spermaceti candles floated in them. Spanish dancers in frilly white skirts and fishnet stockings, danced through the try-works, clicking their sharp heels and castanets. Torches burned in their metal stands attached to the masts and the rails.

"Boy," said the captain, looking at the dancers sashaying through the try-pots, "brings a whole new meaning to that old saying about, 'If at first you don't—if you can't get it right—"

"Not again, sir, please, not again," begged Krill, falling prostrate on Wrong John's shoulder. Silverspoon looked down at Krill with his left eye nearly closed and right opened wide.

"Well, anyway, this is the first time I ever aced a midterm," said Wrong John. "Fact is, it's the first time I ever got better than a 'D' without having to *persuade* the professor with a visit from the Pinkertons." He chuckled at himself, inviting the laughter of those around him. "Course I never had a tutor like Krill here back in college days." He turned to his pet bird perched on his shoulder and fed him a salted peanut.

"Aiiieeehaaa!" wailed a mariachi singer, lighting into a raucous polka. The captain took off his big Mexican hat and waved it. Krill danced back and forth on his shoulder, waving his pint-sized sombrero. He had good reason to celebrate. Nobody could deny that his strategy had slain them. He and the captain sauntered across the deck of *Liberty*, with an air of invincibility, both of them shooting personality bullets from their finger and wingtip six-shooters.

The captain and officers circled the deck two or three times, shook hands with the winners, bowed to their wives or husbands, and retired below decks for more intimate games of arm wrestling, turtle races, and distance spitting of chaw. When the captain's witching hour of 10:00 p.m. approached, Basma declared the party over and tucked in her captain. All of the newly elected conservatives went to shore. Once Wrong John was asleep, out came the rum, and the previously formal air turned sour and scoundrely in short order. Krill became so drunk he stood on the helm and screeched, "BRACKing losers! You'll never beat us! Never! You can't fight. Pussies! Squishy liberal pussies!"

"Hey!" said Chief, also loaded. "Let's have some fun. Pinch! How much money is left from the China heist?"

Pinch fingered her abacus with careless flicks. "Oh, crud, I donno, maybe fifty gazillion yen or so. Why?"

"Why? Why? Because we kicked their ass, that's why. America owes us—owes us for saving their tax dollars from the libby piggies." He waved his hand at Yo Yo. "Lower a whaleboat, Gunny Bunny! Hoist the him ham! Chuck the frick slackers! Let's go a'piratin'!"

Chief, Yo Yo, Pinch, Krill, and even Basma, climbed into the whaleboat and rowed to the city. A couple of hours later they returned, two Spanish dancers with them, three guitar players, and two boats stacked with gold ingots towed behind. They rousted a few sailors to stack the gold in a nice pyramid, ten feet tall, on the poop deck above Dagger's quarters. They danced and sang till nearly dawn before passing out around the golden pyramid. I went below for some shuteye in my bunk.

The next morning, Wrong John went out for his 7:00 jog and discovered his officers lying about the poop deck. I arrived with a pot of coffee. An especially thick haze hung over the Potomac. By the time the early sun pushed through it, the color was more blue than golden. Gunny's pants were around his ankles, displaying his white boxer shorts with red hearts. Chief had a bottle of rum and a gold bar hugged to his chest. He lay against the pyramid, his neck at an angle that made it look broken. Pinch lay next to Gunny, a bar of gold stuffed down her cleavage, shirt unbuttoned, shoes off. Krill lay face down on the top of the pyramid, snoring, his little black sombrero on the next level down. Sweet must have changed clothes with one of the dancers and lay in a frilly white dress against the bulwarks, her grease pencil mustache badly smeared. The smell of rum permeated the air.

Wrong John kicked empty rum bottles and slurped his coffee. He called over the bugler to sound revelry. The officers came to, groggy, yawning, reluctantly getting to their feet in the presence of their captain.

"What the hell happened here?" he asked, pacing back and forth before the disheveled, unshaven officers who stank of booze. "Is this what you're really about, underneath it all? just a bunch of undisciplined *liberals?*" They winced at the severity of his insult.

"What are you doing with the gold? This better not be your *personal* tax relief, or I'll be really pissed." Wrong John continued to pace, stubbed his toe on a bar of gold, and swore.

Dagger would have none of it. "We killed them in the midterms, damn it! and to the victor go the spoils."

"Ah, Jeez, Chief, when's enough enough? At some point we gotta stop the bleeding here and quit begging transfusions off the Chinese."

"The Great Communicator proved hemorrhaging is *good* for The Economy, healthy, like a nice bloodletting with leeches."

"Ah, Jeez. I don't know," Wrong John said, pacing, scratching his head. "Maybe we ought to put it back this time, keep a little aside for a rainy day."

The Chief's hand went to the dagger strapped to his waist. He yanked the blade from it sheath. "Don't mess with my legacy! I've got to do something *memorable*. A good politician is forgotten in a generation. But a *pirate?* His name lasts *forever!*" He stalked at the captain, upper lip curled on the right side, glistening dagger out in front, shooting hate bullets from his bloodshot eyes. I pulled Peacemaker and backed him down. Silverspoon looked at him with hurt in his eyes, unable, it seemed, to believe his Chief would turn on him. Wrong John looked at Sweet in her pretty white skirt.

"Basma? You too? And dressed up like a *girl?*"

"Sir, I'm—it wasn't my, well, I was—. Oh, damn it! Do you know how hard it is for a black wom—man to break in with the good old boys?" She placed her left hand on her hip and tilted her head to the same side. I offered a dose of Matthew.

"What does it profit a man if he gains the world but loses his soul?" The officers ignored me, except for Basma, who looked up sheepishly, then turned away. God, Jesse James, I thought, you are a hypocrite.

"That's right, Ish. You tell 'em, gunslinger. Unleash your faith on 'em." Wrong John put his arm around me. Krill clicked his black tongue, and a whisper whistled from his perch atop the pyramid.

Sir Yes Sir arrived, breathless. "I heard the bugler. Is the morning prayer early?" He looked around the deck at the empty bottles, up at the ten-foot tall pyramid of gold, and scanned the disheveled officers. "What's all this?"

"Some certain somebodies helped thereselves to the cookie jar last night," said Wrong John.

Sir Yes Sir covered his mouth with his hand and squeezed his cheeks. His hand came to his chest. "It's an old tradition after a big victory, isn't it, Chief? Rob, pillage, some R&R. But if you're going to keep it, at least get it off the ship. We're supposed to be the honest ones, remember? We don't need this lucre lying around. Go and bury it on Pirate Island." Chief gritted his teeth and shook his head.

"Do it!" screamed Wrong John, leaping in front of him. Dagger turned away from him and slowly took down his pyramid. The other officers loaded the gold bars in the boats, and, with several sailors, rowed to Pirate Island.

Silverspoon cupped his hands around his mouth and yelled. "And I want a copy of the goddamn map!"

Later that day, a skip came alongside *Liberty* with members of the Washington press corps that had gotten wind of the midnight raid. "Look," said the captain, addressing them off the starboard bow, "we've always been about tax relief for working-class Americans. Any tax relief that was taken last night is just like a direct transfusion into the bank account of my—of the average American."

"But, Mr. Captain, there's no blood left to draw. How can you take what isn't there?" asked an older woman wearing small, round glasses.

"Well if it isn't there, how'd we take it?"

"I don't know."

"Let me tell you something. Just because it isn't there doesn't mean it isn't there. It's neither here nor there whether what's not there is here. We stick to principle in this administration. We keep our word. And there's one word we stick to above all others: tax relief."

"But, the cupboard's bare. You've had to slash federal aid to states so severely, many of the basic services of government are almost nonexistent."

"That's right. We're getting government out of people's lives, so the free market can set the tone and meet their needs in a healthy, competitive environment." Silverspoon winked at me and said, behind his hand, "Ol' Ahab's gonna get that Dick this time," and he winked at me.

"But businesses are about making a profit, not about—"

"Did I call on you?" He pointed his finger menacingly at the reporter. "Did I say no-limit questioning? Does this look like a free-speech zone?" Wrong John pointed at the black coffin hanging from the yardarm. "Christ! I am sick to death of this never-ending liberal bias. You come out here making accusations. Don't you know we're at WAR? You don't attack your government when you're at WAR. You attack the enemy. The Giant Squid is *everywhere!*" The redness of his anger moved down from the tips of his ears, through his lobes and across his pointed face. Tosspot and Tom Thumb arrived and conferred with the captain. Thumb pulled a squid from his pocket and threw it at the reporters.

"Code Red, assholes," he said in his sonorous voice. "You better run off and pretend to be a hat rack or something till the danger passes."

"Or, if you prefer, there's a pleasure boat leaving for The Tropics in an hour," added Tosspot, using his new euphemism for Batguano Castle. The reporters quickly rowed away. TP ordered the small artillery on deck to fire a few "rounds of encouragement" in their direction.

A couple of hours later, a longboat filled with angry legislators approached *Liberty*. Wrong John could not be bothered to address them, but had Tom Thumb read a statement. He stood on the rail and spoke the following:

"I've said all along that I trust the judgment of the first and second mates of this ship. That's why I hire the best people for the most important positions, because I trust them to use their best judgment and make the good decisions.

The president is not a hair splitter. I can't be bothered with the details of what my staff is doing. How would I get anything done? I became president so that I didn't have to explain myself to anybody. Which is what I intend *not* to do to you."

Another hour or so later, a boatload of corporate lobbyists came alongside *Liberty* and boarded without permission. They ran to the cannon battery and grabbed a souvenir ball, wrote the new regulatory guidelines for their various industries, left the documents and a bag of gold on Wrong John's pillow, and helped themselves to lunch in the galley. Our lookout in the crow's-nest sighted them later going ashore at Pirate Island, greeted by *Liberty's* midnight raiders of the night before. I had gathered by then that it was essential for corporations to receive handouts from the government, but if poor people got anything it would ruin their moral development.

That afternoon the conspirators returned from the island, contrite and apologetic. Chief convinced Silverspoon that his medication had been off, and that he intended him no actual harm. Wrong John accepted the explanation, almost with tears in his eyes. Krill scrambled to his usual position on the captain's shoulder and whistled a forlorn *Star-Spangled Banner*. Basma promised to do her penance with him during their bedtime prayers that night. All, it seemed, had been forgiven, but I don't know, Frank, it didn't seem to me the proper response to a near mutiny. Wrong John didn't want to trouble himself with it and instead fell into planning with them one final act of public persuasion in preparation for the invasion of Iraq.

They called it the Preemptive Pre-rade—a sort of preemptive-emptive pageant, a history of the future as they were certain it would be; they just wanted a little dress rehearsal. In line with the Silverspoon Mandate they were all about pre-diction and pre-vention and pre-monition and pre-caution and pre-emption—it was pre- this and pre- that, and all I could think about was pre-mature ee-jaculation, as they pre-pared to celebrate victory in a war they had yet to fight.

Krill strongly advocated for a parade route through lower Manhattan, along the path of destruction inflicted by the suicide storks: that way, not only would the captain and his mates be able to preempt the future, they would also be able to revisit and reclaim their position as the saviors of the North's greatest city.

The day of the pre-rade brought sunny skies to New York, with a cool but not uncomfortable breeze from the north. Enormous American flags hung from buildings as they had since shortly after 10-10. For some reason, however, the usual protocol of raising and lowering the flags at dawn and dusk, and folding them punctiliously, had not been followed, and the weather had ripped and tattered them, to the extent they looked like oversized red, white, and blue rags. All across America, I heard, Old Glory had been hung on porches, draped from bridges, flown on carriages, flopped out of windows—and forgotten. People told themselves it was a testament to their patriotism, but in my way of thinking, it cheapened the symbol of democracy to have flags thrown about everywhere like so many party decorations. The more I saw them everywhere the less seriously I took them, and the more I thought Americans no longer understood their flag at all. Fact is, the more I saw them, the angrier I became. We would *never* have treated the Confederate flag like that.

Patriotic New Yorkers filled the streets, dressed in sweaters and light jackets, cheering, waving—you guessed it—little flags, everyone well stocked with preemptive roses to shower Wrong John and friends in anticipation of how they would be showered in Iraq. The pageant began with a company of marines in their dress blues, led by the Marine Corps Marching Band, playing *God Bless America*. Two healthy bull elephants, the small-eared Indian variety, pulled the first float that followed the Marines and carried the name "IraqiCo the WonderFoe," sponsored by Cannon Fodder, Inc., *We love your hate, it makes us great!*

The float was something of a miniature of Baghdad, with small temples and palaces, their minarets and onion towers flying both the Iraqi and American flags. Muslim-like women were dressed in black and red embroidered *kaftans* and *burka* face scarves. Men wore *dishdasha* robes and turbans, or *ghutra* headscarves. They danced on the platform and threw roses and daisies at the feet of American soldiers, who carried laughing children on their shoulders. A small camel mischievously stole a bite of apple pie from his cheerful keeper's plate. A group of traditional Arab musicians played a song that American soldiers danced to with veiled Iraqi women. Every so often, one of the "Arabs" would suddenly shout, "We love you Captain Silverspoon!

Praise Allah, you have liberated us from that butcher! Our country is your country, take whatever you wish." Another shouted, "How can we ever repay you for bringing us democracy?" And still another screamed, "Now that Shalong is gone, we love all Jews and will be their friends forever!"

After that came a long float pulled by a team of brown jackasses and titled "Appeasers Beg Forgiveness," sponsored by Cheese Importers of America, *Sure they're cowards, but gosh! they still make great cheese!* It contained people costumed as Germans and French, on their knees before a red, white, and blue figure of Uncle Sam. They pleaded with him for mercy, and he sprinkled them with fairy dust and said, "I accept your apology for disagreeing with me. You can't be expected to have the courage and foresight of an American; after all, you are old and decrepit. I understand that you were scared, but now that we have shown the way you may join us in doing the right thing—just don't expect any rebuilding contracts! Ha ha ha ha ha!" He laughed, causing a ripple of laughter among the spectators.

Agents of Homemade Insecurity circulated through the crowd, randomly frisking grandmothers for nail clippers and small boys for slingshots. They blew their whistles and chucked small, purple squid at suspected terrorists. Any traitor caught with a protest sign was arrested. Wrath of God missile defense balloons floated ominously among the tattered American rags high up in the buildings, their sticks of dynamite and precision-calibrated fuses hanging below like kite tails.

The next float rolled through the street carrying an oversized likeness of Shalong, with his dark moustache, dark hair, and swarthy complexion, wearing a green army uniform, on his knees before a group of American generals, his hands clasped and begging for mercy. It was called "So Long Shalong," sponsored by Mercy Nary, *Pirate Security for the Public Good.*

"Please, I'm sorry," cried the Shalong character. "I won't build anymore Weapons of Mass Hysteria that can incinerate an entire city in a single blast. Please, I was just kidding."

"So long, Shalong," said the generals in unison. "You had your chance to disarm, and you didn't. The Bubba days of lying and stringing America along are over." Shalong had a big sack of money he carried over a shoulder, and he offered big handfuls of it to the generals, who refused to take it. "This money belongs to the Iraqi people," they said.

On the far side of the float stood a dark edifice fenced with barbed wire. American soldiers broke it open and freed the people inside, who kissed them and placed flower garlands around their necks and thanked them for liberty. The prisoners complained of the horrible abuse they had endured simply for refusing to hang a painting of Shalong in their living rooms.

"Don't worry," said the American soldiers, "state-sponsored torture and rape, the mass graves, and random violence are *over!*" They sang a new version of *Yankee Doodle* that went: "Silverspoon a'came to town, a'riding ammunition, stuck a pickle in his pants and called it liberation."

Another float followed with characters dressed as Koreans, Iranians, Syrians, and Libyans and was called "Maypole of Murder," sponsored by WongMart, *Lowest wages, always!* On it, the characters came before another Uncle Sam and begged him for mercy. "Please, we beg of you, don't hurt us. Now that you completely thrashed Shalong we promise to do whatever you say because you are so mighty." They reached into bags carried by camels and donkeys and handed Uncle Sam the guns and bombs they would now give up to avoid the wrath of America. "Here, take our weapons, please. We will never again consider acts of aggression that have not been preapproved by the Silverspoon Mandate. We're sorry for having offended thee. Please spare us." Uncle Sam stroked his beard and pondered what to do with them.

After that came a float loaded with wooden barrels of blubber labeled "Sweet Iraqi Crude," sponsored by BlubCo, *Blubbering Up for a Better Tomorrow!* the barrels were draped with a big, bright banner that read, "Thanks for the freedom, Captain Silverspoon! And Let Us Pick Up the Tab!"

Streams of tickertape and confetti flew from the windows of the high rises along the parade route. Young women screamed and mothers cried. Men stood at attention and saluted. An insecurity agent threw an old man down on the sidewalk, spread-eagle, and searched him. "Aha! Sneaky old terrorist!" said the agent, holding up a pocketknife.

Another float rolled by that held a big tank of marine mollusks. Squid, cuttlefish, octopi and limpet squirmed, fluttered, and inked around the fish tank. Every so often tentacles shot out, and one squid pulled another mollusk into its sharp, pinching mouth. The crowd booed and hissed and threw rotten

308 ~~ James E. Churches

lettuce and tomatoes at it. This was such an odious float with no real "up-side" that it had no corporate sponsor. Squid-bandoleered insecurity agents stood guard over the tank, holding a banner that read: "The Squid Alert is Code Blue. Enjoy the Pre-rade, but Remain Guarded."

The Terrorist Czar, Dick Little, ran along the front edge of the crowd, hollering. "It's not about Squid Alerts, or storks, or poison frogs, or exploding cornbread! That's all a big *distraction!* There are no yellowcake bombs! We have to go after the source, the hatred and violence at the core of Al Quota." Agents of Homemade Insecurity tackled him and smeared him with squid. "Smells like a terrorist to me!" one of them yelled. They handcuffed him and dragged him away. I found out later Mr. Little had been fired for his breach of loyalty.

Around the corner marched the Masturbation Corps, chanting to the beat of two base drums, hanging from the shoulders of a young man and a young woman on either end of the front row. "Sex is a sin. You can't win. Don't go to bed. Save it instead. If you can't wait, then go ahead and masturbate!" Terrorists in the crowd pelted them with bananas and ran, chased by whistle-blowing insecurity agents tossing purple squid.

Next came the Clown Criers on tall stilts, wearing huge papier-mâché heads in the likeness of Al Quota and Shalong, one with a big white turban, a long dark beard, and a white robe stained with blood, the other typical of Shalong, mustachioed and clad in his green army uniform. They walked hand-in-hand on only three stilts, as if they were Siamese twins. Among them on the ground other clowns juggled flaming torches. Some rode too-small tricycles, clanged bells, and yelled: "Hear me! Hear me! Evil! Danger! Horror! Must attack Iraq!"

A float pulled by black mules carried a dozen men and women in stocks, labeled with scarlet letters saying: "I am a traitor. I blamed America first." They wailed, moaned, and begged forgiveness. "We understand you can *never* negotiate with evil. Trying to understand terrorism is *weakness*, and it encourages them to slaughter you." The pilloried liberals pledged to stop complaining about the loss of civil liberties and get to work uniting the country behind its holy crusade.

The captain and his officers brought up the rear atop powerful camels, to whose saddles had been affixed tall poles waving big American flags. The crowd cheered and showered them with roses. Yo Yo caught one and held it in his teeth, striking a dashing pose. Pinch pulled up beside him and pinched his butt. The captain smiled and waved, gave the thumbs up, and pretended to personally know people in the crowd, whom he shot with his finger bullets of love.

Every five minutes a flock of white doves was released from cages carried on rolling platforms in front of the camels. The captain took a bead on one with an invisible rifle and shot it, mugging for Dagger and the others behind him, who laughed and waved at him. Sir Yes Sir shot the captain with a finger bullet. Tosspot waved a ten-foot-tall cross wrapped with an American flag.

Private "contractors" from Mercy Nary—the same sort of humanitarians who would later build churches and demolish inefficient state-run factories in a free Iraq—dressed in black and heavily armed, kept the crowd from approaching the officers. When an Unidentified Airborne Enemy Combatant (it looked to me like a confused pigeon) flew too close to the captain, several of them quickly took aim and blew it to smithereens.

A float of Tax Relief brought up the rear of the parade. Speck and a few of the *Liberty* swabbies grabbed handfuls of coinage from black treasure chests and flung them into the crowd. I noticed the dole was no longer silver or gold coins, but pennies and nickels, which were still eagerly fought over by the impoverished New Yorkers, many of them Negroes who had been out of work a year or more.

One of the black spectators threw a handful of pennies back at Speck and yelled, "I'd rather have a job!"

"In times of war, certain cherished traditions have to be sacrificed," said Speck, repeating one of Marshal Tosspot's favorite sayings.

Further on, a group of protesters lay down in the pre-rade path and attempted to disrupt the festivities, their bodies covered by a banner that read, "The innocent women and children of Iraq." It seemed they were prepared to be trampled rather than get out of the way. Homemade Insecurity agents quickly surrounded them, blew their whistles, smeared them with squid, and carted them away. Many were invited to take a vacation in The Tropics.

We found out later there had been hundreds of protests that day all over the world—the largest outpouring of humanity in history to stand against the aggressive actions of a single country—and that country, so reviled and despised, was the land of the free and the home of the brave. All the sympathy from 10-10 had been turned into antipathy. Instead of allying with us to stop terror, the world had allied against us, like never before in our history.

Some days after the pre-rade, news of the protests reached *Liberty*. As I helped the captain prepare for bed, I ventured to ask what he thought of the dissent. He stood at the white enamel washbasin in his blue and white striped pajamas and brushed his teeth. He didn't seem to mind the timing of my question and answered while brushing and spitting, his mouth white with foam.

"Well, Ish, it's like this. I'm the guy who's got to make the difficult decisions. It's not a popularity contest. If I let myself be swayed by the opinion of fifteen million people, how does that look? Does that convince our enemies of our resolve? Does that frighten evil back into its cave? No, it does not." He brushed and spit into the white basin on his dresser. "I'm actually glad those people are against me on this. It just shows we're on the right course."

"How does the bitterness of the world—and a bunch of Americans— show you're on the right track?" I waited for him to finish, a white towel draped over my forearm.

"Ish, God tests you. That's how I know. If there wasn't a test of faith, if it was too easy, that would mean it was the work of the devil." He gargled with water, spit it in the basin, and brushed his tongue with his toothbrush.

"So you reckon Satan tricked fifteen million people into marching for peace?"

He took the towel from my arm and wiped his mouth. "Wadn't the Tooth Fairy."

You know something, Frank? I was starting to believe, by the way he had split the nation, and the world, that Captain Silverspoon was willing to cause another Civil War in order to pursue the full extent of his mandate. His reasons for doing so would, in the end, be little different than the reasons we had for seceding from the Union in 1860. Or going back further, for the argument among the founders as to whether George Washington should be our first president, or our first king.

It was the argument, Frank, the *central* argument of our nation, and that's why I think you're right about Mr. Melville and his *Moby-Dick*. It *will* be recognized as an American classic some day, because Mr. Melville understood the argument at the core of America. He saw there was a White Whale of aristocracy, feudalism, and domination by the white-humped minority that was about to shatter the *true* American dream. He understood the reason Ahab *had* to risk everything to kill Moby Dick. If he hadn't, then there would be no hope for the ideal of equality, free expression, privacy, civil rights, fairness, and justice.

America put itself right in the middle of that argument. We agreed to work it out on our own soil with our own blood. We would attempt the experiment that goes hard at the natural instincts of the human animal to achieve dominance, to enjoy the privilege of his and her position, and to never give it up. We agreed to tangle with our most primitive urges, to fight if necessary—as we did in Missouri—brother against brother, sister against sister, white against black, wealthy against poor. We would stand up to those deep, ancient instincts and say to them, "No! You must stand aside and stand down and yield to this ideal of democracy."

So hats off to you, big brother, and to your hero, Captain Ahab, who lost a leg to the White Whale. He put in once for the ideal of freedom, made it his mission to bring the monster to justice at the end of his sharp lance. He put in twice, and a third time, and was dragged to his death by Moby Dick with a whale line around his neck. Like the man that reminds me of him, the man I once hated with all my heart, Abraham Lincoln—a man with the same long face and slim beard and deep-set eyes and steely resolve—Ahab was crushed by the White Whale and killed by it. But does that mean he should not have stood up to it? Does that mean he should have laid down his harpoon and let the monster lord his might over the world forever?

BOOK III

Honeymooning in Babylon

Chapter XXXVII

Operation Castration

I T TURNED OUT TATANKA was right about the night eagle following us. In
the days after Silverspoon's Preemptive Pre-rade, that grizzly, rasping,
pecking sound on the hull returned. Night watchmen commonly cried out
about headless snakes reaching for them in the dark. None of it mattered.
The Silverspoon Mandate had fixed on Shalong of Iraq as the Giant Squid.
He was *out there*, far away, and deserving of all hatred. The officers of *Liberty*
concluded their portrait of evil with a masterstroke of irrefutable, final,
inescapable reasoning. Yo Yo released the following statement to the Mandate
Media conglomerate and a thousand vengeful Clown Criers:

"We can't risk the discomfort of Americans in the brutal conditions of
an Iraqi summer. It's dangerous enough over there without the threat of heat
stroke, cancer causing sunburns, painful particulates in the eyes, and nasty,
sand-blasted raspberries on the skin. We've got to get in there now while
it's still cool and not too windy. Besides, revenge for 10-10 requires dramatic
results. You blow up an Afghan cave and you know what you got? A bigger
cave. Not very impressive."

His argument convinced the powerful leaders from the island nations
of Samoa, Vanuatu, and Bora Bora to throw their armies (150, 75, and
14soldiers, respectively) in with America and its British vassal in forming a
broad Coalition of the Sancho Panzas, willing to follow Wrong John Quixote
in his crusade against the squidmills of Iraq.

Gunny Yo Yo deemed the invasion Operation Castration, so named
because he expected to preempt the preemptive war by castrating Shalong
before the war actually began, thus removing the balls of Iraq and spurring
an early shower of roses on our troops. "It will be glorious!" he assured the
captain, "like Napoleon arriving in Moscow, hailed as the great liberator that

he was."

Operation Castration was the most secret of top, top secret missions, and was to be done by the sudden, awe inspiring, and deadly accurate *fling* of a razor-sharp marshal arts throwing star by a Special Forces commando dressed as a Persian concubine. I only knew about it because, on the eve of the invasion, Wrong John awoke from a nightmare and stumbled into the galley in a panic. He calmed down over goat milk and shortbread, and described his nightmare. "There was the wind up, and the pitch, but the razor-sharp marshal arts throwing star turned into a boomerang on its way to Shalong's *huevos*. It circled around and came right back at *my huevos*, and was just about to neuter me when I woke up."

In anticipation of the mass surrender that would occur in a nutless Iraq, U.S. troops amassed on ships in the Persian Gulf and on Iraq's southern border with Kuwait. A surprise betrayal, however, botched up the northern front. The Turks refused Silverspoon's demand that American troops be allowed to amass at their border. "Well, shee-it," Wrong John said, "we'll borrow a pile of gold from China and give it to you. Just let us amass, *amigos*." The Turks refused. They felt loyalty to their Muslim brotherhood that pre-dated the Silverspoon Mandate. It was a loyalty not for sale.

About when the Turks betrayed her, *Liberty* began to take on water. The chief engineer blamed it on the same enemy that had severed the ship's anchor and set her adrift some months ago. Round-the-clock pumping began in earnest, but the Irish engineer preferred to dry dock and make repairs. The captain would have none of it.

"How can we be leaking?" he asked petulantly. "Idn't this the lead ship of our great nation? We oughta be leak-proof—ain't that right, Krill?"

The parrot whistled a quick doorbell singsong. "Leak-proof *Liberty*. "BRACK! Stick to principle. Hold to message."

"Well, sir," the engineer informed the captain, "some bloody thing has been tearing at us, and has riven gaps in the hull."

"Some *bloody* thing? What do you mean, *thing?*"

"Based on the accounts of the night watchmen, and the nature of the gashes in our hull, our best guess is—ahem—the, um, the Giant Squid." The engineer rolled his eyes skyward and tapped his foot on the deck.

"Giant Squid! You're doin' that blarney thing, ain't ya? takin' a piss on me—or however it is y'all put it. Everybody knows the Giant Squid lives a league under the sea and has never been seen. Ain't that right, Ish?"

"Hell, ought to be a *good* thing if it is the big squid," I said, pointing with Peacemaker at the brown-grained nickel he had nailed to the mainmast. "You got us all fired up to find it with that hickory nickel up there, Ahab." I fiddled with Peacemaker, opened the cylinder, and found another bullet missing. Who's taking my bullets, I wondered?

"Huh," Wrong John grunted. "The Giant Squid's just a *mandato enchilato*. Nobody expects we're gonna *actually* eat the damn thing." He faltered and almost fell over, as if the squid had grabbed the ship and shaken it. Nobody felt it but him. "God damn it! Just get down there and fill the hole—I don't care what with." The engineer saluted and went below.

"There's a hole in the bottom of the ship, a hole in the bottom of the ship, there's a hole, there's a hole, there's a hole in the bottom of the ship." Krill sang a child's walking-home-from-school song. "There's a squid in the hole in the bottom of the ship, a squid—." He took a flick to the beak.

Despite what Chief called "Turkish pusillanimity," the U.S. continued to amass its troops in Kuwait and the Persian Gulf, and wait for news of Operation Castration. If the secret agent was successful and preempted Shalong's abominable seed, the invasion of Iraq would truly be a parade, requiring no combat, but merely a janitor to sweep up the roses. On the eve of launching Operation Castration, Wrong John hosted a ceremony on board *Liberty* to inaugurate the Silverspoon Mandate as a foreign policy platform. The invasion of Afghanistan did not count, because it was a "retributive strike, not a preemptive one," the gunner explained, "very Bubba, but a necessary prelude."

Speck had opened the try-works and filled the silver pots half full with oil and lit them. The three fires acted as massive lamps at the center of the ship. The crew stood in formal dress on either side of the try-works. Wrong John and his officers gathered on the quarterdeck, where important legislative allies, members of the Supreme Court, and important corporate sponsors also stood. A crescent moon hung above the shoreline forest; a bright star, possibly Venus, dangled between the sharp points of the crescent. A lone trumpet played the The Star-Spangled Banner. Everyone on deck placed his hand over his heart. Some sang along quietly. The try-pot fires reached up with flickering orange-blue flames and made a low rumble.

When the song finished, Wrong John nodded at me, and I stepped forward from my position among the laborers along the mizzenmast. Tatanka had given me a prayer he thought would be nice for the occasion. It looked good to me, so I agreed to read it. The Sioux was not at the ceremony, having kitchen work to do for the dinner to follow. I hadn't asked him which book of the Bible it had come from, but it didn't seem important to me. I cleared my throat and read.

"When the sky is torn
When the stars are scattered
When the seas are poured forth
When the tombs are burst open
Then a soul will know what it has given
    and what it has held back
Oh, O human being
    what has deceived you about your generous lord
who created you and shaped you and made you right
In whatever form he willed for you, set you

But no. Rather. You deny the reckoning
that over you they are keeping watch
ennobled beings, writing down
knowing what it is you do

The pure of heart will be in bliss
The hard of heart will be in blazing fire
the day of reckoning, burning there—
they will not evade that day."

I looked over at the captain, who nodded at me sternly and said, "Thank you, IshcaBible, trusted servant of captain and ship. You have once again inspired us with a beautiful verse from our most holy book. It is indeed, my countrymen, a day of reckoning for Shalong and Al Quota. It is a day when they pay the price for the actions they have chosen. America will not be shy about serving the Lord in bringing down his sword of justice." He bowed his head and closed his eyes in prayer.

The rest of the officers and crew also bowed their heads and shut their eyes, except for TP, Chief, and Basma: the marshal narrowed his eyes at me, Chief—though I could not hear it—held his mouth as he did when sucking teeth, and Basma raised her eyebrows. She pulled her head back and tucked her chin. Hearing myself read the prayer aloud, I realized it hadn't come from the Bible at all at all. The three eventually closed their eyes and bowed, and I was free to sneak to the galley and find out the source of Tatanka's mysterious verse. It was one thing to be a coyote preacher with the *actual* Bible, but quite another to be the coyote preacher biting at the darkness. I found the Sioux peeling carrots and humming softly, alone at a washbasin in a dark corner of the galley, working by candlelight. His long hair, braided thin on the right with an owl feather at the end, hung down and shielded his face.

"Tell me about this prayer, Tatanka." I said. "I know it's not from the Bible. Is it a Lakota prayer? I thought it quite powerful."

"You're wrong, Ishcabibble. It is from a most holy book, from the Holy Land," he said, continuing to peel the carrots.

"Okay, so what book is it from? The style is certainly Old Testament, but the language is rather odd." I drummed my fingers on the stained, knife-scored table on which he worked. "I need to know, the marshal and Chief are about to grill me over it. I can see it coming."

"It is Suras 82, 'The Tearing.'" He continued to peel. Thin pieces of orange flesh flew into the white basin. I noticed his whale tooth carving sitting on the table next to him, beginning to take shape—some sort of four-legged critter.

"Suras? I've never heard of Suras. That's not a book in any Bible I've ever seen."

"It is from the Koran."

I nearly busted a gut. Tatanka looked back at me and laughed. After a minute, I caught my breath. "You mean to tell me Captain Wrong John Silverspoon sent his troops on a crusade to Iraq with a prayer from the Muslim holy book?" I laughed some more, as did my Indian friend. "Damn you, Injun. Those pirates will send me down the plank for this."

Tatanka washed his hands and wiped them on his soiled apron. He regarded me with a warm smile, the flickering candlelight soft against his deep brown skin. He reached into his back pocket and pulled out another piece of paper. He handed it to me and said, "Give me 'The Tearing.' This one is from Revelations. Tell them you read this one. Do not waver. Remind them that to pursue this would embarrass Wrong John. Would bring him shame at the hour of his greatest glory."

We exchanged papers, and I ran back up the stairs and onto the deck and tiptoed to my position aft. The silent prayer was still in progress. TP, Chief, and Basma had their eyes tightly closed, but I supposed it unlikely they hadn't peeked. When the silence ended, TP broke into song. I could see by the way the captain wagged his head and rolled his eyes that the musical number had not been part of the program. Honestly, that marshal's voice chilled the bones, but that did not discourage him. He bellowed *Onward Christian Soldiers* with everything his trilling tenor could muster.

> "Onward, Christian soldiers, marching as to war,
> with the cross of Jesus going on before!
> Christ, the royal Master, leads against the foe;
> forward into battle, see, his banners go.
>
> Like a mighty army moves the Church of God;
> Brothers, we are treading where the saints have trod;
> we are not divided, all one body we,
> one in hope and doctrine, one in charity.
>
> Onward, Christian soldiers, marching as to war,
> with the cross—"

The captain stopped the song by giving TP the sign to "cut"—several quick slashes across his Adam's apple with the tips of his fingers. Wrong John thanked us all for attending the prayer service and blessing our military as it headed into battle. The formal part of the ceremony ended, and everyone milled about waiting for dinner. As I expected, TP and Chief approached me together, cross looks on both of their faces. I recalled their sneak attack of me on the Preemption as we coursed through the North Sea fog on our way to Gravenhage. At least this time they had the decency to approach me head on.

"Where did you get that prayer?" Chief asked with a scowl.

"It's from the Bible, of course. Where else would I get it?" I said, trying to sound indignant.

"That was *not* from the Bible!" hissed Tosspot. "I know the Bible intimately, and that verse was not biblical."

I shrugged my shoulders. "Guess you don't know your Revelations, lawman." I held up the paper from Tatanka, folded in two, between the middle and index finger of my left hand. TP snatched it from me and started to read it to himself.

"Read it out loud," demanded Dagger. TP read the passage.

"The beast that thou sawest was, and is not;
and shall ascend out of the bottomless pit,
and go into perdition:
and they that dwell on the earth shall wonder,
whose names were not written in the book of life
from the foundation of the world,
when they behold the beast that was, and is not,
and yet is."

"That's not what you read!" Chief asserted, shaking his finger at me.

"Sure it is," I answered. "Works pretty good too, if you ask me. Tells of the evil Wrong John's out to destroy. You know, the many-armed, color-shifting beast that is, and is not, and yet is."

A flock of Canadian geese flew across the starred crescent moon, honking, their wings whistling. The try-pots hummed and flared blue-orange. I heard Wrong John's distinctive breathless laugh, and Krill on his shoulder cackling. Basma stood at the bow, leaning over, comforting the wounded figurehead, I imagined.

"There was something in the one you read about *reckoning*. Where's the reckoning now?" Chief said, shooting his hate bullets at me through bloodshot blue eyes. TP jangled his leg irons and glared at me. I, of course, reached for my natural defenses holstered at my sides. Reckoning? he had asked. I imagined there would be some.

"It's implied," I said. "You're just so good with scripture, you filled in the blank—right there where it says 'whose names were not written in the book of life.' Wrong John did it too."

"Horse feathers!" cried Tosspot. "Silverspoon can't tell the difference between the Bible and Mother Goose, but *I can*. There were no 'thous' or 'shalls' in what you read. It had a very foreign sound, very idolatrous." He lowered his eyes at me and slapped his hand with the counterfeit passage. "It's better to confess these things, Ishcabibble, than to force us to extract the truth from you tooth by tooth."

I couldn't believe it; he had called me Ishcabibble, as in "scribble." None of them had *ever* called me that name, not once since we left Squid Roe in Galveston. I nervously ran my tongue over my teeth. If there was one thing I treasured, it was my strong straight teeth, not a one of them chipped or filled with silver. I did not take kindly to the pompous preacher's boy threatening my pearly whites, but he had called me Ishcabibble, and that was a sign that he was closing in on me. I tried to throw him off with my closeness to the captain.

"Let's bring it up with Silverspoon. I'm sure he'll want to circle everybody up again to discuss the verse. How did he put it? 'Trusted servant of captain and ship. Inspired us with a beautiful verse.' Let's go see what he thinks." I smiled at them and walked toward the captain. Neither of them followed me. I heard TP slap the prayer, and Dagger's squeaky mouth, but that was it.

"You know, Ishcabibble," Tosspot said, raising his voice. "A Pinkerton man received a report that Jesse James took a ride in our pre-rade. Can you imagine? He's supposed to be dead, and yet, he managed to crash our party."

"Some legends just don't want to die," I said over my shoulder.

"Maybe not, but all *bad* things must one day end."

I walked away, remembering how he had examined my six-shooters at

Great Abaco Island, and had asked me about the initials "JJ" inscribed in the silver caps of my pearl grips. Had he put that together with the sighting of Jesse James in New York City? And just who had sited me, anyway? Who could have recognized me, all tattooed, and bald, dressed up as a sailor? There weren't too many, and nine out of ten who could would have to be Misery boys. God, Frank, I needed you then. I needed you to watch my back like you always had. Sweat came out on my forehead and I couldn't keep my eyes from wandering to that hung coffin, dangling from the yardarm.

Something has surely changed, I told myself, as I wiped the sweat from my brow with a folded red handkerchief from the back pocket of my snakeskins. *Liberty* is taking water and I, IshcaBible, the Good Book with legs—and a gun—have been called Ishcabibble, as in "scribble." And Silverspoon has launched America's first preemptive war.

Chapter XXXVIII

Operation Pantywaist

News of Operation Castration did not arrive back in Washington for several weeks. The entire time, Silverspoon could not be pleased on the most trifling matters. He sent his morning eggs back to the kitchen if they had even a hint of hardness in the yolks. He measured the strength of his coffee by holding an eyedropper of it to the light—and sent it back if the hue were too dark or light. He complained that his shirts and coats no longer fit, and he ordered a tailor to redo his entire wardrobe. Krill volunteered for the job, having still retained some of his human talents as a tailor. No one spoke it, but it was obvious his clothes no longer fit because of the growing hump on his back, now the size and color of an albino grapefruit.

Krill measured his shoulders and back with a cloth tape, a stubby pencil in his beak. He wrote the figures on a small pad of yellow paper, muttering and clucking to himself.

"Those the measurements of a king?" I asked, returning from the kitchen with the proper shade of joe. "Or is it a better fit for Quasimodo?"

"Not the cut of the cloth, Ish. Not the cut of the cloth that matters. No no. No no. It's the story *behind* the fabric, yeah, the weaver and loom. That's what counts." He placed his cloth tape along Wrong John's arm and wrote down the numbers on his yellow pad, whisper whistling in soft chirps.

"How's the search for your sweetie coming?" I asked him, concerning his lost love, turned by that frog into a stork.

He snapped his little red head at me and raised his left eyebrow (or whatever it is that birds have). "Don't know. Don't know. TP may have already killed her. Don't know. Have to hope. Have to hope she left America before 10-10. Have to hope she went out, like she wanted, to see the world. See the world."

Finally, one calm morning—the bankside forest shining light green with spring leaves, and splashed with showy blooms of flowering dogwood, wild plum, and hawthorn—word arrived that a military envoy was on his way up the Potomac. Our usual clan of airborne ambassadors circled in the air above the ship. Not Pinch, nor anyone else, hailed them any longer as signs of God's blessing, and must have accepted them for the honest buzzards that they were.

Silverspoon, whose new shirts had not been finished, walked on the deck in a T-shirt and carried a baseball glove. Krill was not on his shoulder, but probably down in the carpenter's workshop, sewing. "Hey, Pinch!" he called. "You got that Brouthers ball I gave you? Let's toss it around. Spring training, girl!"

Pinch waved and smiled her big grin. She hustled below and returned a few minutes later with her prize Detroit Wolverines baseball, signed by Big Dan Brouther—greatest slugger in the majors. She dropped into a pitcher's stance, wound up, and smoked one at her captain. He caught it with a loud pop. "Dang me, girl." He took his glove off and shook his hand. "You got some pepper, tell you what." Pinch smiled, blew on her knuckles, and polished them on her chest.

"Gunny! Chief! SYS! Basma! TP! Thumby! Grab your mitts. Spring training. We got the Sha-long Squid comin' to town. Let's be ready." The other officers looked back and forth at one another, squinted, shrugged, and slowly wandered off to find their baseball gloves. Ten minutes later, all of them were back, wearing mitts—except for Tom Thumb, who tottered out of the hatch carrying a short baseball bat. "I'm the designated hitter, captain," he said, taking a swing with his bat. "I'll be on the poop deck, practicing. Call me in if you need me." He walked aft to the golf platform, tossed a small squid in the air, and belted it into the river.

Wrong John threw the ball to Chief, who tossed it to Gunny, who threw underhand to Sir Yes Sir, who skipped one to Basma. She fired one right at Tosspot's head, and he barely covered it with his mitt. The other officers looked at her with raised eyebrows. Pinch's mouth dropped open. "That's hot sauce, marshal," she said. "Good thing you blocked it, or you'd be headless and smoking from the neck!" Basma turned away and crossed her arms. The marshal picked up the baseball and examined it, considering, I imagined, whether or not to confiscate it as evidence of Sweet's terrorist intentions. Wrong John waved at him to throw it to him.

From a down-river bend, a four-masted, square-rigged dreadnought steamer chugged up the Potomac, a trail of black smoke in its wake. It turned out to be the *Shokanaw*, commanded by Admiral Tucker "Yarn" Olive, so nicknamed for his renown as a storyteller. He anchored the big gunship thirty yards downstream of *Liberty*, and came to her in a longboat. Speck and the quartermaster helped him aboard. He stood at attention and saluted Silverspoon. The captain saluted him casually and flipped the baseball at him. The admiral caught it in his right hand and rolled it in his fingers.

"Got a little something for me in your jewel case, Yarn?" asked Gunny, rubbing his hands together. Silverspoon and the other officers gathered in a tight circle around Olive.

"I've got *something*, that's for sure, but the scrotum color is not an *exact* match," said Olive, his voice deep, gravely, sincere. He flipped the baseball at Dagger.

"We're not looking for riddles today, Yarn. Tell us what you've got," said Chief, throwing the baseball hard into his own mitt, pulling it out and throwing it again.

"Our agent got into his palace," Tucker Olive said. "He was dressed as a harem girl, veiled, wearing a sheer silk kaftan, white as a newborn lamb. The first night in his chamber the commando went into an exotic belly dance, had Shalong down to his skivvies, then got him out of those, and *ZING!* Nailed him between the legs with his razor-sharp throwing star."

"So where are they? Where are the *cojones?*" the captain asked. Dagger continued to slap the baseball into his mitt.

"They weren't his." Olive dropped his head.

"What? What do you mean they weren't his?" asked the captain, his voice raised an octave.

"Apparently Shalong has hired numerous look-alikes, who are virtually identical to him," answered Admiral Olive stiffly.

"Then how do you know it wasn't him?" asked Dagger, leaning forward, the baseball clenched in his fist.

"We have it on very good authority that Shalong has a distinguishing mole on his scrotum. This man had no such mole."

"He could'a had it removed," said Wrong John. "Or maybe it just fell off—warts do that, you know." He reached behind himself, trying to scratch the lump in his back, but couldn't reach it.

"Well, there was another sign." The admiral cleared his throat and looked side to side. "Shalong is known to have a very large, uh, cannon down in the black forest there and—"

Captain Silverspoon grabbed himself in the crotch. "Yeah? Well I ain't exactly packin' a pea shooter."

"—and the guy we got didn't have much to brag about, especially—"

"I don't care about the rat bastard's cock, for God's sake!" exploded Dagger. He spit his words so violently he ejected one of his gold canines, and it bounced off the admiral's chest. Dagger hauled back and heaved Pinch's baseball far out into the Potomac. She watched it land, swallowed hard, and covered her mouth with the fingertips of her right hand. Basma walked over and touched her shoulder. Pinch batted her eyes, and they filled with tears. None of the men seemed to notice what had happened.

"We relied on the very best intelligence in the world to prove our case for war," Chief fumed. Sir Yes Sir coughed and turned away. "I expected the same level of detail applied to Operation Castration. We planned to take the bastard out, right from the get go, and I want to make sure we either *got* his balls or we did not *get* his balls!"

Admiral Olive stared at the ground. Krill, who had come up unnoticed from the hold, snuck in and grabbed the gold tooth in his beak, then skittered away. "As it turns out," the admiral said, "he—the imposter—was wearing a fake mustache, and when the special ops commando removed it, the phony had a cleft palate."

"You mean to tell me the most sophisticated special operations task force in the world was fooled by a guy wearing a fake mustache over a hair lip?" Dagger paced the deck in a tight back and forth, his steps heavy, almost stomping. Yo Yo stepped back and hid behind the foremast. Chief paced, and fumed, "That's inexcusable, absolutely inexcusable." Wrong John, imitating him, paced and rubbed his chin.

"*BRACK!*" squawked Krill, his words garbled. "Inexcusable, absolutely inexcusable. *BRA—*"

The Chief was on Krill instantly, lifting him by the neck from the deck. "Shut your goddamned mouth, you stupid, insolent—." Dagger stopped himself, but continued to hold Krill by the throat. "Spit out the tooth, you little klepto." Krill stuck out his black tongue and let the gold tooth drop from the end, into Chief's outstretched palm. He dropped the parrot to the deck. Wrong John stepped beside his first mate, and kicked Krill out of the way. Boy, I thought, the ride from hero to goat is a short one on this ship.

"Order another strike!" yelled Silverspoon. "Use some nunchuks on him this time. I don't care. Just beat him to a bloody pulp."

"I'm afraid we can't do that, sir."

Silverspoon did a double take. "That was not a purty please, Admiral Olive. It's an order!"

"It can't be executed."

"Excuse me?"

"We're ninety-nine percent certain Shalong has gone into hiding, down into a labyrinth of tunnels and secret chambers below Baghdad."

"God damn him!" screamed the captain. Chief Dagger ground his teeth, shook his head at the admiral, and shot him with poison hate bullets from his deadly eyes.

"The other thing—our agent, who was able to smuggle out the one message about her—uh—his mission, has gone down in the labyrinth with him, and if she's—he's— still alive, has been absorbed into Shalong's harem," said Admiral Olive in a somber tone.

"What do you mean, "he—she?" What sort of games are you playing?" questioned Chief, his finger pointed at the admiral's face.

"The agent, to get in there—that close—had to be a woman."

"You sent a woman in to do a man's job?" asked Wrong John.

"Well, I'd say it *was* a woman's job, you ask me," said Pinch, an angry tone to her voice.

"That's right, ma'am," said Olive. "And this agent is probably the most proficient martial artist in Army Special Forces. If anyone can make it through, she can."

"But in his harem? I mean, he could be putting his hairy paws all over an American female individual. That disgusts me." Silverspoon stuck out his tongue.

"She understood the risks, sir. Besides, the news from Iraq is not all grim," Admiral Olive added quickly. "Simultaneous to the castration strike we began to bombard them with our destroyers. They have already retreated from the coastal cities and our troops are ready to invade."

Yo Yo popped up from behind the foremast. "Not so fast," he said. "Before we put troops on the ground I believe we can get the Iraqi army to preempt itself."

"I'm all ears," said the captain. He thumped his baseball mitt with his fist. A gust of wind flapped the furled sails and fanned the corporate flags in the masthead. The lookout fired his rifle at a snowy egret plying the shoreline for fish. The officers looked up at him. "False alarm," he said. "Thought I saw a squid."

"Well, as I've said," Yo Yo went on, "modern military strategy is more about persuasion than it is about actual fighting. Battle, it turns out, is not ten percent inspiration and ninety percent perspiration, but it's actually one hundred percent disposition. It's *psy-ops,* psychological operations, not primitive sword fighting."

"Spare us the lecture on military theory, Gunny," said the captain. "What are you going to *do?*"

"Having closely studied the Arab mind, its inclinations, its predilections, I am aware of an inbred yellow streak." He straightened the lapels of his jacket, smoothed back his slick brown hair, adjusted the patch over his left eye, and walked between the officers of *Liberty* and Admiral Olive. "Let me introduce a little psy-ops beauty I call Operation Pantywaist. It involves dispatching unmanned drone blimps, each pulled by a couple of vultures, over the skies of Iraq. Each blimp is equipped with a sophisticated niner-fiver, alpha-tango-walnut, psy-ops leaflet dribbler doodad."

"Oh shut up with the phony field commander lingo," said Sir Yes Sir curtly.

"What?" asked Gunny.

"I've seen your weapons systems in operation. You probably still have a headache from the field test of your balloon bombs."

Gunny came at the diplomat, who responded aggressively. Chief got between the two and kept them apart. Sir Yes Sir turned away. Gunny adjusted his monocle, pulled on his gold nose ring, and continued, "The drones will dribble thousands of leaflets inviting the Iraqi army to surrender before the war begins—what I call 'Self-preemption for Self-preservation.'"

"And we think that'll work?" asked the captain skeptically.

"The Arabs have historically shown themselves to be shiftless and disloyal. They'll pledge a blood oath to follow you into the fires of hell—Jahannum, they call it—but as soon as it gets too hot, they cut and run." Gunny sliced the air with his hand. The captain nodded and winked at him. Yo Yo's erect index fingers went beside his head.

"Your father knows about that from the first Gulf War," added Dagger. Wrong John's eyes brightened at the mention of his pa.

"You got a sample?" asked Wrong John. Yo Yo reached into his pocket and retrieved a square piece of paper the size of his hand, and handed it to the captain.

"It's in Arabic, dodo." He wadded the flier and threw it at Yo Yo.

"I can translate." The gunner picked up the leaflet, uncrumpled it, and placed a monocle over his good eye. "It says:

'Praise Allah. Do not be afraid. We will not hurt you. We want only to kill your leader and take over your country. Lay down your weapons, tie yourself to a tree, and wait for us to come and arrest you. We will be merciful, as is Allah. We will provide you with a new American name, such as Jack, Bob, or Fred. You will be happy, prosperous, and free. You will be allowed to vote for the political candidates we choose for you. Democracy is great, as is Allah.'

That's it."

The captain shrugged. "So they're pretty sold on this Allah guy?"

"They think he's the cat's pajamas."

"Likin' it. How many you think we'll get with the notes?"

"We're estimating a psy-ops conversion average of point-three-o."

"The captain is not a statistician. Give it to me regular."

"One in three."

"That's great. How many troops you reckon it will take to go in and mop up?"

"Ten."

"Ten? Ten total troops to, you know, to go in there and march to Baghdad, lay siege to the city and bring it, and Shalong, to their knees?"

"Twenty-five, tops."

"You mean divisions, right?"

"No, I mean individuals."

Sir Yes Sir shook his head. "You need ten psychologists to examine your thick head. That's what you need. troops!" He expelled a gust of air through his lips. "You couldn't capture a herd of goats with ten troops."

"Like I said, twenty-five, then." Gunny looked at him through the monocle, his one good eye enlarged and fishlike.

"Twenty-five? That's ludicrous. Twenty-five men—what do you think this is, guard duty at Girl Scout camp? And your psy-ops program—it's an insult. You might get a few deserters, but one in three? Come on." Sir Yes Sir crossed his arms and shook his head. His half-closed eyelashes fluttered.

Yo Yo looked at him through his magnifying monocle. "Well, if you would have done your job right at the UN, maybe we'd have a few French Foreign Legionnaires to pad the numbers."

"What do you say we send in a few divisions, Yo Yo, just as a show of force and a little insurance," Chief advised.

"Fine, whatever you say, but let me tell you, gentlemen, the modern military is not about divisions and regiments and all of that tired strength through numbers nonsense. Modern military is mental. It's about perception and disposition. You shock them, you awe them, you humiliate them, you win the psychological battle very early on. What follows is rather like the act of a good hypnotist—bark like a dog! bark like a dog!" Gunny growled and woofed in the air.

Sir Yes Sir sighed, turned, and walked away. Pinch and Sweet followed him, and the three had an animated discussion behind the try-works. Krill sat next to the quarterdeck rail where the captain had kicked him, and hung his little head. He seemed to be counting his gray toes with the tip of his wing. Tom Thumb continued to bat small squid into the Potomac, every so often yelling, "Stee-rike three! Code Red! You're outta here!"

"Of course your foot soldier," Yo Yo continued, "will also help administer the rebuilding protocol, which, in my opinion, is best handled with private contractors."

"Hell yeah!" said the captain. "Get government out of war's way. We'll *piratize* the military. Imagine a military that answers to nobody but the opportunity of the global marketplace. Perfect marriage of the War on Squid and *Congreso Mandato*—endless war and endless plunder. All financed by a chicken population that will pay any amount for its precious safety."

"Brilliant insight Mr. Captain," said the Chief. He nodded at Admiral Olive. "With all due respect to the admiral, the U.S. military is a government agency—run like one—slow, wasteful, inefficient. Piratizing the military would make it less expensive and would eliminate the nuisance of public accountability."

"No cumbersome congressional approval," said Yo Yo.

"Simple majority vote of the board of directors," added Silverspoon.

"Quick check on the profit and loss statement," said the Chief.

"Bing, bang, boom! War for fun and profit. Let's piratize!" The three exchanged hearty handshakes and slapped one another's backs.

The admiral cleared his throat loudly and scuffed his shiny black shoes on the deck. The others looked at him, seeming to be surprised that he was still there. "I've got an update on Afghanistan."

"Afghani-who?" mocked Silverspoon. "I thought we done blew away all them tents already." He kissed his hand and blew across it.

"Well, we've completely lost track of AQ and his gang of bad guys in Afghanistan. We've had to divert our attention and Special Forces units to Iraq. So, well, it looks like we may not get the hoodlums for awhile." He could not look at the captain and his chief, but looked straight ahead, out across the flat Potomac.

"Don't sweat it," said the captain. The admiral snapped his head up and back, frowned, and looked at the other officers. They looked casually at Wrong John, not the least bit surprised.

"But I thought it was your mission to bring in Quota—slay the Giant Squid, rid the world of calamari," said Olive.

"What I said and *what* I said are two differ'nt things. That's what I meant, and is very different from what I *actually* said." The captain adjusted his balls and sniffed. "What I actually said is what I meant, 'Wanted, Dead or Alive.' Is he not one of those at this very moment?"

"Yes, uh, yes, sir, I suppose he is."

"Then we're still on message, ain't that right, Krill?"

"Brack," said Krill weakly, still sitting where Wrong John had kicked him.

"You got to understand somethin', Olive. This War on Squid, it's kinda, well, convenient. You see that gold coin I nailed to the mast?" He pointed to his hickory nickel. "That shows I'm serious about squid huntin'. But win or lose, it's all in how you play—it's a matter of, of—the way you do it, that's, that's how you play the game."

"No-ho-ho, noooo, please, not another quotation," Krill wailed.

"We need the Giant Squid out there, on the loose, layin' low for the Great White Whale," Wrong John said. "It keeps Moby Dick sharp. Keeps folks patriotic, willing to follow orders, to stay in line. You give us regular news of an AQ sighting, or a near miss—so everybody knows we're still on his ass—and just, you know, round the sombitch up about two, three weeks before the election. *Comprende?*" Dagger and Gunny nodded. The admiral shrugged his shoulders.

"Okay, sir. I was—." Admiral Olive hesitated again.

"What is it?" asked Silverspoon.

"It's—well, we've had a couple of little accidents in Afghanistan. Not just two, actually, a number, but these have been the worst so far."

"What? Friendly fire?"

"No no no—fog of war sort of stuff—their side, pretty much SOP, but, kinda ugly."

"Well?"

"It seems we left a few hundred of AQ's Afghan allies in an airtight livestock shed with no food and water."

"And?"

"And they were discovered several days later, very smelly, and very dead."

"And? I mean, they were enemy combatants, right?"

"We think so, some of them anyway. They were, well, we just kept rounding up anyone who looked suspicious and cramming them in there, for, you know, to interrogate them, and then, well, our boys got distracted shooting artillery at wild asses and whatnot, and forgot about the—the detainees, and then, you know, we found that mess."

"That's well within the bounds of the mandate," said TP, making a note in his small book.

"War's an ugly thing," said the captain flatly. "Nobody's perfect. Besides, America is still really, really torqued about 10-10. The people want raw meat, Silverspoon Mandatewise, and I aim to grill it for them." He pulled a golf club from a bag leaning against a halyard and waggled at an imaginary ball, his baseball mitt still on his left hand. "You want to let Quota harbor in your country—just as bad as joining him. Far as I'm concerned, there idn't an innocent person over there, not one." He took a practice swing with the club. "Get me?"

"Yes, sir. I'm glad to hear you say that, because, well, there were other— there were several of these sorts of misunderstandings, but, the one—the worst one—some—there were some boys—some boys," he choked up and had to brace himself before he could continue. He dropped into a yarn about the incident, his deep sandpaper voice that of a grandfather telling a bedtime story.

"A company of light armor—Delta Company—had come upon a small town of mud brick structures, fractured by artillery and eroded by wind and rain. It looked more like an ancient ruin than a city inhabited by the living. The mid-morning air was crisp, and blowing from the northwest, and had kicked up a dust storm of fine brown silt. Sharp mountains, broken like vandalized windows, surrounded the high, treeless plateau.

"Delta Company crept into the shattered town as quietly as could a company of light cannon and Gatling gun, pulled in heavy, horse-drawn wagons, escorted by two platoons of infantry. They had been separated from the main battalion and were lost, hoping to encounter a kind stranger who would point them toward the rendezvous in Kandahar. The wind moaned and whistled through the windowless mud structures that appeared to have been abandoned. About half the company had come around a corner when they were fired on. The Gatling guns spun on their turrets and reeled off a thousand rounds in less than a minute, reducing the mud building to a heap of brown clods. Infantry searched the debris but could find no trace of their attackers. Where had the gunmen gone? How many were there? Had the company rolled into a trap? What if they became pinned down with no way out? The wind picked up. Fine dust got in behind their goggles and made their eyes water.

"The captain gave orders to withdraw, drivers yelled, 'Hya!' and their bullwhips went hard on the backs of big black Belgian draft horses that reared back and neighed in a jangle of harness and steel traces against whiffletrees, then the snap of leather straps, lunged against by the mighty Belgians. The heavy wagons groaned and rattled with the sudden surge of force and speed, followed by the pounding boots of jogging infantrymen.

"Delta Company rumbled through town without encountering another attack and made hard for the open plain ahead. Just at the outskirts of town, they passed through a bombed-out neighborhood inhabited by a thin donkey and a couple of scroungy chickens. The road narrowed and was gouged by explosions, which forced the company to slow down. Just as the road opened up, and Delta's captain gave the order to advance to open ground, the men heard to their right what sounded like small arms fire coming from an open field. Through watery eyes and the haze of brown dust, one of the young privates saw what he thought were men holding riffles in the air and running at Delta Company. He shouted, 'AQ fighters at three o'clock!'

"Our men at the Gatling guns spun on their turrets with a high-pitched grinding and opened fire on the fighters in the field with pounding fifty-eight-caliber rounds. The Gatling guns reeled off round upon round upon round in a deafening roar. Empty casings flew in all directions like wood chips from a furious mill, bouncing off the men and the wagons and the horses and landing in the dusty road. When finally they stopped, the field was quiet, except for the wailing wind.

"Our boys slowly approached the clearing. What they found made many of them sick to their stomachs. Blood and body parts and mangled corpses and broken sticks littered the clearing, which was, in fact, a playground, and the AQ fighters, children playing war with sticks for guns. We had mowed down fifty of them."

Admiral Olive concluded his story with a deep sigh and stood at attention.

The captain turned and looked aft of *Liberty*. He bit his lip and screwed up his face and hit his thighs with his hands. Nobody seemed to know what to say. Dagger sucked his teeth and blinked furiously. Yo Yo pretended a sudden emergency on the cannon deck and excused himself. After a minute, the captain turned back to us.

"How did we—? I mean, their parents, their moms and dads, how did we, did we—how did we break the news to them?" He bit his lip and grimaced.

The admiral stood at attention. He had fallen back on his discipline as a military officer to control his emotions and report the facts. "It is not the responsibility of the United States Army to track down the enemy's next of kin after a hostile encounter."

"Hostile encounter? Hostile? What? A schoolyard of kids playing army?"

"Sir, with all due respect, Mr. Captain, you ordered us in there to punish and remove that regime for its part in 10-10. You advised us to be aggressive and ruthless and to preempt any sign of danger. When our soldiers roll through a strange neighborhood and hear what they interpret as hostile fire, they are required to respond with extreme prejudice. They were simply doing their duty."

Something unseen jolted us from below. An engineer scrambled through the hatch and onto the deck, and called all hands to the pumps. I noticed the fluted edge of a huge brown tentacle slip into the river. The jolt knocked several of the crew to the planks, including the captain, who did not move or attempt to get up, but just sat cross-legged and hung his head. Krill waddled over and sat in Wrong John's lap. Admiral Olive regained his footing, gave an abrupt salute, returned to the *Shokanaw* and steamed away, back to the Persian Gulf, to implement, I assumed, Yo Yo's "psy-ops beauty," Operation Pantywaist.

Chapter XXXIX

The Dangerous Mumblety-peg Trick

Basma, Sir Yes Sir, and Pinch came to the galley later that afternoon and asked about the news from Afghanistan. "None of the officers will give us a straight answer," Pinch said. Tatanka, Roberto, and I had prepared a robust chili that cooked on the cast-iron stove and filled the small kitchen with a piquant aroma. Tatanka carved on his scrimshaw. I polished and cleaned the baldheaded iron twins. Roberto cracked piñon seeds on the table with the edge of a glass and munched the sweet nuts. Chickens, geese, and turkeys clucked and gabbled and pecked at the seed in their pens. The clang of laborers working the pumps rose from the hold.

I told them the story of the children in the playground. When I was finished, no one spoke. Pinch sniffled and wiped her eyes. Basma looked at the floor. She squeezed the bridge of her nose between her thumb and index finger. Sir Yes Sir fell into his training as a soldier, as had Admiral Olive, and became stiff, not yielding to his emotions.

"This is what happens when you count yourself a victim," I said, as much to myself as anyone in the room. "You just make more victims. Nobody takes responsibility, and so it can never end. They attacked you for no reason. You attacked them for no reason. The bloody revenge goes on and on."

Silverspoon poked his head in the galley from the doorway. "Anybody want to hit a few squid with me and Thumby?" The three officers stared at him in disbelief. "Suit yourself—but I gotta tell ya, those little hummers make a satisfying 'thwack' when they hit the bat." He turned and bounded up the stairs. Basma lowered her head and shook it slowly side to side. Sir Yes Sir walked with Tatanka to the cookstove, and the Lakota stirred the steaming pot of chili. "God damn it," Sir Yes Sir said. "This is why military force is always the *last* option. It can *never* be first—never. These mistakes are inevitable, but they can't be justified if you started the damn fight." Tatanka nodded, grunted, and stirred the chili. The clang of bilge pumps tolled from below.

A few weeks later the *Shokanaw* steamed around a downstream bend in the river and cut a trough to *Liberty*. "Thar she sails!" shouted the lookout. "She flies the banner of a naval commander!" Everyone had been anxious for the return of Admiral Olive, and soon after the lookout's cry, the deck swarmed with sailors and officers talking loudly and pointing at the mighty dreadnought.

Olive came aboard, and, pleading fatigue, asked for a few hours of rest before telling the tale of Operation Pantywaist in Iraq. "But are we winning?" blurted Wrong John.

"Yes, yes we are," said Olive, raising his hands. "The war is over—I think. Or it never started—perhaps. Either way, we have taken Baghdad and control of the country."

"Huzzah! Huzzah! Huzzah!" cheered the crew, shaking their fists in the air and hugging one another. They chattered noisily and surrounding the admiral. He made his way to the rail and returned to the *Shokanaw* to rest until after supper.

"God, I *love* my mandate," said Chief, pulling on the lapels of his tight blue jacket. Wrong John cocked his head and glared at his first mate. Chief sucked his gold canines (the dentist had replaced the one he spit out at Olive during his last visit) and tugged on an earring. "Oh—*our* mandate."

After dinner, Krill orchestrated a convivial gathering around the try-works for the heroic tale anticipated from Admiral Tucker "Yarn" Olive. Krill had Tatanka fire up the try-works and pop corn in the round silver pots. By the time Olive came aboard the officers and crew sat on the deck, passing around bowls of popcorn, visiting playfully. The admiral walked in, smiling, as would a storyteller entering a receptive gathering. He was about to begin when Wrong John preempted him. He got a boost up the red brick try-works and stood on top.

"A'right. Now before we get into the whole conquest odyssey, let's play Post-War Planning Lottery." He clapped his hands together and rubbed them, and turned his front-to-back, blue humped hat sideways. "I'm thinking of a number between one and twenty. You officers get to make a comment on post-war Iraq. If your total word-count adds up to the number I'm thinkin' of, you win the prize." Tom Thumb handed up a small fish tank, about six inches square, sealed on top, holding a small blue-spotted squid.

"It's a desktop Squid Alert Christmas tank," said the captain. He turned it over, shook it. The tank filled with a flurry of tiny snowflakes. "A'right, let's do this. Crude?"

"Capture the blubber plants. Put some American Ingenuity to them. Boost efficiency and profit. Yankees skim the cream," said the Oil Czar in a flood of words.

"Seventeen. Pinch?"

"*Piratize*. Water, sewer, power, roads, hospitals, colleges, cemeteries, state-run factories. Sell them off to the lowest American bidder."

"Like it. Nineteen. Thumby."

"Squid Alert. Keep them scared. Code Orange, every day. Martial law," said the little man in his deep, resonant voice.

"Check. Eleven. Basma?"

She shook her head and looked at the deck.

"Balk. Runners advance. von Shlop?"

"Pizzle, puzzle, where's the muzzle? Dizzle, dazzle, keep them frazzled. Herky, jerky, serve them turkey."

"Science, huh? Fifteen. Sir Yes Sir."

"Captain, with all due respect, this is not what I had in mind when I suggested a thorough post-war plan for Iraq. I meant detailed analysis of at least twenty contingencies. The variables are limitless, but we should try to anticipate them. That, *also*, should be part of your *mandato*, shouldn't it?" The diplomat's hands went to his hips. He pursed his lips and raised his eyebrows.

"Fifty one. Busted. TP?"

"Private prison system. Expect a liberty *backlash*. Let's control it, and also make a buck off it." He flicked his silver star and nodded sharply.

"Good for the goose, good for the gander. Seventeen. Gunny?"

"Overwhelming outpouring of gratitude. Some fresh-democracy hijinks. Just let it go."

"Crisp twelve. Nice. Big Chief?"

"Rebuilding contracts. Some companies made good bucks from the destruction. Others don't get a payday until we rebuild what we broke. It better happen quick, or we'll have a riot on our hands."

"Busted by thirteen. Want to buy back a dozen?"

"How much?"

"Ten apiece."

"Pass."

"What do you mean, riots? Iraqis goin' crazy for water and lights?"

"No. American companies angry they won't make their second-quarter profit projections."

"Check." He picked up the Christmas tank. "Pinch, it's yours. Nineteen was the number. Hope this makes up for what hothead did to your baseball." He shot a dirty look at Dagger. Pinch stepped forward and accepted her mini-Squid Alert, smiling broadly. She shook it and held up the small squid -in-a-blizzard for everyone to see.

"Planning. Very important part of my job. You happy now, SYS?" Wrong John grabbed a handful of popcorn from a try-pot and got help down from the try-works. The diplomat, who sat on the quarterdeck, hung his head between his knees, and pulled his short, curly hair.

Olive climbed up and sat on the edge of the squatty red brick structure, smoke rising from the rear of the furnace. He laced his hands together, and said in his low, warm, purring voice, "Once upon a time...

"There was a war in Iraq. It was against a dictator named Shalong. Everyone knew he was a bad man—a very bad man. He had killed his own citizens, ruined his nation's natural resources, started dangerous wars, lied to the world. America decided to make him pay for his crimes, and so it brought a great army to his shores and to his borders.

"Before America attacked his army, it tried to trick his soldiers into surrendering. Big black vultures flew over the country—hundreds of them. They pulled big balloons that had contraptions attached to them. These contraptions were filled with tricky, very persuasive leaflets inviting the soldiers to surrender, or risk the full wrath of America's mighty military. Very few accepted the invitation."

"What?" asked Gunny. "That can't be true. I know the Arab mind. I know it."

"The few that tied themselves to trees had their throats slit. The other Iraqis must have thought it dishonorable to give up like that. So, anyway, the vultures flew over and rained down their white leaflets. They were the biggest snowflakes anyone had ever seen, and they might as well have melted when they hit the ground."

Tatanka walked up from galley and began to do tricks with his long yellow jackknife at the bow end of the quarterdeck. The blade stuck in the wood with a "thonk" after every successful move. I noticed Silverspoon craning his neck to see what he was up to. The crew passed metal bowls around and munched on popcorn as Olive continued his story.

"After the leaflets melted, we realized an invasion would be necessary. And so we marched into the Cradle of Civilization. First we encountered a marshy plane, well grown with date palms and reeds, the rivers and canals plied by strange round boats called *guffars*. The guffar is the oldest watercraft in the world, maybe eight thousand years in use. It has no rudder, and is woven out of the marsh reeds, then sealed by a thick pitch on the outside. We watched these round rudderless boats, just whirling around and bumping into one another, as they floated along rivers and canals. Sometimes they held barley or rice in bags, figs, dates, pistachios, other times goats, sheep, donkeys, horses—even camels!

"We still believed the Iraqi people would be very happy to see us, happy to be liberated, so we took great pains to make a good entrance in the first Iraqi city we came to, Nasiriya. Nasiriya is an ancient city of mud brick buildings, domed mosques, cultivated orchards, butcher shops, grain and spice merchants, camel tack stalls, a thriving *bazaar*. We surrounded it and bombarded it with artillery. A day or two into it, the white flag went up. It was time for our grand entrance. We decided to let a trick rider from Springfield, Missouri, Private Joe Simms, lead us into town. He stood on his saddle, wearing a perfect blue cavalry uniform, his back arched, head thrown back, hat hanging from his neck, arms spread out and away from his body, ready to receive the shower of roses.

"The Iraqis gathered on narrow balconies projecting from the upper floors of mud brick buildings in various shades of brown and blonde. Gateways of ornate iron led to hidden courtyards. Men sat on the two-tiered benches of the coffee shops and puffed sleepily on the tubes of their brass *hookah* pipes. They dipped tin cups in clay urns and drank water with their small cups of dark Arabian coffee. Young boys kicked balls in the alleys, dressed in blue and white, vertically striped robes. No one uttered a word.

"The men stared at us in their *dishdasha* robes and head scarves wrapped in camel-hair rope. Women covered in bright red, brown and golden *kaftans* and *burkas* revealed nothing but their orbs of coal, glaring at us. I don't know what happened to the Iraqi army. It must have taken on the attributes of a squid and disguised itself perfectly as ordinary Arabs.

"Simms opened his eyes and straightened up. He became incensed that there was no celebration, no explosion of gratitude, no dancing in the streets, no trays of candied figs, no urns of *arrack*, the sweet, fermented palm sap, no proclamation by the *mufti*, no feast of *halal*.

"*There was no shower of porcelain-white Abyssinian roses.*"

Admiral Olive left the words to dry in the air. A sudden breeze rustled the sails and rattled the binnacle compass. All eyes went to Gunny Yo Yo, who had jumped to his feet and stood like a bull ready to charge, snorting, all but scraping his hooves against the deck. "That's impossible! They were cheering—you—you just couldn't hear them. The Arab has a quiet spirit, not demonstrative like we are in the West. But I can read his mind. He was rejoicing deep inside—throwing roses in the garden of his soul." He looked quickly among the other officers. None of them would make eye contact. The captain had his arms crossed, his lips drawn down in disgust, and stared over the Potomac. Chief pounded on his forehead with the thumb end of his fist.

Sir Yes Sir rubbed and squeezed his hands as if making a meatball.

Wrong John expelled a gust of air that vibrated his lips. He walked over to Tatanka and joined him in his game of mumblety-peg with the long yellow jackknife. Tatanka winked at me and smiled.

Olive continued. "The trick rider Simms straightened up, dropped his arms, opened his eyes, and yelled, 'What's the matter with you people? We saved you from Shalong and this is the thanks we get? Well you can go to hell, then. You hear me? All of you can go to hell!' A single rifle fired. Simms fell from the horse, dead, shot through the heart."

A ripple of shock, disbelief, anger, and pain rolled through the crew. Gunny walked to the far rail and turned away from Olive. The squeak of Dagger sucking air across his gold canines pierced the air like sharp fingernails on a blackboard.

"BRACK! Carpe diem. Carpe diem. There are no setbacks—no setbacks. Call out the Clown Criers. America liberates Iraq in record time! Most impressive military operation in history—in history! Get them out. Every street corner." Krill hopped up and down on the quarterdeck rail, flapping his wings and whistling. "Page one, Mandate Media: 'Silverspoon Mandate Scores Its First Victory!' Hoorah! Hoorah!"

Gunny turned, smiled at Krill, and gave him a thumbs up. Admiral Tucker "Yarn" Olive continued his tale. "The cavalry company panicked, shot wildly in all directions, screamed, horses snorting and whinnying, and charged out of town.

"On the outskirts of Nasiriya, a *wadi* dropped away to a green vale. A copse of pale, gray-green olive trees stood in a field of lavender, their trunks entwined by jasmine, blooming with white flowers. The combination of the two aromatic flowers gave me a welcome, sweet breath after the tragedy we had just endured."

Wrong John attempted the difficult knife trick called "Shave the Barber." He placed the jackknife in his left palm, snapped it into the air with his right, and flipped it end over end. It stabbed into his right foot. He jumped up and down, rubbed his wound, and swore. Basma rushed toward him but he waved her off. "If our brave American troops must stand in harm's way, so can their commander-in-chief," he said.

Olive looked over at him briefly, then went on. "A lone Bedouin sat under an olive tree in his white robe and hood, a few scruffy, black-faced sheep lying at his feet. He ran a rounded bow over the single, single horsehair string of his *rebaba*, a square-bodied violin regarded as the ancestor of all stringed instruments. The song I cannot describe, for I have never heard anything like it before. I can only say how it made me feel: lost in the desert, parched, frightened, lonely. How did America end up here? I wondered. How could a young nation such as ours, a mere child, subdue this untamed birthplace of human culture? What could we possibly hope to accomplish that hadn't been tried here a thousand and one times before?

"We rolled on to Baghdad, horse hooves clopping, artillery wagons groaning and creaking, some of the men smoking and humming folk tunes. Up ahead stood an ancient city, abandoned, worn down, and broken from a thousand years of neglect. From a mound near the center rose a round tower, peeled of its bright colors and protective skin of mortar, worn unevenly on its flat top, as if bitten by a snaggletoothed Titan. I thought of ancient Babylon and the famed Tower of Babel. I wondered, as in the legend, what common language we would use now that we were in Babylon, and how we would understand one another? Would we build our Silverspoon of Babel in the desert? or would we fall to the same confusion as the laborers of Nebuchadnezzar?

"Up ahead we came to a pontoon bridge over the Euphrates, made of wooden boats lashed together and covered with a cedar boardwalk, fingers of purple and red in its grain. It put off a wonderful smell. Empty guffars were tied off near the bank, looking like a collection of brown bubbles. The sound of artillery bombardment boomed from the city. Clouds of black smoke rose from the center of town. We crossed the pontoon bridge and took up positions outside of Baghdad. Our cannon joined those of the other companies surrounding the city. On into the night the bombardment continued. Iraqi artillery responded sporadically, but was ineffectual."

Wrong John, following the masterful Sioux, attempted the mumblety-peg trick called "Tony Chestnut." He balanced the knife on his forehead, flipped it up, and stuck it in his right foot. "Son-of-a-bitch!" he yelled, reaching down to pull the knife out of his boot, already bloody from his first mistake. Basma again approached. He put her off, his sharp nose flared, ears red with fury. "I'm prepared to make the ultimate sacrifice for my country. Leave me alone!"

I looked at Tatanka. He did not smile or wink. His eyes held a coldness, and distance, that should have been a warning to Wrong John—except he didn't notice. I remembered my conversation with Tatanka in the small cabin when we were just beginning our adventure. He had called his Moby Dick the white snake, the never-ending white snake of settlers' wagons. Was he going to get even with them for taking his land, killing his namesake, the buffalo, massacring his people? Was he going to take out all that anger and hatred on Wrong John Silverspoon?

"The next day, we marched on the city. Just like in Nasiriya, we encountered no soldiers. It truly was a War on Squid, for we could not see the enemy. It only came out at night, and struck with quick darts and jabs, like the springing of many tentacles. We set up bases and got to work hunting down Shalong, his sons, and generals—and of course finding his Weapons of Mass Hysteria.

"In the spirit of psy-ops, winning the mental battle to humiliate and intimidate our enemy, we gave Shalong's generals the nicknames of women's undergarments. We called them Garter, Bloomers, Panties, Corset, Silk Stockings, and Lingerie. Shalong, the biggest prize, went by the code name of Chastity Belt."

"That's good," said Silverspoon, pausing in his game. "It's important to mock and ridicule these people."

"Why is it important to do *that?*" asked Sir Yes Sir.

"Why? Because we got us a mandate to be tough. That means making an example of bad guys, showin' folks what to expect if they go agin us."

Yarn paused, then went on with his story. "The second prong of our post-conquest strategy was to seek and find the Weapons of Mass Hysteria. We searched every cave, every *wadi*, every *ziggurat*, every *yashmak*, every, garrison, outpost, suspicious tent, and palace—the stables, kitchens, poultry pens, gardens, cisterns, sewers. We wanted those yellow cakes. We wanted to find the hideout of the poison-dart frogs. We wanted their swamp, and their leader, the evil chemist, Ali Baba, and his forty beakers.

"And we wanted that vulgar Garter, and the Silk Stockings, and most of all, the Chastity Belt. Sadly, these distractions prevented us from securing the country. Mobs of free Iraqis went on rampages through the cities, looting museums, palaces, government offices, state-owned factories. They stole, burnt, or otherwise destroyed anything associated with Shalong's rule. Huge bonfires broke out, fueled entirely with the frames and canvas of Shalong portraits hung on every available wall in Iraq.

"Sadly, they also stole or destroyed some of the most valuable articles of antiquity the world has ever known: Sumerian bronze urns, Assyrian stone tablets, Babylonian bone carvings, tapestries of Persian sultans, things that belong to our shared heritage as the people of the world. We should have protected the museums, at least."

"Democracy is messy business," said Gunny from across the ship. "Freedom is about being free to make mistakes."

"It must have been a frightening discovery when you came upon those tins of poison-frog-frosted cornbread the size of football fields," said Chief.

"It would have been," said the Admiral, "if we had."

"What do you mean, if?"

"We haven't found anything." That one, too, Olive hung out like long johns on the clothesline. Only the black coffin hanging from the yardarm seemed to fit with what had just been said.

"Ouch! God damn it!" There was Silverspoon, the big yellow jackknife sticking for a third time into his right foot. He seemed unable to pull it out, just bounced on his foot, howling and cursing. Nobody went to his aid. Something about his silhouette, with the newborn hump on his back, and that long yellow knife sticking out of foot, made me think again of Captain Ahab. "Whosoever of ye raises me that white headed whale," he said, "with three holes punctured in his starboard fluke—look you, whosoever raises me that same white whale, he shall have this gold ounce, my boys!" I looked from Silverspoon to his hickory nickel nailed to the mast, and back again at the darted captain of *Liberty*.

"But the Shah," exclaimed Basmati Sweet. "We toured the country. He looked in his crystal ball. The weapons were in there—even I saw them. They've got to be there. I won't be able to live with myself if—"

"Take a deep breath, Second Mate Sweet. The weapons are there. We'll find them. Just keep looking, Olive. Turn over every stone. Follow the tracks of every jackal through the desert. Find the goddamned weapons." Dagger stood and walked to his quarters. "Okay, kids. The show's over. Get some rest. We've got a lot of work to do."

Chapter XL

Mission Impossible—Er, Accomplished

Wrong John's mumblety-peg wounds required six stitches—two for each cut. He threw his cowboy boots overboard, disgusted at the punctures in the right boot. "Feed 'em to the fishes," he said. His mood reflected the attitude of *Liberty* after Admiral Olive's visit. The invasion had either gone very right, or very wrong, and no one could tell for sure which was true. Krill, of course, seized the day and spread the word that America had achieved a stunning victory, one of the great military operations in history.

Ah, Frank, you know what had happened, don't you, brother? American had not won a war. It had not even begun to fight one. Its enemy had recognized it could never stand toe-to-toe with the power of America. Similar to us Missouri rebels in the Civil War, the Iraqi rebels—who I'm sure, like us, thought of themselves as grand patriots—faded into the catacombs of Baghdad, and all those ancient cities, and prepared for a long, agonizing, cat-and-mouse bushwhacking.

At the time, however, none of the officers—except the diplomat, who confided in Tatanka he thought it premature to celebrate a victory—recognized, or *wanted* to recognize, what had truly occurred. The very day after Yarn's story about the invasion, Silverspoon and his parrot set about arranging a ceremony on *Liberty* to honor the achievement in Iraq. They had Tatanka open the try-works and get the three silver pots going with spermaceti fires. All officers were required to wear dress blues and to assemble in ranks on deck at nineteen hundred hours.

The bugle sounded that evening, and brought about the usual thunder of boots that signified the sailors lining up in their rows. The sun poised above the western bank of the river, half under the forest, half over, and seemed to hang there like a ripe orange ripped in two. The cool spring air bit into my skin. I looked up at the masthead and noticed Old Glory looking a little faded, while the corporate flags around her seemed brighter than ever. I pointed it out to Speck. He wasn't surprised to find the stars and stripes fading. "Made in China, Ish. What do they care about our colors over there?" he asked. I had the impression, looking up there in the twilight, that Old Glory was the fat belly of a razorback, and those other flags were ticks, sucking its blood, and growing fat and bright from it.

The captain came out of his quarters, Krill in his usual spot on the right shoulder, Basmati Sweet to his left, holding an ornate wooden box. He limped to his position on the quarterdeck, his right foot bandaged so thickly it appeared to be a small white pillow. His officers arrayed in their half moon behind him.

"Hey, ya'll," he said, in a casual, breezy tone, "it seems pretty clear the American military showed its absolute might in defeating Shalong."

"Huzzah! Huzzah! Huzzah!" cheered the crew. Wrong John nodded, his lips sticking out and drawn down at the corners. "Fling us a one-liner, would ya, Ish?" he requested.

I stepped forward from the mizzenmast, ready with something from Ecclesiastes. "One generation passes away and another comes: but the earth abides forever. I have seen all the works that are done under the sun; and, behold, all is vanity and vexation of spirit." I took my cue from Admiral Olive, and left the words to dry in the air. After a minute, I said, "Congratulations on the easiest victory in the history of warfare. It's got to feel mighty good to march through the battlefield and trounce somebody that didn't bother to show up." I returned to my position next to Tatanka, among the laborers—many of whom were not present, as they were occupied pumping the bilge. Evidence of their industry could be seen by the steady flow of water out a pipe from the hatch, and the drainage of it through the scuppers.

"That's right, IshcaBible. It does feel good. Damn good," said Silverspoon. He puffed his chest, raised his chin, and saluted at the tomb of the unknown enemy, somewhere in the Arabian Desert. "War is hell, though, and it was tough on me. I sustained several deep wounds during the battle, as you may have noticed." He held up his overly bandaged foot. "It was tough, but I stayed the course, and Baghdad is ours." He paused and the crew cheered, though somewhat reserved, given the tall tale he had just told. Wrong John squinted and looked out over the Potomac. The irregular light of the try-pot fires rummaged over his sharp face.

"In honor of our nation's great achievement, the hard work and sacrifice of everyone involved, the huge investment of time and resources on the part of so many, the sacrifices of our citizens, the steadfastness of our Congress, I now present myself with the Purple Heart for wounds received in battle." He moved in front of himself and turned as if to speak to himself where he had been standing. Basma opened the box, and he removed from it a Purple Heart medal, clipped to a red, white, and blue strap.

"To you, the honorable Captain Wrong John Silverspoon, son of Wrong John Johnson Silverspoon, I present the Purple Heart. Even as the fighting grew heavy and lesser men would have fallen to retreat, you held your ground, sustained mortal wounds, and brought down the evil regime of Shalong." He switched places, bowed his head, and placed the medal around his neck.

"God BRACK America!" Krill screeched. "God BRACK America!"

Sir Yes Sir had such a look of disgust on his face I thought he might have to run for the rail. The Chief blinked several times, removed his thick glasses, and rubbed his eyes. Gunny grumbled and groused that he wished he had been wounded in battle. Basma tilted her head to the side and squinted, as if trying to see something far in the distance. TP saluted and held his left hand over his chest. Crude and Pinch didn't seem to understand what they were witnessing. Krill stood on the captain's shoulder, and if a bird could smile, that's what he did.

"Thank you, Captain Silverspoon," Silverspoon said to his imaginary self. "Without your strong leadership, making the difficult decisions, taking bold action in the War on Squid, I wouldn't be here today receiving this honor. This victory is for freedom and democracy, to protect our way of life so hated by Shalong, and is truly a great day in the history of our great nation. Thank you, sir. Thank you very much." He saluted to himself, switched places, saluted back to himself, switched places, raised his fists and smiled on us all.

A splash came from the river. "Man overboard!" shouted the lookout. We rushed to the rail to find Admiral Olive, madly swimming for the *Shokanaw*, anchored fifty yards downstream of *Liberty*.

"Don't go runnin' off!" yelled Silverspoon, hands cupped around his mouth. "Got us a mission for you in New York City!"

The next day the captain and I went by train to New York with Gunny, Basma, and Krill. Silverspoon spent most of his time in private quarters with Yo Yo, going over a new, top-secret military weapon. None of the rest of us was permitted to see the new weapon, nor learn anything about it, except to find out from the captain that *he* would personally test it.

I sat in my sleeper car, watching the landscape of Maryland go by, green and rolling, filled with dairy farms and hardwood forests, crisscrossed with a hundred fresh streams and dotted with bright lakes. We passed through the station at Belair, and at Churchville and Level, then crossed the great Susquehanna River and chugged on to Philadelphia. All along the way those chintzy "Made in China" American flags hung off of bridges and buildings, the fabric faded, weather beaten, ragged. I wished someone would show them the kindness you would a stray dog, and invite them in out of the rain.

That evening after dinner, alone in my cabin writing down my thoughts, I heard a knock on my cabin door. I slipped the lock open and cracked the oak slider a few inches. There stood Basmati Sweet, wearing one of her bright red, flowered silk bandanas, and a new collection of copper and silver baubles in her ears. There was no fake mustache penciled above her lip. She had on a softly draping, white cotton shirt with a long cut down the chest, and no buttons. I saw a V-shaped shadow down the opening of her shirt. The white fabric was nudged out by the tips of her breasts.

"Evening, Basma. Come on in," I said, feeling that familiar tingle in my groin and rush of blood across my face. She walked in, sat on the couch, and crossed her long legs.

"What did you think of his ceremony?" she asked.

"What's to think?" I sat next to her. "Hell if I know. What did you think of it?"

"Oh, I don't know. I can't let myself think what I really think. If I do, it will mean trouble for me. I don't need any more trouble in my life." She looked up at me with her deep brown eyes, and blinked with her long lashes. I followed the line of her jaw, down her long, supple neck, down to that shadow between her breasts. I looked back in her eyes, and leaned toward her. She closed her eyes, the long lashes lying down on her luscious, chocolate skin. I closed my eyes. Our lips met. A current passed between us and feathered through every part of my body. My left hand cupped under her soft, round breast, and floated gently over her tense nipple.

She pulled away and stood abruptly, brushing back her shock of black hair and smoothing the front of her shirt. "Well! This is—that was entirely, not at all becoming of, of an officer." She constricted her throat and lowered her voice. "We can't—IshcaBible, as you well know. I mean, you're white. I'm black. You're a man—and so are you—am I." She walked toward the door, turned, walked toward me, started to sit down, turned again. "I thought we should discuss the captain, the potential that he's well, that he's, he's—. I've got to go." She slid the door open and strode down the corridor.

I watched her walk away, swaying, elegant, and felt that rasp of shame again, sanding a flat spot on my heart. I had crossed a line I hadn't crossed since that day Momma Zee found me in the barn with that Negro slave. I was not supposed to feel what I was feeling, not allowed to. How can it be, I wondered, that I can shoot a man straight through the head and feel nothing, but I kiss a black woman and I can hardly breathe from the guilt and shame? "You're a sinner, Jesse James," whispered that bent bullet next to my heart. "You can *never* be forgiven."

Sometime during the night we arrived at Grand Central Station. The captain and Gunny rushed away in a coach to an undisclosed location on Long Island. The rest of us were to gather on Bedloe's Island, and, as Wrong John said, "Prepare to be dazzled." We took a ferry to the island, and watched Lady Liberty rise up before us. She had come from France to celebrate the Centennial of 1876, and had just recently been placed upon the granite pedestal that made her two-hundred feet tall. Beneath the pedestal stood Fort Wood, a star-shaped harbor outpost no longer in use. Basma stood beside me on the ferry as it cut through the harbor, steam engine clanging, a big cloud of black smoke chuffing from its stack. Her hand slipped down my elbow and forearm, over my wrist, and entwined with my hand. I looked down at her and she smiled up at me, then she let go of my hand and turned away.

"That's what America is all about. Right there," she said, pointing at the statue.

When we arrived on Bedloe's Island, it was overrun with soldiers, wearing their dress blues, crisp angled black hats, white gloves, and spit-shined black boots. They were all new recruits, eager, fresh, young, anxious for the excitement and glory that can only be had with war. Krill climbed on Sweet's shoulder and joined us in our wade through the crowd to see the inscription on the statue. Basma read out loud the poem by Emma Lazarus.

> "Not like the brazen giant of Greek fame,
> With conquering limbs astride from land to land,
> Here at our sea-washed, sunset-gates shall stand
> A mighty woman with a torch, whose flame
> Is the imprisoned lightning, and her name
> Mother of Exiles. From her beacon-hand
> Glows world-wide welcome, her mild eyes command
> The air-bridged harbor that twin-cities frame.
>
> 'Keep, ancient lands, your storied pomp!' cries she,
> With silent lips. 'Give me your tired, your poor,
> Your huddled masses yearning to breathe free,
> The wretched refuse of your teeming shore;
> Send these, the homeless, tempest-tost to me,
> I lift my lamp beside the golden door!'"

The excited cries of the soldiers diverted our attention to a huge blimp floating in the sky above the harbor. On its side a giant American flag had been hung. From behind the island, the *Shokanaw* steamed in front of us and anchored fifty feet off shore. A brass band on the *Shokanaw* blared *The Battle Hymn of the Republic*. Something fell from the blimp, at first appearing to be a package, then, with arms and legs flailing, was clearly human. It fell for a second or two, when a large U.S. flag seemed to burst from its back and remain attached to it by thin ropes from the corners of the flag, which suspended its fall by the wind it caught.

"My God," said Basma "What is it? Who would do such a thing?"

The flag allowed whoever it was to float slowly toward the bay, toward a landing on the *Shokanaw*. I don't suppose there was any way to steer the thing, and it drifted away from the dreadnought, which lowered a lifeboat to pick it up where it splashed into the bay. The lifeboat rowed with its wet passenger back to the *Shokanaw*. On the deck of the ship, a man dressed in a dark three-piece suit, and wearing a top hat, had come up from the hatch to join Admiral Olive. The lifeboat came alongside the ship and unloaded its passenger. When the blimp diver came to our side of the boat, it was clear who it was.

"Mission impossible—er, accomplished!" yelled Wrong John Silverspoon, wearing a soaked, one piece, olive drab jump suit, a black, rubber galosh over his wounded right foot. The applause, whistles, whoops, and cheers of the young soldiers were so loud I had to cover my ears. Silverspoon quieted the crowd with his hands in the air. "Wadn't that a great stunt?" he said, gesturing up at the blimp that still floated overhead. The soldiers roared their approval. "That's what we call a blimp-o-chute—brand new invention—and it's another example of how American military technology will be brought to bear in the fight against squid. Wherever they try to hide their nests, in whatever deep-sea trenches or underwater caves, we will spy on them from the sky, drop in on them, and smash their eggs before they hatch!" The GIs went absolutely berserk.

"Some doubted the wisdom of invading Iraq. Some said it was too dangerous, too far away. Well to them I say: *Eat my dust!* The war is over and we have prevailed!" The approval was again deafening. After the noise died down, the man in a suit stepped beside Wrong John.

"This here's Prime Minister Toady of Great Britain. We share this great victory with Britain, the only country besides us to throw some real manpower at Shalong." The prime minister stepped forward to address the crowd, tipped his black top hat, and adjusted his red tie.

"Today, in Iraq, we have taken the fight to terror," he said in his upper-class English accent. "America and Britain have predicted the squid's desires and we have prevented those desires as a good parent would an unruly child. We have removed the worst tyrant in the world, and he is now on the run and will be hunted down for the rapacious wolf that he is. We have been bold, we have been brave, and the world is a safer place because of it. We have chosen action over appeasement, courage over complacency, bravery over fear, boldness over timidity, and thereby averted a catastrophe of unimaginable proportion!" Prime Minister Toady paused, prepared for the applause he rightfully expected, but there was none. The soldiers were silent. I reckon he used too many big words for Americans. Wrong John stepped in front of the Brit.

"You wanna see my scars?" he yelled. Clown Criers and the Mandate Media had spread throughout the land a story that Wrong John had received deep wounds from a covert operation launched on *Liberty* by an AQ/Shalong spy.

All around us the soldiers screamed, pumped the air with their fists, and chanted, "U-S-A! U-S-A!"

Wrong John peeled away his black rubber boot, tore off the exaggerated bandage on his harpooned foot, and pointed his toes at the crowd. The soldiers whistled at him as if he were a showgirl. The attention got him so excited he wiggled out of his olive drab jumpsuit and did the cancan in his skivvies to the rhythmic clapping of the crowd. The Navy band joined in with spontaneous dance music.

Basma looked away and covered her eyes. "Oh my God," she said. Krill became so distressed at the spontaneous dismantling of his carefully constructed presidential persona, he attempted to fly from Basma's shoulder to rescue his boy. He didn't get more than a few feet before he crashed into the back of a soldier's head and fell to the ground. The soldier turned and kicked him. Basma picked Krill up and cradled him in her arms. "It's my fault," he whimpered. "Never leave him unsupervised. That's the rule. It's my fault."

"What, you may be wondering, will your captain do next? Well that's a very good answer, and I intend to question it. Thing is, we won a battle, but the war goes on. Shalong may be on the run, his country now liberated from him, but evil knows no borders. It slithers, like the squid, wherever it damn pleases, disguising its sinfulness in whatever color or pattern best suits it at the time. But rest assured, America, I got the mandate, and I will not rest until every squid has been destroyed, and evil, bad thoughts, sassy backtalk, rude gestures, lying, the sticking out of tongues—and let's not forget calamari—have been eliminated from the earth." Again, the soldiers roared their approval. I had never seen people cheer so enthusiastically.

After the ovation the soldiers went back to their bases—awaiting their assignments in Iraq— and we boarded *Shokanaw* with Admiral Olive and the captain and sailed out of New York Harbor. Not more than ten leagues on from Cape May, a Navy cutter intercepted us with news of a dastardly betrayal. Dick Little, who had lost his job over his outburst at the Preemptive Pre-rade, had been quoted in a damning article about Weapons of Mass Hysteria, printed by a "Benedict Arnold newspaper," as Krill put it:

'Fraud!' Says Terrorism Czar, 'There Are No WMHs in Iraq!'

New York—Former Terrorism Czar Dick Little stepped forward to refute *Liberty*'s claim that Shalong of Iraq had acquired large quantities of yellow cakes from the Congo, and Amazon poison dart frog serum, in order to make the most destructive weapon known to man.

"First of all," said Little, "the yellow cake TNT enhancer is very difficult to come by, and is produced in very small quantities by Pygmies in the Congo, who use it in their initiation rites to conjure the spirit of the serpent. Besides that, a close examination of the documents meant to prove Iraq had smuggled yellow cake from the Congo, have clearly been forged. The names, locations— everything—were entirely fabricated."

Regarding the Amazon poison-dart frog serum, Smith claims similar results. The frogs are very elusive, he says, and, again, deadly poisonous, so milking from their skin even enough toxin to down a single monkey requires a great deal of time and effort. The delicate work can only be done by indigenous people, who are not inclined to give up their frog juice after they've worked so hard to get it.

"To get enough of this frog juice, to, say, blow up a yellow cake bomb and atomize the poison, thus killing hundreds, perhaps thousands of urban dwellers, would require approximately a thousand years, at current production levels," says Smith. He goes on to say that, once again, the documentation of the smuggled frog poison proved to be entirely fabricated.

"I believe the American people deserve to know the truth. They need to understand that their government deceived them about the reasons we went to war. Experts in all branches of government, not just me, were ignored or silenced if they expressed any opinion with the potential to block or stall the march to war."

The captain threw the newspaper to the deck of the ship and ground his foot into it. He clenched his fists and stomped to the edge of the bridge. If there was one thing completely intolerable to Captain Silverspoon, it was disloyalty. When we arrived back in the calm waters of the Potomac, the Chief was waiting in his sparse cabin. He too had read the story.

"What're we gonna do about this, Chief?" asked the captain. He and the other officers stood around Chief's plain oak desk. Chief leaned back in his chair, his hands clasped on top of his head.

"I've got some ideas," Dagger said. "But first, we can't give the story any credence whatsoever. We discredit Chicken Little—Krill can come up with some story about how he's just a disgruntled employee, upset that he lost his job."

"BRACKsolutely, sir. Can do, will do," said Krill, saluting with his wing. "Stay on message. No matter what. Weapons of Mass Hysteria! Shalong and Al Quota! Evil squid brothers. Horror! Destruction! Thank God for the Silverspoon Mandate! America has been saved!" Krill waddled off to summon the Clown Criers and the Mandate Media.

"Okay, but what else?" asked Wrong John, limping back and forth on his white-bandaged foot. "I want Smith's head for this. I want him strung up. How are we supposed to win the War on Squid if he feeds our cornbread to the cuttlefish?" asked the captain. "He's got a one-way ticket to Batguano, I'll tell you that!" fumed Tosspot. "We'll get a confession out of him, find out who put him up to this. I don't care how many BLT's and games of leap frog it takes—he will pay for this crime!"

"Not so fast, TP," said Dagger. He leaned forward in his chair and held up his hand at the marshal. "We can't touch Little directly. He's too high profile right now. There are better ways to punish him."

"Name one," said Wrong John.

"His wife."

Basma's eyes went wide. She raised her head and looked around. Pinch did the same thing, and when she made eye contact with Sweet, moved beside her. Sir Yes Sir, looking shocked and ready to explode, somehow held himself in check.

"What about his old lady?" asked Silverspoon.

Chief looked at Sir Yes Sir, Basmati Sweet, and Pinch. "Sweet, SYS, Pinch, I need you to cook up a secondary plan. Go to the roundhouse and work one up, we'll compare notes later." He shooed them out with flicks from the backs of his hands. None of them moved.

"That game is over," said Sir Yes Sir, crossing his brawny arms over his chest.

"Fine, but if there are any outbursts of female or Negro sympathy, you will find yourself sleeping tonight with the rats in the brig. Do you understand?" The three nodded. Tosspot jangled the leg irons on his belt. 'Okay, good. Here's what we do, Mr. Captain: Out Mrs. Little."

"Who cares if we out her? What's she doing that would make any difference to anybody?"

"It just so happens, Mr. Captain, that Martha Little is an agent in covert operations. We out her, and that's the end of her career. With the old man blackballed for his treachery, and her handout from Unka-Sam Fatass over, they'll have to move to China to find a job."

A few days later, a Mandate Media mollusk changed his color and shape into that of a reporter, and broke the story of Mrs. Martha Little, wife of Dick Little, who was a covert operator for the U.S. government. The story proclaimed Chicken Little's status as an inept federal bureaucrat—his first government job, after all, had been with the Postal Service—a no-talent hack with a powerful wife who got him his job. He had attempted to leverage her influence further to receive an unwarranted promotion and raise, but had been denied, and went from there to invent his fabrication about the forged documents. He was also not very colorblind, and resented having to report to a Negro man, Basmati Sweet. The article ran with a photo of the Little's from their wedding.

Chapter XLI

Treasure Map for Peace

In the days that followed, the Giant Squid grew more bold in its fingering of *Liberty*. There wasn't an evening went by that a sailor didn't see an undulating brown tentacle squirming along the deck. Sometimes it latched on and rocked the ship gently back and forth for minutes at a time, as would a mother singing a lullaby to her child in a cradle. I honestly preferred the sticky arms to that damn grinding beak. I didn't like the sensation of being broken into, like my head was a filbert. At least with a tentacle, you could get a bead on it, shoot the damn thing, run from it, something. That other way, though, that was the road to insanity.

One morning Wrong John caught a sailor prying loose the hickory nickel he had nailed to the mainmast. Silverspoon had just started his jog when he lit on the thief. Wrong John was ready to call the marshal and have him arrested, but the sailor insisted the plug nickel was his. "I've raised the Giant Squid—or it has raised me, sir. The nickel is my reward!"

"Oh have you now?" said Silverspoon, sneering. "Like it's possible for the Giant Squid, who lives half a league under the sea, to be here, in the Potomac, not more than fifty feet deep." Silverspoon jogged to the rail and looked in the water. "So where is she? Huh? Where's the squid? I don't see no squid. Here, squidy, squidy. Here girl. Huh. She didn't come." He jogged back over to the sailor. "You put that gold doubloon back, and you leave it there until *I* say you've seen the Giant Squid." He ran off down the planks. The clanging pumps rang from the hold, and water continually surged through the black iron pipe sticking out the hatch.

Whether he would acknowledge it or not, however, Silverspoon had grown uncomfortable on *Liberty*. None of the officers, it seemed, enjoyed the ship's company either, ever since Chief Dagger's slanderous revenge on Chicken Little and his wife. The officers always seemed to have business in the capital, or some far off place, and were seldom seen. I did not have a good feeling about it either, and talked it over with the Lakota on more than one occasion.

"That photo of her. All those newspapers. Not good. Not good to put out a photo of your own spy," he said to me one day in the galley, scratching on his scrimshaw with his jackknife. I agreed with him. It was one of those bridges, that once crossed, offers no return. I wondered by what name Martha Little was going by in her secret mission. Where was she? Did her assignment concern the War on Squid? Wherever she was, whatever her assignment, I agreed with Tatanka: not good.

Silverspoon pestered Krill to find something important for him to do now that he had kicked Shalong's butt. What I think he really wanted was an excuse to get away from his occupied ship. Krill came to his aid, as usual. He conjured a mandate-friendly game he called The Treasure Map for Peace.

"How do you play?" asked the captain, a true lover of a good game.

Krill stood on the dark aged wood of the helm, walking back and forth among the spikes of the wheel. "War to peace. War to peace. Turn the war in Iraq into Middle East peace."

"War to peace? I thought the mandate was about me *startin'* wars whenever I felt like it." Wrong John slurped his steaming cup of coffee. The Squid Alert tank behind him shone blue—guarded, which hardly seemed the proper color when the Giant Squid was very possibly directly below the ship, dining on Silverspoon's cowboy boots.

"Wrong, John. Wrong, John. We started the war to save the peace, save the peace. Conquered and occupied Shalong's country to *prevent* a war. BRACK! Started a war to stop one. Had to. Wrong Peace Silverspoon." Krill hopped up to the binnacle and rubbed the brass lamp with his beak. Watching him stroke that lamp reminded me of his dream to find Aladdin's lamp in Arabia. He believed there was magic in those desert sands. Maybe he was manipulating his captain in order to get *himself* out there.

"Oh yeah, that's right. I'm the peace president. I start wars to prevent peace—I mean *preempt* peace—that is to say, I give peace a chance to happen before it happens." He scratched his head, and slurped his coffee. "You know what? I deserve a re-ward for all the peace I'm preempting. Why don't you guys nominate me and Toady for the Nobel Peace Prize? Wouldn't that be swell?"

"Bit of stretch, that one, bit of a stretch."

"Idn't that what we're about? Takin' risks and kickin' names?"

"Okay. You'll be nominated. You'll be nominated. But what about this Treasure Map for Peace. Carpe diem, boss. Seize the peace. Find the Treasure Map for Peace in Israel. Peace in Israel."

"Israel? I thought we wanted to de-Bubbafy Israel, get rid of the phony handshakes and the kissy-kissy and just let them fight it out like men." He slammed his fist into his palm with a loud pop.

"We did. A masterstroke, a masterstroke. Bloodshed in the Holy Land. Would make King David proud. Make him proud." Krill hopped down from the binnacle lamp onto a spike of the helm. He pecked madly at an edge of the wheel.

"Nailed that one. Bull's eye." Silverspoon pretended to throw a dart at a board.

"Think about contrast. Think about politics. A muscle flexed. A tummy rubbed. Silverspoon's got it all. He's got it all." Krill gave two quick wolf whistles.

"I did tell the people I was a humble guy, a compassionate guy, so yeah, I sorta like where you're headed," the captain said, scratching his cheek. From that conversation, and consultations with the Chief, SYS, and Gunny, the captain was shortly dispatched to Israel via the *Shokanaw*, to unveil his humble side and demonstrate the gentleness that complemented his brutal manhandling of evildoers. He might just sew up the Nobel Peace Prize while he was at it.

We boarded the *Shokanaw* for another trip across the big water. Only I, Basma, and Krill went along with the captain on the trip. *Shokanaw* powered down the Potomac, into the Chesapeake Bay, and out into the open water of the endless Atlantic. *Shokanaw* was my kind of ship. Four-masted, steam engine, heavily armed, deep keeled—it plowed through storms, split waves, rent swells, and nothing seemed to slow it down.

Maybe I had gotten used to sailing, or maybe Olive's dreadnought was just very fast, but it didn't seem to take but a few days to pass into the Mediterranean, and follow the coastline of North Africa to the ancient port of Jaffa in Israel. Along the way I had many pleasant conversations with Basmati Sweet, but we did *not* kiss again, both of us seeming to have decided against it.

The *Shokanaw* docked along the limestone seawall at Jaffa, fronting a great fortress rising up from the shoreline and culminating in a sharp, scalloped tower. Fishing boats lined the waterfront, and with their sails down and single masts sticking in the air, I thought them a floating forest striped of its branches. Piles of nets rested along the shoreline, dotted with the cork floats that helped the nets to spread. The prime minister of Israel, Ishmak Cordon, greeted Captain Wrong John Silverspoon with a brass band, a battalion of Israeli soldiers, flag bearers waving the American and Israeli flags, and ten young women holding extravagant flower bouquets. Silverspoon smiled and waved, and plugged Prime Minister Cordon with a volley of love pellets. I was a little surprised the president of Palestine was not in attendance. One of Cordon's guards told me that he had caught his *kaffiyah* headdress in the bobbed wire surrounding his compound and could not extract himself in time for the celebration.

After the initial reception, the leaders traveled by carriage straight to old Jerusalem, and to the Western Wall, *ha-Kotel ha-maàraui* in Hebrew, the most holy of holy sites in all the world, referred to later by Muslims and Christians as the Wailing Wall. Coal-dark, Arabian stallions, glistening and svelte, pulled the landau coaches across the dry plain between Jaffa and Jerusalem. In a few hours we arrived at the ancient site of the Temple Mount, Moriah, where Abraham—father of Judaism, Islam, and Christianity—confirmed his faith in God with his willingness to sacrifice his only son, Isaac. The mount had at one time been the location of King Solomon's temple, which had been twice destroyed, and was now crowned by the golden mosque of *Caliph Add al-Malik*, built in 690 A.D., and called the Dome of the Rock, or *Qubbat al Sakhra* in Arabic.

The prime minister had ordered a stage erected where the Western Wall, or Wailing Wall, ended at its intersection with another portion of the old temple rampart. There were two narrow passages to the stage falling away from it at right angles. One passage went north and south along the Western Wall, and the other led away from the old city and into Palestine. The alley along the Western Wall had apartments to the west. Wooden poles draped with bright, freshly washed robes stuck out from the windows of the apartments several stories high.

Silverspoon and Cordon took the stage and stood before the massive quarried limestone monoliths, believed by many to have been taken from King Solomon's original temple, some of them weighing forty tons and more. The pale white stones had been stacked, torn down, and stacked again over thousands of years, and showed their age by the rough surfaces eroded from millennia of rain.

After a brief introduction from the prime minister, Silverspoon came forward and spoke. "Here we have gathered at the Whaling Wall, which is very, very important as a symbol of the international trade in blubber," the captain said. "We must always remember, as the Whaling Wall reminds us, that energy is what powers the great economies of the world, and above all else, we must protect the sources and supply of energy—which we have done by freeing the blubber of—freeing the people of Iraq."

Loud, contrary rumblings arose among the onlookers. Krill, who sat on Silverspoon's right shoulder, whispered something in his ear.

"Oh, uh, well, as with all of God's creatures," said the captain, stumbling over his words, "whales too shed tears, as we all do, and have, and will again, here at the Wailing Wall. Too much sadness has been shed here, over the centuries. Too much pain has been shed. Too many cats have shed on the sofa. But at least there's one less snake to shed now that Shalong's mass graves have been filled with the bodies of liberated Iraqis." He paused and stared at the crowd.

"Because of our new strength in the world, bad guys are scared of good guys again, the way it should be, as taught by America's great comic book writers." He paused for the approval he had come to expect as automatic, and seemed perplexed when the reaction was muted. He adjusted his blue-humped hat and gave a half grin to Krill.

"A'right then. It's like this, bitter tribal conflict that goes back a really long time, and has caused untold grief and suffering, can still be fun. You people have been taking yourselves way too serious for way too long. That's why today, courtesy of your friends in America and the good people at the Easily Broken Toy Company, we bring you an exciting new, realistic, ethnic rivalry challenge called *The Treasure Map for Peace*." Again, he waited for the applause, which came in a smattering. He leaned over and said to Krill from the side of his mouth, "This is going about like Yo Yo's shower of roses." Krill grumbled and ruffled his feathers.

"Can we have the contestants approach the stage, please?" said the captain. The crowd standing in the right-angle alleys parted to allow two groups forward. One came from the west and included five bearded men in white robes, wearing the traditional red-and-white checked *kaffiyah* with a colorful cloth band to hold it in place. The other group walked in from the south, and included five bearded men in robes of white, brown, and rust-red, with yarmulkes on their heads. The men of both groups wore leather sandals.

Wrong John looked down on them, as they had likely been looked down on by men from Egypt, Greece, Babylon, Rome, Persia, Turkey, and Europe for the last three thousand years. "Okay, so here's how it works. Each team gets directions to a specific location. At that location you will find instructions for a task. You must complete that task as instructed, and return here with evidence that you completed the assignment. You will be given another clue, which will lead you closer to The Treasure Map for Peace, which is the Grand Prize, buried out there somewhere in the desert."

Krill hopped to the Western Wall and pulled two sets of directions from gaps between the worn stones. He hopped back to the captain's shoulder and held one set of directions in his beak, the other in his right claw. I noticed the Jews in the crowd glowering at Krill, and several women covered their mouths with their hands. He didn't seem to notice, or have any awareness that prayers were inserted by Jews in the gaps between stones, and it had appeared to them he was stealing prayers.

"Okay," said Wrong John, "everybody ready? Get set, on your mark, go!"

Krill handed the Palestinians and the Israelis their instructions, and the two groups of men hustled off in opposite directions. "I'll put five bucks on Israel," the captain said to Krill.

"No way. I'm not taking the Arabs," said Krill. The captain grabbed a handful of peanuts from his pocket and hauled back as if about the throw them.

"Okay, okay," Krill squawked. "I'll do the five bucks, but I want odds—two-to-one at least. Two-to-one."

"Done."

After the contestants vanished, the crowd also dispersed, and life at the Western Wall went back to normal. Men and women approached the ancient limestones, placed their written prayers in the gaps, and recited their devotions. When they finished, they kissed the wall and walked away. As soon as one finished, another arrived, in a continuous stream throughout the day. On stage, Basmati Sweet brought out a large box of dominoes. She, Wrong John, and Krill set about building an elaborate pattern in white-dotted, black dominoes. I couldn't tell what the pattern was meant to be, but when it was complete, the captain, Krill, and Basma stood back and admired it.

"It all began with Iraq," said Basma.

"Now Israel falls into place," said Krill.

"Treasure Map," said the captain, slapping his hand with a large, rolled and bound cloth scroll.

"The fundamentalists in Iran fall," said Basma.

"Replaced by secular free marketeers. BRACK! *Mandato Capitalistas*," said Krill.

"Bringing down Syria's bad guys," said Basma.

"King of Jordan stubs his toe," said Krill. "He stubs his toe."

"Inviting a democratic rebellion."

"Freeing all of Arabia! All of Arabia."

"And on to Pakistan, Turkmenistan and every other Stan, Dick, and Harry in the region," said Wrong John. "All because I cornholed Shalong." He leaned down and flicked the first domino with his index finger, and the chain reaction began. In less than a minute, the Silverspoon Mandate had completely reordered the Middle East. When all the dominoes had fallen, I stepped back and could see the pattern spelled out two words: Middle America. It was just that easy. The three exchanged handshakes and hugs and smiles of glee.

About that time the Arab contestants came around the corner pushing a wooden handcart with rickety, squeaky wheels. They galumphed to the stage in a flurry of white robes and unloaded from their cart four rifles, two kegs of gunpowder, three sticks of dynamite, and two cannonballs. They bowed in unison. The one with the longest, grayest beard spoke for the group.

"We have completed the first challenge. It was not that hard." He reached to his head and adjusted the tie on his headdress.

"BRACK! Comin' around the backstretch. Look who's in the lead! It's Pretty Palestine by half a length. BRACK! Half a length."

Wrong John poked Krill in the stomach with his index finger. The parrot coughed and wheezed. "So this is it?" asked Silverspoon of Team Palestine. "These are all the weapons?"

"Yes, this is everything. The *intifada* is completely disarmed."

"Seems a little light to me."

"It is all, everything, the total." The leader bowed slightly and gestured at the small pile of weapons.

Silverspoon pulled his head back and away. He looked at them sideways, one eye closed. "Well, I don't know." He turned to the parrot. "I guess for the sake of the contest, we'll have to take you at your word. Okay, Krill, give them the next clue." The parrot jumped from the stage up to the wall and retrieved another clue. He gave it to the team, and they went away in a flurry of waving arms, rustling robes and loud, quarreling voices.

Not long after, a rumble of horse hooves and heavy wagons rolled in along the south end of the Western Wall. Supplicants praying had to squeeze themselves nearly into the cracks in the rock to avoid being crushed by the heavy wagons. The Jewish team, in their colorful robes and black skullcaps, rolled up to the stage in the wagons loaded high with long wooden boxes. Two of the men pulled a box from a wagon and threw it on the stage with a bang. They pried it open and stood back for Wrong John to examine the contents. He pulled a pump-action rifle from inside.

"Nice lookin' Winchesters," he said. He pumped the handle and aimed down the alley, directly at a tall Arab carrying on his head a long tin loaded with round loaves of bread. The Arab dropped to the ground, scattering his bread on the tawny stone path. "Sorry, bud!" yelled Wrong John. "We're doin' peace this time. May you be fruitful!"

He lowered the gun and waved at the frightened baker. I immediately thought of the prisoner at Batguano whom the interrogator had called "The Baker."

"So you found the money?" Wrong John asked Team Judea. The Jews nodded. "Good. And you decided to use the aid money to buy Winchesters?"

"Yes," said the man with the longest and most gray beard. "As you have shown us, peace can only be achieved by a show of strength, and by attacking your enemies before they attack you."

"Hell, bud, we didn't show *you* that. Israel wrote the book on preemption." Silverspoon tipped his hat at the Jewish leader. He bowed back. A woman about fifty feet down the wall wailed and pounded her fists against the ancient stone. We all looked over. I wondered what had caused her such pain, but there was no way to know.

"In the War on Squid, peace has to be attacked before it attacks you. That's one'a your basic fundamentals of the mandate." Wrong John pressed his lips tight and nodded.

"Yes. We can only hope to be as successful at it as you have been."

"Good luck," said Wrong John. He sent Krill for another clue in the wall, and, after they received it, off went the Jewish contestants in a flurry of waving arms, flapping robes, clapping sandals, and loud voices.

The day grew sultry as morning passed into afternoon. The small crowd that had gathered dispersed. Only one or two people prayed at the wall. We took refuge under large canopies erected over the stage, and drank cool green coconut juice. A rug merchant slept in his faded wooden cart along the shady side of the alley, next to the Western Wall. A long-necked black Egyptian cat tipped up a small basket and crawled under it to escape the brutal sun. Almost two hours passed before the Palestinians showed up—missing two team members. The three remaining contestants arrived bloody and bruised, their robes torn and one of them missing his *kaffiya*.

"I figured this one might be a little tough," the captain said to Basma as an aside. He turned to the contestants. "So, d'ya get the clue?"

"Yes," said the taller, less bloody of the three, "and we attempted to carry out the instructions, but the militant leaders did not believe we had the authority to arrest them, and they beat us up. Two of our team defected and began also to beat us. They said we were traitors to go along with America and Israel."

"BRACK *up* two spaces. Do not pass Go. Do not collect two hundred dollars." Krill pushed the backs of his wings at Team Palestine. They looked at him with a mixture of confusion and hatred in their eyes.

"Look," said Silverspoon. "We can't help you until you help us. We need a victory in the War on Squid, and that means you roundin' up your bad guys and bringing them to justice. The treasure's out there for you, lots of it. You just got to stop the terror first. Now go back there and arrest the terrorists," the captain instructed. The three turned slowly and shuffled away, heads lowered, arms hanging limply at their sides.

Twenty minutes later, Team Judea rumbled north along the Wailing Wall. They drove four big wagons, loaded with fence posts and barbed wire.

"You find the money?" asked the captain. The five wise men nodded enthusiastically. "Great. Great. So what's all the bobbed wire and fence posts about?"

"We believe the best way to move forward with preemptive peace is to erect a fence between us and Palestine."

"Really?" asked Basma, hands on hips.

"Yes. We have to keep the extremist elements at bay. Monitor their movements to and from here to there. This way we won't be threatened and our enemy will be contained."

"Sounds like a concentration camp to me," said Basma. The captain elbowed her in the ribs. She gasped and doubled over. I wanted to coldcock him—but then I remembered he thought she was a man, and that was the way she wanted it.

"Okay," Wrong John said to the Israeli contestants. "Up to you, but don't get carried away with the fencing. You know, out in Texas, a rancher or two been known to extend his holdings by running the fence 'cross another guy's dirt."

"We wouldn't think of it, Captain Silverspoon," said the leader, stroking his long white beard. The other four tucked their chins and stroked their beards as well.

"Super." Wrong John turned to Krill, who provided the next clue, and off raced the Jews. A swirling dust devil spun through the street, throwing sand and stones in every direction, knocking over tents and market stalls, causing the onlookers to cover their faces with shawls, veils, and edges of robes. After a moment it hit the Wailing Wall, blew down the American and Israeli flags, and pattered the stone blocks with pebbles and grains of sand. Wrong John coughed, wiped his eyes, and took a drink of water from a goatskin.

"Mmm, sweet water they got over here," he said, and let another stream of the liquid pour from the goatskin into his mouth. Krill and Basma looked at each other and grinned. They knew it wasn't water, but wine. It probably wouldn't have surprised the captain; by that time, he would have believed himself capable of turning one into the other. He swallowed deeply and looked down the narrow street stretching west. Around the corner stumbled a single contestant from Team Palestine, his white robe torn and smeared with blood, headdress twisted, nose and mouth caked in red. He weaved down the road until he stood before the stage.

Wrong John crossed his arms. "Look. I can't give you another clue until you stop the terror. So where's the squid?"

"I am a dead man, a dead man. Please, can you protect me?" the frightened man pleaded.

"Not my problem, bud." Wrong John held out his hands and shrugged. He looked up the West Wall, then down the northern rampart. "A'right, since you're such a good sport, we'll give you another clue—but get it right this time." Krill hopped to the wall, pulled out a clue with his beak, hopped to the edge of the stage, and spit the paper at the Arab. He bent over and picked it up with his shaking hands and read. He wadded the clue, and threw it to the ground, turned, and staggered off in the direction of Gaza.

"They expect us to give 'em a country? With an attitude like that?" asked Silverspoon, raising his eyebrows.

Basmati Sweet dropped from the stage and picked up the crumpled clue. "Go to your president's quarters. Surround it and do not allow him to leave until he confesses to his terrorist crimes," she read.

"Is that askin' too much?" asked Wrong John. "We just so happen to be at *war* around here. Shee-it!"

A magpie landed on a corner of the stage. Krill skipped over, and the two birds chattered back and forth. I was surprised at the voice of the Arab magpie. Unlike the American black-and-whites that cackled noisily, this one squeaked, more like a mouse than a bird.

A platoon of soldiers in the Israeli Army strode our direction along the Western Wall. Wrong John called them to the stage. He took the clue from Sweet and handed it to the sergeant. "You guys think you can handle this one?" The sergeant looked at the paper and nodded his head without hesitation. "Go for it," the captain said.

The sergeant barked his orders and the platoon trotted off toward Gaza. A short while later, the Jewish contestants pulled up from the south in a single wagon loaded with broken timber, bricks, window sashes, broken glass, and cracked, terra cotta roof tiles. They stopped in front of the stage and approached Silverspoon. Behind them, a crowd of Jews walked along the wall and filled the narrow alley.

"We have complied with the rules. All settlements on the West Bank have been dismantled, and the Jewish settlers relocated," said the elder of the group, twisting the black skullcap on his head.

"This is it?" asked Silverspoon, looking at the loaded wagon. "That's the debris from all your illegal settlements?"

The contestants bowed and promised all at once they had taken down every home in the disputed territories.

"I don't believe you," Wrong John asserted. He stood back and put his hands on his hips.

"You wouldn't be calling us liars, would you?" asked the elder, pulling on his beard.

"I might be. Deal is, you gotta give a little here."

"Are you advocating that we negotiate with terrorists?"

"Hell no! I'm advocating that you play by the rules of the Treasure Map game. You want the treasure, you play by the rules."

"By whose rules? Who said you get to make the rules?"

"I did. End of story."

The contestants began to yell and proclaim their distaste for the rules, and their doubts about the treasure, and their anger at how many of their people had died only to have their deaths debased by giving up what they fought so hard for. The anger spread from the five contestants into the tight gathering of Jews positioned in front of their most holy place.

From around the opposite corner, a crowd could be heard chanting, "Where's our treasure? Where's our piece? Where's our treasure? Where's our piece?" They marched down to the stage from the west, waving sticks and broken bottles, and filled the narrow street. The last of the Arab contestants stood in the lead.

"I cannot arrest our patriots," the contestant said. "To many Arab men are wrongfully held in prison already." Wrong John held up his hands, waved them at the Arabs, and backed up.

"And what does your contest say about Jerusalem?" the Palestinian said. "How will you honor the claim of both peoples on this holy place?" He pointed up at the golden Dome of the Rock, shining behind us, glistening with an incandescent, golden light from the setting sun. Then he gestured at the other end of the wall, where the dark dome of the *al-Aksa* mosque rose above the parapets.

"And what of our people who were displaced by the Jewish invasion?" cried the Arab. "Where will they live? How will they be compensated for their loss?"

The leader of the Jewish group shouted, "Compensated? For killing our children? For wishing to drive us into the sea? For denying our ancestral rights to our homeland?"

"And you can assassinate our leaders and we're supposed to do nothing?" shouted the Arabs.

"They are evil terrorists!"

"And what of your murderers?"

"Are they to do nothing when you kill their people?"

"You started it."

"It's our homeland. Look at the Torah!"

"It is our homeland. Look at the Koran."

"We claimed it first."

"You left!"

"We came back!"

"We stayed!"

"*Haram-esh-Sharif! Haram-esh-Sharif!*" chanted the crowd of Palestinians, speaking their name for the Temple Mount.

"*ha-Kotel ha-maàraui! ha-Kotel ha-maàraui!*" chanted the Jews, speaking their name for their most holy site. The chanting grew louder. Fists and sticks and broken bottles thrust into the air. The crowds began to shift and yaw, lean and sway, pushing against the stage, making it groan and pop. Krill flapped his wings and spoke to me in his shrill voice. "Ish! Help us out here! Help us out! Throw them some scripture. Quick! Or they'll cut us up for *shish kebobs!*"

I pulled Widowmaker and fired a couple of rounds into the air. The crowd stilled and quieted and cast its collective eyeball at me. "This most holy site reminds me of the story told about King Solomon. You know the one. Two women came to him with a dispute about a child—both of them claiming to be the mother. Solomon said it was only fair then to cut the child in half, and give an equal portion to each woman. One of the women agreed to the idea, believing the king most wise. The other turned pale. Her lips quivered, and she handed the baby to her rival. 'She is yours. Take her, please. Do not harm her, wise king,' she pleaded. Well, by that Solomon knew she was the baby's true mother, and took the young'un away from the imposter.

"I ask you now, people of Palestine, people of Israel, what shall we do with this child, Jerusalem? Shall we tear her apart? Or will one of you show yourself the true mother, and give her away to your rival?" All was silent. Then came a rustling of robes. A sullen murmur coiled in from the two passageways that reached at right angles away from the stage. A collection of small peach-colored clouds dropped to a fiery red-and-yellow sunset, casting a golden-pink halo over the ancient wall.

Krill clawed his way up Wrong John's leg and stood on his shoulder, bobbing his head forward and back and side-to-side. The captain leaned toward him and said in a stage whisper, "It's gettin' ugly. Better am-scray." He reached back to Basma, who handed him a large scroll. He unfurled it slowly and showed it to the crowd. It was a map of Israel with a big "X" west of Jerusalem.

"Friends of the Holy Land, 'X' marks the spot where you will find a treasure—two states, two states buried in the desert. Can't say exactly where, but they're out there. Just keep diggin' till you find 'em. Really, truly, enjoyed the show. Best of luck, see you in the funny papers, and we'll catch you down the road."

A shriek came from somewhere in the crowd. "My baby! Someone has stolen my baby!" Shrill voices shouted. The crowd shuddered. Rocks began to fly. Yelling broke out in Arabic and Hebrew. Glass bottles shattered against the wall. Staffs slammed against other staffs.

Wrong John threw the map into the crowd, turned, and exited stage left. I glanced over my shoulder to see the Jews and the Arabs ripping the Treasure Map to pieces. I gathered Basma close to my chest, pulled Peacemaker, and fired into the air. That opened a path for us along the limestone wall leading west. A company of Israeli soldiers met us halfway and escorted us to our waiting landau. The shining, black Arabian stallions reared back, neighed and snorted and snapped at their traces. In a rush of clopping hooves, we shot away from old Jerusalem.

Chapter XLII

The Fisherman and the Jinni

When we reached Jaffa, Admiral Tucker "Yarn" Olive had *Shokanaw*'s engine stoked. Black smoke rose from the stack. He set full sheet and pushed away from the stone seawall. We were on our way west toward Alexandria when Wrong John approached Yarn on the bridge and ordered him north. The admiral asked for an explanation, to which the captain said he had hatched a scheme. "I'm gonna sneak into Iraq, goose the troops, hunt down Shalong, and bird-dog those WMH's." He winked at the navy man. "You want a job done right—"

"You gotta do it yourself," Krill interrupted breathlessly, saving himself from another painful misquote.

"That whole Treasure Map deal, that didn't cut it," said Wrong John. "Those A-ribs and Jews act like they own Jerusalem. We Christians got a thing or two to say about that, I'll guar-an-damn-tee ya," he said in a snit. "'Al-hash-mash-kibosh,' chants year A-rab. 'Ick-mack-nicknack-paddywhack,' chants yer Jew. How about, 'Our Father who art in heaven,' huh? How about that?"

Krill stomped back and forth on his shoulder, the sea breeze fluffing his neck feathers. "Whose got a mandate? Them or us? Preempt the Second Coming, will you? We'll show you. *BRACK!* We'll show you."

We arrived at the shore of Lebanon in the middle of the night, and docked at Beirut. We boarded a train and took out across the Syrian Desert on our way to Baghdad. Basma procured Arab clothing for us at a stop in Damascus, in keeping with Wrong John's desire to sneak into Baghdad unnoticed. We men stopped shaving so that we looked like natives by the time we got there.

"My beard's too thin to ever pass as an Arab," Basma told us one day. "I'll just go as a belly dancer." It surprised the captain and Krill that she dressed in the costume right away, and traveled the entire five hundred miles in the sheer, baggy pants and short blouse that revealed her smooth stomach, and her dark, oval belly button. She still scribbled on her grease pencil moustache, but she did not tied down her breasts. I imagined that it must have been a great relief to stop pretending to be a man and just be a woman for awhile—even though she still lowered her voice.

One afternoon as we shared lunch, Wrong John whispered to Krill, "Boy, Basma's got some realistic hooters there, don't he?" Krill gave a soft wolf whistle in reply.

We stayed in our sleeper cars the whole time because Wrong John didn't want to be recognized by Iraqis and get overwhelmed with gratitude and adoration before he was ready. For the next three days and nights we traveled across the most desolate desert I had ever seen, mile upon mile of flat boulder strewn plains, punctuated after long intervals by a camel caravan, a dusty outpost, a company of American troops, or the rare *wadi*, a depression in the desert that often held some greenery, a small spring possibly, and a few palm trees. Sometimes, a few listless oryx lay in the shade, rubbing their long straight horns on the tree trunks.

It was a very long three days, locked up like that, all of our meals brought to us, and not exactly American fare: lamb stews and bean dishes and flat bread. I often waited up after the sun went below the flat, cloudless plain, hoping to hear a soft knock at the cabin door, but it did not come. All for the best, I figured. That one kiss with Basmati Sweet was something to savor for a good long while—and to take it any further was to risk getting that old, beat up bullet next to my heart all riled up.

The four of us took our meals together, but I didn't have much to say. I missed the Lakota, who understood the pleasure of an unspoken conversation. I tried to ignore Krill and Silverspoon, yammering about the adventure ahead of them. It annoyed me that they were always looking forward to the next great thing, and never reflecting on what had just happened. Then I remembered my outlaw days, and that was pretty much how it worked when you were on a spree of robbing. To stop and ponder what you had been doing would have very likely stopped you—and then what?

"I want to look Shalong in the whites of his eyes and tell him he's a coward," said Wrong John over dinner, sopping some gravy with a chunk of fry bread.

"Wait'll we find those weapons. *BRACK-A-DOODLE-DO!* We'll be heroes. Heroes I tell ya," crowed Krill. He took a bite of papaya he held in his gray claws.

"Go down in history," added Silverspoon.

"You'll be going down...somewhere," I muttered. I had gotten out my Indian toy, and pulled on the string between my hands, making that shiny emerald, pearl and brown-striped abalone button whirl one way, then the other, until it pulsated with a power all its own. Every time it reached the end point of one direction, the button seemed to wink at me, before instantly spinning the opposite way. I became fascinated with the dynamics of it. The harder I pulled in one direction, the harder *it pulled* in the *opposite* direction. When it reached the end point of its spin, there was no choice but to be turned by it, to switch directions—*no choice*.

As we neared Baghdad, and the valley of the Tigris and Euphrates— ancient cradle of civilization—the scenery began to green up. I felt like I had already been there—Olive had painted such a vivid picture. Fields of green barley swayed in the breeze. Almond and apricot trees showed the first signs of fruit. Clematis vines twined up jujube trees and bloomed purple and violet, in contrast with the small yellow flower clusters of the trees. Geese and ducks went butt-up in shallow ponds. Date palms lined canals and leaned over the water with their sweeping trunks and clumps of long, saw-toothed, green leaves on top. Those round boats Yarn had described, *guffars* he called them, swirled down the streams. We came through the ruins of ancient Babylon, crusty, tumbledown, and no more impressive than a sand castle at high tide. It was hard to believe this had been home to the fabulous Hanging Gardens, one of the Seven Wonders of the World. I looked for Yarn's Tower of Babel, but nothing stood very high. I wondered if he hadn't made it up.

Groups of women carried baskets on their heads, overflowing with dates and figs. Merchant carts pulled by donkeys hauled raw wool, sacks of grain, chickens, and crates of oranges and bananas. Basma knocked on the door and handed us an umber body paint she said would stain our skin brown, and would eventually wear off, but would last for a week or more without the need of a second application. Obviously she hadn't needed it, already in possession of deep, coffee skin.

Wrong John and I painted the umber dye on our white skin, then donned black turbans and dark robes. Sweet put a dark shawl over her skimpy outfit, and wore a *burka* over her head and face, so that only her deep brown eyes could be seen. Krill wore a little *kaffiyah* with a red band around his forehead, and put gold rings on three of his toes. He was so active on Silverspoon's shoulder, craning his neck to see out the window, skittering left and right, the captain finally pushed him away. Krill perched on the window frame and rubbed his beak up and down against the glass, muttering, "Open Sesame. Open Sesame."

The train whistle blew and we entered Baghdad and stopped at the station, where a bazaar was erected all around. We got off the train in our Arab disguises and waded into the market. Merchants sat under tents with Persian carpets, hookahs of all variety, and bags of spices—cinnamon, cardamom, ginger, anise, cloves, nutmeg, frankincense. The smell of strong coffee, tobacco smoke, and the rich spices hung in the air. We passed carpets laden with scarves of great beauty, *burkas* made of muslin or silk, bronze vessels, and copper oil lamps that looked like short, stretched out tea kettles. Krill ran up to the first lamp merchant he saw and bought a dozen shiny, new lamps. He had them tied to a length of camel hair and dragged them behind himself, calling out, "New lamps for old! New lamps for old!"

The merchants and customers pointed at him and laughed. I doubt if they understood his English, but he continued offering his wares.

"You fail Economics 101?" asked Silverspoon of the parrot. "New lamps for old?—if that ain't dumb as dirt."

Krill ignored Wrong John and spoke to me from the back side of his wing. "Momma always told me. Listen to your magpies, son. Listen to your magpies." He continued to drag his clanging chain of copper lamps along the dusty plaza. Life appeared at first to be very normal. A woman haggled over the price of a blanket. A man traded three goats for a horse. Children in blue-and-white, vertically striped robes held hands and swirled in a circle. Men sat on the two-tiered benches of the coffee shop, sipped their brew, and smoked their *hookahs*. Wrong John bent over a lamp merchant's table and picked up a bright copper lamp. He rubbed it, and looked at it expectantly, eyebrows raised. When no purple smoke arose from the long spout, he tossed it back on the table.

"Hell, even if I did get three wishes, I wouldn't know what to do with 'em. Kicked Shalong's butt. Set Iraq free." He opened his arms and turned in a circle. "Looks like liberty's takin' hold real nice." He slapped his stomach. "Israel's now at peace, thanks to me. Average Americans got tax relief; *we* got our Ellis Outland. Got my No Child's Behind, my Masturbation Corps, my God Arrest America Act. Got my mandate, my Squid Alert, my media monopoly. If that jinni pops out I'll just have to auction my wishes to the highest bidder."

Krill continued along through the stalls of the bazaar, calling, "New lamps for old. *BRACK!* New lamps for old." The Iraqis pointed at him and laughed, but he didn't seem to mind. A young woman in a blue *kaftan* embroidered in gold approached him. She wore a cloudy quartz crystal on a silver chain around her neck. I could only see her raven black eyes and the hint of her round face beneath her scarf, but everything about her spoke to me of beauty. She leaned down to Krill, patted his head, and gave him a pistachio. He happily worked the nut free with his pitted beak, and spit out the shell.

"What do you have, pretty Polly?" she asked, her English perfect, accented British. She ran her lithe, brown fingers over the bright copper lamps. "They

are so lovely. All of them. And you will trade one for my tired, old lamp?"
She slipped her right hand up the loose folds of her blue *kaftan* under her left
wrist, and pulled from within a dingy, dull lamp, dented and scratched, its lead
stopper poorly fitted and sitting at an angle.

Krill stared at the old lamp, his head weaving, wings quivering. He
dropped his chain of new lamps and held out his wings. "Yes. Yes. I will trade.
I will trade," he said in a quiet monotone. The young woman chose the lamp
on the end of his string, and set down her trade. She patted Krill on the head
and skipped away.

Up ahead, a group of men with black shawls wrapped around their faces
scrambled through the bazaar. Their long rifles pointed into the air. Rounds of
ammunition in bandoleers crossed their chests. They knocked over stalls and
tables of fruit, baskets of dates, figs, and pistachios. They trampled over piles
of rugs and blankets and kicked copper lamps with their heavy boots. Gunfire
broke out, and we dropped to the ground. Two of the masked men stopped to
return the shots, then broke into a run. I reached under my robe and pulled
death and destruction from my holster.

Shortly, American soldiers ran through the market, wearing their blue
uniforms and black cowboy hats, knocking over tables of glassware, pots and
pans, wicker furniture, and racks covered with leather sandals. They stopped
and kneeled here and there to shoot at the Arab bushwhackers. Silverspoon
started to stand, but Sweet pulled him down to the ground. "What are you,
crazy?" she asked, urgently. "You're in disguise, remember? An Arab stands up
right now and he's going to get shot."

"Oh yeah," he said, rolling onto his stomach. He touched his face with
his fingertips as if it weren't his own skin.

The remainder of the American company followed the lead troops and
spread through the bazaar. One of them got shot. He fell over a coffee roaster,
screaming profanities. He pulled his revolver and fired off random shots into
the various stalls around him. The entire company flew into a rampage of
cursing and shooting, breaking tables, knocking down tents, bashing Iraqis
with the butts of their rifles. An oil lamp somewhere caught a tent on fire, and
a conflagration erupted in the market. Merchants and their families screamed
and ran. A bucket brigade tried to form, but the Americans continued

randomly shooting and yelling and running around, even more confused and angry with all the smoke.

The black-masked Iraqi militia popped in and out of view, took quick shots, and disappeared. Americans screamed, "I'm hit!" and cried out in pain and fell writhing to the dusty ground. A company of cavalry arrived in a racket of hooves, sabers drawn, cutting down fleeing Iraqis left and right. The fire spread and the shooting intensified. Shouting in Arabic and English mixed in a cacophony of pain and confusion and fear.

Something inside of me snapped. I flew off my hinges and regressed instantly to pure wild-dog Missouri guerrilla. I didn't know if I was in some Clay Country ditch with Bloody Bill Anderson, Arch Clement, and you, Frank, or if I was busting out of Northfield, Minnesota, with the Youngers and Charlie Pitts. I only knew one thing: nobody, not nobody ever born, outguns Jesse James.

I let loose with a bloodcurdling rebel yell, and unleashed hellfire from the barrels of Peace- and Widowmaker. I gathered up Basmati Sweet and backed out of the bazaar to the far side, away from the train station. Wrong John scurried after us on his hands and knees, Krill sitting on his humped back, riding him like a Brahma bull, and clutching his ancient lamp to his chest. A steam whistle blew, and a bell clanged. The bluecoats had us pinned against a brick building pitted from grapeshot. I reloaded quickly. Gunshots blasted around us, tearing holes in tents, pinging off pots and pans.

The fire spread quickly and filled the plaza with smoke and crackling flames. I counted it a blessing and used the cover to work my way along the wall, toward an opening in the line of structures. I got us down to the gap, and was relieved to find a donkey cart parked there. Two men in white robes with black shawls wrapped around their faces ran crouched from the front of the cart, lifted some blankets in the back, and motioned us under. The four of us snuck into the cart. One of the men gave some command in Arabic. The donkey brayed, jerked at its harness, and pulled us away down the alley.

I looked out from under the blanket to try to get some idea where we were going. It was impossible. One crooked ally poured into another in a maze of passages and pathways between buildings faced with narrow balconies that nearly touched in the middle. We passed lop-eared brown sheep, stray cats, and old men asleep in doorways. The alley became so narrow I though the sides of the cart would begin to scrape the pocked brown surface of the buildings. Finally we reached a dead end, and the donkey stopped. One of the black-hooded men spoke a code in Arabic in front of twin verdigris doors, each with three round windows stacked in the center. The sound of bolts sliding, chains slipping, and locks opening came from within. One of the men escorted us inside, while the other removed his black scarf, handed over his rifle and ammunition, and donned the tattered brown robe of a common peddler. He turned the cart around and drove it up the alley.

We hurried down a musty hallway, past rooms with odd, spicy smells, up a twisting, stone stairway, through a door, and over the top of a flat roof. We shinnied down a rickety ladder on the face of a building, crossed an alley, passed through a weathered, wooden door, and hurried down another musty hallway, lit by a candle in an iron cage. We climbed another set of twisting stairs and walked through a half door into a room stacked with bags of rice and lentils, and baskets filled with cinnamon, ginger, nutmeg, cardamon, and clover. An Arabian oil lamp lit the room with a flame out the narrow spout. Behind the bags of grain a small sleeping area had been arranged. Fluffy pillows decorated in elaborate Persian scroll sat on the floor. We sat among them, and were soon given strong coffee and rich pastries from a bent woman carrying a silver tray.

"Hot damn!" said Wrong John. "Ol' Gunny was right about how thankful the Iraqis would be for their freedom." He took a big bite of the pastry and a slurp of the strong coffee.

I drank my coffee, and it was a mighty good feeling in the belly—that warm, rich brew. I so much felt like I had just escaped to one of my Clay Country, Missouri, kinfolk after robbing a stagecoach. God did I love the feeling of getting away with something.

One of the men who had rescued us returned, his face scarf open and hanging along his shoulders. He spoke to me in Arabic. I put my hand to my ear and shook my head. "Americans," I said. His eyes grew wide and he quickly covered his face with his scarf. He hurried from the room, and we were left alone.

"Here we go," said Wrong John, shaking his head and grinning. "They recognized me and now its gonna be Silverspoon time—all signin' autographs and gettin' my picture taken with everybody and his pet goat."

"Shut up, Silverspoon!" I snapped. "Don't you know where we are? This is a bushwhacker hideout. They thought we were resistance fighters—that's why they saved us. If they figure out who you are, it's Silverspoon time all right—to die." Wrong John gulped and crossed his hands in his lap. Krill snuck off with his lamp and secreted it away in an empty grain sack. Basmati Sweet rubbed her forehead with one hand, the other kneading the fabric of her pants leg.

A few minutes later the rebel returned, accompanied by a smaller man. Both of them wore black shawls wrapped around their faces. The smaller man spoke in broken English. "You are Americans? What are you doing here?"

"We disagree with Silverspoon's war," I said. "We come from Arab ancestry, and have traveled all this way to help you in your battle for freedom against American oppression."

"Oppression?" said Wrong John. "We're the liberators here, Ish. Shalong was—." Sweet's hand shot out and clamped over his mouth.

The smaller man spoke to the other in fast Arabic. The other replied. They went back and forth for a minute. The smaller one turned to me. "It is not safe to be an American in Baghdad. Whether you are of Arab, Persian, or Pakistani descent, you are American. You can only help us by going home. Tell your leaders we do not want America here. We have our own ways. You do not understand us."

I nodded at him. "If that's how we can help, we'd be happy to oblige."

He spoke to the other man quickly. He nodded at us, made a sign over us, and the two walked from the room. We were left alone for several hours. Wrong John had to piss so bad he snuck in a corner to relieve himself. Not long thereafter, a young woman arrived with a pot of lamb stew and a bowl of rice. She sniffed the air, drew down her lips, and squinted. Wrong John rolled his eyes and looked away.

"Is there a bathroom nearby?" asked Sweet. The woman showed us to a room across the hall. We returned and ate our meal. The others hardly ate, but I took on a good feed. A good gunfight always made me powerful hungry.

We settled down in the soft pillows to rest. The young woman, who spoke

decent English, asked if she could tell a story. No one objected. She lit a piece
of myrrh in the lamp flame and placed it smoking on the edge of a brass plate.
She spoke of the Fisherman and the Jinni, from the *1001 Arabian Nights*.

"A poor fisherman with three small children went to the sea to cast out
his nets. A devout man, he never threw more than four times, and paused at
the proper times of each day for prayer.

"One day, he cast his net three times, and thrice he pulled in heavy loads.
None of them, sadly, included fish, but instead contained an ass, a basket of
stones, and a pile of mud and shells. On the fourth throw, he pulled in a copper
lamp, its lead top stamped with a sacred seal. He opened the lid and purple
smoke rose from the lamp. It formed into a giant that stood before him.

"'Prepare to die, for I must kill you,' the giant roared.

"'Kill me? But why? I have just liberated you. I am your savior. I have
brought you from oppression into the light of freedom.'

"'It makes no difference, fisherman. I must kill you anyway.'

"'This is a mistake. It cannot be so. You should be grateful. You should
shower me with flowers and gifts for the great favor I have shown you.'

"'You must die. There is but one gift I have to give: you may choose the
manner of your death. Shall I cut off your head with my scimitar? boil you
in oil? throw you into a pit of cobras? tie your arms and legs to four different
horses? You decide.'

"The fisherman broke down and cried. He wailed for his three children
and his wife who would never see him again. He begged for mercy, but the
giant would not budge. 'Well then,' said the fisherman, 'by the power of that
god whose name is stamped into the lid of your lamp, tell me why, at least,
before I choose the means of my death, must you kill me?'

"The giant consented. He spoke of how he had defied a tyrant sheik who
tortured and killed his own people. He raised a secret army to defeat the sheik,
and was promised help from a great foreign nation, but was betrayed. He was
captured and, through magic, imprisoned in the lamp.

"For the first hundred years of his captivity, he swore to shower his
redeemer with untold treasure. During his second hundred years trapped in
the lamp, he swore to make the gems of a thousand kingdoms his savior's
alone. During the third hundred years in the lamp, he promised to make his

liberator a king, and grant him three wishes every day for the rest of his life.

"'But even after four hundred years had passed,' said the giant, 'no one came to save me. I became bitter and hateful. My yearning for freedom twisted and coiled inside of me, until all I could think of was killing the fool who came to set me free.

"'My only concession, which I offer you today, was to let my liberator choose the manner of his death. I shall take great pleasure in providing you a most wonderful demise, exactly as you request it, and I shall glory in the sight of you taking your last breath.'

"The desperate fisherman, now certain he would die, decided to try one final approach. He would attempt to convince the jinni there was no possible way a great spirit such as himself could ever again fit into such a tiny lamp. 'Whatever sorcery was at play all those hundreds of years ago is no longer of this world. It would be impossible, in these times, for such a vastness as yourself to fit in that small, small vessel.'

"'In that you are wrong,' boasted the jinni. 'There may be none other than I, in these modern times, who possesses such powers, but indeed I do!'

"'I'm sorry, but you boast. It is okay. I am a dead man. Still, you boast.'

"'You are not yet dead, and I will prove to you my greatness!' The jinni turned himself into smoke and flowed from a great purple cloud into the lamp, until he was completely gone.

"The fisherman quickly popped the led stopper onto the lamp and threw it back into the sea. He moved his family to the very spot, and every day he warned fishermen to never open a lamp that showed up in their nets from those waters."

Krill whistled a muffled tune and pushed his cloaked lamp to the side. I thanked the woman for the story. She bowed, blew out the lamp, and left us to rest. Not more than minute passed before Silverspoon was snoring. I could hear Basmati Sweet's quiet breath. I wanted to lie with her, but I did not.

Chapter XLIII

Proconsul Blackbeard

The next morning, our liberators fed us a tasty goat cheese omelet, strong Arabian coffee, and flaky, cinnamon-honey pastries. They read to us from the Koran, which was translated by the English-speaking woman as follows:

> Suras 105, The Elephant
> In the Name of God the Compassionate the Caring
> Did you not see how your lord
>   dealt with the people of the elephant
> Did he not turn their plan astray
> Did he not send against them birds of prey,
>   in swarms
> raining down stones of fire
> making them like blasted fields of corn

They blindfolded us and led us out of the labyrinth of hallways, passages, stairways, and alleys, to a busy cafe on a bustling street. When our blindfolds were untied, we looked around and there was no way to know who had brought us to that place. All the men and women appeared to be ordinary Iraqis having breakfast. Everyone wore their robes of various colors, and their headdresses, be they wrapped turbans, loose scarves, *fez*, or *burkas* that left only the eyes exposed. We walked outside, directly to the street (there were no sidewalks). Across the road a *halal* butcher slaughtered sheep on a platform in the manner prescribed by the *shari'a*. Next to him a tack shop sold the strange pillow saddles that were common to horse riders of the city. Donkey carts passed back and forth, along with camel trains and men on horseback. From next door came the sound of a cockfight: men shouting, urgent flapping of wings, squawks and screeches. Krill cringed and wrapped himself in the grain bag that held his lamp. A proud man, tall and regal, head wrapped in a thick black turban, walked by with a falcon on his forearm.

From around the corner came a bugle call and the roar of cavalry horses. The street cleared, and an American cavalry company charged toward us. Wrong John jumped in front of them and waved his arms. The man riding with the captain pointed at Silverspoon and the two rode toward him. "Olive, thank God it's you," said Silverspoon. "We've been through hell. Get us to HQ, pronto."

Olive brought us to Shalong's Baghdad palace, where the American civilian leader of Iraq had taken up residence. It must have once been a very beautiful place, but the facade had been nearly destroyed by artillery. Flowery tile mosaics in bright blue, gold, and red contrasted with geometric stone and brickwork—and had been smashed by cannonballs. Thick columns supporting pointed archways had big holes blown in their sides. The cupola above the third tier of burnt orange roof tiles had its left side shattered. We walked through a dark, pointed portal to an inner courtyard. It felt like entering paradise. No damage had been done to the inner courtyard. Double stone pillars capped by carved imposts marked a series of perfect arches that formed a gallery on all four sides of the courtyard. An intricate arabesque of bright tile and sculpted stone filled the area above each arch. Small bushes stood amid a grassy central square, anchored by a stone fountain ten feet across, burbling with clear water, and encircled by white, marble lions.

A man walked toward us through a wide arched entry, across the gallery and into the courtyard. His long mangy hair stuck out from a tattered leather tricorn hat. He wore a long scraggly beard, was missing a top front tooth, and wore at least ten gold bracelets of various sizes and shapes on either wrist. He was the first of Silverspoon's pirates to actually look the part. He walked directly to Wrong John Silverspoon, removed his hat, crossed his body with it, and deeply bowed.

"Greetings and salutations, Captain Silverspoon. It is an honor to serve ye here in Baghdad. I am Proconsul Blackbeard, named by me dear mum for the famed terror of the Carolina coast. Aye, they called him Blackbeard but his Christian name be Edward Teach."

Wrong John leaned back, turned to the side, and regarded his proconsul from an angle. "You're runnin' the show over here?" he asked.

"Your wish is my command, skipper." Blackbeard bowed again. He turned to Olive and said, "He's rather more swarthy than I expected."

"He's been under cover, disguised as an insurgent to get an inside look at the new Iraq. That's the type of guy he is," Olive said, spinning another yarn.

"I'm plumb tuckered, proconsul," said Wrong John. "How 'bout you scare us up a bed and give us a brief debriefing at dinner, say 6:00 sharp?" He didn't bother to introduce us to the pirate. I could tell by the way Blackbeard looked at me that he recognized immediately our common outlaw heritage.

"T'would be a pleasure." Blackbeard turned and led us through the gallery, into a corridor, and out into another gallery and a more intimate courtyard holding several pink-marble tables, a flowing pond with blooming white lotus, date palms clattering in the breeze, jasmine vines twining up the stone columns, and mango trees heavy with fruit. On the far side of the pond, a flock of eight storks rested on the grass.

"Oh my BRACK! They were right. He did have storks," Krill screeched. He dragged his lamps across the lawn and fell directly into conversation with the storks. I looked over at Basma, who gave me a weak smile. She looked exhausted. Blackbeard clapped his hands and veiled women in white robes came immediately to his side. He instructed them to take us to our quarters and make us comfortable.

"Would it give ye any pleasure, sir, to sleep in the very bed of Shalong?" inquired the proconsul of the captain.

"Ya darn tootin! I been wantin' to fart in his sheets every since he came after my dad."

At six o'clock a servant girl called us to dinner in Shalong's private dining room, a lavish hall filled with luxurious pillows and thick Persian carpets. Trays of food in brass bowls sat on low tables among the pillows. On the wall, a sequential wall mural depicted the history of Baghdad, from ancient Sumer through to present day. All likenesses of Shalong had been painted black. I lay down in the soft pillows and looked up into the vaulted ceiling at the most intricate tile work I had ever seen: bright red roses, surrounded by a field of cobalt blue, enclosed in a double flower-bud shape, surrounded by pink glass beads, enclosed in zigzag stone inlay. Designs within designs mesmerized me as

I lay in the pillows, fed peeled grapes by lovely Arab women in creamy robes of sheer silk.

Basma sat on her pillow with her arms crossed. She refused the offer of grapes, instead requesting a glass of white wine. "I find it a little slimy that we've set up headquarters in Shalong's palace. Doesn't that create the immediate impression they've just traded one dictator for another?" she asked sternly.

"Basma!" said the captain.

"*BASMA!*" squawked Krill, spitting chunks of green grape from his beak.

"It does not confront me, skipper," said Proconsul Blackbeard. "We're simply followin' the grand traditions of the people here, Mr. Sweet. If ye don't occupy the former ruler's castle, well then, ye haven't truly vanquished him."

"We're not supposed to be conquerors, proconsul."

"We aren't? Then what was the point of it all?"

"That's right, Basma. The main thing is, we're in here, enjoying the good life, and The Chastity Belt's in a hole somewhere, eatin' corned beef from a can." He caught a dribble of grape juice that ran down his chin.

"Aye, captain 'tis a pleasing thought by all accounts," said Proconsul Blackbeard, "And rest assured, sir," Blackbeard continued, "we're a'huntin' Shalong at this and every moment of the day, gaining good nose of his stench, and presently will be upon him to pounce!"

The captain squinted at him and asked, "That mean you're gonna catch him?" The proconsul nodded and tore a hunk of lamb meat from a roasted leg. "I want a souvenir," added Silverspoon. "We might'a missed his family jewels, but I want some trophy of his manhood, Blackbeard."

His mouth full of meat, Blackbeard replied, "The very phallus with which he relieves himself shall be laid upon ye tiller." He doffed his ragged tricorn hat and bowed his head.

"*BRACK!* Spare us the dick. Give a gun. Give a sword." Krill whistled like a train. Wrong John nodded in agreement. Basma sat on her pillow and slowly nibbled a piece of goat cheese.

"Suit ye taste," said the pirate. He bit full into a ripe mango.

"You gettin' this place good and piratized yet, Blackbeard?" asked Wrong

John. He pulled a square of beef from a skewer with his front teeth.

"Aye, aye, we call it Order Nine... Order Nine, a simple declaration turning over all public assets to the office of the proconsul. That'd be me!" He slapped his chest hard with both hands. Bits of food flew from his fingers. He swilled from a goblet of red wine—drinking openly in front of the teetotaling captain. "Our first business, of course, has been blubber. Ah, skipper, the whales here, they beach themselves by the hundreds. Day by day they swim up the Tigris and Euphrates, and roll over, fins out, in the shoreline muck. Arab's aren't whalers, though, like us Yanks. For every pound of blubber harvested, two are wasted. We'll bring it round, sir, fear ye not. We'll bring it round."

"You finding any WMHs?" asked Wrong John.

"They saw us coming, skipper. Must have buried them all in the desert. Fear ye not, though, fear ye not. We've got our bloodhounds on it." Blackbeard swilled his wine and belched. "Oh, and good on ye, sir, for scupperin' that dirty Chicken Little. We've seen the photo of he and the missus in the Arab papers 'round here. 'Twas good as posting the scoundrels head on a spike at harbor entrance."

"Thanks. Speakin' of heads, what about Quota's and Shalong's? America grows impatient with me."

"Shalong's in our sights. That's for sure. But Quota, he's a slippery one. We likely won't find him in Iraq,"

Blackbeard hoisted his golden goblet and sloshed down another big draft. He snapped his fingers, and one of the servants hastened to his side. He gave instruction close to her ear and she skipped away, to return with a large rolled cloth. Blackbeard unfurled it on the geometrically perfect, red Persian rug beside us. There rested a flag in the colors of the United States, with the same red and white stripes, but in the field of blue that would house our stars stood a crescent moon with a single star beside it.

"We've changed their symbol for 'em, skipper. It will help 'em steer clear of the shoals if they stick to the red, white, and blue," he winked at us and smiled, his missing top incisor a black rectangle in his mouth.

"Hang on there, partner. Don't the Iraqis feel allegiance to the old flag? You can't just change their flag on 'em." He popped a date in his mouth. Krill pushed a grape around the pillows with his beak, gabbling to himself, "Sim sim salabim. Sim sim salabim."

"A point well taken, indeed, skipper. I just assumed ye preferred all remnants of Shalong's regime hunted down as lady's undergarments. The other flag be his. Would ye want me flyin' bloomers over our new holdings?"

The captain ground his teeth. "No! Torch the old flags. Scare up a big pile of wood and send the flames clear to heaven!" He threw his arms up at the ceiling.

"Shall we throw a few of their dusty books of history on the pyre as well, skipper?"

"Hell yeah. We're givin' 'em a new history anyway—a hell of a lot better one than they had—an American one—brief and blubbery."

"Aye, skipper, we'll heave to it straight away. A fine demonstration it shall provide of the new freedoms awakened by the fire of democracy. Brilliant, skipper, brilliant!"

The next day Proconsul Blackbeard asked to take us on a tour of Baghdad. He wanted to show us the excellent progress he had made in rebuilding the country. Silverspoon readily agreed to the invitation, but asked for a little extra time to scrub away any remnants of the dark skin that had saved his life. He called me into his room, where he sat in a tub of steaming water and was fed de-pitted pomegranates by demure former servants of Shalong.

"Make me white again, Ish. I can handle this colorblind thing—but not when it's staring back at me in the mirror." As I scrubbed him raw, he pontificated about his stance on the dark underclass.

"Ouch, Ish, you don't have to take it down to the bone," said Silverspoon of the loud roughing up I administered to his brown-stained skin. "Interesting thing, that everybody's bones are white. Deep down, no matter what our surface color, everybody's got white bones."

I soaped up the rough-hewn brush and bore down a little harder, avoiding the white lump in his back. I could not but glance at the unnatural, albino growth, except to notice that it had a dark spot emerging in the center.

"And that's a good thing, is it, Wrong John?" I asked. "Everybody being white deep down?" I was thinking of Mr. Melville, Frank. He devoted a whole chapter to the subject of whiteness. In great detail, Mr. Melville studied the color that is no color, the purity of it that is divine, and the emptiness of it that is death.

> "It was the whiteness of the whale that above all things appalled me...Therefore, in his other moods, symbolize whatever grand or gracious thing he will by whiteness, no man can deny that in its profoundest idealized significance it calls up a peculiar apparition to the soul."

"Sure it's good, Ish. Everybody wants the same thing: to be white, Christian, all holy and pure, in the whiteness of angels, God and heaven. When you get down to it, we all believe in the white ideal, the American ideal. We all want to pursue prosperity."

I took the brush to his neck. "What about life, liberty, happiness?"

"Don't color the issue. Prosperity is the measure. White are the stones of the path. Look at Sir Yes Sir and Basma: they've disregarded pigment, left behind the victim mentality, and stand with us in the very heart of power."

"So this whole thing in Iraq's just a bleaching, is it? a cleansing? the making of dirty wood into clean white paper? on it to compose a new love poem to the Silverspoon Mandate?" I slopped soapy water in his face so he had to shut his eyes. I couldn't keep myself from looking once more at the pale growth on his back. I had to agree with Ishmael: even as whiteness is "the very veil of the Christian deity," it is, at the same time "the intensifying agent in things the most appalling to mankind."

I left him to dry himself and prepared to go on tour with Proconsul Blackbeard. .Wrong John, Krill, Basma, and I met on the west side of the palace on a fortified bridge that arched away from the main palace to a secured blockhouse leading to the city. A domed building rose before us, ornately tiled in an Arabesque geometric pattern of blue and white. Minarets stood above it and, because of the time of the day, carried the magical voices of the *muezzin* calling the faithful to prayer. I listened to the beautiful song and wondered if Islam would be allowed in the new white American Iraq.

Blackbeard stormed out of the massive, arched dark wooden doors of the palace, surrounded by a security detail of the most scurvy band of feral dogs I had ever seen. He advised the captain that his experience at the bazaar would never be repeated in the protection of the proconsul's private militia.

"Shouldn't our guy in Iraq be protected by good old American GIs?" the captain asked, raising his left eyebrow at the mob surrounding Blackbeard.

"Not if we wish to preempt the terrorists lurking after every corner, sir. All due respect and all, but government soldiers are mostly dark-skinned wastrels with nothing better to do, or poor white trash in the same boat—exceptin' the legacies, sir, many with fine military pedigrees." Blackbeard doffed his hat and bowed. "Me boys here, now, they're professional warriors, sir, men with well-seasoned black hearts and a taste for blood." He looked around and smiled at his merry band of "private contractors," some of whom smiled in return with gold, silver, or missing teeth, others who just sneered, checked the sharpness of their daggers, picked at their ears, or adjusted their balls.

"Let me introduce ye to me mob of rascals. These two here, Rohumba and Arandi, be genocidal killers from the African heartland." Two large, muscular Africans nodded at the captain and slapped their dark machetes. "Over here we've got Lars, Gunter, and Hilda, former members of the Apartheid Enforcement Agency." The three burley blondes—two men and a woman, I believe (though there was no real evidence of that besides the name)—had shaved heads; two had nose rings while the third sported a bone pierced through the lower lip. They stared ahead blankly, as if they were not of this world. "To me right, meet me hired guns of the Slavic region, Ethnic Cleansing Specialists Milan, Slobodan, Ravdan, and Creuton." The four Slavs, two squat and bald on top with long straight hair on the sides; one tall, thin, and buzzard-nosed; the fourth gargantuan and wearing an iron helmet and facemask that made him look like an executioner. They thumped their chests with their fists.

"These ones here, Enrique and Umberto, previously roamed the highlands of Central America, hunting down the impediments to American policy in the region. And on the vanguard, you'll find the Mongolians, Altai and Kublai, whose lineages require no further explication."

The captain looked around at his proconsul's band of thugs. He nodded and drew down his mouth. Krill also nodded and looked among the hired guns.

"As ye have suggested, sir, the array of manpower before ye bespeaks in volumes the wisdom of a handpicked team of mercenaries over a random lot of volunteers. Before ye stands the future of America's armed forces." Blackbeard spread his arms and bowed. "Once again, skipper, ye be spot on, truly, spot on."

The compliment and credit achieved their desired result on the captain. He relaxed his face and smiled at the detail. "America, land of the free, home of the brave—and the contract killer. I couldn't be more proud of you for joining our cause." He went around and shook hands with each of the team, with Krill, on his shoulder, whistling *The Battle Hymn of the Republic*. Basma stood with her arms crossed, head tilted to the side, a nauseated look on her face.

Proconsul Blackbeard gave a whistle, and the men lead us across the bridge and through the blockhouse, out on the road, and into town. Our first stop was at the former Iraqi Ministry of Blubber, a complex of boxy buildings that had miraculously been spared the bombardment of our artillery. Out front, the newly christened Endrun Iraq already flew Iraq's redesigned flag, the stars and stripes with a crescent moon and stars in the upper left field of blue. In the tradition of Silverspoon's *Liberty*, the Iraqi flag was surrounded with the corporate flags of American blubber companies. American soldiers painted the building's facade a dark green with large, circular brushes.

"Aye, skipper, 'tis a mighty struggle we face to save their whales. One day we make an improvement. The next day they blow it up."

"Who blows it up?"

"Shalong loyalists, foreign terrorists, Shiite radicals, stray cats from the Ottoman. We know not who, how, or why. Truly 'tis a squid, sir—a well-chosen name indeed—for it seems to have innumerable arms, changes color at will, vanishes, and strikes again where we least expect it. When we lop off an arm, it just grows a new one back."

"Listen, Blackbeard. That deal about the squid? that's just a marketing tool for the folks at home. The real thing is, it's, it's a, uh—"

"White Whale," said Basmati Sweet. "You've got to chase down this insurgency and kill it, so we can get the blubber. Without it, the great ship that is America will be stove and sunk."

"*BRACK!* Kill their white whale to save the Great White Whale."

Wrong John looked at Krill on his right shoulder, then over at Sweet to his left, and across to Blackbeard in front of him. He didn't seem to understand what they were talking about.

"Whether it be whale, squid, porcupine, or marmot matters not to me. We follow the Silverspoon Mandate. Regardless of what happens, it serves our aims, makes us stronger and more convinced we are right," said the pirate. "Each and every time one of our boys gets killed, or loses a leg in a surprise attack, we take it as positive signs that we're rooting the rats out of their nests. Whatever they do, it is the desperate act of cowardly villains well on their way to defeat."

Our detail lounged against the side of the blubber headquarters. A flag-bearing drummer from the U.S. Army approached the giant, iron-helmeted Slavic and asked for a smoke. Without looking at the American soldier, the contractor pulled papers and a tin from his pocket and handed them to the young man in blue (he was really more of a boy). He rolled a smoke, put a match to it, and tried to engage the mercenaries in conversation.

"Come, they told me, eh?" said the drummer, with a northern accent, his words embodied by the smoke that went with them. He flinched when a loud explosion went off not more than a block away, a dark cloud of smoke rising in its wake. The Slav shrugged. "Thought I was signing on for a celebration," said the drummer. "Somebody forgot to tell the host." He shook his head. "These Iraqis, whew! Can't tell friend from foe. Not hardly worth it, at less than a buck a day."

The tall, skinny, hawk-nosed one, Creuton, replied gruffly, "Buck a day? Not in my army. I make ten dollar a day, plus incentive and bonus for preempting squid attacks."

The American whistled. "Well, I'm not in it for the money." He pounded a quick rat-tat-tat on his snare drum. "I'm here because this is the right thing to do. America won't let thugs and tyrants run loose in the world. No sir!"

The giant Slav lifted the iron mask from his face and spit a gob of tobacco juice on the ground. "That what they tell you? How noble your mission!" he said in a deep, throaty voice. He spit another brown gob to the dry, dusty ground. "How many wars you fight?"

"This is my first, but I'm glad to do it. Freedom's no guarantee. You got to fight for it." He blew a snort of smoke through his nostrils.

"You are a child. A believer of fairy tales. You cannot fight for freedom on another man's soil. Your own soil—that alone is the ground of freedom. Such is the American hero—a fool." The big man spit again and ground the spit into the dry dirt with the heel of his heavy black boot. "The only soldier who profits from war is the one who kills because he loves it, who fights because it is his passion, who wins in the only way that counts: by the weight of his gold sack and the number of ghosts dancing to his fiddle."

The drummer boy threw his cigarette to the ground and stamped on it. His face fell into a grim frown and he glanced around at Blackbeard's black hearts. I couldn't tell if he was angry, or about to cry. He placed his flag in the leather holster at his waist, positioned his sticks above his drum, and walked away, playing the haunting rhythm that accompanies criminals to the gallows.

One of the South Africans, I think it was Lars, drew a bead on the GI with his rifle. Hilda pushed the barrel toward the ground. "He won't last a week," Lars said.

Blackbeard strode over and said, "Avast, ye scurvy dogs! Train ye mugs on the enemy, would ye?" He continued the tour through town.

Up from a crooked alley loped what looked to me like a long-eared, pug nose, red coyote, with a spotted back and a black stripe down its side leading to a bushy, black-tipped tail. I realized later it was the Iraqi version of a coyote: a jackal. It had something in its mouth, I couldn't tell what, until it sprinted past. It was a blackened human hand, fingers curled, as if it had made one, last, desperate grab for life.

We walked along the dusty streets, baking in the sun, past the rows of shops, apartments, coffee houses, banks, and restaurants. Silverspoon looked across the street and raised his hand to wave at someone. "Hey, idn't that the Shah? Makmoud Cherubic? It is him. Hey, Shah!" Wrong John started to walk toward him but Blackbeard grabbed his arm. "Avast, skipper! Don't go near that one."

"Why not? He's our guy, next Shah of Iraq, been a pirate longer than me."

"No, sir, he's a traitor. Been telling us lies just to stay on the dole and set himself up to rule."

"That a problem?"

"The dirty bastard may have been part of a wicked plot with Iran, to send us after Shalong so they wouldn't have to, then build a Shiite government very hostile to democracy, open markets, hootchy-cootchy shows, and the open selling of liquor in the streets—very un-American."

"Why that no good, lousy cheat! I ought to pop him in the nose right now!"

"We'll be gettin' to that for ye, skipper." He pulled the captain away and we continued on.

On the site of a large outdoor market, called locally a *souk*, one that was said to have been on that ground for perhaps a thousand years or more, the army was building the largest WongMart in the world. All the merchants, the proconsul informed us, would have to purchase permits from WongMart to have their goods sold in the store, and if, for any reason, they were unable to fulfill an order, WongMart would absorb their companies to insure consumers a constant and cheap supply of the goods. "We're building the store for WongMart with taxpayer dollars to support the free enterprise system," Blackbeard confided. "Sadly, though, a pattern of ungratefulness has set in. Iraqis prefer their pitiful public factories and locally made goods to the better, cheaper stuff we can bring in from China. Every day, we try to build the WongMart. Every night, they tear it down." He lowered his eyes and shook his head.

Along a bank of the Euphrates, we noticed a group of American soldiers throwing Iraqi men and boys into the surging water. The captain inquired of Blackbeard what it was about. "We've developed a foolproof way to determine if a man be terrorist or not. It's a system perfected in Salem and other early colonial towns, skipper. Ye throw them in the water, and if they sink, well, lucky for us, they aren't terrorists, but if they splash around like a whale under harpoon, well then, they're certainly evil, and we don't let them back to shore."

"What happens to the ones that sink, the good guys?"

"They drown, skipper." He noticed the troubled look on Wrong John's face. "Well at least they perish with a clean conscience. And skipper, a wench accused of witchcraft—she ain't sayin' her prayers to the Virgin Mary, if you know what I mean. The same be true of these bilge rats. Sink or swim, they're all praying to Allah for the destruction of America." That seemed to comfort the captain.

Basma scowled at Blackbeard. "You can't be serious."

"And why not?"

"We're supposed to be winning hearts and minds, showing the values of democracy, the contrast of American liberty with Shalong's casual brutality."

"As ye wish," said Blackbeard, doffing his hat and bowing. "Avast there! Take ye prisoners to stand trial." The soldiers looked at him with blank expressions and didn't reply. Blackbeard continued his tour.

Eventually we came to a small black market that traded cart and wagon parts in an alley off a main road. Wooden wheels, axles, seats, bridles, and all manner of frames lay about in odd stacks, watched by hooded men in dark robes. When they spied Blackbeard, the men scattered, trying in vein to take some of their goods with them. "Round them up, boys! Terrorists all! Bucking the system. Damaging the profit margins of good American patriots. String up the thieves!"

Rifle shots sounded all around, and Blackbeard's mercenaries fanned out and spread through the area as if of one mind. I could appreciate their precision, tried experience, and cold-blooded resolve.

Captain Silverspoon ignored the raid—he had hatched another scheme, a big one, to unearth by his own undercover work Shalong's hidden Weapons of Mass Hysteria. With Blackbeard busy chasing down the bushwhackers, Wrong John took out a magnifying glass from his pocket, got on his knees, and examined the ground for signs of cornbread. He crawled to a doorway in the narrow street. "Ants," he said. "Look at the string of ants. He followed them through the doorway, down a hallway lit by a single candle in an iron cage, until the passage ended at a green door. Krill hopped along beside him. Sweet had waited outside. I grabbed the candle from the holder and brought it along.

"Open, Sesame," said Silverspoon, standing at the chipped, green door, chuckling at himself. He pushed open the door to a storage room piled high with dry goods. He followed the chain of ants walking to and from a large cardboard box. He reached inside and pulled from it a smaller paperboard box. I brought the candle close to the cover of the box. On it was an illustration of a bright, white, blonde-haired, blue-eyed American girl with a sparkling smile and a measuring cup in her hand, overflowing with flour. "Little Judy's *Instant* Yellow Cake Mix" the box read. "Just add an egg, a little milk, pop it in the oven, and presto! Dessert is served!"

The captain's jaw dropped as he read. He shook his head in disbelief and, with lips moving, read again. " 'Little Judy's *Instant* Yellow Cake Mix.' Damn! Can you believe it, Krill? Right here in the middle of Baghdad, not but a little ways off the main road, a whole warehouse full of deadly yellow cakes. Did we find the WMHs, or did we find the WMHs? Or did *we* find the WMHs? Or did we?" He held the box delicately to his chest, as if he feared dropping it would cause one of the greatest explosions in the history of civilization.

Krill looked closely at the box. He read the ingredients and even licked a little white powder from the top corner that had been slightly torn. "BRRREAK an egg. Break an egg. But maybe not the *deadly* yellowcake of the Congo. Something important! Something very important! Crumby dessert. Crumby dessert." The captain tweaked his beak.

"Point is, says right here, 'Yellow Cake.' Found in Baghdad at a secret weapons lab of Shalong's. I'll go home and talk it up. If later on it turns out to be regular cake mix, so what? Point's been made. Anybody who refutes me is just a divisive partisan traitor—way un-American. Push comes to shove, we'll tell 'em our assessment was the best we could do with the available intelligence."

"Works for me."

And so we took the train back to Beirut and boarded the *Shokanaw* with a case of Little Judy's *Instant* Yellow Cake Mix, the final, ultimate, irrefutable "smoking gun," as Krill said, that proved Shalong's guilt, and justified the speedy invasion and destruction of his evil regime.

Chapter XLIV

Pip

I had always felt the Great Plains to be a vast ocean of grass, but crossing the endless blue Atlantic for the second time, I had again a much broader understanding of vastness. Along the way, the spouts of several whales were sighted from the masthead, causing much excitement in Wrong John, who wanted to go after them. Admiral Olive refused, telling him to chase whales would be completely contrary to his mission. Wrong John begrudgingly accepted his reasons. His mood became even more sour when, a week out from the port of entry, *Shokanaw* ran out of chocolate. In order to feed Silverspoon's insatiable sweet tooth, the cook had to dig into the case yellow cake boxes just to prevent what Krill called a "meltdown," a term I associated with a child's reaction to his ice cream falling on a hot sidewalk. After the chef served the first yellow cake, I had to admit, it did have a rather explosive lemon flavor in the mouth.

One morning over coffee and cigarettes, Basmati Sweet thanked me for saving her life in Iraq. I tried to tell her I didn't believe she would have died in the Baghdad bazaar.

"I didn't mean then," she said, taking a sip of strong coffee, then a puff of that smooth Turkish tobacco I had gotten at the bazaar. "I meant when the captain started mouthing off to the rebels who rescued us. I don't think he would have listened to anybody but you."

"Thank you, ma'am. Sometimes he sticks his silver foot in his mouth." She laughed. Krill came running past, carrying his scuffed and battered copper lamp, grousing to it about something I couldn't understand. If I didn't know better, I would have said his girlfriend *was* the lamp.

I decided that night to face my demons, to stare down the voice of Momma Zee, and go against all of my upbringing and everything I fought for my entire life. I went to Sweet's cabin and knocked on the door. She opened it a crack and looked at me. "IshcaBible," she said in her gentle alto women's voice. "Ahem, uh, IshcaBible." She dropped to a forced tenor.

"Basmati," I said in my regular voice. "Basmati." I lowered to a strained bass. "May I come in and visit?" I continued in the falsely lowered tone.

She half smiled, half grimaced, opened the door, and let me in. I brushed by her. She closed the door and slipped the bolt into the clasp. "It's nothing special, but make yourself at home." She spoke in her normal tone. The small bed next to the curving hull was no bigger than a child's. A glass lamp hung by a wire from the low ceiling and rocked with the wave-tossed ship. The low thud and rumble of the steam engine came through the wainscoting of the back wall. A small desk stood against a portal. On the far wall was a blue armchair.

I laid my holster on the desk, and started to sit in the wooden chair, but she stopped me with her hand on my elbow. "Sit there. It's more comfortable. I'll sit on the bed," she said, directing me to the armchair. She quickly closed a black gear chest. I noticed frilly, lacy women's things inside. She sat cross-legged on the bed. She wore black pantaloons and a loose, collarless madras shirt—purple and gold. She was barefoot and did not wear her usual bandana. She still had on her grease pencil mustache, and I could tell that her breasts had not been unbound from their day's labor at manhood. I would have expected the bandage was the first thing to go when she retired to her quarters.

I wore my usual black bowler, the snakeskin pants, a denim shirt, leather vest, pointed black boots, and, of course, the baldheaded twins at my hips. I took my hat off and set it in my lap. I rubbed my shaved head and looked everywhere but at her.

"So, what's on your mind?" she asked, fondling the hem of her shirt.

"You. You were on my mind. I—ever since that time in the train, on the way to New York City, when we—." Why couldn't I say it? Why couldn't I say the word "kissed?"

"I thought we agreed," she said. "That was a mistake. I'm a man, and so am I—are you. And there's the race issue."

"Please, don't insult me, Basma. You and I know there's only one man in the room." I licked my thumb, leaned over, and rubbed the silly mustache from below her nose. "That's better." I leaned back in my chair.

"What else do you know about me that nobody else knows?" She rubbed

398 ~ James E. Churches

her mouth with her delicate hands.

"I wouldn't want to presume."

"Please. What else?"

"I don't know. Maybe something. Maybe nothing. You mentioned the problem with race. I'm a Missouri boy. I grew up with slaves. I fought for the Confederate side. And when the war was over, I kept fighting, on and on until Reconstruction ended."

"Ku Klux Klan?"

"Here and there, shortly after the war, then no."

"You kill black men after the war?"

"Here and there."

"You rape black women for fun? Here and there?" She fiddled with the shrunken head hanging from her belt.

"No. Never."

"So you feel guilty that a nigger-hatin' white Southern boy kissed a black woman? And you came down here to make yourself feel better?" She scooted away from me to the far corner of the bed, crossed her arms and gazed toward the rough pine door. I sat back in my chair and looked out the small portal. Lightning flashed from a faraway storm.

"You remember when we first met?" I asked. "Down in Galveston?" She nodded but didn't look at me. "You said I didn't look like the type who ought to turn down a chance at redemption. Remember that?" She nodded. "Well, this is it. There's nothing else in this pirate caper that holds any hope for my lost soul. Except you." My throat got tight. I blinked my eyes hard to hold back the tears.

She looked over at me, her eyes moist, a sad wrinkle in her brow. She scooted closer to me, brought her knees tight against her chest, and held them with her hands, then rested her chin on her hands.

I could no longer block the tears flowing from my eyes. A drop ran down my left cheek. "Basmati Sweet, I am sorry. I am sorry for what I done all those years against the Negro race. I am sorry for fighting, and killing, and scalping my brothers, in the pitiful devotion to slavery. I am sorry for the robbing, the running, the hiding, and all the lying I done all those years. What was the matter with me? Who could have ever wronged me so badly that I made so much misery in the world?" I reached into my back pocket for my red kerchief and blew my nose. I wiped my eyes with the back of my hand.

"I don't expect you to forgive me. I don't. I only want you to know that you have taught me my hatred was wrong. You have shown me the beauty, the grace, the intelligence, and wit of a charming woman. You bring honor to all African Americans, all women, by the way you carry yourself in the world of arrogant men. I am sorry you have to hide who you are. And I am sorry for the way you have had to betray your principles in order to fit in."

A wave crashed against the *Shokanaw*, tipping it to port, leaving foam to slide down the glass of the portal. The lamp swayed back and forth, creaking, casting shadows that grew and shrank, grew and shrank. Sweet's eyes overflowed with tears. Her lips trembled, and she wept. I moved over to the bed and held her. She laid her head against my chest and cried. I stroked her cheek and told her it would be all right.

After some time, she looked up at me. I dried her tears. She pulled away and got a hanky from her chest and blew her nose, them came back and nuzzled my neck. "You know," I said, "you don't need to bandage something that isn't wounded." She looked up at me, sat up, and slipped her bright shirt over her head. White gauze covered her entire ribcage. I stood her up and found the taped end of the bandage. I turned her slowly around, unwrapping her, like we were doing a Christmas waltz, a dance of healing, a dance of true freedom, a dance of honesty, and forgiveness, and truth. She slowly turned, her eyes closed, those long thick lashes lying against her chocolate skin. Her lower ribs came into view. I could see them lifting and falling with her excited breath. Then her breastbone showed, and the lower curve of her breasts, then her nipples and the valley between and the hollows under her arms.

She tilted her head back, eyes still closed, and spread her arms. "Ahhh," she sighed.

I leaned down and kissed one breast, then the other. I softly kissed her brown, pillow lips. She slipped her arms under my leather vest and lifted it off my shoulders. She unbuttoned my shirt. I slipped her pants over her hips, down her legs, and over her feet. I slipped off her pink underthings. She unbuttoned my snakeskins. I wore nothing underneath. We fell to the bed, naked, kissing, our legs entwining, rubbing together at the groin, hot, hard, and moist.

We made love in the swaying ship, chugging west somewhere in the vast Atlantic. We gave ourselves to the overwhelming desire for touch that neither of us had felt for so many years. We grunted, moaned, kissed, fondled, rubbed, caressed, tickled, laughed, and in the end, snuggled like two tired kittens. That old bullet, hunkered down beside my heart for all eternity, whispered to me, real quiet: "Okay, well, that's it then, Jess. The war is over."

Sweet purred and kissed me under the jaw. "Roll us a smoke, would you, Ish?" she asked. I dug through my discarded snakeskins and found my pouch and papers. I rolled two smokes, placed them both in my lips, and stroked the white tip of a stick match with my thumbnail. It popped and flashed to life. I lit both cigarettes and handed one to her. She took a deep draw and blew out a thin jet of smoke, followed by two perfect, round gray circles.

"You said you might know something about me, but then you only talked about yourself—typical man. Tell me, IshcaBible, what do you see?" She snuggled against my chest. I took a draw of smoke and tried to blow rings. I never could do that.

"Well, Miss Sweet, I only know what those wiser than me have taught. On my own, I am as ignorant or more than ol' Wrong John Silverspoon. Left to my instincts, I'm nothing but a fool for gambling, liquor, fightin', easy money, and jackass thrills. My big brother, Frank, he tried to bring me round. I'm happy to report a few shards of wisdom finally did work their way through my thick skull."

"Oh yeah?" she said, tickling my ribs. I laughed quietly through my nose. "And what *did* those shards whisper to your brain? Wouldn't happen to be scripture, would it?"

"Yes, ma'am, from the Bible of whaling." I took a puff from my smoke and flicked the long ash on the floor. "Now I'm going to follow the mandate here, and preempt your displeasure by apologizing in advance for any spite this may stir in you." She poked me in the stomach. I grunted.

"Oh, please," she said. "Mandate, my ass." She reached down and grabbed my balls. "You know, Ish, the best things in life can't be planned or anticipated. You've just got to close your eyes and let them happen." Two perfect smoke rings floated across the room.

"Amen, sister. So, gettin' back to *Moby-Dick*. There's this one character, a Negro boy named Pippin. Pip's a slight lad who usually does not go on the hunt, but is left on board the ship. One day, though, a whaler gets hurt, and Pip has to man the oars. The whaleboat strikes out after a spermaceti and lances it. The whale slaps the boat with his tail, and Pip gets scared and jumps overboard. He gets tangled in the line, and to save him, the harpooned whale has to be freed.

"Pip now, he's branded a coward, a "poltroon" they call him, and when he later leaps again in fear from the whaleboat they leave him to float alone in the limitless sea. This drives Pippin mad, for in that vastness, his small, human soul becomes overwhelmed by the power, and indifference, of God."

Basmati Sweet's fingernails dug into my ribs.

"The Pequod eventually reaches him, and picks him up, but he is no longer the merry, dancing, singing Pip, who entertained the crew with his tambourine. He roams the ship, calling out senseless things. 'I look, you look, he looks; we look, ye look, they look,' he says."

I reached for my snakeskins again and found a few sheets from the book that I had torn out for the occasion. "Listen to this one from old Pip:

'And I, you, and he; and we, ye, and they, are all bats; and I'm a crow, especially when I stand a top of this pine tree here. Caw! caw! caw! caw! caw! caw! Ain't I a crow? And where's the scare-crow? There he stands; two bones stuck into a pair of old trousers, and two more poked into the sleeves of an odd jacket.'

"Ahab takes pity on the crazy black lad and makes it his mission to protect him from the scorn of the crew. He takes him into his cabin and looks after him." I looked through one of the torn sheets. "Here, here he tells the boy: 'Thou touchest my inmost centre, boy; thou art tied to me by cords woven of my heart-strings... Come! I feel prouder leading thee by thy black hand than though I grasped an Emperor's.'

Sweet laced her hand in mine and squeezed my fingers.

"Even as Ahab takes Pip under his wing the lad's attachment to him begins to ease him off his quest to kill the White Whale. How can he take down that pale, humped beast of dominance that wants to make the world a slave, if the one he hopes to free by it does not want his freedom? 'No, no, no!'

says Pip, when Ahab leaves him for the hunt. 'Ye have not a whole body, Sir; do ye but use poor me for your one lost leg; only tread upon me, Sir; I ask no more, so I remain a part of ye.'

"'They tell me, Sir,' Pip continues, 'that Stubb did once desert poor little Pip, whose drown bones now show white, for all the blackness of his living skin. But I will never desert ye, Sir, as Stubb did him. Sir, I must go with ye.'

"'If thou speakest thus to me much more, Ahab's purpose keels up in him,' says Ahab. 'I tell thee no; it cannot be.'

"'Oh good master, master, master!' Pip cries.

"'Weep so, and I will murder thee!' Ahab exclaims. And then he goes off to hunt Moby Dick, Pip safe, he assumes, in his cabin below. Of course, as you know, nobody is safe, and the White Whale destroys all the whaleboats, and sinks the ship with Pippin inside. Only Ishmael survives."

Basmati Sweet sat up and came around in front of me and sat on my lap facing me. I was so delighted to see the softly curving lobes of her breasts, free, hanging down, yet also pulled up, in the buoyancy and tension that is the great allure and beauty of that feminine shape.

"Do you think I am *Liberty's* Pippin?" Sweet asked urgently. "Have I been a coward and leapt overboard midway through the hunt? Have I gone mad and mute and become a silly servant girl hanging on her master's coattails? Is it true, IshcaBible? Is it true?"

I grabbed her and pulled her close to me. Her legs reached around my waist and locked behind my back and squeezed. I did not know what to tell her. Who was I to say her place on *Liberty*, or her place in history? "I don't know, Basma. I can only say that you redeemed me. It's not too late to do the same for yourself."

Chapter XLV

Seven Come Eleven!

When *Shokanaw* finally arrived in Washington, Silverspoon could not wait to announce his personal discovery of the missing Weapons of Mass Hysteria. He invited members of Congress and the press to an important announcement from the deck of *Liberty*. Their small, packed boats arrived and anchored starboard. Wrong John stood at the rail, his officers beside him, somber, crisp, alert, aside from his second mate and diplomat, who stood away from the rail. Sir Yes Sir did not look good to me: he appeared weary, thin, and jaundiced.

Silverspoon held up the last box of Little Judy's Instant Yellow Cake Mix. His sweet tooth had demanded the remainder of the case be baked before we reached port. "Yep, we found the banned weapons. This here's a box of yellow cake I discovered at a weapons storage facility in Baghdad. There are literally thousands of boxes just like this one, packed with explosives intended for the shores of America."

"Looks like a regular box of Little Judy cake mix from here. Can we have a sample to run some tests on it?" asked a senator from Massachusetts.

"No. We'll do the testing and we'll let you know," the captain replied.

"It should come from an independent third party, don't you think? You do have some bias in the matter," countered the senator.

"See, now there you go, with your liberal bias, trying to bias me against myself when all I care about is the safety of our great nation." He slipped a finger under his collar, pulled on it, and strained his neck. The lump on his back had grown to the size of a football. Krill had tailored his shirts and jackets so that it had its own pleated pouch—a very nifty bit of scissor work from the old haberdasher. "There may be hundreds, even thousands of mobile yellow cake bakeries cooking evil on the corners of every Iraqi city."

Somebody yelled, "Yeah, they're called street vendors."

"What if it turns out to be an innocent cake mix, and not explosives?" asked the senator.

"What's the differ'nce? You see—here's the deal—Shalong had the will, the means, the plans, and the intention to purchase and use yellow cake. As the commander-in-chief, I couldn't risk the safety of my people based on what he actually did or did not do. I had to act on what he might or may have considered doing. I had to get ahead of the curve, stop him dead before he did the dirty deed."

"You mean before he added the eggs, or after the milk?" The senator laughed, as did the others gathered alongside us. I and several on board *Liberty* tried to suppress our glee, but a few snorts and sniggers escaped.

"Ha ha. That's so funny I forgot to laugh." Wrong John's nostrils flared and his sharp ears grew red. "Let me put it to you this way. It's nice that you can be jaded and cynical in the safety of a safe America I've made safe for you, but just remember one thing: you can't have your yellow cake and eat it too. Our boys in Baghdad don't have the luxury to laugh about these matters, not after 10-10, nor do me—nor I are—not me may—a'right?

"I can't sit around and hope that Shalong and Al Quota are only exchanging cookie recipes. I've got to read their minds and act decisively on the clairvoyance. That's the science behind my new mandate, and that's what we'll be basing American foreign policy on until calamari has been eliminated from the earth."

"So we'll be attacking other countries on the basis of hunches for as long as evil exists on the earth?"

"That's pretty much it."

"Doesn't that strike you, Mr. Captain, as a little, well, evil?"

"Absence of absence is not evidence of evidence." He had tried to quote a line Gunny used in the run-up to the war, but turned it into a nonsense Wrongism. "You know what your problem is? You can't tell the differ'nce between good and bad. That's why you're out there in a little boat, listening to me, and I'm up here in a big boat, ignoring you. Thanks, everyone. May there be peace on earth, and God Arrest America." He turned, as did his officers, and walked away.

After all this talk of war and Weapons of Mass Hysteria, everyone on board needed a little break. It came in the form of a trip to the Regulatory River Boat, a paddle wheeler afloat in the Chesapeake Bay that had become a sort of clearing house for government red tape. On a crisp October evening, we set sail for the bay.

The low sun cast a pumpkin hue over the swirling waters of the dark Potomac. All down the shore, hardwoods of maple, oak, ash, hickory, walnut, larch, and locust milked every drop of light from the fading sun into their scarlet, golden, amber, rust, and salmon tinted leaves. *Liberty* passed through this still parade of exuberant color, on her way downstream to rendezvous for a night of good food and drink, relaxation, and a little good, honest gambling. A murder of boisterous crows accompanied us most of the way, several times landing on our topsails and carrying on quite a conversation.

I wondered if Krill, being a bird, might understand their language, and asked him so. "Crows are tough, Ish," he said. "Don't actually speak—not the bird tongue. They cross over. Material to spirit. Talk in the tongue of angels. The tongue of angels." He walked away with his copper lamp, muttering, "Don't worry, sweetie. I'll get you out of there. I'll get you out of there."

Not more than three leagues on, we received another mighty jolt from below. *Liberty* quaked in the aftermath of the blow, alarm bells clanged, men scrambled to battle stations, and Gunny ordered a spray of cannon fire in a broad pattern across the water, but on the wrong side of the ship. Tatanka had been standing with me, enjoying a smoke, when he noticed a'starboard the long curved arm of the Giant Squid.

"That critter seems to come at us all the harder the more WJ chases his mandate," I commented, taking a pull off my smoke. From the watch pocket of my snakeskins, I pulled the Indian toy he had given me. I looped it between my fingers, gave it a twirl, and tried to get that pulsating, whirring engine going. That abalone button would not get started—just went flat after one rotation, time and again.

"You have to work hard to start a cycle like that," said Tatanka, noticing my frustration.

Finally I got it going, spinning and pulling my hands in and out as it whirled one direction, winked at me, and reversed. "See? See how it works? The harder I pull out, the harder it pulls in. It feeds off of my energy. The more I pull against it, the stronger it gets." The toy whirred and buzzed.

"Captain asked for this battle. Now he's in it. Once these things begin, few people ever get out." He pulled out his yellow jackknife and carved on his scrimshaw.

We sailed on, the captain and officers locked away in his cabin, preparing their money belts, I assumed, for the festivities ahead. Well into the night, *Liberty* came alongside a pure, white riverboat with two huge black paddle wheels aft, her rigging decorated with innumerable lanterns so that she glimmered as a constellation, fallen whole to earth. Dixieland jazz escaped from the interior, mixed with a jumble of excited voices. A makeshift gangplank linked *Liberty* and the riverboat together, and our officers sauntered on board.

Wrong John took the lead with his customary knuckling-dragging ape walk—a little more bent, I noticed, than it used to be, from his deformity. Krill perched on his shoulder, wearing a small, round, straw hat with a red band. Chief Dagger came next, gold hoop earrings gleaming, his body turned to approach the experience in the furtive manner of a crab. Yo Yo followed, head high like a proud horse, silver nose ring shining, black eye patch and monocle in place. After him came Tosspot, walking stiffly, eyes lowered, searching, suspicious. Pinch was next, blue eyes bright, and eager, her long, heavy legs and arms flopping about awkwardly. Crude waddled beside her, licking his translucent red lips and adjusting his odd pile of hair. Sir Yes Sir lagged behind, hands stuffed deep in his pockets, a tired look in his eyes.

Basmati Sweet was last. After our time together she had stopped binding her breasts, wearing a grease pencil mustache, or tucking a rubber hose down her pants. She did, however, continue to speak in her false tenor. She had avoided me since our return. I suspected the reason, but I didn't figure she was interested in further guidance from Mr. Melville.

Our group entered the main cabin, a grand ballroom, and came face to face with a Squid Alert tank ten feet across and ten feet tall. The four squid inside, red-and-blue-striped three-footers, cast a green glow: all clear. It was the first and only time the alert had ever recorded green. I supposed it was related to the "mollusk agenda" that had been described down under Washington at the conservative fish tank. Control the message, and you control the pigment of the squid.

From the ceiling of the ballroom hung crystal, gaslight chandeliers. A lush red carpet covered the floor. Next to the fish tank stood a marble bust of the captain and his chief mate. The place smelled of cigar smoke and whiskey. Barmaids in slinky undergarments, stockings and garters sashayed past a big roulette wheel in the center of the room. There were craps tables, blackjack, and poker tables on one end, and hundreds of gamblers yelling, placing bets, whooping and whistling.

The Pirates of the Potomac entered the ballroom. The music stopped, all games suspended action, and all eyes turned to Silverspoon. The captain looked up and waved. The room erupted in applause. He gave the thumbs up and plugged people with .45-caliber personality bullets. He nodded and scooted people back to the games with a few flicks of the back of his hands.

My first instinct was, naturally, to figure out a way to rob the place. It was, after all, the greatest of all pirate victories, dating to Captain Kidd, to steal the booty of another pirate. With that thought foremost on my mind, I set about exploring the casino.

A huge roulette wheel in the middle of the room was the first attraction that lured me in. I came upon it to find a clergyman at the wheel, shouting, "Round and round and round she goes, and where she stops, nobody knows." I noticed a sign next to him that read: Holy Roller Roulette. He sent the steel ball in the opposite direction of the spinning wheel. It made a slow, whirring descent to the numbers, hit the dividers, and began bouncing in a loud, uneven staccato contrasting with the steady whiz of the wheel's gears. Players rooted for their numbers until the ball finally settled into a slot. "Nineteen, nineteen!" shouted the clergyman. A short chubby woman squealed and bounced up from her chair, "That's me! That's me." She ran up and hugged the minister, who pulled an envelope from a tray next to his seat and opened it.

"Congratulations, ma'am, you have won an affidavit prohibiting your most despised liberal Catholic politician from receiving communion at his or her favorite parish. Simply present this document to the priest before mass and he will—you're gonna love this—shame the baby-killing liberal for his sinful policies as he approaches the altar. Shame him, or her, in front of the entire congregation, for undermining the faith and giving agita to the Pope! How 'bout that, folks?" The players clapped and whistled, and the woman who had won bounced up and down.

I stuck around for a few more turns of the wheel. All around, at the different gaming tables, people screamed and shouted, whistled and whooped, danced or threw tantrums. The band of black musicians didn't notice the gamblers—they just played their Dixieland. At the roulette wheel, a dapper man in a pin-striped suit hit on seven and won the honor of being a judge at the National Creation Science Fair, at which he would judge the merits of such childhood experiments as, "Why Did God Create Fossils? Proving Darwin Was a Heretic," "Why Is the Sun Hot? God's Love or a Red Hot Nuclear Furnace? Prove It in a Diorama," and "Reducing Blubber Consumption or Prayer?—Do the Math on Global Warming."

A slender white-haired woman in a cherry red dress won the honor of dinner on *Liberty* with Captain Silverspoon if she could convert ten or more Muslims to Christianity. A Mexican man won six faith-based charity credits, allowing him to reduce his personal tax burden by fifty-percent if he promised to pray for the people who would lose the services his money had provided. A pot-bellied man with greased dark hair, combed straight back, hit on ten and won a weekend retreat with the Masturbation Corps at Camp K-Y. It was a rare chance, as an adult American male, to preach the virtues of abstinence to one hundred nubile virgins. He squeezed the coupon in his puffy red hands, licked his fingers, and slicked back his hair.

I wandered over to the poker tables and observed a game, trying to decide if I should sit in. It appeared to be somewhat like the poker I had played at saloons in the West, but I didn't understand the betting, which wasn't with money but a strange set of commodities I could not comprehend. In one game of seven-card stud, I witnessed the following exchange, after the five players received their first two hole cards and one up:

"I'll bet two tons of mercury," said one man, peering furtively at his hole cards.

"I'll see your two tons of mercury and raise you half a ton of arsenic," said the man next to him.

"Fold," said the next, "too toxic for my blood."

"Call," said the next, shoving in a stack of Promissory to Pollute notes.

"See your mercury, your arsenic, and raise you two environmental regulation rewrites."

The first player threw his cards on the table. "Christ! How can I stay in with somebody who's obviously planted an employee in the bureaucracy?"

"Snooze you loose," said the heavy better, flipping his palm up and tilting his head to the side. The man next to him threw his cards down and folded. The only guy left called the bet, and, to everyone's astonishment, raised a fish kill fine waver, apparently very hard to come by.

"I'll call," said the only player remaining, "but it doesn't take a poker genius to figure out you're either sitting on a department head or yanking somebody's chain on the deck of *Liberty*."

The other guy held a stern poker face, and the next cards went out. The first guy had a jack of hearts and a ten of hearts showing. The second had a two of spades and five of diamonds. Both checked instead of betting and took another card. The first added a king of hearts to his royal family. The second got no help on an inside straight.

"I'll bet twenty-five leaky drums of hazardous chemicals."

"To hell with you," said the one. "Twenty-five drums—you think you can buy the pot, is that it?" His competitor did not react.

"You ought to stay in," said the last guy to fold, "you know, just to keep him honest." That got a laugh all around.

"All right, I'll call your twenty-five leaky drums, and raise you a midnight dump at the local sand pit." He threw some coupons into the pot, muttering under his breath, "Hell, if I loose this thing, I'll have to set up shop in Mexico. Down there they figure a fiery salsa can offset any damage from poisons."

"Before I call him on the midnight dump, I just want to check with the dealer, make sure it's a legal bet," said the crafty industrialist controlling the action.

The dealer, whose nametag read Bob Benson, Environmental Investigator and Card Shark, responded, "Guys, guys, gimme a break. Do you realize I'm now the *only* investigator left? me, solo, the Lone Ranger. Legal bet—ha! There's no such thing as *illegal* when nobody's watching."

"Wow," said one of the guys who had folded. "I didn't realize Silverspoon's Mandate had come so far."

"They've preempted government snooping and pointless disruptions to productivity—put an end to state sponsored terrorism against business?"

"Sure they have. Which would you rather have, a factory in America that's a little sloppy but providing jobs, or one that moves to China where the Mandarins understand the importance of a seamless partnership between government and business."

"Not that anybody's going to stay put anyway—labor market and all."

"The workers terrorize us mercilessly: higher pay, longer vacations, better healthcare, stronger pensions, safer working conditions. It's about time to kick the mandate up a notch and start preempting these labor rights terrorists before they unleash their squiggly squid against our bottom line!" He chewed on his cigar and slammed the table with his fist.

"Easy, killer. All in due time," said the high roller. "Silverspoon is well on his way to starving the beast of the federal bureaucracy. Call it a tax cut, call it looting the treasury, call it whatever you will. The point is to get the country as deeply in debt as quickly as you can, until everyone is absolutely insane to balance the books. 'Sorry,' you say, 'had to slash the Boreal Toad Protection Department to get the deficit back in line.' Then you go in and mine the copper that you couldn't get at because of the friggin' toad."

"That's right," said another. "Same deal with the labor rights terrorists. When there's nobody watching over our shoulder, nothing prevents us from busting up their terrorist plots like we always used to."

I walked away from the tables of Pollution Poker more than a little impressed with the sophistication of the game, feeling completely overmatched as a poker player and a thief. I could not hope to compete in this parlor of the wealthy elite. I still lived in the world where money paid for things, where cash got somebody's attention and gained you respect. Out on the Regulatory River boat, money was never seen, but always lurking, hidden in slippery *assets*, squidlike things that could change color at will, slip through the tiniest opening, and disappear.

I wandered over to a craps table where big money rode on the hot hand of a Montana mining czar who couldn't miss. "Seven come eleven!" he yelled, and threw the dice. They tumbled across the green felt, bounced off the far rail, and landed on five and six. A jubilant whoop rose from the players at the table. The dealer pushed around more of the surrogate money certificates. I couldn't tell what they were until the Montanan, on his next turn, hit an eight on the third try, gathered in his winnings, and walked toward the bar. I approached and asked him how he'd done. He was reluctant to speak with me until I informed him I was IshcaBible, assistant to Captain Silverspoon.

"Oh, so you're IshcaBible. Heard a lot about you. Is it true you can quote a Bible verse for every occasion?" he asked in his low, gravely voice through a hedgerow of rusty whiskers over his lip. He continued to walk directly to the bar.

"Those that exalt themselves will be brought down, and the humble will rise," I said with a slight bow.

"Damn, you are good. Where'd he say that? Sea of Galilee? Sermon on the Mount?" he asked.

"It's from Luke," I said. "You were pretty hot on the table, mister. Must have walked away with some nice prizes."

"You know it, son. Some real beauties. Sort of thing I really love about the Silverspoon era—adventurous and profitable. Just a lot of good fun. What'll you have?" he asked as we reached the bar. I looked around to see if the captain was near. He was still convinced of my virtue, and it was a hole card I intended to keep. Not seeing him, I ordered scotch with a twist. The mining czar, who introduced himself as Montana Mike, drank from a tall tankard of beer, white foam sticking to his bushy auburn moustache. He thumbed through his stack of certificates. "Hmm, let's see. Healthy Forest logging permit, mineral rights to a mountain goat sanctuary, dredging clearance on Clear Creek, permit to build a damn on the Salmon River—not really much to brag about," he said, pausing to take another pull on his tankard, licking the white foam from his moustache. I took a drink of strong scotch, grimaced and coughed—it had been a while.

He continued to thumb through his stack of promised booty. "Oh wait, here's a nifty one: 'CIA Covert Operations Dream Vacation, An All-Expenses-Paid Coup for Two,' that's all it says. Shucks, that's a nifty one. I'll have to go over to the cage and see what it's about."

I walked with him to the cashier. Montana Mike handed her the certificate and said he wanted to cash it in. She handed him boat tickets for two to Caracas, Venezuela, and the deed to a property on the island of Trinidad and Tobago. "How's this deal go?" Mike asked, smiling. The cashier pulled a gun. She wasn't smiling. My hand went to Peacemaker, but I didn't draw. The woman escorted Mike and me below decks to a small room, dimly lit and smoky. Several pirates dressed in black stood smoking fat brown cigars on one side of a small round table. They wore black leather bandanas, black face masks, black silk shirts, black britches, and black boots. The cashier shoved us to a table opposite them, and left.

"Hey, what's the story here, guys? I'm just a happy miner, digging in the dirt for chunks of silver and gold. I don't want no trouble," said Montana Mike, his voice shaky, hands trembling. "You know I've already raised fifty-grand for the next election. What's that make me, a Girl Scout? a Sodbuster? a Shylock?—oh, I forget the categories."

"Okay, buster, we're onto your tricks. You cashed in the dream vacation, right?" said one the pirates, in a high, earnest voice immediately familiar to me.

"Well, yeah, but, I don't need it—I mean if there's some problem with it, I'll, you know, give it back."

"Yeah, there's a little problem," said another pirate, a short one, again, in a voice I was sure I knew. "By cashing in that voucher—delta-tango-vulva—you signed on to foment a military coup in Venezuela, with the intended outcome to topple a democratically elected leader so we can piratize his blubber operations."

"I didn't—I wouldn't have, have done anything—anything illegal, or dishonest. I mean, I just wanted to have a little fun," he stammered, his low, gravely voice suddenly high and fragile, knee trembling against a leg of the table, causing it to rattle on the wooden floor.

"A little fun, huh?" said another of the gang. I knew by the way this one sucked his teeth exactly who it was. "You think it's fun to rip open the belly of a sovereign nation? to cause chaos and ruin? to displace thousands of people from their homes? You think that's *fun?*"

"No no no! I think it's awful. It's wrong. I want nothing to do with it. I'm out. I'm sorry. I thought we were all friends out here," Mike stammered. "What is this, some sort of a sting? You guys—Silverspoon backstabbing his buds? What the hell kind of a—"

One of the pirates who had been standing with his back to us turned quickly and peeled the black mask from his face. There in front of us stood Captain Wrong John Silverspoon, a big smile on his face. The other pirates pulled off their masks, and Mike gaped at them open-mouthed: Gunny, Chief, Tosspot, Crude, and Pinch. Krill popped out of a broom closet and squawked, "BRACK! Trick or Treat, Mikey." The miner almost tipped over in his chair, but I caught him.

"What'a ya mean, 'I think it's awful?'" chided Wrong John. "Take a look at that deed you're holding. Trinidad and Taco is where we're building you a refugee camp, old buddy. We get the blubber and you warehouse the human refuse. Uncle Samuel J. Fatass picks up the tab, you set the price per head, and it's bases loaded with Mighty Mike up to bat." The captain bounded around the table and put Mike in a headlock. The others laughed and jibed him with friendly insults about what a weasel he was. Mike laughed and playfully punched Wrong John in the ribs. "Oh, and by the way," the captain told him, "the bushy moustache thing is *definitely* out. It's just way too Shalong, Mikey. You don't want the nickname of Chastity Belt, do ya?"

"You sons-a-bitches!" Montana Mike exclaimed. "You really had me going. CIA dream vacation—I shoulda known." He chuckled and received a good joshing from the officers of *Liberty*. The captain pulled me aside and thanked me for picking Montana Mike for the gag—an old friend of the Silverspoons, families going back for generations, a "good man." I told him it was no problem at all, I was happy to help out. Truth is, I had no idea Montana Mike was a friend of the family, but truth on Silverspoon's *Liberty*, I had come to realize, looked and felt a lot like a rubber chicken.

Wrong John winked at me and said, "Sure is good to be back with our own kind, idn't it?" I took it as a reference to Iraq.

I winked back at him and replied, "Treat your neighbor as you yourself would like to be treated."

"That from Matthew, or Mark?"

"The *golden rule?* Ye ought to know that one, *skipper*," I answered, imitating Proconsul Blackbeard.

The captain turned and said to the others they had better get back to the ballroom, that there was some sort of shooting contest about to begin. When we came back upstairs, a crowd had gathered around a thirty-foot-long contraption that had been unveiled behind the Pollution Poker tables. A sideshow hawker called out to the onlookers. "Step right up, ladies and gentlemen. Step right up and take your best aim at the most rare animals in the world. Step right up, don't be shy. These exotic creatures have been shot at for millennia, that's why they're endangered! Step right up!"

The first two contestants took aim at the menagerie of odd specimens. The critters had been lashed to small platforms attached to a clattering conveyor that carried them behind oscillating fake bushes and rocks, waterfalls with running water, artificial clouds that rose and dropped, and stage sets of sand dunes and mountain ranges. The animals shivered and moaned: a rare Madagascar lemur, a New Zealand blue duck, a baby white rhino, an American crocodile, a black-footed ferret, a Bengal tiger, an orangutan.

The contestants, a man in a tuxedo and a lovely woman in a long white dress, took aim but could not shoot. "I just don't see the sport in tying these animals up like this and humiliating them and killing them," said the woman. "We should set aside sanctuary for them and carefully guard them."

"Of course we should," said the hawker, "and that takes money. We handsomely pay the governments of the countries where these animals live, so they have the capital necessary to purchase game preserves and hire wardens to protect the animals. What's wrong with our friends having a little fun and getting a trophy out of it?"

"So we're going to kill them to protect them?" asked the man.

"That's right. It's the Silverspoon way: preempt extinction by killing them before they all die off. It's the logic of proactivity and pirate market capitalism. If there's no exchange of money and goods, you're looking at the evil of false generosity, the sort of ain't-I-swell mentality that helps liberals sleep at night."

"Well I'm not a *liberal*," scoffed the woman. "I just don't see the wisdom of killing endangered species to save them. I sounds to me like another scam to exploit the last refuges of wilderness."

"You, madam, are a heretic. And I shall call security on you." He waved over an agent of Homemade Insecurity. The chubby guy ran over, blowing his whistle.

"Have you discovered a slug trail in the carpet, sir?" the agent asked.

"This woman has blasphemed against free-market capitalism," said the carny.

The agent pulled a squid from his bandoleer and pitched it in the woman's face. She screamed and stepped back. He moved to slap her in handcuffs. Several people gathered around the agent and dared him to try. Somebody else snuck into the works of the shooting gallery and cut loose the pitiful creatures, which began to run about, knocking into people and gambling tables, flying into the lights and breaking them, tripping people. The roaring, charging tiger caused a stampede toward the exit. People screamed, flames and smoke filled the ballroom, and animals and people ran higgledy-piggledy for the exits.

I ran for *Liberty*, where our sailors prevented panicked gamblers from clambering on board but recognized me and allowed me to pass. *Liberty* soon pulled away, and we watched the riverboat go up in flames, gamblers jump into the cold water of the bay, lifeboats lower and row from the paddleboat.

"Help!" a woman screamed from the water. "Something's got my leg!" There was splashing and yelping on all sides of the Regulatory Riverboat. *Liberty's* bilge pumps clanged, and she set sail back to the flat Potomac.

Chapter XLVI

There's a Loop, All Right

In the weeks that followed, *Liberty* continued to take on water, and it began to look as if the ship would sink. Things began to go badly for the pirates on several fronts at once. Their war in Iraq, which they had claimed as a victory, had, it appeared, just begun. Hundreds of U.S. soldiers were being killed, and the newly liberated and democratized Iraqi people seemed to have unending hate for their liberators. Proconsul Blackbeard retaliated by shutting down an Iraqi newspaper that had the audacity to describe him to its readers as a pirate. When friends of the paper marched in the streets to protest, he sent in the cavalry to disperse them, which caused a riot that claimed many lives on both sides. Second Mate Sweet asked the captain if he thought it a problem that Blackbeard had, at one fell swoop, violated every precept of the First Amendment.

"Thatn's in *our* constitution, not theirs," he said. "Besides, it's a war over there, Basma. Free press is a luxury of *peacetime* democracy. They want to express themselves, they better learn to behave—like good Americans."

Perhaps he was right, but the Iraqis didn't see it that way, and a rebellion spread throughout the country. Many in Congress and the previously complacent press began to question the wisdom of America's continued presence in Iraq. "We see the escalating violence as a very positive sign," Yo Yo told a gathering of the press one afternoon. "Democracy is messy, messy, business. Freedom means the right to screw up, as well as do right, and the Iraqis are just taking off the training wheels. There's going to be a crash or two."

"But what about the violence against Americans and our allies? That can't be a positive sign," noted a *real* reporter, a non-member of the Mandate Media.

"Sure it can. It shows the desperation of a few thugs and terrorists attempting to derail the *Little Engine That Could* on its way to freedom. They can't stop it. Freedom beats too strongly in the breast of every Iraqi. It thinks it can, it thinks it can."

Others in Congress called for more U.S. troops to stabilize the situation, but Gunny stuck to his guns. "I'm actually considering reducing our forces in Iraq," he told a troubled congressional delegation. "More troops just means more targets. Our job is to control the psychological battlefield. Do we do that by number of bodies? Is it achieved by number of guns? No, it's achieved by fear and intimidation. I know the Arab mind. We bring in more troops, the Arab mind perceives that as weakness. We just need the soldiers that are already there to growl a little louder."

It was vintage Silverspoon Mandate, straight out of Krill's doctrine requiring that any event, no matter how bad it appeared, be twisted into something good. Although Gunny, Dagger, and Wrong John seemed to believe the story, fewer and fewer outside of central command continued to go along. *Liberty* was almost daily besieged by the Congress, the press, former supporters, even leaders of business, with questions about Wrong John's policy and the direction he was taking the nation. One of the worst blows came through Chief's negligence.

It seems that when Dagger "outed" Chicken Little's wife, Martha, he hadn't checked on the nature of her assignment. Somebody in the *real* media, uninitiated in the opiates of *Congreso Mandato*, dug up the fact that Martha Little was none other than the secret operative designated to remove Shalong's balls in Operation Castration. Martha Little's picture, the reporter noted, had been broadcast all over the world. I remembered Blackbeard saying it had run in the Arab press of Iraq.

One night, under the cover of a cloudy November sky, Dick Little, former Terrorism Czar, once again penetrated *Liberty's* perimeter and boarded her some hours after midnight. Having spent the better part of twenty years hiding from either Union soldiers or the law, I never slept more than an inch or two deep, and heard the first boot steps above my head. I came out on deck with Peacemaker and Widowmaker and found Little had already bound and gagged the lookouts, had lit a lamp, and was preparing to roust the officers.

"Mr. Little," I said, surprising him from behind a storage chest. "Have you discovered another threat to the people of America?"

He turned and gawked at me, a wide, insane glimmer in his eyes. His previously ruddy face had gone sallow and ghostly. In his hand dangled the severed head of a woman. "IshcaBible, well, you're right about that. I've discovered a threat all right. It is the officers of this bloody ship!" He lifted the head by its matted red hair and thrust it in my face. "Meet Martha Little, my dearly decapitated wife," he said through clenched teeth, voice quavering. His curly blonde hair was greasy and disheveled, his clothes wrinkled, his face with a week's growth of beard.

I looked at the ghastly head. Time and weather had drawn the wrinkled skin down to the bone and made it a deathly gray, darker in the sockets that had once housed eyes, the desiccated lips retracted from the mouth to reveal a full, ghastly smile. I recoiled, imagining a teardrop had run down its cheek— then I realized it was a crawling maggot. Little's gang continued to climb over the rail, despite my threatening pose with Peacemaker and Widowmaker aimed at their leader.

"Are you pure fool, Mr. Little, attempting to take the commander's ship like this?" I asked. "Even if you get the culprit, you'll hang for your crime."

"I'm a terrorist now, and I've got my quota to fill. Life means nothing to me. My mandate, Mr. Bible, is to kill—and that's what I intend to do," he seethed. I didn't know what to do. I knew how I would feel if somebody did that to my Zerelda, and yet—there was the night with Basmati Sweet, and the bullet beside my heart. "The war is over," it had whispered. How could I advocate for Dick Little? How could I any longer stand on the side of more killing?

"I know you want revenge, Mr. Little," I said. "It's a terrible thing that's been done to your family. I just—I'm in no position to tell you anything. I just wonder if more killing is the answer."

"There is no answer," he hissed. "That's the problem. That's what goes wrong when something like *this* mob takes over your country. You can't do anything to make sense of anything. Life and death no longer occupy the opposite ends of a long pole. They stand together like husband and wife." He brought his wife's head to his chest and held it and kissed the matted red hair. He looked at me again with those too-wide glimmering eyes. "You're either with me, Mr. Bible, or you're with them that sold out my lady."

I pledged to help Little, if he promised never to reveal that I had—or to hurt Second Mate Sweet. He agreed, and I positioned Little's men where they could quickly capture the captain and his officers, then I had them tie me to the foremast, outside of Wrong John's cabin, and give me a couple of blows to simulate a scuffle. After that, it was left to fate if any justice was to be served.

Just as Little and his men were ready to go after *Liberty's* officers, the crew roused itself from below and burst through the hatch with sabers drawn. Little and his men fell upon them and a melee broke out from stem to stern. In the soft lamplight I saw lunging forms on either side of me, heard the shuffle and thud of heavy boots, the crash of steel against steel, the grunts and growls of the men in combat, the cries for help, the curses and damnations. The captain awoke and called out my name, but I did not answer, from my pretense of having been knocked unconscious. Men screamed and bodies splashed overboard. Swords clanged and clashed. Guns went off.

"You traitorous blackguards!" yelled Sir Yes Sir, joining the fight, and probably the only officer to do so. I could not see Dick Little, but imagined him fighting like a mad wolf with his wife's head tucked under his arm, his long, messy yellow hair flying in his face. He would want that she witness the avenging.

The battle lasted no more than ten minutes—these things never take much time—and I could hear from the loud voice of Dick Little, to my left on the foredeck, that he had subdued our crew and had *Liberty's* officers at sword point. I also noticed the flashing of a signal light from the cannon deck that told me someone had notified our escort we were under attack. Little's gang had several torches going, and he walked from officer to officer and dangled his wife's head in front of their eyes.

"Take a good look at them darling. These are the heartless worms that sold you out to punish my honesty—my honesty. Me, and my ignorant honesty." Little grimaced, closed his eyes tight, and hung his head. He shoulders drooped and his legs wobbled, and I imagined he might topple to the deck. After a moment, he must have recalled his purpose, braced himself, and brought his wife's head face-to-face with the officers lined up in front of him. "Look into their pitiful eyes, my Martha, and tell me if there is even a glimmer of soul inside." He held the dark shriveled head nose-to-nose with Tosspot, then Dagger, Gunny, Pinch, Crude, Sir Yes Sir, Basmati Sweet, and, finally, the captain, who had Krill perched on the shoulder of his crisp white nightshirt.

Little drew back and bellowed, "Which of you is the villain who betrayed this daughter of liberty?" I had not seen eyes that wide, and insane, and unrepentant since Bloody Bill approached those unarmed Union regulars on the train in Centralia—unarmed, released on furlough, Missouri boys most of them, just like us—and shot them down one by one.

"I'm outta the loop here," said Wrong John. "Can somebody bring me up to speed?"

Little jumped at him and thrust his wife's head into Wrong John's face. "You're out of the loop, are you, Mr. Captain? The loop?" Little's voice cracked and tears welled in his eyes. He held Mrs. Little's head to his chest, cradled it like a child's, stroked the mangy red hair. He cocked his head back, panted, breath agitated, irregular. Little shook his head, blinked his eyes, and bit his lip. A spasm of agony racked his body, after which his eyes flew wide open, and he looked around as if he had awoken from a nightmare. "There's a *loop*, all right, that you should be in. A loop—hah! The very noose made round by the hangman's knot!"

Before his words had finished, a boy stepped forward. He was on the verge of manhood, hair long, blonde, and unkempt, a boy, I guessed, about the age I was when I joined you, Frank, to ride with Quantrill's Raiders. In his hands he held a thick coil of hemp rope. "Here, Dad, let me—let me string him up for you—for Mom, let me," said Little's son in a shaky voice. He showed some skill with a rope, despite his anxious fingers, and wove the hemp into a sturdy noose. He opened the loop to a suitable diameter and held it up for his father, who nodded his head. Dick Little grabbed Wrong John by the collar and jerked him forward, causing Krill to fall from his shoulder to the deck. Little's boy threw the noose over the yardarm and secured the end to a cleat. Men from Little's gang held the officers at bay with the tips of their sabers against their gullets.

Dick Little grabbed Wrong John by the hair and pulled his head down. The hump on his back stuck up above his shoulders, looking like a second head cloaked in a white sheet. Young Little threw the noose over Wrong John's head and drew it snug around his neck. "I'm the—your commander," said Silverspoon, his voice cracking and choked. "And I order you to release me, and to—." The back of Little's hand came hard against his mouth. Silverspoon trembled, and a line of blood ran from his split lip.

"My commander? My commander? You call yourself that? You claim a position of leadership? You're nothing but a pirate and a thief, a murderer, a liar, and a fraud. How does it feel, governor, to have the coarse hemp against your privileged skin?" He looked hard at Wrong John and pulled up on the rope, causing Silverspoon's eyes to bulge and face to turn red. Little turned, his wife's head in his left hand, the taut rope in his right, and addressed an imaginary crowd.

"Hail the gathered ghosts with us to witness your lynching. Hail the Texans hung in your gallows. Hail my dear, sweet Martha, and the butchered Afghan children, and the Iraqi mothers, and the American soldiers, and the victims of 10-10—all the ghosts whose souls will not rest until you feel the full weight of your decisions against this noose, and this rope over the yardarm of Liberty."

He released his grip on the rope and signaled with his hand for young Little and his helper to hoist Captain Silverspoon into the air. They heaved to the rope, which brought Wrong John's hands to his throat, trying to assuage the rough choking. The tips of his toes lifted from the deck, and his eyes bugged out, and the veins on his forehead bulged. He began the famous hangman's waltz, tiptoes dancing against the unforgiving planks.

"*BRACK!*" Krill leaped up from the deck and clamped down with his beak on the hem of Wrong John's nightshirt, as if to pull him back down, but instead went up along with him.

Dagger should have had something to say, a confession to make (it was him, after all, who deserved to hang for betraying Martha Little), but all he could do was squeak, "Please, I don't want to die."

"So, it was you, Chief?" Little leapt at him and lunged with his sword. "You're the yellow cur?" Dagger stumbled backward and fell on his ass. Dick Little waved his sword at the row of officers and thrust Martha Little's head in their faces.

"We could have *preempted* the attack of 10-10. We had the evidence. There didn't need to be a war. Shalong could have kept his balls—he had no seed." He brought the wrinkled head to his chest and kissed it. "But you didn't. You didn't. You did nothing. Why? Why, I want to know? Hah! I'll tell you why. You wanted your mandate. You let Quota do the dirty work for you. Hah! You had an enemy to preempt all right!—the very spirit of American democracy!"

The next instant, a company of U.S. Navy sprang over the rail from all directions and set upon Little and his gang before they could get Wrong John aloft. The boy lost his grip on the rope, and Silverspoon fell to the deck. Little's gang hadn't a chance and were immediately subdued, disarmed, and locked in leg irons. Through it all, he cradled his wife's head in the crook of his elbow. The officers had gathered around their captain and tended to his wounds. He rubbed his throat and breathed deeply. It didn't take him long to regain his usual form. He walked up to Little, punched him in the gut, and as Little doubled over, kneed him in the mouth.

"You're a stupid bastard, Chicken Little. You never know when to shut your goddamned mouth! Do you?" He glared icily at the man bleeding profusely from the mouth. "You blabber on and on about the sky falling. Well guess what? It just fell on *you!* Now you're going to die, and so is your boy. You are a traitor!" He turned his back on Little and threw his hand into the air. "Take 'em up, boys."

As men from our crew came forward with ropes, Little pulled out a photo he had tucked in his shirt. "You might want to reconsider, Wrong John. I've got photos here of our boys torturing Iraqi citizens. It's really sick, considering we're the good guys, over there to demonstrate the virtues of democracy, due process, fairness, and all that—educating the heathen Arabs as to our advancement over the barbarian Shalong. There are lots of these that could start popping up in newspapers the world over."

Silverspoon turned on a dime and lunged for the photo. He looked at the image, then at his officers. "This is a fake. It has to be. America would never act like this. That's not who we are."

"Oh, it's real, Wrong John, just as real as Al Quota, and the love I had for my lady." Little's head dropped, and his face disappeared behind the messy blonde locks of his hair.

"We wouldn't do this, would we, Gunny?" Yo Yo stepped forward, took the photo and looked at it closely through the thick monocle of his one good eye.

"That's not torture, *per se,* it's more like, uh, teasing, being mean, you know, roughing them up. It's not *exactly* torture, in the truest sense of the word, because it's psy-ops, like I've been saying. Right, TP?" He handed the photo to Marshal Tosspot, who looked at it and stroked his pale jowls.

"That's correct, Yo Yo," TP said. "This image is a lark, really, not even close to the sort of severe bodily or mental harm required for it to be 'torture.'"

"Sure, I mean, come on, this guy didn't end up in Jahannum for jaywalking," said Yo Yo. "He's a bad guy, and in order to stop his squid buddies, we've got to know what they're up to. It's tough, I'll grant you, and it's mean, but not torture—not *exactly.*"

Silverspoon looked at Yo Yo and TP, his brow wrinkled, lower lip sucked into his mouth. Sir Yes Sir and Basma stood behind him, but looked away, off the bow, unable, it seemed, to embrace what they had been a party to.

"Is it torture?" Dick Little said, mocking the discussion. He paused to spit blood. "I don't know. Does it matter if you violate every international agreement on the matter? God help us! Of course it's torture, pure and simple, or if you wish, call it *terror*. You use it for your aims just as your enemy uses it for his. It's just a technique, right? a way to get what you want? I just wonder, in your eagerness to defeat evil, do you intend to carve away the darkness in your own hearts before or after you murder all your enemies?"

Wrong John walked past Little on his way to his cabin. In the doorway, he turned and said, "Let Little go. Burn the photograph. And Little, I want you to turn over any and all pictures of Jahannum in your possession, or I promise you, your son will die."

I went down the hatch and into the small cabin I shared with the Sioux. The image of Martha Little's severed head would not leave my mind. I almost wished that pecking thing would pry open my skull and lift that image from my memory. It brought me to the butchery of Quantrill's Raiders, the beheading we did, the scalping, the cutting out of tongues, the mutilation. Every time I closed my eyes, heads without bodies floated around me, their mouths moving, as if to speak, but nothing came out. I looked to our friend Mr. Melville for some comfort, a kindred soul who might understand the language of decapitation. I found something in Chapter 70, "The Sphynx," when Ahab looked upon the severed head of a sperm whale, hung from the side of his ship:

> Speak mighty head, and tell us the secret thing that is in thee.
> Of all divers, though hast dived the deepest... where in her
> murderous hold this frigate earth is ballasted with bones of
> millions of the drowned... Oh head! thou hast seen enough
> to split the planets, and make an infidel of Abraham, and not
> one syllable is thine!

Neither also did the head of Jane Smith have anything to tell me. Yet, to know old Ahab, like me, had stared at a severed head, and wished for it to speak its secret, brought me some comfort I would not have had alone. And

424 ~~ James E. Churches

while Silverspoon dog paddled on the surface, his secret agent had gone on a deep, deep dive, and had seen the bones in the belly of the whale.

Chapter XLVII

The Bare Yolks

The next few days were among the most somber I had spent with the Pirates of the Potomac. The captain locked himself in his quarters, took his meals there, alone, and conducted no meetings. The only other time he had been so withdrawn was after the 10-10 attack. The officers went about their business in Washington, leaving only Second Mate Sweet and Krill on board. It didn't look like Pinch was going to save Wrong John this time with baseball metaphors. She was busy on a major offensive for Dagger and Krill: cooking the budget numbers on a massive federal program to supply Mug-Wump and Frog-Gob liniment to every American citizen over the age of sixty. She had also been recruited in the War on Squid to spear the monster with American investment power.

Basmati Sweet had also locked herself in her cabin, and I did not see her. When I knocked on her door to inquire of her welfare, she told me to go away. More pumps had been brought to the bilge, and the clang of their action dominated the atmosphere day and night.

One evening after dinner, I lay in my bunk making some notes. Tatanka was in the kitchen, finishing up the dishes, banging pots and pans around. Someone came down the hatch. Whoever it was didn't say hello, or strike up a conversation, but only added to the clatter in the scullery. I knew by the wordless conversation it was the two black oaks, rooting and sun reaching in the silent melody of trees.

I lay in bed and considered my three years on *Liberty*. I had seen much and learned a great deal. I yearned to hear your voice, Frank, to wrassle with Jesse Jr., and hear a story from my good Mary. I wanted to sit with you, Frank, and share with you my idea to write a book about my latest adventures. Don't laugh, brother, I was serious!

All I wanted by then was to be away from *Liberty*, to be free of the madness of that voyage, to retire into a simple farming life with family and good friends. I had participated in enough pirate follies by then to have lost any taste for it. I had at last recognized the emptiness that blossoms from proud, wrathful desire. Revenge was how I had justified twenty years of robbery and violence, telling myself it was because of what the Union had done, what the Union had done, what the Union had done. Oh, they destroyed our simple farming ways, brought the coldness of machinery into our quiet, peaceful country. Tatanka, though, taught me our peace was pure charade, erected on the backs of African slaves and the Indians whose land we had taken. There can be no abiding peace built on a foundation of suffering and despair. So where, I wondered, was this elusive peace? Where was the home of solace and grace? Could it be found anywhere in America anymore?

All around me the War on Terror continued unabated. Explosions crackled over the river several times a day, because of threats, I presumed, detected by the Wrath of God airborne defense system. Militias patrolled our streets in search of the squid that were everywhere, and nowhere to be seen, lurking, plotting, preparing to kill us, only because of who we were. Boats full of supplies and troops sailed to the Middle East in a continuous stream of commerce for war. Boats full of blubber traveled the same route, so thick in the sea they were like stepping-stones from America to Arabia. Squid Alerts went to Code Orange, and mollusks flew like penalty flags at a football game, but aside from a few reports of foiled attempts, nothing happened. I could only guess that Tom Thumb received his wages through some new science invented by Dr. von Shlop—some new sort of barometer that measured the weight of fear in the air.

All manner of favors were bestowed on the friends of *Liberty*, in the name of Silverspoon's Mandate, which permitted any and every swindle so long as it was explained as a program to preempt an economic recession, preempt a diminishment of Christian values, or preempt a threat to our safety. Safety, that was the word, the all-powerful emblem of our brave new nation, under siege from omnipresent evil. Safety, we agreed, mattered more than anything,

anything, anything at all, as if we could, by building the walls of our barricades thick enough and hiring enough security forces to patrol them, prevent death itself from passing through.

I felt smothered by it. In my stomach, a knot had formed, and it never went away, a knot of sickness, of dread, for the life I would never have lived had my purpose been to avoid danger. In this new Silverspoon America, it seemed to me most lives were hardly worth living, for they contained no adventure, no risk, no recklessness, no whimsy.

I smiled, recalling exactly what Sweet had said that night on the *Shokanaw* when we made love. "You know, Ish, the best things in life can't be planned or anticipated. You've just got to close your eyes and let them happen." Those words, and nearly every other one that she or I had spoken that night, had become for me a new epitaph. I would be a less troublesome ghost one day because of them.

In Silverspoon America, everybody seemed to agree that nothing should be done with wild abandon. It had to be planned, protected, and made safe. Yes, safe, always and above all else safe. So safe it was safe from living, and ended up something in between this world and the next. In this sadly safe new world, outlaws were outlawed, and we would never know another James and Younger Gang, or a Butch Cassidy, Billy the Kid, Calamity Jane, or a Molly B'Damned. It struck me funny that the full course of the safety game would be for Silverspoon to outlaw himself—he *was* a pirate, after all. In this safe new world of Silverspoon's, the marshal was right to remove the dangerous breasts of Lady Liberty, to cut off the fullness of their mystery, the fearless longing in them, their impossible, perilous beauty.

But in the end, the one who wants to outlaw danger, outlaw impulsiveness, excessive passion, mysterious squid, and the wild beast within us all, has to be questioned. We have to wonder, to what end does this person want us to be so passive, docile, domesticated? What does this person gain from pacifying us, if not, as had come to be, to rob us and turn us into slaves? Anyone who says he wants to make you safe, don't trust that man. What he really wants is to control you and manipulate you, and get you to do *his* bidding ahead of your own. Don't trust this man, who says there is danger only he can protect you from—especially if *he* is the source of the danger. That's when the hackles should go up and the sword of doubt made sharp.

From the kitchen, the two black walnut trees had settled in at the kitchen table. I could hear them sipping coffee. Finally, one of them spoke a human word.

"You know, Lakota, when that rope went over the yard for Silverspoon, I wanted to put my head in the noose," said Sir Yes Sir slowly, his voice somber, grating, like gears calling out for oil.

"Wasn't you betrayed his wife," replied the Sioux in his flat, low voice.

"Wasn't it? I was there when the scheme was hatched. I didn't object. I'm the one who presented the phony war evidence to the Common Countries. If we hadn't gone to war in Iraq, Martha Little would have never been ordered into the Chastity Belt's palace. I've given my voice, my authority, my credibility, to everything we've done." His chair slid against the floor, as if he had pushed away from the table.

Tatanka sipped his coffee. A match popped and hissed. Tobacco smoke wafted into my small room. The bilge pumps provided a constant, uneven, troublesome rhythm underneath their conversation.

"Honestly, Tatanka, I'm a complete failure as a diplomat. They gave me a title, but it might as well have been 'boy.' They preach the gospel of colorblindness. They're not colorblind. They know damn well I'm black, and my blackness is a tool for them. My military service is a tool. Trot out the big black man. Give him a fancy title. Everybody will believe him." His chair fell back and slammed against the wall. I could hear his heavy footsteps pacing the small galley. "It makes me sick."

Another chair slid. I could barely hear Tatanka's soft steps. He walked over by the stove, then back to the table. "Here. I made this for you."

"My goodness. It's amazing. I couldn't. You've worked too hard. I can't accept this." I could picture that piece of scrimshaw he had been scraping on with his yellow jackknife these last months.

"There was never any other purpose. It is yours."

"My gosh. Thank you. Thank you so much. It's so amazing. I've never seen anything like it."

"The white buffalo calf woman came to my people, long time ago. She brought the sacred pipe. It is the center of our religion. I do not know the answer for you. I do not know how you can find your lost honor. I offer to you only what the white buffalo calf woman offered to us—the way of prayer."

He moved back to the table and sat down. I had never heard him speak so many words. And he was not yet done.

"There is all this talk of White Whales, dark squid, evil this and evil that. There is only evil that lives in the hearts of men. That is the *only* place to hunt it. In my way, we talk about the sacred hoop, the wheel of life. It has all the colors on it: red, yellow, black, and white. None is better than the other. None worse. All people. We are here together. The earth is mother to every one of her children. The sun of *Wakan Tanka* shines down on each of us with equal light, equal warmth. It does not decide who deserves love. You are here, and blessed, Sir Yes Sir. I do not judge you. Find your prayer way. Find your peace."

I don't know how Sir Yes Sir reacted to the Lakota's words. He did not speak. I can only say that his blessing found its way to my heart, and would be welcome to live there beside that rusty old bullet for as long as I lived.

Three days later, Wrong John Silverspoon emerged from his cloister wearing those shiny blue pants and funny pillow shoes that told me he was going for a jog. I polished Widowmaker—careful, as I always was since my youthful accident, to make sure she was unloaded—and watched him take off on a run across the deck. He continued on, teasing and taunting everyone he encountered. I shook my head, knowing his good spirits meant only one thing: the pirate adventures of Wrong John Silverspoon were not yet finished.

After his jog and a little weightlifting, the captain retired to his quarters to clean up and take his breakfast. I served his coffee and asked as to his spirits.

"Ish, I'm an optimist at heart. I just can't help—like the Great Communicator—to look on the bright side of life. Yes, we've had some tough times, and they aren't over, but I have to keep the focus on the positive. That's just my nature." He jabbed at the bare yolks of his sunny-side-up eggs with the sharp corner of a crisp piece of toast.

I almost dropped the pot of coffee. "But you were nearly lynched less than a week ago. And your agent, Mrs. Little—they took her head because you wanted to get even with her old man."

"I'd like to have the luxury to linger on the negative. That dudn't serve the American people. Am I leading by example if I stew about this or that secret agent who blew her mission? No, I am not. I lead by leading, which is to say, do by doing. If I'm not doing by doing then who's going to do it?"

I wanted to dump the steaming coffee over his head. I had seen this pattern too many times not to understand the sort of pathology at play with him. I had seen it in Quantrill and Bloody Bill, and Clel Miller and Archie Clement and—okay, Frank, I'll admit it—Jesse James too. I had come to think of it as becoming unhinged, when the purpose of the mission becomes separated from the actions of the man. He stands there, backward at the helm, but thinks he's facing forward. He tells himself what he does is for the mission, but there is actually no longer a connection to it. The action is unhinged, has no link to his values, to anything that makes him human. These men, these unhinged ones, had a few things in common: they had lost the ability to feel, they had lost the capacity to consider themselves or their actions, they had surrounded themselves with people who feared them and would not risk attracting their ire.

Before I could respond to Wrong John's pablum about leadership, the ship's engineer stormed into the cabin. "Mr. Captain, sir, begging your pardon, but we've got to find dry dock. We simply cannot continue like this or the weight of the pumps alone will take us to the bottom."

"Did we have an appointment?" asked Silverspoon, working a toothpick between his teeth.

"No, but sir, this is an emergency."

"A'right, gimme the details. Twenty words or less."

"If we do not seek repairs, the ship will sink."

"Ten to spare. You want to purchase for reserve or use 'em up?"

"Captain! The ship will sink. Glug, glug, glug. Understand?" He made a circular motion with his finger as of water going down a drain.

"Used 'em up. Your choice." He took a big slurp of coffee. "You see, Ish. This here's exactly what I'm talking about. I got a fella standing here can't see past a problem. Pure negative. Not my style. I see a hole and wonder what good will come through it. He sees a hole and says the ship will sink. Night and day."

430 ～ James E. Churches

The engineer hyperventilated, clenched his fists, jerked his head to the side, and stomped out of the cabin. Silverspoon continued to pick his teeth— unhinged, like I said, not able to be touched. I wasn't about to attempt any influence over him concerning the imminent sinking of his boat. He simply did not want to hear it, and by not wanting to, he didn't. How can I condemn him, brother? How obstinate was I about going up to Minnesota to punish that Yankee Radical, Adelbert Ames, when we knew nothing about Northfield country and had none of our friends to help us? I can only comment by the nature of my own flaws what I saw in Wrong John Silverspoon.

I carried his breakfast dishes out of his quarters, and while on deck, saw a long boat rowed by twenty strong men approaching *Liberty*. As it drew closer, I could see it contained Gunny, Tosspot, and Dagger. At the same time, another boat, a small steamer, bore down on *Liberty* from the south. The two arrived at almost the same time, and as the officers came aboard, I noticed a third approaching, another longboat, that flew the flag of the press corps.

The officers gathered on the bridge to discuss a new plan the three had conceived. They had just gotten into it when the officers from the steamer came on board with bad news from Iraq. Several major bombs had gone off in Baghdad, the worst of which had destroyed the Common Countries headquarters and killed the lead diplomat. The CC had decided to pull out of Iraq, not to return until its safety could be assured.

Gunny threw up his hands. "We never said we'd protect them. They want to be in there, they've got to secure their own headquarters. I mean, really, how can you keep the peace when you can't even protect yourself?"

"Worse than that, they've given a victory to the terrorists. They've said, 'Hurt me, and I'll run.' Exactly the wrong message to send to AQ and Shalong," said the Chief.

"How many was that?" asked the captain.

"How many what? Bombs? How many dead? What?" replied the Chief.

"No, words. How many words? Did I set a limit yet?"

The other three looked at each other. Gunny cleared his throat. TP puts his hands together at his chest and looked toward the sky. Chief sucked his teeth and tugged on the gold hoop in his right ear. "How about we play no limit, Mr. Captain. Just take the lid off the whole Scrabble game."

"Risky, Chief. You got the cash to cover it?"

"Come on, sir, remember me, former CEO of Hellbent Industries, chairman of the shadow board. Can I cover it? Come on."

"Okay, great, so who's next?"

Tosspot spoke up. "I just think these events show the complete bankruptcy of the peace process with these heathens. They are a Godless, evil race, and they can only be dealt with by the harshest of hands."

"Gunny?"

"Intelligence, sir. It's all about information, resources, data. This isn't a matter of TNT ripping apart buildings and bodies. It's an idea that somebody, somewhere hatched, and we've got to beat it out of them just exactly who and where, before it happens again."

"Preempt, good. Like it. Chief?"

"As I said, they're playing right into the hands of the squid. It's whole point is reach around behind you and tickle your back—bring up the hackles. I say let the CC run. It's just one less nose sticking into our business."

"Agree." I informed the captain a press boat had pulled alongside. "Damn those ticks! Can't we just, you know, exterminate the pests?" I shrugged. He strode over to the side of the ship, beneath the grisly free-speech zone, and addressed them. "What the hell do you want now?"

"We heard the news about the bombings in Baghdad and were just wondering how concerned you are that the CC headquarters was destroyed."

"Well, I'll tell ya, I'm not concerned at all. Proconsul Blackbeard sees it as a very positive sign, and I agree with him. Shows we've got the Giant Squid on the run."

"But this had nothing to do with squid. It was a wagon of wool with explosives hidden in it," said the reporter.

"And where do you think wool comes from? There's some naked squid running around Baghdad, I can guarantee you."

"How is this a positive sign?"

"Gunny? You want to volley that one?"

"Sure, captain, I'd be happy to." Yo Yo stepped to the rail. "People, you've got to understand the Arab psyche to appreciate the extraordinary success this represents for us. Your Arab respects you when you can bring your enemy out of the shadows, lure him out like a rat to a trap, and make him show his hand. These bombings are a clear signal that the enemies of freedom hold a weak hand, that they're desperate, hopeless, and lost."

"It doesn't look that way to me," said a reporter. "It looks to me like they're determined, strategic, and emboldened. It begins to look as if we're losing control of Iraq before we ever got it."

"Chief?" said Wrong John.

Dagger did not hesitate. "Do you think it's your job to demoralize our fighting men and women in Iraq by suggesting they aren't doing their job? Does it make you feel good to criticize those willing to make the ultimate sacrifice for their country?"

"I'm not criticizing the troops. I'm questioning the thinking behind our campaign in Iraq. I totally support the troops. I have a cousin over there."

"Sure you do," Dagger continued. "Why don't you call on Dick Little and tell him his wife died for no reason, that it was a lost cause. Go tell *him* she wasted her life attempting to stop evil in its tracks." Now there was a guy with some balls, I thought,—after what had happened with Dick Little, to mention him and his wife *in support* of your point—that was sinister.

"Okay," said the captain, "that about covers it. Now if you'll excuse us, we were in a meeting about how to protect America from terror."

"But we're not done. Speaking of Dick Little, who was it on *Liberty* that outed his wife?"

"And what about the rumor we've been torturing Iraqis?"

Wrong John drew his pistol and fired a shot over the reporters' heads. "Are you deaf or something? When I say it's over, it's over. That means no more questions. Not one more word. Now beat it!" He turned and walked into his quarters.

Chapter XLVIII

Two Thousand Shares in Tamil Tigers

After his conversation in the galley with Tatanka, Sir Yes Sir disappeared. I did not know if he was on assignment, or had quit, but I didn't see him for quite some time. News from Iraq continued to be grim. The war had indeed begun, and it was ugly. I had been to Baghdad, down those narrow streets and alleys, those labyrinthine corridors. I could not imagine trying to fight an enemy that knew its way through those timeless mazes. At home, Ellis Outland, and the tax relief program began to cause economic problems. The national debt had spiraled out of control, and jobless people were getting angry. *Liberty* needed a—as Wrong John liked to say—"pick-me-up."

Less than a week later, we were back in New York, in the heart of the stock exchange just minutes before the opening bell. Krill had orchestrated the event as an exercise of the *Congreso Mandato*, a foray into the world of friendly mollusks, where a positive reception could be counted on.

A stage had been set up against a bank of windows—the very ones, I learned, through which several suicide storks had flown the day of the attack on America. A broad American flag hung behind us, and two more flags hung from stands at either end of the stage. The rail of the stage had been decorated with red, white, and blue ribbon, patriotic starbursts, and blue vases stuffed with red and white roses. The tickers clattered with news from foreign markets; loud chatter reverberated off the high ceilings and resonated from the oak floor stained with sweat; the place oozed an intoxicating smell, one that reminded me of the inside of a bank vault. I liked it.

I had never been in a beehive of so much excitement. Men in dark business suits and black top hats or bowlers milled about the floor, arguing loudly about the day of trading ahead. I was told the exchange was always like this, but even more so on a day when the captain of *Liberty* intended to unveil some unexpected new financial boon. The head of the exchange pounded his gavel, quieted the crowd, and introduced Captain Silverspoon. The captain waved and received a nice round of applause.

"Hey, I'm honored to be back in New York, at ground zero, where I heard you ask me to punish those who attacked America. I have done so in spades, and continue to do in triplicate. Soon we'll have the entire wardrobe of ladies lingerie strung up in the closet. Today I'm back, in the financial capital of the world, to kick a little more tar out of the bad guys. As usual—you know me by now—I'm going to hit them before they hit us. This time the weapon is not assassins, or secret retribution centers, or military operations. This time I'm going to get 'em by unleashing the power of capital and profitability. I'm going to let you, the financial barons of Wall Street, bust their balls by making a buck off of them. I'd like to introduce my financial chief, Pinch, to give you the details."

Pinch stepped forward, smiled genuinely with her large, crooked teeth, wiped imaginary sweat from her forehead, smiled again, coughed a couple of times, and began. "Thank you, Mr. Captain. What a leader, huh?" She pointed at him with both of her hands, palms up. The investors applauded generously. "Boy, I'll say. What a guy. So, yes, as he said, we've got a real opportunity for you at the opening bell today, a whole new market, a whole new game, that puts you, our greatest weapon, on the front line in the War on Squid."

She pulled at the edges of her blouse, which was just a little small and didn't quite reach her skirt. "You and I know the squid are out there, plotting and planning, ginning up their next big caper against America and our allies. Now, we're going to stop most of them, but nobody's perfect, so now and again, they're going to pull one off. Your job is to throw your market savvy, your analytical talent at predicting trends, against their devious minds, and lay down capital predicting what they will do." The crowd reacted with a mixture of excitement, surprise, wonder, and, I detected, some anger.

"It'll go month by month, so, starting with May, you invest in the Terror Futures Market by saying when, where, and who will commit an act of terrorism. You gamble on how—and how many will die. For example, let's say you're convinced Hezbollah is going to launch a mortar attack on an Israeli border outpost on May 15 that will kill three Israeli soldiers. You contact your investors, raise the capital, and throw it into the market. If the attack happens as you have predicted, big time pay off, up to a thousand, even ten thousand, percent return overnight. Another time, maybe you think it will be a Moscow train bomb by Chechen separatists, June 8, killing fifty Ruskies. Raise the capital and invest." Now the traders raised their voices, and jostled one another on the packed floor.

"Hear me out. Hear me out," said Pinch, raising her long thin hands. "Just imagine the fury of the terrorists when they find out savvy American investors made some nice coin off of their devious act of savagery. Boy, will they be peeved, and our wager is, a lot less likely to try it again in the future. As everybody knows, money talks. So let's let our money do the talking!

"Captain Silverspoon, ring the opening bell!" The captain took up the ceremonial hammer and slammed it into the bell. Nobody moved. There was total silence. He grinned nervously and banged the bell once more. Nothing. I looked out over the crowd and did not see a single face that appeared excited by the new opportunity. Those faces, unmoved and vigilant—it was Northfield all over again, Frank. I've told the story. Rather than hide from us the way we were accustomed—our sawed-off attitude was by that time legendary—those Minnesotans stood their ground and fought us, and won. The same sort of faces looked back at Wrong John from the trading floor that morning. I didn't know what to expect, but I instinctively lowered my hands to the pearl butts of my guns.

"What are you waitin' for?" asked Wrong John. "Where's that New York minute we've heard so much about?"

This was apparently the cue for our shills dispersed in the crowd to grease the wheels. "I'll take a thousand shares of Tontons Macoutes, political assassination, Port-au-Prince, Haiti, June 5, three dead," hollered Speck from the left side of the floor.

"Sold!" said Silverspoon, banging the bell.

"Five thousand shares of Armata Corsa, September 11, train bombing, Nice, France, eight killed," yelled the quartermaster, twenty feet to the left of Bill.

"Excellent investment," said the captain, again, hitting the bell.

"Sixty-five hundred in Hamas, November 6, suicide bombing, Tel Aviv, Israel, public bus, seventeen dead," hollered the second Bill, fifteen feet to Bill's right.

"Slam dunk. You just *know* they're gonna do it." Wrong John banged the bell. After that, no one spoke, and the determined, seething brokers stared at the captain. "So who's next?"

"Two-thousand shares in Tamil Tigers, December 25, sniper fire, Negombo, Sri Lanka, seven de—." A punch to the stomach stopped Speck mid-sentence. The quartermaster bravely attempted to put forward an offer for the Columbian National Liberation Army but was thrown to the ground.

Someone yelled in a loud baritone, "This is truly depraved, Silverspoon. Have you completely lost your mind?"

"Hey, nothin' personal. It's just business, right?" he replied.

Another yelled, "I lost my brother in the attack of 10-10. Do you think it would soothe mom to know somebody got rich predicting it would happen?"

Said another, "What's to prevent the terrorists for investing in their own crimes?"

"Well see, that's just it, that's the trap," said Silverspoon. "We'll track their financial activities, and when a lot of money shows up behind a certain evil commodity, we'll know it's them, and—and, we won't pay them, see, we won't pay them even if they hit."

The Chief stepped forward. "What he means is that we'll know where they're going to strike by following the money. That way we can preempt the attack before it happens. Just follow the money."

"But then you're interfering with the market," said a small man in a nasally voice. "If I've got a million dollars riding on the New People's Army to bomb a bank in Manila, I don't want you getting in the way."

"We'll compensate you for the loss," Dagger said. The small man threw his notebook to the ground and walked off the floor.

"Compensate? Come on," said the baritone. "The very idea is gruesome. Only a scurvy pirate could feel good about making money off of terror and death."

"Look. I didn't invent the Giant Squid. It's a terrible thing, and terrible things must be treated in terrible ways," said Wrong John. He dropped his notes and bent over to pick them up.

"Oh my God!" someone shouted. "What's that growing on his back?"

"He's turning into some kind of a monster!" shouted another.

"It's a curse!" yelled the baritone. "He's cursed, and he's bringing a curse on all businessmen. He's making it so we're ashamed to admit we do business for a living."

"Some of us still care more about our country than we do about making a buck!" someone yelled.

"Tell you what," said Silverspoon. "Just as a favor between friends, we'll provide 'undisclosed' access to intelligence reports."

"You can't be serious. Insider trading tips to encourage investment in terror?" roared the baritone.

"What're friends for?" said Silverspoon. The baritone retorted with a stream of epithets. Someone else swore back at him and questioned his patriotism. The two yelled back and forth.

Someone else interjected, "What about breaking up their operations? What about stopping the killing? Shouldn't that be your priority?"

"Yeah, and what about developing better relations with the Muslim world?" cried a man with a raspy voice. "What about treating them like human beings and trying to better understand their grievances? That's the only way we'll ever end this madness."

"Where are Shalong's Weapons of Mass Hysteria?" bellowed another man. "That was the whole reason we went to war."

"What about Al Quota?" someone yelled. "Isn't he the one who attacked us?"

"Shut up!" a young man yelled. "We've got to stand with our president. Not tear him down."

"Why should we? He's ruining the country," said an old man.

"Then go ahead and leave! Move to France where they love tyrants," the young one countered.

"You move. This is *my* country," retorted the old man.

"Stuff it!" snapped another Silverspoon supporter. "We need to reorder the Middle East for the safety of the world."

"And what about 10-10?" interjected a small man with an Indian accent. "How can we trust a commission headed by Dr. Henchman? He should be on trial, not pretending an investigation into your negligence. When are you going to take responsibility?"

"You want to know where the buck stops? Huh? That it? It stops right here." At that, Wrong John reached into the breast pocket of his jacket and pulled out a black leather billfold. "When it lands in my wallet!" He chuckled in loutish grunts, mugging to his officers. I quietly pulled Peace- and Widowmaker and held them at my sides.

"You know what, Silverspoon? *You're bad for business!*" shouted a trader, giving Silverspoon what Pinch told me later was "the ultimate insult."

Some of the brokers booed and threw pens and pencils and notepads at us. Others cheered and pledged their support for their captain. Arguments broke out on the floor and quickly degenerated into a brawl. Traders yelled and screamed, punched, kicked, bit, pulled hair. A few angry men rushed the stage and tore at the railing, snapping wood and the red, white, and blue ribbons. Another group attacked them and advised us to get away before it was too late. All the while, the ticker tape rolled on, clacking out the latest news about the flow of money in the financial fish tank of the world.

Pinch lifted Tom Thumb onto her shoulders and he pitched small, purple squid at the rioting businessmen. "Unsportsmanlike conduct! Pass interference! Encroachment! Elevated Squid Alert! Code Red! Duck and cover! Too many players on the field! Illegal block! Half the distance to the goal!" he boomed in his deep voice, slapping the brokers in the face with floppy, fishy, purple squid. I found it odd to have a pitching frenzy of squid into a fish tank of friendly mollusks—an unexpected blurring of the lines between friend and foe.

I fired half-a-dozen rounds into the air, and ran for the back door. Silverspoon followed me. I piled into a waiting coach. Silverspoon and his crew clambered in after me. We escaped at a full gallop, hooves clattering on the cobblestone, wooden wheels banging and creaking, the driver yelling, "Clear the way! Mandate emergency."

"What did they mean about me turning into a monster?" Wrong John said, his voice shaky from the bumpy road. "That wasn't very neighborly." He looked out the window.

I wasn't going to explain. He had a growth on his back bigger than a football, and he didn't know it was there—or at least refused to admit that it was. You can't talk to a man like that.

"Bad for business?" he questioned. "Kiss my grits. I'm in the business of business. Whether I am or am not bad for business is my own damn business!" He punched the door of the coach. "From now on I speak to military audiences only—good patriotic folk who can follow orders."

Chapter XLIX

Ding Dong Shalong Is Gone

I was starting to have the feeling, after our hasty retreat from Wall Street—one place you would assume "the CEO president" would be well received—that there was nowhere left to hide for the Silverspoon gang. It was that all too familiar feeling an outlaw gets after he realizes he has pulled one too many jobs in too close a succession, providing too fresh a trail for the posse. Even though I was a desperado for twenty years, I never much liked the feeling that wherever I went, some Pinkerton, marshal, bounty hunter, or vigilante, might turn up round any corner and try to gun me down. That's why my best hideouts were in my hometown of Kearney, Missouri, as I've said, in and amongst my people, under the simple alias of Tom Howard. Down in Kearney, folks saw me not as a criminal, but an avenger of injustice for the Old South. I was beginning to wonder if Wrong John Silverspoon had a Kearney anywhere in America, where he could become an Ishcabibble, like Tom Howard, and just blend in and be left alone.

Where he ended up was aboard *Liberty*, a ship now entirely occupied with pumping bilge water, incapable of sailing as a ship of state, not even as a vessel in a whaling fleet—nothing but a big, fat, waterlogged, corporate bordello. I can tell you, having outrun a posse or two, the last thing you wanted was to be a sitting duck, fat and slow, out in clear sight, but that's what we were on *Liberty*. Delegations of concerned citizens, reporters, congressmen and women, foreign dignitaries, you name it, harried us every day. Up in the sky, buzzards circled, grown to a flock of more than twenty. Corporate lobbyists treated *Liberty* like a private yacht they had hired, and could be found any time of the day or night loitering on deck, climbing up to the crow's-nest to "take in the view," raiding the kitchen, firing cannons for kicks, furling and unfurling the sails, competing to see who could raise his corporate logo higher up the masthead, writing new regulations for their industries as if composing love poems to a favorite mistress, while they casually chewed sunflower seeds and spit the husks on deck—even getting drunk, despite Silverspoon's strict prohibition of alcohol.

Wrong John tolerated the lobbyists—what else could he do? they represented his employers—but he had completely lost his patience with the intrusions, and almost never deigned to answer anyone's questions—unless Krill had cleared them as somebody who could be counted on to cover for him.

To say Wrong John could use a piece of good news about that time would be a serious understatement. What he needed was a miracle, and he got one: the capture of Shalong. News arrived via the *Shokanaw*, and our guardian angel, Admiral Olive. He chugged alongside in his beefy, four-masted steamer, flying a crisp American flag, with a complement of sharp sailors, shining cannons, a spiffy deck, metal polished and looking very precise, very military.

Shokanaw hailed us and asked permission to come aboard—quickly granted according to Krill's new Presidential Access Guideline Matrix. The officers interrupted a campaign strategy meeting in the captain's roundhouse to receive the admiral. Silverspoon ran to the rail and welcomed Olive aboard, even gave him a big bear hug, which the admiral stiffly received, hands at his sides. "So, tell us, Yarn, to what do we owe the leisure of your company this fine evening?" Silverspoon asked.

The admiral smiled. A couple of lobbyists barged in and asked for Olive's autograph. He scribbled his name in their books and asked them to leave. The remainder of the officers arrived and gathered forward of the try-works.

"Sir, I have some very good news for you," Olive said.

"Spell it out, swabbie," Wrong John said.

"The Kurdish militia captured Shalong near Tikrit, and they're ready to hand him over to us for certain 'assurances.'"

"I got him? You mean I got him?" exclaimed Wrong John. Olive nodded. "Yeehaw!"

"Assurances?" asked Gunny, looking lizard-eyed through his monocle.

"What do they mean, assurances? We've been protecting them from Shalong for ten years."

"Well, sir, that's true, but they want us to assure their autonomy in a future Iraqi federation."

"Christ, Olive, tell them whatever they want to hear," said Dagger. He sucked his gold canines and shot Olive with small-caliber displeasure bullets from his bloodshot eyes. "Then you tell them we want a little quid pro quo. Tell them to stick Shalong in a hole somewhere and let the Americans capture him—get a lot of photos, spin off a couple of new American heroes. I want Proconsul Blackbeard front and center. We don't get mile one out of the Kurds capturing the Chastity Belt for us."

"*BRACK! Mission Accomplished II.* First we took his country. Then we took his soul." Krill flapped his wings and whistled *Hello Dolly*. He jumped from Wrong John's shoulder to his copper lamp resting on a bench, and mumbled, "What's the key? What's the key?"

"Did you get my souvenir?" asked the captain, so excited he bounced up and down, splashing in the water that flowed from the bilge pumps, out the iron pipe, and across the deck. "Did you get it? What did you get me, Olive? What did you get me?"

Olive snapped his fingers, and a smart sailor presented him a wooden case carved with intricate floral designs. Olive opened it and removed an antique Persian scimitar in a golden scabbard. He withdrew the sword, and presented it in the palms of his hands to Wrong John Silverspoon. The handle was decorated in shining gold and glittering rubies and emeralds. The long, curving blade was inscribed with flowing hieroglyphics.

"Yes, sir, we did manage to get something from the Kurds especially for you." He handed the sword to Silverspoon. "He was wearing this when they captured him." Wrong John greedily took the sword, shoved it back into the scabbard, and attached it to his belt. He pulled the blade, and placed his right index finger above his lip, pretending a thick moustache. He strutted back and forth before the try-works.

"I'd like a statue of me there," Silverspoon said, voice lowered an octave, pointing with the sword. "I want a mural of me on the side of that building, all calendars to be Shalong every month of the year, all hotel bath towels with me embroidered on them, uh, a song about me to be sung every morning by the children in school. Oh, and you over there, go dig a mass grave for yourself and your family. And, you, over there, you're arrested for having too few paintings of me in your house. You will be tortured until you confess your love for the ayatollah, at which time you will be killed, as will all of your family, and placed into a mass grave. And you, little darling, shall be set aside for my pleasure whenever I feel like it—then tortured, killed, and thrown in a mass grave with all of your kin." Wrong John dropped the fake finger moustache and chuckled and gloated at his officers. He slapped the sword against his thigh, as if it were the bottom of an under-achieving student in his No Child's Behind act.

"Has the thing got a name, Olive? You know, like Excalibur or something?" asked Wrong John.

"Typical of him, he named his sword after himself."

"What? You got to be joshin' me. I got Shalong's *Shalong?* God damn! Who needs his *cojones?* I got his friggin' bat!" He hooted and jogged quickly in place.

"I know this is a sore subject, sir, ever since Chicken Little made such a fuss, but, we need to find out what the Chastity Belt is hiding," said Yo Yo.

"And?"

"I'm not advocating we *torture* Shalong, *per se*, but I don't think we should play pat-a-cake with him either."

"God, don't start up with cakes again, not after the way they skewered me over the Little Judys. Jiminy Christmases!" Wrong John played at drawing his sword and thrusting at an imaginary opponent.

"You're right, Gunny," said the Chief. "We've got to work him hard, find out where he hid the WMHs, get him to rat out these holdouts so we can piratize the blubber trade and make this whole deal worth our trouble."

"It's legally not torture," said TP, "if you *accidentally* hurt the individual. Our guys just say, 'Sorry I broke his nose—slipped on a banana peel.' Furthermore, when all's said and done, His Majesty the Commander-in-Chief is not beholden to any quaint treaty or law on the matter. His sovereign right is to do what he sees as best for national security, so—"

"Mess him up," said Wrong John. "The sombitch tried to kill my daddy."

He parried an imaginary opponent. "Break his leg, break his arm, I don't care. Just don't break the law." He winked at Yo Yo and Tosspot, and dispatched Admiral Olive back to Baghdad with orders to depict a graphic capture of Shalong by Proconsul Blackbeard—and permission to "do whatever it takes" to get information out of him. Olive saluted and strode away.

Krill jumped from his lamp onto the try-works lid. He flapped and waddled across the ivory presidential seal. "*BRACK!* Call up the Mandate Media. Ring in the Clown Criers. 'Silverspoon Catches the Evil Chastity Belt of Baghdad. Huzzah! Huzzah! The Squid is in the Slammer!' Get 'em out here. We've got a re-election to sew up." Speck jumped in a whaleboat and rowed to Washington. He returned two-and-a-half hours later, followed by two longboats crammed with reporters and photographers, loudly speculating on the scoop at hand.

While the specksynder had been out gathering reporters, Wrong John and Krill rehearsed the *Mission Accomplished II* show. By the time the audience arrived, they were ready. Members of the press knew the news had to be extremely positive when they were invited on board and seated in chairs instead of being left to bob in the river.

The captain stepped to the quarterdeck rail to address the reporters gathered before the try-works. He pulled Shalong's sword and pointed it at the group. "What I am holding is what you call your sword. Not just any sword, but the sword of a very nasty *hombre*. Can anyone guess whose sword it might be?" He slashed and thrust at an imaginary opponent.

"Shalong's?" asked a woman reporter at the rear of the group.

"God damn it!" shouted the captain. He slammed the sharp edge of the sword into the rail, sending off a spray of wood chips. "Did I call on you? Huh? Did I?" He pointed the sword accusingly at the bespectacled older woman. "Well, did I?—whatever your name is—didn't I tell you people to wear name tags? Well, did I?" Reporters nervously scooted and scratched their chairs away from him.

"Uh, no sir, you didn't. But, well, it sounded like an open-ended question. So—"

"So you just thought you could break the rules because you're *so* smart. Well you can't. The rules is there to protect the rules, and to make sure the rules remain rules as long as rulers rule them. Now, who has a legitimate guess as to whose sword this might be?" Several hands went up.

"Bob?"

"King Henry the Eighth's?"

"Way cold. Shirley?"

"Ivan the Terrible's?"

"Warmer. Bill."

"Genghis Khan's?"

"Heating up. Joanne?"

"Alexander the Great's."

"Ouch! Hotter than a pancake griddle. Jer?"

"Hannibal's?"

"Who the hell's that? Char?"

"This is just a wild guess, but Al Quota's?"

"Whoa! Scorching me alive. Ahh, I'm melting—but no. Brenda?"

"Could it be Shalong's?"

"Bingo. You got it. Ding dong, Shalong is gone. You get the prize, a—"

"Hey, no fair. I picked Shalong first guess," said the bespectacled older woman.

Wrong John pointed his sword at her and stared at her with his narrow, intense eyes, nostril's flared, ears reddening, sword hand quivering. Mercifully, two sailors grabbed the woman and threw her overboard before Wrong John skewered her. The captain calmed down after he heard the splash and cry of "Help! I can't swim."

"Yes, folks, this is the sword of a thug, the rapier of a tyrant, the cutlass of a madman, the scythe of a sicko, the blade of a butcher—you get my drift. I may not have got his 'nads, but at least I got his stinger. Shalong's *Shalong*." He ran a finger along the sharp edge of the sword. "Ouch!" He licked the blood. "Get me another purple heart, would you, Basma!" He shook his hand, grimaced, and jerked his head sideways.

"Thanks to me, evil no longer runs loose in the streets of our cities. No longer does it have free rein to distribute Weapons of Mass Hysteria to the minions of Satan." He slashed wildly at the air, turned, and accidentally (I think) severed a rope that held a block and tackle from a yard. It fell from the rigging, landed on one of the reporters, and knocked her unconscious. Silverspoon continued.

"No longer, ladies and gentlemen, can Numb Nuts build yellow cake bombs laced with poison frog juice for delivery to our cities. No longer can he play bridge with AQ, and gloat with him about the slaughter of 10-10.

"And so, as I said before, only this time I mean it, Mission Impossible!— er, Accomplished!" He thrust Shalong's sword into the air. The crew cheered enthusiastically. The reporters clapped respectfully. "I got him, folks. I captured Shalong. Got him on ice in the hoosegow. This means an end to the terrorist insurgency by his remnant followers. It means big-time wedgies until he tells the location of his banned weapons. It means peace, prosperity, and safety for America, Iraq, and the world."

"How can you have captured Shalong when you're in America, and he's in Iraq? Don't you mean Proconsul Blackbeard captured Shalong?" asked a reporter.

"What's the differ'nce? Proconsul Blackbeard is my proconsul. As his president, he is mine, and therefore everything he done, I did. He is me and I am he, the two of us as one in saving America."

"Do you think it's possible the inspectors may have been right, that there were no illegal weapons left in Iraq?" asked another reporter.

"I done covered that one already—'member the box of yellow cakes?"

"That has been entirely invalidated by Dick Little," the reporter retorted.

"Oh yeah." He looked down and scratched his cheek.

"*BRACK!* Piddle, diddle, Little. Nothing but a liberal patsy," said Krill.

"Now hold your horses, there," said Wrong John, pointing his sword over the press corps. "Who gave the signal to dog pile on Silverspoon?"

"There wasn't—I didn't see any signal. It's just that, well, traditionally, when we get invited out here it's understood that what we do is ask questions."

"Understood, is it? Funny, I didn't get that memo. I thought it was: Wrong John talks, you listen, and if he's in the mood, you get to ask a polite question—if, and only *if*, he calls on you, one question, twenty word limit. Did he call on you?"

"Well, no, but—"

"No buts. The captain didn't call on you, so shut your gob. Any further questions?" He looked idly at the fingernails of his right hand. "No? Okay, great, now run off and print your little stories about how I captured Shalong. Already got my purple heart, see?" He showed the medal he had given himself after Yarn's story of the Iraqi invasion. "Shoo, shoo." He scooted the press away with a dusting from the backs of his hands, then turned and sauntered into his cabin.

The reporters stood from their chairs and moved to the gunwale. "Look!" one of them shouted. "It's Dr. Henchman!"

Wrong John ran to the rail and waved. Henchman stood at the bow of a longboat, waving. He wore thick black glasses on his nose, a dark suit, and had his wiry gray hair slicked back. He waved at Silverspoon and smiled.

"Back to your seats, class," the captain said. "Looks like Dr. Henchman has finished his report on 10-10." The reporters returned to their folding wooden chairs. Dr. Henchman came on board and got a boost on top of the try-works from Speck. He stood above the reporters as if he were Moses, returning from Mount Sinai with the Ten Commandments.

"I have finished zee study of zee 10-10 attack. I am happy to report zer was no shenanigans on *Liberty*. Zer was only a lapse in intelligence. Bubba should not have slashed zoz budgets. Zee solution is more and better spies. More spies wis more power to search, to seize, to arrest, and to interrogate. Here at home, and everywhere in zee world. Zis will preempt any such attacks in zee future."

Tosspot cracked his bullwhip above the reporters. They flinched and cowered. One of the crew jerked the rope that held the black coffin aloft to the right of the reporters. It swayed and turned, showing the words, "free speech zone," painted in white letters on the side. A reporter near the middle of the pack raised her hand slowly, and not very high. Dr. Henchman pointed at her.

"I'm sorry, Doctor, but—I was just—I was wondering. Where's the report? Can we get a copy?"

Dr. Henchman held his right elbow in his left hand, and held his face with his right hand. He paced back and forth, deep lines between his eyebrows.

"Zat is a funny sing. Zee report. Ha ha. I recently rescued a St. Bernard from zee animal shelter, ant—zee foolish animal, poorly trained, mistreated—he snuck into my office and ate zee report. Ha ha."

"You expect us to believe your dog ate your homework?" scoffed a reporter.

TP cracked his bullwhip again. "You heard the man."

Wrong John slammed Shalong's sword into the quarterdeck rail, sending off another spray of chips. "There's that got-damned liberal bias again. I am so sick of you America haters. Here we have one of our great patriots, a man who has given his life to serving his nation, and all you can do is sass him."

Dr. Henchman held up his hands and pushed them at the reporters. "Don't vorry. I have been blessed wis a photographic memory. I can assure you, zee findings are clear. Captain Silverspoon did everysing humanly possible to protect America. To help him preempt anozer such attack, we must provide him more spies, and sacrifice zee Bill of Rights to zee War on Squid."

"We can't go back and report about the report when there is no report. We'll be fired," said a reporter. Damn, I thought, the disease of Wrongism is spreading.

"Gosh, lady, that really breaks my heart," said Silverspoon, placing his hands over his heart and batting his eyes. "Who do you think you work for? Us, or them?" He gestured over the Potomac toward the city. "A'right, class dismissed." He gave Dr. Henchman a hand down from the try-works. The two of them and the officers retired to Chief Dagger's quarters below the poop deck.

Chapter L

Massage at a Bath House

In the weeks that followed, the insurrection in Iraq did not abate with the capture of Shalong. It intensified. One morning after prayers I overheard Sir Yes Sir telling Basma that it was a mistake to imagine the guerrilla war in

Iraq as the futile actions of a few remnant thugs. He said it was an organized rebellion against the American invasion and it would not end until we were out of the country. "We can call it terrorism, tell ourselves Iraq is the big squid in the war on slither, but the Iraqis don't see it that way," he said. "They feel invaded by an imperial power, and are fighting for their independence." Basma nodded absently. She leaned against a halyard, almost as if lying in a hammock.

"The actual War on Terror," added Sir Yes Sir, "is being neglected. I can only pray that we get our priorities straight before another tragedy happens." He looked at Sweet for a reaction, but got nothing. He made an excuse to leave, and went by whaleboat to the city.

Sweet wandered up to her favorite place, leaning over the bow, commiserating with her bandaged sister, Lady Liberty. I came up behind her, reached under her arms and hugged her to me. I squeezed her soft breasts in my hands. She did not resist, but relaxed into my arms.

"I been proud of you for not putting these beauties back in prison," I said, gently kneading her breasts. She sighed and leaned her head back on my shoulder.

"Oh, IshcaBible, it is so difficult. It is so difficult sometimes, to be who I am, to see myself as I want to be, and to know the concessions I've made."

"We all face that, Miss Sweet. I didn't mean to judge you with that story about Pip." I took a deep breath. "I been wantin' to thank you for that night. I hope there isn't something wrong between us. You haven't spoken to me."

"No-no!" she said urgently, pulling away from me and turning. "Don't think that. It was beautiful—too beautiful. I didn't know what to do, so—so I did what comes naturally to me. I pulled away."

I smiled at her and tipped back my black bowler. "I'm mighty glad to hear you say that. Our time together meant so much to me. It felt like a long festering sore closed up that night. All my people shared that wound, and you helped it close up for all of us."

She leaned back against the rail. A black hawk flew over, calling out in its shrill voice. Somebody on shore worked a saw back and forth on a tree trunk. Water splashed onto the deck from the black pipe sticking through the hatch. The water spread out, drained out the scuppers, and dribbled into that great river.

"Roll us a smoke," she said. "Would you, Ish?"

I pulled out my tobacco pouch and twiddled a couple of quick cigarettes. I gave us both a light and waited for her smoke signal. She did not disappoint. We smoked for a few minutes, neither of us speaking, she just standing there against the rail, the bowsprit with it narwhale horn sticking out behind her, the mutilated figurehead unseen below the bulwark.

Finally, she took a quick breath. "IshcaBible, I—I also want to thank you. My heart had been closed for a very long time." She twirled the shrunken head dangling by a gold chain from her belt. "You made me believe I could love again. You made me want to love—want to love *you*." She looked away, and took a deep pull on her smoke, then blew her smoke rings.

"I can't though—can't love you. I don't want to have to hide my love— and we would have to—a black woman and a white man—we would have to." She looked away again.

"I understand, Basma. I understand, and it's okay."

"And what you said about Pip, I'm not angry about it. It has given me long pause, long, long pause. I don't want to live like Pip. I don't want to live in fear of the open water. I won't." We finished our smokes, and she walked away—oh, how she did walk away with that graceful gait of hers.

That afternoon, more bad news arrived from overseas. Sir Yes Sir's observation was validated by a number of terrible bombings in Turkey and Bali that killed hundreds of innocent people. Yo Yo and the captain called a press conference to discuss what they called "the recent victories in the War on Squid." They took their usual places along the starboard rail and addressed the reporters waiting below in small boats.

"You can tell by the desperate actions of evil-doers in Bali and Turkey that we are scaring the cockroaches out of their dark corners," said Wrong John.

"It's very, very gratifying to have these bombings so obvious and out in the open," added Gunny. "No more secret bombings from an enemy we can't see. We've got them scared and desperate, running around bombing in broad daylight."

"When has a bombing ever been a secret?" commented one of the journalists. Gunny and the captain ignored the remark.

"Like I've been saying, it's a war, and war is ugly," said Wrong John. "It's always the last resort, unless of course, you're me, and you got yourself a mandate, which makes it the first resort—actually a pre-resort, the vacation *before* the vacation. I'm just thankful we're smoking them out, and it's taking place in Turkey and Bali and not Tulsa and Boston," said Wrong John.

"Yupper," said the gunner. "Each time innocent people are killed like this, we're all the more convinced our strategy is right on the money. We almost feel like saying, 'Go ahead and kill people. The more the merrier.' Because with each senseless death, we know our final victory in the War on Squid is one explosion closer. It's remarkably gratifying work."

"Almost? Almost feel like saying? Heck, Yo Yo, I'm just gonna say it. *Bring it on.* The more you kill, the more certain we are that people are dying. Without dead people stacking up all over the world, how can we enforce the Silverspoon Mandate? So bring it on. We need the dead as much as they need us."

"It seems the War on Terror is only creating more terror. Wasn't the idea to stop the insanity?" asked a cheeky female reporter at the prow of a rowboat.

"What'd I just say?"

"Excuse me?"

"Didn't I just re-irritate the Silverspoon Mandate?"

"Yes, but I was just—just trying to understand your strategy for reducing and eliminating terrorist attacks."

"Look, we never said word one about terrorist attacks. We said 'terror.' Big differ'nce."

"I'm not clear on the distinction."

"Who the hell are you? Did I call on you? Somebody shoot that gal, would you?"

Tosspot walked to the rail and drew a bead on her. The reporter held up her hands and shook her head. "No no no!" she said. "I retract the question. I'm sorry, Mr. Captain, truly, I am." Silverspoon slapped the air with the back of his hand and walked away. The marshal fired a round into the water next to the reporter. Speck walked up with a Squid Alert tank.

"Sorry, folks," he said. "Party's over. The little guy's turning yellow." The reporters turned and rowed away slowly in their small boats.

It was in this very positive climate that Krill launched in earnest the captain's re-election campaign. I suppose, looking back, Silverspoon had always been in "re-election mode," as he put it. If there was one thing he kept as a solemn vow, it was to outdo his pa, and that meant, more than anything else, getting elected to a second term. At this point, re-election was looking to me a far sight less important than staying out of jail, but bullheaded old Wrong John was hell-bent on a second term, despite the gathering storm around him.

His seeking re-election was, to me, about the same as if I had ran for mayor of Russellville, Kentucky, after robbing the Nimrod L. Long & Co. bank in March of 1868. I simply could not imagine campaigning on Main Street, shaking hands, and kissing babies, with everybody knowing I had their hard-earned savings stashed away in my saddlebags. Maybe I'm just skittish, but I would have had some trouble settling into the campaign, fearful a vigilante would ambush me, or a lynching mob would rise up while I was on the stump claiming the inviolate sanctity of the town's financial institutions. Not Silverspoon, though, he could grin and look them in the eye, knowing he had picked their pockets, and not even flinch. Equally as surprising, most Americans didn't seem to mind, or take the time to notice that he had drained the public watering hole.

I was happy when Krill sent the captain on a fundraising tour of America. Anything was better than sitting there with a bull's-eye on our backs stuck in the middle of the Potomac. I didn't much like the fundraising—found it boring, the same dry speech night after night. The money part of it was intriguing, I will admit. I could never quite reckon how Silverspoon threw out the same tripe night after night, and every time the crowds of his supporters filled up his collection baskets to overflowing.

I must say, he did have a following, and they truly loved him. I don't imagine there's anything he could say or do to lose the loyalty of his, what Krill called, "base." No matter how badly things went, they just dug deeper and deeper to pay for his re-election. Now some of them, I understand, benefited directly from his style of governing. These were the wealthy industrialists, the investors, the venture capitalists—the ones that got invited to his golden pyramid parties on Pirate Island. They had good, hard cash reasons to stand with him.

But I couldn't quite grasp how it was that salt-of-the-earth country folk got so excited about him. From what I had observed of his policies and practices, they had nothing, *absolutely nothing* to gain by his winning a second term— and a lot to loose. I reckoned it was the power of the *Congreso Mandato*—all those conservative fish tanks planting slugs and piss clams all over the place, shaping the debate through the Mandate Media, and the incessant droning of the Clown Criers—that convinced them he spoke for their values. And then, of course, he spoke the old "God is on our side" sermon. I wished people would stop paying attention to what was spoken, and look at *what was done*.

He went around the country, now exclusively to military bases, military schools, veterans groups, or military contractors, and delivered speeches about how he had bravely fought the War on Squid. He wore Shalong's *Shalong* from his belt at all times, and flourished the lavish scimitar at every opportunity. He cited statistics about how many thousands of squid he had *shish-kebabbed*, how much safer America was because of him, and how important it was that he had captured the Chastity Belt. He constantly derided the "wishy-washy liberal flip-flopping" of his opponent, Lieutenant Jerry.

One thing he did struck me funny. He came up with an Amazon poison-dart frog that sat on his shoulder. His parrot savant had been left behind to plan the campaign, so there was a vacancy. The new tenant's skin radiated a vibrant red from its back, and had large black spots on its sides and legs in a field of turquoise. It wasn't any bigger than the tip of his thumb, but when it croaked, it resonated like a trumpet.

"Yep," he said, during a stump speech, "found the Weapon of Mass Hysteria hiding under a log in Shalong's backyard." He pointed at the bright red and blue spotted frog on his shoulder. Someone had trained it to croak on command, so whenever Wrong John said, "Shalong," it croaked so loudly people in the audience jumped. "Don't worry about your president, folks," he added, "I'm immune to the poison of Shalong."

"*CROAK!*"

An aspect of the campaign I did find interesting was the undercover work of scouring Lieutenant Jerry's life for the sordid, the unseemly, the decadent misdeeds of his sinful past. He was a man, after all, so there had to be one or two things he might not want the world to know about. I learned pretty quickly that it wasn't so much what he had *actually* done but the *appearance* of misdeeds that was important. I knew the game. As I have said, we played it like a jew's-harp with Johnny Edwards all those years, twanging out our jingle about the evil Union and its Missouri puppets.

I convinced the captain I could do him more good helping Krill with the *real* campaign than standing by him on the red herring tour. If he was one thing, Captain Silverspoon was a wicked campaigner, and he recognized immediately where my services would be of the most value to his re-election.

I joined Krill as he skulked the alleys and back doors of Washington to conduct the "research" necessary to put our opponent on the defensive. TP had gathered together a motley cast of snoops who knew people, could get into any building, pick any lock, shake down any potential source of data on the challenger. I was paired with Krill and two of the snoops, Itch, a skinny, short, red-headed Irishman who stank of whiskey, and Scratch, also thin, but dark-complexioned, a Cuban, who always had a cigarette dangling from his lips. Krill chose him as his horse. Together, the four of us embarked on a "fact finding" mission to benefit the campaign.

It came as no surprise to me that we ended up at the city dump—down an eroded red bank along Rock Creek north of town. The local garbage man—well compensated for his insight—pointed out to us where he had dumped the most recent load containing Lt. Jerry's trash. We dropped into the dump, startling hungry seagulls that screeched at us for interrupting their feast. "Brack, yourself," said Krill from his position on Scratch's shoulder.

"Over there, Ish," said Krill, pointing with his stubby, red wing. "That's the stuff. Let's play archaeology. Find the past to kill his future—kill his future. *BRACK!*"

Itch, Scratch with Krill on his shoulder, and I wandered over. Krill jumped into the heap of trash, grumbling and whisper whistling to himself. He picked through with his beak and claws, finding, every so often, some tasty bit of dried fruit to chew on. Itch and Scratch also dug, as did I—something I had never done, and would have looked down on as the work of a bottom-feeding Pinkerton. It took almost two hours before we got into the refuse that belonged to Lieutenant Jerry. "Here's his stuff," said Krill, waving his wings in front of his beak and squinting. "Reeks of indecision."

We dug around, found a discarded quill pen, socks with holes in them, wine and gin and beer bottles, an old pair of shoes, a bicycle wheel with broken spokes, a magnifying glass, a bowling trophy, banana peels, carrot ends, potato peels, and the leg bone of a lamb. Itch pulled up from under a horseshoe a receipt he found worthy of comment. "Must be bloody fine to soak yer arse at the Russian bath," he said. "Likely be us poor gobs buying his massages with our tax dollars." He wadded up the receipt and tossed it.

"What in the BRACK? Did you say 'Massage at a bath house? Massage at a bath house?'" asked Krill. He flapped his wings and scampered through the trash toward Itch.

"*Pobre ihito*," Scratch said, flicking the butt of his cigarette. "Poor little rich boy."

"Find that receipt!" screeched Krill. Itch went after it, and with the help of Scratch, found it tucked beside a brown banana peel. He handed it to Krill. The bird held it tightly in his scabrous gray left claw. "Coup de grace! Coup de grace! Flip Flop takin' a dive, takin' a dive. Ouch! Belly flop!" He cackled, whistled, and gabbled to himself. The noise was so loud and complicated it could have been a flock of parrots, sitting in a tree in Georgia, debating when the peaches would ripen.

Chapter LI

Size Matters

Tosspot and his crew of Pinkerton creeps rendezvoused with us in an abandoned dairy on the waterfront. I walked to the tack room in the back that smelled of musty leather, the walls filled with cracked saddles, old halters, leather straps, and bits, the floor stacked with milk buckets, mops and push brooms, barrels of sawdust, and empty bottles of ammonia. I got introduced around, and noticed a dusty portrait of Abraham Lincoln hanging on the wall, spider webs from the ceiling. Clerestory windows let in a feeble light. Even though I kept my head shaved and wore the Polynesian tattoos, the Pinkertons always seemed to look at me a minute longer than was respectable, like they were trying to place me. They seemed especially to notice, and cross reference in their minds, the contents of my holster, Peacemaker and Widowmaker. Those were some rather famous guns, with their pearl handles I had custom fitted to them, no doubt described in the Pinkerton dossier on me. So far, though, no one that I was aware of had put two and two together.

One of them stared at me more intently than the others. He wore a thick auburn beard and a ten-gallon hat pulled down low on his head. Every time I looked at him, he looked away. Something about him—the way he carried himself, the sharpness of his nose, his shifty eyes—reminded me of somebody, but I couldn't say who. He whispered in Tosspot's ear after eyeballing my weapons. Tosspot looked over at me with a sour smirk.

"Whatta ya got, TP?" asked Krill, trying, I thought, to act nonchalant, when I knew he was dying to crow about his discovery.

"Some excellent material," said TP, reaching into a brown leather briefcase polished at the grip from hand oil. "Now here's something you might think insignificant at first glance, but look at this." He held up a pack of chewing gum with three pieces unopened. "Three pieces out of seven, just thrown away."

"That's the pattern," said Krill to Itch from his perch on Scratch's shoulder. "Flip Flop. Careless. Wasteful. Can't make up his mind. Can't see clearly. Can't remember. Is the pack half full, or half empty? Just tosses the whole thing. Putz ain't even a decent liberal—a decent liberal. Liberal gives the last three sticks to a bum. Gives them to a bum. Pats himself on the back. 'What a good boy am I. What a good boy.'" Krill rubbed one wing across the other and whistled like a sad violin.

"Observe this trinket," said TP, holding up a flattened nickel. "We got this out of his desk in the Capitol." He handed it to Itch, who turned it over and passed it to Scratch, who gazed at it through the gray smoke from his cigarette and handed it to me. I noticed the flattened face of an Indian on one side and a buffalo on the other. Flip Flop must have set a nickel on the train tracks just like I had as a boy. Krill took it from me and rolled it in the talons of his claws. He tossed it in the air.

"Heads he loses, tails I win." Krill watched the flat nickel clang on the rough plank floor. "Sorry, Flip Flop, you loose. Changed your mind one time too many. One time too many." Krill flipped the coin back at Tosspot.

"The man respects no institution, no standard, not even money. He's practically an anarchist." The marshal returned the coin to his briefcase. One of those Pinkerton boys lit up a cigarette and stared at me through the smoke.

"Boy, TP, you *really* scored," Krill whistled with mock admiration. I could tell he was itching to disclose his find.

"What did you get?" TP asked Krill.

The parrot crawled down Scratch's mid-section, reached into his watch pocket, and pulled out with his beak the receipt from the Russian bath. "Oh, nothing much. Nothing much. Just this RECEIPT FROM A BATH HOUSE! BRACK!"

"Let me see that!" Tosspot ripped the receipt from Krill's beak. He read it with quick, darting eyes. "This is fantastic. Almost as good as this." He snagged from his briefcase the patient log from a doctor's office. "It confirms Flip Flop's appointment with a cosmetic surgeon. Seems he was inquiring about a procedure to augment his diminutive phallus."

Krill hopped from Scratch's shoulder, across the wobbly table, and scrambled up TP's chest to his shoulder and examined the registry. "Ho, baby, this is unreal. Unreal! Got to be a flip-flopper. Got to be. Can't make a stand when there's nothing to stand on." Krill clicked his tongue and muttered and whistled. "What a story line: 'Dickless Flip Flop Seeks Approval at Gay Bath House.' Unbelievable! It's O-VER. Can anybody say, 'Four More Years?'" In his excitement, Krill jumped from Tosspot's shoulder to the table, danced a jig, and sang a ditty.

"Got him good. The magic lamp said I would. Thank you sweetie. Got him tied up, real nice and neatly."

I opened the cylinder of Widowmaker—another bullet missing. Tosspot reached into his briefcase and got that horrible little notebook of his. He licked his pencil and lowered his eyes at Krill. "Not to get off the subject *too far*, but what is it with you and that lamp, Krill? You speak to it as if it were alive."

"*BRACK* you, marshal! Peter Peter pumpkin eater. Had a wife and couldn't keep her." He hissed and stuck his black tongue at Tosspot. The marshal raised his hands and backed up a step.

"Okay. Okay," he said, sliding his book into the leather folds of his briefcase.

The meeting adjourned. Krill's next step was to lure the victim to his doom. This came about through a bit of prestidigitation on the part of Krill's friends in the Mandate Media. One of the better known in their ranks, Ben Smite, an old hand well respected for his incisive personality profiles, invited Lieutenant Jerry to an interview. The candidate readily agreed, as it was commonly understood that a positive portrayal by Smite was a major boost to your campaign. Smite met Lieutenant Jerry—escorted, as presidential candidates always are, by a retinue of advisers and body guards—in the Capitol rotunda and brought him to a waiting coach, pulled by a team of strong chestnut Morgans. Flip Flop didn't want to be separated from his team, but Smite assured him they would follow closely in a second coach parked behind the first. "We need as much one-on-one time as possible," Smite told him.

The two got into the lead coach, and the driver cracked his whip. The second coach followed, driven, unbeknownst to the passengers, by one of our crew, who made a wrong turn along the route. The solitary Lieutenant Jerry, happily jabbering about a Civil War battle he had fought, fell into Krill's snare, located in the same abandoned dairy along the waterfront.

Lt. Jerry walked in with Smite, who ushered him to the rear of the building, into the area formerly reserved for milking. Jerry was a tall man with a long face and thick, neatly groomed salt-and-pepper hair. He had deep-set eyes, bushy eyebrows, and one top front tooth longer than the other. Smite sat him down on a three-legged milking stool, one leg shorter than the others, the seat boards separated from age. The same wan light passed through the clerestory windows. Rusty milk buckets littered the white tile floor, stained with the waste of many an old cow.

The reporter excused himself and disappeared into the tack room. Krill,

Tosspot, and the rest of us were in there to listen. I let Krill stand on my shoulder so we could both see the action through a popped out knothole. A moment later, several Clown Criers and reporters from the Mandate Media escorted Smite back out to the milking room.

"Smite, what the hell is this?" asked Lieutenant Jerry, his deep voice salted with anger. "I agreed to a one-on-one, not an inquisition."

"Sorry, Flip, but the stakes are too high. My publishers have a position, and my future is attached to that position," Smite said.

"You're a journalist, man! You're *position*, and the reason it is protected by the Constitution, is to provide accurate information to the people."

"Don't give us that stooge food!" yelled a fat clown with a big, red, rubber nose on his face. "We feed the *mandato molluski*. And it feeds us—well." He rubbed his big belly.

"Krill! Where is that flea-bitten parrot? I can see his grimy claw marks all over this thing." Krill snickered behind his wing from the tack room.

"Never mind him," said Smite. "Do you deny your regular attendance at the St. Petersburg Bath House on Fifth and K?"

"What? Why should I—what difference does that make?"

"So you don't deny it?"

"Of course not, why should I?"

"No reason," Smite said, conferring with a Clown Crier. "So then you also don't deny your receiving a weekly massage from Percy Willins, who works there?"

"Why would I? He gives a great massage."

"I'm sure he does—and whatever else strikes your fancy."

"What the hell—"

"Here's a statement from Percy, quote, 'He was constantly asking for my opinion of his penis, wondering if I thought it was big enough, attractive enough. He often complained of groin pulls, and asked for extra attention to that area. Then, after he became aroused, he would ask if I thought his penis more attractive. I don't know how far he would have taken it, and I didn't want to find out. I already have a boyfriend.' End quote. Percy Willins, a man, friends, a man." The gathered reporters and clowns scribbled notes in their books.

"That's absurd! I've never, for one moment, wondered about or asked questions about the size or quality of my penis. If anything, I've worried I was *too big*, too meaty and potent. My penis and I have always been cordial, and on good terms, since my boyhood in the hills of Massachusetts, hunting for frogs and chasing butterflies, a carefree American youth, spent—"

"Spare us the campaign commercial, senator." Smite received a piece of paper from a clown. He placed his reading glasses on the end of his nose. "This is a patient registry from a Doctor Donkeydick, with your name on it."

"That's—let me see that." Flip Flop lunged for the paper. Smite pulled back.

"Ah-ah, hands off the prima facie. Do you deny visiting Dr. Donkeydick to discuss the possibility of engaging the good doctor's services in his specialty, the transformation of earthworms into anacondas?"

"That's—I would never—My inquiry concerned reduction. I was wondering—just curious, really—whether he could help me with the discomfort of *excess* manhood."

The clowns and mandate reporters guffawed. "As if! As if!" said the fat, red-nosed clown. "A man has never been born—*never*—who would ask for a smaller dick." They all chuckled and made notes in their books.

"The question we now have to ask ourselves, that all of America wants to know, is, on what side of the trough are you feeding?" asked Smite.

"What do you mean? I'm—I've had enough of this charade. You'll be hearing from my lawyers." He tried to get up, but the Clown Criers pushed him back on the stool. He struggled to his feet, but fell back after someone cocked the trigger of a gun.

"I guess, senator, what it comes down to is this: for whom are you having your dong extended, the missus, Percy the queer masseur, or, in what would have to stand as the greatest flip-flop in political history—*both!*"

The lieutenant's face went red with rage. His legs trembled so the uneven legs of his stool rattled on the stained tile floor. "This is libelous! I will not stand for it. Only the most disreputable scoundrel would print such drivel." The journalists did not look at him, but scribbled in their notebooks.

"When it comes to running the greatest, most powerful country the world has ever known, a country on a mission to rid the world of evil, *size matters.*" Smite tucked his pencil behind his ear. "Let him go." Lieutenant Jerry stumbled out of the dairy. The journalists worked with Krill to fill in the details of the story, and ran off to meet their deadlines. That one Pinkerton with the bushy auburn beard stood in the corner with Tosspot, the two of them talking quietly and pointing at me.

The following piece, printed in the *New York Daily Mandate*, typified the coverage:

Sex Scandal Rocks Flip Flop Campaign

New York—The candidacy of Lt. "Flip-Flop" Jerry appears headed for a flop of monumental proportions, with news today of a scandalous secret homosexual relationship.

It seems that for many years, Jerry has been a weekly visitor to the notoriously queer bathhouse in Washington, the St. Petersburg. He has paid for erotic massages by one Percy Willins, who claims the senator has a chronic obsession with the size of his penis.

"He's always asking me to look at it, and tell him if it's big and pretty. He suggests I massage his groin and asks if I like him better now," said Willins. "I'm embarrassed by it. I already have a boyfriend, and, with Lieutenant Flip-Flop's blessing, we're getting married next month. I would hope he appreciates my desire to save myself for the night of the wedding."

Lt. Jerry denies any amorous desires for Willins, stating that when it comes to sex, unlike almost every other matter, he *does not* flip-flop, but stays with his woman, on his back.

Flip-Flop admits to consulting with one Doctor Donkeydick, a cosmetic surgeon who specializes in penis augmentation. As Mr. Willins confirms, Flip Flop's obsession with the size of his penis is not without reason. Amazingly, Lt. Jerry asserts that his problem is not a small penis, but one that is *too large*.

"In all my years as a cosmetic surgeon, I have never once had a man come to me and request penis reduction surgery. Not once," says renowned Washington doctor Ben Dover.

Some would say it is irrelevant whether or not the

Commander-in-Chief is well endowed. Some would say Flip Flop's penis envy, like Bubba's fellatio exploits in the Oval Office, is not material to his leadership of the nation. Others would disagree.

"It's dangerous to have a man with deep-seated self doubt in such an important position," said renowned psychologist Sarah Genics. "A man who's afraid to be seen naked in the locker room probably won't show up well on the world stage."

President Silverspoon, campaigning at the International Anti-terrorism Training Camp in Georgia, formerly known as Mercenary Mountain, had this response when informed of Flip Flop's genital impoverishment:

"I'm sorry to hear it. I thought we were going to have a good fight among men, but come to find out, he's just a boy, or worse, a girl. I—you know, I don't fault the man for what God did or did not provide him with—long as he's not parking the horse on both sides of the street. I just—it's—when you're taking on the bad guys of the world, you don't want them pointing at your crotch and laughing.

"Truth is, we're at war here. I started it, and I aim to finish the job. I don't care how many people have to die for me to get there. It's a dangerous, dangerous world. America has lost its innocence. We live in a climate of constant threat. You can't *hunt* the Giant Squid unless you're *packin'* a Giant Squid. *Size matters.*"

Chapter LII

Any Terror Happens

Krill had himself a campaign theme he called "one for the ages," the ultimate macho slogan of a modern dragon slayer: *Size Matters*. To drive home the point, Krill leaked intimate details of the captain's bedroom prowess to influential gossip columnists at leading American newspapers. It became the common currency of the land that, while Silverspoon made love in the missionary position—always on top—Flip Flop flip-flopped all over the place, attempting to make his inferior tool function as intended. The story-line served the campaign strategy nicely, and Krill delighted in the captain's steady rise in the polls.

Lieutenant Jerry attempted to counter the growing resentment against his "martial deficiency" through the difficult-to-believe claim that he was *too big*. At a rally in Durham, North Carolina, he claimed, "I'm *too* infused with masculine power. It's dangerous to be so well hung—and hell on zippers!"

Krill cackled every time he heard of Jerry bragging about his excess virility. "*BRACK* me in the ear! He's playing our game—our game. Nobody, but nobody, outguns Wrong John Silverspoon in the big gun contest. Nobody!"

To reinforce the *Size Matters* theme, Wrong John began to adjust his genitals whenever he addressed an audience. I asked Krill if it was part of the strategy, or if he had gotten crabs from sleeping with a disreputable teddy bear. "Watch it, Ish. Little respect for the boss there."

"Come on, Krill? How can playing with yourself in public be a re-election strategy?"

"Boss has the nose for these things. Has the nose. Doesn't fart without smelling the political fallout. Crotch game's a symbol. Perception of virility, power, assertiveness, control." He scratched himself rapidly under his chin. "Right tool for the right job. Always handy, ready to perform. Big hammer, Ish. Big hammer. Not easy to cram in a tool belt. Little uncomfortable."

Wrong John snuck up behind Krill and grabbed him. He brought the bird in front of his face. "Where you been sneakin' off to every night, tiger?" he growled.

"Who-who? Me-me? Nah-nah-nah-nah-nah!" Krill jabbered. A bullwhip fell onto the deck. The three of us looked up to the crow's nest, and there was Tosspot, hand over his brow, pretending to study the shoreline for squid.

"You dropped something, marshal," I said. He looked down, smiling, and waved. What a klutz, I thought—captain of the spies—God help us.

All the dick-wagging in America may have captivated voters, but it riled the Giant Squid. Al Quota hit Spain with a series of bombs on busy commuter trains, leaving several hundred dead, and two thousand injured.

The government of Spain, a staunch attendant to the Silverspoon Mandate, tried a parrot game of passing the rotten peanut to an indigenous Basque separatist group (the ETA), but was found out to be lying—all of this just days before the Spanish presidential election.

When the terror strike first happened, a boatload of reporters showed up wanting comment. Silverspoon and the Chief greeted them at the usual receiving area off the starboard bow. The black coffin hung above them, warning ominously about the fate of those overly free with their speech. The men at the deck cannons rotated them in the direction of the press corps. Wrong John walked to the rail, opened his arms, smiled and nodded, dropped his arms and said, "It's a great day in Spain! *Viva la mandato!*"

Chief stepped beside him and shook his hand. "Perfect opportunity to demonstrate our resolve, show them we can take anything they dish out."

"Why do you say, 'us?' Isn't it the Spanish who took the shot?" inquired a reporter.

"Listen, it's our war," Wrong John said peevishly. "Any terror happens, we get the credit for it. We're the ones who get to feel good about forcing evil to the streets of Madrid, instead of weakly waiting for it to land again in Manhattan."

"We just hope the Spaniards recognize the wonderful opportunity that has been laid on their doorstep," said Dagger, his voice deep and grave. "They now have the chance to follow our lead and tell the terrorists to pound sand. They can show their resolve by staying the course, re-electing the tough-on-terror Conservative Party, and making a stand against squid that will make me proud."

"But the conservatives lied to them," came a voice from a small boat.

"So?" Wrong John said. "What makes you feel safer: to be in the hands of somebody bold enough to lie to your face, or to hope an honest shrimp dick won't faint when the squid jumps him in a dark alley."

"I'd rather have one that is honest, and tough."

"Can't have it both ways. Shame on you for your greed. Your children will pay the price for you indecision," Dagger said, wagging his finger at them.

"Any condolences for the families of the victims?" another reporter questioned.

"You bet. Let me just say to the families, I'm the guy who wipes the noses and changes the diapers, so if you need any of those things, give me a holler," Silverspoon said. "Otherwise, *Felicidades España!* Congratulations for making the ultimate sacrifice in the War on Squid. Spain has shown itself a great ally by taking a bullet for America. You have preempted an attack on Manhattan, Mobile, or Minneapolis by steering evil to the streets of Madrid. In so doing, you have shown yourselves worthy of a healthy rebuilding contract in Iraq. Some might call it blood money. I call it smart money. You threw in with Uncle Wrong John, and this is what you get. The world is a little safer today, thanks to your dead. You make us proud, and all the more convinced our strategy is picture perfect." The captain and his first mate waved to the reporters, turned and walked to the roundhouse.

Some weeks later, a messenger arrived with news the Spanish defied Silverspoon and elected the liberal democratic leader their next president. He pledged to withdraw all twenty-seven Spanish troops from Iraq, and leave the guarding of the new Najaf Endrun Energy office to the Polish. This incensed the Silverspoon team so much they declared Spain a Friend of Terror and canceled the inaugural Running of the Bulls, a new festival in Basra, created in a free and liberated Iraq to celebrate Spain's devotion to the mandate.

When members of the media arrived for comment about the Spanish election results, the captain and his chief could not be bothered to address them. Instead, they released a terse statement that read as follows:

"The Spanish have betrayed the mandate. Their cowardly decision to run from Iraq gives a victory to the Giant Squid. They have sold their sovereignty to her. Al Quota now holds the keys to the kingdom. Spain has given an election victory to terror, and has emboldened squid the world over. All because a few insignificant people died."

Throughout all of this, Wrong John Silverspoon campaigned relentlessly under his new theme: *Size Matters.* In the spirit of his mandate, as explicated by his parrot savant, he did not allow the tragedy of Spain to drift into the negative, but seized it as further proof he must soldier on with his lonely crusade to slay the Giant Squid. As he put it one day to a group of ROTC at the University of Maryland, with his tiny blue and red Weapon of Mass Hysteria perched on his shoulder, "Heck, I don't like to see an ally like Spain go soft like that, but I can't let it get me down. I've got to set the tone and stick to principle. It's like this, folks: we're number one, we've got the big gun." He grabbed his crotch. "Hey, I didn't start this fight, but I aim to finish it. And when it comes to the ultimate destruction of evil squid, *Size Matters*."

"CROAK!" said Dart, the captain's new pet frog.

The campaign of Lieutenant Jerry responded by trotting their candidate out and proclaiming *"Size Matters More."* Jerry, they said, not Silverspoon, had the resolve necessary to win the War on Squid. "I'm going to kill the terrorists with bigger, more explosive bombs," Jerry told a gathering of mothers, devoted above all else to playing soccer. "I hate them much more the Silverspoon does. He just pretends to hate them, but I really, *really* hate them." He adjusted the bulge in his pants. *"Size Matters More."*

The bad news continued to pour in. It seemed to me the more Silverspoon pretended it was good news, the more his hump grew, as if it was a storage depot for self-deception. He could no longer stand up straight, and had started using Shalong's sword as a cane. He also became plagued with nosebleeds. They started for no apparent reason, and would not stop without Dr. von Shlop stuffing his nostrils with gauze. This further exaggerated the grating effect of his high-pitched twang, making it even more difficult for me to be around him.

A week after news of the Spanish election, another messenger arrived with dire news from Iraq. In the town of Falluja, rebels attacked a convoy of American contractors (I could picture Blackbeard's malignant bodyguards) as they passed through the city. Five had been killed, their bodies mutilated, burned, and hung from a bridge. The press arrived for comment on the "good news," and Yo Yo gladly obliged. He climbed out on the foremast yard and lowered himself to the black casket. He received the press corps while sitting on the coffin.

"Have we reached the stage yet in Iraq when we can begin to use the word 'tragedy?'" asked a reporter at the bow of a red skiff.

"Absolutely not. I'm thrilled about the aggression in Falluja." Gunny pumped his legs and began to swing to and fro on the coffin. "We've got a big fish on the line over there. And we aren't going to let it go." He held onto the ropes holding up the coffin, kicked his legs, and swung harder.

"There's seems to be a growing hatred of America."

"Not true. There are a few thugs and criminals trying to disrupt the democratic process. That's it. The more they attack us, the more certain we are that freedom will reign."

He swung a couple of more times, then started bouncing up and down. Sir Yes Sir had a hold of the rope tied off at a cleat on the deck. He leaned against the rope with his strong shoulders and thrust against it with bursts from his legs.

"Hey! What are you doing? Can't you see I'm conducting a press briefing?" Gunny shouted.

"Oh, I'm sorry," said the diplomat. He let go of the rope and the coffin crashed to the rail. Gunny fell forward into the cold river. He splashed and spluttered in the water.

"Let's see now," said Sir Yes Sir. He placed his left foot against the bulwark and stroked his chin. "How does this work? If it floats, that means it is evil, and we can't let it back on board. If it sinks, it's not a warlock, and it drowns with our blessing. Wasn't that the deal, Gunny?

"Help! No! You can't do this to me!" Yo Yo yelled, bobbing in the icy water, his urgent breath like jets of steam from his mouth. "I'm the commander of the military. You can't treat me like this!"

"It's not torture, *per se.* You fell in there by accident, and I'm letting you drown as a program of psy-ops. It's not about you turning blue and your lungs filling up with water. That's old school. This is just a mind game. And, after all, you're not in there for *stealing donuts.* Now, if you want to come in, confess." Sir Yes Sir picked up a bundle of coiled hemp rope and draped it over his shoulder.

"Confess?" Gunny went beneath the surface, then bobbed up, thrashing. "Confess to what?"

"Confess to your crimes. Confess to the lies that brought us to war. Confess to the poor planning, the bad judgment, the arrogance, and cocksure bravado that promised everyone a shower of roses."

Gunny went under. He didn't come back up, and it looked as if he was innocent of witchcraft. Then he popped up, twenty feet downstream, cursed. His face was pale and lips blue. Sir Yes Sir threw him a rope. Gunny latched

on, and the big black man hauled him close to the ship. He let the rope grow
slack, and Gunny started thrashing again.

"Confess, 'detainee,' admit your evil intent," Sir Yes Sir demanded.

"Evil intent?" Gunny went under. The diplomat hauled him up with the
rope.

"Don't lie to me! Confess! Confess!"

"I confess! I confess! Please! Let me live!"

Sir Yes Sir hauled in Yo Yo. He pulled him, shivering, over the rail. Yo Yo
fell on the deck, exhausted, and curled up in a trembling ball, coughing and
wheezing.

Dagger walked up, carrying a golf club. "Interesting, isn't it? how the
abused become the abusers? how the downtrodden, at the first opportunity,
tread upon their oppressors?" he said to Sir Yes Sir.

The diplomat's fingers rolled into tight fists. "Very interesting, Chief," he
growled. "Interesting, isn't it, how the enforcer becomes a squeaking rat when
he is confronted with his treachery? How he's willing to let his captain, for
whom he pledges undying devotion, hang for a crime *he* committed?"

"You're suspended until further notice." Dagger leaned down to check on
Gunny. "Dismissed."

Sir Yes Sir saluted. He went to his cabin, gathered his things, and rowed
to shore.

I dropped into the galley for some solace. There stood Tatanka at the
washbasin, peeling potatoes for fish chowder. He did not look up. I rolled us
both a smoke, walked up, and gave him one. I gave us both a light. From my
pocket I pulled that button toy. I flipped it around and pulled. It didn't go. I
tried a few more times. Finally things came together and it started whirring
and pulsating, spinning one way, winking at me, reversing, gaining power with
every pull, until it felt like I was just a witness. It pulled my hands in and out.
I had no choice.

"Look at this thing, Tatanka," I said, cigarette dangling from my lips, toy
whirring like a hummingbird. "I pull it out. It pulls me in. I pull harder. It pulls
back harder. In and out. There can be no end. Look at the damn button. It's a
buzz saw, Injun." I ran the spinning button on the table. It rattled and whizzed
against the surface, making a gouge in the wood.

"You see? Look at it tear. I pull, it pulls, they pull, we pull. On and on it goes. I kill, you kill, they kill, we kill. On and on and on." The button whizzed and popped, whirred, and rattled as I slashed it against pans, against the wall, against the chicken pens, making the birds flutter and cluck.

"It never ends and we are doomed, doomed for having started it, doomed because now we have lost control. The toy is running on its own power, using us, just using us, driving us on to kill, and run, kill, and run, push-pull, push-pull. War on Terror—terror. War on Terror—terror. Back and forth and back and forth until we are entirely and completely insane. Insane! Insane! Insane!" I screamed.

Suddenly Tatanka was beside me with his long yellow jackknife. He slashed the string, and my whirring demon fell to the ground. It tottered, rolled unevenly a couple of turns, and fell over, a button—a pretty, emerald, pearl, brown-striped button from an abalone shell.

Chapter LIII

Consorting with an Enemy Combatant

One evening, just after dinner, I leaned against the windlass and picked my teeth, Tatanka by my side with his redstone *chanupa,* preparing to go into prayer. The captain was out campaigning and had been on the road for a week with Pinch—and his Amazon WMH, Dart—touting his miraculous economic plan that had bankrupted America in record time. Tatanka elbowed me in the ribs and pointed to the try-works.

Krill waddled up to the iron door of the furnace with his dull copper lamp, grumbling and whisper whistling to himself. He looked left, then right, pushed up the handle, and snuck into the furnace. The door shut behind him with a clang. Tatanka and I tiptoed over and kneeled next to the iron doorway through a wall of red brick. We put our ears against it. The first thing I heard was the tolling of bilge pumps, resounding through the ribs of the ship, vibrating every part of her with a low-frequency alarm. Then I heard Krill's bird voice.

"Oh, sweetie," Krill moaned. "I can hear you in there. I know it's you. I don't know how to get you out. I should have asked in the Baghdad bazaar. I should have, but—somebody would have stolen the lamp. Everybody wants the magic. I should have trusted, found out the secret. Oh, sweetie."

Tatanka and I, face-to-face with our ears against the iron door, looked at each other, both of us perplexed and amused by the parrot's love affair with the Arabian lamp. The grating sound of something sharp against metal came to my ear. Krill must have been rubbing the lamp with his claws.

"Open Sesame! Open Sesame! Open Sesame," said Krill. That grating sound grew louder. His voice had gotten shrill and desperate. It resounded off the hollow silver try-pots. "Sim sim salabim! Sim sim salabim! Praise Allah! Pass the hummus! Fly, oh magic carpet. By the gates of Ishtar, I command thee! Open! Pickle relish! Open! Let my jinni out! Brack, brack, brack, brack. It's not working, honey. I can't get you out. What's that? Oh, damn. I can't hear you. Speak up. Stupid lamp!" I heard the clanging sound of hollow copper against the iron floor of the furnace. He must have kicked the lamp.

"I can help him," Tatanka said. He pulled open the iron door and crawled into the try-works furnace. I followed, then closed the door behind us. Tatanka lit a candle. Krill had backed up into the far corner. He spread his wings and tail to conceal the lamp behind him.

"What's this? I miss dinner? There a media emergency? Code Orange? What's up?" he chattered, covered with the soot of old rendering fires.

Tatanka took a leather pouch from over his shoulder. He opened it and withdrew his redstone pipe. From another pouch, he got tobacco. He offered it up to the sky, and to the earth, and to the four directions. He filled the pipe, cradled it in his arms, and looked at the parrot.

"I know your struggle, flying one. You want to receive the magic of the lamp. It will not come out for you." Tatanka spoke in his flat, low voice, his dark purple-brown face, and long, black hair shining in the candlelight. I breathed in the smell of fresh tobacco, mixed with the odor of burnt whale flesh.

"Whatta ya mean, magic lamp? I'm just working on a new campaign slogan. 'Wise Wrong John Frees the Arab Jinni, Saves the World.' You like it?" Krill stammered.

"It is hopeless, flier, hopeless. She will *never* come out. You waste your time—and mine!" Tatanka turned and crawled toward the door.

"Wait! Okay. I'm sorry. I just—nobody can be trusted. Everybody lusts for the magic. They lust, and will kill me to get it. Kill me," Krill wailed, looking directly at me. I turned quickly away from him, realizing my hands were stroking the smooth leather of my holstered guns. He was right. I could have used a wish or two.

"I have my *own* magic," said the Lakota. "You want help, or don't you?"

"Yes. Please. How can I do it, Injun? How can I get my baby out?"

"You cannot. She is trapped."

Krill dropped his small red head and cried.

"The only way out is for you to go *in*."

Krill raised his head and looked at Tatanka with teary, pleading eyes. "But how?"

"Do as I say." Tatanka placed the copper lamp between them. He flicked a match against the iron floor of the furnace. He lit his *chanupa*, blew smoke up, down, and in the four directions. He held the pipe in front of Krill and told him to smoke. "Pray for a way in, flier. Pray for the spirits to let you come in." Krill puffed on the pipe, his eyes closed tight, and muttered under his breath. Tatanka handed me the pipe and I smoked. Tatanka sang a quiet song in his native tongue. He shook a buffalo horn rattle in a steady rhythm.

Krill continued to mumble, eyes tightly closed. He began to rock back and forth. Tatanka shook his rattle in a steady rhythm. He sang his Lakota medicine song louder, the high notes cracking, quickly falling to low chanting, then back into the sky. I began falling into a trance. I did not want to get lost, so I kept my eyes open and tried to see my reflection in the bottom of a silver try-pot.

Krill fell over and lay on the iron floor vibrating. Tatanka's song went soft, but his rattle continued the same steady rhythm. Krill shook and quivered. His wings fluttered, as if he were taking a dream flight. The copper lamp began to vibrate against the iron floor. It became still, and Krill too settled, his body trembling only a little. He stayed this way for a while—I don't know how long.

Finally, he shook himself and opened his eyes. Tatanka's song slowly trailed off. He stopped the rattle. Krill sat up and leaned against the brick wall. He breathed hard, blinking his eyes. Tatanka waited for him to catch his breath.

"What have you learned, flier?" he asked.

"Oh, God. She was in there. She was there. Oh, thank God. She was beautiful, but I could not touch her. The pain of it. To be with her, but not be able to kiss her." He wept into his wings.

"Did she speak to you?"

"Yes—yes! She had her voice back. But I couldn't understand her. It was a foreign tongue."

"Do you remember the sounds?"

"Yes—so melodic, so beautiful."

"Speak them to the lamp. From your heart, speak them."

Krill walked to the lamp and spoke, his voice more smooth and tender than I had ever heard it before.

"*Ghar man mirma marâ biyârid shûmâ,*
Mûrdeh be neghâr-e man sepârid marâ.
Ghar bôseh dahad bar lab-e pôsîdeh-e man.
Ghar zendeh shavam âjab madârid shûmâ."

The lamp vibrated against the furnace floor. Golden smoke poured from the spout. It swirled around the lamp more and more tightly, then flashed. There before us stood a radiant stork, white as an angel, wing tips a glimmering black, beak and long legs vibrant red, eyes a piercing bright yellow. It spread its wings, filling the small space, then wrapped them around Krill. Tatanka nodded toward the door. We crawled out the square of iron.

Tatanka closed and latched the door. We walked together to the bow. I had hoped Sweet might be there, speaking with her sister, Lady Liberty, but she was not. Tatanka and I smoked a cigarette. I had many questions I wanted to ask him, but did not trouble him. He had done enough. What could possibly be added by answering my *wasichu* questions?

After we finished smoking we went below to clean up the dinner dishes. Twenty minutes into it, the sound of fast footfalls above us signaled that something had happened. We rushed up the hatch.

Tosspot and his men surrounded the try-works. Krill's high voice squawked from inside the furnace. We ran over and found Tosspot halfway in the door. He scooted himself out, Krill tightly gripped in his right hand. He clapped him in miniature irons around his thin gray legs and backed him up against the brick wall.

Basma must have heard the commotion and arrived from her quarters. She wore a red nightshirt that revealed just enough of her supple shape to instantly kindle my longing. I yearned to wrap my arms around her, and draw her against my chest, but could not. I thrust my hands into the pockets of my snakeskins.

"What now, Tosspot? Another witch-hunt?" she asked, hands on hips, chocolate skin glistening in the golden torchlight.

"Perhaps it's against your principles, *Basma*, but I just so happen to be upholding the law."

"*BRACK!* What's the charge, what's the charge?"

"How does consorting with an enemy combatant grab you?"

"What?" asked Basmati Sweet, shooting me a questioning glance.

"You heard me. Mr. Krill has been caught having amorous relations with a stork. A stork that is no doubt a spy, and one that has been using him to gain valuable intelligence against our great country."

"*BRACK!* Message mix up. Got his stork tangled in a squid."

TP pointed a long, accusing finger at Krill's face. "Oh, you're good, aren't you, Peckerhead? Threw us off track with your squid ploy, all the while protecting your jihadist waterfowl friends. Saudi Arabia has no national bird— save perhaps *al Borak,* that mutant flying horse of Muhammad. Silverspoon may have fallen for your ruse, but I never did, and now the farmer's ax is sharp for parrot pie." Krill jumped up, rattling his little irons, and bit TP's finger. Tosspot pulled back his bleeding index and sucked on it.

"Remove the little pecker to a holding cell on shore. Send him to Batguano on the next available ship!" Basma turned to me with a worried look. I shrugged and tipped my hat back; what did she expect me to do? I knew by then the marshal wouldn't be happy until he arrested *somebody* close to Captain Silverspoon. Krill at least had a magic lamp to help him. What did Jesse James have?—except a record longer than the beard of Methuselah. Far as I knew, Krill hadn't robbed any banks or killed anybody. He'd find a way out of it.

Krill noticed Sweet's concern and winked at her. She looked back at me and shrugged. "BRACK! Tatanka! Avsa the ampla," Krill said in pig Latin. Tatanka nodded at him. We stood by and watched as TP and Speck were lowered in a lifeboat and rowed away with their prisoner.

"I do not speak his language," Tatanka told me later as we lay in our bunks. "Do you know the bird tongue? Avsa the ampla?"

"It's a silly code, Injun. It means save the lamp." He tapped something hollow with his fingers. I looked down and saw the copper lamp sitting on his pillow.

Two days later, Wrong John returned from the campaign trail to rest and catch up with business on *Liberty*. After a nap, he came out on the deck for some fresh air. The bright red-and-turquoise poison-dart frog sat on his right shoulder. The bilge pumps clattered and clanged, louder than ten tinkers loaded with pots and pans running down the street. A thick rope of water ran from a pipe out of the hatch, spread across the deck, and drained out the scuppers.

"Where's that damn bird? I had that frog sittin' in his place the last week, and he's got a whole new take on the mandate. Thought I better run it past birdbrain before I go to bat for Dart." His voice was high and nasally from the gauze stuffed in his nose. The bleeding problem must not have improved. The little frog, the size of Wrong John's thumb tip, shot out its pale green tongue, a long sticky muscle twice the length of his body, and nabbed a flittering mayfly.

"Krill's gone," I said, idly polishing Peacemaker with a swatch of gray felt.

"Gone? What do you mean, gone?"

"TP tossed him in the hoosegow. Intends on shipping him to The Tropics."

"What? He can't ship Krill off to the farm club. Take *me* out to the ballgame, will you? Get me the marshal!" I holstered Peacemaker and went to find Tosspot. We arrived together a few minutes later. He was halfway through shaving, and had cream over the left side of his face, a white towel tucked in the front of his shirt, and a razor in his hand.

"More trouble in the latrine, Sire?" Tosspot asked.

"You could say that, marshal. Turns out, you're in the shitter."

"*CROAK!*" blatted Dart.

"Pray tell, Sire? Have I offended thee?"

"You damn straight you offended thee. Where the hell's thee pet bird?" He pointed his finger at TP, and it was *not* loaded with a love bullet.

"I had to arrest him, Sire. The God Arrest America act requires the immediate detention and interrogation of spies."

"Spies? Shee-it. Who *idn't* a spy to you anymore?"

"You, Sire; myself; the Chief; Gunny Yo Yo—"

"That was a rhetor-a'frickin' question, dummy. How in hell'd you ever settle on Krill being a spy?"

"I'm sorry to have to break the news to you, Majesty, but we caught him consorting with a stork, a female stork, on our list of suspicious foreign animals. To get in bed with the enemy—*We're at war with storks!*—is high treason and must be punished with death." Tosspot's flaccid face shook with rage, spraying the deck with gobs of shaving cream.

Wrong John pulled Shalong's *Shalong* from his belt and leaned on it like an old man on his cane. The bulging hump on his back stretched his blue coat so that the sleeves pulled above his wrists. He scowled at TP with a tight-lipped frown. Something was off. I blinked my eyes and squinted at him. His chest rose and fell, and yet his nose was plugged and mouth closed. How was he breathing?

"The war is on *squid*, dummy, not storks," Silverspoon said to the marshal.

"Who was it that couched it in those terms, Majesty? Think back. And who attacked us? Did squid grow wings and fly through New York with bombs in their tentacles? Huh? I think your friend Krill has been spying for storks a *very* long time."

"Aw, nuts, TP. He's my right-hand bird. Can't you cut him a break?"

"Not when he abets the enemy, Sire. It's the law of the land. I am duty bound to uphold it, whether I like it or not. If you wish me to tender my resignation, I shall do so." He dropped one leg behind the other and bowed profusely.

Wrong John fumed and fidgeted at the brass buttons of his crisp navy coat. "CROAK!" said the vivid red-and-turquoise frog. Wrong John tipped his head in the direction of his tiny Weapon of Mass Hysteria. He nodded and grunted and whispered words to the bright amphibian on his shoulder, its body pulsating from rapid breathing.

"Okay, TP, let's move on. Dart's got me covered consultant-wise. I can't let that horny parrot drag me into a scandal at this point in the race. We move on, don't skip a beat, until we rescue the White House from perversion!"

"Uh, Majesty, that was last election's theme."

"Right, right. What I said was, 'Until we rescue America from squid!'"

"CROAK!"

TP came to attention and saluted the captain. "*Size matters!*"

Wrong John saluted and adjusted his pecker.

Suddenly the ship lurched violently side-to-side. I saw the tip of a tentacle from the corner of my eye, the exact brown of the hull, and heard the smacking of suction cups pulling away from the wood. I rushed to the side but the Giant Squid had already fallen invisibly into the water. Thirty dark men and women—Mexicans, Puerto Ricans, Cubans, Nicaraguans—streamed from the hatch, their eyes wide, jabbering in Spanish. The chief engineer followed them and rushed to the captain.

"Sir, I can't keep the workers down there! The thing has grown bold. It reaches into the hold with those slimy arms and grabs their legs." The engineer's arms flailed above his head. "It's impossible, sir. They call it *la diabla*, the devil, and it terrifies them." The absence of pumping stiffened the air, and it seemed to become glass, easily shattered by the first harsh word. I could feel the water pouring into the ship, weighing her down, swamping her hold. My legs got heavy, as if I too were filling from a hole somewhere in my feet.

"I'll handle it," said Wrong John. He turned to the Latino workers. "*Hombres y mujeres, no es necesario get scardo. El monstro es muy softo, squishimundo. Es un spongo."* He wrung his hands together as if squeezing out a sponge. The workers raised a din of protest in Spanish, shaking their heads, crossing themselves, and pointing toward the hatch. Wrong John drew his pistol and aimed it at them.

"I damn sure ain't going down from a strike. God, they wouldn't let me near a tee box at the club once that'un got around. Back to work, everbody. *Trabahando, muchachos! Ahora!"*

The brown-skinned workers continued to protest. Wrong John fired two rounds into the air, and they shuffled to the hatch and returned to the pumps. The engineer looked at me with such a wrinkled brow, it might as well have been he that Wrong John wrung.

Chapter LIV

The Return of Blackbeard

In the days that followed, news came to *Liberty* of two tragedies. First, it came to light that Lieutenant Jerry's campaign slogan, *Size Matters More*, was "gaining traction" with the voters. Jerry had somehow been able to expand the notion of masculine potency into other areas of policy besides the War on Squid. Voters were becoming convinced his "bedroom politics" might be stronger than Silverspoon's. They began to imagine he could use his big stick to get better and cheaper medical care, that he could stop the emigration of jobs at Ellis Outland, and that he could wave his abundant wand at the energy industry and shift the heat from blubber to renewable sources such as wind and sun.

Jerry even quoted from, of all things, *Moby-Dick*, and was especially fond of a line in "The Tail": "Real strength never impairs beauty or harmony, but it often bestows it; and in everything imposingly beautiful, strength has much to do with the magic." People began to doubt the stories of his tiny pecker. They began to wonder if the man belittling his opponent's dong might very well have a trouser deficit of his own. Jerry climbed ahead in the polls.

The second tragedy involved Chief Dagger. He had been dispatched to preempt Lieutenant Jerry's momentum, and seemed to be gaining ground. Tom Thumb raised the squid alert to Code Orange. This shifted attention away from the campaign. People instead boarded their windows and stacked sandbags around the local bank. Jerry's momentum began to fade. Chief turned the heat up on him during a speech at a blubber facility of his former employer, Hellbent Industries. Dagger stood on the platform around a boiling blubber vat and delivered a brutal attack on Lieutenant Jerry.

"A vote for Jerry is a vote for squid. Put him in office, and watch him run from Iraq. It will be back to Bubbaville, holding summits and kissing butts to avoid the hard realities of war. You saw how AQ punished the lisping Spaniards. Well get ready for worse—far worse." He pulled on his collar, stretched his neck, tugged on his gold hoop earrings.

"Why do you think the Squid Alert is at Code Orange? America on the verge of an attack?" Dagger asked. "Because Jerry's dick is *too small*. The Giant Squid senses it. That's why the alert has gone up. Jerry caused it with his dickless flip-flopping. His wishy-washy, weebly-wobbly, namby-pamby limpness is an open invitation to the Giant Squid: 'Come, mollusk. Attack us. We will do nothing to *defend* ourselves.'"

Despite the event being closely choreographed, a non-mandate journalist managed to breach the cordon and stand near the front of the press corps with the Clown Crier's and corporate oysters. She was later identified as the same reporter who years ago had confronted Wrong John in New Orleans about his military service, alleged opium smoking, and crooked business deals.

"Isn't it true that the company you used to run, Hellbent Industries, has profited by millions of dollars through the war in Iraq?" she charged.

Chief, caught by surprise, stumbled backward a few steps. He fired hate bullets from his bloodshot eyes, but they had no effect on the plucky reporter.

"And what of this news that Slick of Endrun Energy has orchestrated the biggest corporate swindle in history? He's a major contributor to your campaign, an old friend of the Silverspoon family, and reportedly the *biggest voice* on your secret energy committee."

Dagger stumbled backward another few steps, dangerously close to the bubbling golden blubber. "Slick? Slick who? We have no prior relationship with anyone named Slick. The name alone is *way* to slippery for honest men like the captain and me."

"Oh really?" said the woman. She brandished a Christmas card with the baby Jesus in a manger on front. "Here's a Christmas card. It says, 'Dear Chief Dagger, You old sidewinder. I count our friendship one of my best. Your position in government has been the best thing that every happened to Endrun Energy. Keep up the good work. Merry Christmas. Yours always, Slick. P.S. Don't forget to check your stocking.' How do you explain that?"

Dagger backpedaled some more and then tumbled into the vat of boiling oil. He was dead within seconds. I thought it a fitting end to his "immortality project," one that played well with the everlasting tragedy he hoped would carry his name forward through time.

The news hit Wrong John like a sucker punch to the belly, midway through his morning jog. He doubled over and fell to the deck. He was unable to catch a breath and quickly became deathly white. The quartermaster could not resuscitate him. I thought he would die, but his new pet, Dart, rubbed up against his cheek and croaked in his ear. The toxin in its slimy skin shocked Wrong John. His body convulsed and he began to breathe fitfully through his mouth. A few minutes later, he was breathing normally and regaining his color.

Dart worked on him for the next hour, sitting on his shoulder, speaking a language only the captain could hear. Wrong John stood and wobbled to his roundhouse. Again he withdrew for many days and would not come out. No one attempted to rouse him.

One fair day the pale blue sky radiated animal clouds on a one-way merry-go-round, a haze of blubber smoke lay low and gray over the Potomac, bilge pumps clanged below, and I spied a three-masted schooner approaching, the Star-Spangled Jolly Roger waving from its mast. It came alongside and hailed us. I immediately recognized the captain as Proconsul Blackbeard.

"Ahoy!" he shouted.

"Ahoy!" returned Pinch. She ran to the captain's quarters with news of Blackbeard's arrival. This must have brightened him, for he soon emerged, blinking in the sunlight, and walked to the stern to welcome Blackbeard

"Permission to come aboard," hollered the pirate.

"Granted." The captain stepped back from the rail. "The return of Blackbeard. Wow. That's a good thing, right?" Pinch nodded, but not very convincingly.

Proconsul Blackbeard lowered a longboat and came alongside with his giant Slavic guard, Creuton, wearing his iron mask; the two big Africans, Rohumba and Arandi; and Lars, the herculean blonde South African with gold hoop earrings and a bone through his lower lip. Speck dropped a rope ladder and they came aboard, landing heavily on deck with their clunky boots, backs strapped with swords, pistols, crossbows, and hatchets. Blackbeard's face had grown gaunt and sallow since I had last seen him. His scraggly beard seemed thinner and grayer, but he swaggered nevertheless, his cutlass waving, wrist bracelets jangling, and smiling with that big, black gap in his front teeth.

"To what do I owe the leisure of your company, proconsul?" asked the captain, offering a hand. Blackbeard shook it and smiled with his meager teeth.

"I've given Iraq her sovereignty, skipper, and so I've brought me crew back home."

"Sovereignty? You mean—it's—that's it? You've got Cherubic installed as the shah?" asked the captain, Dart perched on his shoulder, panting. Silverspoon pulled Shalong's sword and leaned on it. His hump now forced him to bend over like an old hag.

"Cherubic? Not that blackguard! He's swabbing the walls of Jahannum, that one. A true turncoat, him—back-stabbing villain! Not fit to call himself a pirate. Not in my book." Blackbeard spit on the deck. "Have ye got any grog, sir? We ran dry off Cape Hatteras, and me boys be a might grumpy by now." The surly band of feral dogs gathered around Blackbeard, leering at Silverspoon and fondling their weaponry.

"Oh, sure. Whatever. Pinch, call down to the galley for pints all around." She licked her lips, slapped her hands together, and hollered down the hatch. Silverspoon continued. "Who's the shah then? I mean, you can't just—just give them back their country like that."

"Indeed I can! Indeed I have! I've got the most bloodthirsty of the lot running Iraq for us, skipper. He'll be right. And let him have the flea-bitten mongrel of a land, too. There's nothing left for us, sir. It's a waste, pure and simple. A complete waste. Anything worth me time's loaded on me ship there, the *Coalition*, set to be portioned among me good crew here." He looked around at his band of dogs. They thumped their chests and grunted. "And ye, sir, ye of course as well." Blackbeard took off his tattered black leather, tricorn hat and bowed.

"Time out there, partner. You can't just leave. I give the orders around here. I'm the commander."

"*CROAK!*" added the frog.

"Beggin' your pardon, sir, but it's time we moved on. Shalong had the place completely ruined, skipper. Baghdad's a shantytown from hill to vale, chockablock with bilious people impossible to tame. They're leaving the whales to rot in the sun. Won't let us near the beasts. No, sir. Iraq's hardly a prize worthy the great Captain Silverspoon. We need a new enemy, sir, someone fresh and fat and ready for the slaughter. Might I suggest the Persians, skipper?"

"*CROAK!*" The captain tilted his head toward his frog. He nodded and grunted.

"Dart likes it, so what the hell. Wrong John's my name, regime change my game."

"There ye be, skipper! There ye be!"

Pinch arrived, followed by Roberto carrying a tray loaded with frothy beer mugs, and Tatanka toting a second piled with sliced ham, yellow cheese, and rounds of rye bread. The pirates set upon it like pigs, snorting, sloshing beer, tearing hunks of meat and cheese with their broken, crooked, brown-stained teeth. They belched and farted, and banged into one another's swords, crossbows and armor. I elbowed my way in and got a cold brew and a slab of meat. Pinch was right in there, swilling beer with the best of them.

A half-dozen corporate lobbyists piled over the rail and sauntered over. They wore the fine foppery of upper-class gentry: shining tricorn hats with ostrich plumes out the back, sleek chiffon britches, black shoes with brass buckles on top, white shirts with flouncy dickeys running down the front.

"I didn't know it was 'Pirate Night' on *Liberty*," said the tall fresh-faced one in the lead. "I would have rolled a bum for the proper attire."

"Is this *all* you've got, Wrong John?" asked another, scowling at the plate of food. "Stale beer and rancid cold cuts?"

Wrong John cast them a wan smile. "Hey, fellas. I don't know what else we got. Talk to the cook."

"Talk to the cook?" said the leader. "We don't talk to *cooks*."

"Unless we need an accounting report," interjected another, to the chortles of his mates.

"Who's the head waiter around here?" the leader asked. "You there, with the pretty earrings. Take my order."

Lars turned slowly. He squared his broad shoulders, narrowed his pale blue eyes, and ran his upper teeth over the bone stitched into his lower lip.

"Who be these dandies?" questioned Blackbeard, slapping a hand on Lars' leather clad shoulder.

"Who be we?" the leader said. "We *be* your boss, dirt bag. Now fetch us the good scotch, would you?"

"Bugger off, ye wanker." Blackbeard turned to the captain and frowned, his tongue working at something stuck in a molar. Wrong John shrugged his shoulders.

"Bugger off? I don't think you get it. We *own Liberty*. This is *our* ship. Now you'd better just—"

Blackbeard pulled on his right earring—the signal for his mob to break out. They dropped their mugs of grog and set upon the lobbyists. Creuton grabbed one in each arm and tossed them overboard. Lars lifted the leader over his head, spun him a couple of turns, and threw him in the drink. The other lobbyists ran for the rail and jumped over, chased by Rohumba and Arandi, waving their bone-pitted machetes.

The pirates returned to the feast laid out on the capstan, laughing and slapping each other's backs. Roberto came up from the hatch with a fresh tray of frothy mugs. The pirates hoisted grog, clanged mugs together, and chugged them, suds dribbling down their chins.

"Best to not mix ye pirates, skipper," Blackbeard said from behind his hand. "Makes a bloody mess of bones and booty. Always gets ugly." Blackbeard tore into a hunk of ham and pointed to the captain's shoulder. "I see ye put ye fat parrot on rations. Well done, sir. I prefer the cut of his jib, sleek and slippery with a poison back for good measure. Where be the parrot, by the by?"

"Got himself arrested. Caught in the sack with a stork, if you can believe it. Stupid bird." Wrong John leaned on his sword.

"He has something of mine—a lamp. Know ye where it be, skipper?"

"Nope."

"Keep an eye peeled for that bleedin' parrot, boys. I want me lamp."

"You must have huge hole below," said the giant Slav in his broken English, his girth broad as two men, iron mask tipped back over his head. "The pumps—they sound like sword battle."

"Hungry barnacles. No big deal. Got 'er under control." Wrong John pulled a hunk of ham from the platter and joined it with a slice of cheese and bread. Blackbeard ripped off a chunk of yellow cheese from a thick round, grunted, and cleared his throat.

"The bloody Arabs, skipper, they fight dirty, let me tell ye. They've made a stand in the graveyard, sir. Lured us into stomping the bones of their ancestors, they have. The spirits be much restless over it, skipper. Much restless." Blackbeard shuddered and took a long draw of brew.

"No one can beat that army," added the monstrous Slav with a deep belch. "Those the deepest cemeteries the world over. Two hundred generations deep. Who can fight an enemy such as this?"

"The by-God American military, that's who!" said Silverspoon defiantly.

"CROAK!" added his frog.

Blackbeard and his pirates looked at each other and shook their heads. "The final straw, skipper, be when the bloody coalition lost its nerve." He beat on his chest, sending shards of yellow cheese flying. "It breaks me bleedin' heart, skipper, to report to ye the victory our so-called mates gave to Quota when they let him grab the tiller and steer their ships of state. First there be the Spaniards—cowards all they be."

"No kiddin'," said Wrong John. "And I used to *like* tacos."

"Then come the kidnappings, skipper. Friends helping us rebuild: Japanese, Koreans, Turks. The villains swore to take their heads if their countries didn't withdraw their armies. Can ye imagine, sir, me true chagrin when Satan's angels captured a wagon driver from the Philippines? I wanted him back, sir, that I did with all me heart. The monsters scrawled a note, demanding every soldier of the Philippine army leave Iraq at once, or they would lop the lad's head."

The captain swallowed hard, tugged at the collar of his shirt, and craned his neck. I supposed he had recalled the decapitated Martha Little. His tropical frog sat impassively on his shoulder, pulsating from its rapid breath. The other pirates munched the tender meat, grunted, and sloshed their grog.

"I begged the Philippine commander not to curtsy for the squid. I told him the mandate forbids negotiating with terrorists. The general tried to stand firm, but the sheepish queen of that country, sir, she handed him his balls—bloody wenches! they've never mixed with piracy, that's why the code has *always* banned them, ALWAYS! The saintly crone ordered all her troops home, every last one—a great moral victory for squid the ocean under." He removed his hat and placed it over his heart and bowed his head. His men followed suit.

"What?" asked Wrong John, leaning forward on Shalong's sword. "They up and left? That's not allowed. Silverspoon Mandate states very clearly, Chapter 6, Verse 10: There will be no—no, there won't be any—uh—you can't leave or change, the, uh, the thingamajig—until I say so."

"CROAK!"

"Alas, skipper, they defied ye, and we came to utter defeat. The lady, sir, the Queen of the Islands, she ruined it, mucked it up with her mercy, and bloody hell, skipper, the jig was up and home I come, a done pirate, skipper. Scuttled I was, by that one daft, gentle lady. She ended the war, skipper, for the sake of one simple peasant man—a lowly pilot, that is all, of a mere supply wagon." Blackbeard squeezed the edges of his hat and bent them in two. His men looked down and fell still, neither to drink nor to eat, but only to look down and utter not a word.

The pirates quietly finished their food and drink and retired to their ship. That evening I parked myself at the bow, hoping the second mate would pay a visit to her sister. I smoked a cigarette and gazed at the bright star rising to the east. It must have been one of the big planets, Jupiter or Saturn, it was so full and bright above the tree line. I felt a hand on my shoulder, and turned with a smile—dropping instantly to a frown.

"Well, well, well. Ishcabibble's up from the dungeon. How do you sleep down there with all the racket, *Ish?*" asked the marshal, his voice sticky with superiority, holding a hurricane lamp.

"I sleep fine, marshal. How do you sleep after what you done to Krill?" I puffed on my cigarette and blew the smoke in his face. Tatanka silently walked up and stopped about ten feet behind Tosspot. He looked at Tosspot, brought his fist to his hand, then opened his hands and tilted his head to the side. I could tell he was ready to jump the marshal. I gave him one quick shake of my head.

Tosspot side-stepped to the starboard rail and leaned against it with his elbow. "Funny you should mention the parrot. Now that he's behind bars, I can turn my attention to public enemy number one." He slapped his bullwhip.

"I never heard of a lawman arresting himself."

"I more had in mind Jesse James. Have you seen the rascal anywhere?"

"We already been through this, marshal. I never run across the James brothers."

"That's funny," he said dryly, stroking his jowly cheeks. "Charlie Ford says you're the spitting image of Dingus."

That's when it clicked. That Pinkerton in the dairy, the one kept eyeballing me. I knew he was familiar. Tosspot had recruited that traitor to finger me. Well, I told myself, the old bullet next to my heart may have said the war was over, but it looks like one more will have to die. Then an ally showed up.

Up behind the marshal waved six or seven monstrous tentacles. The two longest ones with wide, paddle shaped ends, seemed to have some sense about them, like antennae. They felt the air around Tosspot and closed in on him.

"Better watch your back, marshal."

"Is that a threat?"

"No, it's a fact. The Giant Squid's about to give you a kiss."

He turned slowly, just as that flat paddle, covered with sharp suction cups, was about to wrap around his throat. He leaped away, into my arms. The tentacles shot out and pulled on him. I pulled back. Tosspot screamed. He struggled to free himself from the grip. The Giant Squid and I had a tug of war with Marshal Tosspot. I was losing.

Then came a flash of steel. Tatanka's jackknife sliced into a tentacle. Brown goo oozed from the cut. The tentacle slipped away. The Lakota sliced the other. It too oozed the brown goo and pulled back. A slippery splash came from the river. Tosspot panted, his face dripping with brackish river water, whole body shaking.

I pushed him back against the foremast. "Here's the deal, marshal. You forget about Charlie Ford. You forget about Jesse James. Or we feed you to the Giant Squid. What's it going to be?"

He held up his hands. "Fine. Fine. It's forgotten."

"Good. Now you go on and face your fear, Marshal." I drew Peacemaker and escorted him to the whaleboats. Tatanka and I lowered him and watched him oar frantically toward shore.

Tatanka handed me a smoke and smiled at me. He gave us both a light and didn't speak for a minute. "Out there in the North Sea, you said Tosspot was a dead man."

"Well, I prayed on that, Injun. The white buffalo woman, she said there was another way."

"Huh. Maybe so."

Chapter LV

Eat the Squid, Skipper

In the following days Blackbeard grew close to the captain. He regaled him nightly with tales of his worldly adventures. He spoke of cities sieged and conquered, rampages along the Spanish Main, wild debauchery in old Saint John's. Wrong John fell to staying up late and sleeping in. He stopped jogging, and I believed he wasn't long away from tippling a bottle of rum. Blackbeard and his gang certainly did, every night and half the day. All the time Silverspoon's poison frog could be found squatting on his right shoulder. Wrong John wore a flask of water over his shoulder and doused his new consultant every so often. Dart thanked him with its one word, "*CROAK!*"

So complete was the slide into irreverence, Silverspoon discontinued the morning prayer to start the day, and the evening prayer to end it. Tatanka stepped in privately and lit his *chanupa* at dawn and dusk to welcome divine guidance into our days.

Night after night Blackbeard croaked in Silverspoon's left ear, Dart croaked in his right, and Wrong John Silverspoon slowly transformed into a bonafide buccaneer. He stopped shaving, stopped cutting his hair or brushing his teeth or bathing. He gave up his crisp navy coat for a pigskin vest Blackbeard gave him. He consented to a piercing of both ears and his naval, and took to wearing gold hoops in all three. "Now that Chief's gone," he said, "somebody's got to carry the little golden thingies."

One evening after dinner, Blackbeard's men stormed the captain's quarters and pinned him to the wall by the tips of their sabers. They forced him to strip to his skivvies and wait for further orders. I did not even flinch toward the twin terrors at my sides. Whatever happened to Wrong John Silverspoon from that point forward I reckon he deserved. I went out on the deck and found Blackbeard and his other pirates filling the try-pots with water, and lighting a fire in the furnace. Another placed spermaceti candles all around the kiln.

Just before midnight, Blackbeard ordered the candles lit, along with several torches placed off the masts and rails. By then the try-pots boiled. Vapors of steam rose from them, filling the air with the strong smell of fish guts. Smoke chuffed from the roaring furnace. Tatanka had dumped three- and four-foot long squid tentacles into the try-pots. They had been cooking for more than an hour. To starboard of the try-works, the crews of both *Liberty* and the *Coalition* had gathered in an unruly cluster. Gone were the days of precise ranks on either side of the deck. None of *Liberty*'s crew dressed in their navy uniforms; they instead wore baseball caps and jerseys emblazoned with the marks of corporate sponsors underwriting the voyage.

"Bring me the scallywag!" roared Blackbeard.

Speck delivered the message to the roundhouse. Blackbeard's African pirates, Rohumba and Arandi, dragged Wrong John out to the try-works and stood him before the boiling vats of squid. The tips of rubbery legs poked into the air, waving and jostling in turbulent water. I stood with Basma and Tatanka on the foredeck and watched as the humped captain, wearing only his skivvies (and his frog ornament), kneeled before the pirate Blackbeard. Wrong John's eyes darted in all directions, searching, it seemed, for someone to protect him.

Blackbeard banged his cutlass against the brick structure and looked down at the captain. "Well, matey, it's been nigh four years of ye dancing arm's length with the devil. It's bloody well time to end this charade and make ye a consecrated buccaneer." He flashed his gap-toothed grin.

"*CROAK!*" said the neon frog.

Blackbeard turned to the try-pot and skewered the two-foot tip of a brown-streaked tentacle. He turned and held the limp arm in front of Wrong John's face.

"Eat it, skipper, and be who ye truly are. Eat it, and be made strong by the flesh of ye enemy. Bite, captain, bite hard, chew good and swallow. Make the battle with evil ye own battle. Take it back from the curs of Al Quota and make it ye own. Eat the squid, skipper. Swallow it deep."

He wiggled the squid arm in front of Silverspoon. Blackbeard's men pounded in unison on their scabbards with their fists. The golden candlelight flickered and flashed in the blue eyes of Wrong John, against his dirty, unshaven face, against the wet tentacle of the squid and Blackbeard's sharp sword. Silverspoon licked his lips, and looked quickly around. He brought his fists to his chest and rocked his head back, squeezed his eyes shut and bared his teeth, and pounded his chest with his fists.

His head came forward and he leaned in toward the squid, but he didn't open his mouth. He turned his head to the side and spoke to Dart. "I can't do it. It's dirty. It's ugly. We don't eat squid. God no! We hunt squid, kill 'em and burn 'em. The captain does not eat squid."

"*CROAK!*"

"No, Dart! I won't do it! I eat that squid and I become evil—a little part of me becomes evil, and it grows. I'm the good guy. I want to stay good." He looked over at me. "IshcaBible! Throw me a quote, *amigo.*"

"Sorry sir, the only reference that seems apt has to do with the Eucharist, and to compare the body and blood of Christ with the present menu, well sir, would that not be sacrilege?"

"Aw, jeez. Hell if I know. Just give me somethin' holy—anything!"

"Okay, captain. Here's John 6:53-56:

> Then Jesus said unto them, Verily, verily, I say unto you,
> Except ye eat the flesh of the Son of man, and drink his
> blood, ye have no life in you.
> Whoso eateth my flesh, and drinketh my blood, hath eternal
> life; and I will raise him up at the last day.
> For my flesh is meat indeed, and my blood is drink indeed.
> He that eateth my flesh, and drinketh my blood, dwelleth in
> me, and I in him.

"Jesus is not a squid!" screamed Silverspoon. He looked around for mercy, but saw none reflected back at him. "What in tarnation am I gonna do?"

"Eat the squid, skipper," said Blackbeard. "There be no other way. Eat it and be saved. Take back from it ye power. Claim ye own murderin' ways. Give them not to squid, nor terror, nor evil, nor any other curse. Make them ye own and turn them to the good."

The pirates pounded on their scabbards. The metal handles of the bilge pumps banged against their casings—a jangle and clash rising from the hold that sounded like a prison uprising. Two long, slippery tentacles slithered through a scupper on either side of the ship along the deck, and wriggled toward Wrong John Silverspoon. Basma reached over and grabbed my arm. Tatanka's stern face looked as it had during his mumblety-peg game with Wrong John. Blackbeard glared at Silverspoon along the sharp edge of his sword. Wrong John carried on an urgent whispered conversation with the silent poison frog.

Basma released my arm and strode down the quarterdeck stairs. She walked up to Blackbeard, and stretched her long, elegant neck toward the tip of the tentacle. She stuck out her soft, sleek red tongue and pulled the brown squid arm into her mouth.

"Basma!" shouted Silverspoon.

She bit down and pulled away a chunk of meat. She closed her eyes and chewed slowly, deliberately, softly groaning.

"Basma, no! You're pure. You're one of the good guys. We are children of the light—of the light. We cast all evil out of us when we opened our hearts to the Lord. Don't let the evil back in!" He reached out to her, but she drew away from him, closer to Blackbeard.

"One of the good guys?" she asked, her voice natural, unstrained, womanly. "You think I'm one of the *good guys?*" Her eyes spoke sharp fierceness into him. Wrong John shrunk back. "You think I'm pure? Just one of the pure old good old boys?" Her hands went to the buttons at the chest of her pleated muslin shirt. She grabbed the folds of her shirt and tore it open. Her fine, soft, vibrant breasts spilled out of the fabric, glistening with sweat in the pulsing candlelight, black nipples erect, breasts rising and falling with her strong, fast breath. Wrong John stared at them. He blinked hard. The squid arm rocked slowly back and forth from the end of Blackbeard's sword.

"I am a woman, Wrong John Silverspoon! I am a black woman! I reject your colorblindness! I reject your pale, bland, lifeless world. I am black. I am *colorful*. See me! I hold all colors, all emotions, all dreams. Every painting that has ever been made lives in this skin." She slapped her chest with both hands. "Do not wash me out! I am dark. I embrace the hidden—all possibility awaiting birth in the dark, feminine womb. I open my heart to love. I open my heart to the unknown. I want to live, and to live means to get dirty. I did not come into this world to be pure! I am here to live, to get dirty, to take risks. I am here to love." She looked up at me, tears in her fierce eyes, tenderness in her vulnerable breasts, rising and falling with her breath. She leaned to the squid, took another bite, slowly chewed, and swallowed.

"I am not pure, Wrong John. Nobody is." She pulled the shrunken head from her belt and held it up for all to see. The squid tentacles squirmed closer to Silverspoon from the sides of the ship.

"This shrunken head is a fake. It is a wooden carving, painted by a make-up artist to look real, like that wooden nickel nailed to the mast. It is a fake, like my voice, and my mustache, and my rubber dick. I thought I needed them, to make me more than I am. I didn't think a woman—God forbid, a *black* woman—had enough to stand on the ship of power. BUT I WAS WRONG! I am enough! This mission is not worthy *of me!* It is beneath *me* to go along with this lie. I divorce myself from this cursed mission. I divorce myself from servitude, from the need to be controlled by the white master. I am not Pip. I choose freedom. I choose *LIBERTY!* I will to ride the open ocean of my true destiny."

She reared back and threw the wooden head over the ship and into the Potomac. She looked at me and smiled, walked to the opposite side of *Liberty*, tore off her shirt, climbed out of her pants, threw off her silk bandana. She climbed the rail, dove into the water, and swam for shore.

All eyes went to Wrong John. He licked his lips, squinted, leaned toward the squid, shaking, his hump quivering, and took a small bite. He swallowed it without chewing. He had his mouth closed, and his bloody nose plugged with gauze, yet he breathed. Was his T-shirt rising and falling above the hump? Nah, I told myself, that's impossible. The Giant Squid's tentacle that had slithered inches from his foot withdrew, slipped along the deck and out the side. *Liberty* trembled from a shake by the squid. The pumps clanged, clattered, and the water poured from the pipe out the hatch.

"*CROAK!*" said the frog. Blackbeard thrust his sword into the air. The pirates ripped loose with three "Huzzas!" Tatanka looked at me and shook his head.

Chapter LVI

A Squid in Every Pot

Next morning a gaggle of vultures fought at the try-pots over the leftover squid soup. When Tatanka and I rose from the forecastle they barely noticed us and wouldn't shy off even as we ran at them and yelled. We finally gave up and left them to their rubbery, tentacled feast. Wrong John and Blackbeard gathered in the roundhouse to plan a trip of re-election plunder on shore. Several days later they rallied in the early evening for an event at Mt. Vernon, the estate of George and Martha Washington. *Liberty* weighed anchor and sailed north of the city to the estate on a bluff overlooking the river.

I was about to climb into a longboat to go ashore when Tatanka grabbed my arm. "I have to get Krill his lamp," he told me. "Next boat to Batguano leaves today."

"Okay, brother," I said, smiling. "I'll see you later."

"Maybe not." His face was grave. "The night eagle—it rises. The ship cannot withstand it. Do not go back aboard."

"Okay," I said, turning. I got into the whaleboat with Wrong John and the pirates. Blackbeard's mercenaries put their strong backs into rowing us to shore. A flock of noisy vultures continued to fight over squid parts on the try-works. Just as the whaleboat reached the small dock at Mt. Vernon, the pumping crew on *Liberty* poured silently from the hold and into whaleboats on the far side of the ship. It looked to me like a prison break. They lowered and rowed away. I noticed the tall Lakota among them. I placed my hand over my heart, grateful for our friendship, imagining it was the last I would see of him.

Wrong John and Blackbeard, intent on what was ahead of them, fixed their gazes to shore and didn't notice the desertion. I had felt the brief tidal surge in *Liberty's* bowels when the pumping crew threatened a mutiny, and was certain that when Silverspoon completed his program he would return to a sunken ship.

A group of citizens had gathered on the sweeping bowling green that separated Washington's Mansion House Farm from the Potomac. This was not a carefully managed rally, as Krill would have orchestrated, exclusive to partisan fans. It was a Dart rally, organized around survival of the fittest. They appeared to be mostly Silverspoon supporters, but there were a few *Size Matters More* placards on display. Off to one side the newly reprised *Mutual Masturbation Corps* signed up new recruits to its popular platoon, "The 69 Club." The crowd chattered nervously and held an edginess that reminded me of an elk herd catching the first whiff of a panther. I could see why as the pirates cut a swath through the crowd on our way to the front piazza of the mansion. There on a two-story, skirted platform between the white pillars stood a twenty-foot- square Squid Alert tank. Of the ten or so five-foot-long mollusks undulating through the water, five were bright orange, and the remainder were orange, blushing red.

Tom Thumb stood on the platform with a megaphone explaining the reason for the Code Orange-Plus. "The Great Communicator has died! Our inspiration, our crusader, is gone. Squid everywhere are emboldened! Code Orange-Plus! Half a click away from devastation! Look around you. Who looks evil? Be vigilant! Search the suspicious for bombs or Lieutenant Jerry pamphlets!" Fights broke out in the audience as vigilant citizens preempted terror by attacking men who had a vaguely Arab scent to their mustaches. Agents of Homemade Insecurity added to the melee by blowing their whistles and slapping the unpatriotic in the face with small purple squid.

Wrong John and Blackbeard went behind the black-skirted stage and climbed the ladder. They stood beside Tom Thumb, both of them at least twice his size, and waved to the crowd. Wrong John and Blackbeard appeared to be brothers. Both wore tricorn hats, faded blue frocks, knee-high black leather boots, and cutlasses at their waists. They had scruffy beards, earrings, and bracelets at their wrists. Wrong John's nose was stuffed with blood-soaked gauze. He used Shalong's *Shalong* as a cane, and had Dart poised on his shoulder. He placed his hand on the fish tank and closed his eyes. His body began to shake.

Tom Thumb drew back, mouth gaping and eyes wide. "Look!" he boomed through the megaphone bigger than him. "The heir apparent has calmed the squid!" Magically, the paddling marine mollusks translated the rainbow of alarm from orange-red, to yellow-orange, to light blue, and all the way to solid, steady green. A collective sigh arose from the crowd. I could hear the agents under the stage working the colored film in and out of the hidden slot beneath the tank.

"It's a miracle!" Thumb roared. "Code Green! The terror threat is *low!* Captain Silverspoon has joined his mind with that of the squid. He has *communicated* with it—Greatly Communicated. He has exuded the power that sends it shrinking to the darkest depths." The crowd whistled and cheered.

Wrong John turned to them, smiling and waving, though bent over from the hump and leaning on his sword. "We all grieve the loss of the Great Communicator. God rest his silver tongue. His legacy is in the hands of this mouth." He pointed at his open maw. "When it comes to chewin' the fat, I am the king of gristle. I'll be speaking in accord with my mandate, *preemptively*—that is to say *before* I think. If you want to start callin' me Great Communicator II, well okay. Just don't call me late for supper."

"*CROAK!*" Dart blatted.

"The legacy lives on!" shouted Tom Thumb. "The legacy lives on! The legacy lives on!" He chanted, and the crowd followed him. Wrong John bowed his bent form even lower.

"My God!" someone shouted. "Look at the size of that hump!" A wave of anxious whispers rippled through the crowd.

Wrong John righted himself as best he could. "Let me say a word about my competitor. 'Word.' There, that's about all he deserves. He's all talkin' about *Size Matters More*. That shows his complete stupidity concernin' the War on Squid. Look at my Weapon of Mass Hysteria." He gestured at Dart. "He ain't big—but he's damn dangerous if you don't know how to handle him. What's the most dangerous critter in the world? A spider, no bigger than my thumb. But what's even more dangerous than that? Disease, friends. It's so tiny you can't even see it. *Size Matters More*—shee-it! What a *more-on*. I know these squid—know how they think, how they operate. They don't buy into boasting about the size of your organ. They judge you on your true character. If you ain't got it, you ain't got it." He grabbed his crotch.

"With me today is my new first mate, Blackbeard, fresh from a stunning victory in Iraq. He turned over sovereignty, and the world is a safer place because of it. Our mission to liberate and democratize Iraq is complete. It's on to bigger and better enemies." Blackbeard doffed his hat and bowed.

"One of my first initiatives is to declare a new national holiday to be celebrated on 10-10 of every year," Wrong John said. ""It's called National Squid Day, and Blackbeard will tell you all about it. Blackbeard?" Wrong John stepped back and Blackbeard came forward.

"Thank ye, skipper. 'Tis a fine day here at the home of President George Washington. 'Tis a day to deepen and make more clear our common purpose as Americans. 'Tis a day to make the tragedy of 10-10 a tragedy not to be shunned, but one to be celebrated. We thereby declare the anniversary of the stork attack National Squid Day in America.

"There shall be a squid in every pot, and all of us together shall on that day break bread and tentacle together. Verily, we shall share a meal of terror, and by eating terror we shall not fear it, but shall rather overcome it, swallow and digest it, and make it our very own. Only by eating squid shall we know evil. Only by knowing evil shall we defeat it. There is no beating the Giant Squid, invisible in the darkness a thousand feet beneath the sea. We must coax it up, let it wrap its tentacles around us, dance close with us under the full moon, make it our friend and, finally, our flesh."

Blackbeard's men clapped their scabbards, causing a wave of applause to pass through the crowd. Wrong John patted Blackbeard on the back and stepped in front of him. "National Squid Day," he said. "Got a nice ring to it. Hey—eat your squid with a silver spoon! Had some myself just the other night. Strange flavor. It let's you be who you really are." He tilted his head toward the poison frog and nodded and grunted.

"*CROAK!*"

"Here's the deal. Eat your squid and gain the strength, like I did, to admit you're a pirate. It's an initiation we all gotta do. Eat your squid and admit you love money more than anything else. Admit with me you're willing to do anything to keep your big house, your big horses, your big wagons, and your big debt. Chew the squid and relish the truth of America's pirate way. Admit we take most of the blubber in the world. Admit we take human and natural resources wherever we can find them easiest and cheapest. No one can challenge us because we've got the biggest military and the fattest wallet. Hell, it's a nice position to be in."

The crowd seemed perplexed by his words, unsure how to react to them. It was not the sort of speech Krill would have allowed, but Krill was in prison and Dart held the place of honor. The frog was not at all like the parrot. He came from the wet hollow of a tree, deep in the Amazon rain-forest. To touch his slimy red and blue back was to die.

"You see, folks, it's like this. You really did give me a mandate. You said protect our stuff. Do whatever it takes. Keep us comfy and cozy, you said. That's my mandate. Now some of you may complain, say I've gone too far, but after you eat your squid, you'll get it. We're all pirates. We plunder the world. We take what we want and enjoy it, because that's what you do when you rule the seven seas. Simple as that. But I'm not gonna stop there."

He walked across the stage to Tom Thumb and pulled a squid from his pocket. Wrong John threw it into the crowd. "I'm going for the *BIG mandato enchilato*. Squid may be squid. They may be ugly and gooey. But there's a worser enemy out there—way more terrifying than any squid. I'm declaring war on it. Hear me now: America declares *WAR ON DEATH!* We will hunt death down and kill it wherever it hides. We will show death no mercy, and will not rest until death has been eliminated from the earth!"

He walked back to the fish tank and banged it with Shalong's sword. Black jets of ink squirted out the butts of frightened squid that shot away. "Anybody dies in Silverspoon America, they will be subject to torture. We will burn them with hot irons. We will drive nails into their fingers. We will pull their teeth, one by one, until they confess! until they tell us *why they died!*"

He put his arm around Blackbeard, who smiled nervously and looked around for his band of scoundrels.

"I will erect a death shield around America—far superior to our current missile defense. I call it 'Laugh of God,' and it will be impossible for the dark angel to breach. Yes, it will cost billions of dollars and drain the treasury for generations to come. So what? You gave me a mandate. I will not rest until death has been eliminated from America!"

"CROAK!"

Wrong John turned and climbed down from the platform. The crowd, it seemed, had been paralyzed by the magnitude of Silverspoon's new war. He pushed his way through them, bent in half, using his head as a ram. Blackbeard and the pirates followed him across the bowling green to the dock.

Chapter LVII

Make That Third Wish

The pirates boarded their longboat and rowed back to *Liberty*. Seven redheaded vultures perched silently on a yard of the main mast. Corporate flags hung limply in the calm. Old Glory had faded so completely it had gone colorblind, and hung like the white flag of surrender. Someone had taken the black coffin that was roped to the yard. Well, Ishcabibble, I told myself, there goes your life-buoy. We came aboard and something was immediately different. I knew it was the lack of pumping, but it took Wrong John and Blackbeard a while to recognize the change.

"Awful quiet out here," said the captain.

"That it is, skipper, that it is," added Blackbeard softly.

"Thing is, we ain't sinkin'. I guess the leak fixed itself. I've always been lucky that way. Things work out for me, just because I'm me."

It stayed quiet for a while, then that awful gnawing sound rose from the hold. I could picture the black beak of the Giant Squid chewing through a rib of the hull. Wrong John and the pirates gathered around the hatch to get a better listen. A huge tentacle shot out and wrapped around Lars, the big, blonde South African. He screamed and tried to pull his knife, but the squid had his arms pinned. He kicked and fought, but the squid constricted, reeled him in, and pulled him down inside the ship. The captain and the others leapt away from the hatch. The leak hadn't fixed itself, but had only been plugged temporarily by the gooey body of the Giant Squid.

"Dang it," said Wrong John. "*Liberty*'s been occupied."

Blackbeard and his gang backed further from the hatch. "Well now, that's another kettle of fish," said Blackbeard. "We'll be on our way now." He doffed his hat and bowed to Silverspoon. He and his men walked toward the longboat.

"Wait a second," said Wrong John. "I thought the squid was good, that we wanted it close, so we could feed on it and make it our own."

"Sure, skipper, sure we do, but we don't want her takin' the ship. Blimey! That shows ye've waited too long to wrestle with her, sir, that she's grown too bold. All is lost when she's moved into ye home and outgrown ye supper table."

"But I took a bite. I did it. I came clean."

"That little nibble? Lordy, skipper, that was hardly the banquet of a man ordained to rid the world of evil. We'll be off now to dry dock the *Coalition*, make repairs, and celebrate with our loot from Iraq. Fare thee well, skipper, fare thee well." He turned and leaped over the rails, caught hold of the rope ladder, and climbed down to the longboat. His men followed.

The gargantuan Slav paused at the mainmast and pulled off the hickory nickel with his teeth.

"Hey!" shouted Silverspoon. "That's for the lad raises me the Giant Squid."

The big man spit the plug nickel into his hand. He tossed it at the captain. "Keep your eyes open. She may be close." He turned and climbed over the rail.

Wrong John caught the nickel. He watched them row away, his eyes small and sad, mouth drawn down at the corners. Blackbeard stood at the prow of the longboat leaning forward, one hand on his hip, the other edgeways above his eyebrows. Wrong John opened his mouth, as if to say something to him, but no words came out, only a puff of air that pushed up the back of his shirt. The vultures in the rigging kicked up a ruckus pecking at one another, flapping their broad black wings, and squawking. From the hatch, seven or eight tentacles of the Giant Squid wriggled in the air, undulated and gyrated as if dancing to some deep ocean drum-beat. Silverspoon looked over at them and shook his head.

"Well, IshcaBible, looks like it's just you, me, Dart, and the Giant Squid. Talk about your Apocalypse. Holy shee-it!"

I looked at him, bent over, using his vanquished enemy's sword as a crutch, the hump on his back well advanced in its conquest of his body. I thought of all the miles we had come together, all the trials we had endured, all the suffering, the foolishness, the endless games. I did not know how to feel towards him. Despite everything he had done, I could not hate him. He seemed too innocent for hatred, like some critter in nature that only grew dangerous because it had been cornered. I took off my bowler and rubbed my bald head.

"Would it surprise you if I said my real name isn't IshcaBible?" I asked him.

"Not IshcaBible? You funin' me?"

"Nope. I'm really not IshcaBible. I tried to tell you all along, It's bibble, as in 'scribble.' Ishcabibble."

"Scribble? That's a little bit biblical."

"I'm no preacher, Wrong John. You tried to make me into that. In truth, I'm a bushwhacking Southern rebel who lived for the terror he could spread.

That's who has been witness to your story." The squid tentacles dropped down the hatch.

"Huh," Wrong John grunted. He reached behind himself to scratch his hump, but he could not touch it. He leaned toward Dart. Wrong John nodded and murmured. He whispered something to Dart, and paused while it apparently said something only he could hear. They went on like this for a while, not noticing the sound of oars against the water from an approaching lifeboat. When the boat drew close, I could see the banished junior officer, Bill, rowing, and Krill holding his lamp to his chest. Tatanka had made the delivery.

Krill set the lamp down, grabbed it in his claws, flapped mightily, and flew from the lifeboat to the edge of the try-works. He looked around at the mess of squid parts, half empty mugs of grog, chunks of meat and chewed bones, bread ends, and urine stains across the deck of *Liberty*. "BRACK *almighty!* Look at this place." He waved a wing in front of his nose and squinted.

"*CROAK!*" blatted Dart.

"Who are you?" said Wrong John.

"Captain!" Krill cried. "It's me! your old buddy, Krill."

Krill looked at me and ruffled his feathers. "Oh, this is bad, Ish, real bad." He nuzzled the copper lamp with his cheek and spoke the words he had learned that night in the try-works furnace.

> "Ghar man mirma marâ biyârid shûmâ,
> Mûrdeh be neghâr-e man sepârid marâ.
> Ghar bôseh dahad bar lab-e pôsîdeh-e man.
> Ghar zendeh shavam ájab madârid shûmâ."

The lamp shook and rattled against the metal plate capping the furnace. Golden smoke poured from the spout. It swirled into a tight circle, flashed, and there stood the radiant white stork with glistening black-tipped wings, vibrant red legs and beak, and shining yellow eyes. Wrong John blinked his eyes and rubbed them. He walked closer for a better look.

The madly writhing legs of the Giant Squid sprouted from the hatch. Krill jumped back and shuddered. He looked over at the captain. His small bird eyes shut halfway. "Sir, try to remember. It's Krill, you know, Peckerhead, Blabbermouth. I used to be the one. You turned to *me* when the squid was on the loose. Now you're listening to a frog? *BRACK me!* Completely off strategy, sir. Not sticking to principle, *at all*."

"*CROAK!*"

Wrong John looked at Krill with empty eyes, not a trace of recognition in them. He leaned over to the frog, frowned, nodded, grunted. Suddenly, the stork leapt from the rail, shot out its long neck and sharp bill and grabbed the bright frog. She pushed off of Silverspoon's shoulder back to the try-works, the little weapon wriggling in her beak. She tipped her head back and swallowed Dart whole.

"*BRACK!* What a gal!"

Wrong John gawked at the stork, then at his shoulder, and back at the stork. He closed his eyes and rubbed his temples. He lifted his tricorn hat, brushed his hair back and shook his head like a dog shaking off water. He opened he eyes and looked fondly on Krill. "Peckerhead, you made it. How'd you git out of prison?"

"Tatanka brought me the lamp, sir. The one from the Baghdad bazaar." He pecked the copper lamp and it rang like a bell. "My sweetie, she was in there. It was a curse. She had been living in Shalong's palace. Gone off to see the world. She tried to help the agent, Martha Little, escape after the castration scheme went bad. Shalong's sorcerer cast a spell on her. He put her in the lamp, and she could only come out if the magic words were spoken with true love."

He put his wing around her long red legs. "Now she's a jinni. She gave me three wishes. For the first, I wished for freedom, and I was out of jail. For the second, I wished to be with you, wherever you were, and I found you. Now there's a wish left. One wish. You can have it if you want." He smiled at Wrong John as only a toothless parrot can.

Silverspoon frowned and put an index finger over his mouth and nose. He tugged on a gold earring and turned his leather tricorn. He stared at the Arabian lamp sitting on the try-works next to Krill. After a minute he dropped his hand, shrugged, and raised his eyebrows.

"Jeez, you know I can't think of a single thing I would change."

I could not believe it. Aladdin's magic lamp sitting in front of him, and he couldn't think of a single wish? There had to be something. "What about the capture of Al Quota," I said. "You could wish for that."

"Got Shalong. Same differ'nce."

"What about *Liberty*? Why not wish for the hole to be fixed?"

"What for?"

"So she doesn't sink."

"Let 'er sink. See if I care. Got me the mandate. Got what I came for."

"The hump!" I exclaimed. "You could wish for it to go away!"

"What hump?"

I paced the deck, rubbing the shiny leather of my holsters. "Think big, Silverspoon! Why not take the grand prize, the one you say you were born to fulfill."

"Likin' it."

"One-up the Prince of Peace. Do what he could never do."

"Still with you."

"Rid the world of evil, Wrong John! Make that third wish. *Ask for peace on earth.*"

"*BRACK!* Guaranteed place of honor in history! Guaranteed!" Krill whistled the preamble to *Charge!*

Wrong John scratched his head and kicked at the deck of *Liberty* with the tip of black knee-high pirate boot. He looked at the madly waving arms of the Giant Squid. The vultures in the rigging flapped their wings and tore at the edges of the sails. The stork preened her long, white, black-tipped wings.

"I don't know, Ish. I got me the mandate. That's what I came for. If I wish for peace, what good's the mandate? What am I gonna preempt if everybody's gettin' along? Ain't no fun in that." He looked at me with a half frown.

"*BRACK!* That's the spirit, sir. Peace is boring. Got no action, no intrigue. Stick with the mandate. *BRACK!* Stick with the mandate." Krill jumped from the rail and landed on Wrong John's right shoulder. "We've still got a campaign to run. Keep that third wish for an October surprise. I had some great ideas in prison. Disappearing ink at all the polls. Got to happen. No record. No recount. And Flip-Flop, we gotta stay on him. Get some folks on the streets. Take a simple poll: 'If you knew Flip-Flop was a regular at a queer bath house, would it change your vote in November?' Simple stuff. Stick to the basics, *BRACK!* Stick to principle."

"Wait a second, Krill. I'm—it's—*Liberty's* going down, and—well, I'm the captain. I should go down with her." He crossed his arms and set his jaw. Krill crawled down his arm and stood on his hand and looked at the captain.

"Step down, captain. Step down. She was never yours to begin with. Step down, sir. The ship is lost, but you can still be captain."

"What do you mean, Krill? I can't be the captain without my *Liberty.*"

"Sure you can, sir. *Liberty* was *always* a hopeless fantasy—from the very start. Founding fathers were starry-eyed liberals. To hell with 'em!" He climbed back up Silverspoon's arm.

"We'll get a new ship, call her the *Avarice*, or the *Dominator*. Maybe we'll call her the *King John*, or *His Highness*. One of your friends will give her to us. A good *pirate* ship of state. We'll sail on, take the victory. Nothing can stop us!"

Krill hopped the rest of the way to Wrong John's right shoulder. *"BRACK!* On to victory!" The stork spread her broad, white wings, lifted from the try-works, and landed on Silverspoon's left shoulder. The captain walked to the rail, leaned on his sword, climbed over, winked at me, and saluted. He descended to the waiting lifeboat. Bill put his strong back to the oars, and the keel cut a line through the smooth surface of the Potomac.

"Krill!" I called. "Did you ever figure out what those magic words meant?"

"Yeah," he called back. "They were from the Persian poet, Rumi:

> If I should die,
> I bid you carry me
> To where my love doth lie;
> There let me be.

> And if one kiss
> On my cold lips she give,
> Wonder not, that by this
> Again I live.

Then it was me, Frank, alone on *Liberty* with the Giant Squid growing inside of her. I was foolish enough to think I might do battle with the monster. I pulled my 45s and cocked the triggers. I was ready to unleash terror and destruction on it.

Click, click, went the triggers of Peace- and Widowmaker. I flipped open the cylinders: no bullets. Of course not. Of course not. The war was over.

For no apparent reason, the tentacles dropped through the timbers, down into the hold, and were gone. I saw some movement on the port side of the ship. I looked over to see a huge black squid eye, and then a jet of black ink. The squid shot off in the direction of Wrong John's lifeboat.

Presently, a whaleboat came round an upstream bend. The whalers heaved to at the oars and pulled the boat smoothly down the Potomac. "Thar!" shouted the captain at the tiller, a tall, gaunt man with a thin dark beard, pointing in the direction of Silverspoon's lifeboat. "Thar blows one with a hump like a snow hill!" The harpooner, a powerful, tattooed Polynesian without a shirt, left his place at the oars, grabbed his dart, stood in the prow, and hoisted his harpoon high.

Liberty began quickly to fill with water. I could feel it weighing her down, taking her buoyancy, the emptiness inside of her, and filling it with heavy brine. The river pulled her under, soon to drown the splintered mutilation of her figurehead, and me along with her. The gunwales lowered to the water, and for a moment, when deck and river surface were one, I had the marvelous sensation I could walk on water. Then I began to sink, up to my knees, my waist, my chest, the weapons that had saved me all those years—Peacemaker and Widowmaker—the ballast that would take me to my death.

A slow silhouette bore down on me from upstream. It was Tatanka in the black coffin. When the try-works went under, I noticed the magic lamp that had been left on top. It bobbed in the river and floated away. The ship bubbled and groaned. Water swirled around my neck. There was Tatanka. He said not a word, but hoisted me into his two-man tomb, and paddled left, then right, past the gurgling shipwreck, down the silky Potomac toward the sea.

ACKNOWLEDGMENTS

There are so many wonderful people who have come together around this project. Susan, my wife, and Sam and Franny, my sons, have endured an absent husband and father for the last nine months. Thank you for your love and patience.

I appreciate the love and generosity of my mother and father, Bob and Lillian Churches, my brother Tom, and sisters, Kathy Fair and Ange Odievich, my ninety-three-year-old grandmothers, Tomacita Mares and Elva Churches—and my brothers by marriage, John Fair and Daniel Odievich. I appreciate the sacrifices of all of my ancestors, who I have felt standing with me and behind me throughout. I have been grateful for your desk Grampa Mares, and your picture, smiling at me. How I wish you were here. I am especially grateful to my sister Ange, who has given so much encouragement along the way.

Thanks also to Sue's side of the family, Bob and Jane Davis, and my brothers and sisters-in-law.

Here's to ye, David "Cutthroat Coly" Colson, editor, buddy, soul brother. Your compassion for the characters and the story gave so much life to this piece. What fun to have done this together.

I appreciate the fine eye for detail of Michelle Asakawa, who caught so many mistakes. Many thanks to Lisa Trank, who cares deeply about this effort, and the dream of American democracy. Hats off to me hearty, Don "D" Harris, web master, *compadre*, and man of deep convictions.

A deep bow to my brothers in the Moon Belly: Christian Glover, Edward Eamon Duffy, Timothy Murphy, Lee Kimja Hansen, Aeric Leonardson, Seth Dream Seeker Braun, and the Moonsnake. You all have stood with me so strongly. I am honored to know you.

Thanks to my fellow mollusk, Tom Daly, and to the master shadow dancer, Keith Fairmont. Deep appreciation goes to Jeffrey Duvall, who made that first passage with me into publishing. Thanks also to Mike Massa, Ned head, friend, financial wizard, and also Todd Buchanan, Eldora activist, who helped many ideas to gel.

Again, I'm grateful for the support, emotionally and financially, from John "Jack" Madden, Jr., a true Renaissance man. I give thanks for my mentor and friend, the late Marvin "Swede" Johnson, a man of deep character. I miss you "Swede." To the late L.W. "Mike" Michaelson, my college fiction teacher, I wish you were here. To the other teachers at Colorado State, David Clark and the late Cecil Neth, you helped me so much. To the late John Gardner, thanks so much for your high standards and deep regard for the power of fiction. And to Miss Baker, my third-grade teacher, thanks for seeing something in that hyperactive little boy. Sorry about the trick with the snow boots.

I want to thank the Y2L group, and the late Steve Cannon, whose death challenged me to cross this threshold. Bless your soul, brother. Also, I'm grateful for the brilliant needle work of Jeffrey Dann, oriental doctor, who got me through the labor pains.

My heart goes out to the late Wanabi Hoshila, the Lakota elder and holy man who guided me so kindly. I feel your spirit.

I wish to honor the lineage of Tai Chi Ch'uan, including Master Waysun Liao, Master Dave Mishlove, Master Richard Eversley, all of my teachers over the years, and the students in the Nederland group. I am thankful for this art.

Bless all of my old buddies in the poker circle: Kenny J, Hz, Scooter Mac, Harry, the Ant, D, and Coly. I'm grateful for the safety net here in Nederland, especially Beth Fitzpatrick and Dave Ritt.

I want to acknowledge the brilliant work of Herman Melville, and his classic American novel, *Moby-Dick*. I honor the life and times of Jesse James, and the people who told his story, especially the wonderful book by T.J. Stiles, *Jesse James Last Rebel of the Civil War.*

I also want to express my deep respect and appreciation of the Bible, The Koran, and all the holy books of humanity.

So many great writers and brave souls have inspired me to do this work. There are too many to list them all, but a few who have made an impact on me include: Al Franken, Michael Moore, Molly Ivins, Jim Hightower, Ron Suskind, Lewis Lapham and the staff of *Harper's*, William Rivers Pitt and Truthout.com, Amy Goodman and Juan Gonzalez of Democrac Now!, David Corn, John Dean, Paul Krugman, Bob Woodward, Thom Hartmann, all the writers at *The Nation*, American Progress Action, James Moore and Wayne Slater, Rush Limbaugh, Matt Drudge, Ann Coulter, *The Weekly Standard*, The Heritage Foundation, The American Enterprise Institute, The Kato Institute, and all the wonderful conservative fish tanks of America.

Finally, I am grateful to history for presenting me the pirates—what great material to work with. This time in history got me fired up to do something. This is my small pebble tossed into the pond.

About the Author

James E. Churches is the descendant of Colorado pioneers on both sides of his family. His father's family settled in the Golden area in 1858 and ran a stage stop. Rawhide Churches, the original pioneer, is said to have broken every bone in his body taming broncos. His mother's family came to Colorado with Spanish missionaries in the early 1800's and received the first certified cattle brand in the territory. The Ortiz family married into the Native American community, giving Churches a strong affinity with their ways. Churches is proud to trace his ancestry back to Thomas McKean, the first Governor of Pennsylvania and signer of the Declaration of Independence.

He has been married to Susan for fifteen years. They have two boys, Samuel, 8, and Francis, 5, and live in Nederland, Colorado, a mountain town west of Boulder. He is the co-author, with Jeffrey Duvall, of the non-fiction book, *Stories of Men, Meaning and Prayer*. He is also the author of the novels *Horse Pictures*, and *The Pumpkin Prophesy*, and a book of poetry, *First Poems of July McNair*. When he is not writing, James teaches tai chi to area seniors, and runs a design and writing studio with his wife.